I0642787

City of Angles written by Stefan Gagne
(copyright 2013)
Artwork by Allison Barraza

Thanks to J. Norburn, the Franklin W.
Quackenbush Home for Displaced Rainforest
Monkeys, and all of my awesome Kickstarter
backers for making this possible.

Keep supporting free web novels!

//001: Starting Out Sideways

88:88 a.m., by the clock on the end table. At least until he fumbled to turn off its shrill alarm; then it snapped properly back to nine in the morning.

Waking up on a mattress which had, during the two years since initial purchase, been gradually assuming a U shape. Difficult to stay horizontal when the universe wants you to sink into it, hammock-style.

Dave Smith was not one for literary metaphors, so the irony of it was completely lost on him. Which was a shame, given how accurately it described his day-to-day living as of late.

He'd interviewed for permanent positions on a regular basis since graduating, but had yet to land one. The problem was and wasn't his commercial art portfolio; *very solid work*, they would say, *clean and neat*. What they would not add was *inspiring and creative* or *shows amazing promise to grow and develop*, because he did not. He was merely solid, clean, and neat. They had a name for people like that... "temporary contractors." Nobody you really needed or wanted an ongoing personal relationship with.

As a result, he'd been telecommuting while completing a number of random tasks for a number of random clients, many of whom he never saw again after shaking their hands at the start of a project. Oh, but they'd email him, they'd email him quite a bit.

Peeling himself out of the U-shaped bed, Dave didn't bother changing out of his t-shirt and pajama bottoms—no need, really. Instead he went right to his computer, tapping a key to bring it back to life, to check his email. His apartment was his office was his life, after all.

We'd like the lower lines to criss-cross and then reconnect, his current client suggested. *And can you make it more like a Celtic knot?*

Funny. Dave could've sworn that a few days ago, they'd specifically asked him NOT to make it look like a Celtic knot.

He'd designed and redesigned and refined this silly company logo dozens of times. Every day, new emails would come in from Lucid Technologies with new "design suggestions." By this point, he was used to them contradicting each other. The design had long ago stopped looking like a logo and started looking like one of those mazes they put on kiddie placemats at fishstick restaurants. But, fine—he would spend today working on the new suggestions, mail the results back, and tomorrow repeat the process anew.

But first: ham sandwich. An odd choice for breakfast, but he ran out of

English muffins yesterday, and leftovers would have to do until he felt like leaving the apartment for a shopping run.

Add some old mayo, scarf it down with 1% milk.

Step out of the apartment to grab the newspaper.

As usual, his hallway was dead quiet. Presumably his neighbors had real jobs, real places to be; he never saw them, at any rate. Didn't even see who delivered the newspaper. Didn't even READ the paper (who read newspapers these days?) but someone kept delivering it, so he figured it'd only be polite to bring it into the apartment every morning.

Work on the design a bit. It was taking shape... what shape that was, he had no idea. But it FELT like it was taking shape. Hopefully Lucid Technologies would finally be satisfied this time, and send him the stupid paycheck for a job well done...

Bounce a tennis ball off the wall, ponder design.

Work on the logo.

Sit down to play a dungeon crawler on his video game console. He'd been stuck in the same labyrinth and fighting the same chaos elementals for a hell of a long time, with no end in sight. This killed a few more hours as he pondered the design.

Work on the logo.

Maybe read a bit, or watch a movie.

Bedtime. Sink back into the U, close your eyes, and wait for the next day. Just how things are.

Sleep.

Dave Smith could, by many metrics, be considered the least interesting person alive. He had no "life" in the 1990s definition of it, i.e. "Get a life, you loser." He had little personality to speak of, unless blandness was coming back into fashion, 1950s-style. The universe would have casually overlooked his life and death without really missing out on much.

In fact, the universe did exactly that. Fortunately for Dave Smith, "the" universe was not the only universe paying attention to him.

This would prove to be tremendously important when the very next day, he'd meet someone who'd change his path forever, his apartment would be destroyed, he'd lose everyone he ever knew or loved, and he would nearly be killed in the most horrific manner imaginable.

All of this because Dave did not realize that his city was not his city anymore, and hadn't been for some time.

Blissfully unaware of his impending doom, Dave snored away as his spine was deformed by the bed. If it were capable of independent thought, that spine would have been satisfied to know the horrible mattress was going to be shredded into so much stuffing and springs in eight hours' time.

88:88 a.m., by the clock on the end table. At least until he fumbled to turn off its shrill alarm; then it snapped properly back to nine in the morning.

Waking up on a mattress which had, during the two years since initial purchase, been gradually assuming a U-shape. Difficult to stay horizontal when the universe wants you to sink into it, hammock-style.

Peeling himself out of the U-shaped bed, Dave didn't bother changing out of his t-shirt and pajama bottoms—no need, really. Instead he went right to his computer, tapping a key to bring it back to life, to check his email. His apartment was his office was his life, after all.

There's still a lot of work to do, but it'll have to wait.

That was new. Lucid had delivered a fresh round of changes to implement every single morning, until now. Seemed he had the entire day to himself. Infinite possibilities stretched out before Dave Smith—go to the movies, head to the park and feed the ducks, learn hang-gliding. Or at least take a shower and go shopping. Not that he'd do any of those things, but it was nice to know the options were there.

But first: ham sandwich. An odd choice for breakfast, but he ran out of English muffins a couple days ago, and leftovers would have to do until he felt like leaving the apartment for a shopping run.

Add some old mayo, scarf it down with 1% milk.

Step out of the apartment to grab the newspaper.

Step out of the way as two people run past him, directly into his apartment. They shut the door behind them—locking him out, as he heard the mechanism firmly latch shut less than a second after the wooden frame shook from the impact of the heavy door being slammed against it.

This left Dave standing in the hallway, holding the newspaper. His house keys were inside, of course.

Despite his extremely rapid home invasion, he wasn't shocked. That was just how Dave Smith rolled.

Instead, his concern came from the fact that the lights in the long hallway outside his apartment were starting to flicker... and go out, one by one, in the distance. *pop. pop. pop.* The superintendent was going to hear about that, certainly. Not safe to walk down the halls without light—

The door to his apartment opened just long enough for an arm three times stronger than his own to grab Dave by the back of his university t-shirt and drag him back into his own apartment.

Dave staggered into the apartment, roughly yanked in and released by the man. No sooner than he was clear then his DIY Swedish bookshelves were being shoved in front of the door, to barricade it.

"All you've got is a lousy knob lock," the man grumbled, while bracing the shelves diagonally, testing them to see how much give they had. "No deadbolts, no chains. Are you looking to get killed? And here I am, out of door spikes... Penny! Exit check!"

A young girl bounced by, just under his immediate field of view.

She threw open the door to his closet, with bare plastic clothes hangers rattling around from the force of it. Dissatisfied with his wardrobe, next she checked the bathroom—where the ratty shower curtain and old toothbrush were there to greet her. And... that was the end of her door-seeking quest, as Dave's apartment barely qualified as a closet, what with the living room and bedroom and kitchen sharing elbow room with each other.

"No connecting exits," she replied, quickly. "There's the window, I guess, but..."

For lack of a better option, Dave stood around looking confused. And studying the two uninvited guests.

The one who tossed him casually aside was pretty impressive for a guy approaching middle age. Graying around the sides, true, but otherwise he'd pass for one of those action heroes you see sneaking up behind terrorists armed only with a combat knife and an endless supply of vengeance. Not a beefcake 80s action hero toting an M-60, but one of those lean-yet-athletic nothing-to-lose action heroes who favored a quick neck snap twist.

Dave's reason behind immediately jumping to movie imagery was because the man dressed the part, as well. He had on cargo pants no doubt brimming with MREs and extra ammo clips, and an authentic-looking bulletproof vest. The genuine firearm and—yes, that was in fact a combat knife!—sealed the deal.

An armed intruder would be worrying to many. Dave instead was curious about the contradiction offered by the girl plus the man, working as a team.

Because she was not a tough-as-nails hitter chick action heroine to go with her action hero dad. She was probably about thirteen years old, skinny rather than buff and brawly, and dressed like a mountain climber... backpack brimming with useful gear, rough climbing boots, kneepads and elbowpads. No body armor here, just an ordinary t-shirt and khaki shorts. She also lacked the gent's neck-snapping musculature, and his grey hair; what he could see peeking underneath an old-timey explorer's pith helmet was ordinary red hair pulled back in two short pigtails, to stay out of her way. A shining example of youth and boundless energy, as she desperately searched Dave's little four-walled world for some way out...

Of course, eyeing the girl was probably not going to make the guy very happy. Maybe that was the reason why Dave now had a knife to his throat.

"Erm, excuse me," Dave felt the need to say in his defense.

He didn't dare turn his head, but did catch frantic movement out of the corner of his eye—the girl waving her hands, trying to interrupt this before the walls got painted red.

"Dad! Dad, whoa!" she exclaimed. "What're you—"

"Back off, Penny," the man warned—not angrily, just sternly. "Right. Who're you? How'd you get here? You with that thing that's hunting us down? I warn you, go cubist on me and I'll—"

"My name's Dave Smith, I moved here two years ago, I'm not sure what thing you're talking about or why it's hunting you down and what's an avant-garde art movement have to do with any of this?" Dave asked, smoothly providing the answers the man sought. "And if this is a robbery, my wallet's over there, although I've only got twenty-three bucks since I haven't hit the ATM recently..."

The girl (apparently named Penny) dared to put a hand on the arm holding Dave at knife point.

"Dad, calm down," she spoke... sternly but gently, similar to her father's prior command. "He's not one of them. He must be an import! This is his home."

"Horsecrap. Nobody can *live* in the Sideways," the father warned. "This guy's gonna Picasso on us any second, just you watch..."

"Fine. Then you can deal with it when and if that happens. Meanwhile, we've still got the first Picasso to deal with, don't we...?"

Slowly, and hopefully not reluctantly... the man backed down, pulling the knife away. Keeping an eye on Dave right up to the last second, before he turned and focused on barricading the door by trashing more of Dave's furniture.

To distract the furniture's owner from the ongoing destruction of his home, Penny decided to play welcome wagon.

"Hi, I'm Penelope Yates, and that's my dad Gregory," she introduced. "Sorry for barging in on your home like this. You're Dave, then?"

"Yes? I mean, yes, I'm Dave," Dave said, because it was true.

"I have to say, you're taking this experience remarkably well, Dave! Better than any other fresh import we've run into," Penny said, with a smile that was like a reassuring pat on the head of a small child. "That's very good, very good for you. Bodes well for your future in the city. Assuming we survive, I mean. I mean, we *will* survive, most likely, because hey—it's not our first run-in with a wild Picasso, you know? We survived those and we'll probably survive this one. All we need is an exit, they lose track of you eventually, bad visual acuity because of the distortion field. So, *relax!*"

"I am relaxed," he stated. Because he honestly had no idea what was going on, which meant there was no point in becoming unrelaxed over any of it.

"That's good, because as I noted before, it bodes well for your future. Although I'm not entirely sure how you're relaxed because to be honest I am kinda *freaking out* right now," she added, maintaining the strained smile. "Dad? Door? We good? Did it leave?"

Greg was about to respond, when the door responded for him.

A gentle rapping. Light, like someone's knuckles hesitating mid-knock, before resuming. Trying to be polite, trying not to disrupt the gentleman who lived here.

And more knocking. More knuckles. Three hands worth, which implied more than one person.

Then one hundred knuckles total. Still gentle, still polite, but far too many of them going simultaneously to sound polite. Dozens of people knocking on your door at once, which meant a feat like packing in a clown car, given Dave lived at the end of a narrow hallway...

At this point, even Dave was starting to worry. Too many things he didn't understand were happening for him to take his usual approach of not worrying about it. On the other side of his front door, what sounded like a horde of very polite people were very, very eager to get inside. And judging from his new companion's reactions, those very polite people would then likely murder everyone.

The doorknob began to rattle.

Slowly... Greg backed away from the barricaded door. Which meant he did not have much faith in the barricade.

"Out. We need to get out, *now*," he emphasized. "You, college boy. Got a rear exit in this dump? Anything non-obvious?"

"It's... uh, the rent isn't particularly steep because it's just a one-room apartment," Dave supplied. "There's only the door. And the fire escape, I guess — wait, what—?"

The other doorknob had begun to rattle. Because his door now had two doorknobs.

It was periwinkle blue, made of that fake crystal glass you'd find on doorknobs at grandma's house. The second knob had appeared slightly above and to the left of the original, and just below a third knob, which was stainless steel. Briefly his eyes hurt, and then there were six doorknobs. All of them different, all of them rattling...

"It's going to keep twisting the door until it grows a knob that's not locked, and then we are boned," Greg explained. "So. Fire escape. Now. I'll go first to make sure it's safe."

He brushed past the pair, grasping the bottom of the window and yanking up hard. Since Dave had never opened the window before, it gave a creak of protest before giving up and awkwardly slotting upwards.

"Dad! Wait wait—you said never to go *outside* when we're in one of the Sideways!" the girl protested. "We don't know what the space will be like out there..."

"No options, honey. We're going out," he said. "College boy, you go last. If it eats you, at least my daughter and I can get away while it's distracted, got it?"

Dave didn't even respond. He was busy getting ready to leave.

After all, even if you were caught in your pajamas with morning stubble and bed hair, you didn't leave the house without the essentials. Smartphone, check. Wallet with twenty-three dollars and his ID, check. Keys, check. (He had four keys on the ring—a key to his father's house, a key to his apartment, and a key to his old dorm room. Might be a good idea to check in on Dad, after today's madness was done.)

His bare feet hit the cold metal of the fire escape just as his front door split into fifteen smaller doors and fell apart. He was tempted to look behind him to see what exactly was breaking into his home, but suspected if he did that he'd finally understand what it was he was supposed to be worried about. And then, he might go completely crazy.

When Dave was very young, his mother and father took him to see a themed attraction park owned by a major motion picture corporation. He got to experience a simulated earthquake, he got to watch a simulated tornado, and was nearly eaten by a simulated shark. Back then he was easily startled, so an endless series of brushes with simulated certain death had nearly driven his eight-year-old brain into a dark corner to hide and suck its thumb.

He rarely gave any thought these days to those incidents. The one takeaway from his vacation experience was instead a curious simulation which was not promising horribly painful death, but instead a puzzle of sorts.

They were buying a hot dog from a street vendor, on a simulated city street. In the distance, Dave saw the rolling hills and buildings of San Francisco... stretching impossibly far, all the way to the horizon. Which didn't make sense, because he knew the theme park wasn't that big. He tugged and tugged at daddy's coat sleeve, begging to go get a closer look. Eventually, his parents gave in, and the race was on to see how far the road went.

It dead-ended in front of an elaborate multi-layered optical illusion—a series of painted wooden panes, flat as the boards they were made from, which only looked like a distant city when you yourself were at a distance.

And now, someone had plunked down one of those elaborate paintings outside his apartment window.

Dave wasn't sure how he hadn't noticed it before now, now that he was desperately scaling a fire escape in his bare feet, trying to escape an unknown horror that was intent on very un-simulated murder. Despite that threat, it was the illusion before him that grabbed his attention and wouldn't let go.

The side streets and buildings past his tiny little window were nothing more than flat paintings. In fact, the entire side of his building appeared to be in fact a large room, with the walls designed to look like they were not walls. It was like another theme park ride, where you sat in a tiny car and were shuttled through dark fake-cities, usually teeming with robotic pirates.

He felt the need to bring this point up, to the two who were doing a much better job escaping than he was.

"Excuse me," he spoke up, "But what happened to th—"

"There's nothing out there and there never was," Gregory Yates barked back. "It's just a stream of connected spaces. Try not to look at it and for heaven's sake, don't look down either! Just keep climbing."

"Yes, but my point is, only yesterday there was definitely something resembling a real city outside my window," Dave replied, while rounding one of the U-turns in the fire escape. "I think there was a city, anyway. Not that I really paid attention but I think I'd have noticed someone replacing my borough with THAT... and why shouldn't I look down? I'm not afraid of heights."

He looked down.

And saw something worth being afraid of.

At first, a splitting headache snapped across his brain pan. The human eye is not very good at processing things which break all known laws of optics.

Soon, his mind told him he was looking at a blurry thing which was completely in focus, so long as you had seventeen different focuses at the same time, all of them several feet away from the actual space of his head. If you could see the entity from all those perspectives at once, MAYBE you could put it together, like a jigsaw puzzle. Instead, you were looking at whatever it was through a multitude of shattered windows.

Whatever it was... it was warping the fire escape, as it scaled up after them. Not bending the metal or rusting it—the fire escape simply got... STRANGE, as it went. Branches started forming which went nowhere, or doubled back on themselves. Perfectly ordinary looking metal structures which were designed by a civic engineer who had gone completely insane, without losing any of his crafting skills.

They bubbled and warped and bent and snapped back into shape as it passed, leaving behind a structure which would do no one any help if they had to escape a fire. Or escape a malevolent, reality-eating monster.

One which had noticed him. And was now trying to speak.

No doubt because his life had somehow turned into a monster movie, it used a creepy little girl kind of voice.

stop // come // wait //
delicious // eat // tasty

Dave stopped looking down three seconds after he'd started. Closed his ears to the thing's babbling and broken voice, tried not to even think about whatever it was.

His current situation was that he was climbing to escape something bad. That was enough motivation, really.

Until they ran out of fire escape.

By this point, the façade on the wall opposite to them had wrapped around to the wall they were on. The side of the building Dave was climbing had stopped being a building and started being a poor imitation of one—crudely painted lines to represent brick and mortar, splotches of blue paint for windows. A smooth surface... and a fire escape that terminated a good ten feet below the actual rooftop itself.

Without a word, Penelope pulled a grappling hook and thick rope from her backpack, passing it to her father. Gregory took two spins with it and hooked the edge of the roof neatly.

"Hope you did a lot of fake rock climbing at the Student Union, boy," he called out, without looking down. He gave Penelope a leg up to start climbing the rope, then was up and over in the blink of an eye after her.

The reason why Dave wasn't afraid of heights was because he indeed did a lot of fake rock climbing at the Student Union. It was an easy way to get exercise in without having your bike constantly stolen. Trying to resist the urge to look down and confirm that the thing was still after him, he grasped the rope, and hoped like hell that he remembered that lesson from his school days more than he remembered Econ 101.

They were lucky the roof even existed. The fake room beyond Dave's window capped off with a ceiling designed to look like the sky—but had included enough headroom for a fake rooftop to go with the fake building. If he stood on his toes and reached up, he could touch that sky...

There was one problem. The roof was completely featureless. A square of black pavement, from edge to edge. Aside from a meager attempt at a surrounding half-height wall, which they'd grappled up and over, there was nothing there of any note.

No air vents to slide down. No access door leading to a stairwell back in. On all four sides, simply sheer drops to the bottom of the artificial play space. Not even any other fire escapes, as a quick glance over the sides proved. The roof was a dead end.

"So we drill through the ceiling or blow it up and then head back down again through the building, right?" Dave asked. "Or parachute down to the street?"

Penelope brightened. Well, she still had a manic panic about her, but her smile desperately peeked through.

"Wow! You know, that's really good thinking," she said. "You're getting the hang of this, Dave! Hey Dad, next time I go out exploring let's bring a drill, some explosives, and maybe a parachute. Except, um, we don't have any of those things right now so I think we're stuck up here..."

Gregory, meanwhile, was loading a fresh clip into his handgun. Because he'd spent two of them already before they even reached the apartment, trying to drive the thing back.

"Pull back to the opposite edge," he ordered, stepping back. "More distance. If I can line up a shot, maybe I can find a vital spot and end this before she makes contact and infects us..."

"You can actually shoot that thing?" Dave wondered.

"In theory. It's flesh and blood, at the core—but getting through the mess of physics it's become is... darn it all. Wish I'd brought grenades this time. Or a shotgun..."

Penelope rested a hand on Dave's arm. Well, hung onto Dave, more like.

"It'll be okay, it'll be okay," she promised. "You don't have to be afraid. Dad's beaten Picassos before. We're going to be fine—"

"*Shh,*" Gregory hissed back, taking a proper non-Hollywood handgun stance, waiting for the target to come in view...

It had walked up the side of the building after them.

Dave couldn't help but look at the thing, now. Flesh and blood, at the core...? He did see a vague human shape in there, come to think of it. Arms and legs, a head. A strange mix of green and brown, actually. Dark brown hair, or at least some mass of particles and strands that animated in a wild fashion around what might be its head. Dark green, of its clothes... a suit? A dress? Some odd triangular shape... with an orbiting ribbon, a sash of some kind which seemed so familiar...

Step by step it approached, flickering and bending as it went. Stuttering and slow, limping as it moved. Moving was causing it physical pain, almost, as it flared with eye-tweaking activity each time it shuffled ahead—

The sharp report of a gunshot nearly broke his focus.

And did absolutely nothing to slow the approach of the creature. If Dave's eyes could've tracked the bullet, it would have seen the projectile pass through the outer edge of the phenomenon, turn thirty-two degrees, continue another two feet, then melt into a tiny wad of liquid metal.

But because his focus wasn't completely snapped by the shot... he could now see what was so familiar about the band of cloth circling around the thing's torso.

It had tiny, tiny badges floating around above it. Like embroidered satellites, across a sea of felt. Merit badges.

He willed himself to pay attention to the thing's babbling.

mister // mister // selling these delicious //
mommy where are you //
made from tasty natural ingredients // mom, stacey keeps putting gum in my //
for a good cause // make it stop // help // flavors you know and love //
make it stop //

Dave physically pushed at Gregory to keep the next attempted shot from hitting home. It went wide, completely missing the little girl. Not that it would've connected, regardless.

In return, Gregory gave enough of a shove to send Dave staggering.

"That's not a gosh darned GIRL SCOUT, okay?!" Gregory shouted. "Not anymore! Now stay out of things you don't understand, brat!"

"You can't kill a kid!" Dave declared anyway. Because it was a universal truth, in his view.

"LOOK at her!" Greg yelled back, taking aim again. "That's not a little girl anymore. She's been Picasso'd! Tortured and twisted by the city into *that*. And if she gets too close to us we may end up just like her! So unless you've got any other brilliant ideas, back the heck off!"

Many people would have raced through their minds, trying desperately to think of a way out of the situation. Panic and fear driving you to scramble for a weapon, a strategy, a tactic—anything that would keep you alive in the face of certain death.

Dave was not many people. There was a very, very simple way to deal with someone selling cookies door to door, after all. Why look any further than that?

He stepped in front of Gregory's gun, and smoothly withdrew a wallet from his pajama pockets.

"I'd like to order two boxes of Thin Mints, please," he stated.

The Picasso stopped advancing.

It crooked what was possibly its head, studying him carefully. Then studying the money in his hands.

"I'm not exactly sure how much they cost, but I remember they were my mother's favorite, so I think I'd enjoy them too," Dave continued, holding out twenty-three dollars, all that he owned in the world. "Let's see... can you make change, or should I call someone at your troop office, or—"

"For heaven's sake—!"

Gregory yanked the cash out of his hands and tossed the whole wad at the young Picasso.

("Hey, that was all the money I had left in the world!" Dave protested, of course.)

The bills, on approaching the girl, began to twist and warp. Denominations shifted, the face of Washington became something unpleasant, and then finally they were deep enough into the cloud of the phenomenon that they could no longer be properly seen.

2.3 tense moments passed.

// thank // you //

Slowly... the break-point in the fabric of reality faded. It grew smaller and smaller, becoming translucent against the painted backdrop of an artificial night sky, until the girl was simply gone.

A piece of paper fluttered to the rooftop, left behind in her wake.

On it was a completely random mishmash of letters and numbers, in wildly varying fonts. Only one word was even slightly legible: RECEIPT.

Getting back down from the roof took far longer than scrambling up it.

The chaos left in the wake of the distorted little girl had rendered the fire escape into something not entirely unlike a vague recollection of a fire escape from someone who had seen one years before. Gregory took lead; he tested each section of the winding iron structure, making sure it was stable enough before he'd let his daughter climb down. (His first suggestion was to send Dave as a canary in a coal mine, but Penelope vetoed the idea.)

There was only one way out of the "Sideways," as the pair had called them —the way they came in. Since they'd been chased down a dead end by the Picasso'd girl, it meant reversing course. Including visiting Dave's apartment again. Or rather, what was once an apartment.

Gregory had overturned some furniture in his efforts to make a barricade. The cookie-seller had overturned the idea of an "apartment" in order to break down that barricade. What was once his front door was now a multitude of smaller doors with many doorknobs, scattered across his entranceway. His bed had been turned into two beds, each triangular in shape. His kitchen was now a bathroom comprised entirely of toilets which was in the shape of a kitchen; any thoughts of being a bit thirsty went away when he saw what had become of his coffee maker. His closet of clothes had been fused together into one giant polyblend lump of sleeves and trouser legs and shoes, which meant he'd be stuck in his pajamas for the duration.

And, much to Dave's disappointment, his computer had been turned into a computer made entirely out of cheese.

All that work on Lucid's corporate logo, gone. He still had a good picture of it in his mind, but it would've been nice to have the files to show for it. Proof that he had not in fact been completely wasting his life, telecommuting out of his dingy little hole in the wall for so long.

Gregory was busy picking through the mess, looking for anything stable and useful enough to take with them. Dave didn't move to stop him from salvaging what was left of the place.

"It's going to be okay," Penelope assured Dave, while they waited. (She'd been doing that quite a bit, even though Dave hadn't shown any signs of distress yet. Not even at seeing the disaster zone that was his home.) "We'll take you back to the city with us. It's MUCH more stable there, not like it is this deep into the Sideways. You'll find a new place to live. Okay? Dave?"

"Would I like the answer if I asked how I could get back home? I mean, back to Earth?" Dave hazarded.

"Ummm... maybe?" Penelope tried. "It depends. I mean, did you *really* like that world? Did you have unpaid phone bills to deal with? Or—oh, I know! Maybe you get excited about embracing bold new life challenges?"

"That means there's no way back, then."

"...yeah. Sorry about that," she said. "Nobody's ever managed to find a road back to your world, and nobody knows how or why people end up here. It is what it is, you know? But... you can make the most of it! Start a new life. Full of exciting and fresh opportunities! I mean, not *here*, this place is a death trap, I mean back where I'm from. The city proper. Very exciting there and not always fatal. Once I'm done mapping out this part of the Sideways—"

"We're heading straight back," Gregory declared, while testing out his grip on vaguely ovoid porcelain knives from the toilet-kitchen. "No more exploring. Adventure's over, Penny."

"But I'm not done," she protested. "It's only been a day and a half and you said we had supplies for five days. Besides, we barely mapped out that hallway network, and I KNOW I saw a storefront through one of those doorways we passed while we were being chased. I could find something really valuable—"

"Do you really think there's only one Picasso out there? Or are you waiting to find out if the rest of her troop is close behind?" Gregory asked, setting the knife aside. "We're done here. It's not worth the risk. Besides, it's going to take us another day and a half to work our way back, and with your new pet here, those rations will be going even down faster. The sooner we dump him in the Department of Orientation for processing, the better. Either that or we toss him to the next Picasso we meet, I guess. Now let's get moving."

Hiking his backpack strap up an inch, Gregory stepped carefully past the multitude of doors scattered across the floor, and back into the hallway.

Sheepishly, Penelope tipped her pith helmet to Dave in apology for her father's behavior.

"He's just really protective," she excused. "He's not THAT awful a person when he's not busy trying to keep me alive during an expedition. C'mon! I'll show you the rest of this part of the Sideways. You'll love it!"

Dave did not love the Sideways.

He didn't hate them, either. They were just... there. And incredibly strange.

The hallway of his apartment building had been copied verbatim into this new, weird world. Where it normally turned right and headed down stairs, though, it connected to the hallway of some other building entirely—from a hospital, it seemed, judging from the labels and chart-holders next to each door. Doors which, despite Penelope's insistence that they map every inch of this place using her tablet computer, had been left closed. If you wanted to survive in a creepy haunted lair, the last thing you should do is investigate hospital rooms, after all.

From the hospital hallway they connected to the hospital cafeteria, which had plastic chairs turned up on plastic tables... a cavernous room, which halfway through started having piles of wooden crates instead of dining tables, until it was simply a storage warehouse for a home improvement megastore. Two rooms, sharing the same space, stronger at opposite ends. A few warehouse offices connected, but with no workers in sight. Which was probably for the best.

After that, it was a long, long haul through a series of bedrooms. All of them were completely mismatched; a children's bedroom would connect to an extremely fancy hotel room which connected to what looked like a makeshift meth lab with a ratty old cot in the corner. Bedrooms rarely had two doors, which meant that they had to progress by going through a door, then climbing through a window into another bedroom, then going through a door, and so on.

All the while, Penny kept chattering about how amazing this place was—how organic the flow of rooms was, how strange the way they all clustered together, the unique patterns she was seeing here which weren't anywhere else in the Sideways. Because she had explored a LOT of Sideways, in the years she'd been doing this amateur urban spelunking.

The Sideways.

The way she'd explained it was like this:

"Have you ever seen something funny out of the corner of your eye, but when you turn your head, it's gone? The Sideways are like that. The whole city is a mishmash but it's not THAT mixed up of a mishmash; you can only find connections this random in the Sideways, and you can only find the Sideways by noticing a flicker in the corner of your eye which isn't there when you turn to look at it. You gotta use mirrors to indirectly look, and THAT'LL show you the door for real. And you can find all sorts of amazing things in there!"

"Like what?" Dave asked. (He wasn't actually that interested, but it helped pass the time, and the girl seemed to enjoy talking about it, so...)

"Well, the thing which is funding, like, EVERYTHING we do is the Crackers," Penelope explained, as they were climbing through yet another bedroom window. "Ah, that's the name people gave to the slightly cracked smartphones. We found a shelf in a store somewhere in the Sideways, and there's ONE phone on the shelf. It's got a crack in the upper right corner, but otherwise it works fine. And if you pick the phone off the shelf... it's still there! You can grab another and another and another and never run out! That's why everybody and their dog has phones, even though, um, there's a lot of poverty out there. They're cheaper than air. And Dad and I made a hefty bounty off them! Great find, right, Dad?"

Gregory spoke up, to add his two cents.

"A great find, although we did have to give a Picasso the slip to get it," he said. "Some irate customer who was there to complain about her data plan to sales clerks who didn't exist anymore. Glad the Department of Resources took over after that..."

"Bottomless phones and another Picasso?" Dave asked. "But... that kind of thing doesn't normally happen in the city, you said earlier?"

"Heck no! You need to be in a REALLY weird place for causality to go that strange on you," Penelope emphasized. "And the weirder the place, um... the more likely it'll infect you with cubism. At least, that's what the Department of Safety says. But the phones are totally safe, and they made us a mint!"

"I guess you can make a lot of money looting places like this, then."

"Well, yeah, but... that's not really why I do it," Penelope admitted. "Um. So! ... so. What about you?"

"Me? Uh. What about me?" Dave asked, puzzled when the focus suddenly shifted to him.

"What's your thing? What's your deal?" she asked. "It helps to have a thing or a deal. Means you can find a place in the city to make your own. What's yours?"

He had to think about about that.

"I draw stuff for corporations," he summarized.

And that was it. Which took Penelope a few moments to realize was in fact the start and end of it.

"That's all?" she asked.

"Well... I was never good at fine art, and I can't cartoon, and... people pay for you to draw logos and adverts and fonts and stuff. So, yeah. I draw stuff for corporations."

"Do you like it?"

"People pay you to do it," Dave said, with a shrug. "I mean, they PAID me to do it. They don't anymore, I guess, now that I'm trapped here forever. ...I am trapped here forever, right?"

"Well... explorers like me are always checking unchecked roads and routes, trying to find a way back, but... in, um, practical terms, for all intents and purposes... yes," she admitted. Again. "Are you SURE you're feeling okay...? I'm not an Orientation Officer, and technically I've lived here all my life so I don't know what it's like to lose everything, but you've got my sympathy if that's worth anything which I'm not sure it is so, umm... um. Yeah."

"I'm fine," he replied.

"Dad? I'm not sure Dave is really fine."

Which was the last straw for Gregory Yates.

Not that he was angry at his daughter. "Anger" and "at" and "Penny" were three words which never found confluence in his mind. He could be frustrated with her, he could be annoyed, but there was never anything close to hate there for the only thing left in his world he truly loved. Of course, his flavor of love could be a bit tougher than others, but the situation called for it. Especially the current one.

It was nighttime in the Sideways, and they were camping down in two adjoining bedrooms. Gregory was very insistent on the arrangement. Penelope would get the queen sized bed in the comfortable room, where he'd sleep on the barcalounger next to it. As always, she'd packed her pajamas and even a teddy bear which she was probably a few years too old for—but when you slept in the Sideways it wasn't a bad idea to embrace what comforts you could, Gregory felt.

Dave, meanwhile, would be in one of the bunk beds in a kiddie bedroom which connected to it. Most likely because Daddy was not happy about a boy several years older than his daughter sleeping within arms reach of her. And yet, despite being out-of-sight / out-of-mind... Penny kept talking about him. Hence, the last straw.

"Penny, it doesn't matter if Dave is really fine," Gregory explained, while arranging some quilts around the edges of his sleeping chair. "Dave is not, in fact, our problem."

"But we saved him from being stuck forever in the Sideways! We're his rescuers!"

"Yes, we saved him. And that's the extent of our relationship to Dave Smith," he clarified, having a seat. "Look. You said it yourself, earlier; you're not an Orientation Officer. Dave's probably so deep into shock that he's not even responsive to the craziness of his new situation. He's going to need their help, not ours."

Penelope sat up in bed, pouting. "I don't think the city's crazy..."

"No, but you didn't come from where he comes from. ...I'm from his world, remember?" Gregory said. "It's a very orderly place, compared to here. Everything makes *sense* there. So when I first got here it took me a long time to accept what happened; I needed a lot of help from the Department of Orientation. I was about his age when it happened, too. Right now, we are not what Dave needs. Once we get home... we've got to leave him in the hands of professionals. That's the mature thing to do."

"But—"

"No buts. Keep your distance, Penny, because Dave will be going away soon. It's better for him that way... even aside from orientation, you know the life we lead is dangerous. And I don't just mean the Picassos."

"You keep me safe just fine. We haven't had any problems in ages..."

"Discussion's over, Penny. Now. Did you brush your teeth?"

She crossed her arms, and grinned manically to show off shiny gums before glowering in protest.

"Let's bunker down and get some rest, then," Gregory said, pulling a quilt over himself. "We've still got a hike ahead of us before we're out of the Sideways. No time for naps tomorrow. Night, honey. I love you."

An hour later, and Gregory was asleep. He slept lightly, of course; ready to spring into action at the slightest noise.

Fortunately for Penelope, she'd long since learned how not to make the slightest noise when she wanted to sneak out of bed.

No more home. No more job.

His father, left behind. Everyone and everything he knew left behind.

Stuck in a place which was completely alien and weird. No matter how much she claimed the "rest of the city" was less weird than this particular spot of it.

A weird place where people could wake up insane and distorted and wander endlessly in cubist agony for the rest of their lives, and accidentally bring that ruin onto others.

And Dave felt... nothing.

You're coping remarkably well! the bubbly Penelope had said. She did 90% of the talking, really, while Dave said nothing. And felt nothing.

He didn't feel tired, for starters. Despite hiking all day, climbing in and out of windows, scaling piles of furniture whenever they hit a particularly unorganized abandoned space. No, right now he felt like lying there and staring at the bottom of some other kid's upper-tier bunk bed.

No home, no job, no family, nothing.

No thoughts. Nothing to say on the subject.

Until she popped up out of nowhere and nearly sent him rocketing into the wooden flats holding up the bunk above him.

"Hiii," she whispered. "Shhh. Dad's dozing away. Stay quiet."

Dave regained his wits quickly... and instinctively backed away from her, scooting against the wall the bed was pressed against. Because if Gregory stopped snoring and caught him with her, he'd probably have a new mouth in his neck in seconds.

"What're you—?"

"Dad wants you to go to the Department of Orientation when we get home," Penelope explained. "So we'll have to part ways. ...he's right, I know. But... I don't get a lot of chances to make friends, you know? He keeps folks away from me, and, um, sometimes there's good reason for that, but it still sucks. So yeah, okay, sure, you're a really old guy—"

"—not THAT old—"

"—but even so, you've been to that other world! And now you're here, and that's really fascinating to me! So if you gotta go soon, I wanna talk s'more before you gotta go. Okay? I mean... I'll leave you alone if that's what you want, I guess..."

Dave settled in... sitting cross-legged, across from her. This would likely take a while. And it wasn't like he was sleeping either, so...

"So I'm a sensational new find, like those cracked phones?" he wondered.

"Don't be like that," she said, assuming it was a verbal pout. "I'm a people person, that's all. I like talking with people, when I get the chance. ...well. Talking *at* them, I guess. In fact I should stop talking at you and just let you talk. Okay? Okay. What's on your mind, Dave? You've heard more'n enough of what's on mine..."

He stared at her for a bit, saying nothing. Because he wasn't sure what he was supposed to talk about.

Then he talked anyway.

"It's not that I'm really great at coping with things like this," he stated. "I wish you'd stop saying I was. I'm actually completely terrible at it. That's why I never bother with coping. I just... don't know how to react, so I don't react."

This time, it was Penelope's turn to look lost and confused. She wasn't expecting him to start chatting about something *that* deep. So, in response to silence, he continued.

"I used to have serious anxiety problems, as a kid. I spooked easily. A lot've things have gone wrong in my life. It just got to the point that... well... I was so anxious I came out the other side and everything that went bad on me was just background noise. And now I just don't even care. I just do what I have to do, one way or another. ...I'm not making a hell of a lot of sense, am I?"

"No, it... I mean, that makes sense," she said, slowly coming around from idle chit-chat to serious discussion mode. "So... all of this *is* actually getting to you?"

"Maybe. I guess. I don't really know one way or another," Dave admitted, with a shrug. "But unless there's a way back, then these are things which are happening, and that's that. I can't get worked up about disasters anymore. Like when the Twin Towers fell, and I didn't really have any feelings about it. Or when I found out about Mom's cancer."

"O-oh. Um. I'm sorry to hear that about your mom, Dave."

"It could've been worse, really. In a way, she was glad she found out too late."

And... he was apparently done, because silence reigned again.

"Sooo... you just keep going, then?" Penelope asked, to fill in the gap. "There has to be more than that, though. A reason to keep going. I mean, even when I'm scared, I keep going because I believe... um. You'll think I'm crazy, actually. —or maybe not, since you don't have any preconceptions about the city... okay. Wanna hear my belief?"

"Sure," Dave said, possibly not meaning it. (He was used to making automatic small talk, after all.)

"I think the city has a heart," she said. "Sure, plenty of mappers think there's some pattern to it we've yet to grasp, but I mean something beyond that! Sometimes, I can almost *feel* the way this city feels. And if I map more of it, I'll know that heart. If I manage that... if I can understand the city, right down to the roots... maybe I can use what I learn to help people in this city find hope. —which is *incredibly* silly, and Dad really thinks it's silly even if he doesn't have it in him to say it out loud, but... um. My point is, well. That keeps me going. ...what keeps *you* going?"

It was a question he'd never given serious thought to.

Maybe it was this surreal place. Maybe the late hour, the lack of sleep, the quiet internal desperation. The pleading look in the optimistic teenager's eyes, really hoping that Dave was going to say something which would make her feel better—because knowing his dead reactions were more fatalistic than deadpan wasn't a pleasant thought. Maybe Dave just wanted her to feel better.

Maybe it was the truth.

"I keep going because I'm hoping in the end, it'll all sort itself out," he said. "It'll all make sense and things will be okay."

Suddenly, he was being hugged. In a very little-sistery sort of way.

"It'll be okay, Dave," she whispered. "I promise. For you, and for everyone."

Which is exactly the scenario that Gregory arrived to, when he swung the doorway open.

Quietly, Dave prayed that his execution would be swift and painless. Instead, he heard a stern but patient voice which did not sound like sharpening knives.

"Penny, get back to bed. It's late," Gregory spoke.

Sheepishly, the girl extracted herself, and tried to play this off as a casual and completely unimportant situation. Sneaking away quietly, past her father and back to her room.

"Um," Dave offered.

Gregory closed the door behind himself. And locked it.

With a heavy sigh... Dave sank back into the Star Wars sheets he was lying on previously. A crazy-protective father and a far too personable teenager. Just another thing on top of a pile of things which were, at best, problematic and unsettling...

No home no job no family weird place dangers everywhere.

Still, he found himself sleeping soundly in minutes. Probably just a complete collapse from exhaustion. Probably.

Dave's grand introduction to the city itself came in the form of a basement laundromat in an apartment building. It looked... well, like the dingy little laundry room in his own apartment building, just with the machinery in a slightly different configuration. With no windows and nothing to scream aloud "YOU ARE IN A STRANGE PLACE!", it was almost comfortingly normal.

The abnormal part was that they walked straight out of a wall. But, as Penelope had explained, the entrances to the Sideways were hidden... you'd never find one unless you indirectly looked at it. Or went to lean against a wall and fell in, presumably, which is why the edges of the entrance were marked with yellow and black hazard tape.

DEPARTMENT OF SAFETY — SIDEWAYS ENTRANCE — DO NOT CROSS, the black lettering cheerfully declared.

"Er, were we supposed to be in there at all?" Dave felt the need to ask. "I mean, I know I didn't have much choice in the matter, but you two did and that warning looks mighty authoritative..."

"It's just a yellow-black," Penelope said, pulling her tablet computer out of her backpack, to review the map she'd been making. "The Department of Safety doesn't LIKE mappers going in, but it's not illegal. If it was a red-black that'd mean an official quarantine and, well, yeah, we don't go there. Although I don't see why they insist on stopping us! I mean, okay, it's dangerous. But if someone's willing to take the risk, why not let them in? You could find all sorts of great things in the Sideways that'd help people... new repeaters, new resources, new shortcuts... "

"And you could let a Picasso out into the city," Gregory said, while hiking his sagging backpack up on one shoulder. "Law's there for a reason, Penny. Odds are they're going to black-red this one off after we submit our report, too."

"We could just hang onto the map ourselves," she suggested. "We don't HAVE to file it with the DoS..."

"We're not black hat mappers. It's our responsibility to report a Picasso, you know that. At any rate... we're clear of that mess now," he concluded. "So, Dave, welcome to the City of Angles. I'll give you cab fare to get to the Department of Orientation. Just tell the clerk at the front desk that you're a new import, and they'll put you through the system. Have a nice life—"

"Can't we at least get lunch first?" Penelope asked/begged. "I think Dave's been a really good sport through all this, and we shouldn't just pack him up and ship him out like that. Let's show him the sights!"

"We talked about this, Penny. He needs orientation, not a tour guide. I'm not in the mood to be around when his mind is blown by those sights."

Dave politely raised his hand, wishing to speak.

"My mind doesn't easily blow," he explained. "And your daughter's talked about the city a lot. A LOT. I'll be okay. Also, I am kinda hungry. They sell real food here, right? Not Soylent Green or anything...? Although I spent twenty-three dollars on two boxes of cookies, so, um... if you could spot me, I'd appreciate it..."

Between Dave's earnest calm and his daughter's bubbling enthusiasm... Gregory rolled his eyes and relented. Just as he'd done ever since running into this unfortunate.

Rolled his eyes downward.

And left them there, for a moment. Studying something in the gloom of the laundry room...

"Let's go big! Dad and I know a really great seafood place. It's kinda expensive since, um, no oceans around," Penny chattered away, leading Dave out of the room. "Still, this is your big debut! I'll kick in some of my allowance if I gotta to get you a lobster..."

Footprints in the room's dust. Cigarette butts. Four little impressions, like chair legs, in a neat square. Which matched nicely with a chair that had been moved to one corner of the room for the time being.

The people who lived in this apartment building didn't actually use this laundry room. Ever since an entrance to the Sideways was found here, the room was a no-go zone; sure, your chances of accidentally falling in were slim, but city citizens were not a risk-taking sort. The washing machines were nearly rusted shut and unusable.

Someone had been here, regardless. Having a seat, having a smoke. From the angle of the chair... waiting for someone to come out of the Sideways.

Either they got bored and left, or had to visit the potty and were on their way back right now. Neither option appealed.

"Lobster sounds good," Gregory decided, wheels turning in his mind. "In fact, lobster sounds very good."

The City of Angles.

That wasn't the official name, of course. There was no official name. But the joke had been passed around so long and so often that it had stuck in everybody's head. A city, where everything was at a slightly askew angle to everything else? City of Angles. Sticky, very sticky.

These were the sidewalks that the trio were walking down, now. Finally out in the open—the real open air, not a painted simulation of an open air environment. Dave didn't think he was claustrophobic, but he had to admit a certain sense of relief at taking in a breath of car exhaust and garbage and sweat and humidity. All very familiar smells to a graphic designer who had been living in a city for the last two years...

The best part, hands down, was the sunshine. It was high above his head— hopefully not just painted on a false ceiling—and even at street level there was enough sunlight trickling down to warm his face.

But the differences between the city he left and the city he now had to call home were striking.

The angles, those were obvious. This was what Penelope called "The Zag," a central roadway that zig-zagged along with a series of sharp lefts and rights and lefts and rights. Yet it was certainly all one street, judging from the painted lines on the road, and meant to be taken as such rather than a diagonal slice of city blocks. The sidewalks confirmed it, snaking along and hugging the edges of the asphalt perfectly just as sidewalks should.

The buildings GENERALLY followed the back-and-forth nature of the roadway; sometimes the sidewalk would be too narrow or too thick, as the looming brick-and-mortar structures squatted in positions that would make any civil engineer weep in agony. No Leaning Tower of Pisa effect... but they were rotated a bit, like teeth in a mouth that hadn't seen a dentist in fifty years.

As for the buildings themselves, well...

"So that one's actually a department store," he repeated, pointing to what was obviously a warehouse, with the U-Stor-It logo painted over.

"Yep!" Penelope confirmed.

(Gregory took point, so he could glare at anyone who came too close. Despite being out of the Sideways, he was in bodyguard mode for reasons unknown. At least this left Dave and Penelope to chat without interference— from him, and from anyone who might slow their progress down the sidewalk.)

"And that building which clearly was a shopping mall is now low income housing."

"Yep! Dad and I've traded with the folks there a few times though, so, uh, I guess there are some mall aspects left..."

"And the steps down to that subway station lead to a hair salon."

"I used to get a really nice hairdo there, before Dad started making me wear a helmet for safety reasons. Now I just stick to pigtails, they're easier. And cuter. It's hard to look cute when you wanna be functional."

"Why not just... I don't know, use the buildings for what they were originally?" Dave asked. "Seems like it'd be simpler..."

"You tell that to the fifteen shoe shops I once saw along the same street," Penelope said. "Nobody needs that many shoes. —okay, lame fashion magazines say I do, but I prefer a good pair of boots. Better for long distance hikes."

"Demolish a few of them and put up something else, perhaps?"

"Ooooh... bad idea. The city... ummm... it doesn't like that," she tried to explain. "I read in the history books about how in the 1930s, when things were just starting to get organized, the Mayor tried a demolition and construction spree. Aaand... the district he did it in is now almost completely Picasso'd and sealed off by the Department of Safety. My theory's that you gotta keep the overall shape the way the city wants it—you can fiddle around a bit, but only a bit."

"So, you can't snip somebody's arm off and install a third leg and expect it to work," Dave summarized.

"Exactly! See, you're getting it. New buildings keep arriving, and we have to make the best of them. There's no known pattern or predictability yet. Your vision just goes screwy, and BOOM, something new's inserted itself between two buildings. All the roads shuffle around to make room. The city's always shifting and moving! —okay, not ALWAYS, the Zag's been relatively stable for decades which is why it's so popular, but you can still never be too sure. Maps constantly have to be updated, to keep people in the know. Smartphones are great for that; most mappers sell their data to map-app keepers and can make a great living that way."

All of the nuts and bolts were fascinating, from a technical standpoint. Clearly it excited Penelope to talk about her city, too. But the part Dave didn't feel comfortable bringing up, the key difference, was what he saw in the people.

There weren't as many of them here as there were back home. This was an overgrown and underpopulated city; plenty of folks on the sidewalk, plenty of cars on the road, but clearly not as many as there should be for an urban center of this size. More importantly, the ones who were here had a certain urgency that hastened their steps. Get where you're going, because where you're going may change on you if you don't hurry...

He was familiar enough with anxiety to see it in their faces. Getting by day-to-day here was challenging enough for most, too challenging for others.

No wonder Penelope's dream was to fully comprehend the incomprehensible shape of the city. Living in uncertain times was bad enough, and adding uncertain places on top of it couldn't help. "Making do" was not the same as thriving. Even if Dave had been making do for quite some time, he had enough of an objective viewpoint to know the difference.

"I think I can make do here," he decided to say.

"Really? That's great!" she replied, smiling. "You just watch; you'll be on your feet in no time. Personally? I love the city. It's exciting! It's full of wonders, full of things to see and people to meet. A lot of people, all they see is the downside, you know? Usually imports, like you. Um. No offense. But for folks like me who were born here, well... this IS the world. What's to fear from it?"

Gregory, who had apparently been listening in the whole time, spoke up.

"Cubism," he started, counting off on his fingers. "Starvation. Muggings. Getting lost. Gang violence. Cults. Drug overdoses. Going homeless. Getting arrested. Sickness or injury with no coverage. Accidentally walking into the Sideways. Losing hope and wandering off. Your street rearranging itself and leaving you stranded..."

Having run out of fingers before he ran out of horrors, he gave up at that point.

"Guess if you're lucky, VERY lucky, you can move out to the Suburbs," he added, to show he saw at least a little upside. "You can get there if you know the right roads out of the city, the ones that don't just loop back around. The Burbs are just as random as the city core, but at least they're less fatal. There, the worst you'll have to worry about is having a bad WiFi signal and spotty hot water service..."

Penelope was quick to jump to her city's defense, under that waterfall of negativity.

"I mean, okay, a lot of that happens, sure, fine," she dismissed. "But that's... all of those problems can be solved! Eventually. With the right thinking. With good maps."

"Honey, this city's been here nearly a century. If the Mayor and his Departmental cronies were going to sort things out, they'd be sorted out by now."

"Dad, you're making us look uncool in front of Dave!"

"Don't think Dave really cares. Do you, Dave?" Gregory asked. "You're not the caring-about-things type, ri..."

He trailed off, mid-observational insult. Narrowed his eyes, as he glanced in the reflection off a Plexiglas-covered bus stop.

And reached back to grasp his daughter's hand, right before picking up the pace.

"I'm extremely eager for seafood," he explained immediately, before anyone asked what was up. "It's been a long day and some fish and chips would be perfect. Wouldn't mind seeing your Uncle Archie, either."

"Oh, right! Archie's the guy who owns the place," Penelope explained to Dave, distracted by the chance to explain more about everything to the new guy. "Keep up! We'll be there soon!"

A glance in a passing shop front window reflection confirmed Dave's confusion at this change of pace.

And that the two men in suits were still following them, Gregory sourly noted.

"That Fish Place" was not a particularly inspired name for a restaurant, until you considered that it was just about the only fish place that existed in the City of Angles. Sure, you could get beef or chicken or even venison—thanks to the most distant layers beyond the city and beyond the suburbs, where random grasslands and ranches and rural communities had been mashed together—but no oceans meant no easy access to fish. And yet, That Fish Place had fresh fish daily. If you wanted fish, that was the place to be.

Originally it was a bit of a seedy, rough-and-tumble place that brewed a mean codfish liquor. It had been converted out of a former clothing sweatshop with a highly unique basement; that grim and grimy industrial building was hardly a welcoming locale for an eatery. Fortunately a company that specialized in rebranding and redesigning had worked with That Fish Place to make it into a family restaurant, complete with wacky stuff on the walls and waiters with pieces of flair. Since then, it became an upper middle class destination of choice.

The industrial space wasn't completely revamped, of course—you couldn't simply knock the building down and stick a new one up. The city wanted Thing A in Slot A, and you didn't want to push back too hard on that. But with enough decorations and dividers and elevator music, you could make even the worst rust bucket in the universe look cheery and inviting... even if just under the surface lurked something ugly.

No matter how hard they smiled or how often they tried to shave off the five o'clock shadows, Gregory Yates knew the crowd that ran this place. They had a very valuable resource under their floorboards, and enough of a checkered past to know how to defend it. Nobody had made a move since the upscaling of the atmosphere... but they would be ready to shove, if push came to shove. Which made it an ideal destination for today.

Gregory flashed a rare smile as he walked in the door, breezing right past the couples and families who were waiting to be seated for the lunch rush. Walked up to the Johnny the Maître d' (originally known as Johnny the Icepick) and shook his hand, exchanged pleasantries, made a big show of it.

"Greg Yates! Hey man, it's good to see you!" Johnny the No Longer An Icepick called out, reaching out for a manly hug. "And little Penelope! And... wait, who's that guy?"

"A new friend. We're showing him around. Any chance you can squeeze us in somewhere? A table in the back would be just fine," Gregory said aloud, before moving in for a Manly Hug Where You Hit The Other Guy On The Back Repeatedly.

"*We're being followed by two goons in cheap suits,*" he added quietly, once he was in whispering range. "*Get us out of sight and tell Archie.*"

"I think we can cover you," Johnny said, in response to both requests. Ignoring the pleas of the customers who had been waiting an hour or more, he whisked the trio away on the winds of friendship.

And flicked a hand gesture, which caused two waiters who could easily have passed as linebackers to very, very casually loiter near the door.

Gregory spared a glance over his shoulder, to see the goons who had been lying in wait for them outside the Sideways pause at the window... and move on. Good. But he didn't breathe easily; relief could come when he knew what the hell was going on. And until then, well... no sense worrying Penny, or Dave, for that matter.

After days of being alone in the Sideways with nobody but her dad and her new buddy, Penelope was glad to be back in the city. Even gladder to be at

That Fish Place, which always had a festive and jovial atmosphere.

It felt right, to her. This was a place where families, entire families could come and sit down and peacefully enjoy something they rarely got to experience. The staff, despite looking like extras in a documentary about the Hell's Angels, were friendly and kind and always had a good joke or two to share with the owner's niece. That Fish Place represented the promise of what the city could be, instead of what it was, and Penelope felt that was the perfect way to introduce Dave to the core of the city.

Except Dave wasn't cheerfully smiling. He seemed about as nonplussed and nonchalant as he did in the Sideways.

Dave's probably so deep into shock that he's not even responsive, her dad had guessed.

I never bother with coping. I just don't know how to react, so I don't react, Dave had said himself.

It was probably too much to hope that getting him out of the scary part of the city would be enough to get the guy to both relax AND enjoy himself. She had been holding a glimmer of hope that he'd be able to do it, but... Dad was right. He needed help from the Orientation experts. Maybe they'd be able to get him somewhere he needed to be, where he could feel at home.

Still, she wasn't going to shut down the welcome wagon just for lack of a smashing success.

"Honestly, I'm not THAT into lobster," she admitted—since her dad was gone at the moment, off to visit Uncle Archie. "But my uncle always loves to make me a special lobster chowder when I get here, something off the menu, and I like to make him happy. You can have some too, if you want. Or do you see anything else on the menu you like?"

Dave glanced over the laminated card full of wackily named dishes and zany entrees, trying to figure out what appealed. Not much did. Not much didn't appeal, though. Honestly, he was too busy idly doodling on the back of a kid's menu with the box of crayons they'd left at the table to give it much thought.

"I never really had enough money to sit down and eat somewhere. Usually I got pizza or Chinese takeout or something," he said. "And in college I practically lived off cold cereal. I think I've got the gourmet sensibilities of an alley cat at this point. Sooo... I don't know. I'll go with the chowder, I guess."

Figuring it wasn't worth it to push the guy into expressing his heart's yearning desire via meal selection, Penelope let that one go. Besides, something far more interesting had caught her eye.

She studied the weird design Dave was scrawling away at, using a brown crayon. A twisting, spiraling, tangled thing... at first she assumed he was just scribbling randomly, but...

"What's that?" she had to ask.

"Hmm? Oh. I was working on this before my computer got turned to cheese," Dave said. "Just trying to see if I remember it well enough to remake it. It's supposed to be a logo for some company that makes internet routers, or security systems, or digital sausage makers or something..."

Penelope tried to follow the line work, with her eyes. Each time she did, her gaze just slipped deeper down the center of the mess, like she'd gotten lost along the way. Honestly, it sort of hurt her brain to try. She couldn't imagine it being stamped out on t-shirts and printed on coffee mugs or anything.

"That's a logo? Aren't logos usually snappy and simple? Or maybe with a picture of an animal, or something..."

"Search me, this is what they wanted. My job was to make it happen, not ask what they were thinking," he said, giving up for now. On a whim, he folded up the menu and stuffed it in his back pocket, with his wallet.

"You know you'll never get paid for that job, right?" Penelope asked, making sure. "They're back on your world. No point working on it anymore."

"I guess. But... I don't know. Can't hurt to keep my skills sharp and stay in practice. I'm going to need to get graphic design work here, now. This kiddie meal menu is the closest thing I have to a portfolio anymore. ...where's your dad? Shouldn't he be here? We need to order our food soon..."

Penelope laughed. "Dad always, always eats the same thing. Fish and chips. That's it. Very predictable, like a watch. A food watch. A watch that tells food instead of time, or something. Anyway, he's probably busy catching up with my uncle. They'll be back soon after having a few laughs, just you wait and see."

"Kegstand Greg! You old son of a bitch!"

"Archie! You old son of a... a..."

Gregory offered a helpless shrug, unable to finish his greeting.

All the same, his old friend reached out for an even manlier hug than Johnny the Maître d' offered. It was enough to nearly pound Gregory's lungs out through his chest.

Three hundred pounds of equal muscle and fat, Archibald Tully carefully had a seat behind his official managerial desk in his tiny little wooden chair. He nearly dwarfed his desk, and certainly seemed far too large for the two tiny shot glasses of whiskey that were ready and waiting.

He promptly downed both glasses, while Gregory had a seat opposite.

"Still booze-free and swear-free, huh, Greg?" he asked. "Fine here! More of both for me..."

Gregory set his backpack aside, settling in. "I wish I could say this was just a social call, Archie, but..."

"But it's business, and it's bad business. I know how it is with you, Greg," Archie said, leaning back in the creakily protesting chair, steepling his fingers. "Word passed up the chain from my boys at the door you had company. Didn't get a good enough look. Kind of wild-eyed, they said... could be... *pfeh*. Lord above knows you made enough enemies over the years, from before and after..."

"They were lying in wait for us outside the Sideways," Gregory explained. "We missed them by a hair. Dumb luck. Fortunately my kid wanted to chow down here, so it was good cover. I don't wanna worry her. She has enough things to worry about already..."

"So you brought your problems to Uncle Archie's doorstep, knowing he wouldn't turn away his beloved niece."

"What, you'd turn me away if I came alone?"

"Of course not. We were running buddies and blood brothers. Close enough to family," Archibald noted. "And actually family when you married my sister. I owe you for hooking the old gang up with legitimate work, for finding this place with the Sideways repeater basement full of fishies. I've got plenty of love for you... but I can only stick my neck out so much. That's just practicality. Only so much neck to stick out."

"That implies you have an idea of who was coming along to put an axe in your neck," Gregory recognized. "Wild-eyed guy in a cheap suit. Any idea who it could be?"

Archibald poured himself another glass. He'd need it.

"I hear rumors," he ruminated. "You know this city drives some folks over the edge. Makes 'em believe in all manner of crazy shi... crazy crap. Like those Exodus freaks, the ones who think the Endless Roads lead back to Earth, or to Heaven, or Nirvana, or whatever..."

"You think one of those was tailing us? What'd we ever do to them?"

"Didn't say that. Just... crazies *like* those crazies. Or... like the Bedlamites."

Gregory eyed his old buddy, suspiciously.

"They went out of business in eighty-two," he reminded Archie. "Hunted down by the Department of Safety. Just a bunch of Picasso worshippers LARPing at being masonic wizards or something..."

"Hunted down, or went into hiding in places nobody'd find 'em. Like... y'know... the Sideways," Archie said. "I'm not saying I have proof. I'm just saying what the street's saying. Lotta people out there going cubist, lately. It's really been flaring up in the last decade. Makes people wonder if the Cult of Bedlam's still active. And... since I know you two love to explore the Sideways —"

"She loves it. Not me."

"The Sideways are sacred ground to Bedlamites, folks figure. And you two disturb that shi... that manure on a regular basis, yeah?" Archie reminded him. "Look. We used to be hard, together. One gang of lost boys from Earth, up against the wild of the city. But that time's over, Greg. We settled down, went straight, got jobs. You married my sister and turned pro at bodyguarding, I nailed down an eatery with the help of the old boys. We can watch your back, put you three up for a few days. But you gotta walk out the door eventually, and if there's some cult after you, there's only so much I can do..."

"A few days will be just fine," Gregory said, grateful despite Archie's trepidation. "Enough time to talk to some contacts, figure out the score. I'll offload our third party with the Department of Orientation—no need to risk the poor idiot's life, or to burden the old gang with all three of us."

"And of course, I insist on paying for your lunch today," Archibald said. "No ifs, ands, or buts. Now, let's go say hello to my favorite niece. I've got her favorite lobster chowder already cooking up in the kitchen!"

By the time Gregory got back to his daughter, it was too late.

They were caught, and there was no escaping. Not from this. Because he'd been so focused on what strange new enemy could be interested in him, that he'd forgotten about the traditional enemy of all who mapped the ins and outs of the City of Angles.

Two men with non-shabby suits were sitting at the table, with a nervous-looking Dave and Penelope. Not the same men who had been following them —but just as dangerous, and twice as unavoidable.

They'd been polite enough to wait for Gregory's return. One flashed his badge, on seeing Penelope's father arrive.

"Officer Cartwright, Department of Safety," he said, with a cat-eating-canary smile. "Gregory Yates, you are under arrest for violation of the Advanced Quarantine Protocols Act of 2006—specifically, venturing into a red-black section of the Sideways. You have the right to remain silent."

DEPARTMENT OF SAFETY OFFICIAL RECORD --
DO NOT REPRODUCE WITHOUT PERMISSION OF AN O-2 LEVEL
SECURITY OFFICER

ARRESTING OFFICER: Security Officer Cartwright (O-3)

DETAINEES:
Gregory Yates (Quarantine Violation)
Penelope Yates [MINOR] (Quarantine Violation)
Dave Smith [UNPROCESSED IMPORT] (Violation waived due
to extenuating circumstances pending cubism
evaluation)

ARREST INTERVIEW FILE 001: PENELOPE YATES
INTERVIEWING OFFICER: Security Officer Jensen (O-4)

[Jensen] Penny, do you know why you're here?

[Penelope] *silent*

[Jensen] Would you like a soda, or maybe some candy?
I can ask the desk sergeant to get you some. Have you
eaten in a while? You were in the Sideways. I can't
imagine you'd find any good things to eat there. Does
your father--

[Penelope] You're not going to make me say my Dad's a
bad Dad. I had a good breakfast. And I was going to
have lunch before you grabbed us, you jerks.

[Jensen] Penny, you're here for your own safety.
You've been in a very, very dangerous place. We're
trying to help you. We're your friends.

[Penelope] I'd have something to say about that, but
Dad doesn't approve of swearing. Instead, I will use
this gesture. *performs an obscene gesture*

[Jensen] We know your Dad's been bringing you to
dangerous places. Sometimes past the known and stable
edge of the city, sometimes to the Sideways,
sometimes to recently imported buildings... all sorts
of dangerous places. Didn't you see the red and black
tape on that Sideways entrance?

[Penelope] It was a yellow-black, not a red-black. We
checked. We didn't break the law!

[Jensen] According to our records, that entrance was
marked red-black, and has been for two weeks. You
would have seen that it was off limits. Witnesses
placed you going in that laundry room and coming out
days later. I'm afraid it doesn't look good, Penny.
Now... why does your Dad insist you have to go to
dangerous places like that?

[Penelope] Don't pin this on him. I'm the one who
makes him go there.

[Jensen] I rather doubt that, Penny--

[Penelope] You call me Penelope. Only Dad gets to
call me Penny, because I'm always gonna be his little
girl. And I'm done talking about this stuff, so I'm
gonna sing the theme to Spongebob Squarepants until
you let me out of this room.

[Jensen] Now, Penny--

[Penelope] WHO LIVES IN A PINEAPPLE UNDER THE SEA?!
SPONGEBOB SQUAREPANTS! ABSORBENT AND YELLOW AND
POROUS IS HE *subject continues to sing until well
after Officer Jensen departs*

ARREST INTERVIEW FILE 002: DAVE SMITH
INTERVIEWING OFFICER: Security Officer Jensen (O-4)

[Dave] Finally. Listen, I'd like to lodge a
complaint. I've done nothing wrong, and--

[Jensen] We know. We've been observing you long
enough to make an initial determination that you are
not experiencing cubism. So, you're free to go.

[Dave] Oh. Well. That's very understanding of you.

[Jensen] I've asked the Department of Orientation to
send over a bus for you. Welcome to the city. They'll
take care of your temporary housing and training
sessions, to help you get acclimated. I take it the
Yates have informed you of where you are?

[Dave] Yes, and in fact, where exactly are--

[Jensen] Someone will be by shortly to show you to
your ride, and your things will be returned to you.
Apologies for the inconvenience.

[Dave] But what about Penelope and Gregory?

interview ends

ARREST INTERVIEW FILE 003: GREGORY YATES
INTERVIEWING OFFICER: Security Officer Cartwright (O-
3)

[Cartwright] Good to see you looking healthy,
Gregory. How have you been lately?

[Gregory] *silent*

[Cartwright] Frankly, it's amazing to see you looking
healthy. You've been spending a lot of time in the
Sideways over the last few years, with your daughter.
How old is she now? Thirteen? Fourteen?

[Gregory] *silent*

[Cartwright] Bit of a dangerous hobby to drag your
own child along on, isn't it? Exploring in forbidden
places. But... I guess that's par for the course for

you, isn't it, Gregory? Even after your gang banger days are done, you find new ways to cause problems.

[Gregory] *silent*

[Cartwright] I've been following your file for some time now, waiting for a good chance to catch you where you're not supposed to be. We've been tightening up quarantine qualifications for years, just to keep people like you from throwing your lives away stupidly. Sooner or later, we'll have every dark corner under lock and key before you can get there. Then what'll you do with your life, I wonder?

[Gregory] *silent*

[Cartwright] You know, you're something of a legend around the Department. Nobody's ever been able to nail you down for anything. You play it safe, lately. Untouchable. Personally? I'd love to send you up for murder. Shame all the evidence is tucked away deep under the city, isn't it.

[Gregory] *silent*

[Cartwright] I bet even if I did find some way to drag up those thirteen-year-old charges, the jury would pull it down to manslaughter. After all, your wife DID consent to join you on that little venture into the Sideways. Brilliant mapper, by the way; her data's still quite pricey on the market. A lot of folks miss her. Do you?

[Gregory] *silent*

[Cartwright] You were lost for a full year down there, according to the records. Went down with a wife, come back without one. Got a baby girl out of the deal though. Now, that's just the public record on the subject; what I'm curious about is--

[Gregory] Susan's Law.

[Cartwright] Excuse me?

[Gregory] Violation of quarantine protocols is acceptable in the event that another's life is in immediate danger. Put into effect as a samaritan law, when Susan Mathers lost control of her baby stroller and it rolled through a red-black door to the Sideways. The court accepted that her breaking of quarantine was acceptable as it resulted in the rescue of another human being, with the caveat that the Department of Safety and City Council was not to be held legally responsible for any risks taken in the process.

[Cartwright] Yes, I am familiar with the law. Being an officer of it.

[Gregory] You can't hold me or my daughter. We were simply following the letter of that law when we went into the Sideways to rescue someone.

[Cartwright] I'm sorry, who exactly...?

[Gregory] Dave Smith. He's in the next room, isn't he?

[Cartwright] Let me see if I'm interpreting you correctly. Stop me if I'm getting it wrong, please.

[Gregory] Will do.

[Cartwright] You're saying that your purpose behind breaking quarantine in the first place... was to save the life of one Dave Smith.

[Gregory] Correct.

[Cartwright] A young man who you never met before now, and who was apparently LIVING in the Sideways for some time without realizing it. Someone you couldn't have possibly known was in need of rescue.

[Gregory] The end result is the same. We saved his life. Susan's Law says nothing about intent.

[Cartwright] I'm... fairly certain the intent is implied--

[Gregory] And, if you insist on claiming I'm abusing my daughter, I'm going to add "following my child into the Sideways to save her as well" on top. The media will love it, believe me. I'll also point out that the entrance was in no way, shape or form a red-black.

[Cartwright] I have the records right here, Gregory. It's a red-black. I sent an officer down there just to verify, and confirmed the color of the tape outline.

[Gregory] I'd love to see a lab analyze that tape, to figure out how fresh the glue is. But you're missing my overall point. If you really want to paint me with a nasty brush, well, two can play that game. I have to wonder what your dirty laundry is like. And you know I have the connections to dig it up, don't you? Since you're such an expert on me. How far do you want to drag this, Mr. Officer? Are you so convinced of your case -- and your own standing -- that you want to play ball with me? Knowing exactly how far I'll go for my daughter's sake?

[Cartwright] *silent*

[Gregory] So, Susan's Law. We walk. Today. Now, I'm going to call my attorney, who will back up everything I just said. If you'd like to waste everybody's time and taxpayer dollars, we can sit here and stare at each other until he repeats my claim, word for word -- in front of a Judicial Officer if need be. Or, we can leave now and save you a lot of paperwork. How spiteful are you, I'm wondering?

interview ends at request of Officer Cartwright (O-3)

The first thing Penelope did when she rejoined her father was jump up, grab onto him, and not let go.

All three of them were being released, pending further review of the charges. Gregory was short on the details, and Penelope didn't question it; clearly he'd had a rough day, a rough COUPLE of days. and all that mattered was that they were free now.

They stood at the steps of the local Department of Safety offices, which were half a block away from another local set of Department of Safety offices, thanks to the city's tendency to mock the carefully laid plans of men. All that was left was to wait for the bus which would whisk Dave off to his new life.

"I want you to call after you get settled in," Penelope insisted.

"Okay."

"And don't let them scare you. The city's not as bad as some folks in Orientation claim. It's not actively trying to kill people or anything!"

"Okay."

"Once you get a new address let me know and I'll bring a housewarming gift."

"Okay."

"I'm sure you can find work. Lots of new businesses pop up all the time in the city. They probably need logos and things and people to draw them!"

"Why do you care so much what happens to me?"

Which floored Penelope's endless stream of enthusiasm. Or put it on pause, at least.

"I don't mean to be rude, just... I still don't get it," Dave said, hands in the pockets of his pajamas (still the only clothes he owned). "You didn't know me a few days ago. I'm not a very personable person, I know that much. Your dad hates my guts..."

(Gregory cleared his throat. "I would define it as pragmatic indifference, actually," he said in his defense.)

"...so why do I matter to you so much that you want to stay in contact and make sure I'm doing well?"

Now, Penelope had to pause her rambling thoughts to really think. And answered with a question.

"Do you want to stay in contact?" she asked. "I mean, wouldn't you like a friend?"

She was just a kid. She wasn't related to him. There was no connection there, beyond the strange confluence of circumstances that brought them together in the first place. Dave couldn't think of any sound logical reason why he should care one way or another. If anything, life would be much less complicated without someone around who routinely went spelunking in the darkest corners of Hell. He would be better off just moving on without dealing with any of this, like he always did when things felt uncertain.

"I guess I wouldn't mind having a friend," he answered, instead.

The Department of Orientation occupied a slightly substandard motel, a dozen blocks away from the central Zag of the city.

Dave barely paid attention as his Orientation Officer explained how the government's temporary hostel worked. What the curfew rules were, why they didn't want new imports wandering off until they had completed the seminar, when meals would be served and so on. He soaked it all in for later consideration without really considering any of it.

Hours later (even if it felt like minutes) and Dave was sitting on a bed in a semi-lousy motel room which would be his home, until they kicked him out into the wider world of the city to sink or swim.

Not really his home. His home was gone. His apartment, his city, his world, his job, his family, everything that was his. He had a phone, an empty wallet, and a ring of keys to his name. Somewhere along the way he'd even lost the kiddie menu he'd scribbled a crayon drawing on.

Alone in a horrifying new place where insanity was infectious, he could accidentally step through the wrong doorway and be lost forever, and nothing he'd taken for granted would ever be true again.

Briefly, very briefly, the pang of panic surfaced.

He thought he had problems before, back in that world. Mother, gone. All his art ambitions collapsing around him because he just didn't have the talent. Struggling to keep grades up. Living from contractor paycheck to contractor paycheck, alone in a city where he knew nobody, where he was surrounded at all times but lonely as hell...

All of that, he'd trade all of this for all of that in a heartbeat. Those were first world problems compared to being stuck in the City of Angles. And unflappable Dave Smith was becoming flapped very rapidly, sitting alone in the motel room, listening to the air conditioning, waiting for taskmasters to pour dire warnings on his head for several days about all the ways he could die.

Anxiety attacks were a thing of the past. He just didn't bother with them anymore. Until now.

But just as he felt that rising swell, that initial sense of complete unease... something green caught the corner of his eye. Something which wasn't there a second ago.

Two cardboard boxes, decorated with smiles and good cheer. Green, and full of tiny brown cookies with a chocolatey, minty taste. Girl Scout Thin Mints.

A note had been left on top of the boxes.

thank you, i feel better now.

The instructors who were there to help Dave get used to how things worked in the City of Angles would've likely recommended he run away immediately, notify a Department of Safety official, and have the boxes of cookies destroyed with flamethrowers to prevent any possible chance of cubist infection from having the slightest inkling of a notion of possibly taking place.

Instead he ate the delicious cookies, and felt tremendously better about his place in things.

The report had been filed. There wasn't anything more to be said on the subject; the case just wasn't airtight enough to bother the judicial system with it. He'd get back to it later, would find other charges, would make it stick in the long run. Officer Cartwright always got his man, in the end. So why say any more than that?

Apparently someone did have more to say about it, which is why Cartwright (an O-3) had been called before the primary Security Officer himself, the O-1, holder of the Department of Safety seat on the City Council. A man that Cartwright had never met before, being a full two ranks over his pay grade.

Being the first visit Cartwright had made to Officer Seth Dougal's office, he didn't know if it was good or bad that Dougal had called him in after working hours. He'd heard that Dougal worked late and in isolation, without a secretary or deputy assistant of any sort. Even heard that Dougal never actually *slept*, which was silly.

At least the office was nice. Carpeting was fresh, desk was mahogany, floor-to-ceiling windows showed a nice expanse of the city. The abstract art hanging on the wall behind Seth Dougal's desk was a bit sketchy, given the natural aversion most in the city had to anything resembling a cubism, but surely someone that high up on the food chain could be afforded a few eccentricities.

As for Dougal himself...

A serene-looking fellow. Dark skinned with a contrastingly white suit that cost more than Cartwright's weekly paycheck. Nice manicure. Green power tie. Every inch a sensible and well-grounded fellow.

"I understand you're the one who brought in the quarantine violator today," Officer Dougal opened with, while sorting through the papers on his desk.

"Yes, sir. And I assure you, I'm not done with this Gregory Yates character," Cartwright insisted. "He's a menace to public safety, and always has been. Since the anonymous witnesses who reported the incident have, ah, vanished, and certain facts regarding the accuracy of our record keeping on red-blacks have come to light—"

"There's no sense chasing after some young fool who's become an old fool, Cartwright," his superior declared, pushing the papers aside for now, and getting up from his seat. "What's done is done. The ones who violated the sanctity of the Sideways slipped our grasp, but in the end we've learned a great deal. It's time to shift our priorities..."

From his coat pocket... Seth Dougal withdrew a small piece of waxy paper. A children's menu. He unfolded it carefully, and set it on the desk.

Cartwright squinted at it, unsure as to why some crayon scribblings were even slightly relevant to the Yates case. It looked like nothing important to him.

"I don't expect you to recognize the importance of this," Dougal stated. "Few do. But when I tell you this is the single most important piece of evidence to emerge from today's fiasco, I trust you to believe me. We stumbled across it completely by accident, but that's how it goes, doesn't it? It's like the city. One thing connects to something completely different, which connects to something far stranger indeed..."

"It's a crayon drawing, sir. What could that possibly have to do with—"

"This... Dave Smith, yes? An import. Who was *living* in the Sideways, for who knows how long. He was close to the core without realizing it, in tune with it. He even managed to lure one of her beloved children away from that dark place... that's why I sent two of my agents to follow them. A task they failed at completely, but... perhaps that was for the best. We need to watch him carefully. Keep our distance, as the map he's making is not yet complete, but watch him all the same."

"Sir, what are you talking about? What agents? And, well... he seems like a complete nobody. The real target should be Yates. That man is—"

"Tangential," Seth Dougal stated, folding his arms. "Related, connected in strange ways, but... no. *This* is the key. Speaking of which, didn't you notice the discrepancy in his arrest report? The contents of his pockets...?"

"A smart phone, a placemat, a wallet, and a ring with three keys on it. So what?"

"Not the report. The photos of the objects," Seth said... reaching into his coat for the second piece of evidence he'd stolen.

A photograph of four keys on a ring. Or maybe three. Or maybe four...

Cartwright was an experienced officer in the Department of Safety. After years of sealing off dangerous parts of the city, you got a sense of impending cubism, of approaching Picassos. The hairs standing up on the back of your neck, bits of your brain starting to race. He was seeing an impossible thing, a static photograph which was in flux between two images, and that likely meant...

"I'll... I'll contact a quarantine team immediately and send them to his Orientation Center!" Cartwright declared. "We'll seal it off and destroy the object immediately and determine if the boy is corrupted—"

"You'll do no such thing. I just told you, we need the boy to finish his work, unhindered. Besides, you no longer have the authorization to commandeer departmental resources in any form whatsoever," Seth Dougal declared... extending a hand towards the other man. Smiling. "You tendered your resignation five minutes from now. I could have use of your unusually personal knowledge about the Yates case, and besides, you've seen far too much already to remain in the dark. It's time for you to join a new organization, Cartwright... and your orientation begins tonight."

A blur. Snap focus. Things coming apart while still being together.

Cartwright tried to back away, instinctively, but he wasn't moving in Euclidean space anymore. He was moving towards Dougal... through him, phasing, shifting. Past the desk, past the man.

Through the abstract art on the wall and into the Sideways.

Where he was not alone.

She smiled at him with six million mouths, each with six million teeth. And in the face of Bedlam, Cartwright no longer remembered how to scream.

//end

Buildings next to buildings, askew or aligned. Buildings sometimes intersecting buildings, for that matter. Walk down a hallway, end up in a ballroom, double glass doors to a subway station, third exit on the left goes to a lending library. It's inadvisable to ask if they use the dewey decimal system.

There's no rhyme or reason to any of it—we've got streets which lead to dead ends, roads which criss-cross and loop back around, highways which go nowhere. Literally nowhere, as in "anybody going down that road is not coming back." This is not a good place to wander off unless you like wandering off forever...

Nobody knows where the city came from. Nobody knows how we got here. Nobody knows why any of this is happening. But it's happening. The city exists. We are here now. It's growing every day, and bringing new people with it.

We live a life amidst the twisted yet familiar.

If we're going to survive this, if we're going to stay alive and thrive, we need to learn to live in the City of Angles.

...here's an angle to consider...

Dave Smith is an ordinary joe, one who epitomizes the word "ordinary." Ordinary in every way, shape and form, except for the critically important ways in which he is not. His entire apartment was juxtaposed into the city without him realizing it—and then promptly destroyed by a wandering Picasso, a person fallen to chaos.

He's made friends along the way, including the young mapper Penelope Yates... but being a newly arrived refugee, he has a series of emotional hoops to jump through before he can take his place in the city. Now he's on his own, running the gauntlet of the Department of Orientation...

//002: Orientation Express

Sunlight streamed in through the cheap plastic blinds, illuminating a room which could at best be called shabby.

That alone wasn't enough to wake up Dave Smith. It never had been; he'd been using an alarm clock since he was a kid, having to get up before the crack of dawn to make the school bus. If he had his druthers, he'd sleep in until afternoon. Not that he was naturally narcoleptic or anything, he just rarely had anything compelling enough in his life to wake up for.

Of course, that was back on the Earth he knew. One he'd never be going back to, now that he'd landed in the City of Angles.

This wasn't his home. This wasn't his bed, or his window blinds, or his pillow. He was all alone without a penny to his name in a world which had been actively trying to kill him. That should have been enough of a compelling reason not to sleep in... but on the other hand, sleeping in meant dreaming away this nightmare, which was enough of an upside to stay snoozing until the alarm clock buzzed.

His hand fumbled for the clock, knocking an empty carton of previously delicious cookies aside in the process.

Yawn, sit on edge of bed, stretch. Scratch at his butt through the pajama bottoms he'd worn ever since departing the smoking ruins of his life. Hopefully the motel had a laundry service.

Shower, dry off, brush teeth using the tiny samples of nasty green toothpaste.

Slippers had been provided by the door, along with a note. *Please See Front Desk to Complete Registration, and Welcome!!* With two exclamation marks.

He was here to become oriented, apparently. People cared about his well-being and wanted to make sure he was ready to join the vibrant society of the city. All he had to do in return was sleep and wake and listen to what they had to say several times in a row. Dave could manage that. He'd been coasting long enough that coasting through this weirdness was achievable. Ride it out, and hope for the best.

The analog wall clock made of stainless steel was ticking loudly enough to be heard over the receptionist's tinny little radio, which was playing some sort of smooth jazz ear pap suitable for any office.

"Name?" she repeated, to catch his attention away from the retro-style timepiece.

"Dave. Dave Smith," he added.

The woman with the beehive hairdo wrinkled her nose. Between that and the horn-rimmed glasses, she seemed to fit in nicely with the ridiculously outdated motif of the motel, at least.

"*Full* name, please," she clarified.

"...Dave Danger Smith."

She had been glaring at him before, but that glare now sharpened and flattened out simultaneously.

"I had a very eccentric mother," he explained. "I'm actually not dangerous. I'm the least dangerous person you've ever known and I avoid danger like it was... um... danger."

With a sigh, she jotted down his name, trying very hard not to sketch in quotation marks around his middle name.

"Full names of your immediate family members?"

"Richard Allen Smith."

The receptionist allowed another exasperated pause, to egg him on.

"That's it," he stated. "My mother died some time ago. It's just my father, no brothers or sisters."

"Mother's full name, please," she said. "This is for the official genealogical cross index records. I need both of them."

"Oh. Ah, Annabell Valentine Smith. Originally Annabell Marie Valentine, if that helps. Neither of them are over here, though..."

The receptionist kept her eyes down as she wrote, which was something of a relief. Those sharp looks had been gradually flaying off Dave's flesh.

"The Department of Orientation will make sure of that," she said. "The records have only been digital for the last few years, and honestly those idiots can barely keep track of the letters of the alphabet much less the entire population of the city, but... if any relatives are here, we'll let you know. Probably. ...any food allergies?"

"No."

"Any medication requirements?"

"No."

"Any psychological issues so far? We do have a more advanced track for people who are unable to cope. Are you unable to cope?"

"No...?"

"Anything even remotely interesting about you that I should be writing down here?" she asked, cutting to the chase.

"I... ah... no, probably not," Dave admitted. "I'm not very interesting. People often tell me so."

"Previous occupation?"

"Graphic designer. Artist. Um, freelance. I didn't really have any steady work, except for this one contract which—"

"So, commercial artist," she said, ticking off a box. "That it? Any other special skills?"

Dave considered this one.

"Some people say I can keep a level head in a crisis," he suggested. "Not that you can earn a living doing that. I mean, nobody pays you to not react to things. ...nobody pays you to do that in this city, right? Or is there a burgeoning non-reaction industry out there?"

Glad to be done with it, the receptionist slammed the bottom of the form with a rubber ink stamp, and handed it over along with a laminated card and freshly printed schedule.

"That'll get you past the Department of Safety officials at the gate, assuming they show up for work today," she said. "Not that we recommend leaving the motel compound until your orientation is complete. The Department of Orientation assumes no responsibility for any harm or hazard encountered beyond the compound. New clothes will be provided for you tonight and the Burger Buffet Bonanza™ adjacent to the motel is free if you present your laminate. This orientation course is optional and you're free to leave any time you like, although personally I'd suggest you stay put, shut up, and listen to what the instructors tell you. Also, job placement services will only be available to those who complete the course."

His head nodded the whole way through, like a bobblehead in a 1.3 Richter scale earthquake.

He had no intention of leaving before they made him leave, of course. What little he'd seen of the city proved that stepping past a certain line was a bad idea—and learning where that line existed was a good idea.

While Dave had taken corporate courses to learn about illustration software and such, those typically happened in swank hotels or business learning annexes. There would be preprinted name tags, comfortable chairs, coffee and bagels, and sometimes even chocolate chip cookies on Tuesdays. The atmosphere was professional and the surroundings modern.

The Seaside Sandy Shores Motel was neither professional nor modern. Nor even seaside.

The city had deemed fit to yank some tacky motor lodge up by the roots from a Mid-Atlantic tourist trap, and likely yanked it up during the 1960s. The whole thing was painted varying shades of teal and pink, with plaster seashell designs over every door. Which did not fit at all when it sat like a low-lying pile of kitsch amidst towering brick structures taken from an inner city slum, on all sides. The roar of traffic was no substitute for the roar of the sea.

With no real reason for people to WANT to rent rooms here, it had been taken over by the Department of Orientation to use as a halfway house for people like Dave. He'd noticed a few others in his situation, huddled in their rooms or wandering the outdoor terraces aimlessly. He supposed being shaken by the whole experience of being yanked into this world was completely understandable. The tacky and inappropriate surroundings did little to comfort them.

On the plus side, there was a swimming pool. Few corporate learning annexes had swimming pools, in Dave's experience. That meant he could enjoy his free Burger Buffet Bonanza™ Breakfast Burrito while sitting in a plastic reclining chair, and enjoying the reflection of sunlight on the rippling surface.

Being one of the few refugees who was apparently willing to go enjoy the poolside experience instead of curl up in a ball and whimper made him stand out, however. Which meant he was immediately approachable by those who were waiting for someone to make the first move.

He was just finishing up his breakfast burrito when his mentor and wizened sage for the week wandered up.

The guy wore a very tacky white suit straight out of the 80s, with a white tie and a pastel flower print shirt. Popped collar, of course, and a pair of snazzy sunglasses hanging from the neckline. The smell of the grease holding his styled coif in place was nearly as strong as the smell of the burrito Dave was munching. The retro look meant he fit in perfectly with his surroundings, however, which meant maybe he wasn't as badly dressed as he might've been elsewhere.

Unlike Dave, he was in fact wearing a name tag to this training seminar. It read "Hello, My Name Is (Hollister) And I Am Here To Help!!" which meant whoever slapped two exclamation marks on Dave's welcome note probably designed these, too.

"Hey hey!" the man greeted. "Dave Smith, right? Hollister Avenue, Orientation Officer. I'm your camp counselor, as it were. Fancy seeing you out here so early! Y'know in the years I've been in this gig, I've never seen someone come poolside first thing in the morning...? Usually they sit in their rooms until their session's up..."

"I was hungry," Dave suggested. Holding up the burrito for emphasis. "And the weather's not bad. Sooo... seemed to make sense. That's all."

"You know, this is a fabu idea, just fabu," Hollister said. "Good thinking, Dave. You're a sharp cookie. —funny, people don't think of cookies as sharp, so why do they say sharp cookie? One of life's many mysteries, Dave, one of life's many mysteries. But! You know? Let's go with this. Hang on, wait right here. I'll be back in a few."

And then he was gone, scampering off across the empty parking lot and towards the motel rooms.

For lack of another option, Dave finished up his greasy tube of unidentifiable foodstuff and then... waited. Because the strange man had told him to wait, and he seemed like he was in charge.

Minutes later, and Dave was no longer alone at poolside. Hollister had dragged along three more refugees to meet him.

He only had a brief moment to get first impressions, as the energetic man in the suit quickly rearranged the plastic furniture into a rough circle, encouraging everyone to sit down.

The largest of the trio was what the media would probably pointedly not specifically refer to as a Scary Black Man, even while reporting on whatever alleged crime spree he had been on. He had all the right trimmings, with the baggy clothes and tank top showing off impressive musculature, and a ball cap which he was adjusting to keep the sun out of his eyes. But the eyes, well... they were just as uneasy and nervous as anyone's in this place. There was nothing actually scary about him; what he was going through was plenty scary to himself, it seemed.

Next was a stick-thin blonde with clothes which were very possibly stylish, but Dave (who typically spent all day in his pajamas) knew absolutely nothing about style. To him, they just looked colorfully horrible. She had an equally colorful and horrible purse with her, which contained one horrible little dog— which Dave at first assumed was a plush doll, until it snapped an angry bark at him. Its owner cast an equally disparaging look at Dave, to solidify their mutual pact of instant dislike.

And then there was the totally ordinary woman in totally ordinary clothes who was completely in over her head. She stayed near the back, and didn't move until Hollister physically guided her over to one of the cheap poolside chairs. She had a look about her which said that whatever the universe was doing to her at the moment, she was patiently hoping it would stop soon.

"Okay, so, that's Jayden, Brittany, and Sarah," the guidance counselor identified, in order. "And this is Dave. Together, you're Group Four. And you know me, I'm your good buddy Hollister. Welcome to Orientation! Let's hear it for Group Four, people!"

Nobody cheered. So, Hollister coughed politely, and moved on.

"For the next few days I'll be teaching you fine folks all about the City of Angles," he said. "That's ANGLES, not ANGELS. Common rookie mistake, but you, you're not common rookies, right? When we're done you'll be rip roarin' ready to go and start your new lives! Like Dave here. Dave came right out of his room and decided to enjoy the pool, isn't that right, Dave? It was all his idea that we hold our first session out here, instead of that musty conference room. Good thinking, Dave! Let's hear it for Dave!"

He tried to start the applause himself. Nobody clapped. So, Hollister coughed politely, and moved on.

"Now, I know what you're all thinking," he said, despite being in fact completely wrong about that. "You're thinking, this Hollister guy, he seems like he's got his act together. What's he doing in a dead-end job like being an Orientation Officer? Well, I'll tell you. I'm a *people person*. I actually like this job. I like to get people things they want, things they need. Hook-up Hollister, that's what my friends call me—and I've got a LOT of friends. Like you! I'm here for *you*, to make sure you're ready to go, to make sure you're happy. Best way to do that is to get to know you, REALLY know you, as people. So we're going to start out not by cracking open one of those boring three-ring binders and getting right into the lessons, like the Department wants. We're gonna get to know *you*. —Jayden? You want to start?"

Jayden blinked in surprise, taken out of his thoughts by the sound of his name.

"Huh?" the young not-actually-a-gangsta replied.

"Let's get to know you, Jayden," Hollister repeated, leaning forward into Jayden's personal space to show how much he cared. "Tell us about yourself. Who you are, where you're from, what you want out of this city."

"Oh. Well... if I gotta. Name's Jayden," he said, despite being called by name three times already. "I'm... be honest here, may as well be given the situation I'm stuck in, I'm just some kid from Sacramento. —I'm not a kid, I mean, I'm twenty-one, got the card to prove. Raised by my aunt until she went, then back to my moms. Learned tough after that. Uh, but I'm not really lookin' for any trouble or... lookin' for anything. Nothin' specific. A job, I guess. They get you a job if you sit through this thing, right?"

"That's the plan, my man," Hollister promised. "I mean, they'll try. Things can be tricky. But you? I think you'll go places. I barely know you but I've got a good feeling, you know? Right here. Gets me right here."

"That's your stomach," Jayden pointed out.

"Here," Hollister corrected, pounding on his chest over his heart. "Sorry. I missed breakfast. So, how did you get to the city, Jayden?"

"I was just down by the corner store with my boys, you know, just hanging out," he said. "Summer, you know? No school, nothin' to do. Anyway, went in to get somethin' to eat, and I was busy payin' for it when BAM! everything went weird an' the whole store got moved to this crazy-ass city. Took me and the poor old bastard who runs the place with it. ...where's he now? Mr. Fong. He doin' okay? I was figuring I'd meet up with him when they said new folks go to Orientation, but..."

Now, Hollister was the one looking uneasy. "Ah... well... some adapt better than others," he explained. "I saw his file when I was reading up on you folks, and... Mr. Fong, it's cool, it's cool, he's getting the treatment he needs. He'll be able to accept the transition eventually, don't you worry. The Department of Resources may even let him work in his store again! He's like family to you, huh?"

"Naw, I just know him, s'all," Jayden said, with a rolling shrug. "Doubt I got any family here. And if they're right, and there's no way back... well... damn. There's no way back, right?"

"I really hate to bear bad news, but no way back, that's right, correctamundo," Hollister replied. "It's harsh to say, I know. But people have been looking for decades, and nobody's found a way back to Earth yet. That's why we've got Orientation, so you can learn to embrace your new lives—"

"This is utterly ridiculous."

The voice of dissent coming from the leggy blonde with the purse poodle. Which yipped twice, in agreement.

"Assuming I haven't gone completely insane and am imagining all of this," she suggested, "I'm not the slightest bit interested in your ridiculous summer camp. I don't need adult career counseling, I HAVE a career. I'm a star! ...how is it none of you have recognized me yet?"

She glared around at the group, getting only blank looks in return.

"Hello? Brittany Geneva?" she introduced. "Winner of America's Top Voice, season three? Beat out all eleven other survivors in Lost Without a Passport: Brazil? Star of my own reality show, Brittany's All That? ...come on! I'm famous! Don't you people watch television?"

"Can't afford cable," Jayden offered.

"I mostly watch Netflix," Dave said, with a shrug.

"Um," Sarah the totally normal person offered, feeling she had to say something but not really up for saying anything.

"I don't believe this. I'm trapped in some insane-o world with the only three people who've got zero cultural taste," the TV starlet exclaimed, rolling her eyes. "Well, fine! I don't need you three. What I need is contacts. Media contacts. You, Hollister, you say you have friends in high places?"

The counselor in the white suit did his best not to look cornered. "*High* places, well, to an extent. I mean, it depends on how you define 'high.' If there's an altitude scale vis-à-vis social importance and power—"

"And you DO have television in this city, yes?" she continued. "So, call up some television executive and tell them Brittany Geneva wants—no, *insists*— on a meeting. They'll know me. I'm famous. I can get out of this ridiculous motel and back on the air where I belong! —or better yet, have them send a camera down here! Four mismatched refugees arriving at a new city, living in a kookily designed building? That has reality television written ALL over it!"

Unused to being pressured by the wide-eyed new arrivals, Hollister did his best to play it cool. "Television, media, yeah, I think I know some guys who know some guys," he suggested. "I mean, I *think* I do. At the very least I can make some calls and see about—"

"Good, you do that, whatever," Brittany stated—getting to her feet. "Meanwhile, I'm going back to my room to watch what passes for TV in this backwater world. And if you're really so good at getting people what they want, you can get some gourmet dog food for Miss Mittens here! She's starving."

The dog got off a few more agitated barks, before her owner turned on a heel and stormed off in a huff.

Hollister waited until Brittany's motel room door slammed shut behind her before continuing.

"Sooo... Dave and Sarah," he continued, eager to get the meet-and-greet back on track. "Let's get to know you. Which one of you wants to go first?"

Neither of them wanted to go first.

"Sarah, then," their team leader picked at random. "From your file, it says you're from Georgia...?"

With attention firmly on her... the middle aged woman withered.

"I... I want to go home," she mumbled. "Please. I have a family, I have children. They need me..."

This, Hollister was more used to working with. He reached over, put a hand on her shoulder. Adopted his most comforting voice.

"I know this is hard to accept, Sarah," he said, "But you're here, now. There's no going back. But I promise you, I swear to you, your family will be fine. You don't need to worry. Right now... what you have to focus on is your own life. It's a new day, a new start! What you do with it is entirely up to you. ...ah, just, it can't involve going back."

"But, but my husband, my children..."

"You've got a loving husband and good kids. I read your file. They're going to be fine—and so are you. You're a strong woman, Sarah. Wife of a pastor, pillar of her community, supporter of charities and champion of the homeless, yes...?" he said. "Some people, when they come to the City, they're complete unknowns. But your works echoed even here! We've got reports from people who came to this city before you that know who you are. Do you remember Yvonne?"

The name brought her out of her momentary despair. Mostly because it was a point of confusion.

"Yvonne? Here? Are you sure? I just saw her a month ago," Sarah said. "We've been working at the city shelter together for the last year. She was getting back on track after losing her house..."

"I know, and her orientation records had your name in them as a possible point of contact," Hollister said, with a grin. "See? You're not totally alone here. Listen, she's working out in the Suburbs at the mo', but I'll put in a call and see if she can spare some time to visit. Okay?"

Still unsure... Sarah offered a tentative little nod. Which Hollister took to be a gleeful nod of assent.

"That's the spirit!" he said, removing his hand from her shoulder (so he could offer a thumbs up). "Right. Okay. I think we've all got some culture shock, and really, that's totally reasonable. Personally, I think the standard orientation course throws you into the deep end too soon, you know? Here's an idea—let's break for the day. I've got binders you can bring back to your rooms and study at your leisure. We can pick up tomorrow, nice and fresh. And today? Just focus on resting, relaxing, getting used to things. You need anything, anything at all, I'm staying in room 3F. Just down the hall from Sarah's room. Okay? Okay. I'll drop by with your binders in a bit. And hey— I'll find you all swimsuits, 'k? Enjoy the pool."

He started shaking hands, and offering general words of comfort and support, before the group disbanded to wander off to their rooms.

Except for Dave. Who was still sitting poolside, having been completely overlooked in the meet-'n-greet process.

Which was fine, really. He wasn't particularly memorable, and he knew it.

GETTING TO KNOW YOUR GOVERNMENT!!

The unusual nature of the City of Angles means a more unusual approach to government. Like the old world America, we are a democracy -- however, our branches of government differ.

- **THE DEPARTMENT OF ORIENTATION!!**
    - Immigration: Acclimation, Housing (if available), Job Placement (if available)
    - Growth: Geneological Studies, Census Taking, Sociological Data
    - Health: Psychological Services, Welfare & Insurance Systems

- **THE DEPARTMENT OF RESOURCES!!**
  - Economics: Financial management, fiscal policy
  - Acquisitions: Annexation & redistribution of newly arrived resources
  - Public Works: Power, Water, Communications
- **THE DEPARTMENT OF SAFETY!!**
  - Police: Law Enforcement
  - Justice: Courts, Legal Development
  - Security: Quarantine, Mapping
- Assorted cross-departmental task forces (Disease Control, First Action Response Team, etc.)

Representatives from the City, Suburbs, and Outlands are elected bi-annually to join the Mayor's City Council and manage these three departments. Mayoral elections are held quad-annually--

knock knock.

Dave Smith looked up from his three-ring binder, to notice that it had gotten dark outside. Also, that he had a guest.

On opening the door he found Jayden holding up a six-pack of beer, from an unrecognizable brewery. Probably some local brand.

"Hollister got this for me. Probably wasn't supposed to, but the guy's damn eager to keep us happy," Jayden explained, letting himself in. "I was gonna get drunk in my room but figured, hell, what's the point in that? May as well share. I doubt Brittany'd give me a second look and Sarah's still a bit squirrelly, sooo... that leaves you."

While not a particularly big drinker, Dave accepted a can tossed his way. After all, what else was there to do? He'd already watched some of this world's television, already got his phone updated to work with local networks, and already read most of the binder. Probably more than the others had accomplished, since Dave had accepted his fate by now. That meant a drink to celebrate wasn't out of the question.

On tasting the foul brew, he almost changed his mind. His new drinking buddy made a similar scrunched-up face of distaste.

"Either Hollister got the cheap stuff, or this is actually the best the City can produce," Jayden said. "Ugh. Still, beer's beer, right?"

"I'm not sure this legally can be classified as beer," Dave suggested. "I hope there's something like the FDA here. I'm not done with my book, but I haven't read about one yet..."

"You actually reading that thing?" Jayden asked, settling into a guest chair, while Dave sat at the edge of his bed.

"Why not? Beats not knowing how things work," Dave said. "Whoever wrote this thing was way too fond of Powerpoint, though. And Comic Sans MS. My inner designer is freaking out at all those adorably rounded corners..."

"Don't seem like you're freaking much."

"I don't really freak out externally," Dave explained. "It's a long story."

"Me, I'm freakin' pretty hardcore," Jayden admitted. "Gettin' antsy. I may just run for it, comes to that..."

Dave finished off the last of his beer and opted not to reach for another. "I thought you wanted a job?" he asked, setting the empty aside.

"Assumin' they give me one. Assumin' they don't ship my ass off campus and into foster care..."

"I don't follow."

Jayden pulled off his hat, swiping some sweat off his shaved scalp.

"My I.D.'s a fake," he said. "Says I'm twenty-one just so I can buy booze. I'm still in high school, man. Big for my age, but I'm still in school. Those search and rescue guys who hauled me and Mr. Fong outta there, they just took a glance at it and sent me along, but... well. What's that binder of yours say about refugee kids?"

Dave's mind flipped back a few dozen pages, to a section on immigration processing.

"They seem to be... relatively on the ball when it comes to adults. Maybe their foster care system's not so bad," he offered. "I mean, most people end up here without any relatives or friends. They have to have some way of putting kids in a safe environment—"

"I ain't a kid and I don't wanna be treated like one," Jayden said, waggling a beer can at Dave. "If I'm here on my own, if I don't got family, then... you know what? Fine. I'll go it alone if I gotta and call it a blessin' in disguise. I came from a goddamn war zone of a hood and I'm lucky to be alive right now. City of Angles is my fresh start. They get me somewhere to live and a job and I just keep pretending I'm an adult, I work hard, and maybe I can get somewhere better than I was, you feel me?"

"I feel you," Dave said, with a nod. "Well. I mean, I'm not *feeling* you, as in physically feeling you or anything, I mean..."

"But I get sent to some greedy family lookin' for a handout for takin' care of a 'fugee brat, maybe that don't happen. Maybe I just end up back on the streets.

Here, I got a locked-in chance. Out there, chances could drop. I'll go with the devil I know. —you won't snitch on me, right?"

Dave shrugged it off. He couldn't think of a reason to report this to the authorities; not out of some manly bond or loyalty, but just because it wasn't his business. Still, an idea tickled the back of his brain.

"You haven't finished high school, then?" he asked. "Could be rough out there. And no family to back you up..."

"That's just how it's gotta be, right?" Jayden said. "I'm not gonna call some strangers family. So... it's all on me. Live or die, sink or swim, it's all on me. ...not sayin' I'm thrilled about it, or that it'll be easy. Scares me outta my mind, honest. But that's the City, feels like. A lot like home."

"It was that bad back on Earth for you?"

Jayden finished off his current drink, and tossed the empty aside.

"Truth be told?" he said, leaning forward in his chair. "I was in Mr. Fong's place to rob it."

"Seriously...?"

"I ain't proud of that. Gang initiation, is all. Either I get in with them, or they just keep beating me up every day until I agree to get in with them. I didn't have anythin' against Mr. Fong. Hell, when everything went screwball, when those First Response guys showed up... I was glad. Meant no matter what else, at least I was out of that situation for good. Timing was perfect, I hadn't even pulled my piece yet; I dumped it fast and made like an innocent bystander. No more Earth, no more living in gang turf, no more troubles."

"New troubles to replace the old, though," Dave pointed out.

"So? At least they're different troubles. I'll take 'em over the streets I came from," Jayden said. "Wasn't any way out until the City of Angles gave me one. Not everybody's lucky enough to get in one little fight and their mom gets scared and says you're moving with your auntie and uncle in Bel Air. ...'sides, my auntie died in a car crash few years back. I was alone and screwed back there, maybe I'm alone and screwed here, I don't know, but... hell. Can't be worse."

Alone and screwed. Dave chewed on that, for a bit.

He'd arrived in this City alone. So had most people, it seemed... alone, now hiding away in unfamiliar motel rooms, being given little comfort beyond binders of printed slides and one enthusiastic teacher of arguable competence. Brittany, forever cut off from the adoring public that made her world make sense. Sarah, having left loved ones behind and now facing a life of isolation. Jayden, trying to figure out the best way to move forward with what was given to him...

And then there was Dave. Plowing onward, doing what was asked of him, in hopes that it'd all sort itself out in the end. An empty and useless hope, in the face of all this weirdness.

The only one who had been able to make him feel like that hope was justified was some kid he'd met along the way. With all the radical shifts in scenery, that chance encounter felt like a dream he'd once had rather than something that actually happened to him.

It'll be okay, Dave, she'd told him. *I promise. For you, and for everyone.*

"I think I'll have another beer," he decided. "And propose a toast to your future. And mine. And, well, anyone else, I guess. Let's just call it a toast to the future, in general."

The younger man cracked his first smile, pulling the aluminum can from its rubbery ring binder and tossing it over. One tinny *clunk* later, and they were drinking to good health.

"So, what job do you hope they'll find for you?" Dave asked, curious.

"I think President of the World'd do me fine," Jayden joked. "I used to practice making speeches in my bathroom mirror, as a kid. How 'bout you? What're you hopin' for?"

The best possible job they could find him was a stable and well-paid job in graphic design, in a well-established corporation. He could draw neat little lines and impersonal company logos until the day he retired fat and rich, if he landed just the right position.

"I always wanted to be a fireman when I grew up," he remembered.

On a fake rooftop, underneath a fake sky. Fake stars spinning slowly in a spiral design, over head.

Television antennas, everywhere. That was silly; over-the-air broadcast was a dead concept. The idea of an apartment building roof covered in spindly, wiry, weirdly bent antennae was an anachronism. And yet, there they were... dozens of them, all rotating at strange angles. He could feel them brush inches away from his skin, like metal brambles that tangled and tore across an urban landscape...

Oh, right. This is why I don't like getting drunk, Dave thought to himself. *Nightmares. Of course.*

He could only think it, because Dream-Dave was silently screaming. Dream-Dave usually was screaming and trapped in a weirdly-ordinary-yet-menacing version of the real world.

chirp

"This is a really weird nightmare," Penelope Yates said, hovering just over the lip of the rooftop, sitting indian-style across from Dave. "Are your nightmares usually this weird?"

It's not really that weird. It's just scary because it's completely out of control.

"Oh? You prefer being in control?"

I wouldn't say I'm fixated on it or anything. But given the alternative, I would prefer to have enough control to not be lost in a forest of spiky metal wires, yes. Wouldn't you?

chirp

Penelope considered, and nodded in agreement. "Guess that's a valid point. Why not take control, then? You realize this is a dream, so can't you make them go away?"

His trembling body continued to barely avoid being scraped and clawed and eviscerated by the gleaming wires, while he considered that. They pulsed with a million broadcast signals, flowing in and around and through him like wind, threatening to throw him into the tangle... but never quite strong enough to do so.

I've never been able to before, he thought. *That's just not Dave Smith. Dave Smith enjoys feeding himself these nasty things whether he wants them or not, because he's used to worrying. Always has been, whether it shows or not. But if I ignore it long enough, I'll wake up and that's that. Good enough, right?*

chirp

"Who says you have to be that person anymore?" Penelope wondered. "Everything's changed. I mean, look up at the stars. Those are your stars, aren't they? You made them. A guy who can make the stars can be anything he wants, not just the person he thinks he has to be. Look up."

So, Dave looked up at the brilliantly lit stellar pattern.

Then he looked down at the rooftop, which finally jumbled itself into a meaningless bundle of razor wire. Without him in it, because now, he was in the stars.

"Much better, yes?" Penelope asked.

"Considerably," he agreed, with his voice now returned to him. "Hmmm. Is because of the City? Does it give you strangely coherent yet incoherent dreams?"

"Maybe. Maybe not. I'm part of your dream, how would I know?" the girl asked. "I'm the client, you're the designer. You're supposed to have the answers and I'm supposed to have the questions. For instance, where's that chirping noise coming from?"

chirp

"That's my phone's text message beep," Dave said. "Someone's IMing me while I'm asleep. Only person in this world who has my number is you... um, is Penelope Yates, so I guess she can't sleep and she's texting me. Which... you knew already, since I know. Okay, I get it."

Settling down among the stars, Dave had a seat on nothing and tried to make his headache go away. It wasn't fair, being hung over during a dream. But even without the rooftop peril, this WAS a nightmare, so some suffering was probably a reasonable expectation.

"I wish I wasn't so drunk. I could wake up and reply," he continued. "I totally forgot to call her after I settled in, like I'd promised to do. Poor kid. She can't have too many friends, constantly living on the go like that..."

"Like Melinda from third grade, you mean?" Penelope asked.

"Right. Only knew her for three months, before her dad got his deployment orders and they had to move away again," Dave said. "I worried for weeks about how she was doing, overseas..."

"And now you're worried about your father."

"He's going to be all alone, without me there anymore. I'm trying hard not to think about it. It's hard to keep my head together, with the craziness going on..."

chirp

"Penelope promised you it'd be okay," the imaginary girl reminded him. "That everything will make sense in the end. Of course, it's not like she has any real say in that. The whole universe spins the way it wants to and nobody can change that, right? It's out of control, especially in this city. All you can do is hope for the best."

Dave shrugged in agreement. "Guess so."

"Or you can look up, and go to the stars instead of being stuck down in the mire," she reminded him. "Like you did, just now. You want things to make sense in the end? Then make sense of them. Do it. I mean, look at the stars!"

"Uh, I already did that. I'm here, aren't I?" he asked, pointing them out.

"No, no. I mean LOOK at the stars. Look at them."

And his perspective shifted.

Not to the rooftop, to the craziness and menace of the city. Not to being within the sky itself, too close to see it for what it was. There was a third perspective... somewhere else, somewhere outside, looking and truly understanding...

The stars had been arranged in a shape resembling his unfinished Lucid Technologies logo. He'd recognize the twists and turns of that spiraling knot-like shape anywhere.

Instead of a chirp, the next sound was his alarm clock sounding bright and loud. True to form, Dave Smith snapped awake, and probably forgot everything he just learned in the process.

Dave's hand knocked a few empty beer cans off his end table, as he fumbled for the button which would make the annoying sound go away.

With throbbing agony in his head encouraging him to do otherwise, he pulled himself upright and tried not to think about the previous night's festivities. Step one would be to track down some water and aspirin, step two would be to try to avoid throwing up, and—

—that should have been made step one, he thought in hindsight, after returning from an emergency session praying to the porcelain god. But at least it was over with.

Take a shower. Brush teeth. Brush teeth *again*, to get the taste out. Get dressed; Hollister had obtained some Department of Orientation sweat pants and t-shirts for him yesterday, which meant he would be once again wearing telecommuting garb. At least this time, he'd have shoes...

Check his phone. Instant messages. For some reason, he knew there'd be some waiting for him.

PennyLane: hi u there?
PennyLane: i can't sleep. can't call, trying not to wake dad.
PennyLane: he says we have to lay low a bit, after that brush with the cops. i'm planning my next adventure, though!
PennyLane: guess you're still asleep.
PennyLane: it's ok. you need your rest. call me when you've got time but no rush k? and don't let orientation scare you. life in the city isn't terrible. you can make whatever you want of it! you're a new person and it's all up to you! i know you'll do ok.

Fumbling with the phone through the haze of his hangover, he thumbed in a reply.

DaveSmith: Doing OK. Getting breakfast, will call later. Haven't really seen anything scary yet.

On his way out the door, intent on getting more greasy foodstuffs, his gaze lingered on a blue thing.

Someone had slipped a blue piece of paper under his door. Some kind of leaflet. Assuming it was more orientation notes, Dave pulled it out of the door jam, unfolded, and read.

YOU ARE NOT BEING TOLD THE WHOLE TRUTH

The Department of Orientation is keeping something from you, out of fear of how you will react. We think you deserve to know the reality of your situation.

YOU DO NOT EXIST.
THIS PLACE IS NOT REAL.
YOU ARE ONLY AN ECHO OF WHO YOU THINK YOU ARE.

This was proven beyond a shadow of a doubt in 1968, with the arrival of Elvis Presley in the City of Angles -- and confirmed in the years that followed.

Do you wonder why nobody on Earth has raised an eyebrow at what would surely be a rash of missing persons cases? Enough people are taken to the City each year that surely it wouldn't go unnoticed. Especially if a major public figure like Elvis vanished overnight...

PEOPLE WHO CAME TO THE CITY AFTER 1968 SAID HE NEVER LEFT!
THE REAL ELVIS DIED ON EARTH IN 1977.
THIS CITY'S VERSION OF ELVIS DIED IN 2002.

EVERYONE HERE IS ONLY A COPY -- THE REAL YOU IS STILL ON EARTH

THE "YOU" THAT IS HERE IS ONLY AN **ECHO** OF THAT REAL PERSON

The Department of Orientation holds this truth back, until they feel you are ready to accept it. They claim this means your family and loved ones will not miss you, because you never left, and that means you don't have to be afraid. No gaping holes are being left in society because nobody is being kidnapped by the City of Angles.

Those who are "born" in this city are figments of the City's diseased imagination -- they never existed on Earth, they were never real in the first place. These things occupy government seats, they rule over your tortured life in their streets. The Department of Orientation isn't run by refugees, it's run by natives, and the nightmares *want* you to suffer.

Every day you exist in this nonexistent place is a day of suffering. You do not have a soul, you do not exist, there's no reason for you to keep enduring this just because they say you have to.

YOU ARE ONLY AN **ECHO**. YOU DON'T HAVE TO ACCEPT THIS CITY'S LIE.

Embrace the teachings of Echo. She is the path towards your salvation. She can help you embrace non-existence and finally be free of the City of Angles and the pain it brings. We love you, she loves you, and we promise to help those who accept this truth.

There wasn't any time to ponder the truthfulness of it, the implications if it were true, or how Dave might feel about all of this.

Like the alarm clock which pulled him out of slumber, another sound pulled him away from this latest oddity. The sound of a woman screaming.

He immediately dropped the flier and ran out the door, towards the person in distress.

At least today, Dave had proper shoes on. That meant he could double time it up the concrete outdoor steps of the motel, to the third floor.

Quickly, his mind was putting together information. He knew exactly what to expect, by the time he arrived on the scene.

One, the screaming was coming from the end of the row of rooms—where Sarah's room was.

Two, he'd seen blue leaflets sticking out from underneath other doors along the way. Someone had been through here in the dead of night, slipping them all the cheaply printed flyers.

Three, Hollister had assured Sarah yesterday that her family would be fine despite her arrival in the city... but didn't say WHY. And if the flyer was telling the truth, now Dave knew why—and so did Sarah.

By the time he arrived at her room he knew exactly what he'd be seeing: Sarah, screaming at Hollister. Who was unfortunately quartered in the room right next door, and now bore the brunt of her distress.

The mother of two and devoted wife was shaking a slightly leaflet at him.

"Is it true?" she demanded to know. "Is it TRUE? Is this what you've been keeping from us?!"

Given the broken lamp near the door, likely hurled at velocity, Dave decided to enter the room without saying a word... but ready to get between them if need be.

The chaos had attracted more than Dave's presence, however... a quick glance confirmed Jayden at the door, and Brittany nearby, although after one look at the situation she departed. Likely to continue the phone call she was in the middle of. Other refugees from other orientation groups were also starting to gather, drawn by the noise...

Which put Hollister on the spot. Everybody had the same question, even if they were less aggressive in asking. *Is it true?*

"Goddammit, those Safety goons were supposed to keep those nutbag cultists and their propaganda away from here..." he grumbled.

"Don't you take the Lord's name in vain," Sarah warned. "Don't you *dare*. Now tell me if it's true! Are we just copies? Are any of us real?!"

Clearly, this was something Hollister was used to explaining... even if he was used to explaining it under more controlled circumstances. He had a prepared speech and everything.

"All we know is what we can observe," he explained. "It started out as rumors, people who knew each other on Earth confused about why personal histories didn't match up. The Elvis thing confirmed what many suspected... that when you come to the City of Angles, you never really leave Earth. So, yes. Refugees are, it *seems*, copies. Just like the copies of buildings and places that get pulled in here. And that's the farthest extent of what we know about it —anything else is someone's interpretation."

Sarah's anger drained out, in an instant. Because the implications were far too horrible in and of themselves to focus on anything else.

"Then... it's true," she realized. "We don't exist. We're just echoes. We don't even have souls—"

"Whoa, who says that's true? Who?" Hollister asked. "No souls? I don't buy that for a minute. We are here. We are *alive!* I was born here and I certainly believe I've got a soul, that I *exist*. If you want to look at it from a religious perspective, who says this isn't part of His plan? We can't know for sure. All we can do is work with what we're given. We were given a life here, for whatever reason—"

"This could be Hell," Sarah reasoned. "We could be dead, and this is Hell..."

"I don't buy that. You know why? Because they left out the rest of the story on that flyer," Hollister stated. "It doesn't suit the crazy doom philosophy of the Echo Chamber to tell people what REALLY happened to Elvis—"

"When he found out how he died on Earth, he turned his life around," Dave guessed, interjecting himself into the discussion.

All eyes, inside the room and loitering outside the room, turned to the person they had completely ignored.

"I mean... it just stands to reason," Dave said, feeling quite on-the-spot. "Elvis was a drug abuser headed on a path of self-destruction. One way he could have lived to the 21st century is if he saw what happened to the 'real' Elvis as a wake up call. ...am I right? Okay, I'm swinging in the dark here, but —"

"No, no, you got it!" Hollister confirmed, thrilled to have someone on his side. "That's the thing about the City of Angles, right? It's a new beginning for all of you! Your life here may play out completely differently, but that doesn't mean it's a life of endless suffering like the Echo Chamber claims. It's not *Hell*, that's for sure. Whatever it is... it's ours to make the best of!"

On a roll... Hollister turned to the crowd gathered just beyond the door, watching through the window, listening in on the confrontation.

"Nobody knows why the City of Angles exists, or how it works, or what exactly we are," he said, throwing a bone to the flyer's claims. "But that's the thing. It's unknown. It's unknowable. Where does that leave us? It leaves us with what we have. And that doesn't have to be terrible! That's what Orientation is for, in the end—to give folks hope. Life here will be different, it will be challenging, and you'll be a different person as a result. But trust me... stick with the program, give it a chance, and you'll be ready to take those first steps. Okay? Okay. ...okay."

Lastly... he turned to Sarah. Who was nearly in tears, lost and confused by all this conflicting information.

"Yvonne will be here soon, okay?" he promised. "I gave her a call yesterday and she's arranging for a ride into the city. She got here a few months back, so she'd love to reconnect. A familiar face may be just what you need to bridge the gap between your old life and your new one. And like I said before... your family is safe, and well. You never really left them. Everything's going to be just dandy, I promise. Okay? Okay!"

He offered his biggest, brightest, most confident smile.

It took Sarah three moments to form a coherent response.

"Get out," was all she could say. Not harshly, not sadly, just... stated.

Sensing that the moment had passed, and not wanting to make things even more awkward than they already were, the crowd dispersed. Some to slink back to their rooms and consider for themselves what this new revelation meant, some to give up thinking about it and go get breakfast.

The only ones that stayed, leaning against the guardrail a few doors down from Sarah's now closed-and-locked door, were the rest of Group Four.

"I've been pushing for them to reveal the 'copy' thing earlier in the curriculum, you know," Hollister admitted to his students. "It's too hard to dance around the issue for days. But the headshrinks feel it's better to spring it on you guys after you've had a chance to accept your circumstances... I don't know. Maybe it's good, maybe it's bad. Cat's out of the bag, now."

"So what happens next with Sarah?" Dave asked.

"If we can't reach her... Mr. Fong may have a new roommate," Hollister suggested. "There's limited space in the Department's therapy wards, so they keep letting folks who need serious help slip into the general program. Not surprised they sent Sarah here, but I'll push to get her the help she needs if I gotta. ...what about you guys? You all got the flyers, right? How *you* doin'?"

Jayden pushed away from the railing, looking out across the parking lot, the pool, the Burger Buffet Bonanza™... the whole span of the city, or at least the span that was immediately visible.

"Kinda sucks, since... well, I was hopin' I was out of that hellhole for good. Now it sounds like some of me's still back there," he said. "Feel bad for that Jayden. But *this* Jayden's ready to get movin' on all this. Have been since the start, so I guess nothin' changes for me. As for Heaven and Hell and souls and shit, man, I don't know and I don't got time to think about it. I'm still game."

"My Dad's not going to be alone," Dave said. "Leaving him was the only regret I had. ...well, I regret getting stuck in a city that keeps trying to kill me, but... I guess nothing changes for me, either—"

Brittany snapped a finger, to steal the attention spotlight.

"Yes, yes, giant pity party, psychobabble, whatever," she said. "Poor, poor Sarah. Now—do I have a meeting with a TV executive or not? You said you were going to make calls for me, Hollister. Or are you too busy cooing over some washed-up MILF to pay attention to your main star?"

This would be the other major topic Hollister had wished to avoid talking about. But after confronting an understandably terrified and angry woman, why not go all-in and confront a would-be celebrity with a spiteful streak...? He committed to that course of action with some bitterness.

"I'm not in the mood to sugarcoat this, given I'm more worried about Sarah than you," he admitted, straight away. "So, yes. I made those calls. I know guys who know guys; I passed word up the food chain. And I got no bites. Not a single one. Nobody cares."

"Impossible—"

"It took hours for someone, *anyone* to get back to me who had ever heard of you before. The only time the city gets its hands on television shows from your Earth is when a video rental store or a warehouse full of DVDs gets dropped in here, and with everything switching to Internet streaming, that doesn't happen often anymore. And here-today, gone-tomorrow reality shows? Even less often. So, no, almost nobody had heard of you. And the one guy who had? He said he's more interested in pushing people seen on *local* cable stations than a refugee celebutante who feels entitled to the spotlight. Sorry."

In the face of a ragingly livid celebrity, Hollister put his hands in his pockets, and adopted an uncaring expression. One which said, *too bad honey, that's show biz.*

So she kicked him directly in the crotch, and walked away without a word.

By the time the stars passed from his eyes, Hollister was being helped off the floor by Dave and Jayden.

"...m'gonna get fired," he mumbled, trying to swallow the agony down. "She'll probably walk out now. Sarah'll go to therapy. Crap week. ...you two wanna walk too, I'll understand... I'm a lousy teacher. I know it. Wanting to help's not enough. I'm no damn good at any of this..."

"Let's get him to his room," Dave suggested to Jayden. "I'll go get a bag of ice from the ice machine for his groin. And I'll grab my three-ring while I'm at it; we'll do today's seminar lessons in Hollister's room. Sound good?"

Jayden helped shift the wobbly Hollister's weight onto Dave's shoulders, accepting the room card key. "Sounds good. I'm on it," he agreed, heading off to finish the errands.

"You don't actually have to bother with the apple-polishing, you know," Hollister said, as Dave helped him limp along towards his room. "It's not like there's a test or anything. They'll still try to find you a job, because the law says they have to. But the Department doesn't really care about refugees; they only offer this lousy course to *pretend* they care..."

"You actually care," Dave said. "That's good enough for me. So, I'll care in return. Besides, I've got some questions about the stuff I read in the binder, may as well clear them up before we're kicked out into the city."

Hollister focused through the pain, trying to read Dave's perpetually neutral expression.

"I'd say you're more ready for this city than most people who pass through my classes," he admitted. "But... okay. Let's do this up right and actually teach the book. Get you two started out right. Fabu idea, just fabu."

The normal orientation course consisted of several days of sitting around in an emptied-out storage room of the motel, listening to your instructor read the slides aloud, bullet by bullet. Occasionally he'd bother answering a question or two, but it wasn't likely. Meanwhile, the refugees would stare into space and wonder just what the hell they'd gotten themselves into, and eventually they'd be shoved out the door with instructions to report for duty at a laundromat or something.

And for most of the groups at the Seaside Sandy Shores Motel, that's exactly what happened. But Group Four, despite being fragmented and on the ropes, was actually getting something done compared to the other groups.

By the time the bag of ice had melted, Hollister was feeling more like himself and less like he was going to throw up. Despite losing two of his students along the way he was in better spirits, and coloring way outside the lines when it came to official city living instructions.

"It's not really where you live, it's who you know. Where you live changes all the time. One day, might take you five minutes to walk to the corner store for a quart of milk; next day, it's a block further away; day after that, you're going down two side streets to get there. ...not that it shuffles up THAT often, but you never know, right? So, you get to know who sells the best maps online —don't trust the official Dep of Reez maps for that, they're not on the ball— you're good. Know the right people and you'll know where you're going."

"So... there are districts, and there aren't districts?" Dave asked, confused. "Why bother marking off parts of the city by district lines if it changes so often?"

"Gerrymandering, my man. Gerrymandering in full tilt swing. That's about all locality is good for—and even that's a dodge. The city shuffles up on a regular basis since new buildings get inserted between old ones. That means even if, like... okay, here's a working example: Italian-Americans tended to gather around the Spindles in the nineties, right? But then in 1997 this giant apartment complex from a largely Latino southwestern town showed up right in the middle of the Spindles. Brought two dozen refugees with it! Suddenly, *bam!*, culture clash, shifting voting patterns, nothing's certain. Can't rely on locality to mean anything, socially speaking."

Jayden thought this one over. "Great American melting pot," he recited. "Stupid song from the sixties or something, they showed us a cartoon about it in school when I was a kid. Never really worked like that, but guess here, it ain't optional..."

"Right. City's been like this so long that folks are used to it. Equality forced on us from on high. Or from below, or from the great cosmic spaghetti monster, or whatever," Hollister agreed. "Not like there's universal acceptance, but... with each new generation you get more. Only way to survive is to deal with your own shit and not waste time hating on the neighbors, yeah? That's the idea, anyway."

"City that much of a death trap?" Jayden asked. "I hear stories, I've seen the news on TV, but..."

Hollister paused before answering, to think that through.

"Nnnnot always," he decided on, in the end. "Not as much as folks fear. It's not like evil woogums roam the streets eating people on a regular basis. But fear is a powerful motivator and the media and politicos rely on it to keep them in the green. Realistically... if you learn the lay of the land and aren't afraid to shake some hands, you'll do fine. It's the ones who wander off alone that get in the mess. Having a good friend to keep you grounded is enough, I say."

Which sent up a red flag reminder in Dave's mind.

"I need to make a call," he said, closing his book. "It's getting late and I keep putting it off. Sorry; I'll be right back."

"Hey, take your time," Hollister invited. "Anyway. Jayden, to answer your earlier question, if you wanna score the best lap dances you definitely want to avoid the Zag; those joints bill themselves as cheap and sleazy but honestly, they're upscale and pricey. I recommend Pileup Intersection or the Crossway Points for the best dives..."

Dave loitered by the door, where reception was best. Penelope had helped him load new backdoor software on his phone, which re-connected him from his now nonexistent service carrier to the city's public grid—*not the best*, she explained, *but free's free*. It meant he had to be as close to the open air as possible to do more than send a few text messages, but...

Before he could flick down the contact list for Penelope's number, he caught a glance through the motel room window of someone loitering by the other side of the door. Even in the dim of the setting sun, he could tell who it was.

Cautiously, Dave opened the door.

Sarah hadn't knocked yet. She might never have, really... stuck in the moment of indecision, to approach or not to approach. So, Dave did the approaching.

"Hey," he greeted.

"Um... hello," she said, in reply. Awkwardness rising. "I... couldn't help but hear through the walls. Are you doing the lesson plans...?"

"Sort of. Kinda. In a way," he said. "Do you want to join us? I can get a chair from my room for you."

The answer was obviously *no*, judging from her pensive body language. Not just *I'm unsure*, but flat out *No, I do not want to be here, I don't like what is happening to me, I wish it would all go away...*

Ultimately, though, she offered the slightest of nods.

"May as well," was all she could agree to.

By the time Dave returned to the room, carrying a semi-lumpy guest chair on his back, he'd forgotten all about the phone call he was going to make. The surviving members of Group Four continued their discussion (with the lap dance point of interest hushed up promptly) until it was time to get their horrible dinners, and retire for the evening.

Ring.

Ring.

Ring.

"Hiii! I can't pick up my phone right now," Penelope indirectly replied. "Either I'm out of reception range, or it's on mute because my Dad doesn't want me drawing attention, or I'm being chased by a Picasso, or I'm peeing. Anyway, leave a message."

Beep.

And he had no idea what to say.

"Ah, hi. I'm doing fine," he got out immediately, because that beep was quite pressuring. "Sorry I didn't ring you earlier, and sorry I forgot to reply to the text messages, it's been very strange. But I'm doing fine. Soo... just letting you know. —this is Dave, by the way."

Touch the virtual button, hang up the phone.

On the whole, that was not one of Dave's finest answering machine drops. He'd dialed her up in a rush, having realized it was edging on midnight and he'd once again completely forgotten to ring up the only other person he knew in the city... and then had no idea what to say to the recording device. Unfortunate.

His day was long done. Yet another meal of fast food turning uncomfortably in his belly, a change of clothes back into his freshly laundered pajamas, and nothing left but watching TV or cruising the Internet. Except, of course, he had no idea what to look for on this world's Internet... www.google.com just returned a big page reading "LOL FUGEE NOOB." Which left television.

Sadly, television here was just like television back home—the names were different, the shows were different, but it was the same vapid array of sitcoms and reality shows and dire portents in the evening news that never really interested him back home, either. Even worse, it was the low budget late night deep cable offerings you might get in some backwater state, not any major network polish.

Commercials for "Jerky Bob's discount free-range beef by the pound!" slotted into every other break; apparently whoever this Jerky Bob was, he was very keen on making sure every family squatting at home for fear of going out had plenty of frozen cow chunks on hand. There was a standard Strangers In a Strange House Are Eliminated One By One reality show, except it took on a bit more menacing of a tone than Dave was expecting... the people who got voted out genuinely looked upset to have to leave.

Finally, in the late evening news, there was an interview with the head of the Department of Safety.

"Mr. Dougal, researchers have pointed out that the number of quarantined entrances to the Sideways has tripled in the last five years," the reviewer noted from his teleprompter. "Do you see this sharp increase being attributed to more holes in the city appearing than normal, or simply more efficient techniques for identifying the gaps?"

The charming gentleman offered his most convincing and compassionate smile.

"I would say it's both," Seth Dougal replied. "The Department of Safety is ever vigilant in informing the public of dangerous areas in the city. We are dedicated to keeping the population safe from the threat of the Sideways, and we are working tirelessly to ensure every trouble spot is identified clearly. That said, there is a distinct increase in the number of openings to the Sideways being created in recent years."

"So you see this as an ongoing trend?"

"Yes, and it's one we need to be concerned with. Now, it's part of my reelection platform to obtain more funding for researching the Sideways, to determine the cause of this. I believe with proper study, we will one day have nothing to fear. But should my opponent take my seat on the City Council... I don't know if she would have the dedication I would have towards investigating this issue."

"Then my follow up question to you is this," the interviewer said. "Maps are being drawn of the Sideways every day. In fact, she's likely out there right now, out of reach, in harm's way—all to make sense of the city, and keep people safe. Is this a fool's errand?"

"Oh, absolutely," Seth agreed. "A child's whimsy is hardly any sort of noble crusade. It doesn't matter that she has a rather scary father—this city's nightmare isn't something you can shoot in the head. He'll die, and likely die screaming. Then, she'll be pulled into the unending horror and be twisted into something unrecognizable. It's inevitable, really. The entire city is going to fall to perfect chaos eventually."

"I see. And what of her new ally, Dave Smith?"

The man with the sharp green power tie laughed and laughed, his mouth opening a mouth.

"'Ally'? That's really reaching, don't you think?" he asked, through both sets of lips. "In ANY given situation, what good is having Dave Smith at your side? He's hardly proper big brother material for that poor doomed child."

"What makes you say that? "

"Well, let's run down his defining attributes," Seth suggested, counting them on six-jointed fingers. "He has no skills or talents whatsoever. He's a failed artist. He's mediocrity incarnate. He's three inches from a mental break, and that's on a *good* day. He knows, deep down, that he'll never amount to anything—and he's gratefully accepted that, taking refuge in the stability of the mundane. *Comfort*, even. Why reach, when you risk in the process? No, no... Dave has purposefully chosen to be nothing. What exactly do you think that nothing of a person can possibly do for little Penelope Yates?"

"So you're saying that if this pale echo of Dave died in his sleep, the world would go on without any great gain or loss?" the interviewer asked, curious.

"Oh, I didn't say that. Dave will become, much to his own horror, quite important," Seth assured him, with multiplying smiles of razor wire and concrete. "But once that purpose is expended, that singular strange connection and the end result of Lucid's influence is realized... well... I don't mean to sound cruel, but Bedlam will enjoy pushing him three inches to the left and directly off the edge of his own sanity. Just to show him how weak he truly is, in the face of her nightmare. No, no... Dave Smith sealed his fate when he made best friends with her sworn enemy. She can be quite spiteful, as you know."

"Indeed I do," the interviewer said, before being pulled apart at the edges by the chaotic dark which rushed out of the television set and consumed everything Dave cared for in life.

To his credit, Dave didn't wake up screaming. He woke up silently, with the blare of his alarm clock the only sound to be heard.

The clock continued to ring for a good twenty-three minutes before Dave got up, shaved, brushed his teeth, showered, dressed, and wandered off in search of breakfast.

"Jesus, Dave, you look like crap."

This time around, they were using the actual storage room they were meant to be in. Hollister had done his best to tidy it up—straighten out the chairs, get rid of the litter left by other orientation groups, change the bulb in the overhead projector. He'd even brought in a few boxes of coffee on his own dime, to get everybody up and ready to face the day.

Nobody looked like they were up and ready to face the day. Jayden hadn't gotten much sleep. Sarah was... continually unsettled. And Dave, unflappable and unmovable Dave, bore dark circles under his expressionless eyes.

"I'm doing fine," he insisted, accepting the offered cup of coffee. "Thanks. What's the lesson today?"

"Honestly, I have NO idea where we are in the syllabus at the moment," Hollister admitted, taking his seat at the front of the room. "I was thinking of going totally off the book and telling you about what to expect from your first housing assignment. I've been making calls—let it not be said Hook-up Hollister leaves his peeps hanging! I managed to land you in a decent fringe building. ...ah, and I do have one big surprise to drop on you! Jayden, specifically."

Jayden, who was just sitting down with coffee in hand, hovered halfway over the surface of his chair.

"Uh. Surprise?" he asked, glancing towards the door, in case he had to bolt.

"Hey, hey, be cool, it's good news," Hollister promised. "Well, half good news. See, problem is we know you're a minor, so this is the end of the road for the orientation program for you—"

Coffee spilled on the floor.

"My I.D. is legit! I told you!" Jayden declared. "I'm down, I'm ready to start in the city. Just let me—"

"Your aunt confirmed your age for us."

That put pause in Jayden's protests.

"My auntie's dead, Hollister. That's cold," he declared, narrowing his eyes.

"Car crash, right? That was back on Earth. Not here," Hollister explained. "That's the upside of the echo revelation, see? She got copied here two years before you lost her, so... you didn't lose her! Department was matching your records to find some relatives, and they got a hit. She's alive, and she's ready to take you in; she'll be by later this morning to pick you up."

A pause was inserted in the pause in Jayden's protest.

"You serious about this?" he asked, not sure if he wanted to get any hopes moving in an upward direction yet.

"Sure I'm serious! Okay, okay, I did a big TV-drama reveal, mea culpa," he apologized. "But hey—you've got family, man! That's more than most people get. What's more, I pulled some strings of my own—Department wouldn't be happy, but whatever—and found you an admittedly crappy part-time job in the same district she lives in. Just 'cause. You're all set, Jayden. You get your fresh start AND you get some roots to grow on. Congrats."

Being used to life throwing a continual series of curve balls right to the noggin, it took Jayden a few moments to fully swallow it all. Especially difficult since he had been burning the idea that he was alone and about thrown against this new world head first.

But in time, he came up smiling.

"Well... huh," was all he could say. A pleased sort of puzzled noise.

"Huh indeed, my boy, huh indeed," Hollister said, with an equivalent grin. "Right. Anyway, enjoy your coffee, feel free to hang around—you can learn up all you like until the Department makes you amscray with your auntie. So! Let's get this last day of training underway. I was thinking we'd... wait, where's Sarah?"

She'd taken a chair near the back of the small storage room. Her binder and coffee cup and pencils were neatly arrayed in front of that chair... but she wasn't in it.

And the door was quietly latching shut, having finished its hinge swing open and closed behind her.

At one point, perhaps the windows of the Seaside Sandy Shores motel offered a brilliant vista of sparkling sands and pounding surf. Transplanted into the City of Angles, the large windows instead afforded you a lovely view of a brick wall, and a sheer drop into a back alley between the motel and a block of flats.

A sheer drop that Sarah was looking over, sitting in the open window.

The pounding at her door confirmed that it was the smart move to lock it. The next smart move would be to jump, before whoever it was could run down three fights of stairs and out around the front of the motel, into the alley below. It would be so easy to just jump... the easiest thing in the world. It wasn't even jumping; she just had to let go of the window frame and gravity would handle the rest.

Hesitating wasn't the smart move.

One minute later, and Dave Smith was in the alley, directly underneath.

"Get out of the way, Dave," Sarah called down. "I don't want you getting hurt."

"I could say the same!" Dave called up. "Sarah, don't—"

"Don't what? Commit suicide? I wouldn't. Suicide's a sin," Sarah replied. "But I'm not in the Lord's sight, am I? I'm just an echo. When I'm gone, nothing's lost. You heard Hollister; my real self is back home with her family. She's safe and sound and happy... my family doesn't need *me*. I don't need to be here. I don't need that constant reminder..."

Now, the other two were coming. Hollister, out of breath from making the long run. Jayden, well ahead of him. Good boys. Meant well. She didn't blame them, not really...

"Sarah, I don't think it'll kill you to jump from that high!" Dave warned— before quickly whispering out the side of his mouth. "*Hollister, run back and get the manager to unlock the door.* —all it'll do is hurt really, really badly!"

"So?" Sarah asked him. "This city is painful already. Who cares? This way I have a chance to end that pain..."

"It doesn't HAVE to be painful! It's a new life. It can be whatever you want it to be!"

"I never *asked* for a new life!" Sarah shouted, to the two below. "I never wanted one. I was happy, HAPPY with the life I already had! If this life, if it even is a 'life', can be whatever I want it to be... I want it NOT to be. Get out of the way, Dave!"

"If you jump, Jayden and I are just going to try to catch you, and then I'm guessing all of us are going to the hospital," Dave warned. "Okay? So... just climb back in, and let's talk this over—"

There should have been some sort of last words. That's how it worked on television; there'd be a dramatic life declaration or something, and then she'd jump.

Instead, she simply fell away. Slipping from the window with full intention —no arcing dive, which they would've been able to intercept. More like a puppet with its strings snipped suddenly.

Not that he didn't try to stop it. Dave was hardly a star sprinter, but he was ready and let the reflexes do the rest. Jayden was at his side, ready to move, to catch the falling woman...

And they did. It hurt quite a bit, since it was less of a "catch" and more of a "cushion", but it worked.

He didn't *feel* like any bones were broken. He might've missed a half a minute there from the impact and the darkness that followed, but he was alive. He'd done it, he'd saved her...

She should've had some sort of last words. A dramatic life declaration.

Instead she simply wasn't breathing any more.

When the medics finally arrived on the scene, they determined one lung had collapsed on impact, and her head had cracked against the wall due to the awkward angle of the landing. She didn't have a chance. But Dave and Jayden were essentially unharmed.

Essentially.

Around lunchtime, Jayden left the motel. There was much pinching of cheeks and kissing of foreheads when his auntie found out her favorite nephew had arrived in the city. Hollister handled all the paperwork for the discharge, shook the hands, made friendly.

Given only one student remained—with a walk-out, a disqualification, and a suicide knocking the rest out of the picture—that was the unofficial end of the seminar. Especially since that student was now holed up in his motel room, refusing to come out.

Hollister had left a bag of takeout food outside Dave's door. It went cold soon after.

Unflappable Dave, unshakable Dave. You'd never know it from outside his skin. Look into his eyes and you'd just see limpid optic fluids. He'd sometimes proclaim how close he was to the break point, but it wasn't an easy thing to believe; there was nothing to show he was on edge.

But three inches to the left, and you'll find Other Dave. The one who had disappointment after disappointment, building up in big and small doses, leaving him constantly waiting for the next thing to go wrong. A bad grade. A bully. Falling off your bike and breaking an arm. Your mother's diagnosis...

Dad never really knew how to comfort him. Dave wasn't really sure HOW to be comforted, honestly.

In the end, he pressed a virtual button on a touch screen to reach out at last.

Ring.

Ring.

Click. "Hello?"

The phone trembled in his hand.

"I don't think I'm doing fine," he told Penelope.

The conversation lasted maybe twenty-three minutes. He couldn't even remember what was said. On some detached level, Dave was actually quite astounded at how well a teenage girl was doing at dealing with a broken-down Dave. Maybe because on some level, broken-down Dave was about the same age she was. Everybody's a scared little kid, in their worst hours.

In the end he'd made some kind of promise. He couldn't recall what it was, too exhausted to think straight, but it was enough to level his breathing again.

After the discussion was over, Dave hung up the phone, sank into bed, and fell asleep.

Dreamless hours. No nightmares whatsoever. A blessing.

Wake up. Shave, brush, shower, get dressed.

He moved in a haze, as he approached the receptionist who had "greeted" him on that first day. It was time to be discharged from the program—to find out where he was going.

Seeing that indifferent woman smiling at him was quite... was... quite. Just *quite.*

"Seems you're in luck," she said, holding out a clipboard for him to sign. "We actually found you an entry-level position at a local advertising agency. Graphic design, just like you were looking for. Very old and respected company; you play your cards right, this could set you up for life. Just sign here, and it's all yours."

You kept your head when others were losing theirs, Penelope had explained on the phone, ringing out in his memory through the haze. *Maybe you're not that great at keeping your head when it's your OWN problems on the table, but you did everything you could for that poor woman. Don't forget, you saved us from that Picasso in the Sideways. I think you're stronger than you believe you are, Dave. I think you could really help people... and maybe that'd help you help yourself, in the end. Promise me, okay? Promise me you'll try.*

He wasn't the old Dave Smith. The old Dave Smith was still toiling away in contractor obscurity, clinging to an ordinary life with all ten fingers, desperate to not have to think about anything or worry about anything or be anything. No obligations, no anxieties, no life.

If he was only an echo, a whole new Dave, that meant he could be anything he wanted to be. He could be what he really wanted to be.

He didn't reach for the pen.

"I think I'd like to be a fireman instead," he replied. "Or a paramedic, or a first responder, or something like that. I want to help people."

The woman went back to the suspicious and bored looking person she was on the first day, when she had to resist sketching in quotation marks around his middle name.

"*Really*," she said. "Really? You're seriously turning down the cushiest job offer I've ever found...?"

"I don't care what you find for me, as long as it's something where I'm helping out. I'm okay if it's just volunteer work, and I have to wash dishes in my waking hours. Doesn't matter," he said. "My name is Dave Danger Smith, and I think I'm ready to do something better with my life."

Buildings next to buildings, askew or aligned. Buildings sometimes intersecting buildings, for that matter. Walk down a hallway, end up in a ballroom, double glass doors to a subway station, third exit on the left goes to a toy shop. And yes, all the dolls they sell are excessively creepy.

There's no rhyme or reason to any of it—we've got streets which lead to dead ends, roads which criss-cross and loop back around, highways which go nowhere. Literally nowhere, as in "anybody going down that road is not coming back." This is not a good place to wander off unless you like wandering off forever...

Nobody knows where the city came from. Nobody knows how we got here. Nobody knows why any of this is happening. But it's happening. The city exists. We are here now. It's growing every day, and bringing new people with it.

We live a life amidst the twisted yet familiar.

If we're going to survive this, if we're going to stay alive and thrive, we need to learn to live in the City of Angles.

...here's an angle to consider...

The existential crisis that the city represents is something everyone who lives there has to deal with, in his or her own way. Every place and every person is a copy of something or someone else... you are not who you think you are, the Echo Revelation states. This goes doubly so for natives, who never existed on a world called Earth in the first place.

Some find a way of dealing with that problem. Some ignore it. Others give in to despair and lose their minds.

Some throw their fists in the air and scream at the sky that they DO matter, they DO exist, they ARE here and nobody will convince them otherwise. Torn from roots and torn from family, they form new bonds. Families thicker than blood. They challenge the accepted wisdom of the Echo Revelation, in their own ways. They speak. They write. They make their mark...

//003: Kilroy Was Here

The day started out as always with a progression from one room to another. Wake up in one, move to the other. That'd be the best place to explain what's what, since the progression says a lot about us.

Now when we signed the lease in the first place, the paperwork had tagged these two rooms as bedrooms. The scumbag landlord who rented us this space thought we'd be using it like that, one room for her, one room for me. Two balanced spaces, completely identical in size and shape, with identical windows looking out at nothing in particular. He raised an eyebrow when we told him that wasn't the plan.

If we did that, splitting our lives apart into two cloned boxes, that'd leave only the main living room for fun. And we wanted a lot more fun than one room would allow for. So, we'd both sleep in one bedroom and leave the other room for Whatever.

As an avid reader of body language I could tell the greaseball who was renting this dive was secretly pondering that particular setup and all the dirty implications it held. I'd made a mental note to check the shower each day for pinhole cameras, after that.

It's a frequent misconception that my sister and I are secretly lovers or something like that. I guess it's an understandable if disgusting assumption to make. After all, she's ridiculously cuddly and personable with *everybody* (including me), and on top of that we don't look a thing alike—despite having the same last name, I'm a surly Asian chick, she's a bouncy blonde.

But the simple fact of the matter is that this is what happens when you open your home to a "disabled" refugee foster kid. By blood or not we're family, closer than most but still family, and there are no sordid details to our living arrangement. And if there were, honestly, it'd be none of your damn business.

I don't like it when folks who don't "get" us immediately reach for nasty little labels to stick all over us. They're foul things that ruin our mood. For example:

Marcy Wei (that's me) gets grumpy when you try to stick her with titles like "problem child" or "graffiti vandal" or "cause for concern." People don't like me when I'm grumpy, because I'm typically grumpy already and those make me *super* grumpy.

Vivi Wei (that's my sis) gets sad when you try to stick her with titles like "dummy" or "dirty hippie" or "slut." You don't really want a sad Vivi; she's usually energetic enough to light up a room with her brilliance. Sad Vivi dampens that down to a dim glow. And then I get super *duper* grumpy.

Anyway, all insinuations that ended up being implied in the process aside, shuffling the purpose of rooms around has worked out quite well.

For the bedroom, we bought a queen-size bed which nearly filled the space available. Closet space wasn't a problem, because even if her stylish ensembles took up tons of room my grubby casual duds took up very little. Doubling up in the same bed has never been a problem. The few times I've bothered having boyfriends and wanted some slap and tickle, I went to their place; I didn't drag them back to mine. The room my sister and I bunk down in is a sacred space. It's safe and it's ours.

This in turn left the other room as an open area for anything we wanted. For her, it's yoga and exercising—she stays in shape, has to stay in shape really, to keep pace with the night life. For me, it's writing my words on the walls. I promised the landlord I'd clean the place up if we ever moved, so I could do whatever I wanted in there. That meant I stick to the edges of the room, while she takes the center. Division of space. Works well.

I stick to markers and pencils for most of my doodlings and noodlings in our shared rec room. Spray paint in a confined space is a terrific way to drop dead from fume inhalation—also Vivi preferred her workouts in the nude, and I didn't wanna accidentally give her a pre-layer of aerosol body art before she hit the clubs. (Didn't have to worry about pervs looking in on us; I'd painted a nice sunrise over the window ages ago. Filters the limited light we actually get through that tiny window, makes the room nice and colorful, she likes it.)

Consideration was key when you had a tight living arrangement like we did. Sharing everything also meant not interfering in anything. I gave her space as I worked in one of the corners... swapping between my black book and the marker lines on the wall, studying the way they compared, trying to find the best composition. I'd rolled over this spot with white paint a few hours previous to give me working room, tricky to do when nearly every inch of the walls was covered in remnants of past pieces.

While I stood still with my wrist working the marker back and forth on fills, she did some variety of ridiculous contortions which apparently unblocked your chi or some such bullshit. (She tried to get me into healthy living a few times, but the idea of giving up beer and cheese curls in favor of carrot juice and rice cakes was anathema to me. Also despite being agile enough to run from the cops for half a mile or so, I wasn't exactly the human pretzel she was.)

No words were exchanged as we went about our business, separate but equal... quite normal given the circumstances, though. In fact, I'd completely forgotten she was there until I noticed her out of the corner of my eye, toweling off and studying my work.

Figuring it was about as finished as a rough draft could be, I stepped away, turning to face her.

[What's it mean to you?] she asked me, after flinging the towel over one shoulder. Had to have her hands free, after all.

I was able to explain without too many gestures, thanks to our mutual signing shorthand. No reading lips for us; I'd known sign language since the year Vivi joined our family, and I could mentally translate the clipped and quick sign combinations we favored into full language instantly. I got what normally takes most folks a few sentences to explain out in a shorter span, complete with the emotions I wanted to convey.

Vivi nodded along, understanding perfectly. She was familiar with my art and knew my usual themes; this was a very succinct version of them, but still quite in line.

[You're still planning to paint it in the Defined Tower, then?] she asked, slipping in our personal sign for the Tower. It was like the normal sign, fingers shaping the edges and then tracing upward—but GROSSLY exaggerated and wide. After all, there was only one "tower" in contention for that lofty expression.

I nodded, with a thumbs up. [That's always been the plan,] I replied. [Everybody will see it there. I need to get this word out, far and wide. Plus, I'll be the first one to get up in the Defined Tower. That's going to be great for my rep.]

[You're sure it's safe to reach the Tower, though? I don't like you going past Edge Station...]

Body language was half of sign language; emphasis being placed through a subtle shift in the eyebrows, worried looks, visible concern. She'd been antsy about this piece ever since I told her my plans. Even tried to talk me out of it twice, which she almost never did, knowing my passion for writing. It just wouldn't be the same to throw this up on an overpass or something, not when the Defined Tower was out there, squeaky clean, waiting to be used as my canvas...

[I'll have Slyck with me, like I promised you,] I reminded her—his name being a variant on the sign for "smooth," only more tweaked. Another mutually agreed-on signal. [I won't be alone. He'll watch my back. But I don't think we'll run into any trouble out there, and you know I don't get lost in the city. I'll be okay, Sis.]

Despite one of us being sweaty and the other one still wearing yesterday's clothes, Vivi reached out and nearly crushed me with a hug.

With her arms around me, I could feel rather than see the sign she pressed into my back... thumb, index finger, little finger. Middle and ring curled underneath. [I love you.]

I returned the sign, against her own back.

This was my sister. I was the only family she had—despite opening their home to a refugee foster child, my mom and dad were always distant, never really in her corner. I'd been in her corner since we were very little, and intended to be there the rest of my life. Strange and beautiful Vivi. Stuck living in a world that was a foul and nasty thing. She was too good for this place.

And even if I knew that life was ultimately a cosmic joke, that I was just a dream of an echo and nothing more... if I really thought I wouldn't be coming back from the Distant Tower, I wouldn't have gone that night. No matter how important my words were to me, Vivi was always going to be more important.

Even if I always came back home to her, we had very different lives.

Right now she'd be down at the ZigZag, her home away from home. Either doing a run at bartending to add to the household income, or working as the entertainment director, or simply dancing the night away. She had friends I didn't have, moved in circles I didn't move in. Sometimes I'd drop in at the ZigZag and she'd try to socialize me, but the ridiculously loud and colorful night scene wasn't my thing. I preferred the dark and quiet of the streets. Move on your own, hoodie drawn up, hands in pockets, keeping to yourself. Backpack loaded with spray paint cans. Be unimportant, just a person on the street... until you slip away and do your thing. Like I'd do that night.

Once the sun went down, I made my move.

The subway line expanded recently, with three new completely mismatching stations being added to the red line. Thankfully roads in the City of Angles tended not to plow head on into a wall—they got shuffled around, twisted, extended, but the connectivity remained. The new stations meant the ride to Edge Station was longer than I'd have liked... and less direct. I wouldn't get there until nine. But I'd get there.

As the train made stop after stop, the car I was in gradually emptied. Folks heading out to dirtbag apartments like mine, out near the edges, where the rent was cheap and you had more conditional rules to worry about. (Don't go to floor 23. It doesn't actually exist. There's an opening to the Sideways where the door to apartment 452 should be. The lights are out in the main stairwell and the elevator doesn't go all the way to the top, so have fun walking up there. And so on.) Our place was a haven for new refugees being dumped by the Department of Orientation, and twentysomethings with irregular jobs like me and Vivi. Nobody would honestly care if our semi-broken building started infecting folks with cubism.

A stop before Edge Station, and the only person left in the car with me was a homeless guy who had been basting in his own urine for weeks. Maybe a refugee who lost it, maybe a native who hit the skids, who knew. Wasn't my problem.

With nobody watching, I slipped the silver marker from up my sleeve, popping the cap. Heavy ink, drippy, but perfect for tagging.

Turning in my seat, I scrawled out the word ADVANCE, with an arrow piercing the letters and pointing towards the front of the train. A simple and quick design... signed with my name, my symbol, a tiny cartoony ghost with X's for eyes.

I'd been using that icon-tag for my whole run as a writer. I was the Ghostwriter.

Tomorrow some commuter would see that word. Maybe this car would be headed in the direction it pointed, and they'd think about which way they're going, that they're advancing, moving on. Maybe the train would be going the other way. Then they'd have to think about it a little more...

The City Council saw graffiti as vandalism, pure and simple.

And it is vandalism. It's illegal. You do it in public spaces, you do it where you're not wanted. Graffiti on canvas in galleries is nice, it's positive, but it's also just aerosol art in comparison.

But you don't write because you're a hooligan, a young punk who just wants to do something illegal—you can jaywalk if you're seriously getting off on lawbreaking. You write because you have to. Graffiti is the soul of the city, laid bare in line and form and word and picture, capturing the spirit of an age of those who had no other way to prove they existed.

You've got something you want to get out there... usually just your name, your mark, saying *I was here*. For the first few years, back when I was daring to tag up Suburbia around my parents' neighborhood, getting my name out was enough. My little ghost adorned school lockers and walls of fast food joints.

I was a toy, really—some lamer who did nothing beyond tags and throw-ups, nothing of any importance, like a dog marking territory. I only seriously got into burners and pieces when I got to the city and decided this was gonna be my life's thing.

It wasn't enough anymore to sneak my wacky pirate nickname onto every surface I could find... that didn't prove I really lived, in a world where nobody was really alive. I had to put my thoughts up there, too. The ghost I doodled in my notebooks as a kid was adorable, like a goth corporate mascot, but I tried not to think about why I was so attracted to it. Now, in my twenties, I can grasp it and wear it like a shield. I'm a ghost. We're all dead, unless we can prove otherwise...

Odds were low anybody would see ADVANCE and consider how that related to their life. But it didn't matter. When I saw that bare subway window, I knew that was the word which had to go there. It was already written; I just made other people able to see it there.

A rip-roaring belch distracted me from considering my written statement. The smell of stale urine.

In a voice that was simultaneously raspy and watery, the bum mumbled something in his sleep.

"Green child of madness is comin'," he breathed, loud enough to be heard five seats away. "Gonna crawl down the spiral and into our beds. Bedlam inside you. She's comin' for you. For all of us."

And then he flickered.

It was subtle, like watching a scratched DVD. A brief error, corrected by software which couldn't know exactly what the image was supposed to be. The arm that scratched at his stomach in his sleep blurred, snapped, and the outline of it stayed behind for a few seconds like an afterimage.

Edge Station was only a few minutes away, but I immediately jerked the emergency handle on the door, to move between cars. Wasn't supposed to do that while the train was in motion, but damned if I was gonna sit around a guy who was going cubist on me.

Nobody knew exactly how or why someone went Picasso. Come into contact with one or lurk in an unstable place like the Sideways enough, sure, that made some scientific sense. You didn't want to lick the sheets in a TB ward, either. But some folks never came into contact with anything cubist and still slowly, gradually fell into that doom... no coming back once you were fully bent.

The whispered cant goes: *You give in to despair, let the city crush your spirit, and you'll lose yourself along the way. You'll Picasso.*

Might be true. Might not be. But no matter how gloomy of a ghost I was, I was fighting against that despair tooth and nail. The writing was my way out of just sinking, forever into the pit.

Edge Station, end of the line.

As the city grew in size over time, Edge Station got pushed outward. It hovered at the edge of the city (hence the highly descriptive name), a stone's throw away from where the city stopped being defined.

The City of Angles stretched on forever, as far as anyone could tell. It wasn't like you'd step off a disc and fall into the void for eternity. But after a certain fuzzy line was crossed... the buildings started being less buildings and more suggestions of buildings. Fake storefronts and apartment stoops, with doors made of rough wood that wouldn't open. Windows that were representations of windows, painted on the walls. Shadows that extended too far, during day and night...

Go far enough... and you'd be in a maze of upright brick pillars, the rough shape of a building without being a building any way. And by that point, common sense claimed, you probably weren't coming back. It looked stupendously easy to get lost out there. If you did return, you were probably completely cubist.

Needless to say, few people actually wanted to go to Edge Station. It would've been closed outright if there weren't some housing complexes and shops here, with rent so low that they may as well be squatters' homesteads. When you had nowhere else to live, you lived near the edge.

The open-air platform of Edge Station was a dead zone. At this time of night you wanted to be indoors; anybody who actually lived here was huddled in a corner of a tiny room, desperate and waiting for the daylight. Only a crazy person would come here for fun.

I cooled my heels and sat down on one of the benches. Waited for Slyck to get here.

Waited a good ten, fifteen minutes. Two trains rolled through and nobody got off. I was probably a juicy target, a young and supposedly attractive girl on her own in the middle of nowhere. Wasn't worried, though. The city itself was scarier than its denizens, who were in turn scared off by it and thus left me alone.

I didn't share Vivi's fear of the city fringes. That was a leftover remnant of Suburban living... the fear of what lurked in shadows, be it Stranger Danger or Picassos or who knows what. I'd wandered in and out of the alleys and abandoned buildings of this city long enough that I didn't fear it. On the off chance there was actually an axe-murdering serial rapist with a nervous twitch loitering under a flickering street lamp, I carried a can of mace mixed in with my art supplies. Somebody wanted to screw with me, I'd roll aggro on them in turn.

In fact, I was very much feeling the need to roll aggro on someone. Because Slyck was late as hell.

Giving up on being polite, I busted out my Cracker and dialed him up. It was the cheapest cellphone available, a clone of an outdated model with a crack along the top of the screen—some weird repeater artifact a mapper had found years ago—and I couldn't afford a premium cell carrier, but hopefully it'd work even out at Edge Station.

It worked fine. Except his line rang four times before he picked up, which suggested at the truth of his non-appearance.

"Uh, hey," he greeted, which confirmed my suggested suspicions.

"You're not coming, are you," I stated rather than asked. "Saw my number and hesitated before answering, too."

"Look, Ghost, I like you and all, but... c'mon, you know it's cray, right?" he asked. "Going out to the Defined Tower? I didn't think you'd seriously go through with it—"

"I'm going through with it. Are you coming or not?"

"Ghost, YOLO, alright? You Only Live Once. And to me that means I'm not gonna throw that one life away running off the edge of the map—and neither should you. I worry 'bout you girl, y'know? Look, Racker invited us to a party at his loft, let me get some beers and I'll meet you there and we'll find some other way to kick it tonight. Right?"

I pushed away from the station bench, starting to pace angrily.

"Hanging up, deleting you from my contacts, don't bug me again you goddamn *toy*," I glowered at him over the line. "I can't believe I was seriously considering having sex with you. Bye, Slyck."

"—wait what? I thought you were a—"

In old days, phones were beefy plastic things you had to slam down on a cradle in order to disconnect. Hence, "hanging up." As much fun as it might've been to spike my Cracker into the concrete of the subway platform... they didn't grow on trees. (Well. They sort of *did* in this case, but I wasn't stupid enough to leave myself without a phone all the way out here.) Instead I tapped the red button on the touchscreen with authority, and shut Slyck down.

Another few weeks without a boyfriend. But whatever. Didn't need him. He wasn't serious about the writing.

More important problem than not having someone to throw myself at in a night of drunken frustration: not having someone for my trip tonight.

I could just go on my own. I wasn't going to get into any trouble, no trouble I couldn't handle myself. Vivi would never know...

But I promised. I pinky-swore to her that I'd have someone with me. Maybe it was just for her peace of mind, but... I had to follow through on a pinky-swear between sisters. That's how it worked.

I needed another warm body to fill Slyck's shoes. Someone insane enough to go with me on this strange long trip. Or... someone desperate enough...

Oh, dammit. No. Not *him*.

But this was a code red emergency...

I didn't actually have him in my contacts, because as many times as he tried to slip Vivi his phone number, I'd intercepted and destroyed it. Last time I think I actually ate the napkin. Fortunately, he was on six or seven different social networks, flooding them all with pictures of his kegstanding girl-groping party-hardy lifestyle, with full contact information on each. After all, he was the guy who knew a guy. You had to be able to reach him if you needed something... and sadly, I needed him tonight.

To his credit, he was there in fifteen minutes.

The figure that stepped off the train at Edge Station looked like he'd just walked off the set of Miami Vice. A mismatching pile of fashion tropes that had long since gone out of date... sunglasses at night, a popped collar, and a cologne so thick I could smell it over the axle grease of the trains. Juuuuust enough stubble to look rugged and manly without looking unkempt. Gold chains that sparkled in the glare of the overhead fluorescent tubes.

He wasn't chewing on a toothpick but he probably would've if he'd thought of it first.

The only thing ruining his Vintage Smooth Operator look was the folded up stepladder he was awkwardly carrying under one arm. And his general unease at being here in Edge Station.

Spotting me, he strolled right on up, setting the ladder down.

"Let it not be said that Hollister Avenue doesn't come through in the clutch!" Hollister declared. "The little sister of the ZigZag's Patron Goddess wants a ladder? She gets a ladder!"

"We're the same age," I informed him. "I'm not her little sister."

"Right, right. Sooo... I ducked out on a really sweet party so I could hit up a hardware store and schlep this thing all the way out to the boondocks," he reminded me. "Now, I'm always up for doing a pretty girl a favor, but color me curious as to what this big surprise is you said I'd have waiting in store for me. I've been game to play along, because getting an 'in' with the Wei Sisters is a big plus, but—"

"I need you to carry that thing and come with me. I've got work to do."

"Ohhh.... oh! I get it, I get it now," he said, with a grin. "Babydoll's goin' out to paint the town red, right? Need to get to those hard to reach places? Weeeell... as a duly authorized representative of the Department of Orientation I should be dissuading you from your life of crime, but hey—let's get dangerous! ...but not TOO dangerous. Where're you headed, exactly?"

I pointed.

Hollister dipped his sunglasses down, so he could properly follow my finger to its destination.

At the risk of losing his cool guy persona... he pocketed the shades completely, so he could flash me a look of disbelief.

"The Defined Tower," he replied, flatly.

"The Defined Tower," I confirmed.

Everybody knew the Defined Tower.

It raised a few eyebrows when it showed up a decade ago. In the middle of all those fake brick lumps, beyond the safe zone of the city proper, into the vague and nebulous idea of a cityscape... a thirty-story building had appeared. Poof, just like that. Lit up like a Christmas Tree, spotlights and everything.

Nobody knew why a completely intact building of that size had been copied into the city amidst its least stable structures. That far away from known space, the city was a meaningless maze of concrete and brick... with the Defined Tower being the exception to that rule. It was flawless and perfect and nobody, NOBODY in their right mind wanted to traverse the vagueness to see what was inside.

"You want to go past the fuzzy edge of the cityscape, into the fake buildings, and... what? Write your name on the front door of that monstrosity?" he asked.

"No, I'm going to paint a mural inside the windows of the 20th floor," I explained. "They're pretty tall. I wasn't sure I'd find a ladder in there, so I needed you to bring one. Now let's get moving."

He pointed at me, with both index fingers.

"You... *you* are insane," he declared. "And I am absolutely, positively, utterly, completely, totally, certainly *not* going to waltz into the weirdness just so you can scribble on the walls of a likely haunted tower. And if your sister knew what you were up to she'd probably give you a spanking—"

"She's okay with it," I said, honestly. "We each have our passions, we respect them. But... she made me swear I'd bring someone to watch my back. And that's, against all my better judgment, you. My original partner bailed and you're the guy people call on when they need a thing, right? I need this thing."

"Honey, there are limits to what Hollister Avenue can provide. And there's nothing you can provide in return which—"

"I'll teach you how to flirt with my sister in sign language."

If he was still wearing his sunglasses he'd probably have peered over the top of them at me.

"You're serious," he recognized.

I was. I was disgusted with myself about it, but I was serious.

"You want an 'in' with her, right?" I asked. "As much as I don't particularly like you... I'll teach you how to woo your 'Goddess.'"

I knew his type. Dropping the sleaziest pickup lines, trying to chat up anything with breasts, pretending he was some big shot of the night scene. He was all wrong for Vivi—just some cheap bastard chasing skirt like a lawyer chases ambulances. But I needed to make this concession if I was going to get in that tower.

I was expecting him to either blow me off, or be giddily enthusiastic at the prospect of deafie nookie. He was a man who was led by his lower brain, after all.

Instead he showed an oddly light optimism.

"Do y'think it'd help?" he asked, curious. "Learning sign language, I mean. Would she like that?"

"It can't hurt your chances," I said in all honesty. "Look... Hollister, we're going to be fine. I've been past the edge before and I survived. I've got maps. I know how to navigate and how to lock down an exit strategy. We'll get in, you hang loose an hour while I do my thing, we'll be back before you know it. ...besides, it's now or never."

"Because of the quarantine."

He knew his stuff. But, he did have the inside line. For all his sleazy swindler trappings, he was a civic worker.

"Seth Dougal's about to crank up the border security," he recognized. "Barricades. Guards patrolling the edge. Too many kids wandering off into the mess and not coming back, too many concerned parent groups..."

"And that means I'll lose my chance to make history, yes."

"You know, I really think we can fight the problem with education, not big scary roadblocks. Big scary roadblocks won't deter the determined—they make the prospect of certain doom look edgy and rebellious. I keep telling the Dee-of-Orr folks that we gotta get out there, talk to the kids in a way they can relate to—"

"Are we going or not?" I asked, eager to get moving. "Are you in or out? One night of your time. And then you can make whatever obscene gesture you want in my sister's direction. I am bending my rules for you here, Hollister. Make note of that."

He took his sweet time making up his mind. Probably was weighing the odds of banging my sister against the odds of coming back alive, the scumball. Had to be what was going through that noggin of his.

"Hell, let's do it," he decided, in the end. "What's that thing the kids say now? YOLO?"

I hated that phrase.

It was factually wrong, after all. None of us were alive. We were ghosts, all of us, living in a ghost town.

"YOLO, whatever," I agreed. "Let's go."

I wasn't afraid of this city in the same way Vivi was. Unlike her I was born here, I allegedly lived here, and one day I'd fade away... but the city wasn't my enemy. I knew how to move with it instead of against it.

The undefined spaces beyond the edge were intimidating, yes. But they were less threatening than real buildings, in the same way a model railroad is less threatening than a steam locomotive bearing down on you at full tilt. It's a fake place, a movie set, nothing impressive compared to the original. After a while, you paid the odd feeling of being behind the sets in a haunted house no mind.

But you did respect it. And you worked with it, to leave a trail of breadcrumbs.

I left chalk marks on each building, as I went by. You had to use marks the buildings would accept... hobo signs, primitive graffiti tags, icons representing free WiFi for war drivers to enjoy. Sometimes I sketched a quick hopscotch board. These symbols would keep through the night, because they were a part of the lore of the city.

The theory mappers and explorer kiddies had was that the chalk marks would anchor the buildings down, encourage them to stay still, because now they were more realized aspects of the city. The city has a shape it likes to take on, and fighting against that shape causes disaster... while playing along with that shape can be to your benefit.

I also had a map loaded in my Cracker, but it was already out of date. Without chalk anchors, the undefined spaces shuffle when nobody's looking. Still, even outdated, that map kept me going in the right direction—and it wasn't like the Defined Tower was hard to miss.

It was hard to miss Hollister freaking out as he trailed behind me, lugging along the portable folding ladder.

"This is nuts," he said. "This is nuts. This is nuts..."

"Y'know, that's the kind of attitude that gets you Picasso'd," I told him. "You start to panic, you slip away, and suddenly you've got eight-faceted eyes and your outline's jittery like you're on meth—"

"Not! Helping!" he declared. "I'm calm. I am a calm little lake in the middle of a calm little land next to a calm little tree. ...I am actually looking forward to getting to the tower, compared to this. At least the tower's a real place... y'think we'll be the first people to set foot there?"

"You're the government stoolie, you tell me."

"That's Resources. ...or Safety. Or the FARTs. There's kind of a turf war for who gets to call 'First!'," he explained. "Orientation only mops up the aftermath. And since I haven't seen any paperwork about refugees from the Defined Tower..."

"Not surprised. It's useless to Resources, since you can't reliably run back and forth looting it. And Safety is happy locking down anything even slightly strange."

"For extremely good reason," Hollister reminded me.

"So yes, I'm guessing we'll be the first ones there. Certainly the first ones to do what I'm planning to do. It's gonna be... well, you'll see. Everyone'll see, when I'm done..."

And there it was.

Squeezing through an alley that was narrowing itself right down to the end, there it was.

A fully defined skyscraper. Offices, still with power and light, with spotlights to keep it nicely illuminated. (The City's power grid was a strange thing, in that it looped back on itself with no clear source, yet always provided power. Apparently that extended even this far from the grid.)

People with telescopes had identified it as being some major financial company's property back on old Earth, something famous from a famous city, but I didn't care. All that mattered was the light... and the deliciously large windows waiting for me.

"Island in the sea, eh?" Hollister commented, in about as much awe as I was in. "Beats the hell out of the fake buildings. ...y'don't think there's security guards, do you? Maybe a Picasso security guard or something...?"

"People have been looking at it for ten years from afar, and haven't spotted any," I said. "I did my research on this. The building's completely empty; we should be fine. Doors are locked, so... smash yon ladder through yon glass door there, hey?"

"Might set off an alarm..."

"Big deal. No guards, remember? It's an empty building."

"Even so... let's approach this cautiously, 'kay?" Hollister suggested. "We bash the door in, then wait five. If nobody shows up to greet us, THEN we go in. Look, I know you're brimming with confidence and I really admire that, that's totally awesome, but throw pragmatism a bone here. We need to be able to leg it if the ghost tower has actual ghosts in it."

"I thought you loved risky fun?" I countered, turning to face him. "You've got shots from crazy parties up on your website every week. Aren't you the guy who went skinny dipping in a swimming pool filled with champagne a month ago?"

"...you know a lot about a guy you claim you don't particularly like."

"When it comes to risks, I do my research."

Hollister grumbled a little... but let it out in a long exhale, a relaxation technique.

"I've done some downright ridiculous things in the name of a good time, yes," he agreed. "But this is not what I call a good time. And it's not a ridiculous thing I'm willing to dive into head first—and it's not my own head going in, it's yours, too. I gotta look out for my peeps. So. Break window, await response, and if everything's clear... I'll go in with you. We got an accord?"

Honestly, I wasn't expecting to have to butt heads with him tonight.

I knew his type; dangle boobs in front of him like a carrot on a stick and he'd run where you wanted him to, right? True, going out to the Defined Tower in exchange for boobs was a bit of a stretch, but...

"Whatever," I agreed, in the end.

With a nod, Hollister adjusted his grip on the ladder. Grasping one end, he hefted the cheap aluminum thing up, pointing it like a lance at the glass doors... and lunged.

Glass shattered. No alarm sounded.

We stood in silence for five minutes and were not cut down in a bloody reprisal by an army of security minions.

"Still worth making sure," he decided, breaking the silence. "Right. Let's get in there so you can get your art on."

The building was absolutely, completely solid. The hallways and stairwells were laid out in a logical fashion; no weirdness like you'd see in the Sideways or the crummier parts of the city, where mismatched rooms were connected to each other. This palatial monument to high finance had been lifted wholesale and plopped down intact.

We used the stairwells exclusively, only switching to a new one if we ran out of stairs. A short, direct ascent. Once we got to the 20th floor, we had to leave the upward spiral to find the lobby I was seeking... and that meant cutting through floors full of cubicles and executive meeting rooms, past offices with cat calendars and tasteful Swedish furniture.

Honestly, it was quite boring. Boring enough for us to let down our guard and feel comfortable here. Even Hollister.

"Mid-nineties," he spoke up, as we were crossing through a cubicle farm.

"Hm?"

"The monitors," he said, pointing to the big boxy beige things. (Or at least waving the ladder in their direction, anyway.) "CRT tubes... one-point-three-bar-repeating aspect ratio. Lumpy full size towers, too. These computers are all mid-nineties, and clearly they had money for top of the line. But the building only showed up a decade ago... even by then LCD was coming into play."

"Huh. I'm not much of a computer nerd," I stated dismissively.

"You have a smartphone in your pocket which is more powerful than ten of these things put together and you know where to find my website. *Everybody* is a computer nerd these days," he added. "My point is, this building's older than its birthday in the city suggests. Not much entropy, either. I wonder why..."

"You're the government type, you tell me," I said, kicking a chair on wheels out of the way. Apparently someone had been playing a round of office chair basketball before quitting for the day.

"Orientation, remember? Resources are the guys who study the how and why of the city. And they don't publish their findings," he said. "I've always suspected they don't actually HAVE any findings, and just pretend to be in control to keep folks happy. City's *weird*, plain and simple. ...I doubt Resources would bother studying this place, anyway. Greedy bastards just want new space to annex and new toys to steal, and these toys are crummy."

And then, quiet. Just the air conditioning, our footsteps, and the loose rattle of the folding ladder. And Hollister's breathing, which was quite heavy seeing as he'd just lugged a ladder up twenty flights.

Without a single complaint, either.

"You must want her pretty damn badly," I mused aloud.

"*Huff.* Huh?" he asked.

"Aside from some skittishness at setting out for the tower you've played along quite well," I said. "Even up the stairs when I said we shouldn't take the elevators. A guy who goes that far out of his way for the slightest hint at a chance at nookie is either insane, horny as a toad, or determined as hell..."

Another rattle, as his tired arms hiked the ladder up an inch.

"First? The attitude? Up with it I will not put," he declared. "Second? You don't know me as much as you think you do. If I was powered by my trouser snake there are far easier ways to solve that equation than *this*. Reason I'm taking things so far is because I said I'd take things this far, full stop. I said I'd help you get in the tower and play a combination roadie-and-criminal-lookout for you and that's what I'm doing. Would you prefer I lay down my aluminum burdens and amscray?"

I waved his protests off. "I'm not complaining, I'm not," I claimed. "Whatever your reasoning I'm glad you're being a sport about all this. It won't be much farther now, anyway. Just need to locate the target area, and then it's all on me to get the work done— there!"

It was nearly hidden in the maze of bulletin boards and routing signs indicating the location of executive offices and conference rooms. Every building had to have maps up indicating the fire exits and evacuation routes... doubling as a guide for those who did not in fact work here and did not in fact know where everything was already.

I tapped the map on the wall, to call Hollister's attention to it.

"Welcoming lobby for the firm, three hallways down from here." I explained. "Floor-to-ceiling windows, twenty feet high. That's the one that faces towards the city itself. It's illuminated enough that a piece there will be seen for miles. Almost there, Hollister! Let's move!"

I wasn't the one lugging a folding ladder up twenty flights of stairs. He had every right to call a halt for a breather. He didn't. And put together we had enough energy, especially this close to the end, to carry us both along with great speed.

Perfect. *Perfect.*

Plenty of open space, with only a loose assortment of couches and tables and potted plants. A wall of glass to work with, with only a minor amount of steel window frame to interrupt the flow—nice and modern design, perfect for my uses.

With the fatigue of the trip finally catching up to him, Hollister plopped down in one of the leather armchairs, exhausted. Which was fine; he'd served his purpose in carrying the ladder and now he could chill a moment. Even using the refined and simplified design I'd been practicing on the walls of my apartment, it'd take me an hour to completely finish the piece.

I unpacked my backpack, getting the tools of the trade ready.

Blacks, whites, grays—I liked to work in grayscale for pieces, rather than a more colorful wild style other writers might've used. Stark and straightforward. The message mattered more than wowing someone with a rainbow array of smooth colors. Besides, a full color piece would keep us here for hours, and it'd be easier to sneak back into the city before the sun came up.

Thin caps, thick caps. Different spray approaches and good can control meant I could do a lot with a little, mixing in style without having to spread the color palette around. I'd preloaded caps onto multiple cans of the same shade, so I wouldn't have to swap them around... a corner-cutting time saver, but not one that would hurt the work.

Finally, my black book. Between that and my doodling during my sister's workout routine, I'd finished the piece before I ever got here. It'd be my guide for what needed to be done.

"You're not going to have to climb out the window, are you?" Hollister asked, watching as I gradually turned my backpack inside out. "I'd rather not have to explain to your sister how you fell twenty stories to your death..."

"Reverse glass painting. Legit method. They used to do it in churches, even," I said, shaking up a can. "You do the outlines first, all the tiny little details, THEN the fills. Inside out, no room for error so it's trickier, but doable. I won't be bothering with crazy shaded fills, it'll take too long; some smooth grey will get it done."

"Got this all worked out, huh?"

"I always come prepared," I replied, a bit smugly.

"I'm surprised. I mean, I thought graffiti types just sorta scribble away and then run for it from the cops..."

Unfolding the ladder, I propped it up to the window. May as well start at the top, so I'd get a better sense of scale. I pulled on a paper breathing mask and made my way up, can in hand.

"These 'scribbles' are my words, man. I take care with them," I called back. "Now keep an eye on the doors, keep your ears open. Just in case, I don't know, the Department of Safety comes charging up the stairs with a SWAT team."

As I started sizing up the available space, comparing it to my notebook, I shook up the first can of the evening. The comforting and familiar metallic rattle, plus the white noise hum of the air conditioning and the buzz of the overhead lights, meant we didn't hear the elevator dinging repeatedly in the distance. I could paint away in peace, losing myself in the linework, until it was almost too late.

If you rush art, is it still art?

I hoped like hell it was. I hoped the message and the line weight would be enough, because no matter how confident I was, hanging around in the Defined Tower all night and through the morning was out of the question.

The lines went up fast. Connecting them up and making sure they were balanced perfectly on the first shot was important; this wasn't like a wall, where I could paint over mistakes with fresh design concepts or simply whitewash them out if they were that horrible. Reverse glass painting in a famous landmark had no margin of error. Either you made a masterpiece, or your fumbles would be on display forever.

Fortunately, my muse was with me. (I always suspected my muse, if one existed in the Greek sense, looked like Vivi.) The lines curved and arced perfectly. They connected cleanly. The fills went in quickly, a loose mash of grey that would give the overall shape definition under daylight or moonlight. The finishing touch—the cartoony ghost of the Ghostwriter—I could relax and throw up quickly, because I'd done that icon hundreds of times already. I knew the wrist motions by heart, even when amplifying them up for such a huge glass canvas.

After climbing up and down and repositioning the ladder a dozen times, it was finished.

I awaited review from the art critic I'd brought along.

Who was too busy chillaxin' in a chair, reading some dude-themed music industry magazine to pay attention.

"I'm *done*," I stated loudly, with emphasis, to make a point, etc.

Realizing a girl wanted his attention, Hollister quickly put the magazine away... and noticed the piece for apparently the first time.

It was thrown up there backwards, of course, but if you turned it around in your brain it was plenty readable:

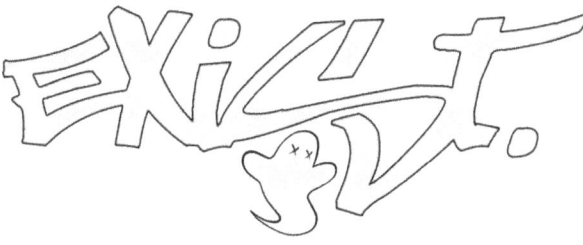

"*Exist?*" he read aloud.

"No, *Exist.* With a period," I corrected.

"Yes, thank you, I can see the little blobby thing at the end," he indicated, pointing to it just in case I needed to know where it was. "I'm just not getting it. We came all this way so you could slap up a random word and... is that

Casper the Friendly Ghost?"

I was planning to leave the ladder here so technically I didn't need Hollister anymore, but throttling him was probably not good sport.

"That's my tag. I'm Ghostwriter," I said. "And it's Exist, with a period. Because it's a command, not a question. I'm not questioning whether people Exist. I'm *telling* them to Exist. You know, as opposed to... you know what? Nevermind. You did your bit already, you don't have to pretend you—"

"It's a defiant stance against the Echo Revelation, while acknowledging it as truth," Hollister said, scratching his chin as he read and re-read the word. "*Exist.* Just do it, just exist. Only way forward is to exist. It's accepting the Echo Revelation but instead of caving in and giving up, it's saying you've got to prove you exist."

Now I was reading him in far more confusion than he was reading my piece.

"... .... what," I stated, flatly.

"You have no idea the week I had recently," he said. "I work Department of Orientation. Refugees usually have trouble with the Echo Revelation. Well, thanks to that and a host of other bungles, my class of four students plummeted to one graduate... and I had someone suicide out thanks to the Revelation. So, yeah. *Exist.* I wish I could've said it so succinctly. Maybe she'd be alive today if I had. You want me to bring the ladder back with us or leave it here?"

I had no response to that. So, he picked it up anyway.

"I don't think you know me as well as you think you do," Hollister said, simply. "Now, if we're all done here, can we please go home?"

I wasn't crying, and yet my cheeks were suddenly wet.

No, seriously, I wasn't crying. Not in one of those deep-emotional-denial sort of "I wasn't crying, there was just dust in the room" deals. I mean suddenly my cheeks were wet when they were not one second ago. And my hair was wet. And my cotton hoodie was rapidly getting soaked...

An ear-shattering series of electronic whistles tore through the room, explaining the sudden indoor rainstorm.

Fire alarm.

Immediately I spun in place, back to my piece...

I used the best paint I could afford, stuff that would stand up to rain and sleet and snow for as long as possible. Even so soon after sticking it up there, even if I was painting it on a slick glass surface, it should've held on under the onslaught of fire suppression sprinklers.

That didn't change the fact that my word was slowly melting downward, into an illegible smear.

I remember screaming, maybe even screaming something like "No no no NO." I tried to push the paint back up the slick and runny glass, messing up my hands in the process. It was too late, of course. Every overhead sprinkler in the room was dumping at full blast, including spraying down the piece and wrecking it in short order...

Faintly, I could see the reflection of orange and yellow flickers on the glass. A fire, somewhere. I didn't care. It was being ruined. My one defiant stance, my tribute to the city, to give people hope and courage to stand up to the Echo Revelation and exist, and it was melting away.

I may as well have melted away, or burned to ashes. It didn't matter. This was the most important work of my life and it was completely ruined. Echo said everything we did was futile and pointless, that life was endless suffering because we were never meant to be here in the first place. She would not be denied.

I could see eyes, wobbly and loose, reflected in the window. Either because I was actually crying or because of a distortion of paint and water, they looked oddly blue...

Torn away from that empty girl's gaze by the hand on my shoulder.

"Leaving now!" Hollister declared. "Fire! Bad stuff! Leaving now!"

Somehow I staggered along, with Hollister leading the way. He'd probably move faster without the ladder, but right now neither of us were in any position to evaluate our situation on such a tactical level. Goal #1 was to GTFO.

Chaos in the cubicle farm. Cloth-covered cube walls on fire. Huge blazing patches here and there, which the sprinklers were having trouble putting down. Maybe the building wasn't about to collapse in on itself or anything like that, but it was certainly a hazard zone for a lone artist and her dudebro companion.

The way back to the stairwell had been cut off completely. As I got my wits back, as I realized I had to focus on the existing I had preciously declared or I would very certainly cease to in short order, I started to rely less on Hollister dragging me along.

I tore the emergency evacuation map off the wall, the one which had led us to the lobby. If ever there was a good time to reference it, this would certainly be it.

"Into the hall and turn left!" I declared. "Another stairwell. C'mon!"

As far as I could see, the path was clear. We'd beat feet down twenty flights in a nicely insulated stairwell, be out the door, and back into the city in under twenty minutes. Fifteen if I could sprint, and I certainly could sprint when my ass was on the line.

It took some distance to get a proper run-up. Dashing out of the cubicle farm and into the hallway, cornering tightly to the left, I was already halfway to maximum speed.

If I'd been at maximum speed I might've run right into my doom.

Apparently whatever dark gods were frowning down on me that night decided that ruining my piece and lighting the building on fire just wasn't horrible enough. No no. They also had to put a Picasso in my path.

To be honest, I'd never seen one in person. And for all my bravado about how I wasn't afraid of this city or its offerings, I can also be honest and say I'd never want to see another Picasso again. They are pants-fillingly terrifying.

It was a mess of blue and grey, a swirl of plastic buttons and chrome-plated shields. There was skin in there as well, hidden somewhere behind the cloud of polyester and nylon. I occasionally caught a flash of pale flesh, like a statue in an art museum might have—framing eyes like clear glass. So many eyes. All the eyes... all turning on the girl who was skidding to a halt on the wet tile floor of the hallway, only twenty feet or so away from him...

Hollister was right. This building did indeed house a Picasso'd security guard. I could see his symbols of office in a blur, orbiting his twisted and agonized form.

Sixteen company-issued sidearms held in as many hands manifested, all clicking menacingly like a Hollywood hit squad.

private property // you see this badge // ugh, don't wanna do night shift again // the hell's that noise // goddamn brat in my building //
*   your last warning // one of these days I'm gonna get to use this gun // patrol is so boring //   kill you // kill all of them one of these days swear to // stupid little chink bitch // KILL*

Oh, yes. Of course. It wasn't bad enough to be killed by a crazed incarnation of reality-bending madness. I had to be killed by a *racist* crazed incarnation of reality-bending madness.

"This way!"

I didn't care who just said that. I just ran This Way.

Bullets zipped through the air where Hollister and I just were. I could see something ahead, two people, an open doorway... something whizzing over my shoulder, towards the incoherent mess that was following us—

Heat at my back. Our rescuers had hurled an incendiary device, landing just short of the Picasso, nearly enveloping it in a burst of flame.

Basic survival skills when dealing with reality-bending abominations—a gun may help a little, but your best weapon is fire. Beyond the distortions, a Picasso is flesh and blood. Dodging bullets isn't too hard for a Picasso but they'll avoid fire, avoid it enough to slow down pursuit. Enough for us to get through the door and to safety.

Even if it also meant that they'd had to set off the sprinklers and ruin my art to save our lives.

My sneakers squeaked fiercely as I slid to a halt inside the corporate lunchroom.

Behind me, the door slammed shut—and tables and chairs were immediately slid up against it. Hollister, working in tandem with whoever our mysterious saviors were. Had to admit, the guy-who-knew-a-guy was on the ball while I was still trying to catch my breath and figure out what was going on...

A quick survey let me take in the pertinent details.

Some guy wearing body armor and a bandolier of what I could assume to be incendiary grenades was piling up tables and chairs, along with Hollister. He didn't pay me any mind, too focused on his current task. Despite being heavily armed and armored he wasn't wearing the dull green of a Department of Safety officer. Maybe I'd be torn apart by a Picasso, but at least nobody was arresting me for vandalism tonight.

The second of our rescuers was a bit less expected. A dude armed to the teeth, okay, that made sense in an action movie sort of context. A scrawny kid with an old-timey explorer's helmet did not.

"Okay, so, I'm Penelope and that's my dad Gregory," she explained, quickly. "We were mapping this place when we spotted the Picasso moving up the elevators and I insisted we try to help you out since you probably didn't know it was coming and now I... have a bad feeling we cornered ourselves because I'm not seeing any way out of this room. Oh! Dad? Ceiling?"

"Ceiling," he confirmed, without looking away from jamming a plastic chair into the impromptu barricade.

"Right! On it!" the girl replied... and looked around for some way to reach it, given all the climbable furniture was gradually accumulating at one end of the room.

In the end she spied the discarded ladder Hollister had hurriedly hauled in here.

"Oh, thanks, that's very forward-thinking of you," she said. "Hey, um, miss? Help me set this up?"

I should probably have stopped and asked what the hell was going on. How they got here, what they were doing here, if they set off the fire alarms and ruined my artwork, and so on. These were all burning questions sitting in the queue behind the most important thing in my brain, which was less of a question and more of a statement, reading I WANT TO LIVE DAMMIT.

So, I helped the kid set up the ladder. She was up it like a rocket once the thing was locked into position—pushing one of the foam core ceiling tiles to the side, to expose the crawlspace of ducts and wires and cables that lurked just over the heads of all corporate drones.

Meanwhile, the big strong strapping menfolk stepped away from their big strong barrier, satisfied with its solidity in a strapping sort of way.

Until the whole thing rattled and shook from the force of impact on the other side of the door. The *ptang! ptang!* of bullets ricocheting off the metal door was also not a pleasant sound.

"Yeah, okay, that's not gonna work," Gregory realized. "We need to go, and now. There's a storage room next door; we go up and over and down into it, then route our way around and back to the stairs. Picassos are lousy at strategy, it'll stay hung up on the door and won't think to double back and find another approach. —the hell are you two kids doing in this place, anyway? Looking for somewhere to get high or something?"

"Dad, sheesh!" Penelope protested, peeking down from inside the ceiling crawlspace. "A) that's stupid and B) not now, okay? C'mon! Leaving!"

Apparently 'ladies first' was not a gold standard for this guy, as Gregory went up the ladder next. Hollister approached, but paused, gesturing for me to go up next. Class act.

After taking two steps up... I paused, to look down at him.

"This is a terrible time to tell you that I only promised to teach you flirty sign language because I knew my sis would never actually sleep with you," I told Hollister.

He stood bracing the ladder, and... peered at me funny.

"...if it's a terrible time to tell me, why did you tell me?"

"Because I'm not sure there's going to be another time. Sorry. Sorry for all this."

Unable to meet his look, I went up, and through the dusty dark, and down the other side into the waiting arms of the pair who had been escorting us along.

The emergency exit map I'd been bringing around with me paled in comparison to the map the kid had on her tablet computer. Even while trying to track down the Picasso as it crawled its way up twenty floors, they had been mapping the whole way. Being, y'know, mappers, and all.

We had time to chat after we ditched the crazy security guy. By kicking the ladder over and replacing the ceiling tile behind us, he didn't know we were one room over—as storage room which connected to a different hallway. That gave us enough rat-in-a-maze distance to work our way around to a different stairwell, and start putting a healthy amount of space between us and the Picasso.

Even if out of sight meant out of mind, we weren't nuts enough to assume the danger was past. The four of us went down those stairs as fast as possible, while trying to avoid tripping over our own feet and rolling all the way to the bottom.

"So the crazy thing is that there's this part of the Sideways in the Suburbs that connects to the Defined Tower!" Penelope Yates was explaining (while trying to keep her voice down). "Suburbs to city, just like that. I knew it! We ended up in the underground parking lot. I think this entire building is actually part of the Sideways, even though it LOOKS completely stable. Entropy's really, really low here. Anyway, we saw the security guard Picasso sleeping at a monitoring station, and were gonna sneak by him when BAM! This alarm went off and all his monitors showed you two at the front door. Took him a while to wake up, we stayed hidden just in case, but he started heading upstairs a few minutes later, and—"

"Are you going to do this every time we run into a helpless stray, Penelope?" her father asked. He had his gun drawn, in case the trigger-happy Picasso somehow showed up around the next bend in the spiraling staircase. "It doesn't matter why we were here or who we are. Better not to go into details. And we're not taking these two out for seafood."

Sensing some hostility, I tried to put emotional distance up. It was a good way to deal with most awkward situations in life, I'd learned.

"Whoever you are and whyever you were here, man, whatever... just... thanks for bailing us out," I said, with exactly as much respect as was needed. "We'll be out of your hair once we hit the front lobby and get out the door. ...evening's completely ruined anyway, may as well go home."

"Really? Why were you two in here, anyway?" Penelope asked. "You don't seem to be mapping..."

"I was... painting a mural," I decided to phrase it, since 'vandalizing a window' rarely goes over well. "Up on twenty. Doesn't matter. It got wrecked by the sprinklers, and no way I'm going back up to fix it."

Hollister, who was still a bit jittery but trying to look cool and confident all the same, showed sympathy.

"K-Kinda sucks," he agreed, with a little stutter when he nervously glanced behind us, looking for guns and blurs. "I mean, it was a nice piece. The word EXIST, with a period, so all the city could see. Very inspirational—"

"No point in sucking up, Hollister. I promised I'd teach you sign language and I will. Not that it'll do you any good."

"Yeah, uh, what exactly did you mean by that, back there?" he asked. "We aren't actively being attacked now, so—"

"*Shhhh.*"

This was one of those times where when someone went *shhhh*, yours was not to question why, it was to do or quite likely die. We *shhhh*'d.

Our merry procession had reached the bottom of the stairwell. One thick metal door lay between us and the open lobby, and freedom from this haunted house. But, even if the Picasso hadn't followed us directly... it might have doubled back and used the elevators or other stairwells, to lie in wait.

Gregory was using a tiny spray can, like a miniature graffiti tool, to oil up the hinges on the door. The less noise they made, the better. After that, he waved for us to press flat against the wall... then drew his gun, stepped to one side, and opened the door a crack.

I couldn't see what he saw, but after glancing this way and that, it must've looked all clear. He waved us through, stepping out first with weapon at the ready.

The front lobby looked much like it looked when Hollister and I first broke in. Scattered furniture, corporate logos, an unmanned security checkpoint and so on. The carpeting was soaked thick thanks to the fires upstairs setting off sprinklers all over the place, but you'd never know someone was chasing a Picasso around with Molotovs just minutes ago.

The broken glass of the front doors was just across the lobby. One straight dash and we'd be home free. But Gregory was moving carefully, leading the pack, continuing to make no noise. *Shhhh* still applied.

We'd gotten twenty floors up despite a Picasso roaming around. I'd taken my sweet time writing a burner which was then burned in turn. If all of that could happen without encountering the monster even once, it meant the thing could move very quietly when it wanted to.

For instance, it could be defying physics and standing on the ceiling just over our line of sight, lying in wait.

By the time any of us (Gregory included) spotted it, the hail of bullets was already airborne.

He'd kept Penelope behind him, just in case. There's not enough time to react to a gunman to make decisions like that after the fact. Planning ahead saved her life.

Eleven of the simultaneously fired pistol shots went wide, missing the group entirely.

Three shots slammed into Gregory's bulletproof vest.

One went into his leg.

One went into his neck.

Gregory hit the damp floor with a mild *squelch*, just as the cloud of smoking guns and malice touched down lightly, blocking our way to the front door. Guns clicking and reloading, ready for a second volley.

Nobody knew what to say, what to do. The one guy who looked ready for war had been dropped in the blink of an eye. Blood from his wounds had splattered behind him—on his daughter notably, also on me, and on Hollister.

Perhaps sensing how terrified we were, how he had us right in the nonexistent palm of his fractured hands, the Picasso took its sweet time to aim his next wave of death. He didn't bother advancing, content to stand in the center of the spacious lobby, to own the space. To own us.

I can't even imagine the look on the poor little girl's face, but I could see the look on what passed for the Picasso's face. All smiles. ALL smiles, no other defining characteristics. Hatred. Smug, smug hatred.

you have the right to remain silent // a paycheck's a paycheck //
goddamn kids act like they're owed // slant and I can have some fun // kill //
you see this badge // you are trespassing //
nobody can stop me now // she's smiling at me // the child of madness // I can
feel // KILL

Penelope Yates was trembling. I could see that much. Almost like her outline was vibrating. ...hopefully not turning Picasso herself...

"No," she whispered. "No... Daddy, please..."

// KILL //

"NO!"

And we shifted half an inch to the left.

Or maybe everything else shifted half an inch to the right. Everything. The lobby, the Picasso, the building, the city.

My eyes were probably just playing tricks on me. A jitter of fright causing my gaze to snap slightly to the side. But it was a slowly expanding shift, outward from the center... from her. From the kid.

One second later and a Buick crashed into the security guard. Head on, from above.

Followed by a van. And a sport utility vehicle.

A waterfall of cars, raining down from above, crashing through the ceiling. All pointed downward, like they were driving down the side of a cliff. Shattered steel and concrete and glass, pouring down in a straight line, right across the space where the Picasso was previously standing. Coming down from above and punching straight through the floor, presumably to crash in the parking lot basement below.

By this point Hollister and I had regained enough of our wits to grab the kid and run for it. He overturned a leather sofa, I wrapped her up tight and slid in behind it like I was stealing home base. Hollister, in turn, covered me. It was a big 'ol duck and cover love-in—and for the best, as I could hear debris clattering against the walls and bouncing off the carpeted floor all around us...

The cacophony went on for a full minute, until it was done raining cars. Only after the worst of the noise stopped did we dare to look over the top of the couch.

The ceiling was gone. Most of the floor was gone.

Looking up through the newly created gap... we saw a parking garage. Delineated parking spaces, overhead fluorescents, reserved spots for corporate CEOs and everything.

Except it was turned ninety degrees on its axis, upright instead of flat, intersecting a dozen or so floors of the building. All the cars apparently had been cozy in their parking spaces until that one fateful moment when they all decided to remember how gravity worked, and went sailing sideways through the "wall" which was in fact the "ceiling" and, well, *whammo*. Dead Picasso, presumably buried under several metric tons of wrecked vehicles.

I'd call it impossible, but the city routinely mocked people who used that word, so. I decided to leave it at highly improbable that we had somehow completely missed an implausibly messed up sideways parking lot in the middle of the building's superstructure.

Also highly improbable was Gregory, who was pushed up against the couch as well, breathing heavily and staring in amazement at what he'd backed away from.

I could see the three impact marks on his bulletproof vest. His leg was certainly bleeding; a basic flesh wound. But the kill shot to his neck wasn't nearly as bad as I thought it was. More of a graze. Ugly-looking, but *just* ugly-looking.

"What in the freaking heck was that?" he pondered aloud.

Thankfully his neck was not bleeding profusely, because it immediately developed a little girl-sized growth. Penelope latched on, hugged and hugged, and was not going to stop hugging for some time to come.

Whole building was really in the Sideways, so who knows why it happened? Just be thankful.

That was the official explanation from our official mapping experts, and it would have to stand. Neither of them seemed keen to talk about how a parking garage upended its contents on the noggin of a murderous Picasso just before it could kill us all.

Gregory was twice as eager to be rid of us after that, but he was too wounded to limp away without help. Fortunately, I had a guy with me who knew a guy. Hollister and I led the Yates pair out of the vague spaces, following the chalk marks I'd left along the way. After that Hollister directed us to a slightly shady free clinic in a tenth-floor walkup at the edge of town. Not a fun trip, but the patient survived, and was being stitched up by a tired-looking doctor we'd roused out of bed not ten minutes ago.

Penelope refused to leave her father's side, even while he was being poked at with needle and thread. She had taken to perpetually hugging a fuzzy teddy bear retrieved from her backpack, however. Small comforts in bad situations, I suppose.

Hollister and I were content to sit in the decidedly non-sterilized waiting room of the doctor's office, looking across the cityscape through windows, and trying to calm down after the night's events.

I didn't realize how tired I was. I wanted nothing, nothing more than to go home and crawl into bed alongside Vivi and feel safe and secure again. Put this whole mess behind me and get on with what passed for my life.

Hollister didn't technically have to stay with me. I didn't have to wait for the Yateses to get out of surgery, either. But we were exhausted, and he was content to be exhausted in my company. I'd just put him through a living hell and he had few complaints...

I owed him an explanation.

"I don't think Vivi's gonna go for you," I said, honestly. "Not for sexy funtimes, anyway. Truth is... she told me once that you remind her a lot of her kid brother, back on Earth. She's an import, you know. Doesn't remember very much about that life she left behind but that was one of the bright spots. A funny little kid brother. And... that's you, now. She likes you, she thinks you're sweet, but... you're her new funny little kid brother. Not one-night stand material."

It was the much-delayed answer to a distant question, one that felt like it was asked days ago. It took Hollister a moment to make the connection.

"No one-night stands, huh?" he asked.

"No chance in hell, no. ...so, I'll teach you to flirt if you still want me to, but... she's not going to be the hot party girl type for you. Sorry. I took you for a ride tonight and for that I'm sorry."

He slid down in the hard plastic seat, thinking about it.

"I wasn't really looking for a party girl," he explained. "Wasn't cruising for easy tail, in general. I've had plenty of that. ...too much, honestly. Sometimes I feel like it's expected of me to be the party dude. I've had all these really thin, short relationships because I'm the guy who knows a guy. I've done the walk of shame too many times. Marcy... *that's* why I wanted to get to know your sister better. Not to hook up with her, just to get to know her. She seemed like someone I'd have a chance at making a real connection with. A genuine and compassionate person. Even if nothing really comes of it, I wanted to try. That's all."

...I don't like it when folks who don't "get" my sister and me immediately reach for nasty little labels to stick all over us. They're foul things that ruin our mood.

The irony was not lost on me that I'd slapped the "playboy bastard" label on Hollister from the moment I met him, and refused to look past it.

He'd done right by me tonight. He went the distance. But plenty of so-called Nice Guys did that, putting in kindness coins until sex fell out—what he did was more genuine. He didn't want my bod, he saw me in need and despite his misgivings went along with my passions all the same. He understood my writing. He showed depth I hadn't wanted to see in him. And in the end, all he wanted was a chance at something real and true. No coy manipulation. Just Hollister, laid bare.

I held up the sign. Thumb, index, ring finger.

"This means 'I love you,'" I educated him. "The context and associated body language is important, though. Vivi likes to use this casually for all of her friends, flashing or waggling it with a grin. Because, well, she loves everyone. It's like saying hello for her. Now, a physical touch with this symbol... well, that's something else. But this is a good place to start."

And life, such as it is, goes on.

I wandered town, trying to get my mojo back with a series of quick throw-ups. Nothing special. I didn't reuse EXIST. It would've been wrong to take something that important to me and toss it on the side of a convenience store.

During the day Vivi and I would take in a movie or hang out at the park. Sometimes Hollister joined us. He'd finally managed to approach her at the ZigZag club without my interference, and charmed the pants off her.

(Not literally. They weren't even dating. Vivi called him "a soul in need," and added him to her entourage of nightlife friends. He seemed more than content with that. If their relationship eventually reached beyond, then... that was her decision. Wasn't my right to step in the way.)

I made up with Slyck, when my nighttime excursions got lonely enough that I couldn't handle it anymore. Boy, did I make up with him. By the time it was over he was left bewildered and I was looking for my pants.

"Sorry I ditched you," he apologized. "I just—"

"It's fine, Slyck, whatever," I accepted. Well, I said it was fine, whether it was or not. "Don't worry about it."

"Was glad to see you got the piece done anyway. Hope it wasn't too rough out there."

I paused in the middle of looking for my left sneaker.

"I like it a lot," he continued. "EXIST. It really says... something, you know? I don't know what it says but I can tell you're really saying something —"

"Slyck, the piece got wrecked," I explained. "It's gone. Just mush on the windows."

After insisting twice more, he broke out the telescope his parents got him when he was a kid, and pointed it at the Defined Tower.

Floor twenty. Floor-to-ceiling windows. Painted bright and true.

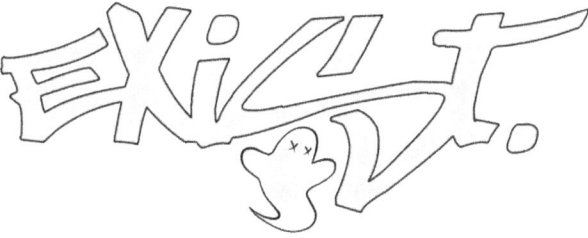

All the line work, all the twists and curves, the light grey fill, and my Ghostwriter tag. All there.

The borders were locked down by the Department of Safety the morning after my excursion. Penelope and Gregory had hopped the train that night, heading inward—going home. They hadn't gone back to paint it. Hollister certainly hadn't.

In fact, according to Slyck, he saw the piece up there the very night I failed to paint it. It was like it had never been erased in the first place.

But I hadn't used red paint. And now, it was red.

No idea what to make of it. So, I didn't. I just got back in bed.

//end

Buildings next to buildings, askew or aligned. Buildings sometimes intersecting buildings, for that matter. Walk down a hallway, end up in a ballroom, double glass doors to a subway station, third exit on the left goes to a donut shop. It's the only place where you can buy klein bottle jellies with sprinkles.

There's no rhyme or reason to any of it—we've got streets which lead to dead ends, roads which criss-cross and loop back around, highways which go nowhere. Literally nowhere, as in "anybody going down that road is not coming back." This is not a good place to wander off unless you like wandering off forever...

Nobody knows where the city came from. Nobody knows how we got here. Nobody knows why any of this is happening. But it's happening. The city exists. We are here now. It's growing every day, and bringing new people with it.

We live a life amidst the twisted yet familiar.

If we're going to survive this, if we're going to stay alive and thrive, we need to learn to live in the City of Angles.

...here's an angle to consider...

Adrift in a warped concrete jungle, a man might sit to ponder the surrealistic horror of his situation. But soon enough, if he wants to continue those ponderings, he'll also need what everybody needs to keep going—food, water, shelter. That means a job, that means money, that means obeying the Maslow Hierarchy. Practicality breaks the back of philosophy. Existential crisis does not put pasta on the plate.

Perhaps the clock you punch in every morning is melting across a Dali landscape, but a punch clock is a punch clock. The chain of survival yokes you down to that grind, burying your face in the trivial and mundane.

In a lot of ways... that doubles as a psychological survival mechanism. If you're putting spindles in boxes for ten hours a day, that's ten hours spent not thinking about the warped abomination lurking in the depths of your subdimensional closet that wants to eat your face.

But for the unlucky ones, the ones who are keenly aware of the weirdness perpetually lurking at the edge of vision... even the drudge of the day won't keep the nightmares at bay. And no matter how far they go, how distant from the center they may journey, they find themselves closer to the core of the matter inch by inch, moment by moment, until...

//004: Turn Left

Dreams, by Cass

Random thoughts light the way down the corridors of dreams, loose and dangling like shoes on a telephone wire, the hare just inches ahead of the fox, the three notes that echo in your head without a title to hang themselves on.

Dreams of the spaces between, hives of madness and horror which are the perfect vision of hell for the Average Joe—but the perfect vision of heaven for Average Joe's mixed-up derivatives,

Dreams of the nightmare engines which exist in plain sight on the evening news, safety and fear dancing hand in hand, reassuring with a pat on the head with one while waggling a finger of disapproval with the other,

Dreams of the holy trinity of Lucidity, Madness, and Oblivion—and within the topmost triangular vertex of the pyramid lies the three-sided goddess of flesh and thought and concrete, known to all yet unknowable,

Dreams of Tommy Westfall, whose spherical dreams in turn encompass everything that ever was and ever will be, the self-reciprocating feedback loop of imagination where reality asserts its own lie,

Dreams of

Snickering.

snickers bars, snacker doodles, snaggletooth, smirks. very funny words.

The smoky haze of the coffee shop / bar / poetry club / bingo on Thursdays trickled into her lungs after that. It sapped out whatever loose forward momentum she had going into it, drained away the impetus. For a moment she considered plowing on anyway... but the words on the page were mocked by the words in the air around that random audience member. Cheapened.

"I don't really feel like reading anymore," Cass announced, flipping her spiral bound notebook shut. "I just sorta haven't got any kind of steam."

Fortunately that incident was the middle of the night; there were two poets up after her, all too eager to snag the spotlight and start reciting with great gusto. By the time the night's session was done and everybody broke for drinks, few people even remembered the derailment of Cass's train of thought.

But she did. The book on the table in front of her, closed, sealed, mocking... that was plenty to keep the localized memory fresh.

Her sour mood was not duplicated by her two table companions, off in their own secluded corner of the club.

Reg (né Reggie) (actually Reginald) was all good cheer and smiles, perhaps trying to elevate Cass to his level. He was all good cheer and smiles for all the poets, really—Mister Encouragement, with his hipster dark glasses (similar to hers) and his hipster beanie (semi-similar to her own baker boy cap). Far too warm and personable to make sense in the cool elitism of the club.

Despite looking like some genetic duplicate of a young Miles Davis recently escaped from a jazz-loving mad scientist's lab, Reggie was a scene rider... a rich socialite producing nothing, soaking in the ambiance, wanting to be a part of it all despite having no ability of his own. He headed up several failing 'zines and poured perfectly good money into art galleries that shut down weeks after opening. Despite being as creative as a kumquat and having the business sense of an avocado, Cass could appreciate his place here. He had a consistent passion and a good ear.

By contrast Fi (because Fiona was too suburban) maintained a cool dispassion and aloofness that rivaled an ice sculpture. She didn't care that Cass had flamed out, one way or another. She was above everything, floating on her own little cloud, daring to touch down only when she felt she had something of tremendous value to say.

A poet's poet, who only spoke in color. The living embodiment of pretension, to be honest, but Cass couldn't hate on her for that. After all, at her worst moments, Cass was just like Fi. Having Fi around kept Cass honest, in the same way a room of mirrors encourages you to comb your hair once in a while.

Two of the three, smoking and drinking. Expected of the scene. Oddly, the club smelt the most of nicotine after Bingo nights more than any other night. Cass herself did neither; she'd had more than her fill of biochemical modification, once upon a time. Which might've been to blame for her shutting down earlier, to be honest...

"I'd say 'Don't let a heckler get you down,' but honestly, I don't think that was heckling," Reg explained. "So someone laughed. So what? It was a funny line. Tommy Westfall! Cool, way cool. You know, even your mentor had them rolling in the aisles from time to time. Howl had plenty of humor."

"Mine wasn't meant to be funny," Cass mumbled. "Though I can barely take it seriously, myself. God. I can't believe I really stood up there reading this crap. Like 'The hare just inches ahead of the fox,' what was I thinking? That's ridiculous. All of it, every last word was too floaty and thin. I need the words to be... I don't know. Heavier. Grounded and real..."

"Yeah, but didn't you say you got most of your words from your dreams? Of course they're going to be floaty."

She held back a twitch.

It was the wrong thing to tell Reg. Cass honestly had no idea why she'd admitted to that, weeks ago. Because yes, most of the words were remembered from dreams... where they had more weight, more value. There was an impetus behind the words while they were in her dream. Putting them on paper seemed to wreck whatever strange magic they once held.

Even the words which came to her in her waking hours had more strength than this... and that was the unsettling part, the part she never told Reg. The waking words...

"Anyway, I thought it was working just fine," Reg said, swerving away from that topic, thankfully. "I never thought I'd hear the name Tommy Westfall in this club. St. Elsewhere, right? Final episode, the entire series turns out to be the dream of an autistic kid?"

Fi's obnoxiously musical voice chimed in, with response. "Interconnectivity," she lilted, in agreement.

"Right. Crossovers with crossovers, leaving nearly all of television in the mind of Tommy Westfall. I like it. Strong image there. I mean, I don't get how it ties into your poem just yet, but I think there's some meat on those bones worth chewing on."

"I guess. I don't know. Maybe," Cass waffled. "It's just too thin right now. Doesn't feel real to me... too out of balance."

"So, do a rewrite. Present again next week. I bet nobody here will even have remembered the first draft by that point."

Cass leaned back in her crappy old wooden chair, dangerously close to tipping backwards. Arms folded.

"That's part of the problem, isn't it?" she said. "The only audience in this city for poetry is a room full of poets. They're all too busy anticipating their turn at bat to bother paying attention to the game itself. —UGH, sports metaphor, no. Point is, none of them are really listening. A reading's for readers and my audience is entirely writers."

"I'm not a writer," Reg reminded. "I just like cheap booze and fascinating art."

"And that's why you're the only person who seems to care about my work. At risk of inflating your ego, I'd say you're the most real person in the room."

Fi wrinkled her nose. "An honest poseur is still honest," she agreed in a backhanded way.

After draining what was left of his tiny little glass of venom, Reg had his say.

"I don't write and I barely grasp any of this. I'll admit that, straight up," he concurred. "No matter how deep I am in the scene I know when I'm in over my head. But even if I don't get what you're trying to say, I get what you're going through. Too floaty? Not grounded? Okay. What you need is to get away from this club for a while. This place isn't healthy for you, and I don't just mean the secondhand smoke. Maybe go on the road, like Jack. Work your day job, soak in the city a bit, enjoy the mundane life the rest of us lead. Then take that back to your writing."

Fi coughed impolitely. "Trust fund baby," she noted.

"Okay, so my life is slightly less mundane than most," Reggie admitted. "But I use my petty cash to work my ass off on promotion and management of the art scene. I serve with both hands and that's something I'm good at; dealing in what *is* so artists have time to deal in what *can be*. Honest work keeps me stable, and I'm thinking it'd help Cass, too."

Cass rocked back and forth on two chair legs, pondering. And trying to ignore the words around Reg's head.

i could tell you some stories, the letters hovering in that haze read, jiggling around lightly in memory-mockery.

Barton Fink, 1991. A highly poetic playwright claims to have his finger on the pulse of the common man, when he actually ignores the common man next door in favor of his own idealized but faux-grounded life. Every time Charlie'd try to speak, *I could tell you some stories*, Barton would interrupt and blabber on without realizing how out of touch he was.

"What the hell. It's not like I have anything to recite next week," Cass reasoned, planting all four chair legs on the floor at last. "May as well earn my keep. Poetry doesn't put food on the table these days."

I was ten years old when I got to know the old man down the hall.

His newspaper had been accidentally delivered to my mother's door. Being a good girl, I timidly brought it to that sequestered door, knocked, and waited to meet the hermit.

Our apartment building was quiet during daylight hours. Kids here couldn't afford home-schooling—my mom worked two jobs so I had a phone tutor, because she was terrified of putting me on a school bus and sending me off into the unknown. That meant I was home alone most of the day, and once lessons were done, boredom set in. That's why the old man and I were the only ones around.

For a hermit, he was surprisingly kind and gentle. I'd been warned of Stranger Danger of course, and started out distrusting him. He offered a cookie and coffee in return for the newspaper, which I declined. He insisted on at least giving me some spare change for a reward.

As he was rooting around in the kitchen for some money, I noticed the tiny black and white book on his end table. Very small, very thin, not a proper book. Curious, I started reading it.

*I saw the best minds of my generation destroyed by
madness, starving hysterical naked...*

He caught me red-handed, reading his book. At first it
looked like he was going to rush over and take it away
from me. He was certainly worried about me reading it...
but stayed his hand.

I asked what it meant, since I didn't recognize most of
the words. He said I'd understand when I was older, but I
wanted to understand now. I insisted. He could compensate
me for my good deed of the day by helping open me up to
this fascinating new world.

That was how the elderly echo of Allen Ginsberg came to
meet a ten-year-old girl, a girl who would forever be
driven by words.

Allen told her once about how easy it was to be a taxi driver in New York, back in his world. It was terrific work for any immigrant fresh off the boat (you had to cross an ocean, like a giant lake, to get there). Fleets of cabs would take you where you wanted to go, and at worst you'd have to deal with someone who didn't know the best way to get around and delayed you a little.

Taxi driving in the City of Angles, in contrast, was serious business.

Not that she'd gotten into it in any serious manner to start with. Cass had become a taxi driver on a lark after graduating with her English Lit degree—she'd always been good at navigating the back streets on her bicycle, thanks to being unable to afford on-campus housing at City University. The commute had expanded seven times in the four years she spent earning credit hours, which meant she had to learn quickly how to adapt to the changing flow of traffic. Taxi driving seemed like a natural extension of that... a way to earn extremely solid money in daylight hours, so she could spend her nights writing.

Most cab drivers drop out after a year, unable to maintain the mental focus needed for the job. Cass could sadly say she'd learned more in four years of cab driving than she learned in four years of college.

Never ride the Buckles; passengers are a surly lot, suspicious of their drivers, and do not like the up-and-down hills of the Buckles. Makes you look like a hotshot. The Spindles were a good and undertrafficked hub, giving you access to all sorts of roads, and worth going out of your way for. Avoid the Zag like the plague after rush hour, because that's where the hungry go to feed in more ways than one, with tons of foot traffic to match the wheeled traffic...

Buckles, Spindles, Zag, Causeway, Pileup Intersection, Crossway Points. Poetic names given to streets which once had other names, before being echoed into the city against their will. Sometimes Cass could see the writing on their pavement, crying out in protest at their repurposing.

Literally, she could see the writing on their pavement. It wasn't something she liked to think about, the literalness of that.

Four days removed from the flameout. Grounding herself on four rubber wheels, getting the job done. Here to there and back again. Reg was right—she needed a break from the cloud if she was going to see the sky. Nestle deep in her comfort zone. Racking up the fares didn't hurt, either. This might've been the first month where she wasn't scraping to make the rent.

Her shiny company cab rolled up to the curb, where some guy in a suit and tie had been frantically waving for attention. No time for idle thoughts; fares, fares, fares. Going to ground. Real life.

He piled into the back seat, briefcase in both hands. The bluetooth in his ear yammered away while he yammered into it. Soon the case in his lap was open, and files were coming out, the seat being used as an impromptu office desk. Cass had already pulled away from the curb and gone a block before he bothered telling her where to go.

"I don't care what Resources says, our copyright should still hold. We're a legal extension of..." A glance up at the driver, through the Plexiglas. "Synergy building, Hammerhead Block. ...yes, that's my point, they can't annex it because we've got the rights to the original works. I don't care what they think they're entitled to..."

She spared a glance to the flurry of papers and folders, to confirm.

"Should buckle up, sir," she called back, loud enough to be heard over whatever angry voice was jammed in the salaryman's ear.

"Should watch the goddamn road, missy," the fare barked back. "What? No, not you, I'm in a cab. Look, the account is registered and fully legal, so there's no reason..."

Typical. But, whatever. Cass watched the goddamn road.

Most cars this deep in the city were cabs, just like hers. Driving was an adventure few city people were prepared to undertake themselves, preferring to take the subway or simply walk. Others dared to hop a bus or entrust their lives to a cabbie. Sure, car accidents happened, but it wasn't like the roads were certain death... it was just fear. Fear and an insane desire for safety.

So, she could let some of her focus drift. There was plenty of city life to take in with her eyes, after all. Things which might work their way into a poem one day. Grounding, feeling, reality, process by osmosis...

Rolling through the Chow District. Street merchants, hawking somewhat sad looking fruits and vegetables. Probably snagged off the back of one of the many rattier-looking box trucks that carted in produce from the sick farms of the Outlands. When you couldn't buy from a branded grocery store like Piggy's, you got your calories where you could.

A mother with a toddler in a harness, with retractable leash, the handle clutched in white knuckles. The kid straining at the end of it, desperate to roam the sidewalk and explore the world.

Glowing typeface appeared, hovering in place.

`cages keep wild animals safe from cities, not the other way around,` the words read, jittering slightly in the haze over the struggling child...

Cass tried to pay no attention to it; she couldn't afford to float off like that, not when she was trying to be as normal as possible this week.

Best way to Hammerhead was down 11.5th street. Traffic was a bit thicker, but this time of day it wouldn't be thick enough to offset the time savings. A good cabbie didn't run the meter out with a scenic tour; folks who took cabs regularly were smart enough to call you out on that crap.

Sure enough, plenty of cabs and buses and box trucks and even some luxury cars on 11.5th. Licence plates with jumbles of letters and numbers.

An expensive BMW. Imported, or rather echoed. Someone forked over enough money to feed a family of four for ages to get that thing. `have a care for people who don't,` the words printed out, glowing and hovering over the rear window of the car. Cass immediately looked away, to a nice safe public bus— `every path leads me to nowhere,` it declared, where an ad for the city's recycling program should have been. Even the haze of chemical exhaust from its high pipeline held words, `the clouds are as real as you make them...`

Finally, the traffic started moving fast enough that she could pointedly ignore the phrases trying to edge their way into her brain. She pushed the accelerator down.

Moving at a fair clip, now. Salaryman would be where he was going in no time at all. And then maybe Cass would pull over, hit a public restroom, splash some water on her face, try not to look in the mirror. The letters enjoyed a good mirror—

`TURN`
`LEFT`

—twisting the steering wheel sharply to the left.

No thought, no consideration. The words large as God's eyes, right in front of her, and that was that.

She should have careened at high speed directly into a taco restaurant, killing herself, her passenger, and countless Mexican food patrons. At best she would've started rolling sideways, hurling herself into some other building. It was insanity to make a ninety-degree turn at speed in this city, especially if you weren't actually turning onto a road, but straight into a wall.

Instead of dying, Cass did a hard left onto a road which didn't exist a split second before she started turning onto it.

And then started rolling sideways.

Unconsciousness kicked in, which made the pain a bit easier to take.

Let's be fair. My earliest poetry was terrible. I was only Allen's prodigy for three years before heart failure took him away from me—three short childhood years. The best I could hope for at that point was roses being red and violets being blue.

Even my high school poetry was horrible. Everybody went through their "dark and gritty" phase. I could ape the motions of the Beat Generation, but it came out trite and angry in a world which had no desire for trite and angry. After all, life in the city is and always was life in the city, comparatively peaceful compared to America in the 50s...

You've never had any wars here, Allen pointed out. *No defining struggles. You copied problems from America, but even those were flimsy strawmen compared to the originals. The Beats never happened here because this world couldn't have given rise to them.*

Only in college did I start to write things which I wasn't agonizingly embarrassed by. And unfortunately, that only happened after my acid test.

I'd managed to avoid smoking and drinking, despite how both ran roughshod through the Beats. Peer pressure didn't hit me very hard, I guess. But when my roomie offered an invite to an LSD party... all I could think about was Allen's musings on consciousness expansion. It seemed like a sure bet for self-improvement, walking in the shoes of my lost mentor.

The little sugar cube opened a door in my head, and the words came out. They hovered, they danced, they commented on my surroundings like footnotes for the real world. The experience was actually quite amazing.

Problem was... the door never closed. Even after the acid faded, the words were still there. When I slept they overtook me like a tidal wave... and when I was awake, distant echoes of them persisted in my vision.

I was too scared to tell anyone. I didn't want to go to Rockford and Greystone, didn't want to suffer Naomi's fate. I knew full well how little this city tolerated madness, seeing it as a stepping stone to cubism.

For a while, I worried I WAS going cubist. I checked myself every day for telltale signs of blurriness or distortion. Edge of my seat living, worried sick about the weirdness, unable to accept it, desperate for the words to go away but unwilling to tell anyone about what I was going through...

I survived despite the persistent hallucinations, and graduated a few years later with most of my marbles. Only once I started ignoring how strange it was to see captions everywhere could I grasp some control over my life again.

And sometimes... they made for really striking poetry. And other times I just couldn't translate what I was seeing in my head into anything meaningful. They tease and taunt me as much as they inspire me. Maybe it's a zero sum game. Maybe the words will never truly help me.

Sirens. Klaxons. Live without warning.

Cass was sitting on the ground, next to an upside down cab. Someone was waving a hand in her face.

"How many fingers am I holding up?" the man asked.

The word three printed itself in front of the blur.

"Three," she replied.

Focus came to her, soon after. An average-looking joe, wearing the brown of a First Action Response Team uniform. The name tag read SMITH, which was a relief, because it was printed text that was not only in her broken brain...

"Good. I mean, there may still be a concussion or something, but... you're alive, which is kind of amazing," he said. "Your passenger's going to be fine. He's on his way to the hospital now. Wasn't wearing a seatbelt, so he's got a broken clavicle... err... shoulder? I don't know, something in that region. You saved his life, turning onto this road. Others weren't so lucky..."

Past the rescue worker... and there was a pileup to rival Pileup Intersection's legends.

A building had inserted itself into the city, right in the middle of 11.5th Street. The street obligingly turned off to the left now, reshaping itself to accommodate the new structure... but it had given no warning of what was about to happen. As a result, a dozen or so cars and a city bus had plowed head-on into the new building.

That was what happened. Cass didn't need it confirmed; she knew how the city worked. These things happen. Insurance companies hate it, mortuaries love it, politicians shake their fingers about traffic safety laws and speed limits, and life goes on.

Especially for her. Because she was the one of the few who had managed to avoid the crash. Cars towards the back managed to veer onto the new side road, having several seconds of visual forewarning of the city change... they made the same call Cass did.

But Cass made the call first. She made it before anyone else could have thanks to two words, four letters each, burning bright. A split second of precognition... but that split second was enough to save her.

Rescue workers, FARTs, firemen and EMTs were swarming over the pile of cars. Department of Safety officers had set up barricades, turning back traffic, keeping folks away. None of them paid much attention to the taxi that had swerved off to the side. The significance of how it survived was lost on everyone, with the far more spectacular pile of wreckage to attend to.

That included the First Action Response Team leader, who angrily called over, waving to the technician tending to her.

"Dave, get your ass back here!" he shouted. "You're only a trainee right now, remember? You're not authorized to talk to anyone! Let the EMTs deal with her."

"Sorry," Apparently-Dave spoke to her. "Gotta go. Sit tight, someone'll be with you soon. It's going to be okay, ma'am."

Leaving Cass to her thoughts, dazed from the crash, waiting for someone to take her to the hospital or something. A living miracle nobody cared about.

Although in her heart, she knew that miracle was probably going to spell disaster. She'd crashed her cab. She'd injured her passenger. Even if they'd survived... this was not good. Not good at all.

The dark man laughs as the hordes of psyches march towards the festering smile of the nightmare child. What's wrong, he taunts? Everything falling apart, nothing making sense? But isn't that for the best? He embraces the thing which shreds and gnaws at the edges of your mind because it pours the vile venom of horrific power into the ego which inflates it to sizes that are not recommended by your pediatrician, and eventually the nightmare and the dream become one and the same and fearlessness is identical to ferocity.

The azure youth watches impassively as the thousands fall in slow motion, tumbling down the sides of buildings and the edges of chasms and through the cracks of society, bouncing off the walls and leaving bloody smears as they plummet in the infinite abyss of nothingness. What's wrong, she asks? Hopeless and bleak in the face of knowing you are nothing? But isn't that for the best? She embraces the nonexistence of the oblivion state because it snuffs out the candle flame that burns and induces pain and passion and encourages you to endure, time out, retreat, it's better to surrender than to lose.

And then there was the third option.

And then there was the third child.

Her herald has designed the hardest road of all, paved with the blood of suffering and trauma, flesh burned bright in ovens of existence before being hammered flat into ceramic red bricks of hemoglobin, the living testament of the ones who live, who with shining lucidity reach out and seize life with both hands, despite the horror, despite the sorrow, despite the weirdness you want to avoid because unfortunately the weirdness is everywhere and there is no avoiding it, no escape, no retreat, the only way out is through, to turn yourself into something new, to turn left, to answer the door because your guest has been knocking for a good three minutes now and you're being a rude little thing.

Cass awoke with a start, cheek pulling from a small puddle of her own drool on the kitchen table.

Which would have been horribly embarrassing if anybody had seen it. Especially since she sat down last night intent on writing some poetry, not intent on passing out at the keys until morning. After finding her glasses, a quick glance showed she hadn't gotten further on her typewriter than "The" before blacking out. How deliciously comedic. Falling asleep sitting up, despite having absolutely nothing exhausting happening during her daylight hours...

No job anymore—the company released her contract, despite saving her passenger's life. If he'd just worn his seat belt, he'd be fine... but no, he had to ignore rule number one of city safety. Instead of blaming himself, he chose to blame Cass for the resulting injuries and slap her with employer a lawsuit.

No self-respecting judge would find her guilty, but the dispatch company didn't care. Cass was just one of dozens of drivers, with more waiting to step up and take her job. Easier and cheaper to settle out of court, cut the problem driver loose, and issue a statement describing the firing as a proactive step towards public safety. It beat tangling with a vengeful lawyer, right? The company didn't owe her anything, they didn't care. Just a replaceable cog in the system.

The only person who gave a crap was Vincent, her direct radio contact in dispatch.

It's a raw deal, I know, he'd agreed. *I can tell you right now, none of the other companies will want a driver who was involved in such a major accident. You don't deserve this mess, so I'll see what I can find for you, but... it's a good thing you have your poetry to fall back on, right?*

No poetry—her antique typewriter hadn't been clacking away through the midnight hour, despite the words that filled her dreams. She felt like a faker before, and without the anchor of the daily grind to cling to, all she had left was being a poetic phony. No confidence. No inspiration.

No progress. No success. No purpose. No...

No knocking.

No, knocking. There *was* knocking. She vaguely recalled being aware of the knocking even before waking up, but the dream had faded by that point, becoming little more than a random pile of vaporous musings. Knock knock at the door, guests arriving, `let me in.`

Quickly Cass wiped up the drool puddle with a sleeve, adjusted her hair to look slightly presentable, and crossed her small apartment to go open the door.

Probably the mailman, or a delivery boy with more severance paperwork. Maybe she ordered food and forgot about it. The landlord, here to demand the rent she couldn't afford anymore. Any number of ordinary city folk could be at her door for any number of ordinary city purposes. Simple and direct and understandable.

Instead, she found a charming old lady in a ridiculously vintage looking dress, with wrinkled skin and a hair bun. Like someone's grandmother from a salvaged 50s celluloid comedy. Which would be funny if not for the very impressively tall and muscular bodyguard-looking type looming behind her, nearly filling the hallway beyond her door. That balanced out the equation somewhat.

"Hello, dearie," the old lady rasped, dry as a bone. "I've come to offer you a job."

Weirdness, Cass thought briefly, her hopes for an ordinary visit leaping spectacularly out the window.

Unbidden, the old biddy waltzed on into the apartment. Had herself a good look around. Meanwhile, the pile of beef that had been following her around chose to fill the doorway instead of filling the hallway. Cass could always jump out the window after her hopes, but that would be the only exit now...

The woman pondered the kitchen table, with its stacks of blank paper and its portable typewriter.

"Oh my. Is that a Smith Corona Sterling?" she asked. "I didn't think they existed anymore..."

"Ah, it's a Clark Nova portable," Cass clarified, moving away from the bodyguard and towards the old woman in a hopefully nonthreatening fashion. "It's... uh. It's a replica movie prop, honestly. I thought it might have mythic resonance but honestly it doesn't type very well. —I'm sorry, I didn't catch your name, Missus...?"

"You may call me Grandma Scarlett. That's Scarlett with two T's, like the actress or the character," the woman noted, holding up two fingers. "It has mythic resonance. Mmm. A bit of a sham, I suppose, like your typewriter. But if this world is a sham, does that make it any less real? Who's to say what's real and what isn't? The answer, of course, is us. No other answer makes sense."

For someone who chose to live in a world of words, Cass had absolutely no words in response to how this situation was developing.

Grandma Scarlett with Two T's, meanwhile, eased herself into one of the chairs at the kitchen table. And gestured for Cass to sit as well, across from her and in front of the Clark Nova. The bodyguard declined to join them.

"Don't mind Jeb, missy, he's just not one for talk," Scarlett said, noting Cass's increasing uncomfortableness with the large fellow. "And he's a big softie, really—though he worries about my safety whenever I need to leave the farm. I visit the city so rarely these days, it's a treat for both of us, really. My word, how this place changes each time I visit! Oh, I don't just mean the buildings, but the people. So many new faces..."

Before she started rambling off in a random direction, Cass decided to wrestle this back to normality. make sense of nonsense, the words on her kitchen wall suggested.

"Said something about a job?" she asked. "Did Vincent at the cab company recommend me for something? Said he'd try to find me work... you run a taxi contract service?"

"A what? Oh, heavens no!" the old woman replied, with a giggle like rustling paper. "No, no. I manage an orphanage, on a farm in the Outlands. The Happy Acre Orphanage! There's so many poor children left stranded in this world, with no family and no one to take them in. I provide a home, a waystation for those who need somewhere to rest and heal. Mm. Well. I have side businesses too, you could say. A delivery business. The business of deliverance. Which is why I'm here today. You are a delivery girl, yes? You deliver people?"

"I... guess you could say that," Cass replied. "I've been a taxi driver for a few years now. Vincent would've given you my resume. You need your kids driven around the city on field trips or something? Because if so, I'm legally obliged to tell you about a traffic accident I was involved in..."

The woman clicked her tongue, in sympathetic disappointment. "Troubles in the past, dear? Well, that's the city for you. So dangerous. Really, it doesn't matter to me; I know in my heart you're the right woman for the job. But I think I've led you to the wrong conclusion. You wouldn't be delivering people, dearie! I have packages that need delivery... care packages, of a sort, handcrafted at my home sweet home..."

Reaching into her purse, the woman withdrew a smart tablet. After some fumbling, not particularly good with the touchscreen interface, she called up a map.

"My orphanage is here, in the Outlands," she explained, pointing with shaking finger to a random spot on a random highway through the highly random rural landscapes beyond the city. "A bit far away, I know, but it's home. You would be making deliveries from my home using a box truck, traveling to various places in the Outlands, in the Suburbs, and even in the City itself. Quite a few stops, quite a distance. An ongoing task as well, week by week, plenty of deliveries to make in the months ahead. I'm afraid it's a long haul, in and around and through... but the pay is above standard for the trucking industry, I'm told. Are you keen?"

Her hopes wobbled slightly. `will you, won't you, will you, won't you`...

First, this wasn't cab driving, it was truck driving. Cargo haulers were a culture onto themselves, rolling through the Outlands with vital loads from factories and warehouses—the lifeblood of the city, since nobody could survive off imported scavenging alone. Her commercial driving licence didn't cover eighteen wheelers, which would've shot this right down... but it did cover box trucks. Still quite beyond her comfort zone. Literally and figuratively.

Cass had rarely driven outside the City (her comfort zone). Technically all of it was the City of Angles, but the "City of Angles" existed in three different "layers" of a sort—Outlands, Suburbs, City. Rural, suburban, urban. If you knew which roads to take, you could safely transition from one space to the next in a non-Euclidian manner.

Taxi drivers stuck to the cramped little roadways of the city, the twisted rat's nest of side streets and major intersections that linked its denizens together. Sometimes you'd be carrying a passenger home to the burbs (safe little bedroom communities), but commuters usually took a bus or owned their own cars. And never, ever did she drive all the way out to the open spaces of the Outlands...

But four wheels were four wheels, and a map was a map. She could read maps, commit them to memory, get a feel for the terrain and optimize the routes. She'd gone from being a collegiate bicycle warrior to a professional taxi hooligan in a few short years. With the cab companies unlikely to knock on her door anytime soon... she'd take whatever work she could get and figure the rest out later.

"I can tell from the series of expressions on your face that you're going to take my offer," Grandma Scarlett said, before she had a chance to take the offer. "With reservations, of course. Understandable, very much so..."

"This isn't really something I've done before," Cass warned. "I drive cabs, not trucks. And not in the Outlands. But... yeah. I'll take it. —what exactly am I hauling, if not toddlers? Apple pies? Knitting? Denture cream?"

"Ahhh. Humor as a coping mechanism. You're a dear one, dearie, just as I thought you'd be. And no, none of that. Jeb, if you please...?"

Now the wall of meat moved from the doorway. But not before fetching a cardboard box, which had been set just out of sight for the big reveal.

Despite saying PAPER TOWELS 6 UNITS on the side, odds were low it held paper towels. Repurposing things was common enough in the city, after all, including containers.

Jeb opened the box, then held it out for Grandma Scarlett. She carefully reached in, and withdrew...

Well, that made sensible sense, at least.

"These teddy bears are hand-sewn by me, with love and care," she explained, setting the adorable flopsy stuffed doll on Cass's kitchen table next to the Clark Nova. "I produce one batch every week. It's been a hobby of mine for over a decade now. Mmm. Not a hobby. More of a calling, I suppose. Sometimes the children help me—not a sweatshop, mind you, but they have a vested interest in this project as well. Once the dolls are complete and... prepared, I ship them out to where they need to be. That's where you'll come in. One run a week, a day or three to complete each run. Lengthy hours but in the end, it's worth it."

Slowly, Cass edged back into her comfort zone. Old widow (presumably a widow) in an orphanage sewing teddy bears for kiddies? That was downright cliché and ordinary. The ordinariness of it, that was exactly what Cass was hoping for. Nothing the slightest bit odd about all of it.

"I'll definitely take the job," she confirmed. "I can start whenever. Got nothin' going on right now."

"Good, good," Scarlett said, with a click of the tongue. "Jeb will transfer the relevant maps to you today. I'm not much with computers, afraid. I have a charming little rented cargo truck you'll be using, which is currently in storage here in the city; I'll give you the keys, you can drive it out to the orphanage as soon as you're ready to fetch your first week's deliveries."

Carefully, the old woman rose from the kitchen chair—Cass could hear bones creaking and hopefully not cracking. She extended a brittle hand to shake... which Cass shook, very, very carefully. we have an accord, the words agreed.

"This is exactly what I need right now, I think," Cass admitted. "I've been trying to get down to earth lately. City living gets to you, y'know. Delivering teddy bears? I can swing that. It's out and out normal. I'll have to thank Vincent for sending you my way."

"I suppose you can if you like," her employer said... with a cartoonish little twinkle in her eyes. "Except I'm afraid I've never met this 'Vincent' person you keep talking about. Good day, miss."

And so they left, without another word.

Presumably they'd seen Cass's name in the news, or something. Or maybe she was more famous in the world of commercial transport than she thought. Or Vincent knew a guy who knew a guy, or something. Plenty of reasonable reasons for that little twist ending.

By the time Cass settled back in to her typewriter, they were long gone—and had left the bear behind.

It flopped adorably against her Clark Nova, as if to say hug me. Well, as if to say and literally to say, with the words in her mind making a return appearance after staying oddly quiet through that discussion.

She nudged the bear aside, letting it topple over and lay awkwardly, while she tried to remember what word was going to come after "The" when she sat down to write last night.

A few minutes later without any words spilling forth, she took the bear under one arm. Not because it told her to or she wanted to or anything like that. Just 'cause.

Having gone without second hand smoke for several days, inhaling it anew was not a pleasant experience. Cass pushed through the haze anyway, identifying her preferred table (on its last legs) and weaving around various hipsters to get to it.

She found Reggie and Fi locked in intense debate over a hot pink sculpture of a penis, which was the opposite of what she wanted to see when she walked in here today.

"I'm just not sure what the piece is saying," Reg pondered aloud, studying the item sitting in centerpiece position of the coffee house table. "Is it a statement about the role of male sexuality in society, or some sort of celebration of neoprimitive fertility? I mean, there's a lot of attention to detail here; it's not an abstract by any means. Is there meaning in that detail? Highlighted aspects which are meant to convey something?"

"Or someone sold you a used marital aid and called it art," Fi suggested.

"Okay, so maybe it's found art, but that doesn't mean it can't be art," he defended. "Hey, Cass, have a seat. Help me figure this out!"

The chain-smoking poet opposite Cass shook her head, sadly. "Reg got played again," she confirmed.

"Can we put the icon of sexuality as portrayed in the media aside for now?" Cass asked, turning her chair backwards and straddling it (before realizing how that played into the current discussion, with a wince). "Got a puzzle of my own to sort out."

"Sure, sure. Besides, it's getting me funny looks," Reg admitted, fetching the *objet d'notquiteart* off the table, putting it in his messenger bag. "What's on your mind, Cass? Still looking for work? You know, I could take you on for a bit hanging paintings at the new gallery—"

"Got a job offer, actually. But... it's... it's kinda... *it's*," she said, unable to find a clever word despite being a poet. "It's a wheel job again, and one I know I can do. A bit out of my usual range, but... ugh. It's cargo trucking. Specifically, long distance cargo trucking of teddy bears in the Outlands."

Neither the pale-faced poet nor the overly enthusiastic hipster reacted badly to this.

"Can either of you seriously see me as a trucker?" Cass supplied, to add her concern to the pile of non-concern. "I'm a city girl. Am I going to need mud flaps with silver strippers on them? Do I have to start listening to country music and wearing big caps reading 'Female Body Inspector'? And to add to the oddity, my employer's like someone straight out of Interzone. A mysterious old bat who talks in riddles and has an ogre for a bodyguard. Also I'm pretty sure she used creepy mutant powers to find me or something."

Fi, who was only capable of laughing if it involved a derisive snort, performed a derisive snort.

"Wild, baby. Sounds like good material for a book to me. Take the job," she suggested.

"But I thought I was shooting for *less* weirdness in my life, not more," Cass said. "Ugh. Hanging paintings would be saner. Or maybe I should just wait tables like every other starving poet out there, or write pulp porno for pennies or something..."

"You're way overthinking this, Cass!" Reg insisted. "It's just a cargo hauling job! Very straightforward. Very mundane. You said you wanted to invest in the mundane, and now it's walked across your doorstep! Teddy bears? Big rigs? Okay, a weird combination, but taken individually they're quite ordinary. I say run with it. I mean, what's the worst that can happen?"

The temperature in the coffee house dropped four figurative degrees.

"...what?" Reg asked, puzzled by the frozen expressions on their faces.

"My god, Reg, you really have no clue, do you," Fi mumbled.

"What?"

"*Never* say things like that."

"Like what?"

Cass buried her face in her hands, picking up the ball so Fi could conserve her words. "She means things like 'what's the worst that can happen.' You're a literate sort, right? How often do things go WELL after that's uttered?"

"Oh, come on! Life is not a Burroughs novel, okay?" Reg protested. "This is what I'm saying about this world messing with you. Life *is what it is* and that's all it is. I don't buy into supernatural superstition. Poetry is beautiful but in the end, the real world is out there. That's how I choose to see it, so I've got nothing to fear from 'What's the worst that can happen.' Take the job, Cass. Everything will sort itself out. You'll see."

A job is a job is a job. In the end, Cass buckled to the need to keep her landlord at bay.

The box truck she'd be spending much of the next few days in was waiting for her at a private lockup, a waystation for rental vehicles intended to do the highway shuffle from A to Z. A decrepit old janitor helped her find the right storage bay, the one with a lock that fit Grandma Scarlett's golden key. what wonders hide within? the words wondered.

Cass was relieved to see the wonder truck itself was completely uninteresting—a battered and dirty thing, boxlike (hence the name) and unmarked. The sort of truck you moved plumbing supplies or the corpses of unsuccessful gangsters in.

She'd spent the previous night memorizing the maps between the rental depot and the orphanage. Not just the specific sequence of turns; that'd land you in hot water if your map became outdated and a turn changed here and there. She memorized the names of roads. She memorized landmarks. She memorized what sort of terrain and what sort of buildings she was going to be passing by. Every single marker that would help her establish where she was could prove useful, in the end.

The key to navigation in the city—and hopefully in the Outlands as well—was to get a feel for your surroundings as a whole. A holistic approach, burrowing a hole through the chaos, coming out the other side. Understand and grasp everything. No mental shortcuts or memorized routes. Grasp what's out there and trust your instincts.

Well. Trust your MAP, first. Then if that fails, trust your instincts.

Even with enough built-up confidence to roll out, she didn't immediately hop Highway Nine to the Outlands. First she eased the truck in and around city traffic, through streets she knew were undertrafficked, to get a feel for it. It felt like navigating a washing machine on skis with team of overly enthusiastic puppies dragging it every which way. Cumbersome, slow, and prone to underturn or oversteer, whichever you didn't want at the time... but after an hour of random meanderings through streets she knew by heart, she had enough of a grasp on the giant lump of iron to make do.

Highway Nine, and out of the City layer and into the Suburbs layer.

"Layers" was a colloquialism. Like layers of Hell, or parallel dimensions... stacked one on top of another in every way except ways which were obvious or visible. You found the right offramp, you could transition from one to the other. The connections were well known, and rarely closed themselves off... Highway Nine had been stable for over seventy years, and was one of the finest ways to get into the smear of middle class housing.

With the scenery getting decidedly less fantastic the farther away from the city she got, Cass busied herself with studying her immediate surroundings.

Someone had hung a cardboard pine tree from the rear view mirror. A hula-girl bobble doll (`aloha!`) from some far away island chain back on Earth swayed back and forth on the dash, forever stuck in a single ukulele note.

Feeling the need to add her own personal touch to the truck, Cass had brought along the teddy bear Granny Scarlett gave to her, and plopped it right down next to the hula-girl. Mythic resonance, indeed. It seemed content to flop down there, basking in the windshield sun...

The last item of note was a strange box in the dash, which had been blinking at her for some time now.

The CB Radio.

Her first hint (beyond driving a dingy truck) that she'd walked into another culture entirely. This was the black box that truckers chattered on, using trucker logo to talk trucker things in trucker ways trucker trucker trucker. The previous driver had helpfully preprogrammed the buttons to various bands, with magic marker scribbles to indicate which was which. PUB. BEARS. SIDEB. LAWL. TRFF. Meaningless shorthand to Cass.

She tried tuning in to BEARS, wondering if maybe it related to her future cargo, but only caught static. Not enough trucks roaming through the burbs to make it worthwhile, maybe.

The channel came alive when Highway Nine eventually bled over into the Outlands.

The neatly curated forestry of the suburbs shifted, transitioning into the wide open spaces and blue skies of the rural landscape. And immediately, the radio came alive.

"—shooting you in the back. Can you cut the reds?"

"Done already. Bear's backing down. Worth every penny, putting in the cutter..."

"Just a baby bear, anyway. Doubt he'd have run you down. But they're getting friskier lately."

"Department's being a pain in the ass with the traps lately. As if I don't pay enough goddamn taxes already..."

"Hear that. See you at Melba's. Over and out."

And that was that.

Briefly, Cass considered reaching for the handheld microphone. Not that she had anything to offer, beyond maybe "Hello?" But this wasn't her element, not yet—she'd be just as out of place as a trucker swaggering on into the coffee house when it was packed shoulder to shoulder with hipsters. Better to leave it on the hook. Maybe permanently.

It wasn't the last time I saw Allen alive, but it was one of the last.

I'd been mentoring under him for three years now, under the guise of a combination of free day care and respecting the elderly. My mother didn't see an ancient gay Jewish man as much of a threat to her little girl, so she didn't mind me spending time with him... and I made sure she continued not to mind, by not mentioning word one of the stories Allen would tell.

And boy, could he tell stories. Stories about the Beat Hotel, or the hippie movement protesting the Vietnam War, or of life in the big cities on Earth. Tales of a world I'd never seen myself and had little understanding of outside of salvaged videotapes.

Then one day, he wrapped up all his stories in a neat little bow for me.

You've never had any wars here, Allen pointed out. *No defining struggles. You copied problems from America, but even those were flimsy strawmen compared to the originals. The Beats never happened here because this world couldn't have given rise to them.*

This world isn't mine. Its problems aren't anything I can get a handle on. I can't live here. Your government pays my rent, hoping I'll be the skaald of their society... but I can't be. My fire died out when I was echoed here. I miss my Peter. I miss my Bill. I miss my world.

If there's going to be a poet for your generation, whatever your generation turns out to be, it's going to have to be someone born here. Someone who is one with this city, ready to embrace it. The longer people here hang onto the grim reminders of America, the less likely they'll be able to live their own lives.

I don't have a place to stand here, Cassy. You do. Make a choice. Make your stand.

Weeks later, Allen Ginsberg passed away. There was no funeral; he had only his government pittance and no family to mourn his passing. It became an interesting footnote in the newspaper, for people who actually knew what he represented. They read that footnote and then moved on.

I published my first poem the very next day, in the school newspaper. It earned me a visit from the principal and a very confused discussion with my mother, regarding exactly what I was up to at that crazy old man's apartment. I was yelled at and grounded and treated as a weirdo by my fellow students, and I wouldn't have had it any other way.

Someone had taken a brightly colored plastic farm you give disinterested nieces and nephews for their third birthday and blown it up to life size. That was the only explanation for the way Happy Acre Orphanage gleamed in the morning sun.

Unlike other buildings in the Outlands, it wasn't the least bit weathered or beaten down by the years. Maybe in addition to looming ominously in doorways, Jeb used his extraordinary size to his advantage and painted the entire building every two weeks without need of a ladder. Regardless of HOW, the farmhouse (candy apple red) with matching barn (also candy apple red) were visible for nearly a mile before Cass actually pulled up to the front of the building in her new truck.

Orphanages were a cottage industry; plenty of refugee children showed up each year without parents, thanks to the echoing process. It was a fortunate and rare thing when an entire family showed up intact. Those who lost that lottery were cast into the Department of Orientation's network of foster homes... some good, some bad. A roll of the dice to see if you find a loving and supportive new family or someone banking in on tax credits in exchange for neglecting a traumatized youngster who just lost everything she loved in life.

From the looks of it, Happy Acre was one of the better options a kid could have. Unless there was secretly a dungeon underneath the place that cranked out handmade sweaters or something... or maybe handmade teddy bears.

If the bears were crafted by conscripted labor and misery that didn't show on the faces of the kids. Of which Cass could see many; faces and kids.

They poured out of the orphanage the instant she threw the truck's parking brake. So many smiles Cass briefly wondered if she'd accidentally found a back lot currently shooting a toothpaste commercial.

At first she wasn't sure if she should get out of the truck. Perhaps they would swarm and devour her.

Soon the sea of kiddies parted, to make way for their matriarch—Granny Scarlett.

The old lady clapped once, a sound like two flimsy pieces of sandpaper coming together.

"Children, this is Cass. Cass, these are the children," she greeted. "Children, it's time to say goodbye to your bears. You know what to do; fetch their favorite things for travel."

In a flash, the mouse army was gone. Back into the farmhouse, presumably to fetch today's shipments of teddy bears. Curious.

Cass stepped out of the truck, to get a better feel on the ground for what was going on. Jeb had already rolled up the door on the back of the truck, and kids were starting to emerge from the house... each carrying one cardboard box, with a teddy bear peeking out the top, sometimes with other small toys or a small blanket to keep them comfortable.

The question already poised on her lips was answered by one of the children, who interjected himself between Cass and Grandma Scarlett.

"This is Daniel," the boy explained, holding his cardboard box high, the flopsy bear peeking out from its depths. "I got to name him myself. He likes lunchtime and crayons. He's scared of the dark, but it's okay, because he's not going to be alone."

"This is your pet bear?" Cass asked. "And you're giving him away...? Aren't you gonna miss Daniel?"

"A little," the boy admitted... but through a smile. "Daniel's being adopted, so it's okay. And I'll have a new bear tonight, just like every week. Miss Scarlett makes sure of that. I think I'll name my new bear Cassy!"

With that he shoved the box into Cass's arms, and scampered back into the farm house.

Grandma Scarlett clucked her tongue, a little chuckle. "Darlings, aren't they?" she said. "I spend every day sewing new bears for the next week's supply. The bears are loved quite intensely, then given away to others who need them. The love... that's important, you see. *Very* important."

"It's important to take a kid's favorite toy away from him?" Cass asked quietly, as the stream of children dried out to a trickle, Jeb finishing the loadout. "If you're gonna sell dolls, okay, but... why give 'em to your kids and then yank 'em?"

"Mmm. It serves a few purposes, teaches a few lessons. It's a very critical process. To share. To accept loss. To grow and raise and care. To love, but be able to let go. To live, but be able to accept change. The city can teach these lessons in a very cruel way; I prefer a kinder way. Aside from that... well. There are no nightmares in my orphanage. Not one."

Cass winced at the sound of the rolling door slamming shut on the back of the truck, sealing the bears inside.

`leaving the nest`, the words hovering over the truck door suggested. The same imaginary words that danced in her dreams...

"Everybody's got nightmares sometimes," she suggested.

"Not my children. They have protectors," Scarlett stated, firmly. "Now, then. You've got a full swath of deliveries to make. Jeb's sent you an electronic mail with the delivery details for each bear... places, times, delivery instructions. Follow them to the letter, it's all very important. You do have time enough for lunch; I understand there's a lovely rest stop just up the highway on the way to your first delivery..."

Lunch. Cass had spent so much time studying maps and getting a feel for the lands she'd be rolling through that she completely forgot about brown-bagging it.

Food would be good. Even if it was some greasy trucker stop, food would be very good. A pile of calories might help her swallow the uneasy feeling in her stomach.

Rest stops were the primary facility type people interacted with in the Outlands. For folks coming in from the Suburbs or the City itself, they acted as waystations between your home and your vacation destination of choice—fuel, fried foods, and maybe a bed (if you needed one). Charter bus lines had contracts to stop at specific rest stops, delivering fresh loads of hungry tourists to distant eateries that would otherwise go uneaten. Plenty of parking for buses. Plenty of parking for the family minivan.

No parking for cargo trucks.

Cass found this out the hard way when she tried easing her bulky bastard of a truck into a space meant for some middle class nuclear family's station wagon. In less than a minute, she was accosted by a Vehicle of Authority... a golf cart with 'SECURITY' stenciled into the side, neatly filled by some guy who clearly enjoyed that fried food on a daily basis.

"You can't park here!" he barked at her. Twice, since the first time, her window had been rolled up.

"I'm just going in for a muffin and an espresso," Cass explained, gesturing to yon upscale food court. "I won't be long—"

"That's a Class C Commercial Transport in a Class A Passenger Transport space," the sweaty fellow declared. "You don't belong in this parking lot. Official Department of Resources policy! You want the commercial parking lot at the other end of the rest area. Move along! Move along!"

"You want me to go park down there and walk all the way back here just to get my lunch?" she asked. "Look, it's tight, but the truck fits fine—"

"MOVE ALONG!"

Not wanting to end up at the business end of a belt-looped flashlight, Cass moved along.

The quaint charm of a roadside establishment rapidly faded as she eased her box truck down the line towards the commercial lot. Without the need to soothe the worries of folks stepping outside their comfort zones, the grass went unmowed, oil spills weren't mopped up, and the asphalt clearly hadn't been resurfaced since the Kent mayoral administration.

Shiny minivans and chromed busses were replaced with filthy eighteen-wheelers and box trucks, haphazardly jammed into whatever space was available... leaving very little for Cass, who had the audacity to show up eleven minutes late to the lunch rush. She managed to find a space light years away from the trendy coffee shop she had hoped to drop in on, which meant a brisk jog back and forth with little time to enjoy herself if she wanted to slog back through the oil and the litter...

Or she could go to Melba's, which was a stone's throw away.

`down home cookin'`, the words suggested to her. just like mom didn't use to make.

The truckers had their own eatery, complete with a flickering neon sign declaring its existence. The word stuck out in her memory from earlier C.B. radio browsing.

Eh, what the hell, she decided in the end.

Within four seconds she understood exactly what a bad idea this was.

Melba's Diner was not her territory. It was the polar opposite of the smoky poet's coffee joint she frequently haunted. Just as dingy and smoky, but a daylight dingy, and packed with people who had likely not gotten beyond roses being red and violets being blue.

A number of heads turned in her direction on entering the doors. The smell of flannel soaked in engine oil choked her nostrils. Sideburns were prevalent. A steel guitar was twanging away on a nearby vintage jukebox, likely wailing about foreclosures and divorces. And there was, in a demonstration of ironic providence, someone wearing a large cap reading *Female Body Inspector*.

Presumably women drivers existed in this industry. Presumably most of the guys here were okay and not raging sexist nutjobs. This was just a chance confluence of events had arranged a picture-perfect tableau of all Cass's worst fears about her new job. She'd stepped into some redneck variant of Interzone. Something to laugh about, really, not to worry about about. Nothing to even think about, honestly. One foot in front of the other.

Eager to get on with this and get some food in her digestive system, Cass pushed on through the thick cloud of noxious odors, right up to the lunch counter. It was tough finding an empty stool—or finding a stool at all, as many had vanished completely up their occupant's backsides—but she managed to locate one near the end of the row.

The only other owner of a vagina in the building wandered in Cass's direction, ready to take her order.

This was the heralded Melba, as declared by the name tag on her apron. An apron which was a war veteran of an apron, decorated in stains, an apron which had *seen things*. Melba herself was wide of girth and full of life, with her hair bunned up tight in a net behind her. Operator and owner, simultaneously subservient to the trucker's needs and the master and commander of their appetites. And looking a bit concerned for the out-of-place hipster chick who had just walked in. Still, a customer was a customer.

"What can I getcha, hun?" Melba asked (with a twinge of sympathy).

"Muffin and an espresso," Cass requested, on instinct.

A few stifled laughs cut through the awkward silence that had dropped over the diner ever since she set foot in it.

"Doughnut and coffee work for you okay?" Melba suggested, trying to be tactful about Cass's failure to adhere to local menu standards.

"Uh, yeah, doughnut and a coffee are fine," she agreed. "And a sandwich. A... um... you know what, surprise me. Whatever you personally like to put between two slices bread will do."

At that, Miss Melba offered a smile. "I think I can whip somethin' up for ya good," she offered. "Back in a jiff."

With the lunch lady MIA, Cass was left to look at her own reflection in a chromed napkin dispenser and hope its gleaming surface was merely a bit dingy. The alternative explanation was that she'd started growing a five o'clock shadow from all the testosterone in the room.

23% of which had just waltzed on up behind her.

Of *course* it was the proud owner of that *Female Body Inspector* hat. Of course that would be the first coworker to speak to her. Of course.

Those who weren't nervously minding their own business studied the scene with interest. The alpha male of the pack had just stepped up to a young wolf, after all. There might be blood. That would be entertaining.

`anything different is bad`, spoke the not-telepathic words over the man's capped head. we fear change. so do you.

It took him some time to figure out where to start in on Cass. There were so many avenues presenting themselves, after all. A woman in an industry which was 3.3% women? A woman wearing men's clothes, slacks and a tie? Obvious dyke. Thick rimmed glasses? You could go for the nerd angle there, that was always a classic.

All choice digs to make, but he decided to open with the safest insult— calling out her dining order faux pas. The rest would likely come along later.

"Well, what do we got here?" he began, because *of course*. "You're a long way from the tourist trap, y'know. You want one of them fancy coffees in the tiny cups you'll want the other end of the rest stop. Name's Eddie; kind of a big deal around these parts. And in case you didn't notice, it's all truckers in here, girl."

Having predicted the specific statement he'd deliver, she had her wallet out —complete with laminated commercial driver's I.D.—and flashed in front of his face without even turning around on her stool.

"I *am* a trucker," Cass replied. "Class C Commercial Transport driver. If you don't mind, I'd like to eat my mystery sandwich in peace."

"Ho-lee...! I'll be damned," Eddie paradoxically declared. "City'll give those out to anyone these days, huh. Now what company in their right mind'd hire some young city slicker like you for an Outland rig?"

And here was where Cass dug herself just a little deeper. Although to her credit, she realized lying would potentially land her in hotter water—and it'd be better to keep things focused on her inappropriate job than anything more personal. Once issues like her ownership of a pair of breasts were on the table, you didn't want to be surrounded by a hundred guys. So far only one loudmouth had made it his business to get up in her business, but... no need to push it. Give 'em a different bone to chew on.

"I'm hauling toys. Contract work. Nothing special," she insisted.

Worked like a charm.

Worked a bit TOO well. The room exploded into laughter. Even truckers who had been ignoring the situation squeaked out a chuckle.

It was like Cass had suddenly put on a clown nose and hit herself in the face with a pie. Suddenly this was less about a visibly different stranger in their midst, and more about the sad and unfortunate joke which had just walked in the door.

"Happy Acre," Eddie recognized immediately. "The old lady couldn't sucker in another one of us, so she's turning to some rube from the city! That is *perfect*. Hey, everybody! Looks like the Cuddlebear Convoy's back in business!"

Drinks were raised in mock salutation, toasting Cass's new job. Well, ironically toasting. Ironic enough that the entire room briefly became soaked in hipsterism.

To further devalue and discredit Cass, Eddie finally put his hands on her... in the form of a paternal pat on the head. Supposedly sympathetic.

"Melba! This kid's lunch is on me," he declared. "She's gonna need every dollar she can hang onto... you poor little girl. You'll be quitting that crazy-ass job within a week. Nobody lasts on the Cuddlebear Convoy for long."

Satisfied that he'd neutralized whatever threat Cass posed to his way of life, Eddie wandered back over to a table of sycophants and resumed eating his hamburger.

Shortly after, Melba arrived with her free lunch. Without a word, Cass scooped up the coffee and sandwich and left the building.

She was halfway through the most delicious pulled pork sandwich she'd ever had in her life when Melba came knocking at her still-parked box truck.

When Cass rolled down her driver's side window, a doughnut was offered.

"You forgot this," the cook/owner pointed out.

The words jittered over Melba's head briefly. `everybody's favorite auntie` they wrote out, supportively.

"It's empty calories, anyway. I don't know why I ordered it," Cass replied, before sipping at her coffee (and accepting the doughnut anyway).

"You've got a long haul ahead. Any calories will help," Melba suggested. "But you'll also be sitting behind the wheel for hours. Not good for your back. Why not eat inside? I keep my stools comfy. Gotta replace the padding every few months, but it's worth it..."

"Not my scene, man. Not my crowd. Not interested in being the official court jester, even if it's better than being the scary outsider," Cass said.

"Honey, if you're working a route, this is your crowd. You're a trucker now, no matter what you did for a living before," Melba replied. "Better to make peace with that. I can't bring your lunch out to you every day, you know."

"Screw it. I can brown-bag. The job's just a job; I don't need to ingratiate myself to a bunch of greasy, fat... okay, no, pigeonholing them is vice-versa, not cool. But point is, I don't need to bother. I can just do my work and be done with it and go home and that's that. Easy enough way to make a living. Comfy."

"Not much of a life, that sort of living. Look... it'll be rough at first. You'll run into Eddie and other Eddies along the way. But they ain't *all* bad. And the sooner you figure out how to fit in the easier it'll be on you in the Outlands."

"I'll be behind the wheel all day, not interacting with anyone. This is a solo job. How do you figure playing buddy boy with those guys will matter?"

Melba stood on her toes, to peer in the window. Feeling a bit sheepish about the wall of metal between herself and the only nice person she'd met at this rest stop, Cass obligingly opened the truck door to make it easier.

In return, Melba reached over, to point out the buttons on her unused C.B. radio.

PUB. "Public channel. General discussion, big forum style." BEARS. "Warnings about speed traps and other cop patrols." SIDEB. "Sidebar. Someone in the pub wants to talk to you semi-privately, you can go here." LAWL. "Jokes. Raunchy as hell, but keeps your spirits up." TRFF. "Traffic reports. Accidents and slowdown. Critical if you want to get your deliveries done on time. You following me so far, hun?"

"I... guess? What's my radio got to do with making nice with the locals?"

"All of these channels evolved over the years so folks out here could work together in the Outlands. Good clear signal, better range than you get on Earth for some reason—we had the Internet before the Internet existed. Good thing too, because the world's spread thin out here. It's not cramped up and tight like in the cities. Without that connection it's just you in the middle of nowhere, friendless. Something goes wrong and you've got nobody in your corner, you're in a bad place alone. We pull together and in the end, everybody lives another day."

Having stretched enough for one day, Melba settled back, adjusting her apron.

"Tomorrow, you come by for lunch. I'll make you somethin' special," she offered. "And I'll have a word with Eddie and the other Eddies beforehand. You got at least me in your corner, come to that."

Cass had no dismissive comment to toss off in reply, so Melba bowed out.

"I better get back to the counter now," she said. "And what Eddie was ramblin' about, your route? You hang in there. He just doesn't want to admit he couldn't hack it running teddy bears. You get this done, stick with it despite the nine kinds 'o crazy you're about to face, they'll respect you in time. Drive safe, now."

With that, Melba ambled back into her establishment. Back to the crowd of hard-drivin' truckers that Cass refused to admit she was in any way related to.

Quickly finishing off her lunch—empty calories and all—Cass fired up the motor with one hand and her cellphone with the other. No sense delaying any more, she had deliveries to make. Jeb had sent a series of emails, one per delivery, arranged roughly in order of closest to furthest out. A to B to C and back home again, that was the way to roll.

And all that business about the job being nasty as Satan's gonads, or whatever... she was *delivering teddy bears*. There was no conceivable way in which that would be unpleasant or strange.

Certainly there had to be a reasonable reason why she was delivering a teddy bear to a construction site.

Cass hadn't read her instructions wrong—the first email from Jeb was very specific, highlighting an address to a building that didn't exist yet. *Department of Resources Construction Site #378, Highway Four. Deliver box marked 'Jerry' to foreman between 1pm and 1:30pm.*

So, here she was, parked just outside a whirling hive of hard-hatted activity. The Department of Resources often tried major constructions projects like these, raising new buildings instead of waiting for existing ones to be imported. It showed forward progress and forward thinking, very good for reelection campaigns... provided the buildings didn't go cubist soon after the ribbon cutting ceremony.

Everybody knew about the New Deal, the massive reconstruction effort from the 30s. It was the early years of the City of Angles, and the Great Depression back in America had enough of a backlash here that drastic steps were needed. Mayor Fletcher demolished several city blocks of imported buildings from Earth, intent on replacing the useless mishmash of clashing building styles with a gleaming city of the future (of the thirties). Ground was broken in September and the buildings were almost ready for occupation two years later...

Overnight, the entire district went bugnuts crazy. Buildings twisted and distorted, workers turned into Picassos, everything completely ruined. Department of Safety had to go in shooting to put down the poor bastards caught in that death trap, then build walls to seal the entire zone away for all time.

Lesson learned—the city knew what buildings it wanted already. Question the ineffable plan at your own peril.

That didn't stop the government from raising new buildings from scratch, of course. Particularly here in the Outlands, where things were spread out enough that it felt "safe" to interject man's works amidst the choosings of the gods. Usually, it worked out okay. Usually.

Still, it put an extra spring in her step, eager to get the box containing Jerry the Bear delivered so she could get back in her truck and drive very far away. It took a few minutes to get clearance from the guard at the gate, and she had to swap her baker boy hat for a hard hat, but eventually she was being escorted through the maze of girders and sweaty workmen to a trailer-hitch office.

Perhaps the foreman was a toy collector. Maybe he asked for the bear to be delivered out here because he was driving home to visit relatives after work, and wanted to take a present with him. Plenty of reasonable reasons...

The spectacled workman behind a desk of messy paperwork did not greet Cass's cardboard boxed delivery with the enthusiasm of expectation. Instead, he deployed a concentrated look of confusion.

"Delivery," Cass emphasized, hiking the large box up a bit in her arms.

"Deliveries go to the resource shed," the foreman pointed out.

"She insisted this had to go right to you, sir," the guard said—he'd insisted on accompanying her. "I tried to explain that you didn't order any children's toys, but..."

NOW the foreman's expression changed to enthusiasm. "Toys? —wait, is that a teddy bear? Tell me that's a teddy bear. You're the new bear delivery person, right?"

"Uh... yes. The new bear delivery person is who I am, yes," Cass replied, setting the box down on his desk. "This is Jerry. He's a bear. ...this is your teddy bear, right? I'm in the right place?"

The foreman eagerly ripped into the box—but used the utmost care to lift the actual bear out of its packaging. He set it down gently, very gently on his desk, propped up against a toolbox. Adjusted the floppy doll's head slightly, to look out the window at the construction site...

"You have no idea what a relief this is," the foreman said, with a smile. "We're eight weeks in on this project and I was beginning to worry I wouldn't be getting a bear this time. Takes a load off my mind, believe you me!"

Neither the delivery girl nor the guard who delivered her looked as relieved as the foreman. As far as Cass knew, teddy bears were not a load bearing structure, so what purpose they could possibly serve here was unfathomable.

"Well... for whatever reason, glad you like your order. I'll pass that along to Grandma Scarlett," Cass suggested. Next up, the clipboard she'd tucked under one arm. "Mind signing here for the delivery?"

The gleeful foreman scribbled out something incomprehensible which was possibly his name.

"Does this mean she's taking orders now?" he asked. "I've tried to reach out to her before, but I got nothing in reply. If she's finally taking direct orders that would make my job SO much easier!"

"Uh... I don't follow. Didn't you order this bear?"

"What? No, of course not. She doesn't take orders, like I said," the foreman replied. "The bears just... show up. Sometimes. I mean, last three projects I've directed, a bear was delivered. Two projects before that I got no bear, and that put my blood pressure through the roof!"

"Okay. Not following this at all. Why, *exactly*, is having a teddy bear at a construction site so important?"

"So the building doesn't fall down, of course."

The silence suggested that further explanation was required.

"I'll grant you this is superstitious hokum," the foreman admitted. "But... I'm not the only one who's gotten bears. Other project directors in the Department got them too, for a decade or so. At first we were like, what the heck? Why is some crazy old lady sending us kid's toys? But when Bob threw away his bear in the trash, I kid you not, the VERY next day his building project went cubist and had to be quarantined. Meanwhile, every project where the bear was kept on site? No problems at all. Still standing strong, even after years. They're good luck charms, and you don't *buy* them, you don't *ask* for them. You either get one or you don't. But now I've got one! This project'll be juuuust fine now. All thanks to you!"

Delivering teddy bears. No conceivable way in which that would be unpleasant or strange.

Delivering creepy dolls hand-sewn by a creepy old lady to people who never ordered them... EVERY conceivable way in which that could be unpleasant or strange.

...no. Not unpleasant, actually. Just strange. It wasn't like the dolls were horrific ruined baby dolls with broken eyes that giggled quietly in the night with busted voice boxes. They were cuddly little bears, unassuming, unthreatening. The fact that they were apparently coveted for their magical luck properties, okay, THAT was strange, but...

Words flickered briefly over Jerry the Bear's head, to remind Cass of Grandma Scarlett's words.

they have protectors.

She left the foreman in his peace of mind, her accompanying guard closing the trailer office door behind them.

"You know he's nuts, right?" the guard mumbled (loud enough to be heard over heavy machinery). "Bet he doesn't break mirrors or let black cats cross his path, either. Buildings don't stand or fall because of some stupid doll. I've worked plenty of jobs without dolls and without problems. It's just a coincidence."

"Nuts. Yeah. Right. Sensible," Cass quickly replied. And then hurried off, back to her truck, away from crazy town.

The next delivery was a strange inversion of the first. Instead of "unexpected and desired" it was a head on crash into "expected and undesired."

She'd parked her truck outside another isolated little house, much like the Happy Acre Orphanage. Not all the buildings in the Outlands were industrial or farmland, after all; plenty of people came to the rural sprawl to get away from the urban sprawl. Much as Melba had said, things were spread out very thin in the Outlands. That became a selling point for some families, which preferred not to have neighbors within eyeshot and earshot and likely would've shot them on sight regardless. Outlands gave them the isolation and mock safety they craved in a world which mocked safety.

Signs like "BEWARE OF DOG" and "NO SOLICITORS" and "NO TRESPASSING" and "someone really needs to chillax" (not what it really said) greeted Cass as she walked up to the front door, with a box full of bear. She was tempted to turn right around and walk away, honestly... especially in light of the revelation that Scarlett's bears were gifts, not orders. Not worth getting a shotgun to the face over. On the slim chance that this bear was in fact expected or would at least be welcomed, she dared to ring the doorbell.

First good sign was that she didn't immediately face the business end of a hunting rifle. But that was the only good sign.

The woman who answered the door looked suspicious from the get go. Cass was clearly unexpected, and judging from the rustle at one of the closed sets of curtains as she walked up to the door, this unexpected visitor had been watched very carefully likely from half a mile away. Plenty of open space in the Outlands. Plenty of distance to see potential risks from.

"We didn't order anything," the woman said right away.

"I've got delivery instructions to bring this teddy bear to your address, ma'am," Cass replied—having already opened the box, so she could show its contents right away, without any motions that could be mistaken for 'I'm going for my gun!'. "It's a gift from the Happy Acre Orphanage. Just a stuffed doll, ma'am. Nothing more."

"We didn't order *anything*," the occupant repeated, as if it was a magic mantra.

"It's a gift, ma'am. As I said. Now, if you'd just sign here, I'll leave this and be on my way off your property—"

"You think I'm not onto you?" the woman insisted. "I read the Department of Safety warning. 'Don't accept unsolicited toys.' They may have anthrax or bombs in them! You turn right around and get back on your truck and get out of here. I'm friends with the local sheriff and he can be here within—"

"Mommy, what's that?"

A young voice, from down the hall. So, the bear had an intended recipient after all.

It was pushing her luck, but... Scarlett had been very insistent on making these deliveries. Given Cass might be running into this situation a lot, the more she could manage to deliver the better. Plus, no hunting rifle. Yet. A solid plus.

"Teddy bear delivery!" Cass announced loudly enough to be heard. It was a truthful fact and safe to announce, she felt... and would get the kid running before mom could shoo her away.

Worked like a charm. An adorable golden curled moppet had smoothly wormed her way around the goalkeeping mother and snatched the box from Cass's hands with fierce strength.

"Aaaaa! She's so cute!" the girl declared, starry-eyed. "The box says 'Janette'. Is this Janette? You are Janette the Bear and you are my friend! Hooray!"

With that the battle was lost, and the mother knew it. Forcefully yanking the supposedly anthrax-stuffed bear away from her daughter would result in a nightmare domestic disturbance. With eyes of angry spite, she glared Cass down in response to her shenanigans.

In return, Cass held out her clipboard and pen.

"Sign here please, ma'am."

The next few deliveries were considerably less threatening, but no less strange.

Three o'clock, a dentist's office. This was a strangely freestanding cluster of offices in the middle of nowhere, a building which would've made more sense in the middle of the city than in the middle of the Outlands; she had to navigate a maze of hallways and elevators to find the exact delivery location. Inside, a disinterested receptionist pointed out that she didn't order a teddy bear (of course) but at least she didn't turn the gift away. It went in the waiting room toy pile, along with building blocks and thick cardboard books from the seventies. Hopefully a child would eventually find little Bobby the Bear in that mess.

Four o'clock, an automobile factory. Not too many garages got copied over from Earth, and annexing (not "stealing") cars for resale meant going through the Department of Resources for a dodgy second-hand vehicle. Outlands were perfect for building local jobs and transport. Although a factory full of robot arms and guys smelling like engine oil was hardly an appropriate destination for a teddy bear, Cass nevertheless left Louie-Louie the Bear with the confused-looking guard at the factory gate. Having no idea what to do with it, he said he'd see if anybody in the factory wanted it.

Five o'clock, dinner. Too far away from Melba's and not particularly interested in opening that kettle of worms again. Fortunately the next rest stop down the road had a drive-through; greasy fast food didn't mesh well with a stomach acclimated to niche little city dining experiences, but it'd get the job done.

Six o'clock, a shipping warehouse for an online retailer, and things got even weirder. "Place the bear in the third open box you find." By this point she was seriously considering dropping the whole job rather than get arrested for sneaking into some paranoid e-tailer's secret stash. She ended up explaining it away as a college sorority scavenger hunt hazing week type thing, correctly guessing the guard as a former frat junkie—he allowed her to poke around a little, under supervision, and thankfully the third box wasn't too far from the front office. And so, Destructinator the Awesome Bear (as his box declared) ended up shipped to someone who was ordering replacement razor blades and vitamins. Pushing luck, pushing what made any sense at all, but...

Seven o'clock.

And if there was a tipping point, it'd be this. Because it made less sense than any of the others.

"Put Daniel the Bear underneath the fifth tree at mile maker 5.4 along Interstate 37. Open the box and walk away."

Daniel the Bear. Loved intensely by that little boy she'd met at the start of this, given away by an orphan in hopes of his surrogate self being adopted. And Cass was ordered by her obtuse and vague employer to dump this bear in the middle of nowhere.

Clouds were brewing tonight, threatening a rainstorm later. Even if she went against orders and sealed Daniel's box shut, the package would be soaked and ruined. And for what? For some mysterious higher purpose? For a crazy old lady's whimsy? What was the *point* of all this?

When mile maker 5.4 was reached and Cass tossed the parking brake... she considered her options. She'd done some borderline stupid things today, all in the name of living up to her end of this job contract. This was actually the least stupid, the least likely to get her arrested or killed. And yet, it felt like the most wrong.

In the end, she decided on a reasonable compromise.

Her last delivery wasn't until nine tonight. She'd leave Daniel here, underneath the tree, and walk away... but only a short distance away, re-parking her truck, facing the tree. She'd wait, and watch.

If it was clear the weather was about to dump all over the kid's precious toy, she'd go fetch the bear, burn rubber to the orphanage, give Daniel back to his owner and tell Grandma Scarlett where to stick it. Life's cruel lessons, indeed—Cass wanted no part of that, if that's all there was to this.

Ten minutes in and the bear in the distance hadn't gotten up and walked away. Her C.B. continued to chatter away, with the background yammerings of truckers. Cass continued to ignore it.

Twenty minutes and nothing. Clouds getting thicker. Even if it wasn't going to rain, this was looking like it'd be one gloomy as hell day. Not improving her mood any.

Twenty five minutes and Cass reached for the parking brake, to drive back and put an end to this insanity. No more weirdness. Time to call it quits and go hang paintings for Reg...

A car had pulled up to the 5.4 mile marker.

She had to strain to see in the setting darkness of the night, but... immediately a kid burst forth from the car, like a cork from a popgun. Judging from the wiggling and panic, he was doing the Pee Pee Dance. The nearest rest stop was miles and miles away... doing your business behind the nearest tree at the side of the road would do just as well as a proper bathroom. (A projection by Cass, granted; but one backed up by the words. `gotta go gotta go too much lemonade` trailed after the kid as he ran for the tree line.)

His father chased after him, less hurried, although likely eager to get back to the road. Mother waited in the car.

Two minutes later, and the kid had a much more leisurely and relieved stroll back to the car.

With a teddy bear under his arm. One he just happened to find during this completely random roadside picnic.

Bear, boy, and father got back in the car and drove away. Daniel had found a home at last.

This left Cass in a bit of a pickle.

She was trying to escape weirdness, to anchor herself to hard reality. Now she felt more adrift than ever, lost in a sea of strange old women and teddy bears and kids who magically find them. Why hadn't she just agreed to help hang paintings for Reg? She could be back in the city, in the filth and noise and hustle and bustle that made perfect sense...

Alas, weirdness was afoot. Weirdness was obviously afoot, but it was solidly and definitively reality-breakingly real weirdness. Scarlett couldn't possibly have known that leaving a bear at that one tree at that one moment in time would result in it finding its way into a kid's arms—that was madness. And yet... there you have it. It actually happened.

The easiest answer was that all of this craziness was a series of complete coincidences. Just like the guard at the construction site said, a mix of superstition and coincidences. Except, of course, the odds were rather steeply stacked against it being a matter of the odds...

Cass would absolutely be drilling Scarlett for answers about all of this. There was still the remote possibility of it all being a hoax of some sort, or a reality TV show. But... did she drive straight to Happy Acre now? Stop the runaway train? She did have one more delivery to make. A delivery which, oddly enough, she had enough time to make even with the stakeout at the last delivery. Almost as if her intentional delay was built right into the schedule.

One more bear. One more box. One more kid in need (presumably).

Fine. She'd already gone farther than she ever intended just to make this madcap episode pay off; may as well see it through to the end. One more delivery and then she could get her answers.

The clock was ticking, the next stop was some distance away. But she'd make it in time. Just in time.

Night had firmly fallen by the time she pulled up to the isolated house. The decorative stars were beautiful in the Outlands, stretching from open horizon to open horizon... but she had her eyes firmly on the ground.

Gravel path. Tire swing spinning in the breeze. Freshly painted treehouse, candy apple red, much like the Happy Acre Orphanage. Fine, so another bear to another kid. She could handle that.

She parked at the end of the driveway, to avoid boxing in a ratty-looking old green pick-up truck that was squatting in front of the closed two-car garage. Today had taught her a valuable lesson in stepping lightly when dealing with Outlanders; no need to look threatening in any way.

Up the path, to the front door. No lights on. Curtains drawn. Maybe the family wasn't home? But there was the truck...

Bracing herself for whatever, Cass tapped the doorbell button.

Nothing.

She could hear the bell clearly; the only noise out here came from crickets and the like. If anybody was home surely she'd hear activity inside—wait. There. Footsteps, coming up a flight of creaky old stairs. Across creaky old floorboards. Closer...

Door locks, being undone in sequence. A lot of them. Maybe another paranoid type? Scrape of a chair or something on the floor, was it propped up under the doorknob...?

Before she could get properly concerned, the door finally opened a crack.

Dark inside. Hard to see the occupant, for that matter... sickly, unshaven, terrible complexion. He wore a third-hand suit under an overcoat, weirdly enough.

the shabby men, the words printed slowly over his head. The letters didn't jiggle or dance around. Very cautious.

"Delivery," Cass announced. "Look, I know it's late and you did not in fact order a teddy bear, but I've got a teddy bear here for your son or daughter, okay? It's a gift. No tricks, just a gift. If you could sign here—"

"No son. No daughter," the shabby man replied. A raspy voice, much like Grandma Scarlett's, but with zero mirth to it. Just... dry. "I didn't order a teddy bear. Goodbye."

"No kids? You've got a treehouse up there," She said, waggling her clipboard vaguely over her shoulder.

"Came with the house. Bought it recently. No kids," he mumbled. "No kids here. Goodbye."

...except there was a kid here.

Now that her eyes had adjusted properly to the darkness, she could see over his shoulder. She could read the situation, read people for that matter; a good life skill to have...

Marks on the corner of a hallway wall. Height indicators, for a growing child. Dates on the lines. 2010, 2012. Bright and colorful crayon lines. A stray sneaker, far too small to belong to this schlub, laces untied. No second shoe. It had been kicked to the side when he approached the door, as if trying to hide it... but not kicked far enough.

But the thing she put the most faith in, despite the source material, was the words.

They hovered over her cardboard box of teddy bear, small and timid. Scared.

she needs me. help. help.

"Goodbye," the man replied again. And then the door closed, locked, and the chair under the knob was replaced.

Panic, as the long-promised rainstorm finally came. A slow and heavy beatdown of rain, content to release itself gradually for the next twelve hours rather than thrash about in fury. Satisfied with its inevitability.

Cass sat at the wheel of her truck, the box at her side, not sure what to do.

There *was* a kid in there, a kid in trouble. She didn't have a single doubt about it despite all the doubts she probably should be having about it. But... what to do about it? Call the cops, obviously. Not that she could get consistent cellphone signal this far out. Department of Safety? Straight to the top, bypass the local fuzz? And say what, that a creepy old man bought a house and said he didn't have a kid? What proof did Cass really have, other than some guesses and the yammerings of the insane babble from her acid-soaked mind?

The smart thing to do would be to turn around and head back to Happy Acre. Get out of this dangerous and surreal job. Phone in her concerns to the cops once she was closer to the core of the Outlands, away from these fringes. Let the powers that be sort this out.

But...

But she had a delivery to make. Scarlett was very insistent that all the bears get where they're going.

—no, that was stupid. Her life wasn't worth a delivery job. Whose life was?

`you know the answer to that.`

She nearly accidentally hit the horn in surprise. Which would have been bad, since she was still parked at the edge of the crazy man's property.

The words were printing themselves on the inside of her rain-soaked windshield, now. The wipers went back and forth slowly, swiping them away, and then the words would reprint themselves on the other half of the windshield. Back and forth. Back and forth...

`we need to talk.`

`we need to talk.`

Her personal hallucination sideshow had only directly addressed her once before in her entire life. It was the day she was lazily rolling along, minding her own business, and a building dropped right in front of her. The words which normally draped life in sardonic color commentary chose that day to tell her to `turn left`, saving her life... and now, for the second time, they were talking right to her.

you have a choice.

everyone gets a choice.

you could give up,
go back,
quit the job,
return to the familiar,
embrace normality.

or you could stand up,
challenge the nightmare,
save the innocent,
embrace what you call
weirdness.

for life in the city
is not weird *or* normal.

life in the city is *both*.
normal is weird is normal.

you can decay in happy
denial.

or live your life, come what
may.

succumb to fear and
take no risks.

or deliver us from evil.

i could leave you alone
forever. no more lucid
dreaming.

or you can become the oracle
that allen always hoped
you'd be.

choose.

choose.

Apex. Top of the hill, up one side, down the other. In one ear and out the other. Event horizon. The point of no return.

Metaphors running through her head, piling up, poetry desperate to get out.

Ever since her one and only experiment with illegal drugs she'd assumed the hallucinations were the result of brain damage; a harmless harm done to her mind in a bout of youthful stupidity. Harmless. Unimportant. But it knew things she couldn't have known. Just like how Grandma Scarlett knew things *she* couldn't have known.

Whoever was on the other end of the cosmic Clark Nova was breaking Cass's fourth wall.

But this wasn't the tipping point, was it? The moment where everything she thought was true upended itself neatly in a pile on the floor. No. That was the day the words saved her life. turn left. She'd been in denial of how critically important that was, too busy focusing on things like career and money and creativity... the world kept turning and she didn't even notice it was always turning on a different axis.

The words were even right there on her handwritten page, so long ago, in a distant coffee house. Visions from her dreams which she thought were deeply nested metaphors that she couldn't un-nest properly, a stacking doll set that was missing a few sizes. *Dreams of the holy trinity of Lucidity, Madness, and Oblivion...*

There wasn't really a choice. Because the alternative was insane. More insane than the insanity she was ready to embrace.

So, she embraced the weirdness in the most normal way possible.

"How do I get her out of there and not get us both killed?" she asked her muse. "Risking myself to save a kid's life, okay, I can work with that. But let's be sensible about it. Get a proper plan going. What do you recommend?"

A Hipster's Plan For Assaulting A Compound Of Weirdness And Possible Kidnappings At The Behest Of Your Imaginary Friend And/Or Mental Illness, First Draft.

1. Park out of sight (but not too far out of sight) and leave the engine running.

The storm was providing good cover, here. If she killed the headlights and parked on the edge of the highway itself, just out of sight from the isolated house, she could cut through the tree line on foot and approach the house from the side. Presumably far away enough not to be seen, but not so far away that getting back alive with a potentially psychotic madman in tow would be implausible.

2. Don't go in through the front door because it would be suicidal and you can't anyway.

Whoever this creepy guy was, he was expecting a full frontal assault judging from the locks and the doorknob gag. Instead, she'd approach from the side.

Like most rural houses this far from civilization, it had a proper storm cellar complete with external access. Best way to run for your life in the event of a tornado tearing through the Outlands, after all. What's more, thanks to Cass's voice in her head (words on her page, anyway) she knew there was a key under the flowerpot he doesn't know about. Hidden there by the former owners of the house, before he presumably started wearing their skin.

As predicted by whatever supernatural force had been passing itself off as brain damage all these years, there was in fact a hidden key to the storm cellar near the door. The parents probably wanted their kid to be able to get in even if they weren't nearby, and burglars were not exactly common out here.

3. Even though you set out this morning to deliver toys and weren't expecting to come face to face with the grim spectre of death, do not stand there like a slack jawed idiot when you find a surreal medical torture dungeon complete with two corpses.

This was the step Cass was experiencing difficulty with.

Over the years, she'd gotten used to the idea of seeing crudely typewritten words hovering over people's heads. She'd also steeled herself against the horrors of the world by watching lots of indie documentaries about the degradation of the environment and social injustice and the wars of Earth that Allen often talked about. She was a poet, which meant she had to be in tune with the sick and strange of the City of Angles, ready to speak its verses of life and death to the masses.

That did not mean she had ever actually been in the presence of a dead body. Grandma's funeral didn't count, because that was a situation designed for comfort and emotional security. Very little murder or aftermath of murder was involved. And while Grandma's last days were indeed in a hospital, full of strange tubes and beeping equipment, that was equipment designed to keep her alive. This appeared to be designed to do the opposite.

Having stepped right into the pages of a Burroughs novel, someone had gone and installed a Facility with a capital F in the basement of this family home. There were machines. There were tubes. IV drips. But also electrodes and wires and metal hooks and things Cass didn't even want to look at. All of it hastily arranged, unpacked from cases that were brought in by pick-up truck, like an impromptu meth lab.

No clear purpose to any of it. If there was a purpose, it was lost in a wall of medical notes and diagrams, hastily tacked up near the bodies—wiring diagrams, crudely written instructions, things like that. Quick reference guides for the madman on the go. Pencil notes on drywall around it all, jotting down numbers, scribbling out unreadable writings. Words which started out coherent but then wandered off towards nonsense...

One word kept repeating. Repeating often enough that Cass could spot it easily, despite trying very hard not to let her curiosity dig any deeper into the wall of crazy.

Bedlam. Bedlam. BEDLAM.

None of that junk really mattered. Leave it for the Department of Safety to investigate. She had a reason to come down here, and it wasn't to marvel at the surroundings. It was a rescue mission. Unfortunately, she was too late to rescue everyone.

Mother and father, dead. Previous owners of the house, before their home invasion experience. Lying on the floor and dead for a few days, from the smell and the look of it. Still hooked up to drains and siphons and worse. The shabby man hadn't bothered unplugging them—he just shoved them into a corner for later disposal. Plenty of dirt around here to bury a body in and no rush to get it done when your nearest neighbor was miles away.

It was perfect, really. Need to slowly and horribly murder people for purposes unknown? The Outlands will provide the ideal victims in the ideal scenario. Too far away from any stable community. Nobody will know. Nobody will care...

The angel on the other end of Cass's golden telephone cared. And for what it was worth, their daughter was still breathing.

Maybe six, maybe seven years old. Malnourished and unbathed for days. Unconscious, but she was alive. Lying on a makeshift cot, some token gesture of comfort, while she ran through a gauntlet of nightmares...

Enough chewing the scenery. Cass was a hipster of action today, and action called.

Quickly she started unplugging things. Left the IV sites and electrodes on, no time to yank them off, but the flimsy tubes and wires could be torn apart or yanked out easily. Disconnect her, grab her, get the hell out of crazy town—

Creaking. Old wooden house, everything creaked. Not the concrete of the storm cellar, but the ceiling above her head, which represented the floor underneath the shabby man's feet. He was on the move now. In hindsight Cass was damned lucky he wasn't down here already when she came in through the side door, but if she wanted to stay lucky, she had to get out before those creaks got any closer.

With the disconnection finished, she scooped up the girl in both arms.

Delivery time. As fast as her feet could carry her.

The girl didn't wake up, even being hauled around roughly through a rainstorm and shoved into the passenger seat of a truck. (Buckled up, always buckle up, sir.) Hopefully she was going to survive this. The typewriter of her brain wouldn't have sent Cass on a rescue op for someone who couldn't actually be rescued, right...?

For lack of a better way to reach her, Cass pulled Jeremy the Bear from his box, and made her delivery. Tucked the bear under the sleeping child's arm. The kid instinctively curled that arm, to hold the bear tightly, so maybe that could be considered a good sign—

Roar of the demon. Light in her hindsights. Headlights. Engines.

Doctor Demento had fired up his pick-up truck, and was coming to retrieve what he had rightfully stolen.

So much for escaping cleanly into the night. Cass didn't bother running around to her side of the truck; she clambered over the child's form and into the driver's seat, strapping in, getting ready to gun it. Leaving the engine running was definitely the right move; headlights on and she'd be ready to bail.

Not that "bailing" at any great speed was possible. This was a damn box truck, not a dragster. It struggled and groaned at the effort of pulling out of the wet roadside dirt she'd left it in... far too long, too much struggling, before she was back on the road. Back on the highway, stretching off into the remote and distant edges of the Outlands...

With rubber on the road, she stabilized the truck and tried not to slip on wet pavement. Then checked her rearview.

Big green truck. Moving at speed. Intent on taking her down.

Pedal down, into the night at the speed of mercy. Whatever she could wring out of this washer-dryer on rollerskates, Cass would wring. It wasn't her vehicle yet, not like her old taxi, an extension of her mind... but no time to become one with the wheels. She had to do what she could with what she had...

She glanced to the wipers, swish-swish.

"I would WELCOME any suggestions, whoever you are!" she called out.

drive, the words suggested.

"This is a lousy time for you to resume being vague!"

drive fast?

Some writers got a muse. Cass apparently got an amusement.

Cellphone. Call the cops. ...who would arrive maybe in an hour, given how far out Cass was from civilization.

Something goes wrong and you've got nobody in your corner, you're in a bad place alone...

Right. Time to break the conversational ice.

Cass grabbed the handset from her C.B. radio, jammed the PUB button, and pushed the red button down nice and firm.

"Uh... breaker breaker... 10-4— hell, I don't know, look, I need HELP," she called out. "This is... it's the Cuddlebear Convoy and I'm on Interstate 455 coming up on Exit 23 and I seriously need help from anyone who can hear me. Please. Anybody out there? Can anyone hear this? Over."

Nothing. Maybe she was out of range? Melba said the radio reached farther than you'd expect, but Cass was near the edge of the known Outlands and there was a thunderstorm going down right now—

"Copy that, this is Eddie in the Hotrod Express—the hell you yammerin' about now, girl? Over."

Cass tried not to groan in despair. A glance in her rear view, at the wildly weaving and honking green pick-up that was still chasing her helped her keep locked into a firm panic mode.

"You aren't going to believe this but listen to me anyway, Eddie," Cass explained. "I was delivering one of those bears and ran into some psycho who killed off a little girl's entire family. I got her out of there and we're headed down I-455 as fast as this piece of crap can go and now he's chasing us and I'm not going to be able to keep this up for long so if you could ring the... bears, or smokey or call a SWAT team or I don't know what I would seriously appreciate it! —over."

"Look, kid, I don't know what drugs you're toasted off your ass on—"

Vector shift. Impact. The box truck rattling from impact, as the green pick-up smashed up against it. Cass swore heavily and twisted the steering wheel, pushing back, trying to re-align with the center of the road.

"Are you or are you not near Exit 23? Yes or no! Simple question! Come see for yourself, assuming I survive that long!"

"Fine! I'll be on there with you in a minute. You're damn lucky I'm so close by. But I find you're stoned I'm tearing that radio outta your truck! OVER!"

"This is Jonesy in the Starlight Runner—Eddie, you seriously going through with this? You know that brat's just pranking you..."

"Yeah, seriously, Eddie. It's probably all crap—"

"Cut the crosstalk and let me drive," Eddie barked back. *"I'll deal with this. Everybody back to work. Over."*

Cass had let the handset drop long before the debate began. She was too busy trying not to die.

The kid somehow was still sleeping, despite the box truck rocking and rolling all over the road. Hopefully she wasn't in a coma or anything... but given the waking nightmare Cass was enjoying right now, maybe being asleep would be best for the kid. The way Cass's head was hurting from the sideswiping impact, she almost wanted a nap, too...

Already rolling at top speed. The green pick-up had fallen back a bit, being less weighty than the box truck and needing more of a head of steam before it could try again—but try again it was going to do. Cass braced herself, waiting for the blow...

The world shook. Her vision blurred. But when it came back... there was an 18-wheeler ahead of her, pulling on from Exit 23. The Hotrod Express, if she was guessing correctly. And yes, it had silver strippers on the mud flaps.

"Jesus Christ, the kid was telling the truth!" Eddie's voice echoed from her C.B. *"We've got a smash-up on I-455! Someone's trying to run the Cuddlebear*

Convoy off the road! —okay. Jonesy, get a bear on your ass, blow through a speed trap if you gotta. Pollock, I want you on your LD with the Department of Safety, tell them there's about to be a pretty damn huge accident. I'm going after that sunofabitch."

"What the hell? Eddie, you're serious about this?" Jonesy replied, confused.

"The brat's a trucker. Whatever else she is, she's behind the wheel so she's one of us—and you know damn well we DO NOT TOLERATE people screwing with truckers," Eddie said. *"Now get on it! Kid—don't reply by radio, focus on your driving—I'm just ahead of you. Here's what we do. When I give the signal you get into the left lane, fast. I'm gonna get in the right lane and jam my brakes. You get in front of me in the center and I'll bitchslap that guy with my trailer. Honk once if you're ready."*

Sparing a glance to make sure the little girl was still there... Cass readied herself for whatever was coming.

And gave a sharp blast on the horn, before veering to the left.

The Hotrod Express seemed to shoot backwards, from a relativity standpoint. It cut through the wall of rain, a wall of steel and wheels that dwarfed Cass's little box truck by far...

She only spared a moment to glance in the rear view, as she pulled out ahead of Eddie.

He'd deftly maneuvered a few tons of metal. The green truck tried to avoid head-on collision, and did so—but not by enough. The front of the vehicle clipped against Eddie's tail, smashing out one headlight, sending it into a spin...

It worked. Cass was going to survive. Insurance premiums were going to go up, Eddie might get in trouble, but she'd survive and so would the girl. Whoever that freak was, whatever he wanted, this was the end of—

Two headlights.

Three.

Four.

Five.

A whirling mass of headlights and chrome, twirling and twisting, rolling along the highway like a cartwheeling pile of shrapnel. Briefly, Cass flashed back to a terrible sci-fi movie she saw once with robots turning into cars and vice versa... piles of disorganized panels and joints and support structures, whirling and shifting and blurring in a visual mess which nobody could really follow...

She heard one word over her C.B., which chilled her to the core.

"PICASSO—!" Eddie called out, in warning—before static cut him off.

The car/driver/picasso tore through Eddie's trailer like a whirling ball of knives through metal butter.

His 18-wheeler split in half, a jagged slice carved right through the middle. The back half careened away and disintegrated—the front half ever so slowly teetered over, until his cab was sliding sideways along the highway. Shattered glass, twisted metal...

...and an unliving monster of shattered glass and twisted metal continuing to give chase to Cass's truck, eager to get at the young cargo inside. Freed from the limitations of physics and the internal combustion engine, the picasso of hard iron could skim across the rain-slick road, gaining incredible speed. She only had seconds left to live.

```
hey

let me help
```

Tiny words, barely glowing. Hard to see them out of the corner of her eye...

A teddy bear. Not the one under the girl's arm... the words centered on the flopsy bear that she'd deposited on her dashboard, next to the eternally smiling hula-girl. The bear Grandma Scarlett had given her, her own personal teddy, no extra delivery required. Cass had been ignoring all day, just another decorative element in the Cuddlebear Convoy... hadn't even given it a name. Immediately she felt a pang of shame about that.

Cass's bear was talking to her, now. Its head had flopped to the other side, to look her square in the eye. Probably just a random confluence of the truck rocking back and forth. Probably.

Her senses sped up just enough for the bear to have his say, despite the high speed picasso bearing down on her.

```
throw me at the shabby man, the bear said. pick me up and throw me.
i'll die. i'm sad about that. but this way, you'll live, and can help
the nice girl in dreams who loves us. i'll be happy with that. it's
okay. i am your protector. throw me at him. i love you.
```

...it was silly, feeling pathos for a stuffed bear. And yet, didn't she watch to make sure little Daniel the Bear found his new home...?

So, she didn't just grab the toy and chuck it out the window, uncaring. She grabbed the toy and chucked it out the window, caring. And hoping.

Instead of watching the road like a responsible driver, she watched her mirror. Watched the impossibly slow arc, the doll tumbling through space, through the rain. It was falling at exactly the speed of gravity... but trailing behind her truck at speed, relatively speaking. And impacted with the twisted sphere of horror dead center.

The twisted sphere of horror turned back into an ordinary green pick-up, driven by a very surprised-looking murderer. Because the truck had re-manifested itself upside down and at a strange angle.

With a horrific sound, the truck cartwheeled off the road, spinning end over end as physics took control of the situation. Last Cass saw of it, it had smashed into a tree line by the side of the highway, and was gone in the darkness of night.

The C.B. radio was on fire with activity for the next hour.

Eddie got his radio working again, salvaging it from the wreck of his truck, and politely asked someone to send a goddamn ambulance because he was losing blood fast and probably broke something. He was relieved to hear Cass somehow survived her encounter with the high-speed Picasso. In fact, all the truckers on the horn were relieved. She was one of them, after all. Far from the court jester, now... she'd survived one of the craziest things the road could throw at her, giving her the stamp of legitimacy. Eddie wouldn't hear anything from anyone who joked about it, now.

For lack of a better idea... Cass drove her cargo back to Happy Acre Orphanage. She was carrying an orphan, after all. The smarter play might've been to wait for the Department of Safety to show up at the crash site(s), to sort things out there, but... for some reason, Cass just kept on driving. No words prompted her. Just a funny feeling that maybe dealing with the Department of Safety wasn't the thing to do tonight.

Her precious cargo was still asleep when she rolled up to the candy apple red farmhouse... but after finally killing the engine after a full night of lunatic driving... she heard a yawn.

The girl roused briefly... snuggled the bear under her arm, smiled, and drifted off into a far more pleasant sleep.

Jeb was there, to help ease the child out of the truck and into one of the orphanage's beds. He had a first aid kit on hand, to aid in removing the IV sites and un-glue the electrodes.

Scarlett was there, to help ease Cass down from her night of insanity. Not that Scarlett's brand of insanity was that much more comforting.

As if walking through a haze, Cass found herself sitting in the quiet and dark living room of the orphanage, with a cup of tea in her hands. Somewhere beyond, the children were sleeping, each with their own teddy bear... including one extra child and one extra bear.

"They'll never come for her, you understand," Scarlett was explaining, as Cass shook herself out of the half-sleep of her collected exhaustion. "No government agent, no Department of Safety investigator will come looking for the girl. The devil never sets foot in a church. She'll be lost in the system. But no matter; she's safe here, safe as houses. And she has her protector to watch over her dreams."

Warm teacup in her hands. Strange night.

"What are they?" Cass asked, thinking aloud.

"Mmm?"

"The bears. What are they. Who told you to make them?"

And Scarlett's chuckle, like raspy paper. Warm and brittle and old, but comfortingly fragile.

"I think you already know that, dear. You know all of this, just as much as I know," Scarlett replied. "You just couldn't find the right words, couldn't write them down. That's because they can't be written down without losing something of their essence. She comes to us in dreams, see. Lucid dreams. She doesn't speak in riddles, not exactly—she speaks in *dreams* the way we speak in English. We see them as riddles, and in the waking hours, something less. That's why Jeb writes down the instructions for where the bears are to be delivered as I mutter them in my sleep. It's not perfect, but it's the best way."

Grandma Scarlett set her teacup down, for now.

"Thirteen years ago... maybe fourteen? It's a bit of a blur, I admit," she said. "Thirteen years ago, a single father came to me with his infant daughter. He had recently lost his wife, you see, and wasn't sure he was capable of raising a daughter alone. He had a bad past. A violent past. Perhaps he didn't feel he deserved this happiness in his life. He wept, you know. He sat where you're sitting and wept, while his infant daughter slept quietly in a port-a-crib... for a time. And then she cried out, and he was there in an instant. A *father's* instincts. I knew then he would be just fine, and told him as much."

As if this explained everything, she paused. Leaving Cass to egg her on, a nod of the head, go on, what does this have to do with anything...?

"When he looked in the crib... it's the strangest thing. The little baby had a teddy bear," Grandma Scarlett said. "Where did she get it from? He hadn't brought it with her. It wasn't a bear from my orphanage. She hadn't pulled it off a toy shelf. Where there was no bear, suddenly, a bear. I named it, you know. Little Penelope's 'Gregory the Bear.' They left that night together, hopefully to grow as a family. I wonder if she still has that bear, some days..."

"And then you started getting the delivery instructions in your dreams," Cass realized. "It was that day, seeing that bear. You started sewing the bears, giving them to your kids to be loved and... I don't know, charged up with love like a battery... and that helps them keep kids safe. Safe from fear. Safe from picassos and all the other insane threats this city offers..."

"I'd like to think my little bears offer some hope against the darkness, yes."

"The one who gives you the delivery instructions in your dreams... I think she's been talking to me for years," Cass confessed. "She saved my life tonight. Saved that kid. ...I'll keep delivering your bears. I promise. I'm sticking with this, at the very least until I understand it more. I thought I was just mildly crazy, but..."

"Ohh, dear, dear... everything's mildly crazy. But only mildly," Scarlett joked... before looking distant for a moment, and then solidifying her expression into something more serious. "And if this world is a delusion, does that make it any less real? Who's to say what's real and what isn't? The answer, of course, is us. No other answer makes sense. Hmmm. Still. It's opportune, I feel, that she led me to you. I'm old and getting older, Cass. What's to come... it's going to take the fire of youth. Your fire, perhaps. And I think you know what's coming, don't you...?"

Lucidity, Madness, and Oblivion.

Bedlam.

The spiral down to the heart of the city.

But one word, above all of those, was coming to mind. A word she'd seen in her dreams, which she tried to express in poetry, tried to shackle down to metaphor and imagery and flowing lines without any success. It stood better on its own.

"War," Cass spoke.

Speeding on in the dark of night.

Soon, she'd be at the Suburbs, and then back to the city. Back to the crowds and the noise and the traffic and home sweet home.

So quiet out here in the Outlands. Everybody asleep in their little houses, far apart from each other, unaware of anything else in the world beyond their tiny slice of it. Maybe aware, but not thinking about it. Same thing in the end.

Cass fetched the handset from her C.B. radio.

"Hey. Cuddlebear Convoy here," she called out across the night. "I'm gonna be over in SIDEB talking a bit, if anybody wants to listen."

Release the button. Switch the channel. Press the button.

And recite the poem. The first true poem she'd written in many a year. A poem of truth.

```
They're coming.

They're coming.

They're coming for all of us, coming down the spiral,
digging and clawing and fumbling in the dark as they
search for the same prize, the heart of the city, the core
of our souls, the root of our existence.

They're coming to tear our sanity apart or to cast us into
the void, to drive us to madness or to despair, to ruin
and destroy and obliterate and take apart everything we
know bit by bit until it's served back up to us in a form
which is completely unrecognizable.
```

They're coming for the quiet ones, the ones that stay quiet, that shut up and move on day by day, shuffling their feet and working their jobs and keeping their heads above water because to do otherwise, to stop and think for even a second about what could be wrong would tip the scales too far one direction or another, because the darkness has already won and destroyed those people inside.

But they're not coming alone.

We're coming with them, we're coming to stop them, we're coming to stand against them, we're coming down the spiral to claim it for ourselves with the help of the one who stands with us against them, she who is the collective unconsciousness, the inner child, the voice of reason, the spirit of living which says we are not alone and never will be no matter what illusions claim otherwise.

We're coming to make our stand with lucid eyes that will see forever.

Are you ready?

Are you ready?

//end

Buildings next to buildings, askew or aligned. Buildings sometimes intersecting buildings, for that matter. Walk down a hallway, end up in a ballroom, double glass doors to a subway station, third exit on the left goes to a used book store. You can find anything you could ever want to read on the shelves, but good luck finding your way back again.

There's no rhyme or reason to any of it—we've got streets which lead to dead ends, roads which criss-cross and loop back around, highways which go nowhere. Literally nowhere, as in "anybody going down that road is not coming back." This is not a good place to wander off unless you like wandering off forever...

Nobody knows where the city came from. Nobody knows how we got here. Nobody knows why any of this is happening. But it's happening. The city exists. We are here now. It's growing every day, and bringing new people with it.

We live a life amidst the twisted yet familiar.

If we're going to survive this, if we're going to stay alive and thrive, we need to learn to live in the City of Angles.

...here's an angle to consider...

Far from the chaos of the city lies the calm of the suburbs. To be a child in the burbs is to be cared for, tended to, provided for, trained extensively, raised to adulthood, and set to repeat the cycle anew with your own children. Coming from money means you have money with which to make money which means the expensive calm of the suburbs stay within reach for generation after generation.

The best way to distract your children—because they will be restless in these calm places, eager for some sort of excitement to punch through the humdrum of the safe existence you bought them—is with consumer goods. Ones that come in a variety of plastics and run on batteries. Which, oddly enough, is also a great way for adults to distract themselves from the canonical emptiness they have taken into their lives.

But all the distractions in the world can't sway the determination of some youth to break free and challenge themselves with new horizons. That's just how growing up works. And in a city which supposedly exists just to chew up and spit out those who seek new horizons, woe be to the parent who has to keep such a child from embracing her dreams...

//005: Wound Up Toys

No moving truck was required.

The Yates family had been living out of suitcases for years now. Mapping out the Sideways for a living meant it was better to pick up and relocate each time you've exhausted exploration opportunities—either that or you had to commute quite a random distance to bop between your home and your work. Better to rent a small, cheap apartment for a few months while you compile up independently drafted maps of the area for sale to the Department of Resources. Once you've fished out all the avenues available, pack up and move on.

Never really any time to get to know the neighbors, of course. Which suited Gregory just fine, as he was a paranoid misanthrope. Penelope Yates knew this because her father got her a vocabulary-building edutainment app on her smart tablet.

But this time around when Gregory announced they were relocating, two things were different.

One, they hadn't finished mapping all the little nooks and crannies of the Spindles. True, there hadn't been a major shakeup in the Spindles for years, but plenty of underexplored backdoor routes in and out and between still existed which nobody had bothered checking. Who knew what treasures they held? They were abandoning ship with maps yet to be drawn.

Two, they were leaving the city proper, and heading to the Suburbs.

Penelope had never lived in the Suburbs before. She'd visited plenty of times, either popping out the other end of the Sideways in some strip mall or tracking down a local legend or two... but LIVING here? Gregory would sooner chew glass than leave the familiar and profitable chaos that was the urban landscape. And yet, here they were.

This left Penelope sitting on the front stoop of a quaint little house, suitcases flanking her to the left and right. Giving dad the silent treatment and refusing to come in to her new "home." Silly, really, and she knew it was silly —she'd go in eventually. Once she had time to chew on her current situation a little. Deal with it.

A house was entirely too large compared to an apartment, separated not by a layer of drywall but by a good fifteen feet of well-manicured lawn from the nearest neighbor. Penelope didn't like houses, and now she was amidst row after row of two-story houses, each with windows all over the place, windows with shutters. (Not that they ever closed those shutters. Purely decorative.)

A quiet and sleepy bedroom community... very quiet. Too quiet. Which, sadly, was probably the point. And was the real reason why Penelope was miffed about all this.

Gregory didn't actually explain why they were going to live with Auntie Karla. Oh, he did explain—catching up with old friends, taking a breather after recent events, things like that. Fresh air and sunshine, good for a growing girl.

But Penelope knew why they REALLY were out here in the middle of nowhere important. Gregory was worried about how things were going down. About the creepy men who followed them home. About the incident at the Defined Tower, the one they didn't talk about, the one he only had a vague recollection of and Penelope wasn't keen to bring up, for that matter... all of it too weird, too dangerous. When Gregory sensed danger, he went to ground and bunkered down. Away from the city. Away from the noise.

No more delving into dark corners and forgotten places. No more tracing the routes in and around and between. She was so close now, so close to understanding the shape of it all, and just like that they were done. Away from the job. Maybe permanently.

It'll just be for a few weeks, he'd promised. *No mapping and no exploring for a few weeks. Focus on your schoolwork. Maybe play with the neighborhood kids or something. Think of it like a vacation. We haven't had much of a vacation since you started mapping, have we? Well, now's the time, I'd say.*

He was never really happy about Penelope taking up her mother's cause, after all. She could read between the lines; why not turn a vacation into a retirement? Maybe the kid'll forget about this stuff and grow to love suburbia. The only reason he let Penelope poke around the Sideways in the first place was because she agreed to do it with him, to keep her safe. Maybe he figured it was time for him to tighten the leash and keep her safe from herself...

Most girls her age would think she was insane for being mopey and depressed about NOT going into the Sideways anymore. But, Penelope wasn't most girls.

And yet here she was. In the Suburbs. Around most girls. And with nothing to do but interact with most girls, she'd have to deal with that culture clash. Because staying indoors all day wasn't going to work, either.

In fact... maybe that was the next step for her. She didn't want to go into the shiny new house? Daddy wanted her to get to know the suburbs? Fine. She'd get to know the suburbs. It was Friday afternoon; kids would be logging out of their online lessons or coming back from public schools around now, ready to face the weekend. The perfect time to get away.

Leaving her suitcases behind, Penelope stepped away from the porch, and into the new world.

He let the curtain drop back, as Penelope got to her feet and began marching with purpose down the street.

"Don't like it," Gregory grumbled. "At least she's not running away. She'd bring her suitcases if she was. But I'd prefer if she stayed in today... safer that way."

Tea, being poured gently from a kettle to a cup. Soft ticking of a grandfather clock.

A far cry from the rambunctious laughter and occasional fistfight that echoed through the air in the old days, the last time he'd seen Cut-ya-up Karla...

Karla was a far cry from how she looked back in those days, too. When Gregory first got to the city, she was a frontrunner in the gang, wearing all the skanky duds designed by fashion companies exclusively to terrify paternal figures now in Gregory's age bracket. And if you called her out on her taste in clothes, Karla'd cut ya up. It was right there on the tin, after all.

Except at forty-four years of age, Karla was hardly a street punk anymore. She looked like someone's matronly aunt, older even than her actual age. Years of hard living accelerating the process, perhaps. It was hard to picture this woman in a sensible sweater and flats back-to-back with a fellow Scavenger, one switchblade in each hand, fighting over the latest find. Pouring tea from a kettle, yes, that was more appropriate.

Even her voice was far more gentle than the grating tone she used to take. But, she could chide Gregory's behavior all the same, even if it was done in a polite way rather than a brutal way.

"You really worry too much, love. She's just off to meet the locals. What's the harm?" Karla Berkowitz asked. "I know the kids around here. Good kids. One of them's been mowing my lawn for some time now while my husband is laid up with his back injury. Heh. Guess I was just too much for him that night..."

"I just don't like having her out of supervisory eyesight. Not now. But... it's inevitable," Gregory admitted, accepting the teacup. "I need to talk to you about that, in fact. I'm not going to be around very much; might not even come home some nights. Whenever I'm out, I'd like you to keep tabs on her. I need to —"

"—investigate the Bedlamites?"

His tea sloshed a little.

"Archie told you," Gregory realized.

"Like he could ever keep anything from *me*," Karla reminded, with a chuckle. "If you wanted to keep a secret, Greg, you really shouldn't have told Archie. He likes to talk turkey, and blabbed right away about how he thought the Bedlamites were alive and well and stalking Kegstand Greg. Thing is... he was right to tell me about it instead of protect me from this mess. These little shits who followed you around, they messed with one of *us*. We're all in this now."

"No, you're not. There is no gang anymore. We all moved on, grew up, got our crap together," Gregory insisted. "And that means no more eye-for-an-eye scrapping. This isn't your fight."

"If it's not, why are you here? You're cashing in on the old gang sentimentality, aren't you?" Karla pointed out. "Looking for a place to lie low, relying on the memories of the good old times to earn you a bed. I'm not saying that like it's a bad thing, mind you. Just saying... you can't have it both ways. Either the Seventh Street Scavengers have your back, or we don't. All or nothing. We may be grown-ups but that doesn't change."

He considered protesting further, but... there wasn't much use. Even if Karla likely wouldn't utilize the rather fine array of knives she had in her kitchen ("I make a lot of pies now, love") to make her point, it wasn't wise to push her more.

"Fine. But it's not like it changes anything," he said. "I have to head into the city and start shaking some folks down for information about the Cult of Bedlam, and I need you to keep Penny out of trouble. ...which may be very long-term, if I shake down the wrong folks and things go south. I just want that up front, that understanding. Between you and Archie there's nobody I trust more with my daughter if she becomes an orphan."

"Then you're going to have to shake down the right people, aren't you? And I think I know where you can start," Karla said, with one of her special vicious little grins. "Which isn't in the city. You need to go to the Outlands."

"What? C'mon. It's nothing but cows and grass out there."

"And Bedlamites. There's a little bastard named Eddie I used to party with, back when I still used to party. He had himself a little truck accident, made the news... and after what Archie told me about your troubles I decided to call my old friend Eddie up and pretend I was worried about him. I think he still thought he had a shot at me, because he told me all about how one of his fellow truckers got hassled by a crazy-looking guy in a bad suit who Picasso'd out right in front of their eyes. He also told me some rumors about a coming war with the Picassos... but, by then he was back to trying to hit on me, so that was that. Even so... sound like a good starting place?"

Again, Gregory had to admit conversational defeat. For someone steeling himself up for a confrontation with mysterious forces, he wasn't as commanding as he wanted to be.

But... he had no idea where to start to look for the Cult of Bedlam. He knew sources, he had friends in low places, but this was deep and dark. Any tip, even one as nutty as a middle-aged gang-banger's trucker boy-toy, would at least give him two feet on the floor.

He had to get to the bottom of it, for Penelope's sake. No choice, really.

Or rather, they'd made the choice as husband and wife thirteen years ago, in the wilds of the deepest and most twisted Sideways. They could have walked away from it all. And been horrible people for doing so, yes, but in those years Gregory hadn't completely shaken the old ways of the 7SS. *Look after your own and screw everyone else.* If they'd followed that mantra and left her where they found her... if, *if*...

No. A horrible thing to even think of. He couldn't imagine his life without Penelope, not anymore. If that meant running headlong into the trouble that came with her, so be it.

"Outland it is," Gregory agreed, raising his teacup. Without extending pinky.

While Gregory was choosing the starting place for his adventure, Penelope was faced with an identical choice. Fortunately, her explorer's street smarts were giving her the starting place she needed.

True, she was out of her element here. The Suburbs were spread out and empty compared to the city; nearly lifeless, particularly these sleepy little bedroom communities. But some things never changed. Kids are gonna play, and they're gonna want to get out of the house whenever mom and dad will let them risk being out in the open in the City of Angles.

For example: kids ride bikes or skateboards, which scuff up the sidewalks on the most popular routes. That meant slopes and downhills. The Buckles, for instance, were a haven for would-be extreme athletes. Not a single sidewalk or handrail went scuff-free in the Buckles. Sometimes you even spotted dark red marks, telltale signs of unsuccessful daredevils who came home with skinned knees. So unless the Suburbs were under 24/7 lockdown with kids chained to their beds, there'd be marks around she could use to track them down, like hunting game in the wild.

Here—dust from a chalk hopscotch board in a driveway. Kids lived in this house, probably a bit too young for Penelope's commercial demographic, but proof they go outdoors now and then. A basketball hoop at another driveway. Plastic rideable cars in the front yard. All good, but no signs of life yet. Around the corner...

There. A nice slope downhill, good sidewalks, not too cracked and lumpy. This would be where skaters and bikers hung out.

If there were any. Which there weren't.

But, as luck or other forces would have it, there was a kid. She wasn't on wheels, which tossed Penelope's theory out the window, but was clearly walking from A to B with purpose. Her pace suggested this was a matter of travel rather than pleasure.

The girl was likely a match for Penelope's age. She came bundled up in a pink jacket, rainbow-hued wooly scarf, and bright red mittens. Which was a bit much, even if it was October and temperatures were starting to drop; it was only 65°F and that level of warm clothing was better suited for 45°F or under. Penelope could see blonde hair peeking out from under her fuzzy hat complete with fuzzy pom-pom on top—

Wait.

No. That was *mapping*, the kind of visual study that Gregory had trained her for. Survival skills in the Sideways, to quickly get a grip on your surroundings and the threat level of people around you. Penelope was out here with one goal, to be an ordinary suburban girl, in mock protest of her vacation. Ordinary girls didn't size up everything around them. So: neighborhood girl. A kid. Done.

It only took her two seconds to study the newcomer, and one second to discard that study and focus on being friendly. She smiled, waved, ran right up to them, and announced:

"Hi, I'm Penelope Yates and I just moved into the neighborhood and I was hoping maybe we could be friends!"

Which was completely ordinary to say, she thought. Despite being a people person she very rarely met new people, but presumably the direct approach would work fine, right? She'd directly introduced herself to Dave weeks ago, and they were email buddies now.

Her new BFF did not react in a directly friendly fashion. She let out a squeaky little yelp and immediately yanked her neck scarf over her mouth.

"You moved here from where? From where!?" the girl demanded, muffled slightly by layers of yarn. "There's a flu outbreak in Hadley's Hearth and chicken pox at Roland Fletcher Middle School. Or the Buckles! Are you from the Buckles? What part of the Buckles? There's rumors of *head lice* there, and — and—!"

"I-I'm not sick! I'm not!" Penelope insisted. "And I'm not from any of those places. My dad and I just moved here from the Spindles. ...is that okay?"

"Don't know. Um. One second please while I check," the girl mumbled... pulling a Cracker phone out of her pocket, trying to fumble the touchscreen through her mittens. Conductive pads in the fingers, hopefully.

After calling up a quick reference app... she nodded, slowly. And started to relax.

"All clear. No major outbreaks or minor incidents in the Buckles in the last five weeks. Anything you had wouldn't be communicable now. ...that's a relief! Hi. My name's Milly. Milly Frisk. What's yours?"

"Penelope," Penelope repeated. "Penelope Yates."

"I'm very sorry for freaking out there, but I've made it two months without getting sick and I'm trying to keep my high score going," Milly explained, while carefully replacing her phone back in a pocket, trying not to let it slip through her giant fuzzy paws. "Mother always says good interpersonal hygiene is the key to avoiding disease. It's also very important to dress warmly! And wash your hands. And... right. Welcome to the neighborhood! So... can I help you in some way, or...?"

"Honestly, I'm just trying to get a feel for the place," she explained. "Maybe meet some kids. I don't know how long we're going to be living here, and I do like meeting new people, soo... here we are! Hi."

"Hi," Milly greeted again.

Since she had nothing else to add, awkward silence made itself known silently and awkwardly.

"Where were you headed, exactly?" Penelope asked, to break through the ice. "You looked like you were walking somewhere. Oh! A sandlot, for a softball game? Or a secret tree fort? Or the video arcade? —wait, those don't exist anymore. The mall? Kids in the suburbs hang out at the mall, right? Seems like it'd be kind of far away, though, and you don't have a bike. I should probably get a bike, if I'm going to be living here. That way we can go to the mall together—"

"I was just going over there," Milly decided to confess, to cut off the interrogation in midstream. She pointed to the next structure down the lane, which she would've reached in seconds if Penelope hadn't accosted her. "To that house. That's all."

"Oh," Penelope said, a little disappointed that it wasn't something cooler.

"But... I'm going to be starring in a movie!" her new friend offered, trying to make it more enticing. "A very special movie for the Internet. We're filming it in the basement!"

"Oh...?"

"Yeah, I'm going to be a damsel in distress. I get to scream a lot!"

"Oh! I mean... wait, what? You're... starring in a movie for the Internet filmed in a basement where you're screaming a lot and in distress?"

"Yeah! And— oh. OHHH. Ohh. Um. That... really does sound completely horrible when you put it that way, doesn't it," Milly realized, blushing as red as the pom-pom on her knit hat. "Trust me, it's way cooler than that and... yeah. Trust me. You'll see. I mean, you want to come along too, right? Maybe you can get cast in a role! —it is completely normal. Honest. For instance, my character is a fish!"

"HIIIYYAAAAAAAH!!" Milly Frisk screamed into the microphone, while instinctively making a karate chopping motion at the air.

If not for the impromptu soundproofing on the walls in the form of foam and egg crates, the scream would've bounced around enough to rattle Penelope's ears. Instead they simply twitched uncontrollably for a second or two.

"...I'm just not sure it sounds authentic enough for a kung fu mermaid princess," Milly complained. "I mean, I'm from under the sea and I'm supposed to be a singer, right? Shouldn't it be a little more melodic and smooth?"

Across the room from the piles of microphone cords and USB cables, a boy was busy setting up the next shot—in which the mermaid-who-was-little dropkicked a terrorist ninja halfway across the tiny cardboard diorama set up to look like Santa's Workshop. He looked up from attaching the green wires for the mid-air combat maneuver (to be edited out in post).

"No no, it was perfect!" he insisted. "Really, y'know, get in there and YAARGH! at 'em. Fierce, like a tiger. See, that's where the funny comes in, because it's completely incongruous with the original character portrayal!"

True to her word, they were filming a movie for the Internet where Milly played a damsel in distress who screams a lot. Specifically, a stop-motion movie with vintage action figures "designed to kick the 30-40 demographic square in the nostalgic nutsack," as Lucas Flynn had so delicately put it.

In stark contrast to the extremely expensive and minimalist adult-world furniture on the floors above, Lucas had taken over his family's basement to turn it into a very expensive and very specific kind of movie factory. Shelf after shelf was dominated by toys across the generations... action figures and dolls, soldiers and bug monsters, robots of every stripe. Every single wall was slathered in expensive toys, from floor to ceiling.

In the center of the room was the sound stage, also known as a table adorned by scale-model sets and a digital camera on a Lego tripod. Lights bright and hot enough to make the enclosed basement uncomfortable hung above, on articulated arms—three of them were flooding Lucas's face as he set up the next frame of the animation, enough to wash him out to white.

Given Lucas's fantastically ginger complexion, that meant he was quite washed out indeed, to the point where Penelope could barely see his face. She assumed he was grinning and grinning big, because he never seemed to NOT smile.

"The whole point is to show a strong female character kicking butt and taking names instead of sitting around waiting for her prince to come," Lucas continued to explain, while affixing a wad of red plasticine to represent the blood spurting from a terrorist's neck stump. "It's a marriage of opposites, vis-à-vis the mise-en-scène and QED. Trust me, just HIYAH! as strong as you can. I know you can do it, Milly!"

Turning back to the laptop computer they were recording dialogue on, Milly took a deep breath... and

"HIYAH!"

loudly enough to rattle the action figures on the desk four feet away.

"YES! Perfect!" Lucas declared. "We got it! Right. Okay, skip ahead to scene three where you tell the evil sea queen octopus lady you're gonna ram a shark up her inkhole. ...Penelope? You sure you don't wanna read for the sea queen?"

"I... think I'm okay just watching the artistic process at work," she decided. "So... you two make movies like this all the time?"

"Flynn-Frisk Funnies! One video a week since, like, ancient times. 2007, I think," Lucas recalled, moving back to the camera to take the next snapshot. "Never missed a week. Tons of subscribers. It's easy, too; you throw some vintage toys in front of a camera, put in lots of blood and fart jokes, and I swear the Internet eats it up like bacon. We make mad ad revenue off our virals."

At this... Milly pouted a bit, uncomfortable. And deciding bringing up an old topic in front of a new person might open the issue successfully.

"I still think you need to keep some of that money, Lucas," she insisted. "You're doing all the work here. I just read from the pages, it's barely even acting..."

Smoothly, he offered his usual justification, without taking his eye off the minute adjustments he was making to the figures. "My folks are rich as crap, I don't need it. I'm more than happy to pass it along, Milly. It's cool, it's cool."

Sparing a glance at the shelving units loaded with old toys, Penelope started to analyze.

"That's why you can afford all this stuff, right?" she asked. "The computers and video editing software, and the microphones and cameras and all the toys...?"

"Yeah, my folks are Grade A nerds, just like me," Lucas said... with pride. "Tech sector entrepreneurs, high end echolocation software apps for the Department of Resources and the like. They named me after Star Wars, you know. I think it's destiny in action that I'm making kick-ass movies—"

"Flynn Audio Systems?" Penelope asked. "Seriously? They made EchoMap? I love EchoMap!"

...except normal suburban teenage girls normally declared "I love Insert Pop Idol Here!" or "I love shopping for consumer goods!" instead of "I love industrial grade echolocation mapping software that costs fifteen hundred dollars in its cheapest edition!"

Milly didn't pick up on it—she was too busy trying to determine her motivation in preparation for next big line reading. (*"You're a part of MY world now, bitch!"*) But Lucas, who knew exactly what Penelope said and why it was such an odd thing for a thirteen-year-old to say, picked up on it immediately. It was enough to almost make him drop the action figure he was posing.

He ducked out from the glare of the lights, so his expression would be more readable.

"You've used EchoMap before...?" he asked.

"Uh... well... yeah," Penelope admitted. No point lying to her new friends, after all. "It's really good."

"You've used software designed for the Department of Resources and the First Action Response Teams to analyze the structure of the Sideways."

"My dad found me a copy for my ninth birthday. Um. Because I asked for it."

"Oh! I get it, just goofing off on a pirated copy for lulz," Lucas decided. "I heard of some high schoolers using it to map out their schools to find good spots to smoke."

"Really? They do that? But it doesn't work very well outside of an interior structure. Works best in tight and winding passageways like you find in the Sideways," Penelope explained, instinctively eager to talk shop. "It's really great when you're on the run from a Picasso and need to know what turns are coming up, to avoid going down a dead end. I mean, the fidelity isn't the greatest compared to standing still and quiet and getting a full survey, but I find if you turn the gain down and increase the pulse rate you can at least get a vague idea of where you're going and that's enough to keep you from getting infected with cubism and turning into a weirdo freakazoid!"

Which was enough to grab Milly's attention, adding her to the Confused Teenager Club alongside Lucas.

Uncomfortable under those stares... Penelope decided to go for broke. It wasn't like she was doing anything *bad*, after all... just unusual. Granted, anything unusual was bad and considered ample fodder for bullying, from what little she knew about real-world social patterns of kids her age, but presumably Milly and Lucas weren't the bullying types. Right?

"I do some... spelunking, you could say," she continued. "Urban spelunking. Exploring. ...I map the city. I'm a professional mapper. I know, I know I'm a bit young for it, but I've got some theories about the nature of the city and the only way I can figure all this mess out is by getting hands-on, and I told my dad I wanted to do it and he was all like 'No way, no how, that's how I lost your mother' but then eventually he decided he would let me do it provided he came along to keep me safe because I was probably gonna go ahead and do it anyway and he wanted to— okay, see, my point is, I use EchoMap and it's really good and please don't think I'm a weirdo freakazoid."

More uncomfortable silence, just like with Milly on the sidewalk. Penelope hated uncomfortable silences. They seemed to imply that she'd done something wrong. Like when Dad was upset at her, but quietly trying to find the gentlest way to explain himself...

First one to break was Lucas Flynn.

"That is... that's..."

And then... he let out a weird little yelping cry and a fist pump.

"SO AWESOME!" he declared. "Oh, dude! DUDE. I mean... dude! That's like something straight off a straight-to-video-movie. *'Penelope Yates: Adventure Gal!'* Excitement! Danger! Kids kicking butt and taking names! I am SO into this idea. ...you're not screwing with me, right? You seriously explore the Sideways?"

"Seriously, yeah, I do," she insisted... pulling out her cellphone, to boot up her EchoMap app. It wasn't as good as the one on her tablet, but she had full access to the maps she's already made in the cloud, which would be enough to prove it. "Look, here's some maps I made in the Spindles a few days ago..."

Determined not to let the image in his head shatter, Lucas scooted around his shooting stage table to peer over Penelope's shoulder at the tiny screen. The zig-zagging network of hallways and rooms illuminated itself there, a translucent pile of polygons that represented SpindlesDelve9b.echomap. She spread two fingers on the screen to zoom out, to show him as much of the map as possible.

...and for a moment, paused. Because she noticed something that had eluded her, even while in the middle of making this map. *It's all very angular, yes, but... there's something of an overall curve to the connecting passages. Arcing around and downward—*

Lucas's sharp inhale distracted her, and the thought fluttered away.

"That... that's EchoMap Pro v23," he recognized. "You can tell from the icon bar. Penelope... that app costs three thousand bucks. The audio mod to your phone must've cost a fortune, too... and you say your dad bought it for your birthday?"

"He likes me to have the best stuff I can get," Penelope weakly explained. "Y'know. To keep me safe."

"This isn't some hobby, is it? You are seriously a pro-level mapper. This is so COOL! Man, the stories you could tell...! The stories I could film...! Of course Milly would have to play you, we can't have someone playing herself, that'd mean it was a documentary instead of a summer action blockbuster, don't you agree, Milly?"

Who was not there.

No blurring, no flickering. That was the first sign, they said—your outline getting strange. She thought maybe she saw her fingers get blurry, but that was just because they were trembling. Again and again she checked them in the mirror, turning them this way and that, just to be sure, just to be safe...

Knocking on the door. Milly nearly jumped out of her skin.

"Milly...? Hey, you okay in there?"

"F-Fine, Lucas! I'm fine!" she insisted despite not being fine. She didn't want to look uncool in front of him, though. "Be out soon! I'm fine!"

Turn out the lights. Any glowing? No. Good. Turn on the light. Anything TOO shadowed where there should be light? No. Good. Check your eyes, tug down on the eyelid, maybe they're wiggly, that's always how they do it in the movies, with camera tricks to show you bugging out a little. Was she bugging out? Maybe. No, couldn't be. Just imagining things...

No cubism. Milly checked out.

But that girl was still out there. And with Lucas. Putting them all at risk.

Knock, knock. They wouldn't leave her alone.

"Milly, um... it's Penelope," the other voice said through the door. In case the identity wasn't obvious.

"Out in a minute!!" Milly insisted.

"I'm not infected with cubism, Milly. I've been to the Sideways, yeah, but I'm okay. I play it safe. So, you're going to be okay too. ...I saw the light flickering under the door, I know the usual checks people make for cubism. Sorry."

Defeated. Milly's shoulders sank, hands braced against the bathroom sink. She was going to look *totally* uncool now. No helping it.

A few moments later and she exited her self-imposed isolationist exile in the bathroom, feeling kind of stupid. The intimidatingly high design decor of the rest of the Flynn household didn't help her feel any less small.

But for what it was worth, Lucas only looked... worried, not weirded out, not disappointed. Penelope, too. Although she was looking around to make sure the Flynns hadn't overheard any of that.

"Look... let's head back down to the studio, and I'll explain," Penelope offered. "There's a lot of confusion out there about cubism. Maybe it'll help you feel better if you knew what I've figured out over the years. Picassos aren't what people think they are..."

The Flynn-Frisk Funnies studio was shut down for the day. More important things than kung fu mermaids were afoot.

Lucas brought another folding chair out of storage; normally it was just him and Milly down here, but it was lecture time with their new guest, and that meant a proper sit-down for all involved. The cardboard set was nudged out of the way, so they could sit around a table to seriously discuss the issues of the day. With a big bowl of puffed cheese snacks and grape soda.

"People say to avoid cubist spaces because they can infect you. And I'll admit, they can be dangerous," Penelope agreed, continuing an earlier point in the chat. "Like the Fletcher district from the thirties which fell apart, or a construction site which twists overnight. And yeah, cubist space is distorted and you don't wanna stick your leg in there any more than you wanna stick it in a blender. But infection? I disagree with that. —okay. Look at it this way.

Everybody knows that the way it works is you get infected, and that means you eventually turn into a Picasso yourself, right?"

"Right. I mean, duh," Lucas said. "Isn't that obvious? It's like zombies. One bite and you're doomed."

"But it's not really like zombies. There's not a whole lot of serious research, but my theory is that there's no virus component at all, nothing spreadable. Maybe that's not how it works. Maybe the infection is just a... a state of mind. A meme or a suggestion."

"Like can haz cheeseburger?" he suggested.

"Not that kind of meme. —well, maybe a little. I mean like an idea—one that's commonly accepted as true even if it's not—which gets stuck in your head and then gets passed on to be stuck in other people's heads," Penelope said, tapping her own forehead for emphasis. "Like, everybody KNOWS if you come into contact with someone who's going cubist or a cubist space, you'll eventually go cubist. That's just what happens. It makes sense."

Milly, who was taking this remarkably well despite her ongoing worry, seemed puzzled. "So... that's just what happens, then? But you said..."

"Right, right, that's what people *know* happens. So when it happens, you expect it to happen! And... it happens. Mind over matter. ...y'know how they say sometimes people just wig out and turn into Picassos when they go insane, even without touching a Picasso in the first place?"

"Like in Psycho Asylum III," Lucas recognized. "Great flick. Lousy effects on the Picassos, though. They just used a kaleidoscope over the lens, but hey, it was when dinosaurs roamed the earth. Like, the seventies."

"Right, but it's not a matter of insanity. It's more like... a state of mind, tied to an infectious idea. Whether you touched a Picasso or not, your own cubism starts to show up when you lose hope. When you give in to fear and worry and everything becomes too much to bear and your life's falling apart and— um. So, it all fits together. Someone thinks they're infected, they terrified about being doomed, they start to FEEL doomed, and soon enough..."

"They end up doomed," Milly supplied. Quietly.

"I'm not saying it's completely impossible to become a Picasso against your will, or that you should go tango with one because you're super awesome and not afraid of anything. There's still a whole lot about them we don't know. But this is how I see it, you know? It's easy to feel that fear, lost in the Sideways, and once you're lost in more ways than one... cubism. ...look, TL;DR, I'm not infected and it's actually harder to be 'infected' than you'd think. So you guys are safe to be around me. My dad and I play it real safe. And I'm *full* of hope for the city. For everyone."

One last bomb to drop, Penelope decided.

"One time a Picasso had us cornered, and we survived because we made friends with it," she spoke.

That had a nicely dramatic impact. Alarm at first, then disbelief, then confusion.

"She was a girl scout, selling cookies door to door in the Sideways," Penelope continued. "Picassos do that. They become... unstuck in their memories. No stable frame of mind, totally lost. She didn't know what she was doing, she just saw strangers and tried to sell us cookies, not understanding that she was a danger to us. Infectious or not, you don't wanna touch something that heavily cubist or your arm could come off, you know?"

"S-So how'd you escape?" Milly asked, trying not to sound like she was scared.

"We bought some cookies."

They waited for the rest of it.

"That's it," Penelope supplied. "We bought cookies from her. That's all she wanted, really. She was scared and alone, maybe for years and years, but she still remembered the joy of selling cookies. We gave her a moment's peace by helping her out, and she left us alone afterwards. Even said 'thank you.' So... I know this is crazy to say, I know the Department of Safety disagrees, but... I think Picassos can be reasoned with. Maybe even saved. Cured, if we could one day figure out how to straighten them out."

With the entire contents of her personal brain file on the subject emptied, Penelope finished off the rest of her grape soda. Her throat was dry, after that little presentation.

Lucas had soaked it all up like a sponge, nodding along, showing the same level of curiosity through the entire speech. The real question was Milly, who had gone into this borderline terrified. Hopefully she found some comfort in Penelope's words...

Milly still looked uncomfortable. But it was a baseline uncomfortable, the sort she seemed to carry around with her at all times. It'd have to do.

"I just hope I never run into a Picasso," Milly decided. "Then I won't have to worry, one way or another. I guess it's not really a problem out here, anyway... there's not many entrances to the Sideways in the suburbs, right? It's the city that's a deathtrap!"

"Uh... I wouldn't say the city's THAT bad..."

"There's nothing weird around here other than the phantom toy store, so I guess we don't have to worry," Milly said, with a smile.

Now, it was Penelope's turn to drop the jaw.

"Wait a moment I'm sorry the what now?" she blurted.

With the door opened, the cows got out of the barn and the cat came out of the bag and the milk was spilled so no point crying over it. But Milly did hesitate long enough that Lucas decided to step in to take the pressure off her.

"It's a local legend. Just a legend," he emphasized. "It's stupid, really. If you stand in one place and do a ritual chant, turn around two and a half times, walk backwards ten paces, and turn around... you'll find a haunted toy store which wasn't there a moment ago. It's garbage, of course. Just like the rumors that some kid from Sunnybrook River went cubist and turned into a giant human pinball machine. The burbs are loaded with stories like that—"

"s'real."

"Eh?" Lucas said, glancing to Milly.

Who was looking at her feet. Well, at her feet through the solid surface of the table.

"It's real," she mumbled. "The phantom toy store. It's real."

"What? C'mon. That's silly. Don't tell me you believe in the Easter Bunny, too..."

"I've seen it."

The storytime spotlight shifted in an instant. But unlike Penelope, who welcomed the opportunity to give an impromptu TED Talk, Milly shifted in her seat like she had to go pee.

"It... I mean... it's on the way home from my school," she told. "Lucas has an online tutor but my folks can't afford that, so I go to Clinton. Home of the fighting Beavers. Um. Anyway... I pass by the spot where they say the phantom toy store is each day, and one day I... I wasn't going to go in! I didn't go in. But I had to know if it was true, and I figured it couldn't hurt to peek, so... I did the ritual and there it was! —and then I ran away."

"You... you never told me about this before," Lucas realized.

"I was too scared to tell anyone! What if my mother found out?" she said. "It's gotta be the Sideways, right? You don't get there through a doorway or anything but it's just like they say the Sideways are, a weird part of the city with weird places and weird things! I was terrified I'd been infected with cubism so I didn't tell anyone and I checked myself for flickers three times a day for a month! ...I was okay, thank God, but..."

But now, Penelope's itch was starting to itch.

Sideways. In the Suburbs. Without a standard obfuscated doorway...

Something like this could go a long way to proving a few theories. Like when she found a connecting path from the city core right to the Outlands, through the Sideways. Or how the Defined Tower was so impossibly huge and out in the open, yet the whole structure counted as the Sideways. How the Sideways were quite frequently NOT the maze of twisty little hallways everybody assumed they were, but something else entirely, like a bruised and tender spot in the city's flesh...

Except Penelope was on vacation, wasn't she? Dad insisted. No exploring. No mapping. Maybe forever.

For lack of a better metaphor, this was like a candy bar you'd just bought from a vendor machine that was hanging on the end of its hook, refusing to drop, tantalizingly out of reach. You could bang on the machine to get it down, and risk the machine falling on you, or just walk way. And Penelope was not the sort to walk away.

It'd serve dad right for grounding her without officially grounding her. And what harm could it do to take a look...?

"I'd like to visit the phantom toy store," she declared. "Maybe go in. Maybe map it out."

Both suburban kids reacted as if Penelope had suggested they go running with scissors and petting strange dogs no matter where they've been.

"Are you high or something? The place could be wall to wall with Picassos," Lucas imagined. "I mean, think about this for a second. Haunted toy store. *Haunted. Toy. Store.* You go in there I guarantee you'll get your soul eaten by a creepy doll or something."

"I don't believe in ghosts. And I can deal with Picassos," Penelope declared, trying to look as firm and resolute as her father usually looked. "I'm a professional. This is what I do. It's my job."

"It's the weekend! People don't work jobs on the weekend."

"All the better. We could head out after lunch tomorrow, poke around a bit, and be back by dinner. Kids go out and play on Saturdays, right? Nobody would know we were doing anything funny. It's perfect!"

"'We'? wait, What we is this of which you speak?"

"Well... I don't know where the place is, so I'd need at least one of you to show me how to get there and how to get in, right?" Penelope said. "And... I dunno, if you want to come along, that's fine too. I guess I could go in alone if I have to. ...I can do that. I don't NEED to have someone come with me. I'm not afraid. Honest."

Not as convincing as she wanted it to be. If someone was going to make *Penelope Yates: Adventure Gal* into a live action TV movie, they'd definitely need a better actress than her.

But... maybe that was the tipping point. Showing that she wasn't some invincible badass explorer. Because from Lucas's expression, he was starting to consider it from a safety-in-numbers perspective.

"It... would be nice to scoop up a few new finds for the studio," he considered aloud. "The store's supposedly been there since the eighties. That means lots of old toys. If I could get some rare find, like a Cabbage Patch Kid or a die-cast complete Voltron lion's set— OH! Oh! And I can film the whole thing! My first documentary! Just like Super Size Me, or Crossway Points of Light, or the Blair Witch Project! Oh God wait no not that last one. Um. I... guess I could go with you. —we'll leave at the first sign of trouble, right?"

"Definitely," Penelope agreed. "I just want to get a map. I can do that with EchoMap nice and quick. Sooo..."

That left one.

Who had returned to her earlier levels of terror.

"You don't have to go," Penelope immediately offered. "It's okay, Milly. I just need one of you to come to help me find the place, that's all. There's no reason you have to—"

"*I'mcoming*," Milly interrupted. Saying it all as one word, so she could blurt it out before being able to stop blurting it out.

"Uh... but you don't really have—"

"If Lucas is going I'm going too and I'm going," she continued. "And you said you're good at this and you play it safe, so... we'll be safe. He'll be safe. Everything will be fine. Besides, I'm the only one who's actually been there, you might need my help. I'm coming."

"...right. Well. Think it over, at least," Penelope suggested. "It's getting late and I need to get home for dinner, so... just... I'll be here tomorrow after twelve. If you want to tag along, be here then. If you don't, it's okay. And yeah... we'll play it safe. You've got my word on that."

The autumn sun, setting nice and quick compared to the lazy days of summer. This was perfect weather for riding your bike home from the sandlot and/or shopping mall and/or nonexistent video arcade, Penelope reasoned. Perhaps she should look into getting a bike, if only so she could make an attempt at enjoying her forced exile from the city... plus, it'd be a fun thing to harass dad about. She wasn't usually vindictive, but watching him dance for her enjoyment would suit her mood today...

Except her dad wasn't at Aunt Karla's house when Penelope got there.

Karla was alone, sitting in a cushy-looking reclining chair. Munching a slice of pizza from a freshly opened box with one hand, holding a beer with the other. She was even watching some kind of bikini contest on cable television. If not for being a late middle-aged woman and the bikini contest consisting of well-built dudes in banana hammocks, she'd be picture perfect for a suburban dad.

"Hey, kiddo," Karla greeted. "Husband's whacked out on pain pills and sleeping upstairs and I didn't feel like cooking today. Come on in and grab a slice. Hm. Your dad doesn't let you drink beer, right?"

"Uh, no," Penelope said—not that she'd lie, given she tried beer once and thought it tasted like what cat urine would probably taste like if she tried tasting that.

"I've got strawberry milk in the fridge, then," Aunt Karla offered. And then, in another token gesture to age-appropriate entertainment, changed the channel to some safe sitcom with a laugh track.

Pizza was tempting. All she'd had since they grabbed lunch on the run at the train station was those cheese puffs at the Flynn-Frisk Funnies basement studio. But more pressing matters came first.

"Where's Dad?" she asked.

"...ah. Now, we come to the conundrum," Karla said, after bracing herself with a long pull on her beer can. "Because I'm sure he doesn't want me telling you where he is, but he didn't supply me with a suitable lie, and I've always been crap at lying. So rather than insult your intelligence, where do you think he'd want me to say he was?"

Ahhh. THIS familiar dance.

Penelope had a seat on the sofa next to Karla, fetching herself some pizza along the way.

"He's at the hardware store, then," she supplied. "Or at city hall, looking at blueprints. Or, in one of his less inspired stories, he's 'seeing a guy who knows a guy,' whatever that means. Obvious lies, right?"

"Does this a lot, then?"

"Not a lot, but... whenever he's doing something sketchy, yeah," Penelope explained. "It's part of our business to have contacts that run a bit underground. Folks who steal blueprints or trade tips about entrances to the Sideways. Dad likes to be a role model and to keep me out of things like that, so... I sit with the neighbors or something while he 'goes to the hardware store.'"

At this, Karla let out a semi-drunken giggle. "He's so clumsy at subterfuge. It's one of the things Lizzie liked about him. He couldn't sneak around and cheat on her. Not that he would, but..."

"You knew my mother, right...? I mean, you were all part of the same gang..."

"Club. Well. Okay, gang," Karla agreed. "And I've got stories about your dad that'd stiffen your pigtails, love. But... bad enough that I'm not covering for his escapade today. I'm not going to dig myself deeper with tales from the glory days."

With that avenue closed off, Penelope focused on her pizza. Too spicy for her tastes, she preferred extra cheese, but pizza was always a welcome gift.

And she began to analyze.

Dad was off doing something shady, and cut her out of the loop as usual. But what could he be doing in the suburbs that was shady? He didn't know anybody out here, aside from a few retired friends. None of them were very shady anymore. From what Penelope knew, the "club" eventually just grew up, tired of having to keep one step ahead of the law and the other gangs. So, nobody out here worth a dodgy story...

Turn it around. He wasn't looking for a skeevy contact out here. He was leaving her out here with one of his most trusted allies because the contact, wherever he was, was TOTALLY skeevy. Like, dangerously so.

And instantly, her anger got as spicy as the pizza.

Two could play that game, after all. He wanted to throw himself in danger without even telling her what was going on? Fine. She had a phantom toy store to explore tomorrow. That'd show him.

Despite eating her Angry Pizza, Penelope actually had a reasonably fun evening. Aunt Karla, belying her matronly looks, was a real firecracker. Especially when drunk, Penelope guessed. For instance, she swore more, and was willing to teach a thirteen-year-old how to cheat at Texas Hold-'Em poker. (Penelope had never been to Texas and didn't know if it was the official game of that nation or whatever, and Karla didn't know either. Fun game, even so.)

After that, she retired to the guest room to chillax in bed and catch up on email and funny cat pictures on her smart tablet.

And another email from Dave.

Dave Smith was Penelope's pet project. If she could help guide this anxious newbie safely into the world of the City of Angles, she could help anybody.

It hadn't been easy. Not one day into his orientation and he'd come face to face with the Echo Revelation—followed by an unfortunate suicide. He'd reached out to her, as low and broken as she'd ever heard him, desperate for something to hang onto... and somehow, Penelope had provided it. It just seemed like a good idea to her at the time, she didn't think it was that life-changing of a suggestion...

Training's going well in the FARTs. (I'm supposed to say the "Response Teams" because the full name's been a three-decade running joke at this point.) They won't let me go in on any new building arrival calls, but I'm studying everything they throw at me, and I get to work with the exterior teams. Sometime soon maybe I'll be in a position to help people like me.

My supervisor, our team's Department of Safety representative, is impressed I am not half-assing it (which apparently is the thing you do around here.) He's even encouraging me to keep working on that corporate logo I was doing for Lucid Technologies. He thinks it'd look good on our monthly newsletter masthead or something.

Enclosed is my latest draft. I don't have any more suggestions from Lucid for changes so at this point I'm just winging it with whatever feels right. It's a good way to pass the time when I'm bored.

Hope things are going okay for you and you were not eaten by a Picasso.

Dave.

...followed by a weird looking spiraling squiggle shape, done in a cheap paint program.

It didn't look like much on her tablet's glowing screen, in the dark of the guest room. If it was cast in bronze and had a nice font under it, maybe it'd work in a corporate lobby. For now at best you could stick it on a T-shirt and look indie, or something. Too weird, way too weird. Maybe that was just an early draft?

Although there was something oddly compelling about the shape, the way the lines curved. Very angular, but arcing around... around, and downward...

Downward, sinking down, spiraling down. Layer by layer. Daylight to darkness, open fields to closed doorways.

Standing alone at the door she'd stood at before, because she was already on the other side. Heart beating fast. The brass knob beckons...

Alone except for her perfect shadow, right behind her and getting closer—

Beepity beep, beepity beep, beepity beepity beep.

Tablet in her lap, screen dark. Must've fallen asleep. The beeping was coming from her smartphone, which was essentially just a smaller version of her tablet with little phone bits baked inside.

Ringtone was a generic. She had personalized tones for her father and for Dave. Who could be calling?

Briefly she noted the time, 2:00 AM, before answering.

"urmhello?" she offered, struggling to pull completely out of her dream.

"Shh! It's me. It's Milly," a whisper trickled through the digital connection. "Milly Frisk."

Oh, right—she'd left her phone number, in case they needed to coordinate tomorrow. And it was... *technically* tomorrow, but...

"Milly, it's two in the morning," Penelope felt the need to point out. "What's up? Something wrong?"

"I'm packing for the trip and I'm not sure what to bring," Milly explained. "What level of sun block do I need? How bright is it in the Sideways? Also, should I take an antibiotic or a probiotic or both? Do you need me to bring an antivenom supply kit for any snakes we run into? Will I need deep-woods insect repellant or will the normal type be good enough?"

Every query blurred together in Penelope's sleep-fuzzy brain, so she decided to generalize.

"Just bring a flashlight and your phone," she suggested. "That's all. I—"

"Flashlight!? It's going to be dark? Oh no, the horror movies were right, it's gonna be a giant dark maze of horrible things jumping out of the shadows!"

"No, it—okay, it's sometimes dark, because not all of the Sideways is connected to the power grid, but—look, my point is, I'll handle any survival supplies we need," she summarized. "Just wear a comfortable and sturdy pair of shoes and bring a flashlight and that's it. Make sure you eat lunch before you go. Okay? ...y'know, Milly, you don't *have* to come along. I said that already, right? It's late, I don't remember..."

"If... if Lucas is going with you, I want to go too," Milly said. "Y'know. To keep an eye on him. To keep him safe. Safety in numbers."

"Actually, statistics show that two people are safer than three in a crisis situation, which is the basis for the term 'buddy system,' and—ugh. Babbling. Tired. Are you totally sure you want to come along?"

"Sure. Totally sure," Milly affirmed.

"Right. So, that means you need sleep, and so do I. G'night, Milly."

"You're not... interested in him, right?"

Penelope rubbed sleep stuff from her eye, not quite catching on. "Whhrr?"

"You know. *Interested.* In Lucas."

"I... no? No," Penelope responded. "No, I'm not. Why—"

"Okay thanks see you tomorrow!"

Click. Well, no, phones didn't click anymore like they did in old TV shows. But Penelope could practically feel the click from how hard Milly must've stabbed that red spot on her phone's touchpad.

Leaving a very puzzled Penelope, sinking back into her pillow with phone still in hand.

So. Milly and Lucas. Lucas and Milly. ...possibly just Milly and Lucas rather than the other way around. Boys don't mature as fast as girls, after all. It is known.

That's the sort of thing ordinary suburban girls do, right? Have crushes on boys and take them out on dates. And go around the "bases," as they are termed. It wasn't like Penelope was a kid anymore, despite her father's opinion to the contrary. She knew darn well where babies came from. She knew about the bases. Even if the actual definitions of those bases tended to be a bit fluid.

Penelope hadn't even batted off a foul ball yet, of course. Hadn't even considered stepping up to the net to score a two-point conversion, or whatever you did in that sport she'd never actually seen. Who had time for boys when you were busy deep-diving into the darkest shadows of the City of Angles? Not that she even KNEW any boys her age, other than Lucas. Besides, no boy would want anything to do with a crazy scary girl like her who actively enjoys poking Picassos with sticks.

Well, okay, Lucas seemed to think it was kinda awesome. And he was kinda cute in a gingery sort of way, which did match Penelope's ginger-ness, but—

No. NOT the sort of thing to get stuck in your head when you're about to go exploring the Sideways without a parental permission slip and with two complete newbies in tow.

She set the phone down on her nightstand, pulled the sheets over her head, and tried to get at least thirty of her forty winks back.

On the plus side, now she had ordinary silly and random dreams with Lucas in them. Which was an improvement over the door and the shadow.

To her credit, Penelope got through breakfast and a lazy Saturday morning without thinking about Lucas. She was mentally preparing herself for a Sideways dive.

Mentally and physically preparing. She'd packed her backpack in secret, stashing the usual supplies for urban spelunking. Flashlights. Night vision goggles. Length of rope, book of matches, climbing hooks, staple adventuring tools. Backup batteries for her phone and tablet. Water thermoses, filled in secret in the upstairs bathroom. Trail mix and other nonperishable foods, leftovers from their last outing...

Not that she was expecting to be out long enough to need an emergency food supply. But once upon a time, her mom and dad weren't expecting to be out too long, and they got lost for a full year. Gregory made sure to drill into Penelope the importance of being ready for a longer stay than you could possibly imagine.

Which led her to having second thoughts. Not about the dive—that was a matter of principle, an indirect contest of wills with a father who dumped her off at her fake aunt's house and then got himself into who-only-knows-what kind of trouble. But bringing Milly and Lucas along, two unproven neophytes... that was dangerous.

She tried to discourage them again, when they met up after lunch. But they'd made their own preparations, and were ready to roll. To varying degrees of appropriate rolling.

Lucas was a one-man film crew. He'd brought a backpack full of detachable lenses and batteries and multiple backup cameras. A head-mounted video harness, for critical POV shots. An expensive-looking digital camera on a leather neck strap rig. Portable lighting worked into his vest. He'd clearly raided his supply of expensive imaging gear and brought most of it with him. On the plus side, he brought enough light for five people, so flashlights weren't going to be needed.

Milly looked like she was ready to storm Mount Everest. She'd dressed warmly and in layers, puffed up like a marshmallow—and with latex gloves on underneath heavy winter handgear. Thick soled boots suitable for trundling through toxic waste spills. Two layers of paper filter masks over her mouth.

And not one, but TWO flashlights; one near-permanently attached by a wrist strap normally associated with motion-based video game controllers, one velcroed to her vest.

It was a miracle their parents hadn't noticed this crazy amount of equipment being smuggled out of the house. Apparently Milly had bundled her gear up in a plastic bag and lowered it out her window at two in the morning, then waited until nobody was looking to sneak out. Lucas just told his mom he was going to go film a documentary and that was enough for them.

That left three junior adventurers standing on the doorstep of adventure, ready to have an adventure. Even if all three had some reluctance to get started.

The doorstep of adventure consisted of a space between a gas station and a store that exclusively sold watch batteries, in the commercial center just outside the neighborhood. Convenient for shopping and exploring.

"Right. So. How does this work?" Penelope said, deciding it was up to her to take the first step.

"Well... legend has it that those who undergo the ritual are granted passage to the phantom toy store, haunted by the doomed spirit of—"

"Just the nuts and bolts, please," she insisted. "This is a scientific endeavor."

"Oh. Well, you stand on that crack in the sidewalk, turn around two and a half times and recite the... actually, I don't know if the poem's really needed, if you're approaching this practically," Lucas decided. "Might be worth trying without it, right?"

"Right. That's thinking like a mapper," Penelope said, with a smile of praise. ...which earned her a funny look from the girl in the breathing mask(s), so she continued quickly. "Turning around two and a half times really just means you're turning to face away from it, right? So I'll try that. Then I just walk backwards, right...?"

She positioned herself on the sidewalk crack, facing the space between the two buildings... then turned, slowly. Took a deep breath. And stepped back.

The Sideways *usually* was an unseen door, an entrance you couldn't spot if you were looking directly at it. An entrance in a wall, that is. An entrance in open air was unheard of, and if it DID exist, it'd be an amazing find. It'd prove that the Sideways aren't a completely contained and indoor phenomenon, that things like the Defined Tower could exist, that anything was possible in the City of Angles...

The air staled. As in, "turned stale," a common indicator of the Sideways. They existed in a low entropy state, locking things in slow or stopped time, and the air was not always pleasant as a result. So even though the sun was shining and the cars going by on the road... Penelope had entered the Sideways.

Two other things confirmed it:

One, her friends staring in horror and disbelief, likely because Penelope vanished before their very eyes.

Two, there was a gigantic toy store behind her.

She'd turned around to look at it. It sat comfortably between the gas station and the battery store, as if nothing was out of the ordinary here. You couldn't look at it and the entire length of road at the same time, of course—no way to verify space was warped here. And if she tried hard enough she might get a headache trying to verify how things twisted themselves around, so, better not to try.

Somehow, she was expecting a creaky old Victorian-era toy store, like you'd see in some creepy horror movie. Probably full of soulless dolls ready to eat your living essence or something.

But no, this was a retail chain outlet, one which had a presence in the city even to this date. It declared, loud and proud, that they were toys and toys were us. If you were a kid of the same persuasion, as their commercials declared, you would be welcome. The architecture and design screamed mid-80s to her, based on her experience with entropy-locked structures to date, but definitely a mundane chain store. Not terrifying at all. Colorful and charming, really.

(Of course, clowns were colorful and charming too, and everybody knew THEY were terrifying.)

She took a step back onto the sidewalk. The relieved inhales told her she'd become visible again.

"Come on in," she encouraged. "The water's fine."

Moments later, three children disappeared from a sidewalk in the middle of a busy commercial street, and were never seen there again.

The legendary phantom toy store lived up to its legend about halfway. Better than completely living up to the ideal of a terrifyingly strange toy store full of weird things that thirst for human blood, but not far enough into the realm of absolute normality to be comfortable by any stretch.

It followed a very retro design for toy stores of its type. The entrance area had railings to keep incoming prospective buyers on one path and outgoing paid buyers on another path. Those who had yet to empty their wallets on the altar of commerce were run through a long hallway, doubling back on itself in a boxy S-like shape... a gauntlet of cheap and seasonally appropriate toys, so your kids will go OOO MOMMY I WANT THIS long before you ever reach the actual toy you came for.

All very normal—but the spooky aspect came from two out of three overhead lights being shut down, to conserve power. The store must've been copied over into the Sideways during an off hour rather than peak business. Also, it was copied in an October, as evidenced by the S-Gauntlet being loaded down in glow in the dark spiders and snakes and witches and ghosts and things staring at them with eyes and eyes and eyes and...

"This is gonna make a killer establishing shot," Lucas commented, getting a nice slow pan over the rows of terrifying plastic goods.

"D-Do you need to use the word 'killer'?" Milly asked. "I mean, do you really need to?"

"It's just Halloween junk. It's not like it's actually satanic toys forged in a factory staffed by six hundred and sixty-six demons dedicated to making murderous action figures that run on AA batteries charged with the blood of orphans—"

"Do you have to use ANY of those words?!"

"Right. Sorry," he said. "I'm just trying to think up a cool backstory for the movie. I'm kinda disappointed; this is just an ordinary store. Nothing weird about it at all. Right? Right, Penelope?"

Penelope spared a glance down at her smartphone, which she'd tethered to the tablet in her backpack. EchoMap had been tracking their progress so far, as well as scanning the space ahead for any anomalies like bent space or intermixed buildings...

"It's actually really ordinary," she concluded. "No cubist distortions or conjoined structures. It's just aisles and aisles of toys. That's all. I'm seeing some side doors, probably to bathrooms and break rooms and warehouses, but the main toy store's completely normal. I'd need to get in deeper to be sure, but I'm also not picking up anything moving other than us. Nothing as large as a person would be, anyway. So, no Picassos either."

"Does that mean we're done here?" Milly asked.

"Since it looks safe, I'd like to map out the main store area completely," Penelope said. "Maybe look in some of the side passages. It's rare for the Sideways not to be cross-connected to other paths; at least one of those doors has to go to somewhere else. ...Uh, we don't have to *fully* explore those paths, but getting some echo maps at the entranceways would give me something I could work on in the days ahead with other dives, maybe..."

No sense pushing her new team into a deep dive on day one, Penelope reasoned. If she was looking for new partners, since her Dad was playing silly buggers, keeping them from being scared off immediately would be wise. Plus, experience had to be built up gradually.

Once through the tediously long back-and-forth-and-back snake aisle of cheap toys, it was into the store area proper, near the cash registers. Signs declared the sales of the season, which Lucas poured over extensively, marveling at all the 1980s toys that were being declared as hot new releases. Milly eyed a candy bar on an impulse buy rack, unsure if it was safe to just take and eat it; she hadn't eaten much lunch due to a nervous stomach...

Penelope, meanwhile, studied a map of the fire exits that had been posted nearby. She snapped a quick photo of it, just in case. It was the sort of thing a customer would completely ignore, since they were too busy shopping to worry about not burning to death in the event of an emergency—surely the store staff would take care of that for you. (Either showing you to the exit or burning to death by proxy so you could be safe.)

Speaking of the store staff, the retail chain had apparently been pushing employees with recognition programs recently. There was an "Employee of the Month" photo wall without a complete year's worth of pictures. The first few months consisted of various bored-looking employees in matching white shirts and nametags... but the last four months were all of the same person. The only one that was smiling.

An older gentleman, probably taking up a job well past retirement years, given he clearly still thought bow ties were in fashion. The bright red of it stood out against his crisp white company shirt. Matching white smile. Happy to be here, compared to the other wage drones.

He was probably long dead by now; this store was from the eighties, back when dinosaurs roamed the earth and they still had steam locomotives. Hopefully he could rest well, knowing he left a tidy store behind, forever locked in time...

Back to the task at hand.

"We'll scout the outermost aisles, checking for doorways," Penelope explained. "Especially ones that don't appear on this fire exit map I copied. And if you see any toys you want and can easily carry or fit in your pack, well... this is all legal salvage, so it's not *technically* theft. Not until we report the place to the Department of Resources and they claim everything for themselves."

The rest of the toy store also proved to be depressingly normal. Poorly lit and creepy, since normally a toy store is bursting with kids and parents and retail workers, but... any toy store at 2 A.M. would have the same effect. A toy store in the Sideways should be creepy for other reasons.

Aisle after aisle of unpurchased toys beckoned to them. Lucas could identify most of the critical brands of the era, having memorized all the manufacturers and their toy lines—he knew which ones had 30-minute tie-in commercials on Saturday mornings, which ones set off sales crazes, which ones were innovative but fell under the radar. His constant chatter of analysis kept the girls company, as both were rather quiet.

Penelope had never really collected toys before. Hadn't considered collecting them. She had an old teddy bear, a memento of some sort from her early childhood, but that was it. Living on the run meant you couldn't own anything that wouldn't fit in your backpack, and living in the digital age meant most of her actual toys were apps on a tablet. She greatly enjoyed matching three gems and making them explode, or raising virtual puppies and giraffes and things. But toys? Physical, hold-in-your-hand toys? They never made sense in combination with her life.

A lot of things kids had when they were growing up—or things teenagers valued in her current phase of life, for that matter—were completely alien to her. She couldn't interject in Lucas's tirade of toys because she had nothing to add. She had very little in common with these ordinary suburban teenagers, in the end. Which was a shame, because she kinda wanted to talk with Lucas today for some reason, and just couldn't figure out what to talk about...

Having Milly around made the situation even weirder. Because while Lucas was studying the shelves, Milly was studying Penelope. Making her a bit antsy. As if mapping the Sideways wasn't bad enough.

"You're seriously saying I can take any toy I want?" Lucas asked. "Like, anything? I thought the Department of Resources claimed everything dug out of the Sideways..."

Finally, something Penelope could talk about. She was the city's most knowledgeable thirteen-year-old when it came to salvage law.

"The Department has to stake their claim before it becomes city property. They haven't staked this yet," she explained. "Lots of mappers and salvage gangs trade tips about unclaimed property in deep Sideways, valuable stuff the government hasn't found yet. There's a big trade for black market maps. But Dad and I always sell our maps to the Department, like you're supposed to do. It keeps the Departments from bothering us. ...usually."

"Where's your dad, anyway? Don't you normally do this with him?"

"Yeah. Normally. —anyway, yes, it's all legal salvage. Take any toy you can carry. But rule is you don't take more than you can carry in a hurry, because... y'know. Might need to hurry."

Legal salvage also meant Milly could in fact swipe that candy bar from the front of the store without running afoul of Johnny Law. But all assumed knowledge said she dare not eat it. Instead she toyed with it in her gloved hands, unsure, while Lucas filmed and Penelope scanned and the trio walked slowly down aisle after aisle.

When asked why she wasn't chowing down, Milly finally explained.

"I don't want to catch any weird Sideways Germs," Milly said. "This store's been here since the eighties! How could a candy bar really be safe to eat after all that time?"

"Low entropy. It's how the Sideways work, for some reason. Hmm. How about some trail mix?" Penelope offered. "I brought some extra in my pack..."

"That's too much roughage! I'm trying to control my diet. I had a bad run of the runs two months ago, and the flu two weeks before that. Threw up everything, all the time. It was awful. I'm trying to be careful."

"And... a candy bar is being careful?"

"Well, it's... I mean, keeping your blood sugar up is good, right?" Milly reasoned. "But I don't want to get sick again. I've gone two months without being sick and that's rare for me. Gotta keep it going—"

"OHMYGODOHMYGOD!"

Milly nearly jumped out of her skin. Fortunately, she had three layers of clothes on over it, which kept her from escaping the epidermis.

With a terrifyingly swift motion, strobing in front of the various lights he had attached to his person... Lucas snatched a blister pack off a pegged wall, holding it forth like a divine relic. Row after row of plastic army tanks rattled on a shelf just above, from the force of the pull.

"It's *Duke*," he explained, pointing to the tiny blonde army man inside. "Duke! Original leader of the GI*JOEs. 1984 carded figure version, third series! Y'know, they were gonna kill him off in the movie, but when kids freaked out over Optimus Prime biting it Hasbro kludged in his survival. But the third series figure was discontinued in favor of a new wave of characters! And this one's even got a manufacturing misprint! Do you have *any idea* how rare this is?!"

The human camera rig swayed a little, when Milly gave him a light shove.

"You scared me!" she complained. "I thought you saw a Picasso or something!"

"Uh... sorry. I just got really excited," Lucas admitted. "I mean... come on, Milly, isn't this so awesome? It's a relic from out of time! It's a free toy store shopping spree! We're on an adventure! Why are you so worried about things like germs and candy bars? We should be having fun with this!"

"The Sideways aren't 'fun'! They're dangerous and it's stupid to go into them and I can't believe you wanted to go in the first place!"

"Well, you didn't have to come along! I didn't want you to come along at all."

"And why's that, huh?" Milly asked, sounding as angry as someone with mild manners could manage. "You wanted go off somewhere alone with Penelope? Is that it?"

(Rather than interject herself in this sudden flare-up, Penelope pretended to be very, very busy studying her echo map. It seemed the safest play.)

"...what? Where'd that come from?" he asked, puzzled. "I didn't want you to come because I know you hate scary stuff like this. And... I don't want you getting hurt just because I like scary stuff. That's all. What's Penelope got to do with anything?"

"Because... because...!" Milly started, trying to find the best way to word it...

Before stopping. Completely. Freezing solid.

"What?" Lucas asked, confused.

"T-tank," Milly mumbled. Eyes locked at a spot just over Lucas's shoulder.

Now, Penelope dared to look up from her map, to see what the fuss was about.

Row after row of white plastic army tanks, with realistic rubber treads and working turrets with springloaded rockets. All pointed forward, in parade procession positioning.

One turret pointed outward. Leveled at them, like an eyestalk, peering curiously. It slid up and down along its joint of articulation.

Carefully but swiftly, Penelope reached out to grasp Lucas's filming harness, and tug him away from the shelf. To turn him to see it, so she wouldn't have to explain and thus make noise and draw even more attention.

The tank had two turrets, now. Then the rockets were made of die-cast metal. Then they were back to being red plastic.

And then the tank rolled off the shelf, treads crawling, as it vertically descended to the floor despite having no battery powered motor of any sort.

The three stepped away, giving the toy a wide berth. It was ignoring them, now... it rolled along the linoleum with purpose, down the aisle and away. The floor warped in its path, bubbling and squirming, black and white tiles mixing together like oil paint... before snapping back to normal, after the tank passed.

Around the aisle's corner, out of sight, out of mind.

"W... was that a Picasso?" Lucas asked. Very quietly. "A Picasso'd *toy tank*?"

"I think it was," Penelope agreed.

"But Picassos are always people, right? I mean, people are big. They aren't little. It can't be a Picasso..."

"There's a lot about Picassos we don't understand. ...and it's high time we found out more," she decided. "This could be important. I'm going after that tank."

"What? But we gotta get out of here!" Lucas reminded her—flip-flopping from the voice of adventure to the voice of reason, after that sobering encounter. "You said at the first sign of trouble, we bail. That's the plan!"

"If I stay out of the thing's way, I should be fine," Penelope reasoned. "Picassos aren't always hostile. Sometimes they can't see you at all. —Lucas, Milly, go back to the front of the store. If you see anything strange, just run for it. I can get myself out of here."

Lucas held up one of his many recording devices. "If you're documenting new facts about Picassos, you need a documentarian. That's me. I've gotta tag along. Milly, you should go back to—"

"I'm going too!" Milly insisted. "I'm an Adventure Gal. I can be just as Adventurous of a Gal. You'll see!"

"But Milly—"

"Okay, look, whoever's coming, come. But come *quietly*," Penelope insisted.

Ignoring for a moment the little voice in her head screaming not to drag these two into her big mistake.

Seeing stop motion in the middle of real life can hurt the eyes. Especially when the toy changed shape every third or fifth frame. A stuttering little thing, walking or rolling or flying along case depending, occasionally growing new bullet point features on the fly or changing into a different toy entirely. If Flynn-Frisk Funnies had early demo reels where they were just starting to get the hang of things, Penelope reasoned those experiments would look a lot like this.

Because it wasn't just a Picasso'd tank. There was a robot dog, barking (and sometimes quacking) as it waddled around. Two remote controlled cars that occasionally tangled up with each other to become one larger car, before splitting up again. White plastic with red racing stripes, with the stripes flickering like flames along a chassis injection-molded in China. A toy helicopter, dangerously buzzing around, sometimes bouncing off shelves and spinning about a bit before snapping back onto its trajectory with a jump cut...

This wasn't just a toy store. It was a haven for lost toys. Creepy lost toys. In fact, Penelope wouldn't be surprised if there was in fact a terrifying soulless baby doll that wanted to eat them somewhere in that mix.

But... the toys were ignoring them, just as she'd hoped. They were moving with great determination towards the back of the store. And three teenagers followed them, crouching low and scooting along, like junior detectives embarking on a poorly animated mystery with the Harlem Globetrotters in tow.

Milly and Lucas had taken Penelope's request for quiet very, very seriously. In fact, Penelope wasn't sure if Milly was breathing at all, but she was muffled behind a pair of paper filter masks.

Carefully, Penelope raised her phone, to use the augmented internal microphone to take another EchoMap pulse snapshot. It was risky, firing it off so close to a Picasso... or a horde of tiny Picassos, for that matter. Although the frequencies used by the software were beyond human hearing, the Yates family had found out the hard way that some Picassos find the noise quite vexing...

The pulse, thankfully, didn't alert the toys. And it gave Penelope an idea of what was going on.

They were converging on a door in the back—a door which didn't exist on her fire exit map photo. So, this was indeed connected to the rest of the Sideways. But what *were* these toys? Too small to be a person. Cubist house pets? ...cubist babies? End result of a Picasso'd daycare center? That was a horrifying thought...

Close enough to the mystery door, she signaled for the others to stop. Not that they knew the hand signals Penelope used with her father on trips like these, but generally people knew an upturned palm meant to halt forward movement. Or it meant "talk to the hand," but she'd asked for no talking, so.

Tank and dog and cars and helicopter stepped at the mystery door. Well, the helicopter tried to stop, but ended up inverting three times before wobbling around in place.

The resounding impact of metal on metal when that heavy door swung open was enough to nearly make Lucas drop his camera.

Darkness. Pure darkness, deep Sideways. The EchoMap pulsed quickly, and Penelope could see a twisting arc beyond it, lots of hard obtuse angles from numerous hallways overlaid and chopped and diced. Maybe seven or eight different hallways jammed in there. The kind of chaos and disorder you only got in the thickest, deepest Sideways, well beyond what should exist in the middle of suburbia...

From this darkness emerged... a tiny educational computer toy on wind-up legs, a pair of action figures joined at the head that walked very awkwardly, and one of those pushable popcorn lawnmower thingies. It popped in a crazy and random pattern as it rolled along on two wheels. Oddly, instead of a rainbow array of hollow plastic balls, it was mostly white and red...

Two waves of toys; one from the aisles, one from the doorway. After a pause, taking in a breath, one single moment of still and quiet... they walked past each other. Tank and car and helicopter and dog into the doorway, figures and computer and popper into the aisle.

The door slammed so hard behind them that it looked like a broken section of a film strip. One moment wide open, the next sealed tight. And that marked the end of the process.

They're taking turns, Penelope realized. *Evening shift replaces the morning shift...*

Eager to share her findings despite her own call for radio silence, Penelope turned to face her friends.

Who had been joined by a new friend.

Because one toy was slow to join the crowd. It made sense; the poor thing was crawling along without any legs, dragging itself with plush arms, its pretty dress scraping along the dirty floors. The tiles silently warped and cracked as it moved, distorting space around it. The adorable little toy looked right at Penelope, behind her unaware friends...

A creepy doll.

Of course.

And then it reached out, and grabbed onto Milly's boot.

Silence shattered by a scream of pain.

Penelope moved on pure instinct. No time for any other reaction, not if Milly wanted to keep her foot.

She gave the creepy doll a savage kick, sending it skittering to the other side of the aisle, amplifying the sphere of chaos around it in the process. That was enough to strip some leather from the toe of Penelope's shoe, but one more second and the results would've been far worse.

With Milly likely wounded, she wouldn't be able to run. Penelope moved smoothly under one arm, Lucas taking the other—thankfully the two of them were on the same page about this, without needing to go over the plan.

The two of them hustled like never before, running as fast as they could while Milly hopped on one leg, to get away. Away from the toys. Away from the danger.

Because that danger was aware of them, now. She could hear the furious sound of plastic popping behind her, the chirps of an electronic speaking toy spelling out fifteen random words aloud in overlapping fashion. Even the dragging sound of cloth on tile, the doll likely wanting revenge.

But getting to the entrance like this... that wasn't possible. They were too far towards the back of the store, and Milly was going to slow them down, screaming and barely able to support her own weight. If they just ran for the door, the toys would catch up to them easily. What they needed was a way to break off the chase momentarily, to recover, and find a better way out...

Fire exit map. EchoMap. She could've consulted either of these.

Didn't have to. She knew exactly where to go without being told. The store was in her head, now, and she intended to make it work for her. For the sake of her new friends, and to make up for her stupid error in judgment, coming here and endangering them in the first place.

Penelope kicked open the door of a bathroom which didn't exist in the first place, and they locked the door behind them.

Too weak to continue screaming, Milly had switched to crying. That wasn't a good sign.

Lucas helped ease her down onto the hard tile floor of the bathroom, while Penelope locked the door. Not that a locked door would hold off Picassos forever, but... maybe they were too small to break through. Maybe Milly would recover, and they could book it through the ceiling crawlspaces, get to the exit that way. Maybe...

Focus. First, Milly.

Penelope squatted down by Milly's legs, while Lucas cradled Milly's head and shoulders, saying something about everything going to be fine. But Penelope was the one who could really assess if it'd be fine.

A mapper prepares and packs ahead. Scissors. Penelope had heavy scissors, capable of slicing through the bent and torn boot Milly was wearing.

"This may hurt a little—but that's just because I'm peeling off your shoe, okay?" Penelope explained. "I'm not cutting you. Trust me."

Working swiftly so there could be no tension and anticipation to add to Milly's worries, Penelope cut through the rubber and leather. Tough work, especially with Milly wearing two layers of footwear. But...

It worked. And the results were promising.

Two layers meant her boots got warped a bit, like the floor tiles the doll had crawled over, but the damage stopped there. Milly's sock was a little frayed underneath, but once that was cut away, perfectly blemish free skin was underneath. The cubism hadn't physically damaged anything important.

Penelope hadn't thought of using clothing defensively like that against Picassos. Sure, her dad wore a bulletproof vest, but that was for the occasional irate salvaging gang they ran into. Maybe she'd have to reconsider tooling around in the Sideways in a T-shirt and shorts, now.

"It's fine," Penelope announced. "It's totally fine. I'm not just saying that, there's no damage at all! Your boots soaked up the worst of it and you're going to be fine!"

The news was not coming as a relief.

"It touched me!" Milly gasped, between sobs. "It touched me oh God it touched me I'm infected, I'm infected with cubism—"

"NO!" Lucas replied—holding Milly tighter, his anxiety rising. "No, that's not how it works, Penelope explained everything! You can't get infected. That's not how it works!"

"Wuh, wuh, what if she's wrong? She said it was a th-theory," Milly replied. "I felt it! It hurt! It still hurts! Oh no, oh no, I'm gonna become a Picasso, I'm gonna... no no no no..."

Someone thinks they're infected, they terrified about being doomed, they start to FEEL doomed, and soon enough...

Penelope tried to ignore the slight flicker coming from Milly's left foot. This couldn't be happening. Couldn't.

And it was all her fault. She defied Gregory's singular order. She took two kids along with her on a snipe hunt. She did something that didn't even need to be done in the first place, and for what? For yet another map of the Sideways? That wasn't worth this risk. Nothing was worth this risk. She could've stayed home, stayed indoors, sat around playing poker with Karla or watching the Flynn-Frisk Funnies being filmed. Ordinary and safe and sane—

"Milly... you are not becoming a Picasso."

Reassuring. But it wasn't Penelope's thoughts. Her thoughts were doom and gloom. These were words coming from Lucas.

"I know you think your life is just one mishap after another, that everything always goes wrong all the time. But not this time, not this way," Lucas promised. A firm promise. "You're going to be fine. And you know why? Because we've still got to finish this week's movie. You have that to look forward to. Just like every single week for the last five years."

Consoling the inconsolable was no easy feat. Milly looked up at him, through her tears of panic.

"Buh, buh, but you don't need me for that," she mumbled. "Not really. I just do voices. And... and Penelope can do voices now. She can go on adventures. You'd rather be with an Adventure Gal, not a Sickly Gal. You don't need me —"

"It's called Flynn-Frisk Funnies because it is *us*, dammit," Lucas insisted. "Not Penelope. She's cool and all, but you? You are *awesome*. I started all this for you! Remember? Five years ago, you got pneumonia, the worst thing you'd ever caught. And I brought my toys and my camera to your house and we made our first movie. We've kept it up every week. Every time, sick or not. I wanted something you could enjoy no matter what. ...because... I kinda want to make these movies every week for the rest of our lives."

The slightest pause in her sobbing, as that sank in. Even Penelope's breath caught in her throat.

"L-Lucas? Are you saying...?"

"I... yeah. You know what? Screw it. I *am* saying that. Mildred Frisk, will you eventually marry me?" Lucas asked. "One day when we've both gotten through college and hopefully landed stable jobs so it's not a completely stupid idea and we can actually afford a nice place to live despite this crapass recession my parents keep whining about?"

"That's the most romantic thing anybody's ever said to me," Milly admitted, in half-shock, half-horror, and half-delight.

"Wow, seriously? Ouch. —uh, at the very least, will you walk out of this toy store with me today without dying horribly?" Lucas requested. "You're not going cubist. The lives we have yet to live are way too cool to allow that."

...and finally, Penelope dared to take another look at Milly's foot.

It wasn't flickering anymore. As far as anybody would know, Milly had just taken one of her shoes off for some reason. The cubism hadn't taken root.

Maybe Lucas was just following Penelope's advice, handed out the previous day. Bolster hope to fight the despair that lets someone give into cubism. Give someone a reason to live, and they'll be able to fight off the "infection." Maybe it was all crap—a marriage proposal at their age was pretty silly.

But... Penelope didn't get that feeling from the boy. The way he held Milly, way he looked after her and wanted her safe and happy...

At least this answered one lingering problem in her mind. She didn't have to ponder Lucas as potential boyfriend material. Why were the good ones always taken, anyway?

That left one last problem to deal with.

Penelope looked to the door.

"You two wait in here," she said... rising to her feet. "I mean it, this time. Stay behind and then run for it when you get the chance. I'm going to give him something else to think about."

"Uh, wait, you're going out there?" Lucas asked, refocusing. "Isn't that... y'know... bad?"

"No, it's living my life," Penelope announced. "I'm tired of running from Picassos. It's high time I got the answers I came here for. And I think I know just how to do it."

She kicked that door open like a boss.

...which kind of hurt, since she'd kicked the door to open it in the first place. But when you wanna make a statement, you kicked doors. That's just how it worked.

The toys had gathered. Two got knocked aside by the door; the others scooted back and away, from the shock and awe of her entrance. Good.

With her presence felt, Penelope dashed away—also to distract the toys from the two who were still recuperating in the bathroom. Time for Penelope to be their focus. Time to deal with this, once and for all.

Two aisles away, and she was at the central bike area. Here, bicycles of all sorts were laid out in neat rows... not for buying, of course. They were floor display models. You took a ticket up to a clerk, and they pulled a fresh bike from the back, and your parents spent the next two days trying to figure out how to put the crazy thing together in secret so you'd find it under the tree at Christmas.

It was still October, but Penelope felt like treating herself to a gift anyway. So she picked a nice bicycle with a pink flowered basket, and yanked the tag.

As the toys approached... she held her retail claim ticket high, like a talisman.

"I want to buy a bike!" she announced to them. "I need assistance on the sales floor. Can anybody help me?"

Approaching from all sides, now. The mutated action figures. Popcorn popper. Slightly damaged doll. And, apparently recalled from whatever task they were on, the remote-controlled vehicles and the computer and tank were back as well. The entire messed-up toy factory was on display, and stalking her...

No. Not stalking. Even when one of them hurt Milly, that wasn't really an attack. She was simply in the way and the Picasso didn't understand the situation. Not all Picassos were violent or cruel; most were just lost and confused. But when a good employee spots a customer on the sales floor, they offer assistance. That's baked in so deeply that it digs through the layers of bewilderment and gives the Picasso focus. Just like it did when the cookie-selling scout was after them.

The toys stopped at a distance, to make that point. They weren't here to fight. They were here for... they weren't sure, maybe. Split in so many directions, a mind can rarely concentrate. So she tried to help them understand.

"Employee of the Month Roberto Vargas," Penelope called out. "I recognized you from your photo by the entrance. White shirt, red tie. White toys with red accents. This is you, isn't it? All these toys. Well, I'm going to need your help, because I want to get a bike. Can you help me?"

A lot to bank on a gut feeling, admittedly. But Penelope knew in her heart she was making the right call. This entire adventure wasn't the right call, sure... but this one moment in time, this was the right call.

Naturally, Milly and Lucas had defied her orders and were peeking around from a nearby aisle. They hadn't run for it. But the situation was in Penelope's hand, now; her friends would be okay. Because Roberto didn't really *want* to hurt them.

Gradually... the toys began to come together. They rolled or flew or crawled or walked, circling, spiraling, piling together. Action figures with rubber tires, tanks with computers for heads. Other toys from around the store joined them, rolling and bouncing and whizzing down the aisles—Penelope stepped closer to her bike, up on the display stand itself, to avoid coming into contact. Roberto could still hurt her even if he didn't intend to, after all.

Soon enough, there was a toy man present and accounted for. A man made of toys, in toys in the vague shape of a man. A true Picasso.

And slowly, with so much effort and pain... the man sat near the bike rack. He held his head made of an educational computer in hands made of felt and plastic. The sharp red of his die cast metal bow tie twirled slowly.

how may I help you today // so tired, I'm just so //
need to search more, more places at once //
    holiday rush is always the worst // can't retire, not with little Miguel
      just getting into day care //
so tired // searching always // help the children, help them //
 are you looking to buy that bike?

Penelope's friends were at her side, now. Stepping carefully around the disembodied sales clerk, but willing to set foot in the lion's den rather than hang back and wait. Lucas had even pulled his camera out again, to film everything.

Where moments ago there was terror and fear, hiding from sight and pondering how they'd ever get out of this terrible place alive... now they had confidence. *Good for them,* Penelope decided.

"What are you searching for?" she asked. "We saw you going into that hallway. Is that why you split yourself up into so many toys? So you could search better?"

The electronic speaking toy craned upwards, looking at Penelope with eyes made of glowing LEDs. They flickered dimly, batteries running low, as his speakers crackled out distorted words.

the little girl // such a strange smile, so strange //
    paycheck to paycheck, this is no way to live //
she's looking for a special toy // special place //
   her heart //
heart of the city, she called it //
 so exhausted from all this //
 so many of me, what's going on, what's happening //
   restocking always calms me, it's like a //
find the heart for the child of madness // a special toy for making new friends

And, unbidden, Penelope's own words floated back into her memory.

Long ago and far away, she told a newcomer why she did what she did.

    I think the city has a heart. Sometimes, I can almost feel the way this city feels. And if I map more of it, I'll know that heart. If I manage that... if I can understand the city, right down to the roots... maybe I can use what I learn to help people in this city find hope...

It was a silly notion. New age crystal stuff. Power pyramids and the Gaia Theory.

But someone else clearly held to the same belief—that there was a heart of the city, an origin point. Someone who manipulated... or maybe created Picassos. The "child of madness." The same one a security guard Picasso had been ranting about, in the Defined Tower...

With a sinking feeling, Penelope asked a question she already knew the answer to.

"Who's the child that wants to find the heart? What's her name?"

The distant memories of Roberto Vargas shuddered. It started at his wheeled feet and snapped up through the cloud of action figure parts and accessories, a pulsing wave.

// bedlam. // she said her name was bedlam. //

That was enough to put a solid fear reaction back into Milly and Lucas, who had been curious and confident just seconds ago. Because even if none of them were alive during the Cult of Bedlam incident during the 1980s, that name carried mythical weight with it. A concept nobody really understood, except to understand it was bad news incarnate.

Penelope decided to wrap this up, fast. She adopted the most authoritative tone she could, solid and adult.

"Roberto, you've been working too hard lately," she declared in a managerial voice. "You deserve a day off. Go home and spend it with Miguel."

With an electronic sigh of relief... Roberto Vargas fell apart.

Toys clattered to the ground, like someone had upended a pile of random charity donations on the floor. Whatever cohesive shape they took before was gone, puppet strings cut sharply.

Odds were the Picasso was merely resting, rather than dead. He'd pull himself together eventually, looping through memories of stocking shelves and satisfying customers and endlessly searching the Sideways. But for now, at least, Penelope had given him a respite from the hell his life had become.

Lucas kept his camera on the pile of toys, the whole time. But he was the first to speak up after the sad story of the Employee of the Month was told.

"Did he say Bedlam? Did I hear that right?" he asked. "Seriously?"

"Seriously," Penelope confirmed.

"I thought Bedlam didn't really exist. It was just Yet Another Crazy Cult, y'know, like the Echo Chamber or others that pop up all the time in the City of Angles..."

"B-Bedlam exists," Milly mumbled. "My uncle, he was in that cult. I never knew him; my parents only found out about it after the cops shot him that night. But they got his diaries and stuff, and, and... Bedlam exists. Definitely."

"And Bedlam's a... kid?" Lucas wondered. "Was I hearing that right, too? She's some little girl?"

Before Penelope could toss in her two cents, something changed.

It was subtle, at first. The dark toy store became the slightest bit darker. Why? Because one of the lights at the back of the store went out. *Pop*, like that, the harsh flourescents went out. And then another. And then another...

A wave, sweeping from back to front. Something coming, from the direction of the fractured hallway into the Sideways.

"We need to leave. *Right now*," Penelope emphasized. And, on impulse, decided it was time to exercise her salvage rights on that bike. After all, she'd always wanted a bike she could ride to the mall with her friends.

They swiped two bikes. One for Penelope to ride with Milly sitting on the back (since she didn't know how to ride a bike), and one for Lucas. There was some initial argument about who Milly was going to ride with, but as the sweeping darkness that was eating up the store got closer, Milly hopped on with Penelope without hesitation.

It wasn't just a blackout. The store was going away, little by little. Whether it was vanishing or just too dark to see for some unexplainable reason, either way they had no intention of hanging around to find out. Penelope had learned more than enough today and was quite ready to take a tactical retreat...

Fortunately she'd ridden a bike before, and they say you never forget how to ride a bike. She hadn't carried a passenger with her before, but that just meant a bit more leg-pumping action. Years of hiking through the Sideways gave her legs that could indeed pump with the best of them.

The front of the store and inevitable freedom approached in rapid order.

Except all the checkout lanes were closed. In fact, someone had doubled up the checkout lanes, filling the empty spaces between them with more lanes, and the empty spaces of those lanes with more lanes, until the lanes were too small to see. A cubist distortion...

"Back out the way we came in!" Penelope announced, making a hard right into the entrance gauntlet. After that, a left and a right and a left and they'd be home free.

Cold, behind them. Cold and dark and weird. It was closing in, now—strangeness at the corners of her vision, as they dashed around the first corner of the snaking gauntlet...

And then, the voice. Distorted and sourceless like a Picasso's voice, but far more coherent, without overlaps. A young girl's voice...

Three // three // three of my friends you've taken from me. The scout, the guardian, and now the toyman. I need replacement friends. You three will be my new friends. Everybody will be my friends, one day. Why not today?

"Don't look back!" Penelope shouted. "Just keep pedaling!"

"I looked back!" Lucas called. "I looked back! Penelope, it's, she's—"

"PEDAL!"

Milly clamped her arms around Penelope hard enough to bruise a rib, having already tasted cubism once today and in no mood to dine on more.

The next corner, and then it'd be a straight run all the way to the exit. Almost home, and...

...and the gauntlet repeated. There was an extra turn, a new aisle of toys, stacked in side by side along with the aisles they just rode through. Penelope remembered for certain there were only three segments of aisles, back-and-forth-and-back, no more than that. But now there were more, and more... an endless series. Long enough to tire them out, or to not make a turn and go crashing into a pile of toys. Long enough for the voice and the shadow to catch up.

Bedlam wasn't going to let them leave.

It struck Penelope as tremendously unfair, first of all. Which was a strange thing to think, that on the verge of falling into a weird abyss, she'd be primarily upset at how bullying it was.

The voice began to hum a jaunty little version of *Row, Row, Row Your Boat*, knowing she need only wait them out now.

Merrily // merrily // merrily // merrily // life is but a dream...

Milly was crying and Lucas was shouting something and Bedlam was singing and Penelope wasn't hearing any of it.

All she could hear was a clear voice in her head, probably her own thoughts.

That dream can be what I want it to be.

and

so

the city

changed.

The bikes slipped through the five-milimeter-wide gap between a fast food restaurant and a coffee shop, and came to a swift halt after plowing into a number of plastic tables and chairs.

This time, it was a bewildered Penelope who was being rescued from peril, as Lucas and Milly pulled her out of an uncomfortable tangle of furniture. A table had pinned her arm, leaving it bruised and sore, but otherwise she'd got off clean for someone who just smashed her bike into a food court at high speed.

The lights were dizzyingly bright, compared to the gloom of the toy store... but after the afterimages swam away, Penelope had a vague idea of where they were. One which was confirmed by Lucas.

"It's the mall," he explained, even if he could barely believe it himself. "We're at the mall! Seneca Creek Mall, two-point-three miles from my house. I don't know *how*, but... Penelope? How'd we get to the mall?"

194

"We... we rode our bikes here," Penelope realized. "Just like I thought we would, someday. ...there must've been a gap, a Sideways entrance we hadn't seen before, and we used it to slip back into the suburbs. —wait, she didn't follow us here, did she?"

Milly, who was continually glancing back at the impossible invisible doorway they'd apparently emerged from, shook her head. "N-No, I don't think so. We escaped. We got away! Wow! I can't believe... I... um... uhoh."

Even if the grim spectre of the child of madness was no longer a threat, they had just rode their bikes around a shopping mall and trashed the food court. And the nice men in the grey mall security uniforms were not happy about that.

"I think we're gonna get grounded until we're fifty," Lucas realized. And raised his hands in surrender.

Mall security was fortunately not quite on the ball as the Department of Safety. When she was hauled in by Safety Officers after a Sideways dive some time ago, they'd kept her apart from Dave and Gregory on purpose—keeping them from getting their stories straight. The rent-a-cops were not clever enough for that, or assumed the kids weren't clever enough to require separation, or likely just were too busy to care.

In the time it took for various parental figures to show up and claim their offspring, the three had conspired to tell a unified tale, which went like this:

"Lucas bought these bikes at a yard sale so we could film an action movie with a bike chase in it—he was following behind us with the camera. But two people on one bike wasn't such a great idea, and Penelope's bike went out of control. Before we knew it we'd accidentally rolled into the mall and crashed."

The story wouldn't hold up to scrutiny—they had no receipts for the bikes, the "film" in Lucas's digital camera could've been checked, the security cameras could've confirmed they ended up in the food court without ever entering the doors, and so on. But it was an ordinary story, overflowing with the mundane and plausible, and nobody really wanted to bother questioning it.

Milly's parents showed up first, with her mother chastising the girl about the risks she took—how she could've got a cut and had it become infected or broken her neck and been paralyzed and so on and so forth. After a tirade of vividly described imaginary dangers, Milly got grounded for three weeks. Lucas would have to get her voice parts by the Internet for the next few Flynn-Frisk Funnies, and the star-cross'd lovers would have to yearn apart, but yearning was a small price to pay for getting away with it all.

Lucas's parents showed up next and were generally uninterested in the story or the transgressions. They just wanted to make sure he got the day's shooting done on his movie. "He's going to go far one day," they declared proudly. He didn't seem surprised by this; having a hands-off angel investor known as

Mom/Dad Productions behind his movies apparently had its upsides. Except now he had to retroactively come up with a script for a bike chase and somehow get the shots he claimed he had if he was going to make this work.

As for Penelope... she knew the story wouldn't hold up to her father's scrutiny. So she was bracing for the worst.

Karla being the one to pick her up from the mall security office meant a slim ray of hope, until Karla explained how this was going to go down (while trying to figure out how to fit Penelope's shiny new bike in her minivan).

"I'm not covering for you," she explained. "Just like I didn't cover for your dad last night. I'm going to tell him what happened here—that I had to drop by the mall and pick you up after you crashed a bike you didn't have this morning —and it's up to you two to sort things out after that. This is your mess and I'm not your janitor any more than I'm his."

Penelope sank in the passenger seat of the minivan, sullen.

"I could just clam up and not tell him a thing," she suggested. "He's not telling me anything about what he's doing, after all. If that stuff's none of my business, then what I'm up to is none of his business."

"You really think that'd help?"

"Help what?"

"Help with what's going on between you two. Help with whatever problems you're facing," Karla said. "Both of you could clam up and sulk in your corners, true. It's a valid response. But think long term about this, Penelope. There's more at stake here than hurt feelings."

Tugging the front of her urban explorer's pith helm down over her eyes, Penelope rode home in silence. And thought.

Gregory showed up three hours later. He'd been out all day and all of the previous night, but on getting a text message from Karla saying Penelope was involved in an incident of some sort—alive and well, but briefly in trouble with what passes for the law in suburbia—papa bear came running home as fast as he could.

He was out of breath and quite angered when he entered Karla's dining room, all tasteful furniture and tea cups. Penelope at one narrow end of the table having a hot chocolate; her babysitter/guardian taking an unassuming but symbolic seat along the long edge of the table, to mediate between the two. A chair opposite Penelope had been helpfully tugged away for Gregory to enjoy.

Feeling oddly as if he'd walked into an intervention, Gregory had a seat.

And winced. Hoping nobody had caught that wince.

"You hurt your leg," Penelope recognized immediately. "You're taking those little baby steps you take whenever you get messed up. What happened?"

"Doesn't matter. What's this about you being arrested?" Gregory asked. "You're lucky it was only mall security and not the Department of Safety. What were you doing? What's going on here, Penelope?"

"I could lie and spin some story, but honestly, I took two friends of mine into the Sideways," Penelope said, straight away. (She'd been practicing what to say, and by the time he got there, she'd been ready for it.) "We ran into a Picasso, and eventually fled on a pair of bikes. Somehow we ended up in the mall. I can't explain that one, I guess we found an exit we didn't know was there. Point is, I broke the one rule you've put down for me—not to go exploring the Sideways without you—and I endangered two other kids in the process. It was wrong, incredibly wrong, and I feel completely horrible about it. We're very lucky we got out safely in the end. And that's the truth."

Gregory Yates had never been angry with her before.

It wasn't really his style. From day one he'd never known quite how to deal with children, so he'd treated Penelope like a small adult—granted, a small adult he was overpoweringly protective of and kept at his side at all times. When she frustrated him, or did something silly, he did his best to stay calm and explain the facts of the matter. Never felt hate. There was never anything close to hate there for the only thing left in his world he truly loved.

Here and now, he was angry. And trying very, very hard to keep it in check.

"How could you... WHY did you... what... HOW could you have been so...!" he tried, backing up and restarting each time, trying very hard not to use the kind of abrasive-bastard words he would've used around Karla and the gang twenty years ago. "You... went into the Sideways alone—no, not even alone, you put two civilians in harm's way!—and... agh. Penny, what were you THINKING?!"

"I was thinking you went off and put yourself at risk without even saying goodbye, so maybe I'd do the same!" she barked back.

"What? What are you talking about?"

"Where were you today? Or yesterday? Last night?" Penelope asked. "You dropped me off on Karla's doorstep and then ran off and don't think I don't know where you went! You're seeing a sketchy contact, or getting in trouble with a gang. You hurt your leg! How'd that happen? Huh?"

"That's... look, it's not important. What's important is that you broke the rules, and—"

"I think it is important!" she called back. "What've you been doing? Huh? Why won't you tell me where you're going?"

"It's none of your business and this matter is closed," Gregory declared. "As for you, you're not to leave this house again for the duration of our stay. Karla, see to it that she stays in her room from now on. If I can't trust you to do the sensible thing, then—"

A hand with garish nail polish, held up palm first to stop him.

"I'm not playing prison warden, Greg," Karla warned. "You both get two hots and a cot, you get my wise counsel and killer tea brews... but I'm not this girl's mother. Nor am I yours, for that matter, which is why I let you go off on your crazy adventure without chaining you to my bed alongside my husband. If the kid wants to go poke wasp's nests—just like you poking wasp's nests, for that matter—I'm not standing in either of your collective ways."

Now, Karla, that was someone Gregory could get properly angry with. Just like old times, the bluntly-speaking she-devil of the Seventh Street Scavengers butted head with the boys quite a bit...

"Karla, gosh darn it, put a *sock in it*," he insisted. "I'm just asking you to be responsible about this, okay?"

"Would you have put up with this kind of treatment at her age?" Karla asked. "Hell no. We were wild and free and got into way worse trouble than she does, and we survived. Reason being that we stood by each other through the whole mess of it, open and clear about the crap we were in. You're not being open and clear. Penelope just laid out what she's been through—it's time for you to fess up to what you've been through. Because I am not playing monkey in the middle any more."

"Those days were different and you know it, dam... darn it! We were idiot kids who didn't know any better. I'm a father and she's my daughter!"

"And we were family too, back then. I'd like to think we're still family, by blood or otherwise. And on top of that... we were in business together, for lack of a better description. So are you and Penelope. You're mappers and explorers, in a partnership. Father and daughter, but partners as well. How well do you think that'll work if you're not being honest? I can't say it's looking great from where I'm sitting. So. How about it, Greg? You gonna tell her... or will I?"

Two against one. It was clear Gregory was going to lose this one; the pain in his hip from where he'd impacted against the street earlier today reminded him that some things couldn't be covered up.

Above all... Karla had a point. Gregory was fiercely independent as a youngster. It was a trait passed on to Penelope... by blood or otherwise. And if he kept this from her, if he was seen as a hostile and controlling overlord rather than someone who cared and wanted to be involved in her life beyond holding it on a leash... he could lose her.

"We're being followed," he explained. "It started the day we found Dave. I've spotted them a few other times, too. It's the times I didn't see them that worry me the most. Word on the street says the... Cult of Bedlam may be operational again. I don't know what they want with us—it may just be a vendetta against anyone who regularly enters the Sideways. I need to learn more to make sure we're safe. ...and I hurt my hip trying to hang onto a car that was speeding away after I spotted some grungy guy in an overcoat behind the wheel stalking me."

The news didn't have as much of an impact as he'd hoped. Unfortunately, that was because Penelope had bigger news of her own.

"Bedlam chased us out of the Sideways," she confessed. "The actual, factual Bedlam. ...I left that out because it seemed a bit too scary to say up front. Um. I was gonna tell you once you calmed down. She's angry at us for taking away her friends, the Picassos we've been running into. She said one day everybody was gonna be her friend... but I think she's after me pretty specifically."

Pieces clicked together, briefly distracting him from any shock at the revelation. Things the truckers had told him. The story of the little girl who'd survived the shabby men's experiments. What little he'd learned so far about the Cult of Bedlam...

Originally, leaving Penelope behind was for her own good, to keep her safe. But even if Penelope avoided the Sideways... there was no avoiding the problem at large. They knew her face, her name. Where was she in more danger? Alone and defenseless with the Cult looming somewhere unknown, or at Gregory's side with the Cult squarely in front of them?

The good old days, the bad old days, the Scavengers against the worst this city had to offer. Back then they'd know which of those two scenarios they'd rather face. Better the knife in front of you than the knife in the dark. Stand together. Come on if you're hard enough. Take it to them before they sneak up on you...

He'd made his decision.

"We need to stay here a few days while my hip sorts itself out. Both of us staying here," he clarified. "Then Penelope and I need to get going, to track down the Cult and find out what they're up to. I'm going to call Archie in on this—assuming he doesn't chicken out—and see what we can scrounge up in terms of safehouses and additional manpower. One bit of good news is that the Outland truckers are with us on this, they've been rallying around some crazy beatnik prophet and are keeping an eye out for Cult activity. So. Penelope... we're not alone. And from now on, we're going into this together. Understand? Both of us. Neither of us running off without the other."

Despite the weirdness swirling around them, the threats of cults and insane gods... Penelope was able to smile.

"You've got it," she agreed. "Thanks, Dad."

Late evening, and once again Penelope was in her room with various electronic gadgets, looking at funny cat pictures. Not much else to do tonight; even with a sinister organization of evil doers after her butt, this was the best place for her to be. True, her dad was sleeping off some of Karla's husband's painkillers, but presumably Karla would shiv anybody who broke into the house.

Her phone beeped away, another generic ringtone. Milly again?

She fetched the phone, sliding it open, and answered.

"Hallo?"

"Penelope? It's Lucas," he identified. "I just emailed you a pic, and, um... I think you'd better take a look right away."

"Okay, uh, hang on..." she mumbled, trying to juggle smart phone and smart tablet at the same time. Booting up her email app, waiting for it to load. "What'm I gonna be looking at here? Proofs for your next video?"

"Yyyyyeahno. This is from the footage I took today," he said. "Remember when you said not to look back and I said I looked back? I was trying to explain something, but... decided I should wait until I had a moment to review the video files, to make sure..."

The email attachment opened, popping full screen.

She had to squint to make sure she was seeing it right. Black on black, barely visible, but the outlines had a distinct shape...

"Penelope? Uh... that was Bedlam, right?" Lucas asked. "The girl that was chasing us in the darkness. I had to run this through some leveling filters, some anti-distortion, but I'm pretty sure this is the clearest and most accurate shot I could possibly get of Bedlam. Soo... why does she look exactly like you?"

Dark on dark, swirls of black and dark green, near monotone shadows in a suggestive shape, but... all of the details were right there. Thirteen year old girl. Pigtails. Even her winning smile.

The face of the child of madness was the same one Penelope saw in the mirror every day.

//end

Buildings next to buildings, askew or aligned. Buildings sometimes intersecting buildings, for that matter. Walk down a hallway, end up in a ballroom, double glass doors to a subway station, third exit on the left goes to a discount all-night pharmacy. It's sheer lunacy to slug back any of the bottled concoctions you find, but since nothing is as it seems, they're actually quite normal.

There's no rhyme or reason to any of it—we've got streets which lead to dead ends, roads which criss-cross and loop back around, highways which go nowhere. Literally nowhere, as in "anybody going down that road is not coming back." This is not a good place to wander off unless you like wandering off forever...

Nobody knows where the city came from. Nobody knows how we got here. Nobody knows why any of this is happening. But it's happening. The city exists. We are here now. It's growing every day, and bringing new people with it.

We live a life amidst the twisted yet familiar.

If we're going to survive this, if we're going to stay alive and thrive, we need to learn to live in the City of Angles.

...here's an angle to consider...

The city shakes and shudders, pulsing with life, growing in size every day. This is the core of the City of Angles, the landscape from which it was named. Concrete and steel and glass and pavement and asphalt and the pounding of so many feet. Despite the terror it represents, the instability and risk, this is home. This is where people live and work. This is where they love and strive and declare they are alive.

But during the hours when most of the safe and sane are huddled under the sheets, when the imaginary sun goes down and the imaginary stars rise, that's when a particularly lively section of the populace makes its move. The night life, the scene, the culture underground. They have their own rhythm, one which stands in defiance of the living dead who refuse to set foot outside their door if they can avoid it. Turn down the lights, turn up the music, and see them go...

//006: Glitch Beat

Breathe in, breathe out.

Random and disconnected thoughts. Floating images and memories. I let them wash over me, turbulent waves, swirling eddies. I saw the ocean, once—it's one of the few sights I can remember from that world. It's not a big blue thing. It's dark and punctuated with white foam, twisting and turning, moving according to nature's whimsy. I felt it between my toes, soaking the sand, and I will never forget it.

The distant past. I remember my brother's smile when he smeared the kitchen with jam. I remember my mother's exasperated sigh, as she dragged him off to take a bath. I remember the sunlight through the kitchen window and the glistening strawberry goo.

My lunch-as-breakfast, three days ago. We were running low on supplies, money tight, but I got some of that jam so I could make my sister Marcy jam and toast. She'd never had it before.

Blue skies and sunshine, the playgrounds of public schools. Warm and calming. Kids everywhere, in motion, swirling like the tides. I remember all these things...

While I let the chaos flow over and around and through me, exercising my mind, as I'm exercising my body. It's muscle memory at this point... a variety of yoga stretches and brief aerobic routines, a little bit of everything. It happens as I think of other things. Limbering up, getting ready for the night yet to come. Unlike Marcy, who camps out on the couch with a box of wheat crisps and licorice for hours, I pay exquisite attention to my form. It's part of who I am and what I want to be.

Breathe in, breathe out.

Pull the random thoughts together, sequence them. Bring myself out of the fugue state. I can feel my heartbeat and I use it to guide me out of the meditation.

Coming to the City of Angles, at a tender young age of seven years. Joining the Wei family, a foster care paperwork error, and staying long past the point I was supposed to leave. My sister's favorite new shiny thing which she wouldn't let go of...

My sister. By blood or not, she had become my sister, and I hers. She was my new life. I was now Vivi Wei, and even as I missed my brother and my mother, I moved forward to become Vivi Wei.

Present day, present time. Deep exhale. And here.

The rec room.

We started our days out here—I ran through my workout while my sister Marcy planned her next art piece. Eventually as the sun set we'd go our separate ways, but this was a joint constant. I could count on it in my life.

Fetching my towel, I dried off from the exertion and wandered over to a corner of the room where Marcy was working.

Or rather, wasn't working. Odd. She'd been staring at the same blank spot on the wall this whole time, with no sketch to show for it.

Didn't need to tap her shoulder or otherwise signal her. She heard me approach, felt my presence. I can feel hers in turn, even if I can't hear her.

My fingers fluttered through the gestures of sign language, after I had her attention.

[What's wrong?] I asked. [Writer's block?]

I could tell she was frustrated; her signing in return was sharp and fast, snapping off the gestures in rapid order and without much flow. Like I'd caught her with her hand in the cookie jar and she wasn't happy about that fact.

[I want to do something big. I want to do something important. I've got something...] and a pause, as she tried to think of how to explain it. [On the tip of my tongue. But I can't figure out what it is. Been having weird dreams lately, and I know they say you can't read in dreams, but I could swear I've seen words there...]

I recognized it immediately, of course. She constantly felt the pressure to top herself, to go big or go home. That drive to create leaked into every aspect of her life, sometimes distracting her to death.

[They can't all be monumental. You're allowed to do smaller words, or just do something for fun,] I suggested, slowing down the signs, deliberately making her slow her thoughts in turn. [Or just skip writing tonight. Come with me to the club! It's going to be a big night for the Zig-Zag. You can invite Slyck, if you like.]

You didn't need to know sign language to know what sticking your finger down your throat and mock-gagging meant. Although I was fuzzy on whether she was gagging at the thought of the Zig-Zag, or of her on-again off-again boyfriend Slyck.

[At least think about it,] I asked. [The invitation's always open. You know that. Come on, let me fix you some lunch. You skipped dinner last night; that's not healthy in the slightest.]

I could shower and get dressed later. Right now, Marcy Wei needed me to keep her straight, whether she liked it or not.

I am my sister's keeper, and she mine. In the early years, when a scared little deaf girl was nearly driven into herself by this city, Marcy was there to keep me safe. She's the reason I was able to level out, to appreciate the city and its wonders, and regain my smile. Marcy was my interface to the world, my ears and voice, and she stood by me when nobody—not even my accidental foster parents—would take a stand.

Now, in our twenties, I was doing the same for her. Without me, she'd float away or sink forever. I know she believes in the Echo Revelation, believes to the point where she somehow thinks she's less "real" than I am. Keeping her spirits up and keeping her attached to life is the key. And it's something I'm happy to do for a loved one.

I'm always up for a party.

As a kid, it was birthday parties. I loved the colored balloons, the party games, the cake with fluorescent bright icing. Dozens of sugared-up kids bouncing around in someone's house, sometimes playing, sometimes fighting, but always in motion. I couldn't communicate very well at these parties and Marcy hated social gatherings, so often I was partying by myself... but by myself within the crowd. It was close enough to inclusion to keep me hooked and yearning for more.

Years go by and the parties start getting more intimate and more crazy, without parental supervision and sometimes with beer if someone's cousin knows a scavenger gang. My communication gets better thanks to writing pads and friends who start learning how to read my sign language. Now I'm in small groups who can understand me, within larger groups overall. Going to one party introduces you to people who can get you into other parties, and so on... until you're a teenage party girl supreme. Having fun, making mistakes, learning from mistakes, growing and loving. By that point, the "disability" was barely disabling anything.

And now that I'm an adult... parties are my life. And my livelihood.

I started out as a bartender at the Zig-Zag, a prestigious position in a prestigious club. The Zig-Zag was square in the middle of the Zag, a back-and-forth winding roadway at the heart of the city which had been completely stable for decades. This was primetime, the main drag, the big show. The only reason I was able to even get my foot in the door was because of my high school connections; a guy I went out with knew someone who knew Gee Bee.

As a bartender, my deafness suddenly became an asset. I could read the lips of patrons no matter how loud the music was—and after I got adept at reading the lips of slurring drunks, I never messed up an order.

Eventually patrons came to know me as a regular, and a sort of signing shorthand emerged... this signal for this drink, that signal for that drink. It became a scenester thing. If you knew how to call out to Vivi from across the room, you were now a deeper fixture of the Zig-Zag than before.

So, every night I'd tend bar, and take breaks to dance.

I've always loved dancing, ever since music finally clicked for me. I eventually came to understand music as an indirect experience... a reaction to someone else's action. Put headphones on me and I won't know what to do with them. But put headphones on someone *else*... and soon enough I'll pick up on the music that's coursing through their body. I spot the patterns, the swells, the rushes. I move in sync. Now, put dozens of people in a room with music, pulsing through the crowd like a wave... and I'm in there with the thick of them, feeling it. It's an amazing experience.

Tending bar, dancing, my star rising... and soon, I'm on a first name basis with the V.I.P.s. I'm being requested by name to handle drinks for parties in the upper rooms. I'm invited to join those parties. Sign language, even if it's just a few specific iconic gestures, becomes the trend of the day with those in the know. I'm included, well and truly.

And one day, Gee Bee up and says "You're practically running things around here anyway, so why not make it official?"

So the on the evening after I made my sister jam and toast for lunch, I was working my sixth straight month as primary entertainment director of the Zig-Zag. I was the breadwinner of our house, the girl of the hour, the star of the show. I made the show happen. And I took great pride in the work.

The hours before opening were hardly glamorous. It took a lot of sweat to make the show happen each night; especially on nights like these, with a live music act about to take the stage. Live *electronic* music, which was even worse, since we had to be ready for whatever crazy array of gadgets were going to be in play. Plenty of wires to check and signals to balance... I used audio monitors with spectrographs to check the levels, but fortunately I also directed a small army of tech-minded scenesters. Together, we'd make sure the show worked.

Gee Bee was on hand, too, making one of his rare appearances. He'd opened the club back in the seventies, and was entering his own seventies at this point. Like everybody's favorite crazy old uncle, he had a comfortable feel about him of a well-worn slipper—granted, a slipper made of leather and wearing a Rolling Stones t-shirt, which broke the metaphor badly.

Communication between me and my boss was often difficult. He couldn't sign to me due to his arthritis, and his vision wasn't particularly great anymore so even if he knew my signs he couldn't read them. On top of that, his dentures meant lip reading was, well...

"Are they hear yes? Your friend and two night's magician," Gee Bee spoke, his lips forming each syllable.

...it was more art than science and not particularly magic. Sometimes it took a second or two to swap out my initial guess with a correct stab at what was really being said—context and expression came into play heavily. Knowing what Gee Bee would be concerned with right now, and given we weren't pulling rabbits out of hats later, I mentally filled in "here yet" and "tonight's musician" immediately after my first reading.

To reply to him, I pulled my smartphone from my purse and flicked open the single greatest app I've ever paid ninety-nine cents for. A few rapid pokes at the touchscreen later, and the phone read my reply back to him through a voice synthesizer. I'm told the voice is actually quite pleasant—I had to test a few different downloadable voice packs on Marcy before I found one that didn't make her wince.

Hollister texted to say he's running late and may arrive after opening, but we're ready for them, my phone told him.

The elder statesman of the club scene nodded his approval. "I'm curious about this new style of music, so I think I'll stick around and watch the show," he said (after a few mental word substitutions). "I don't think I'll be rocking it on the dance floor, not with my hip acting up, but I'm sure you can make up for that. Let me handle the bar tonight—you enjoy yourself, kiddo."

I didn't need my app to express my thanks. A full body hug would do.

I couldn't apply my usual enthusiasm behind it, not with Gee Bee's poor joints, but I hugged him all the same. I like being cuddly and close to people— I like people. I like the warmth and comfort of being around and near people.

He gave me a reassuring pat on the back, and then my earlobe wiggled.

Those weren't related events, of course. I had a bluetooth vibration alert embedded in my jewelry; stylish and functional. Someone was texting me.

After detangling myself from Gee Bee and giving him a big thumbs up of confidence, I turned to dig my phone out of my purse. A few swipes and taps and I was in my messenger app.

Ghostwriter: goddammit Slyck broke up with me

I must've done a whole-body sigh, because Gee Bee took the signal as a suggestion to wander off and give me a private moment. I was thankful for that, as I took a seat by the sound mixing boards for a serious texting session.

Vividly: What happened?

Ghostwriter: little bastard said he was tired of the "booty calls"
Ghostwriter: don't get what his problem is, he's a guy, guys are horny all the time. he should be thrilled when I wanna drop in for a casual screw
Ghostwriter: gave me some crap about wanting more out of our relationship I dunno like maybe he wanted long walks by the lake in the moonlight or something whatever

...which was not surprising in the least. And as much as I wanted to be in my sister's corner, I had to agree with that poor guy she'd been toying with for the past year.

I've had plenty of loves in my life, far more than Marcy. But I've always been honest with them. For some, I've had a deep and lasting spiritual connection which gave us a bond beyond the physical... and for others, it was simply people looking to enjoy each other's company, without inhibitions or promises. But one way or another, I was always clear about my feelings and open about discussing them. We share and love. I've left few broken hearts in my wake.

Marcy, on the other hand... she'll often pick some poor submissive looking fellow as her "new boyfriend," keep him at arm's length whenever she doesn't want to bother dealing with him, and then reel him in whenever *she* wants something. It's a bit cruel, honestly. I've tried to talk to her about it, but she just doesn't seem to grasp how love needs to be a two-way street.

Best I could do right now was console her and try to nudge her away from another episode like this.

Vividly: I'm so sorry to hear that, sis. Maybe it's for the best, though. You never seemed very happy with him, and neither did he. I think this is what both of you need.

Ghostwriter: screw him if he's gonna be a jerk about this. screw boyfriends
Ghostwriter: can you ditch work tonight? let's just rent a movie and get drunk at home or something. get a pizza and some beer and just crash out

Vivdly: I can't, Marcy. It's a big night for the club. Hollister's found someone famous from Earth to play music here.

Ghostwriter: bleh. double bleh. but ok
Ghostwriter: I'll just pizza and beer and movie by myself
Ghostwriter: it's cool, you got your job and your friends, I don't wanna mess with that. see you later tonight.

...which could be a recipe for disaster.

Marcy's idea of "a relaxing night of pizza and beer alone" usually morphed slowly into "a night of self-loathing and externalized anger while getting progressively more and more drunk." Dollars to doughnuts I'd come home to find her in a depressive stupor, unwilling to move from the couch and spending the next day in a hangover haze of apathy.

But... Gee Bee was counting on me. The Zig-Zag was my home, too. I wanted to support them just as much as I wanted to support my sister...

I'd have to split the difference.

Vividly: Honey, I can't leave right away, but how about if you drop by the Zig-Zag for a bit? I think you need to try and have some fun tonight. Once the concert's done, I'll duck out early and we'll go home to watch a movie. OK?

Ghostwriter: eh, ok. but I'm not dancing. and I get to write something on your bathroom wall later. I promise it will be awesome.

Vividly: I'll put a frame around it when you do. See you soon! Hurry over, we're starting soon.

Phone back in purse. Crisis... hopefully averted.

Tonight I'd have to juggle a new musical act, keep the crowd hot, and make sure my sister had as close to a good time as she could. I'd also have rounds to make to greet all my friends who were coming by for the show, and I should really make sure the bar is stocked—and that the bottles with large print labels were near the front, if Gee Bee was tending bar tonight, and...

A juggling act and a half. Honestly, it was hard to enjoy the club when you were working the club, and having a heartbroken sister along for the ride would double the difficulty. But I'd dance from crisis to crisis, deal with it smoothly, and come up smiling. I always did. You just had to find the right beat to move to.

Doors open at nine. Crowds in through the doors, starting to mill, warming the party up...

No sign of the DJ, or Hollister, or Marcy. Not yet. The DJ in particular running fashionably late, considering he was on deck in half an hour. Even without bartending duties, I was wildly running around putting out and stoking fires.

We were easily going to be at capacity tonight, with the high profile musical act that would supposedly be arriving soon—and the doorkeepers were having trouble keeping us at that capacity. This wasn't originally a night club, it was some warehouse space that arrived on the Zag back in the fifties, and that meant a lot of entrances and exits to mind. Not usually a problem, but on a stormy night like this one, the ship tended to leak and take on water.

The crowd was ready for it, but word had spread that the star of the show was missing. I warned the staff to keep a lid on that, to emphasize that everything was (as far as they knew) going to be fine, but word got out. I went around to the groups I knew, trying to assure them and keep them excited for what was to come, all while sneaking to send panicked texts to Hollister...

Vividly: What is going on? Are you on the subway yet?

TheAvenue: Finally got him out of bed and dressed. Think he got stoned or something, sorry. Riding subway, en route, eta 30m. Get things ready so he can hit the stage right after arriving, gonna be cutting it close.

Twenty minutes later, and Marcy showed up.

[Are you handing out free candy or something?] she signed to me, horrified at the size of the crowd. [I practically had to bulldoze my way through the crowd at the door to get to the doorman. He didn't recognize me at first, either. It's not like I haven't ever been here.]

[Sorry, I'm so sorry,] I repeated. [It's a crazy night. The guy Hollister's bringing in was really hot back on Earth. He's a... 'D-U-B-S-T-E-P' artist.]

It occurred to me a bit too late that I didn't know the sign for dubstep. Fortunately, Marcy managed to invent one on the fly.

[You're kidding me. You seriously hired one of those...] Tugging at her cheeks, to mimic the sound I'd heard dubstep was famous for. ['WUB WUB'... guys? Have you even experienced 'WUB WUB' before? I don't think you're going to like it...]

[It's hot and popular right now, and the Zig-Zag's benefiting from that,] I explained. [I book the best acts for Gee Bee, period. Listen, I'm sorry to leave you like this but can you wait at my table? I need to tend to things.]

Marcy looked nonplussed.

[You want me to hang out with your crazy friends?] she asked. [I thought we were gonna 'enjoy' the show together.] With air quotes, of course.

My table, my corner of my club. My friends. Zeke and Joey, the cutest couple you ever did meet. Fi, the poet who deigned to hang out with us every other week. Amanda, who was having so much trouble with her love life...

They didn't get along very well with Marcy, the last few times I'd managed to get my sister to show up at the club. But they knew how much she meant to me, and they could keep an eye on her until everything was calmed down.

[It'll just be for a few minutes, until everything's on track,] I insisted. [The timing's bad, I know. I'll do my best to—]

I froze mid-sign, seeing a flash of light by the backstage entrance. Movement.

Throwing a quick [Back soon] to Marcy, I slipped through the crowd with practiced ease, making my way to the back.

My team of behind-the-scenes ninjas were in hot-stepping mode, now. Doing final checks, warming up, getting ready. That could only mean one thing—showtime was nigh.

I wormed my way around them, careful not to interrupt their work. The backstage area was tiny, as tiny as possible to squeeze in more area in front of the stage. The "green room" matched that, being little more than an oversized closet with a few cheap secondhand chairs for the acts to relax in before their gigs...

Tonight's act had slumped into one of the chairs, and was... no, not meditating. Definitely asleep. His oversized glasses had slipped down his nose, and his long asymmetrical hair was dangling back as he snored away.

This was the first time I'd met the fellow that Hollister had been going on about for days, but that first impression wasn't a great one. The man was pale and sickly, dark rings under his eyes. Unhealthy in every respect...

A worrying sight. Hollister looked equally worried.

I'd known Hollister for some time, in an informal manner—everybody knew Hollister. He knew everyone, or knew someone who knew everyone. He reminded me a lot of the distant memories of my little brother, back on Earth... always smiling, always trying to please, to show off the neat mischief he'd wrought.

Only after a strange evening outing with my sister did Hollister approach me directly, and get to know me directly. Only then did I come to learn that the care-free partying smiles were a front. The real Hollister was a ball of worries, and those worries were very much at the surface tonight.

Even one of my customary full-contact hugs didn't bring him out of it. I was worried as well, so we made a lovely couple in that regard.

Once his hands were free, he explained. His signing was still coming along and we didn't have much time, so he fell back on my lip reading to make himself clear.

"He's been drifting in and out of sleep all day, and having nightmares. I tried getting him some coffee but it didn't help," he said. "His Department case file said he's been having trouble sleeping and I know he wanted to find some work, so I thought this would help him, but... honestly, I'd have left him at home for his own health if I didn't know how important this was to you."

...which left me in a very, very bad place. And Hollister knew it, which explained the guilty look he was giving me.

I needed an act. If this went badly, such a high-profile event, it'd hurt the club. It'd hurt Gee Bee. But if I pushed someone clearly in some sort of psychological crisis into performing just so I could make my life easier, what would that make me? I don't like hurting people, or letting people hurt themselves...

"I'm so sorry. I should have told you more about this before," Hollister continued, since I wasn't replying. "I thought this would help him. I've been working his Orientation case for weeks, trying to help him get back on his feet since arriving in the city. I figured maybe if he could just find a gig he'd comearound, bebetter, so I didn'twanttoworryyou. It'smyfaultyournths mssiptyn—"

A finger pressed to his lips. He was talking a mile a minute now, visually incomprehensible. No sense in it, so I stopped it in its tracks.

I hated having to use my phone app at a time like this. So impersonal, but Hollister didn't know enough sign language yet, and I had to be clear.

I'll cancel the event, I typed. *I'll take responsibility. I don't want to hurt your friend. It's okay, Hollister.*

"No, it's not okay," he insisted. "I wanted to do something nice foryouand I've fkdtallupmsosr—"

A brief flicker at the edge of my sight distracted me from trying to read the mess on Hollister's lips.

Our mutual friend was awake.

His head had jerked forward, before the rest of him slowly followed. Sitting upright, now. Adjusting his glasses.

"Showtime," I think he said, before lurching to his feet and out the door before anyone could stop him.

Momentum carried things the rest of the way through. I tried to chase after, but my team already had their hands on him, running him through the paces. Where to enter from, what his cue would be, how things were going to work. They'd been ready for this all night and stopping that would be like holding back the tide. The DJ wasn't resisting; alert and ready to go, he went along, nodding to the explanations.

I tried keying in *stop* on my phone and making people listen to it, but they were focused on him, now. My little synthesized voice held no weight. Hollister did his part, some sort of argument with the sound technician, even talking with the DJ. I couldn't read properly in the dark and from these angles, people with their backs to me; all that was clear was this show was happening. The DJ shook his head a few times, presumably at Hollister requesting he step down.

This was what he wanted, after all. Like Hollister said, he wanted a gig, and Hollister was the guy who could get you what you wanted. Both as a caseworker for the Department of Orientation and as a dealer in things that need dealing with, he was the one you turned to. He'd done this as a favor to me, a favor I never asked for, trying to prove his worth. It was his default response to the world, a need to justify himself to the ones he cared for. I could have done more to dissuade him, honestly... but a hot act for the club was just so enticing...

We found ourselves at my usual table, minutes later. Zeke and Joey, Fi, Amanda. Marcy. Hollister. Me.

And on stage, a man who needed no introduction. I didn't recognize many faces in the crowd; they were largely imports, people eager for a taste of home. Here was someone they knew, even if I'd never met him before tonight.

On stage, he didn't look like a shambling wreck. He looked alive and ready, reveling in the cheers, soaking them up. Ready to rock their world with his unique flavor of music. I could feel the vibrations through the club floor, the wild appreciation...

Well... maybe this would work out. Whatever problems he was facing, he seemed happy to be up there now. The gig was going off on time, and the crowd was happy. Gee Bee would clean up, and all would be well...

The beat was steady, at first. Dance music. Even without hearing it, I could feel it, see it washing over the crowd. My crew who ran the lighting rigs knew how to sync their work perfectly to whatever sound was pumping through the ridiculously oversized speakers of the Zig-Zag.

As that pulsing wave started to rise... I started to feel my groove again. Later on in the show I could hit the dance floor, enjoy this properly. Show this city I was alive, we all were, and no matter what problems we faced we could face them together. Me, Hollister, Marcy, even our new friend on stage—

Broken beat. Stuttering.

At first, I thought something was wrong. I only felt the impact indirectly, seeing as the cadence of the crowd shattered, fragmented. My lighting crews, not sure what to make of it, started falling out of sync.

Did the speakers blow? Was the DJ's equipment malfunctioning? Was...

No. The crowd was still happy; I could feel their cheering, see their smiles. But the music had become distorted and chaotic. It broke down completely, and strangely enough, that seemed to be what they craved most. The moment they were waiting for.

Wub Wub. I got it, now. That's why Marcy didn't think I'd like it. This was music, but it wasn't music I could experience. It broke every pattern I was able to sense. It worked for the crowd, they lapped it up with a spoon, but to me... it was just chaos. Visual white noise. Glitched beats.

Even as my friends at the table cheered, I sank into the vinyl of my booth. By myself, within the crowd.

I suppose part of me was ecstatic. We'd done it—we pulled off the gig, and the Zig-Zag would rock down to its foundations tonight. Nobody was going home unhappy, they got what they came for. We'd had rock acts before, or experimental music I couldn't get a grasp on. This wasn't really anything new... but after the exhausting evening, being excluded like this didn't help my mood.

Marcy flicked for my attention.

[Sorry,] she signed. Not *I told you so*, just sorry. She knew how crestfallen I felt at this moment, and was sympathetic.

I put on a smile, for her. Maybe for myself, too.

[If they're happy, I'm happy,] I signed back—fingers audible over the likely incomprehensible level of volume that flooded the ears of the club. [I'm going to hit the bathroom. I'll be back soon.]

Gee Bee had a small bathroom backstage, a private one. At the moment, privacy was what I sought. Getting through the crowd to reach it was tricky; if they were dancing and moving in unison, I could have slipped through easily. As is, I had to force my way there through the bedlam.

I had no right to cry.

It was selfish of me to think of this place as my own personal party. In the end, it wasn't for me—it was for them. They were happy, so I should be happy, just like I said.

Of course, that was a line Hollister often used, and I called him out on it each time. He gave of himself and his time and resources perpetually to make other people happy, never once thinking of himself. Generosity is a virtue, but erasure of the self... that could become a vice, in time. An addiction.

This wasn't the same, was it? When I gave to others, I was giving to myself, too. I'd built a nest here, a safe place where I was a participant rather than on the silent fringes. Tonight, after working so hard... my reward was to be pushed back to those silent fringes.

But it was just for one night! Not exactly the end of the world. Not some mass rejection. Couldn't I accept one night of that? Was that selfish? Did I have any right? Did...

Thinking in circles. No clear answers.

This was just one night. It would be over in less than a day's time. Marcy had the right idea in the first place; we should head home, dig in, and let it pass over us. Time gave perspective, and in time, I'd see this for the minor disturbance in my life that it was. I could regain my positivity. Not likely tonight, but soon.

Beyond the tiny staff bathroom, I could still feel the crowd. It felt like a stampede of some sort, crazy and aimless. No comfort to take in it; at last, I knew how others often felt in night clubs, battered on all fronts by too much meaningless noise, driven to headaches. Mine was already forming.

I'd been tucked away back here for minutes. Time to go and face this.

Gee Bee had given me the night off, technically. I'd thank Hollister for his time, say goodbye to my friends, grab Marcy and head home. Simple enough —

In my reversed world of the bathroom mirror, I saw the door fly open.

Marcy.

No words, no signs. Grabbed my arm, pulled hard, hard enough to hurt. I tried a one-armed signal of protest but she wasn't even looking, not looking back, as she dragged me out through the backstage area towards the exit...

Hollister was there already, waving us in. He had been frantically trying to twist the knob, to get the door open. I wanted to explain that it was locked, that most of the entrances to this converted warehouse had to be locked to keep folks from sneaking in. But there would've been a guard back here, who could let her out. Where was everyone...?

He screamed something. Marcy might've yelled back in agreement, because now all three of us were on the move. Jerked back, going towards the stage now. Hollister kicking the push bar on the doors open to—

Chaos.

Lights everywhere. Strobes. The lighting rigs were out of control. In the dark, sometimes a colored beam would pass, and I'd see, I'd see...

Bodies. People running. People being trampled.

The bar, smashed, glass everywhere. The bar was twisted in the center, steel and plastic warped and bubbled like wax under a blow lamp. I saw Gee Bee's face. I didn't see the rest of him. I couldn't and didn't want to...

Marcy pulled and this time I willingly followed. We stayed around the edge of the room, trying to get to the front door, where the crowd was desperately pushing to get out. To get away—

The flickering spectre interjected itself in our path. One moment it wasn't there, the next it was there. Jerking between two frames of a bad videotape, static swirls and color bleeding in its outlines.

The DJ. Still playing, hands on controls and turntables that were swirling around him now. Light and electronics and wires, a cloud of them, shredded and multiplied and twisted and floating free from all laws of physics.

Picasso.

And he was blocking our way to the exit.

His face, I could see so many of his face. Rocking out, getting into his music. Screaming for help. Terrified. Grinning madly, lips pulled back like a skull's grin, reveling in the spotlight. All of it simultaneously...

What truly made me fear, however—the thing that sent me screaming in on myself—was what he said. Because I could hear it.

it feels so good // i can feel the music in me // i want to share this // with // all my friends...

Those were the first words I'd ever heard in my life. I can only assume I heard them; I couldn't lip read that mash of overlapping visuals, and he certainly wasn't signing. The words entered my head, clear and true. Not my own thoughts. Someone else's thoughts, expressed in the way people express their thoughts. With sound.

Backed to the stage, now. Pressed against it. Hollister trying to shield my sister and I, as if that'd really do much of anything.

World going dark. A smothering feeling. Something heavy being thrown on top of me.

Heat, burning heat, stepping right into an oven.

Marcy's arms around me, pressing the sign for *I love you* against my back, hard enough to bruise. Desperate...

...and then, light. The smell of ash and smoke.

Men in fireproof suits, lifting the fire rescue blanket they'd draped over the three of us... while other workers continued to blast the fried body of the DJ with anti-Picasso flamethrowers. The musician had melted into the floor by this point. No longer moving. No longer even Picasso'd.

The Department of Safety to the rescue.

A triage station had been set up on the street outside the ruins of the Zig-Zag.

This meant stopping traffic on the Zag... which had never been done before, not in decades and decades. It was stable, it was the core of the city, it never changed. Sure, the road was famous for worming its way left and right around diagonally twisted blocks of buildings, but aside from that it was the closest thing to normalcy the City of Angles got. Now, traffic was being rerouted around the asphalt in front of the club, while the wounded were treated and men in hazmat suits tromped in and out of the club.

Despite entering into the dead of night, it was bright as day out here. News crews had set up on either side of the triage zone, shining floodlights, capturing every moment of the wounding of the Zag. The Department of Safety wasn't being particularly subtle about this—shutting down the main drag, invading with dozens of health officials and safety inspectors. Plenty of juicy visuals for the news sponge to soak up. People were no doubt watching it all unfold on live cable television... watching, and trembling in fear as one of the foundation rocks of their lives was jackhammered into granite powder right in front of them...

The three of us had been kept away from the main circus, in an isolation tent. The Department officials didn't buy that we hadn't come into direct contact with the Picasso; we were being observed for signs of cubism, even as our cuts and scrapes were being treated.

I was being looked at with suspicious eyes by safety officials, in particular.

After all, my sister was practically growling with anger at not being allowed to leave, and Hollister was actively trying to leverage his civil service cred to get us better treatment. Both of them were fighting.

Myself... I was just sitting there, in silence. Normal for me, but I felt like I'd've been silent even if I could make a sound.

We lost the Zig-Zag. We lost Gee Bee; he was one of the confirmed casualties, along with those who were trampled trying to escape, or those the Picasso had run into head-on. This was a tragedy, a murder, a loss of everything I'd embraced in my life since moving out of my suburban foster home with my sister. Everything, gone, in the blink of an eye...

i want to share this with all my friends, the Picasso said. His voice echoed in my mind. So earnest, so joyful. Picassos were horrible things, suffering and hateful and lashing out, I'd heard. This one was... happy. It reached out to us as a friend, not as an enemy. And yet, it would have killed us all the same... it did kill those I held dear. Everything gone. Blink of an eye. Everything...

Despair is a side effect of cubism. Or maybe cubism is a side effect of despair, nobody knew. Either way, the doctors were watching me for any telltale signs, no doubt. Marcy was, too. Even as she paced and fretted and raised hell, she kept an eye on me.

After what felt like hours, the authority of authorities entered our little vinyl cell.

He didn't wear hazmat gear; instead, he wore a white suit of immaculate tailoring, matching the snow white of his beard. A tall man, dark of skin, composed and perfect like a statue. Comforting and strong. Strange to feel sure of those attributes only seconds after meeting him, but clearly it was a practiced poise—he wanted you to feel comforted by his strength. Being an adept at reading body language, I could see it as a clear and blatant intent.

He spoke to one of the health technicians—turned to the side, so I couldn't fully read. Marcy accosted him, likely asking for us to be released. Hollister joined in. But after a few brief words to them... the man turned to me, focused.

His hands flowed into sign.

[My name is S-E-T-H D-O-U-G-A-L, and I am in charge of the Department of Safety,] he explained in flawless ASL, while speaking those same words aloud for Marcy and Hollister's benefit. [I want to apologize for your treatment. While it is standard policy to isolate those who may have come into contact with a Picasso, the amount of confusion out there has slowed your processing to an unacceptable degree. You haven't shown any signs of cubism. You and your friends are free to go home.]

Marcy replied—she must've been agitated, because normally she's sure to face me while signing and talking. I believe she was explaining exactly where Mr. Dougal could shove his slow processing.

[Please understand, the number of injured is quite high, and the media interest and traffic issues have caused no end of difficulty,] Seth replied. [In addition... this is not the only club we've been called to. Two other nightclubs have had cubism incidents tonight. The deaths are still being counted.]

The chill of autumn in the city didn't match the chill I felt at that moment.

[What do you mean?] I replied.

[There have been three incidents total. We don't currently know what the connection is between them, if there is any connection at all,] Seth responded, to me. [By emergency authorization from the mayor, I am issuing a public health and safety warning regarding similar clubs and social gathering points. We are not instituting a curfew at this time, but we will recommend caution and avoidance of such facilities to improve citizen security. Given the tragic loss of life, this is the least we can do. I'm sorry for any inconvenience.]

He paused briefly, to accept a clipboard stacked thick with papers. Scrawled off a signature in triplicate, then passed it back to a hazmat-wearing technician.

[Your paperwork is processed and you're free to go. Have a nice evening, Miss Wei,] he signed... with a nod of the head to punctuate.

It seemed... sudden. Everything so crazy, all this mess, and then just... sent home. Dismissed. Maybe it was the shock of what happened tonight, but I had no idea how to feel one way or another about this new development.

[That's it?] I asked. [Nothing else?]

[What else would we require of you?] he asked.

[Hollister and I knew the man who went Picasso!] I signed back, some of Marcy's anger leaking into me. [Nobody's asked us anything about him. Why not? We could help you figure out why it happened. I don't believe the club itself was at fault, even if you have had other incidents in clubs tonight. How can you issue some vague "safety warning" without knowing for sure? This should be investigated!]

[And I assure you, any possible causal connections will be investigated thoroughly,] Dougal promised. [The safety warning is simply our initial guidance on this issue. If we require your assistance, we will be in touch, but I ask you to trust us. We are professionals. Thank you for your time.]

And then, through the tent flap and into the night air. Off to important Department of Safety business. Destroying my entire world in one blow, and then gone with a confident stride.

When sunlight reached me again, I felt less urgency to get out of bed and start my day. No need to go exercise and meditate. I did it anyway, but found it harder than ever to pull myself together, to find the beat of my heart and reassemble my self around it.

The Zig-Zag had been shut down; damaged beyond repair. Other clubs were also feeling the sting of this, not just ones which had endured Picasso rampages. Nobody could prove those clubs were responsible for their cubism incidents, but thanks to that "public safety warning" the cable news stations were having a field day. Experts gleefully declaring that there *must* be something dangerous in the music, or the lighting, or the liquor... or simply that the sorts of people who would go to those places surely were cubism time bombs waiting to blow. Strange young people. Loose morals. High on drugs. Dangerous. And the Department of Safety, while saying nothing to support those theories, did absolutely nothing to stand in their way. Their investigation was officially still ongoing.

But all of that, the confusion, the fear, the politics... all of it was just frustrating and worrying. The real depressive blast I was hit with was far more personal.

Gee Bee was dead. The kind-hearted old rocker, the one who wanted to pass his youthful love of music onto next generation, had a closed casket funeral a day later. With few living relations, and fewer club regulars willing to head out of their homes to attend, it was a very lonely service. I attended, Marcy attended. A few from my circle of friends did, but not many. Amanda was there, going through tissue after tissue... and oddly enough Fi, the aloof poet who sometimes deigned to hang out with is, was one of the first to show. But Zeke and Joey, the Zig-Zag's cutest couple, were nowhere to be found.

Nobody had prepared a eulogy; the service itself was hastily arranged by a distant nephew, who didn't even show up for the funeral. Since nobody else would stand up to speak for the dead, it fell on me. I lasted two minutes before I was crying too much to make any coherent signs.

But in the end, I didn't have proper time to mourn. I needed to start hunting for a job, and immediately.

I was the breadwinner of the Wei household, after all. I'd rode on a wave of connections and handshakes right into an extremely cushy position, using the money to keep our modest little apartment stocked with food. Marcy sometimes pulled a part time job when things were tight, but had trouble keeping them. I was the one keeping us afloat... and the rent would be due sooner than later.

Both of us had shiny high school diplomas and little else to our name. I could've flipped burgers or become an entry level typist in an accountancy firm... work a trained monkey could do. But I yearned to be reborn from ashes, and rejoin the world I had been ejected from: to entertain, to dance the night away, to join the party. I was well known in that scene. Surely there'd be SOME work available to me...

...nine days of job interviews later, and no joy.

Hollister tried. He really tried; he felt responsible, no matter how much I tried to assure him he wasn't. But the market for my skills had dried up overnight. No clubs were hiring... most of them were battening down the hatches and running with skeleton crews, or were simply closing down to wait out the tide of public opinion. Even bars and watering holes were keeping a low profile, not wanting to get caught in the negative splash of a high profile Picasso incident.

The few places there WERE hiring, well...

I tried going to the first interview alone. I was a proud and strong woman, ready to make a good impression without needing to rely on anyone else. I was well known in the scene and surely I could prove my worth.

Except, of course, the confused-looking woman who was doing the interview didn't know sign language. I had to use my phone app, which meant a delay between her question and my response while I keyed in my words. Her patience wore thin quickly.

"I'm sorry, but I just don't see how you're going to be able to handle talent relations like this," she explained. "If I could afford to provide accommodations for your disability, I would, but... I'm afraid it's just not in our budget. Thank you for your time."

I couldn't even explain why that wouldn't be needed. She'd waved in the next candidate before I could finish typing.

Hollister suggested a lawsuit, citing discriminatory hiring practices. But the last thing I needed was to make waves.

That was the real problem with my "disability." Or my sex. Or my sexuality, for that matter. Even my general archetype. I could get neatly filed away, assumptions taking place of explorations, and if I tried to fight back... I'd get a reputation as being troublesome. Bitchy. I couldn't afford that, not now, not when I needed to keep my name clean in this shrinking scene.

If I raised hell with a short-sighted potential employer and they passed word on to other potential employers, that'd be even more strikes against me. Then it's not just a matter of hiring some... some deaf-mute hippie, but a deaf-mute hippie who's going to be a royal pain in the ass. Once lawyers get involved, I'd be lucky if I could get a job shoveling fries.

Two failed interviews and five calls without any response whatsoever. Opportunities running thin. Hollister going to the well so much he was coming up with empty buckets... and taking time away from his daily job, working at the Department of Orientation. I didn't want him sacrificing his own career for mine, and eventually told him I'd do my own job hunting for now.

Even aside from aiding and abetting Hollister's city-sized white knight complex, this was a matter of pride. My sister and I set out from the Suburbs against my foster parent's wishes, headed into the city with little to our name. We were determined to carve a place out of the City of Angles for ourselves. If we had to start over from scratch... so be it. I couldn't let this defeat me. No matter what.

Finally I found something vague, but promising.

Dancer needed. No classical training required. Service industry experience a plus, bartending a double plus.

This time, I brought Marcy with me as a sign language interpreter. Lightning fast responses would help my case; she could demonstrate how easily I could communicate under the right circumstances.

We took the subway down to Crossway Points. Not the best part of town, sitting at the juncture of several ridiculously low income blocks known for instability. Every now and then a new road was linked up, making the tangle of intersections thicker and weirder... rent stayed low, people got high, and the Department of Safety was rarely to be seen. But this was my first attempt at finding a job without Hollister's help, and I intended to see it through...

We went by subway during daylight hours, well before the club opened. But even without the facility in full swing, the vague advertisement became highly specific when we opened the doors and saw the stripper poles on stage.

Before I got ten steps in the door, Marcy stopped me in my tracks.

[NO,] she signed. A big No, shaking her head while pinching her fingers shut hard enough to impress a snapping turtle. [No, no. Turn around. We're not at some clichéd daytime-talk-show level of desperation here.]

When she moved to leave... I stood my ground. Refused to budge.

[Rent is due in two weeks,] I reminded her. [And the food's running low. I have to get started on something, and fast. This is...] Paused, to think of a good way to sign it. [Dancing. I can dance, no matter what kind of dancing. It's not ideal, but this is still... close to where I wanted to be. And I'm not exactly modest about my body, sis.]

[I'm not having a bunch of perverted old freaks drooling over my sister's body and stuffing dollar bills up her asscrack. Forget it,] Marcy replied. [You're not some trashy skank, either—]

My sign interrupted hers. Thankful Marcy was signing silently, as other women who were preparing for the club's opening moved around us.

[Don't denigrate people like that, Marcy. That's incredibly unkind. You always say you don't like it when people stereotype us, don't you?]

It probably made her teeth grind, but... she knew better than to belabor the point. Instead, she changed tactics.

[There's other jobs. Catering. Waitressing. Hell, I can get a job too. I'm in this with you, aren't I? We could both go get some crappy-but-paying job. We could beg Mom and Dad for a loan, even. You don't HAVE to do this.]

She was technically right. It wasn't like only one door was open in front of me. But, she was also wrong. Because even if this was left of center, it was still hitting the target I was aiming at. This was the night life. Parties. High spirits. I would be involved in my dream, even if my involvement wasn't exactly ideal...

Fortunately, Marcy understood that. At crisis points, where words were failing us, often we somehow could see into each other's hearts. When she filled the visual silence I left behind, she did so with more calm than her earlier flailing outburst...

[Even if you could live with this, I know it's not what you REALLY want to do,] Marcy pointed out, with briefly flaring emphasis. [And it stinks that you have to settle for something you don't really want to do. You know, someday the public will find some other shiny scary thing to be afraid of... everything'll go back to normal. If only we could wait out the stink of that mess at the Zig-Zag...]

[Well, we can't,] I pointed out. [There's no time, Marcy.]

[If we can't wait, then we should DO something. ...there's something we can do,] she added after a pause. [I've been thinking about it ever since that night. What if we... hang on, let's get out of here. I'll explain outside. We're getting funny looks.]

True. We'd walked right in the door of the club and started waving our hands at each other in silence. Already some of the employees were wondering what was going on, and we'd be approached any moment now if it kept up. If I needed to keep a good first impression I needed to get out of sight, if my sister insisted on an extended conversation.

So, we swapped the smell of cigarette smoke and booze for the smell of car exhaust and open garbage bins in a nearby alley. Not a huge improvement, but standing around outside the building gave us an unusual sense of privacy. Out here we were just loitering and quietly chatting, while the world passed us by...

[Let me walk you through this crazy idea of mine,] Marcy continued. [We have two weeks until the next rent drop, and I bet I can sweet talk the landlord into a delay. Let's see what we can do to improve the situation between now and then.]

I cocked my head to the size, puzzled. [What do you mean?] I asked.

[The media's running wild with the theory that it's all the social scene's fault, that clubs themselves are dangerous, that they caused the Picasso incidents,] she explained, with requisite air quotes. [That fear is what's really between you and a dream job—if there wasn't public pressure on the entertainment sector, they'd be hiring again. What if we could do something to change public opinion?]

Interesting. Marcy was always keen on getting her words out there, having people stop and think about them. What was she proposing? I nodded, for her to continue.

[We can't do that without the facts. The truth,] Marcy continued. [The scene itself didn't cause that guy to lose it. Let's look into what was REALLY going on with that DJ, see what was really to blame. Maybe his apartment was going cubist, maybe he was hanging out in the Sideways, maybe he had a pet Picasso... something we can feed the journos and the cops. How about it?]

...I wasn't even sure how to reply to that. It was silly. Absurd. Completely implausible.

[I'm not exactly N-A-N-C-Y D-R-E-W,] I reminded Marcy. [And neither are you. We should be leaving investigations to the Department of Safety.]

[They aren't doing crap to help us! They're responsible for this mess in the first place, with that stupidly vague "public safety warning." But we're in a good position to look into this—Hollister knew the guy who wigged out at your club. He can point us in the right direction. Come ON, sis. We've got to try. Please?]

It was understandable, of course. The situation was well out of our hands, and Marcy hated being out of control. She wanted to fight, just like she wanted to fight when we were stuck in that isolation tent a little over a week ago. Marcy refused to accept when life threw her snake eyes.

So...

[If this leads to a dead end... I need to take this job,] I warned her. [Even if you don't like it. Even if it's not what I was dreaming of. We have to be practical. Until then... you have a deal.]

[If this doesn't work, hell, maybe I'll stick on pasties and grind the laps of fat losers cheating on their wives,] she suggested.

...a horrifying mental image, there. I could also easily see her taking a broken bottle to the jugular of the first guy to toss a catcall her way.

Sooner or later, she'd have to accept the reality of the situation. But, I supposed it couldn't hurt to play along a bit... if only so she'd feel better about having tried.

We got started immediately. The sooner we began our amateur sleuthing, the sooner Marcy would understand how hopeless this was, and the sooner I could get her consent to take that job. I didn't *need* her consent, any more than she needed mine when she went out into the shadows of the city to practice her art... but in the same way she made concessions to me to help me feel better about that, like taking Hollister with her on her last outing, I'd make this concession to her. Love is a two-way street, after all, even familial love.

She was right in that Hollister would make a good starting point. He knew the DJ more than I did; it tied directly into his day job as a counselor for the Department of Orientation.

When I first arrived in this city, it was the Department of Orientation which found me a foster family. There was a paperwork mix-up—the Wei family was ready to send me back if not for the sudden attachment Marcy had developed for me. From what Hollister had been telling me, mix-ups like that were quite common. Half the Department coasted a wave of apathy from paycheck to paycheck, and little could be done by those who truly cared for the well-being of the innocents who found themselves here against their will.

During daylight hours, when he wasn't jockeying favors and granting wishes for the subculture of the city, Hollister worked a Department job at one of the many orientation seminars the city ran. This week he was stationed in an out-of-place looking motel, adjoining a Burger Buffet Bonanza™. He couldn't take time off the job to meet with us—he'd already taken a lot of time off and bent the rules a tad trying to find me a job. He was playing the exemplary employee to make up for it. But he promised he could sneak away for a time, if we'd meet him at the restaurant.

He offered to buy us dinner. I declined, in part because I didn't want to encourage his extreme selflessness, and in part because the "food" was quite abhorrent. I'm not a vegan, but I disapprove of unnecessary cruelty to living things, and eating these alleged burgers would've counted as cruelty to the human body.

Marcy, of course, took him up on the offer and had a pile of grease in the shape of a triple decker. It sat in its wrapper for now; we had only a few minutes to converse, and she needed her hands and mouth free.

"Seriously?" was Hollister's initial reaction.

"Seriously," Marcy repeated, in word and sign (for my benefit).

"The Department of Safety's already looking into that mess. What could you two possibly find out that they wouldn't have found out already?" he asked. "I know they get a bad rap for being too slow—hell, all the Departments get slammed in the media for being ineffective. But speaking as a city representative myself, I think you two really need to leave this in the hands of the professionals..."

"If there's nothing to find, what's the harm in looking?" Marcy asked. "Come on, Hollister. It's worth a try."

"Even if you find something, what makes you think it'll be a magic bullet that solves your job market problems? It'd have to be some amazing revelation, like being best buddies with the Cult of Bedlam, or something. Even then, there's so many ways they could spin it which wouldn't get you what you want. We're talking a long shot of a Hail Mary of a desperation gambit. I don't get it."

"Because if we don't try, your darling Vivi's going to have to—"

I grasped her wrist in mid-sign. It was enough to get her to stop talking, as well.

Last thing I needed was to tell Hollister about my pending job opportunity. He'd already bent over backwards trying to help me; if Marcy cast me as a poor, desperate girl forced to take her clothes off for money, Hollister would go ballistic. He'd find out eventually, but I'd rather he find out after the fact. It was, after all, my own decision to make and no one else's. No need to complicate things.

[Was he having any issues before that night?] I asked, while Marcy translated my signs aloud. Better that than the phone app, for a quick discussion. [Showing any signs? Did he talk about his cubism? If cubism is brought on by exposure, surely he'd have said what he was exposed to. If it was depression, there would've been signs.]

"But that's the thing, he was doing pretty well," Hollister explained. "Not at first, I mean. I got assigned his case because he was having the usual culture shock new imports get. When I first met him at the craphole the Department had found for him to live in, he was having trouble sleeping. I was going to get him a shrink, but on my next visit... he was smiling and happy. Said he'd found a way to sleep at nights and felt a lot better."

Strange. [He didn't look very well rested the night he died,] I pointed out.

"Maybe he was lying to me, I don't know. Even back then I thought he still looked tired, but... he WAS lively and active, so... I didn't worry. That night was the worst I'd ever seen him. Even then, he was eager to hit the stage and move forward with his life. No hopeless bleak despair. A bit tired, but hell, I can miss sleep and get cranky without turning into a Picasso."

[So if his mood was that high, there had to be some external factor. Maybe we should look into the apartment he was assigned to,] I suggested.

"No way. It's been quarantined by the Dee-oh-Ess. Yellow-black. Could be a cubist paradise, for all I know; I haven't gone back since."

That wouldn't stop Marcy, of course. Normally it'd stop me cold. But something was tugging at me, here...

I'd told myself this was a fool's errand, a way of placating my sister. But the idea that someone in good spirits who was looking forward to his future could turn into a Picasso was... a bit terrifying. Everybody knew cubism led to despair, or despair led to cubism. If you cut out the despair, even cut out the cubism, if anybody could go Picasso at the drop of a hat, what did that mean for people like me...?

All my life I've tried to be a bright soul, working to brighten the souls of others. Parties are a means to that end. That was one reason I agreed to Hollister's suggestion of hiring the DJ in the first place, I wanted to give a fellow refugee from Earth the helping hand that Marcy once gave me. By lifting each other up, this city no longer has to be a place of fear.

Perhaps this was worth looking into. Not that I expected it to lead me back to my comfortable little world as Lord of the Dance—that was unrealistic. But personally, I wanted to know more. I wanted to know why.

[I'd like to visit his apartment, all the same,] I said (ignoring the mild surprise from my sibling interpreter). [I promise we'll play it safe, Hollister. No major risks.]

"I'd feel better if I could go with you," he grumbled. "I'm stuck doing ridiculously long shifts and after-hour client visits lately, to keep my boss happy. ...I'll get you his address. Be careful out there, Vivi. —and you too, Marcy."

Which earned him a semi-playful punch to the arm from my sister, which made me giggle ever so slightly. Even in dark times, there could be some light, I'd always felt.

Space in the City of Angles wasn't exactly at a premium. New buildings arrived all the time—far too many to be filled up with people. The old Earth saying "buy land, because God's not making any more of it" was completely irrelevant here.

So, how do you price real estate when real estate was pouring out of a faucet? Location. Quality. Purpose. True, "Location" was fluid as new neighbors squeezed through the cracks, but some areas were quite stable. For instance, the Zig-Zag... used to be situated smack dab in the central area of the city, its most stable and reliable thoroughfare. That made it expensive as hell— but Gee Bee was old money, thanks to his days in the music industry and his connections. He could afford to buy out the equivalent of Park Place and Boardwalk.

And then you had this place, which was somewhere between Baltic and Mediterranean Avenue. The cheapest spots on the board, the low-hanging fruit you scooped up but never really did much with. Terrible location, poor quality, unsuitable for any purpose.

From what Hollister had explained to me, unless a newcomer to the city was determined to be high value (as assessed by the Department of Resources) they were typically sent to the lowest-rent sections of the city. Pushed out to the fringes, crumbling away, sometimes collapsing into cubism. The idealistic government mandate from the earliest days of the City of Angles dictated newcomers had to be provided for with homes and jobs... but nobody said those homes and jobs had to be worth having.

It was meant to be a springboard—get you on your feet, get some local currency, then get out. When Marcy and I finally reached the front stoop of the apartment building, a stoop with a door almost falling from its hinges, the names places next to each door buzzer were loosely slotted bits of cardboard. Nobody expected them to stay around. Either they'd succeed and move on... or vanish into the night.

I scanned the current roster of the Plaza Arms (oddly named, given there was no plaza around). Y. IVES, K. JONES, D. SMITH, A. GHANEM... and S. MOORE. The surname of our ill-fated DJ friend.

Unlike Marcy, I rarely traveled this deep into the worst parts of the city. I wasn't quite sure about the protocol for approaching places like this. I vaguely remembered from television that you pushed the button for the person you wanted to visit, then waited for them to say something on the intercom which somehow unlocks the door, but that wouldn't exactly work in my case...

Marcy leaned around me and mashed all the buttons randomly. Presumably that worked, because we were in seconds later.

She moved with surefootedness. This was her turf; she routinely journeyed around and through and over outer city buildings, away from the safety and businesslike attitude of the inner city. I let Marcy take point on this one, following rather than being followed.

Unlike our rather nice little apartment complex—complete with a food co-op on the ground floor, a common area where the buskers and hipsters hung out, and other niceties like good wallpaper and no rats—this was indeed a "craphole." It must've been built decades ago, and little renovation or restoration had been done since. So many lights were out that it was practically midnight in its stairwells and hallways, despite being a good hour or so before the autumnal sun would set. No doors were open; no friendly neighbors, unlike the apartment we'd rented with parental seed money. We saw nobody at all. I suspect it would've been deathly quiet to match.

At last... we came to the forbidden door. Lined in yellow-black tape, a well-known sign that you proceeded forward on your own terms and the Department of Safety would not be held responsible for any injury or cubism sustained. I suppose we were lucky it wasn't red-black and completely forbidden; I wasn't looking to break the law TOO much today.

This was quite normal, from what little I knew about safety procedures. A Picasso's home would be sealed off until such time as it was determined not to be a factor in their cubism. Usually, that was a rapid turnover—particularly if the owner had a rather lovely home which the Department of Resources could annex and resell—but nobody was in any rush to repurpose this particular domicile.

Tentatively, I grasped the knob. Which didn't budge. Locked. Obviously, they wanted to discourage people from wandering in, even if it was only a yellow-black.

Apparently that was not stopping my sister. She nudged me, to make way... and then produced what I can only assume were lockpicking tools from somewhere on her person. I don't know why I was shocked; as a graffiti writer she had to get to places she wasn't supposed to be. I only hoped her nightly outings wouldn't one day land her in jail...

I was expecting the place to be a wreck. Not in terms of the quality of the structure, but in terms of all the DJ's personal belongings being overturned and emptied. That's what the police did, after all—they boxed and bagged the evidence, then took it with them. This was indirectly a crime scene of a multiple manslaughter incident; Seth Dougal said there'd be an extensive investigation, which would've taken them through here. There was no need for the Department of Safety to be tidy. We'd be lucky if anything was left other than empty drawers and closets...

When Marcy flipped the light switch, however, I saw a perfectly ordinary low income bachelor pad. Dusty and musty, with the smell of food going bad, but... otherwise completely intact.

Drawers and closets closed, and likely full. No footprints in the dust on the wooden floors. No sign anyone had disturbed this place since that night. Unless the Department of Safety were fastidiously tidy and carried a can of dust for sprinkling behind them as they left, which would've been nonsensical... they'd never been here.

Marcy waltzed right in, taking a quick survey of the room. She'd come to the same conclusion.

[What the hell is this?] she asked, facing me. [Did they just seal the place up and never come back?]

[Maybe they were worried the room was dangerous?] I suggested. [They did tape it up, they had to have done SOME study of the place...]

[People are living on this floor. If the building was going cubist, they would've evacuated. I wouldn't put it past the D-O-S not to be lazy bastards, though,] she grumbled through brisk hand gestures. [At least this makes our job easier. We can search the apartment ourselves—and if nothing else, we can call the D-O-S out on not moving forward with that investigation Dougal promised us. Let's look around.]

There wasn't much to look around at.

Marcy gravitated to a laptop that had been left slightly skew on his desk. I busied myself with closets, drawers, and cabinets... finding things you'd expect to find. The three main essentials in life: food, clothes, medicine.

Food, going bad. Lots of boxed breakfast cereal, plenty of milk that smelled just LOVELY when I dared to open the fridge.

Clothes. Charity hand-me-downs and some official Department of Orientation jumpers, default clothes given to all newcomers. He'd taken the time to dye some of it black, in keeping with his overall style.

Medicine. Some melatonin bottles I recognized from a popular herbalist's store, probably because of his initial sleep problems. Toothpaste, shaving lotion, mouthwash... and a few unlabelled and empty glass bottles, sitting in the waste basket. Maid hadn't come through yet, obviously. I'd have assumed they were originally for cologne if not for the caps with embedded eyedroppers. Maybe eye rinse? Contact lens solution?

My investigation into the mundane details of a DJ's life was interrupted by a flicker in the bathroom mirror. Marcy, trying to get my attention.

Out in the main room, she'd powered up his laptop, hooked to an AC adapter. The battery had probably run down completely in the time since he was last here, after all.

[I was thinking of looking for a diary, but this is the 21st century and people don't have diaries anymore,] she explained. [But I did some research on this guy, and on Earth, he was well known for running his entire life from a laptop computer. So I figured... good place to start looking. Read this.]

She keyed open a file. Most of it was notes on music sketches, audio files, dates and locations for possible club gigs. Contact information for Hollister and others in the Department of Orientation. He was getting his life sorted out, using this document as a scratch pad for his thoughts and things he might need to remember.

Can't sleep. Can't keep from thinking about that other me back on Earth, how easy he's got it. All his friends, everything he has, all of it right there and he doesn't even know I'm here with nothing. I'm freaking out about what's gonna happen to me, about the rumors I heard from others in Orientation about how goddamn dangerous this place is.

I want to move forward like the Orientation counselors say but I can't keep my mind from racing. Tried Melatonin at suggestion of someone in my seminar suggested, didn't help. Orientation guys can't send anybody yet, but they promise someone's coming to help. I'll keep asking around meanwhile.

Not sure about the new songs, I just can't make them gel, I can't make anything work. Tried channeling my nightmares into my music but that's not helping any...

Marcy tapped the touchpad of the laptop, opening the next file. scratch02.txt was a mess, a pile of random notes, nothing really coherent... same with the third file. But the next one had promise.

scratch04.txt

First good night's sleep since arriving, thanks to the N.F. dose. No dreams at all, good or bad. Still feel a little run down but relieved that I could finally catch some z's. Montgomery promised results and he delivered; this is just what I need to help me de-focus from my problems and re-focus myself on my work.

403-2998 montgomery

I think I'm going to get some remixes going -- it's a good foot in the door, playing something familiar but also unique to the City of Angles. Music that other me never would have made. I can make a name for myself here, a new name, maybe.

scratch05.txt

Met Hollister Avenue today. Apparently Montgomery wasn't from the Department of Orientation. I'd assumed he was the guy they were sending since he just showed up with the drugs I needed, but I guess one of the feelers I'd put out myself hit pay dirt. Montgomery never actually claimed to be from Orientation, I guess.

Told Hollister I was sleeping again and would be ready for a gig soon. He seemed surprised. I probably looked a little tired, but I feel awake and in tune with this weird new city. No dreams. No worries. All that stuff vanishes into the dark when I go to bed and gets neatly tucked away, leaving the rest of me to face the day. I wonder if Hollister can get me a gig? I'd love to share this with the world.

scratch08.txt

I'm so tired lately. It's weird, I'm tired, but I'm NOT tired. I get eight hours a night, sometimes more. Montgomery says this just means the N.F. is doing its job, keeping me level. I'm up to 15 drops. A little exhaustion's to be expected. He suggested I take more tonight. I can't sleep without it, so whatev. I've got too much ahead of me to worry about this. New mixes are going great; Hollister found me a gig, too. Get the feeling he's shaking someone's hand while he shakes mine, but that's the music industry for you.

Montgomery wants me to rinse out the bottles and toss them in the trash as I finish them. Less to trace back to him, I guess. Whatev. I'm not gonna stab the hand of my pusher when he's the only one keeping me going.

scratch09.txt

Sleeping so much. Sleeping during the day. Haven't had a single dream. I used to have lots of dreams, all sorts, but now nada. Feels distant, like some part of me's buried away. Can't explain this. Taking more N.F. than usual, even though I'm getting plenty of sleep, don't know why. I'm thinking that pusher gave me something that's gonna screw me over in the end but I can feel her there behind my eyes and she's smiling. Typing on keys I can only see in the mirror now, I don't recognize these letters.

Called Montgomery, told him about the gig tonight. He knew already. He said the time's right for me and the others and to drink the entire final bottle. I did it. I'm not srue why i think i need a nap before the show. i wantot share this witheveryone the laughter so friendly I'm remindd of that video of mine and ishouldbe scared of the dark inside the girl because it will

...which is where the document ended, when the editor autosaved it.

Simultaneously, I felt relief and horror. Selfish and selfless. Selfish relief that there was certainly a direct cause of the DJ's cubism—some drug he was taking, which put him in an unstable frame of mind, ripe for becoming a Picasso. Selfless horror, that this man who just wanted to get on with his life... someone who was excited for the future, who was making plans... fell completely to pieces. He wasn't despairing, not exactly. He was just... falling apart.

I showed Marcy my findings, which linked up to her own. Four small empty bottles, with eyedropper caps. The drug, the N.F., whatever that stood for.

[We have what we need, right?] I signed. [We have testimonial from his laptop which explains what happened, and we even have the drug bottles which somehow caused the cubism. It's a direct link! The Department of Safety can use this to close the case and lift the public safety warning!]

But Marcy didn't look thrilled at this development. If anything, her suspicion had deepened. She shook her head, while replying.

[I don't think so. The Department of Safety never followed this lead even though it was the most obvious thing to do. They never searched his apartment or checked his computer. They could've found all this within hours but instead, they sealed the place up and left. At best, they're amazingly lazy. At worst... I think they deliberately overlooked this.]

[That's crazy,] I disagreed, shaking my head in turn. [They protect the city. Why would they ignore this? If someone's making drugs that turn people into Picassos, that's a huge safety problem!]

[You're assuming that they're trying to solve safety problems,] she replied. [Vivi, you're not out on the streets in the crappy parts of town. I am. There's huge, obvious problems out there the Department of Safety does nothing about. They put up their striped tape and call it a day, while salvager gangs loot new buildings, or people slowly lose their minds in homes that are twisting themselves inside and out... they keep people safe not by keeping them *safe*, but by keeping them *afraid*. Folks on the street *know* this, Vivi.]

[Come on, that's just silly conspiracy talk! I hardly think that level of willful negligence would go unnoticed or unreported. The news loves a good scandal, right?]

[Cable news loves scary stories even more. Scary stories encourage people to stay indoors, to stay afraid, and to watch more scary stories and drive the ratings upward. For instance, taking an incident at nightclubs and using it to effectively kill off all public gatherings. Who needs a curfew when you can spook them into staying home? C'mon! It's not conspiracy, this is just how things *work*. Why do you think I'm out there every night, writing my words on the walls, trying to wake people up? No. They're not here to help us. And they either ignored this, or knowingly swept it under the rug.]

Two words floated to memory: Malice and Incompetence.

It was something Fi once said at our semi-private Zig-Zag booth. My friends and I were relaxing after my bartending shift some months ago, and the conversation subject turned to politics.

Amanda was having some trouble with the Department of Resources, which thought it still owned her apartment and was trying to lease it out to someone else despite her four-year residency. Joey and Zeke argued (in their cute little way) opposite points; Joey thought the government was trying to double down intentionally, Zeke felt it must've been a paperwork misfile...

Fi, the poet of the group, rarely had anything to add on any topic. She was content to sit there and smoke and soak in our discussions, 99% of the time. When she did speak, she used an economy of words.

To wit, she said "Malice or incompetence? Same results."

Whether the Department of Safety maliciously schemed to keep everybody safe by scaring them into being risk-averse or whether they were simply making huge mistakes of oversight, the end was the same—my scene was suffering. It didn't really matter if Marcy was right or wrong, here. The truth hadn't come out. The truth *needed* to come out.

[Putting that aside for the moment,] I suggested, despite Marcy clearly wanting to continue at length, [We need to gather the evidence we came for. Whether we go to the cops or the media or the mayor or whoever, we have to prove what happened here. We have the laptop, but all the drug bottles are empty.]

[And washed,] she added. [Probably because the pusher didn't want anything to trace back to him. The laptop's not going to be enough; we're too biased to be trusted and electronic documents can be faked with ease. We'll also need something physical. If we had some of that drug they could run tests and things on it...]

After a moment's thought... Marcy flipped back a few windows to document four. Highlighting the phone number.

[First one's always free,] she suggested.

This was quite insane, of course. And completely against the promise I made to Hollister. Play it safe, no major risks. Instead, I was sitting in a public park, waiting to meet with the drug pusher who indirectly destroyed my life and murdered Gee Bee...

The plan was Marcy's. She knew the ins and outs of the drug scene, even if she wasn't a user; she knew enough people who were, since she tended to coast around the fringes of society in order to perform her art. Even if our days began and ended in unison, the evenings were spent in very different social circles, after all.

I sent text messages to this "Montgomery" person, using the phone number left behind in the ill-fated DJ's notes...

Vividly: You don't know me but we have a mutual friend, Mr. Moore. I was the director of the club he performed at the night of his death, and he told me about the great medicine you gave him. Ever since his death I've been having nightmares and insomnia. I can't pay much since my place of work was shut down but I'd really like to talk, maybe get some of this N.F. stuff. Please? I'm desperate. I'm not a cop. Help me, please.

There was just enough truth mixed in with the lies to bait the hook. I was using my real identity; this person, whoever he was, could verify who I was. This was a bet on the Malice and Incompetency issue; if his drug maliciously caused cubism and he targeting the night life scene for some crazy reason, he'd have found a prime target in me. If it was incompetence, that he was networking through the scene but unaware his drug caused cubism, I was still making my case appealing.

Later that evening, I got my reply.

(unlisted): Hello. I'm sorry to hear of our mutual friend's passing. I think I can help you. Please meet me at Triple Fountain Park, at the benches near the third fountain, tomorrow at 11am. If this time doesn't work for you let me know. Come alone.

Which meant the next day I was sitting by my lonesome in the middle of one of Triple Fountain Park, one of the less impressive parks the city had to offer, waiting for my new best friend the illegal drug dealer.

The park was a curious place indeed. Supposedly it was originally known as Fountain Park, and was popular with the local families... but then the park triplicated itself overnight, three side by side parks each with their own copies of the original fountain and surrounding sidewalks. That made the place weird enough that the kids stopped coming, kept home by their frightened parents.

According to Marcy, the unwashed masses moved in soon after... fringe people, those who fell between the cracks or Earth imports that couldn't adjust. The only ones who hung out here now were nodding off on substances, drinking from brown paper bags, and/or living in makeshift cardboard empires. The Department of Safety sometimes cleared the park, but it didn't last. These people had nowhere else to go, through misdeed or misfortune.

These parts of the city were alien to me. My sister walked through them constantly... maybe that's why she maintained a foul disposition so often. I'd be disheartened too to know how much people were suffering, scraping by in poverty and homelessness, in the places nobody else wants to go. As much as I wished I could do something for them, as much as my heart sang out sadly as I carefully stepped around cardboard homes... I had to maintain my cover. I had to focus on the task at hand.

Not that I was suited to the task at hand. I stuck out badly here. I'd worn my baggiest, least interesting clothes for this meeting—finding something unfashionable and completely unsexy in my wardrobe was harder than I thought it'd be. Even doing my best to blend in, I drew attention immediately on arrival. Maybe orange wasn't such a good color choice.

For instance, a man in a long and shabby winter coat, going bald but with a scraggly black beard, had... *watched* me on my way towards the bench. He didn't make a move, didn't threaten me, but his gaze stayed fixed on me the whole way there. Something in his eyes scared me, to be honest. His body language was relaxed, collapsed in on itself, but those eyes looked *through* me...

Terrible idea. This was a terrible idea. Even if Marcy was with me, ghosting along ahead me, wearing similarly ratty coats (acquired from her normal wardrobe) and looking like she fit in perfectly. She assured me I was not going to be assaulted, that people here minded their own business. She promised to lurk in the foreground—within my line of sight, but far away enough no one would think we're together—ready to spring into action if anything went wrong. Although if anything went wrong neither of us were exactly masters of self-defense. A lousy plan. Insane. Inadvisable at best.

And yet, here I was.

On some level beyond my fear, I didn't care about the danger. This was something I simply had to do—I wanted to look into Montgomery's eyes. I wanted to see what sort of man would, by design or otherwise, destroy my entire world. I'd say what he wanted to hear, I'd get some of his snake oil, and then we'd make sure he was brought to justice.

When eleven in the morning rolled around, I got my answer.

I could see him coming from the edge of the park. The bench he'd selected for our chat was a fair distance from the entrance; clear lines of sight, with plenty of people able to observe. It didn't seem appropriate for a shady drug deal—or maybe that was the idea, that we'd both feel exposed, so neither of us would try anything funny...?

If I didn't fit in with the homeless and the addicted, he absolutely did not fit in. He reminded me a bit of Seth Dougal... a bright white suit, inappropriate for a park full of scrub grass and dirt and trash. It wasn't quite as sharp of a suit, being a cut which didn't suit his gaunt frame, with the cheap fabrics and awkward lines that pegged it as a cheap imitation. I knew my fashions, after all. This man was aiming for the same sort of class Mr. Dougal carried himself with, and coming up far short.

As he drew closer, I could see other attributes which stuck out oddly. Two-day stubble; not an intentional effort to grow a beard, just a overall lack of effort at personal grooming. His hair was finger-combed and shaggy, originally short and stylish but left like an unmowed lawn for some time. He'd given up on the niceties.

Despite looking like life had been grinding him down... he was smiling, on approach. Took a seat on the edge of the fountain, opposite my bench—a comfortable distance away, not invading my personal space, but close enough for an intimate conversation all the same.

Reading lips through beard stubble could be tricky, but fortunately he wasn't THAT overgrown.

"Vivi, is it?" he asked. "I'm Doctor Montgomery. I'm pleased to meet you and again, I offer my condolences. I've gotten to know quite a few people in your scene. The passing of Gee Bee was the passing of a legend."

I wanted to thank him (whether he was sincere or not) but already had a statement prepared on my synthesized voice app.

I apologize for having to talk to you this way, my phone read aloud. *I'm deaf and mute. I can read your lips and if you allow me a moment to compose replies on my phone, it can read my words to you. Thank you for coming to meet with me, Mr. Montgomery.*

Oddly, this didn't surprise him at all. Usually people react with confusion when my phone does the talking for me. He didn't even need a second to think about it.

"I understand. So. How well did you know Mr. Moore?" he asked, folding his hands in his lap, rocking on the edge of the fountain. "It's so unfortunate when this city takes its most promising new arrivals..."

Not very well. I'd just met him the night he passed. We talked a bit before the show, I responded, mixing in a little lie, to tie myself better to this man's former client... or former patient, perhaps. *He was excited about performing. I was told he'd been having trouble sleeping, but he said he was feeling fine, thanks to you. I was curious about the treatment, so he gave me your phone number shortly before hitting the stage.*

...it took some time to type all of that into my phone, even with the extensive practice I've had with a virtual keyboard. Montgomery sat patiently through it all.

(I could see Marcy in the distance beyond the fountain, behind him... she was keeping half an eye on us, observing. Making sure I was safe and that the plan was unfolding according to, well, plan. Thankfully Montgomery hadn't noticed her yet.)

"I'd asked him not to give anyone my number, actually," Montgomery pointed out. "I suppose he was a bit excitable that night, not thinking clearly. But, no real harm done. After all, now it led me to you. And I'd like to help you, Miss Vivi."

A stroke of good luck, there—my mind was briefly racing to craft a lie which would explain the sharing of a forbidden number. He'd supplied a reason for me less than a moment later.

I loaded another pre-made message, snapping off a fast reply.

I can't sleep. I'm barely eating. I just see that poor Picasso, and Gee Bee's face, and worse. The few times I've been able to sleep I've had nightmare after nightmare. I need to find a job again, I need to get my life on track, but I can't do that if I can't rest. Please, can you help me?

"As I've said, yes, I can help you," he repeated. One disadvantage to pre-written messages. "I've helped a number of people in your... what do your friends call it? The 'scene'? So many problems, so many anxieties and fears. They get in the way of the pursuit of happiness that embodies your scene. What if I said I could take all those fears, all the nightmares, and bottle them up so that they never bother you again?"

I'd say I'm interested, but I've got some worries. How illegal is this? I'm not sure I want to get in trouble with the law, I replied. This was Marcy's suggestion; show some reluctance, to keep things realistic. And look like more of an innocent dupe.

"No, not at all!" Doctor Montgomery insisted. "It's backed by a small investment firm, one looking into alternative treatments for the ailments that run so common in this city. I'm not pushing drugs, Vivi. I'm signing up test subjects for a very controlled and very safe trial run. We're following all Department of Safety procedures, and plan to publish our findings in major scientific journals at the end of the trial. So not only can I help you with your insomnia and anxiety... but you'll be helping others, in turn."

...I found myself smiling, despite my suspicions. He was lying, of course. Very likely lying. But it was nice to think about, that someone was seriously considering the issue of the city's emotional health. I used the dream that this could be true to power my reaction, even if my suspicions ran deep as the ocean.

All my life, I've tried to help others find happiness. Okay. I'd like to participate, I replied. *What do I do? Do you have a sample with you that I can take home?*

This was the critical moment. If he gave me the drug, we could take that to... someone. Maybe Hollister would know a reliable journalist, someone who would hear us out, if Marcy didn't trust the Department of Safety.

Montgomery scratched at his two-day stubble, thinking. A hand went to his pocket... something in there. The drug? Did he bring it with him? The DJ's files said he showed up with the little glass bottles, ready to administer immediately...

"I'll put your name forward as a possible candidate, and ask my supervisor today for his approval," he suggested, after taking his hand out of his pocket. "Let's keep this above board, shall we? There's paperwork and processing and other things to take care of, first. We'll get back to you by text message within a week or two."

Fast. Had to type fast. Had to be believable; play the desperation angle...

Doctor, please, I'm suffering. I don't know if I can hold on another week or two. Is there anything you can give me now? Anything at all?

...and he stepped away from the fountain, to grasp my hands.

It was an attempted show of compassion. A bedside manner technique, to reassure the patient, to show that the doctor cares. Except his hands, they were... jittery. They didn't look jittery, but I've held many a hand, and I know a jitter when I feel one. They almost vibrated with tension he wasn't allowing me to see otherwise...

"I understand your plight. And I wish I could help," he said. "But I'm afraid there's nothing I can do today. I need to be going now. I look forward to possibly working with you in the future, Vivi. Be well."

And then he slipped away. Hands in pockets, turning, walking off.

I tried rapidly typing a response, trying to get his attention with it. I hit the TALK button, held my phone aloft... but either he didn't hear, or he didn't care. Doctor Montgomery didn't turn around.

Quickly, my eyes scanned the end of the park. They locked onto Marcy, in the distance—she'd been sneaking looks through a pair of binoculars now, to check my progress. That meant she knew something was wrong, well before he'd walked away.

[He didn't give me anything!] I signed to her, across the way. [He's leaving!]

I expected her to run back to me, to join up so we could discuss what to do next. Maybe wait it out, try to keep the bait on the hook, see if he took it eventually... a week or two meant I'd need to look at that job opportunity in the meanwhile, but we could still figure out—

Marcy was indeed running. Away from me, and out of the park.

Seconds later and my phone vibrated, with an incoming message.

Ghostwriter: following him on foot gonna see where he goes will report back

My jaw nearly hit the screen. I furiously tapped a reply.

Vividly: NO NO NO come back this is too dangerous we can just wait for him to get back to us!

Ghostwriter: might not get another chance don't worry I know this city this is my city I won't be seen will text you the address when he gets there love you

Insane. Inadvisable. What the hell were we thinking? This was so crazy...

One thing was certain—I wasn't going to wait around in Triple Fountain Park for her reply. I picked myself up and got out as quickly as I could... using the opposite exit from the creepy man in the long coat. Who was, no doubt, still watching me.

Sitting in a nearby coffee house, trying not to draw attention, slowly nursing the same cup which was quickly growing cold. Eyes locked on my phone. Waiting for it to light up with a message from Ghostwriter...

I debated contacting Hollister.

But what good would that do? He'd likely charge to my side, even if it meant ditching his job to do so, ruining his career. And what would he do, once he was at my side? Reassure me? He couldn't do anything more than I could do, which was sit around waiting for Marcy to respond.

...assuming she DID respond. Assuming she wasn't caught. Assuming nothing went wrong, assuming I ever saw her again...

Thankfully, some time after sitting down and as the sun was finally setting... I got the message I was waiting for.

Ghostwriter: Mission accomplished yo. He went to a red-black quarantined warehouse in an unpopulated district on the fringe. No way this doc is legit. I found the perfect spy perch in an office block opposite, perfect view right into his office with no way he can know we're here. Come join me. Grab a taxi, tell them to drop you off at the corner of 67th Ave and 67th Ave. I'll meet you down there.

I read it twice, before replying.

Vividly: Come home NOW. This is getting too dangerous. If he's breaking red-black we can just tell the Department of Safety.

Ghostwriter: Unless they know already. Come on, we can lip read him from this angle through my binocs. It's far away and we'll be safe. See you when you get here.

And nothing more.

Hopping a taxi was easy; convincing them to go out to 67th and 67th was another matter. If you hadn't fallen through the cracks of society, you had no reason to go that close to the defined edges of the city. So, I gave the driver my best kicked-puppy eyes, and nearly all the money I had on me. That did the job.

As promised, Marcy was curbside and ready to greet me. She did so with a tight hug, with an [I Love You] sign. Followed shortly with [Gotta see this!].

I didn't have time to chat—she grabbed my wrist, dragging me inside and up through the bowels of the crumbling old office building. We took the stairs rather than risk the elevator; even with the power on, no sense in trusting an elevator to work properly. (Any new buildings always arrived connected up to water and power, after all. Even if nobody knew quite where the water or power CAME from. The Department of Resources once tried to trace the pipes and wires, only to end up looping back around to where they started.)

She'd found an ideal little sniper nest. With the lights off in the room and the blinds turned just so, anybody who looked up here wouldn't see anything of interest. Eager to demonstrate how awesome her find was, she passed me her binoculars... gesturing to the window.

As much as I wanted to get out of here... there was no sense in not looking, *not* now that we'd come this far. It was all happening so fast, one thing after another, definitely faster than I would have liked. But there was this sense that opportunity was slipping away, and if I didn't take a chance I might lose out on... I don't know. Lose out on knowing the truth. So, yes, I looked. I looked knowing full well the answers may not be pleasant.

The office block overlooked a large industrial warehouse, with red-black striped tape over every door and window. Despite having little to no population out here—at least no registered population—the Department of Safety went out of their way to seal off that building from prying eyes. The lights were on inside, true, but that didn't mean much of anything...

Figures moving past the windows, that certainly meant something.

Marcy signaled for my attention with a tap on the shoulder, and signed [Second floor third window from back and check out who's there with him,] nice and rapid. So, I refocused through the binoculars, to see...

...Doctor Montgomery, sitting at a desk and talking to someone. Interesting.

From the narrow view into his world, I could make out some details. A whiteboard with scribbles and chemical equations. A desk, covered in papers. Filing cabinets. Crumbling walls with peeling paint... he wasn't particularly interested in renovating or keeping the place viable long-term, I decided. Just getting work done.

The strangest part was the person he was talking to. Someone in a white suit, similar to his own. A band of white hair, balding on top. Dark skin...

Marcy's binoculars rattled a little as my grip tightened. The question of Malice vs. Incompetence had been answered. Because even if I couldn't see the face of the man, I knew who it was. I saw that same back walking away from me with a confident stride, the day he destroyed my entire world.

Seth Dougal, director of the Department of Safety.

What little doubt could possibly remain was crushed completely when I shifted my focus, to try and read Montgomery's lips.

"We're still on ?crack?, Mr. Dougal," he said.

(I think. At this distance, through a trick of lenses, lip reading was quite difficult and I had to make some guesses. "Track," maybe? But "Dougal" was spoken clear enough.)

Seth, whose back was turned to me, had a rather long reply. A tiny, tiny shake to his head suggested he disagreed... but beyond that, I couldn't tell what he was describing.

"It won't be a problem," Montgomery insisted. "I had to ?strike? the Nightmare Fuel dose to trigger their ?expectations?, but that won't be needed when her ?affluence? is ?implied?. You can ?commute? without issues."

More words I couldn't read from Mr. Dougal. So I tried to read his body language... and failed. He had the same relaxed composure he had the night we met. If he was upset or angry or happy or disappointed, I'd have no way of knowing.

"Their ?laws? won't impact matters. Between the ?reply? I've stockpiled here and at the ?mother? ?hostilities?, there's more than enough. Granted, I wish I had more time to research and ?define?..."

Finally, more clear body language. Suspicion, I'd hazard. I'd seen the head-tilt Dougal's took on when Marcy was being snarky about something. Dougal must've accused Montgomery of something, because immediately Montgomery grew defensive. A shift to the shoulders, drawing in. Narrowing eyes.

(I reminded myself to thank Marcy later for buying these ridiculously expensive binoculars. At the time I thought they were a needless expense just to find good graffiti spots, but they paid for themselves twice over today.)

"Your men are responsible for those ?seeks?. They were too... unstable. Conscripts and ?admin?. If I had more true believers this would be far quieter. But I've taken care of my own problems, and ?discontinue? to do so. You don't have to concern yourself with me."

Either that placated Dougal's worries, or he was just tired of talking about it. His hand adjusted his tie, it seemed, as he changed topics. A better topic in Montgomery's view, as he nodded along repeatedly... explanations or instructions for what to do next, maybe?

His final statement rang true across his lips, although I almost wished I'd misread it.

"For the coming of Bedlam and the glorious chaos."

With their conversation complete, Seth Dougal walked past Montgomery's desk and straight into a wall.

The wall rippled briefly, peeling wallpaper enveloping him like he'd walked into a freestanding pool. One moment later and the wall was perfectly solid again. Nobody would ever know it was an entrance to the Sideways.

I couldn't take my eyes off Doctor Montgomery, even as he turned his back to me, producing a cellphone to have a chat. Likely because I was still having trouble believing what I'd just seen.

I knew what the Cult of Bedlam was, sort of. Everybody knew some crazy homeless guys had formed the cult back in the eighties. In their heyday they were kidnapping people and sacrificing them to their so-called cubist goddess, Bedlam... but the cult didn't last very long. The Department of Safety, after careful investigation, found their gathering place. There was a huge gunfight. All the cultists died. Presumably.

Except they still existed. And Seth Dougal, the man in charge of keeping the city safe from Bedlam, was running the show. Working with drug slinging would-be doctors. *Causing* Picassos to exist somehow, destroying the social side of the city, pumping the populace with terror...

None of it made sense. But what made sense about a cult that believed Picassos were a good thing to be?

I had no idea what to do with any of these revelations. We obviously couldn't tell our tale to the police; they worked for the Department of Safety. We could try telling the media, but again, what proof did we have? Testimonial? "Oh, I read their lips from a city block away, and we found some computer files." Good for scandal rags to run wild with, but bad for actually making our case and being heard...

A flicker in the binoculars caught my attention. I'd forgotten I was still holding them up to my eyes, honestly.

Doctor Montgomery had finished his phone call, and turned back around to face the window.

To face me. To look directly at me, upwards towards the distant office block.

"I take care of my own problems," he mouthed.

Disoriented, pulling my eyes away from the focusing lenses and back to reality. Turning to warn my sister, but too late.

The man was already in the doorframe, blocking our exit. The same man in the shabby winter coat and scraggly beard, the one whose gaze had fixated on me in Triple Fountain Park. Except this time, he was wearing a gas mask.

I didn't have time to wonder why, as I found my legs not working anymore and the floor rushing up to meet me.

The last things I saw before I blacked out:

The homeless man, flickering and twitching, cubism passing over his surface like a ripple over a pond.

My sister's hand, reaching out to me, trying to reach me... before she passed out as well.

Darkness. Nothingness. Empty. Void.

I'm a very vivid dreamer. Nestled in comfortably at my sister's side, I sleep each night away in peace, across fantastic landscapes of color and light. I wander in and out of my best memories. I feel at peace in that sacred place, my home, my bed. I awake refreshed and ready to face another day.

Void. Nothingness. Empty. Darkness.

The few times I've had nightmares, I need only wake myself and feel the light snoring of my sister to know that everything is in fact all right with the universe. Fears are a matter of perception—they can be conquered by centering one's self. After such wakings, I return to sleep with ease.

Nothing. Nothing at all. Drained away. Can't reach me, she's reaching, but she can't reach me.

Of course, I don't always soak in pleasant dreams or brief nightmares. I have had nights with no dreams I could remember, but I'd like to think I had them all the same, even if they evaporated in the light of morning. My theory is that I've never had a truly dreamless night, only nights where the dream wasn't perfectly wondrous enough to enjoy thinking about during the day.

Gone.

But as I slept, induced into sleep by whatever chemical gas I had inhaled, I had no dreams. None at all.

There wasn't time to ponder why, because when I roused from this empty sleep, I was already in a nightmare. The sort you couldn't wake up from, because you were already awake.

Immediately, a wave of terror hit me. Before I knew what to be afraid of, I was afraid. A primal fear, the kind that soaks the back of your brain, tells you *get out get out something bad is happening* without specifying why. My eyes hadn't focused yet, I hadn't even remembered the circumstances of my unconsciousness, but panic was busy crawling up my spine all the same...

I couldn't focus. Couldn't cut through the fear with reassurance. My eyes swam in the fluids that filled them, ghostly afterimages. Metal, wire, something shining. Writing of some sort. Walls? There were walls, six of them. No, four. A perfect cube of a room. Door, where was the door, why wasn't there a door...?

There was a door. But it was covered in metal. Wire. Mesh. A cage. A cage which lined the walls, a grid of lines, a skintight cell across cracked drywall.

I went for the door anyway.

Pain. My body jerked away in response.

Light caught my attention, to the right.

I WOULDN'T RECOMMEND
TRYING THAT AGAIN.
IT'S AN ELECTRIFIED CAGE.

...handwriting, on a sign. On a television. Someone had left a filthy old CRT tube television in this cell with me, and was holding up paper signs on the screen...

The sign lowered, and seeing the face of my captor helped me draw some conclusions through the absolute terror that still threatened to paralyze me.

Doctor Montgomery. He'd captured us, and thrown me in this cell. Of course, he couldn't talk to me over a loudspeaker, so he went for the next best thing... a closed circuit broadcast, for an audience of one.

Where was Marcy? She wasn't in here with me. I could see clearly now, clearly enough to read, and she was gone. Maybe in another cell? What was going on...?

The good doctor tossed his handwritten card aside, revealing another. He had been holding a stack of them... a prepared speech.

WE'RE GOING TO PERFORM AN EXPERIMENT.
YOU'VE BEEN GIVEN AN OVERDOSE
OF MY NIGHTMARE FUEL.

...and more cards, and more cards...

N.F. IS A FASCINATING DRUG.
PART SCIENCE, PART NONSENSE.
IT SHOULDN'T WORK, BUT IT DOES.

IT INDUCES & ABSORBS NIGHTMARES,
LEAVING YOU DREAMLESS & EXHAUSTED.
THEY BOTTLE UP INSIDE YOU, NIGHT AFTER NIGHT.

BUT AN OVERDOSE...
THAT WORKS SO MUCH FASTER.

HOW ARE WE FEELING TODAY?

ANXIOUS? SCARED? TERRIFIED?

PLEASE BE CLEAR.
THIS IS FOR SCIENCE.

A camera in the room. There had to be. This sadist would want to watch his handiwork.

My eyes darted all over, trying to find one, seeing nothing but endless metal cage mesh. My entire world, pinned and trapped, the room shrinking around me. *Get out. Get out now.* Fight it, stay on top of it, can't, can't think. *Five* sides to the room, no, four, blurred, there had to be... there. Corner of the room...

Shaking hands couldn't form signs. They were too blurry, too indistinct. My muscles jerked and spasmed.

NORMALLY, THE DRUG WORKS QUIETLY, SLOWLY.
YOU SLEEP DREAMLESSLY, UNAWARE.
OF COURSE, IT CAN'T LAST.
EVENTUALLY, THE BOTTLE BREAKS.

YOU ARE OVERWHELMED.
YOU GO CUBIST.
YOU ARE FREED.

YOU'RE GOING TO BECOME A PICASSO TODAY, VIVI.
A MONSTER. A HORROR. PURE AND TRUE TO THE CITY.
AND I'M GOING TO OBSERVE THE PROCESS.

By now, the words weren't on the cards anymore. They weren't on the screen. They were in the room with me.

The reason my hands were blurry wasn't just because they were shaking. They were just... blurry. Cubism. Signs of cubism...

Once infected, there's no going back. Everybody knew that. Cubism was absolute inevitability, a fate worse than death, as you slowly became this *thing* which existed only as a ghost of your former self. The lucky ones get exterminated by the Department of Safety. The unlucky ones wander the Sideways, forever...

Curling up on the floor, hands around my head. Maybe I was screaming, I don't know. Couldn't look at the television anymore; too much, it was all too much. If I shut it out, shut my eyes, maybe I could refocus myself and come back from this, I don't know, maybe, so afraid, so very—

Flashing light between my fingers. The screen angrily trying to get my attention.

Large print on the card. He'd been prepared for this eventuality, and wrote a card in advance.

IF YOU IGNORE ME AGAIN
I WILL KILL YOUR SISTER.

...which effectively removed the option of ignoring what was happening. Slowly I pulled my hands away from my eyes. Faced the television. Made it very clear to the madman watching by remote camera that I was paying attention.

The swimming image of the doctor on the television nodded, satisfied that he was back in control. He reached for a second stack of cards, approaching the camera to begin showing them off.

NIGHTMARE FUEL ALONE ISN'T ENOUGH.
YOU ALSO NEED AN EMOTIONAL TRIGGER.
SOMETHING ANXIETY-GENERATING.

A LOUD AND CONFUSING CLUB, FOR INSTANCE.
OR ALCOHOL AND ENDORPHINS, CONFUSING THE MIND.

OR A SHARP SHOCK TO THE MEMORY,
DISLOCATING IT IN TIME AND SPACE.

SO, WE'LL TRY SOME FREE WORD ASSOCIATION TESTS.

New cards. Single words on each.

MOTHER.

I almost laughed. Anxiety-generating triggers? He'd failed already. After all, I use happy memories of my past each morning, when I left my mind drift during meditation and exercise. I've plenty of happy memories of my birth mother, the one who brought me into this world and cared for me with such love. Many happy memories...

...Mother, sitting alone in the kitchen. Trying to smile, for my sake. So much paper on the kitchen table. Even at a young age, I was an adept reader. I could read words like 'PAST DUE' and 'SECOND NOTICE'. I didn't know what the word 'alimony' meant or why Mr. Vickers, the man in the nice suit, was sending letters about it. The letters which made Mother cry.

Not a happy memory. Not one I even remembered having. But it was genuine. I was there, at that moment in time, looking at the bills and the bouncing alimony checks, things I couldn't have understood as a child. Our tiny little household, constantly on the verge of collapse...

BROTHER.

That little goofball. Smiling all the time, making jokes. He wasn't very good at jokes, he repeated ones he heard without really understanding them. He wasn't as good at reading as I was. Wasn't good at school at all, or learning much of anything. In and out of hospitals, still smiling, always happy to see me when I could visit.

Mother loved him so much. There was only so much she could do to help him get the help he needed, and it wasn't enough.

Despair leads to cubism, cubism leads to despair. Were the sorrowful memories rising because I was infected? Were my memories causing the infection? I couldn't avoid them. They rose up, with each new card shown to me. Mustn't look away, must keep Marcy safe, must—

ALONE.

Always alone at parties. I loved the party atmosphere, kids bouncing around and having fun, but... they didn't want me there. They stared. They made jokes because they knew I couldn't understand them.

It was done as a favor to my mother, out of pity by the other mothers. Either my birth mother or my adoptive mother, the same pity was there. The kids never invited me. She made sure I was included, but I was never really included. I tried, I tried so hard, but...

WHORE.

Written on my locker, in plain view of everyone else at our school.

Finding in-roads to the social scene when I was still learning how best to communicate was difficult. The Wei family couldn't afford home schooling for one, let alone two—we were tossed head-first into the broken social scene of public high school. There, I made mistakes. Sometimes people I thought were my friends were... not my friends. For each genuine friend I found, people I could trust and talk to, I also found liars and cheats. People who took the emotional connection I felt and played me for a fool with it.

I wasn't particularly sexually active, not yet. I was still timid about expressing myself physically and emotionally through love—suburban attitudes beaten into my head about what good girls did or didn't do. But I was active enough to draw attention from the wrong sort of boy, the kiss and tell type. And he told. And told.

When Marcy saw what the other girls did to my locker, she ended up suspended for a week—

SISTER.

—and there was the first chance I had to get out of this with my sanity intact.

The primal fear was pulling up the worst possible memories, even of things I remembered fondly. But with my sister, there were few horror stories to dredge up.

I wasn't supposed to go to the Wei family. A racial mismatch, a cultural mismatch. The Wei's had volunteered to temporarily host an appropriate foster child despite their lower-middle-class income, because it was the "in" thing to do at the time, thanks to a massive public relations campaign by the Department of Orientation. "Open your home to a soul in need," they'd said, back when faith-based charity was a larger portion of the Department. I wasn't even from a strongly Christian background, but they assigned me to the Weis anyway.

I didn't fit at all. They didn't know what to do with a little seven-year-old deaf white girl. But Marcy loved me dearly, right from the start. A temporary stopover as I worked my way through the system ended up being a reluctant adoption, to placate Marcy. She never felt like she fit in anywhere; I was someone just like her, only different. Neither of us fit. If she could reach me, I could reach her, and then we'd at least have each other.

There were fears, yes. But no matter how much I worried about her emotional well-being, no matter how much I feared for her safety and her future... those were fears born out of love.

From this, I had the strength to weakly pull myself off the floor. My hands were still strange, colorful and indistinct... the cubism threatened to engulf me. But I wasn't sobbing through the pain of it. I looked to the television, and stared into the cathode ray tube with more confidence. He would NOT break me.

Doctor Montgomery paused, the SISTER card in his hand. Curious, now. He had other cards ready... but set them aside. Walked out of frame, to adjust the camera. It was time for new tactics.

The camera panned to the left, to something that had been out of frame.

Marcy. Handcuffed to a chair, and struggling. He'd already torn open her shirt.

A car battery, with jumper cables attached and ready.

If memories wouldn't be enough to drive me over the cliff of my own mental well being, watching someone torture my sister would do the job.

Somehow I went from the floor to the door in less than half a second. Grasping for the electrified knob, pressing against the electrified mesh that covered it. Agony, sheer agony and pain. Disjointed time, back to the floor, back to the door. Rewind a few seconds, to the cards. To cards which I didn't even see, but somehow remembered seeing SISTER. ALONE. WHORE. SISTER. MOTHER. BROTHER. SISTER. MUTE. RUIN. DESPAIR. NIGHTMARE. CHAOS. FREEDOM. BEDLAM. BEDLAM.

My arms were light now, light and color. I tried to move through the walls, to will myself to escape and stop this. My sister was screaming and I could hear the screaming, I could hear it, as sure as I heard the DJ's cubist voice so long ago. But whatever part of me was still human couldn't get past the animal reaction to pain, the shock cage. It was designed to keep Picassos in. Picassos, like me.

It had happened in less than the space of two breaths. I could see every wall at once, through an eye I didn't have before. I could feel the erratic stomp-beat of what I didn't know what my own heart. Time slipped, memories jumbled. How long had I been in the room, now? Was Marcy dead already? Did he begin torturing her yet? How did I get there in the first place? Cards. Cages. Memories...

A veil of tears poured, as I wept for what I once was. Normality felt like a lifetime ago.

She brought me comfort. Wiped away the tears, offered a hug. I-Love-You sign to the back.

He hurt you badly. // Very badly, the child of nightmares whispered in my ear. *But he set you free. This prison can't hold you, not really. // Hurt so badly, screaming and afraid. // Why afraid? // You don't have to be afraid.*

My words poured out through my hands, of which I had many.

[my sister // he's hurting her // hurting // please // love her] I frantically signed, over and over and overlapping.

If you love her // then stop him, the child suggested. *You don't have to be afraid. // You are a thing to be afraid of. // He should be afraid of what he's made of you. // Show him why. // Show him your vengeful love, and be free.*

In a gesture of goodwill, the young girl stepped forward... and pulled my cage apart. The wires were such flimsy things, really. It seemed trivial to warp them and shred them, clearing the path towards salvation.

Upright and ready. My dancing shoes laced up tight. The music had already begun.

Light and sound and fury poured out of the experimental cell, flowing down the hallway of the condemned warehouse. I poured like rivers of silver wine through those halls, searching, seeking. Listening with ears I never had before.

My sister's screams. I knew them, I heard them, no matter how far away I was. Turns out, I wasn't far away at all.

Punching through the ceiling which became the floor which became the office of one Doctor Montgomery, member of the Cult of Bedlam, sadist, criminal, madman, ruiner. I shone with brilliant glow, radiant and blood red, my lighting crews timing the pulse of the stage show to the highly erratic beat of my heart.

He'd only just gotten started on Marcy. Less than five seconds had passed between his televised threat and my emergence as the burning-winged angel of love. And judging from the expression on his face, he probably didn't have any pre-written cue cards for this particular situation.

For lack of a better option, the good doctor dropped his jumper cables and made a run for it.

Even this far gone, I wasn't a murderer. I wanted him to stop hurting her; that's all I wanted. But if he escaped, if he told Seth Dougal about tonight night's main event, Marcy would be in danger once more. So, he couldn't escape. So, he didn't escape. I moved at the speed of music, giving chase as the doctor threw open the door of his office, and charged forth blindly...

...right into the arms of the sickly green-black child, who smiled as he spiraled away into her embrace.

I could hear Bedlam's thoughts, or her words, or maybe they were the same thing.

Wondering why? she asked. *True, he WAS helping me. // Helping my friends. // But you're my friend, too. // You're always going to be my friend, now.*

I looked at Bedlam. With other eyes behind myself I looked at my sister, still handcuffed to the chair... and watching in horror, as the thing that was once her sister Vivi Wei hovered there, strange and terrible.

Couldn't move. Couldn't think. It was all sinking in, now—what had happened, what I had become. There was no way back from cubism, and certainly no way back from being a Picasso. I'd embraced it in full force, so I could save her life. The show must go on...

Marcy's handcuffs turned into tissue paper. I'm not sure if I did that or if Bedlam did that. Probably her. Another gesture for my benefit.

It's time to go, Vivi. // You can't stay here anymore, not up here. // You're a danger to her and others. // You don't like to hurt people. // Come home with me, to my special places. // The Sideways. // Climb down the spiral with me, and help me find its heart. // We'll be friends forever in the purity of the city's dream-state.

I knew there wasn't much choice in the matter. That's what Picassos did, right? They eventually drifted off to the Sideways, to roam those halls forever. If I stayed up here... I'd hurt Marcy. I'd get lost. I'd forget myself, and get lost, and hurt Marcy, and hurt everyone, and eventually be boiled alive in the flames of a Department of Safety extermination team. Too late. Too late for me, now...

"NO!"

Her voice. I could hear her screams, before. But now, I could hear her voice.

"Vivi, no, please, no, NO...! Not you. Not this!"

Pleading. I could *hear* the fear in her voice, the sorrow. It was so sad and beautiful, my sister's voice. I'd always wanted to hear it, ever since we first met —her voice and no one else's. It would've been my one regret in life, the only thing I hated about my "disability." When we first met, when the Department of Orientation official was arguing with her parents over paperwork, and—

Snapped back to the present. Almost became unstuck. Would've wandered, mentally and physically.

Come with me. // Come with me. // You can't stay. // You know you can't stay. // Merrily, merrily, merrily, merrily—

—a hand grasping mine.

"If you're leaving, I'm coming with you," Marcy swore, gritting her teeth through the pain as her flesh-and-blood hand clung tightly to what may or may not have been my hand and may or may not have even existed.

Only seconds before her arm would be stripped to the bone, or removed, or twisted around. Her body destroyed, like poor unfortunate Gee Bee—

Breathe in, breathe out.

Her breathing. Her heartbeat. I could hear those, too. Unlike my own erratic half-heart, the heart of chaos, hers was solid and real. And it rang in my ears like the best music I had ever indirectly experienced.

Random and disconnected thoughts. Floating images and memories. I let them wash over me, turbulent waves, swirling eddies.

Pull the random thoughts together, sequence them. Bring myself out of the fugue state. I could feel *her* heartbeat, and I could use it to guide me out of the chaos.

Mother. Brother. Together. Love. Sister. Music. Home. Joy. Dream. Lucidity. Vivi.

My sister. By blood or not, she had become my sister, and I hers. She led me back to who I was, who I wanted to be. I was now and forever Vivi Wei, and even as I missed my brother and my mother, I moved forward to become Vivi Wei.

Present day, present time. Deep exhale. And here.

I fell into her arms, exhausted from the effort. Those warm and inviting arms. Real and human, just like mine now were.

Life was focused, again. My vision clear despite the deep haze that was settling into my mind, an adrenaline crash that was going to take me down into unconsciousness again.

But maybe there was a tiny but of cubism still lurking... because while I could still see the young girl of madness (looking at me in a disappointed fashion) I could see another girl as well. A mirror image, a twin, but formed of white light and the pulsing red glow of life. And she was smiling to me, as I slipped into pleasant dreams.

My fever spiked to 103 that night, but Marcy didn't dare bring me to a Department of Safety hospital. After calling Hollister for an emergency pick-up, she asked him to bring one of his least shady medical men to our apartment.

The doctor had no idea what was wrong, but noted it would likely pass, in time. I just needed bed rest and good food. I suppose feeling under the weather was a small price to pay for coming back from cubism, alive and intact.

I slept quite a bit for the next few days. Always, either Hollister or Marcy would be at my bedside. Marcy had taken a job—thankfully not at the Silken Veil as she'd threatened, but a basic burger-flipper role—and we got a reprieve on the rent. We'd stay aloft a little while longer, as I recovered.

The warehouse burned to the ground the next day, for some reason. The Department of Safety officially investigated it as an arson, but I bet they'd be cheerfully silencing the facts, as usual. Thankfully word of our escape hadn't reached them... Montgomery must not have reported our snooping, keen on taking care of it himself. Our involvement vanished into the night, just as we had when Marcy pulled me from that horrible place and into Hollister's waiting car.

Hollister wasn't sure if he wanted to believe Marcy's recounting of those events or not. If we were lying, it was an insane lie, one which had no rhyme or reason. If we were telling the truth... then not only was the government working with Bedlam, the government he worked for, but it meant I had in fact once been a Picasso. I hoped he wouldn't think of me differently, knowing what I had become...

Three days later, I awoke refreshed and alert. No fever. No fatigue. Oddly enough, someone had tucked a teddy bear under my left arm as I slept.

I shuffled out of bed, putting on a bathrobe. Not quite up to trying my morning exercise routine just yet; I could slack off Marcy-style for now. I kept the teddy bear with me, though. It was comforting, for some inexplicable reason. I never played with dolls as a kid, but...

On reaching the living room of our apartment, it was clear we had visitors.

Marcy was talking with a kindly old lady, who clutched an extra-large purse in her wrinkled hands. Meanwhile, a man about as big as our front door loomed politely in the background.

Noticing my entrance, she offered me a gentle smile. Turned to face me directly, so I could read her lips.

"Rise and shine, dearie," she spoke. "Sounds like you've had a bit of an ordeal, mmm? I know all about it, of course."

[ALL about it?] I asked Marcy, with a few offhand gestures. And got a confused shrug in return...

"It seems we have some common enemies. And some common friends," the lady continued. "A mutual friend by way of a friend. I believe you know a poet named Fi? That means you know a poet who knows another poet who in turn knows me. And when I heard through the grapevine that you'd taken ill, well, old Grandma Scarlett felt just *terrible*. So unfortunate, that business with the serpent and his worm... mmm. Now that you're awake, I suppose I should get to the true point of my visit..."

She gestured for me to sit opposite her, on the love seat across from our couch. Colored curious, I obeyed, nodding for her to go on.

"We have common friends—and as noted—common enemies," she explained. "Enemies in the form of the Cult of Bedlam. I've been fighting it in my own way for years, recently gathering allies to my cause. We were the ones who burned that warehouse, you see. A hateful place, just hateful. If only we'd gotten there sooner... I feel simply awful that we couldn't help you in your time of need."

...the idea of makeshift rebel alliance against the grand conspiracy of the Cult of Bedlam was crazy. About as crazy as the idea that the Cult of Bedlam was running the city. Which meant the two crazies cancelled each other out, leaving me with little left to do but nod along with the nice crazy lady.

"I'd like to make it up to you, in some small way—and you can provide an invaluable service to us in turn. We need somewhere pleasant to hang our hat, when we're in the city. Somewhere the Department of Safety hasn't already traced to us. I understand you used to specialize in crafting pleasant places for people to relax, yes...?"

Now, I felt the need to inject some sanity. Marcy was ready to interpret for me.

[Are you suggesting I become R-I-C-K B-L-A-I-N-E for your... band of freedom fighters? —it's an old movie reference, Marcy.]

"Hah! Rick Blaine. I like that," Grandma Scarlett said, after a soundless giggle. "It has mythic resonance, as a friend of mine once said. Yes, yes, that's exactly what I'm suggesting. Given your experiences, I felt you would be the ideal candidate to operate our 'Café Américain,' as it were. But... there's another side to that metaphor. Like Rick, if you would prefer to avoid this entire mess and to stay out of the fight, I understand. You've endured so much, you poor girl. I won't *make* you endure more. It's entirely your choice."

Insane. Inadvisable at best.

And yet...

[Running a club requires more money than I've ever seen in one place at one time,] I pointed out.

"Really? Hmm. Well, let's see... hmm..."

From her purse, Grandma Scarlett produced three used wadded up tissues, a pack of gum, a small porcelain statue of a cat, and one hundred thousand dollars in neat little stacked bundles. More money than I've ever seen in one place at one time.

"I suppose I'll need to break open a few piggy banks for the rest," she pondered.

Being a Picasso was like living inside a nightmare. The next two weeks were like living inside a dream.

I'd rallied together as many people as I could from the ruins of the Zig-Zag. Most were looking for work, just as I was. Some had gotten out of the business entirely... but enough were still around and still loyal for me to make a tidy little niche for us within the scene. Our club. My club. My own club.

The location wasn't terrific, although that was by design. Being front and center on the Zag would've made us an open target for the Department of Safety's ongoing campaign of terror against its own citizens. Instead we squatted in Crossway Points, halfway between the dire fringe and the pulsing core of the city. Not the most reputable of districts, but it was very much alive with activity. Perfect for running a public establishment which masked a private gathering of rebels in the back rooms.

Running the club both in front of and behind the scenes took a lot of work. Gee Bee had handled a lot of the money matters; here, I was learning fast and hard.

Some of Grandma Scarlett's friends pitched in to help me figure things out —a nice guy who owned a fish restaurant gave me some valuable tips in business management. A guy who looked like he walked off the set of a Die Hard movie helped me coordinate security, both for the safety of the oblivious and happy patrons... and for the secrecy of our little revolutionary club-within-a-club. (Nice guy, if a bit gruff. His daughter was especially adorable.)

For some reason, 'security' also involved hiding teddy bears at strategic points in and around my club. By this point I'd stopped asking why, because the answers rarely made sense. Something about obscuring the vision of the enemy, or protecting against Bedlam's lure, and so on...

Soon enough, on the corner of 23rd Street and 23rd Avenue, the *Lucid Dreamer* was open for business.

I'd gone from having everything I wanted in life to losing everything to nearly losing *everything* to having what I always wanted, in a little over a month. My life swung back around to where it was originally... waking around noon, getting ready to face the day alongside my sister, going to the club to do my thing, coming home to my sanctuary for peace and good dreams.

In the end, all was well. Love drove me forward and love of my dear sister pulled me back from the brink. The universe awarded me for my faith in love with a new home within the scene I adored so much. I could feel hope again, for the first time in so long.

But even this newfound hope was tempered with reality. The reality of what I experienced, becoming cubist, and knowing that someone out there was trying to leverage Bedlam to...

...well, we didn't know *what*, exactly. We had pieces of the story. The drug. The cult. The terrible experiments, in the Outland and the fringes of the City. It was coming together to be a dark shape, indeed. Dark and frightening.

Even with that shadow looming large... I could hold fast to my peace. My love. My home. And in that, I would endure.

Breathe in, breathe out.

His breath had caught in this throat, when he saw it.

So, that would be their opening salvo. Their first public action.

"We'll have it scrubbed off within an hour," some Johnny-no-Name safety officer promised. Dougal couldn't be bothered to memorize the names under his command anymore. "The paint's laid down thick, but we've got solvents that can—"

"It doesn't matter," Seth Dougal recognized. "The morning traffic helicopter caught it on tape. It's all over the news, all over the Internet. We look like a joke. Can't even keep a vandal off the roof of our primary district office..."

A joke. He'd chosen those words well. This officer would pass them down the line, quoting his boss. This was just a bad joke, a tasteless joke. No value to it at all. No truth to be found here. Seth understood media relations—that was half of his war, after all, keeping the media pumping a message of fear into the people. It was important to define the frame, when someone else hung a painting on your wall. Literally, in this case.

If he let on the real reason for his concern... that someone was trying to get the truth out, that someone was fighting against them, destroying facilities and taking out the Shabby Men... well. That would induce panic, which was good, but could also shine light into shadows which needed to stay dark. Not good.

Not long. Not long now, at any rate. Montgomery's death at the hands of these... these ridiculous and backward-looking fools, truckers and gangsters and whatever, they didn't matter and neither did Montgomery, in the long run. Soon, all would be baptized in the waters of Bedlam. Everyone would know the perfect freedom of chaos. The entire city would be restored to what it should have been in the first place.

And even though someone had the gall to paint *this* on his roof...

...it changed nothing at all.

For the coming of Bedlam and the glorious chaos.

//end

Buildings next to buildings, askew or aligned. Buildings sometimes intersecting buildings, for that matter. Walk down a hallway, end up in a ballroom, double glass doors to a subway station, third exit on the left goes to a subway station. Unfortunately it got rotated ninety degrees, so unless you enjoy plummeting down an endless tunnel, don't go there.

There's no rhyme or reason to any of it—we've got streets which lead to dead ends, roads which criss-cross and loop back around, highways which go nowhere. Literally nowhere, as in "anybody going down that road is not coming back." This is not a good place to wander off unless you like wandering off forever...

Nobody knows where the city came from. Nobody knows how we got here. Nobody knows why any of this is happening. But it's happening. The city exists. We are here now. It's growing every day, and bringing new people with it.

We live a life amidst the twisted yet familiar.

If we're going to survive this, if we're going to stay alive and thrive, we need to learn to live in the City of Angles.

...here's an angle to consider...

If words are the hammers and nails of the English language, idioms are the high school shop class artifacts. Stools, chairs, flower boxes, coat racks, common things people make use of to get through their lives. They're binding cultural artifacts which carry weight and meaning which is understood by all, even when the metaphor wouldn't be immediately apparent to a non-native speaker.

For example... "Tend your own garden." "Keep your head down." "Don't rock the boat." "Mind your own business." These are the knick-knacks used to fortify your home against the dangers that the City of Angles throws at you. By focusing on your own problems and minimizing risk, there's no chance of being plowed under by the problems society can throw at you. Enlightened self interest will get YOU through anything, comfy and cozy in perfect isolation.

As for the others around you, there's another coat rack for that.

"Better you than me."

//007: Well Enough Alone

Doctor Carlos Alvarez had operated his neighborhood pharmacy for ten years running. This was his dream, from the earliest age he could remember— to heal the sick and provide for those in need. Getting through school had been brutal, and working up the funds to open his own franchised retail drug store involved taking out loans on top of student loans... debts he may never really get out from underneath. But he'd done it. He made it happen.

Truthfully, at this point in his career he didn't need to work the long hours he worked. It was a small shop by any standard but he did have employees and regular work rotations, so he could take most evenings off to be with his family. But his was a face that people knew, far more than the come-and-go young employees who used his store as a stepping stone towards brighter careers. He liked to be the smile that greeted people when they came through the door.

But aside from the idealistic sense of being a pillar of the community... this was December. Longer hours meant more money for the gifts he wanted to be able to afford for his family. And even though few people braved the cold and ice of a Boston winter to get to his little shop, he was there to serve all the same.

Three hours from closing time, and Carlos was behind the counter, busy watching the weather report on his laptop computer. The storefront windows had iced over, making the street view a blurry mess. He had to make the call to close early and go home before the worst of the storm rolled in, or stick it out for the few customers who might come in. It was a decision he was waffling on, weighing the pros and cons as the little digital man on his video stream talked about low pressure systems and cold fronts...

Until the little digital man stopped moving. A tiny swirling circle of dots indicated the stream was buffering—quite odd, since he'd never had bandwidth problems from this site before...

An error message popped, announcing the connection lost. Also strange. Maybe the WiFi was down? Not that Carlos knew what to do to fix that, beyond unplug it and plug it back in.

Fortunately, he had older technology to fall back on. A television set in the back storage room had been gathering dust for some years, only used as a closed-circuit monitor for the front room. Presumably it would still work for broadcasts. He debated leaving his post at the dispensary counter, but the TV monitor and even the bells over his door would alert him to anyone coming in... and getting one last update on the weather would probably be enough to help him make his decision to stay or go.

Except the television wasn't working, either. It got a grainy picture of his shop just fine, but broadcasts were a no go. Strange. It was old and only standard def, but the set wasn't hooked up to rabbit ears anymore. He'd upgraded to a reliable cable service at the same time the internet went in, a nice two-for-one bundle. And not a single channel was coming in.

Briefly he entertained the idea that classic snowy TV static meant snow was on the way. Like an analog fortune cookie signal, maybe. He could see a shape in the snow of some sort... maybe a human figure... a girl? That might've been the outline of a dress. A smile. Hard to say...

So, rabbit ears, then. That'd help him tune in and be sure. They were nearby, collecting even more dust than the television had been collecting. He'd gotten a fancy new digital over-the-air antenna, so it should at least pick up local stations...

Still static. White noise. Vague shapes and nothing solid. Either every television station in town vanished, or far more likely, this old video junk had given up the ghost.

Well... for lack of better information, he'd have to assume the worst. Not worth risking being snowed in. He'd phone home and let his wife know he was on the way.

No signal. No cellphone carrier.

The entire world went away, some part of his mind suggested. *No, that's stupid,* the rest of his mind insisted.

...jingle-jangle of the bells over his door. Okay. ONE more customer, then he'd head back.

Emerging from the stock room and closing the door behind him, Doctor Alvarez was prepared to issue his usual greeting of a hearty "May I help you?" but didn't finish the sentence.

Three customers. Official-looking uniforms, somewhere between a jumpsuit and a cop get-up. Nothing he could recognize. And one of them was quite clearly and openly armed, with a semiautomatic sidearm at his hip...

"No need for alarm, we're here to help," the one with the gun said, holding up a hand in a greeting / defensive gesture." "City First Responders. I'm O-4 Security Officer Gilt. Please remain calm."

"I... am calm," Carlos tried to point out, realizing halfway through his statement that people with guns asking him to remain calm are either a good reason not to be calm or know a good reason which is why they insisted you be calm.

"Standard sweep," Officer Gilt spoke to his companions. "I'll check entrances and exits. Polk, take inventory. Smith, tend to the import."

"Right. Okay. I got this," the young man named 'Smith' mumbled to himself. He plastered a big comfortable fake smile, and approached. "Hello, sir. My name is Orientation Trainee insert your name here. —Dave Smith. I'm Dave Smith. Ah. And you are...?"

"Carlos Alvarez," the doctor responded automatically, trying to peer around the smiling man at the other two. A man with his hand already on the hilt of his gun, peering out the front door into the street... and another one whistling away as he rifled through the long, straight shelves of Alvarez Drugs. "Excuse me, but are you with the police...? Is something going on I should be aware of? If there a reason I *shouldn't* be calm?"

"Please remain calm," Dave Smith repeated, by rote.

"I am calm. I said that."

"Right. Well, that's one thing in your favor," Dave said. "Most people aren't very calm in situations like this. Honestly, it's a bit of a relief to find someone who IS calm. I mean, last week there was this apartment building, had to be dozens of people, and they only sent our one team in for all those people, it got a bit crazy and—um—actually I guess that's not really relevant to your situation and I'm probably not helping, am I, sorry about this—"

"—excuse me, what do you think you're doing?"

This directed to the one Carlos was genuinely concerned with, the shifty-looking guy who'd been pawing through his inventory since he got here. Polk, his name was.

"Taking stock," the lanky man replied, waving a tablet computer. "Photos, bar code scans, things like that. Man, you got a lotta great stuff here! Resources has been on my ass about trying to track down and requisition more medical supplies. Ohhh, yeah, this is the mother lode. We are talking promotion city—"

"Look, I'd like to know exactly what is going on here," Doctor Alvarez insisted. "This is *my* shop, and I don't know what authority you claim to be from, but nobody is 'requisitioning' anything unless you intend to pay for it, and... and... WHAT is going on?"

An exasperated sigh, from Mr. Officer With a Gun. "Smith, please...?"

"I know, I'm on it," Dave insisted, before turning back to Carlos. "Okay. I don't know any better way of explaining this, because I'm honestly only a trainee and the last guy... left, I'll go with 'left,' before he could train me. But your entire shop just got picked up and dropped in another city. Seriously."

"...seriously," Carlos repeated, obviously not taking it seriously.

"I know. And I'm the guy they picked to explain things to you. Sorry about that," Dave apologized again. "You deserve better, honestly. But this is what we have, you know? —look, if you think you can handle the shock, I know a really easy way to convince you that I'm not crazy. Let's have a look out your front door."

As the Doctor mentally compiled a list of antipsychotics these men clearly needed, he nodded in agreement and moved to follow Dave. If only so once he got to the door, he could make a run for it and try to call the cops.

The windows had iced over, blurring the street view. But Doctor Alvarez knew exactly what he'd see out there—the pad Thai restaurant, a mail order franchise depot, the tree which had been planted by the sidewalk and grown quite tall over the years, etc. And even if it was snowing out, odds were good there'd be a squad car outside the restaurant. It was popular with the boys at the precinct. They'd be able to help him with these madmen...

His feet did not crunch in the light layer of fallen snow. Despite the December cold, there was no snow.

Similarly there was no squad car. No restaurant. No tree.

Other buildings, other signs. Not many signs and buildings far too tall. Even the sidewalk had different pavement... and it ran at a strange diagonal angle, as if the building was askew rather than aligned with the road...

This wasn't Boston. As Dave Smith had suggested, his entire shop had been picked up and dropped in another city. Every signal to the outside world had been snipped off, because the outside world was not the outside world he remembered.

Instead, the city was darker than Boston. Many of the buildings looked abandoned. Carlos didn't come from the greatest of neighborhoods, but there was solidarity to be found there—he had the same spirit they had, to band together against their circumstances. Whoever lived here... if anybody *did* live here... there wasn't any sense of that. Even standing for less than a minute on this slanted street he could feel the place drained of all life. Not Boston. Not the life he knew.

There were any number of explanations, of course. Could all be a dream. Maybe the cold meds he took for his sniffles earlier this morning were having an adverse effect. It was also entirely possible he was undergoing the first episode of latent schizophrenia. Science had any number of answers to offer.

Or maybe Dave was right. And from the sad look on Dave's face, joining him at the door, Dave wasn't happy that he was right.

"Best I can say right now is... sorry," he said, echoing earlier apologies. "I'm new to this city, myself. I know what you're going through. But I'm afraid it only gets weirder from here on out. ...I don't think I'm supposed to frame it that way, but... personally, I figure honesty's as good an approach as any."

"My shop got moved to another city," Carlos decided he was going to have to believe.

"Um. Yeah. There's some fiddly bits and details, which you'll learn about in time, but... yeah."

The next question was a logical progression, and also something Dave couldn't provide an answer for.

"How do I get home?" Carlos asked.

Fortunately for Dave, who had been expressly told to stabilize the import and leave the Echo Revelation for his superiors in the Department of Orientation to deal with, a distraction reared its head in the form of a brief light over his shoulder. Light from an open stock room door.

Polk was already one shelf in, scanning and memorizing, when the pharmacist stormed in on him.

"You can't be back here, whoever you are!" Doctor Alvarez insisted. "My shop. Private property. Hell, there was an Employees Only sign!"

Much to his disgust, the man named Polk snorted back a giggle at the rebuke. He picked up a cardboard box containing a prescription antidepressant, studying the tiny print carefully.

"Dave, keep the import on a leash, okay?" Polk replied, resuming his scans. "I wanna get this place inventoried and my ass out the door ASAP. He's only gonna slow us down. —man, you've got some nice stuff back here! I can't wait to get it hauled off and indexed properly—"

The doctor yanked the box from Polk's hand, placing it back on the shelf.

"I want all three of you out of my shop, *now*," he insisted. "You don't look like any police I know of, no matter what city this may or may not be. And I'm running out of ways to say that this medicine doesn't belong to you—"

"Actually, it does," Polk said, with no small amount of amusement. "Department of Resources Ordinance 14/b, Annexation of Imported Real Estate by Designated City Official. Got to keep the wheels of the city turning, buddy, and there's only so much grease to go around. Plenty of sick people are gonna need this stuff. Public good, and all."

"Are you kidding me? This is America! ...I'm assuming this is America. I'm not hearing any accents here," Carlos reasoned. "And in America, I've got rights. You can't just barge in here like you own the place!"

"Sir... please remain calm."

This coming from the man with the gun.

Not that Mr. O-4 Security Officer Gilt would use that gun on him. Not that he was suggesting as much, or resting his hand on the hilt, or doing anything threatening. He didn't have to make a threat. No look of menace in his eye, not even a steely cold businesslike attitude. Compassionate even, perhaps. But all he really had to do was repeatedly quietly request that Carlos Alvarez *remain calm*. Remain passive. Go along with what was happening to him.

Within minutes, Carlos had been kidnapped, and now he was going to be robbed. Wonderful. The only thing keeping him from going mad was a simple and seething disgruntlement at his situation, and hope that soon he'd be able to get out of here and back to his family. How soon was another matter, but...

Jingle-jangle.

A lousy time for customers. The three men didn't know what that sound meant, but Carlos did. Not wanting to take an eye off the guy sizing up his life's work like a side of beef, he turned to the television monitor. Flipped it to the closed circuit channel, to see who just walked in.

Two people.

With guns.

They wore a uniform as well, although one Carlos instantly recognized. It was universal, no matter which city you were dropped into. Bandanas, hand me down clothes, pistols held sideways. If the nice and sympathetic government trio were legitimate thieves... these two were their illegitimate counterparts. Gangsters. He wasn't familiar with the grey-and-black color scheme they wore, but the way they wore it made gang membership patently obvious.

By this point, his new city official friends had noticed the television monitor. And Alvarez took a tiny and spiteful amount of joy that they looked just as unhappy with the situation as he was.

Dave continued watching the monitor, as if curious about this fanciful thing called a CRT tube. The rest of them, Alvarez included, had a brief pow-wow about what was happening.

"Salvagers," Officer Gilt recognized immediately. He went for his cellphone, in a holster opposite the gun holster, keying some obscure code into an app. "Grey Market Gang colors. Thankfully just two of them, they aren't rolling aggro with their whole crew. Greyscale must've gotten a neighborhood watch tip about the new import. I'm calling in for backup, but we're outer city, so..."

"So they won't be here for minutes. Goddammit," Polk cursed. "This is what my career's come to, is it? Four years and I'm still out in the boonies, getting jumped by Salvagers. Dammit. Dammit. What do we do here? What's the playbook say?"

Cellphone back in its holster. Gun out of its holster.

"Secure the resources, protect the civilians, hold them off until backup comes," Gilt replied. "Dave's not rated for a firearm and neither are you, so that means I'm on it. Doctor, I saw a back door—there's no promise it connects to the alley, not anymore, but I want you and the others through that door if firing starts. I don't care what you see in there, you stick with Polk and Smith and you run. Got it?"

But Alvarez was waving his hands, no, no. "You don't have to shoot at anyone or get shot at!" he insisted—but quietly, just in case. "They don't know we're back here. We just have to lock the door. Backup's on the way, right? To arrest them?"

"Can't risk losing the meds, doc. The city needs them, and it's my job to defend them—and you," Gilt replied, checking his firearm, making sure it was ready. "Two on one, but I'm a professional. Maybe I can scare them off, maybe it'll come to shots, but either way I have to go out there—"

"He's looking for something specific."

This coming from Dave Smith, who had been ignoring the tense discussion completely, in favor of watching television.

"She's scooping up anything she can get, but he's looking for something," Dave explained, not looking away. "He's searching the shelves and not stealing anything. He needs something specific. He's worried, desperately worried. And she's..."

Unsure as to how Mr. Smith could get all that from the grainy security camera, Carlos leaned over to have himself a look. True, one of the two was a young woman who was grabbing every single thing she could—even two dollar packets of band-aids. And yes, the man wasn't touching anything, not yet.

Also, and this made Carlos wonder if his earlier broadcast problems were the result of his TV being broken, there was an odd video distortion effect every second or so coming over the wire. It was isolated to the portion of the picture where the woman was looting... a blurry, flickering snap of electronics going haywire...

When he glanced up, Dave was grabbing Polk's tablet away from him, checking the hastily built index of drugs. Ten seconds later and Dave Smith had a full box of a particular drug, and was headed to the door.

"Orientation Trainee Dave Smith!"

Hand on the knob, paused. Again, Gilt didn't draw his weapon, didn't make a threat. Just used rank and name to stop Dave cold. But the young man wasn't showing any fear, not fear of his boss, not fear of what he was about to do.

"Nobody needs to get shot," Dave promised. "Including me. I know exactly what to do. Trust me on this, Peter. Please."

Not waiting for a response from Officer Peter Gilt, Dave opened the door, and passed through into the main shop. Alone, and closing the door behind him.

Suda suda suda suda suda. She'd been mentally chanting it, ever since they got the tip through back channels. *Suda suda suda.*

That's all this was, to her. A chance to score large amounts of Sudafed, to pass on to other gangs that mixed it up to make crystal meth. Best part was that the score was theirs and theirs alone; Jackie had asked the tipper to pass word of drug store imports directly to them, rather than to Greyscale the bossman. No need to bring the rest of the Grey Market Gang on a private score, no need to divvy the proceeds, more for them, all for them, get the cash, get the stuff, get out, get to bed, sleep, can't sleep, no dreams, dreaming of money, all the money they could ever need to up-stakes and head to the inner city where it'd be safe again...

Honestly, Lonnie had no idea what to grab—she wasn't seeing any boxes clearly labeled Suda. So she was grabbing as much as she could of anything slightly interesting, scooping it all into a shopping basket.

"Grab it, grab the Suda, c'mon Jackie, grab it," she mumbled to herself, to her companion. "We gotta hurry. Farts gonna be here soon. Soon. Gotta hurry —"

"Don't RUSH me, okay?! Christ!" he shouted back. "Don't rush me. I'm looking..."

Testy. Jackie had been testy lately. Something on his mind, Lonnie figured, something weighing. Usually he smiled more. He hadn't smiled lately, not even hearing about this score. This great score. Why was he looking for drug store tips, anyway? Didn't they normally roll 'lectronics? Suda. Who cares. Get yours, get out—

Door. Open door.

Two guns, trained on the FARThead by the Employees Only door.

Scruffy-looking guy, box tucked under one arm. He did his best to hold his hands up, surrendering, without dropping the box he had wedged under there.

"I'm unarmed," the guy announced. "Dave Smith. Orientation representative. Um. Trainee. No gun. It's cool. I'm not here to fight."

Jackie was on the ball, as always. Stepped up, mighty and true. Gun sideways, street style, that Jackie. Lonnie had her gun too but her gun was shaky, very shaky lately, she'd never have hit the mark. Jackie would protect her...

"I'm not here to fight either," Jackie said, which was strange because Lonnie always remembered Jackie itching for fights. "Just stay the hell out of my way and we'll be gone in a blink. You called in backup, didn't you? Your little FART bros?"

"They'll be here soon, yeah," Dave warned. "So you need to get what you came to get, and go. I won't stop you. Actually, I think I've got what you need... just... gonna hold this out here, okay, not a gun, just a box, here..."

Carefully, trying to stay in a surrender pose while simultaneously holding out a cardboard box, Dave offered the item procured from shelves of controlled substances.

"Alprazolam," he explained. "Anti-anxiety benzo. And plenty of it. That's what you're looking for, right? For her?"

Jackie the hardboy, his gun wavering. Lonnie wondered why.

"For my sister, yeah," Jackie replied. Lowering the weapon just slightly, so he could safely and slowly retrieve the box from Dave's outstretched arms.

"I saw her flickering. And I've read the same websites you have," Dave Smith explained. "For what it's worth, I swear by the stuff. It's helped my anxiety attacks a lot. I don't know how long Alprazolam'll effectively fight off cubism incidents, but... for what it's worth... I wish you two the best. You should get going now, before the Department of Safety gets here."

Worried, now. Cubism? What? Lonnie felt fine. Never better. She didn't scream *that* much lately, in the night. Not that much.

"We're going, Lonnie-hun," Jackie said, backing away from Dave slowly. "Going now."

"Too much stuff left to grab, it's a big score, we can't just walk," Lonnie protested. "Jackie, c'mon, big time, this is what we neeeed to get away from the GMGs, we can be okay again, I swear, we can // we can // we can—"

"We're going," he declared.

And they were gone.

Less than an hour later, and the Departments were out in force. Two of them, anyway.

Department of Safety set up tape around the building, Yellow-black, as a precautionary measure to keep anyone from nosing around. People in the City of Angles knew better than to mess with a squadron of safety officers around a yellow-black building. There wasn't much enforcing of safety needed, of course; now that the threat has escalated from a three-man First Action Responder Team to a full-blown import investigation, the Salvagers would steer clear. The gangs weren't crazy enough to attack head on.

Meanwhile, the Department of Resources was busy carting away the entire contents of Carlos Alvarez's drug store. Polk got the ball rolling, but he wasn't in charge, not by far—he was just the first feet on the ground, to pave the way for poachers yet to come. Carlos was forced to loiter street-side, watching the entire process... with the sole representative of the Department of Orientation at his side.

"Not seeing how this is any better than gang-bangers robbing me blind," Carlos spoke with bitter tones.

Dave had no apology and no justification. Best he could was shrug in sympathy.

"You seem like a decent guy," Carlos said, turning to Dave. "Better than this. Courageous, too. I saw what you did for those two. You put your life on the line to get them out of my store safely, so nobody had to get hurt, including them. You didn't even bat an eyelash, didn't panic..."

"I'm just trying to help," Dave offered.

"About the only person here who genuinely is, at that. So. What happens now, Mr. Smith? When do I get to go home?"

And there ended Dave's ability to help.

He could tell Carlos that his family was safe and sound... and that Carlos Alvarez was likely with them now, while *this* Carlos Alvarez had to spend the rest of his future alone in the City of Angles. That would be honest. Honesty seemed like a good concept in general, but...

Nothing Dave could say could really help. In the end, Dave couldn't help anyone, despite taking one of the riskiest jobs the city had to offer expressly to try and do something better with his life. To help others. He had no words for Carlos Alvarez, no comfort, and focused instead on processing the paperwork and putting the good doctor in the system. The best he could do.

Dave Smith stared down the barrel of two guns that night, one of which was held by someone on the verge of going Picasso. He'd nearly died.

But he'd stormed right into that situation without a single moment's hesitation. It was a voluntary flavor of Nearly Died, one without regret: Dave saw what needed to be done, and did it. That was his superpower—while other people were going to pieces, Dave Smith had his act together. It was something a good friend pointed out to him, what seemed like so long ago.

I think you're stronger than you believe you are, Dave. I think you could really help people... and maybe that'd help you help yourself, in the end. Promise me, okay? Promise me you'll try.

Playing hero had some consequences, but one way or another his working day was now done. Time to go back. His apartment at the Plaza Arms wasn't too far from the District 23 First Action Response Team Headquarters, no sense in taking the subway. Other people would be worried about muggers or gangers eager to roll someone like Dave. Dave didn't worry about that.

Back to his crummy and crumbling apartment. Door closed and locked.

Empty and silent.

Breathing. In, then out. Regulate it. Keep watch. Slow and... okay, maybe not very slow, but steady. Keep it steady...

Keep it...

Dave Smith was safe and sound in his own little corner of the world, with no guns and no threats and no risks, and it was here that he finally began to panic.

His panic came from having a moment to himself and his own thoughts and realizing in a single sharp instant just how completely alone and lost he was in the still and quiet and insanity of the City of Angles. A city which ate people alive, which drove a woman to suicide, which pushed people to crime to save a loved one, which took with one hand while patting you on the head with the other. An inescapable city of contradictions.

Life alone had been enough to drive Dave's nervous condition over the edge and out the other side, to the realm of quiet desperation. Now life in the

City was looping his suppressed horror back around to actualized horror. Locked away in perfect isolation in a place they told him was his new home, this apartment, this *cell*, he was losing his nerve all over again.

Fortunately he already had his own Alprazolam, in a tiny little bottle in a tiny little cabinet in his tiny little bathroom.

I'm starting to rethink my career choice.

When I got started in the city, I was offered a job just like my old one -- sit perfectly still all day and draw advertisements. It would've paid the bills and been completely ordinary. I might have even been able to do it entirely from home, telecommuting, just like I used to.

I turned it down because this is New Dave. I wanted to be something more. So instead, they offered me this job with the FARTs.

Don't get me wrong, I'm glad I turned down the art job. I'm a lousy artist, anyway. I keep fiddling with that old Lucid Technologies logo (Officer Gilt thinks it might make a good masthead for the team newsletter) but sometimes I think it's getting farther away from what it should be, rather than closer. Maybe I shouldn't bother.

I'm getting off track. My point is, I want to be something more. You're right about that. If I'm stuck here in this place, I need to make the best of it and the best of myself. But these guys, the FARTs, I don't know if they're right for me. They don't help people, not really. They're damage control.

Yesterday I met a brother and sister facing cubism in the family. I wanted to help them, maybe figure out from security footage who they are, get medical attention for them. You said before that cubism isn't a doom curse -- that you'd even met people who came back from it.

But Polk told me in no uncertain terms A) not to bother, because Safety would just "purge her cubist ass with fire," and B) I should mind my own business if I want to get promoted to a cushy inner city job where the city is stable and there's hardly any gangs. That's the sort of apathy I'm dealing with here.

Anyway, I've got a few days off from the job. I'm the Hero of the Day; Gilt was highly impressed with my "bravery" and he says I've earned some shore leave. Hooray for me.

Maybe I'll meet up with you and your Dad for lobster or something? I know you're really busy with something your Dad doesn't want you talking about -- secret Sideways adventure stuff, I guess -- which is why you can't email too often. If you can't make time for it that's fine, I totally understand. I'll figure something else out. Let me know.

-Dave

On the plus side, Dave hadn't been having nightmares lately. He had a few weird ones in his first weeks here, particularly during orientation, but nothing since. Sure, sometimes he felt like the room was too large or too small or too quiet and he had to regain control of his nerves while awake... but at least that whole "night terrors" problem was somehow solved.

So one comfortable night later, and he was up and moving in this crappy little apartment again. Running through the morning rituals didn't take long. Normally after that he'd be walking over to HQ to sit and wait for any new buildings to arrive in his district... but as he'd emailed Penelope the previous night, he was officially on leave. Even if he half-lied about the reason why.

Gilt did use the word "bravery," and seemed genuinely impressed by Dave's actions. Peter Gilt had been one of the few quasi-friends Dave had managed to make; even if he still stayed professional and detached, at least Gilt seemed to approve of Dave's spunk. Sadly, their superiors up the chain in the First Action Response Team saw Dave's actions as foolhardy and a waste of good medicine, so he was on suspension for a few days. Gilt was the one who suggested he should view it as a reward for courage, even if it was just the courage to buck the system.

"The work we do is rarely pleasant, for anyone involved," Officer Gilt had explained, with a comforting pat on the shoulder. *"All of us do what we can to make the system work for everybody involved, but sometimes that just doesn't happen. Cheer up, Dave. Things would be a lot worse without us around. Take a few days off, enjoy your time, come back refreshed."*

Except routine was what kept Dave refreshed. Without the routine of daily work, he was left with nothing to do but sit around "home." Truthfully, that's pretty much what he did back on Earth, but... it felt different, here. There was more ambient menace in the air. Tension thick enough to cut with a chainsaw. While Dave could hold himself together in situations of obvious external stress, these moments between filled with unidentifiable internal stress were unbearable.

It had been ramping up considerably in recent days, too... that sense of pervasive and nonspecific dread. No clear cause. And unless it was Dave's inability to have proper perception playing pranks on him, the dread wasn't specific to him. It was all over the city. Sure, people moved with fearful purpose any day of the week, but lately... something in the air...

Not that he intended to sit around all day worrying about existential horror. This was New Dave. He embraced a ridiculous career because it was the way forward, not the way backward. So, he'd use today to find some other means of moving forward.

This meant creating a list, to track down causation.

Dave was a big fan of TO DO lists. Of course, he didn't always get around to DOing everything that needed TO be DOne, but making lists, that was a sensible thing to do. So, with a wide-open day ahead of him and no idea what to do with it, Dave decided to take psychological stock of his situation.

Using a note keeping app on his smartphone, he drew up a simple chart.

LIFESTYLE	LIFE ON EARTH	LIFE IN THE CITY
Home	Crummy apartment (quiet, uninteresting, isolated)	Crummy apartment (quiet, uninteresting, isolated)
Career	Commercial art (distant, unsatisfying, underpaid)	Professional FART (distant, unsatisfying, underpaid)
Friends	Only one, age-inappropriate (father)	Only one, age-inappropriate (12yo kid)
Romance	None currently	None currently

Finger tapping on screen. The modern equivalent of a pencil tapping on a pad, in thought.

Maybe Old Dave and New Dave weren't that different. From a glance, both were complete losers with bad jobs and prison cells for homes and no friends within the target demographic and as for girlfriends, well... one extremely awkward prom night experience with two weeks of follow-up fumbling before both drifted off in embarrassment probably didn't count in the long run and certainly not in the short run.

In fact, the only real difference between the two was New Dave's insistence on leading a life that reached beyond tucking away in a corner and plugging away at a wage slave job until the End of Days. New Dave, spurred on by said age-inappropriate friend, wanted to make a difference. Because he could. Because allegedly it was one of the few things he COULD do that others couldn't, actually.

But if he was going to reach beyond for the sake of others, how about for his own sake?

And so, Dave added a new column to that table.

LIFESTYLE	LIFE ON EARTH	LIFE IN THE CITY	TO DO!
Home	Crummy apartment (quiet, uninteresting, isolated)	Crummy apartment (quiet, uninteresting, isolated)	Make this place really feel like home!
Career	Commercial art (distant, unsatisfying, underpaid)	Professional FART (distant, unsatisfying, underpaid)	Figure out how to actually HELP people!!
Friends	Only one, age-inappropriate (father)	Only one, age-inappropriate (12yo kid)	Make new friends somehow!!!!
Romance	None currently	None currently	girlfriend?????

...and drawing a blank again. Because he had no idea where to start with any of that, particularly the farther down the table he got. It wasn't like you could head down to the Girlfriend Store and pick one out, perhaps in a ready-to-assemble flat pack kit.

But... furnishings were available in ready-to-assemble flat pack kits. And Dave's home was decidedly underfurnished and underdecorated. Maybe he wouldn't feel like he was living out of a closet if it felt more like it was his own home. Specifically, New Dave's home.

That was something he could do today. He could go buy furniture. Perhaps personal electronics or digital media, as well. Being a red-blooded American, he knew that the answer to life's existential dilemmas could always be found at the bottom of a credit limit.

Ten minutes later and Dave was bundled up for cold weather, locking the door of Apartment 2B behind him.

With brisk stride and fierce determination, he walked straight into someone loitering outside.

The impact was comical, sending both of them reeling, arms pinwheeling to try and regain balance. A cardboard box fell from her arms, lightly impacting on the grungy hallway carpeting.

Dave scooped up the box that the woman was delivering, holding the cardboard container out for her to accept. Unusually light, whatever it was...

"Sorry, sorry, entirely my fault," he offered along with the box.

"Yeah, thanks," she accepted, taking it back. "That one's 2C, right? The apartment next to yours? Number's been yanked off, can't tell..."

"Uh... I think so. I've never actually met my neighbor," Dave admitted. "I'm in 2B, and I know Mr. Ghanem is in 2A, and... well, if you're looking for Mr. Moore, they taped off his apartment, and—"

Moving past him, she dropped off the box at the doorstep of what was presumably 2C. While glancing at some delivery instructions loaded on her cellphone and muttering.

"Some days I wish things were less gonzo," the woman explained without actually explaining, before turning to leave.

Figuring she might be in a foul mood and following her around would be mistaken for stalking, Dave stayed by his door for a bit before departing for the furniture store.

It was only when he was rolling along in the subway system that Dave realized he'd actually met her before. Some weeks ago, when he was just starting out as a trainee, someone had flipped their taxi cab and he'd checked to make sure she was okay. Good to know everything worked out all right for her, whoever she was.

Life's many unanswerable questions are neatly shoved aside when you're busy grappling with the deeply important decision of what coffee table defines you as a person. In the end Dave got a highly personal coffee table, an individualized entertainment unit, a reasonably nonconformist television to go in that entertainment unit, and a few copies of some old mass-market movies he loved re-watching endlessly. Comfort food, basically. His budget for the month was annihilated and he'd likely be eating peanut butter sandwiches for a week, but at least he could throw on the Matrix or Star Wars and burn off a few hours when things got thick.

Delivery of the goods was going to take a day or so, and he had to be at home and ready to receive them sometime between the hours of 7am and 11pm, but that wouldn't be much of a problem now. Well, it wouldn't be fun to sit around going stir crazy all day waiting for someone to show up Any Moment Now with his goodies, but presumably it wouldn't result in a mental breakdown.

On returning to Apartment 2B, a conundrum had interspersed itself between him and the front door.

Someone had moved the cardboard box from this morning to his doorstep.

He distinctly remembered the discussion with the nice woman in the hipster glasses about 2C, how this box was meant for 2C. Why would someone move it to his door? Maybe they accidentally kicked it? But the box didn't look too damaged. Regardless of *how* it got here, it was up to Dave to complete the delivery. Not quite on par with delivering torpedoes to a two-meter port without a targeting computer and blowing up the Death Star, but it'd do.

Two seconds after knocking on the numberless door of 2C, he remembered he'd never actually met his neighbor.

Two minutes after knocking on the numberless door of 2C, he figured he'd probably never actually meet his neighbor. Maybe he wasn't home? Dave could drop off the box and call it a completed quest, but given it already ended up at his door once, maybe it was better to knock again and make sure this got to its destination...

His knuckles hovered over the door, which had opened at some point between the decision to knock and the attempt to knock.

Dave had to adjust his gaze downward slightly, as a young woman peeeeered at him through the crack in the door, from an apartment of darkness. Although he could only guess at the gender of his neighbor from her voice, given the poor lighting.

"Not buying anything," she mumbled. "Sorry."

"Uh, no, this isn't something I'm selling," he said, hefting the box for emphasis. "I think this is yours. I saw it being delivered this morning, but for some reason it was—"

"I moved it," she interrupted. "It's not for me. See? Says 2B. Turn it over."

Curious, Dave spun the box in his hands. Indeed, APARTMENT 2B was printed on the bottom, opposite to the This End Up arrow. Which was strange —if it was intended to be a delivery address, wouldn't it be on the top...? And the delivery woman was specifically citing 2C as its destination...

"I really think this was intended for you," he insisted. "I was here this morning when it was delivered, and... um. Can I come in and we can sort this out? Maybe open it up, see if it's something you ordered? Feels a little weird to be having this discussion through two inches of doorway..."

"In?" she repeated, as if the word could be misinterpreted. "You want to come in? In here?"

"Um, sure. If it's not a bother. I mean, us being neighbors and all, you can trust me. Not that proximity implies trust, I just mean... I'm... not entirely sure what I mean. Look, I'll just leave this here, and—"

"I'll need to tidy up first," she said. "Wait right here. Right here."

And the door closed.

So, Dave waited right there. Box in hand, its light contents sifting about a bit as she shifted weight from foot to foot.

And waited.

Five minutes later the door opened again, and this time managed more than a crack's width. Not that this helped Dave to see what lurked within; the lighting was terrible, even moreso than the poorly lit hallway of the Plaza Arms.

Honestly, he could've passed the box over and headed back to his safe little apartment. That would be the sensible thing to do. Find some way to kill a few hours, go to bed, wake up and wait for the furniture, watch some movies, watch some more movies, wait until his suspension was up, go back to his job, try to talk a few more people through their life breaking down around them, count the days, get on with it, keep going, and eventually die.

Instead he walked into her apartment.

If Dave's apartment was an underfurnished craphole, this place was an underfurnished craphole with a side order of creeping willies.

She'd gone with the default lamps and furniture, the same minimalist set Dave had started out with. And apparently hadn't branched out much from there; if anything she hadn't changed the bulbs long after they blew. Instead, the place was lit entirely by the glow of various CRTs and LCDs and LEDs.

That was the first thing he noticed, because the only way not to notice it would be to look at it from space. A bank of television sets, of every make and model... ancient tubes with cranky turn-dials, modern high-def sets, big box department store special junkers, and more. They'd been stacked in a roughly pyramid-like shape, using piles and piles of DVRs and VCRs as base bricks for the Aztec temple of video sacrifice. Each one blazed away with light... most turned to the white noise between channels, others showing random TV shows. To add to the weirdness factor, all of them were muted. Silent flickering pictures and flowing snow, begging soundlessly for attention.

On the opposite side of the room, on the standard issue desk where Dave kept his pile of random things he had no other place for, she'd placed a wide array of computing hardware. Like the pile of televisions, it was a mish-mash of all things computer-y from across the generations... two LCD monitors, one giant beige-framed tube monitor, two desktop towers with blinking lights whirring away below. A single keyboard, at least... although it was covered in a tea cozy with a stained daisy embroidered on it, to ensure no portion of the arrangement escaped Strangeville.

It was in the dual glow of video wall and computer pile that he saw her properly for the first time.

A twentysomething, much like him. Baggy clothes, pajamas likely, telecommuting style; some oversized high school t-shirt ("DISTRICT 37 PHS" with some manner of snarling cat head) and baggy sweat pants of generic make. Dave had existed in a similar state long enough to recognize it when he saw it... clothes you wore when you didn't really care to reach the sophistication level of buttons or zippers, and didn't expect you'd need to be part of society anytime soon.

An asymmetric bob of blonde hair—pale enough to be damn near white—swayed as she moved to gather up some empty pizza boxes from in front of the TV, clearing a path for him.

"I couldn't completely tidy up," she explained, setting the boxes on top of other, similar boxes. "Wasn't expecting guests. I don't get many guests. Not many at all. Sorry. Have a seat, mister...?"

"Smith. Uh, Dave Smith," he greeted, in the traditionally awkward manner of his people. The couch was exactly where it was in his own apartment, so he could find it despite the flickering radioactive lighting. "I've been living here since I arrived, but I don't think I've met you yet, miss...?"

"Jones. Kelsey Jones. —sounds like Bond, doesn't it. Bond, James Bond. Why do people do that? —don't really get out much. I do all my work here, so I don't really get out much and... and..."

As if she hadn't been living here untold lengths of time, Kelsey's introduction trailed off while while looking around for a seat Dave knew didn't exist. The apartment mirrored his own, and that meant one couch and one couch only. For lack of a better option, she had a seat next to him... although a respectable distance away.

No coffee table—which is why Dave had bought one today—but he could set the box between them, on the middle seat of the couch. A good, polite barrier.

"Anyway, I saw the delivery person this morning, and she was asking for Apartment 2C," he continued from earlier. "I think your door number got damaged, or something. You should probably call the super about that..."

"Oh, I tore it off. It's like widebanding your true name, if you let people find you that easily," Kelsey explained. "Better to make them work a bit for it. Then the only people who find you are really keen on finding you. Works great. Highly recommended. Really a problem when you need food or toilet paper deliveries but it's worth it, really worth it."

Weirdness is like an invisible line drawn by societal standards. Once you cross it, no comfort can be found, and retreat is highly recommended. Dave was aware, on some primal level, that he had just crossed the Rubicon of weirdness when the girl who stayed inside all day watching a dozen televisions at once admitted to testing the toilet paper delivery man's mettle.

But unlike most people, Dave's tolerance for external weirdness was remarkably high when it wasn't directly impacting his immediate survival. And wasn't he pondering making new friends...? Playing nice with the girl next door meant knowing someone in this city OTHER than your indifferent coworkers, the people you're trying to save who end up hating you, and the preteen Sideways explorer whose father would put three rounds rapid in your head if you looked at her funny. It wasn't a huge step up, but a step up was a step up.

Of course, if he was going to stay and play, that meant a topic of conversation. And Dave was not the most socially graceful of social animals.

Fortunately he'd carried a topic starter in through the door with him.

"What do you think's in the box?" he pondered. "Had you ordered anything recently...? I know deliveries are big business here, so people can stay home all day..."

"Here? Where? Here? Oh. Newbie," Kelsey recognized. "From that other city. The big one."

"Er, from Earth, yes..."

"I track all my orders in a spreadsheet. I use a spreadsheet. It says I don't have anything pending which would arrive in a box of this shape," Kelsey reasoned. "And it did have your address on the bottom. That's really weird. What's in the box? Wait, you don't know. Okay. Let's open it. It might be a bomb. You should open it."

Putting his faith in the likelihood of not being exploded, Dave went ahead and opened it.

Button-eyes stared back at him from the depths of the box.

"It's a teddy bear," he confirmed, pulling the bear free from the box. "Someone sent you a teddy bear."

"Sent *you* a teddy bear," she redirected. "I didn't order a bear. I... I bear-ly ordered... I... no, I can't think of a pun. Sorry. It's yours, anyway. I don't want it. Sorry."

Briefly, Dave considered arguing the point.

But... there was something oddly comforting about the plush toy. It was clearly made with love; even in the dim of the television screens he could tell it was a hand-made craft rather than a mass-manufactured product. It was staring at him with those buttons, which was definitely odd given dolls can't actually stare since they are not alive. A good stare, though. Like it was agreeing with him about something they hadn't discussed yet...

He tucked the bear back into its box, accepting it wordlessly. Probably for the best; Kelsey didn't seem comfortable with the thing, from the way she pressed back up against the opposite arm of her couch, away from it. Instead, she looked to the half-dozen shows airing on the dozen televisions, doing a cursory check of them. Something to occupy her eyes.

"Sooo... watch a lot of television?" Dave asked.

"What? Oh, no, not really," Kelsey explained. "I collect signals. You know."

"Pardon?"

"Ess-Ess. Sideways Signals. The shows between the shows," Kelsey said. "Patterns in the chaos. Things that don't exist. ...huh. You're really new, aren't you? Nobody told you about things like Channel 23?"

"I didn't have a TV until... tomorrow," Dave replied. "I mean, I have one coming tomorrow. And I guess I watched some TV back in Orientation, but there was this thing where I fell asleep with the set on and... yeah. I haven't seen much TV. What's Channel 23?"

She paused, before explaining. Like a video on pause, every muscle frozen. Unsure if she should continue.

In the end... she pulled her legs up, hugging her knees as she sat on her spot of the couch, looking into the flickering static of the video collection jars she'd set up across the room. And told her story.

"Nobody knows. Nobody can find it," she said. "Every single cable provider and all the over-the-air pirate broadcasts, none of them have a Channel 23. You can't broadcast on it even if you try, and if you push 'up' on your remote on 22 you land on 24. It's the holy grail of people like me who poke around in the signals, trying to find the weird things the Department of Safety doesn't like us looking for... can't put a yellow-black around the intangible, but if they could..."

Briefly, her eyes went to the stack of video screens... flicking at each image, looking for something. Pondering the static and the patterns that may or may not exist within.

"I hack cable boxes and inaccessible websites with impossible IP spaces trying to find things like Channel 23," she spoke. "Everybody's got their own theory. Personally, I think it's just a matter of going at it from another angle, maybe from another frequency or amplitude or time slot or outlet or... or... something. Some way through the chaos, working with it to understand it. So. That's the sort of thing I do. I collect Sideways Signals. I know it's dangerous, I know it scares people. Sorry for being creepy."

"So the broadcast space of the City has its own Sideways, just like the physical space?" Dave wondered. "Huh. I hadn't thought of that. How's that work, exactly? And the City's Internet is like that too?"

"It's just that I happen to believe that wait what?"

Kelsey leaned forward, peering at Dave from a funny angle. Her hair did indeed look positively white in the glow of unknowable channel spectrums; white and flickery, from the pulsing static and snow being broadcast onto it.

"I just apologized for being creepy," she pointed out.

"I'm not creeped out," he pointed out. "This is my not-creeped-out face."

"But you should be. Everybody is. It's one of the reasons I don't have guests. Nobody normal likes poking around with Sideways Signals. You shouldn't like sitting around talking to someone crazy enough to do that."

She was right, of course. A sensible person would be politely backing out of the room by now. From Orientation to the grave, the city taught you to fear and respect the many ways the City of Angles could kill you. Rule number one of survival was not to go poking at forbidden places with sticks, be they virtual or otherwise. And the pervasive doom atmosphere was indeed soaking into the fabric of Dave's anxiety...

But that was different from this. This was not that. This was a person. A person very much like Penelope, for that matter... someone with faith and hope in something, and willing to chase it while others were content to let it slip by. Which was more than Dave could manage for himself, some days. Kelsey Jones wasn't something to fear at all.

"I'm not creeped out," he summarized, for lack of better articulation. "Anyway, Danger is my middle name. Legally, I mean, my mother thought it'd be a great joke. Dave Danger Smith. And I'm okay with this."

Clearly, Kelsey wasn't expecting him to be okay with it. It was a confession, not a talking point—she was admitting to sins. But even that didn't explain the wide-eyed reaction Dave was getting...

She stood up from the couch suddenly.

"I need to go wash my hair," she declared. "Excuse me."

The bathroom door closed behind her.

Dave drummed his fingers on the bear-bearing box, not quite sure what to make of this development. The sound of running water suggested she had indeed spontaneously decided it was time for a shower.

Eventually he got up, deciding to bow out for now. Clearly she didn't want the delivery, which was his original reason behind coming here. No sense in overstaying the welcome.

He did, however, fetch the stack of empty pizza boxes on his way out. He'd just drop them off at the dumpster outside the building for her. It was only polite... and about the only helpful thing he could think to do.

So, I met a girl today. My next door neighbor.

Like you, she's an explorer -- did you know that there's a "Sideways" for TV and the Internet? Maybe radio, too. Well, of course you knew, you know everything there is to know about the Sideways. Anyway, that's her turf. She explores the "Sideways Signals." And "Sideways Sites," I guess, to keep the alliteration going. I bet that's what they're called.

It's quite a fascinating idea. After excusing myself from my visit, I spent the evening researching it. But there's not much out there about it, other than dozens of Department of Safety articles discouraging unauthorized cable boxes and such. I found some forums devoted to them, but they're all password protected.

I've been exploring wikis and websites in general for weeks now, burning the boring hours, so I can learn more about this world. Particularly cubism. Our encounter with that Picasso feels like ages ago, but it's stuck in my mind ever since. I knew how to help those two Salvagers thanks to reading a "home remedy" for cubism online. At least, I hope I was able to help them. My theory is that the more I know about this place, the more I can understand it, the less I'll feel awful about being here. That's my hope, anyway.

Didn't get a reply to my last email, guessing you're busy as heck. I hope everything's okay with you. I won't be able to get lunch tomorrow anyway, I'm going to be waiting around for my new furniture to arrive. Well. I say tomorrow, but really it's today, since this is after midnight. You know. I'll go to bed after I hit Send.

Still hanging in here. Still making do.

-Dave

Still calling out. Still ignoring it.

He wasn't having a nightmare. Dave didn't have nightmares anymore, none he could remember. So hearing something that sounded a lot like Penelope's voice, calling out in distress across a great distance? Couldn't be hearing that in his sleep. It would be, by definition, distressing. And he was not having a nightmare. Wasn't having any dreams at all largely. Still ignoring it.

Not safe there. Not with him and his calm assurances. Not with her and her smiling patron of temptation. Not even safe with us and our loud and lucid dreamers.

Very distressing words, which he chose not to hear. Well, he thought he chose not to hear them, but really the choice was made for him. Same effect, in the end. Words landing on deaf dream ears.

Guard the design. Guard yourself. Look to the bear. Let it guard you, and hopefully guide her. That was the best I could do.

And that was just nonsensical, which made it twice as easy to ignore. His pumping blood assured him all was well and he was not in fact in the throes of terror, being swallowed whole. Nobody was. Everything was fine.

I can't reach out any further to help you. If we do, she'll see you. May see you already. I don't know. I can't help. I'm sorry. Be well. Be safe. You're almost done.

Well, that might be a bit of a relief, if Dave knew what he was almost done doing. He didn't, so it wasn't a relief. Besides, he wasn't hearing it anyway. Minding his own somnambulist business. Keeping his head below the pillow. The rush of fluids reassured him. Pumping. Pulsing. Dragging. Thumping. Talking.

What?

Cracking an eye open from his non-nightmare, he slowly focused on the alarm clock. And the stuffed animal he'd dumped on his bedside table behind it.

7:47am. He'd overslept, because the little switch on the top which had four positions and he'd moved it to the third instead of the fourth and he didn't have the volume up so the sounds of Zack and the Wheezer's Morning Zoo Crew did not wake him. The joys of owning a clock radio.

The sound that actually woke him was people in his apartment, moving heavy furniture. Normal people would immediately fear for their safety, assuming someone had broken in and was robbing the place. Dave, despite the sluggish nature of his morning tardiness, guessed correctly on the first shot that the nice people from the furniture outlet had arrived twenty-three minutes ago. They did say they'd be around between 7am and 11pm, after all.

Uncaring about his pajama'd state, Dave emerged from his tiny bedroom into his tiny apartment, where very large men were being directed by a girl with green hair.

"No, two more feet to the left," she ordered, pointing. "Two to the left and eight inches away from the wall. Two and eight, feet and inches. I need enough space to get back there and make the hookups—"

"Kelsey...?"

It took Dave some time to recognize her. For starters, she wasn't wearing slacker-casual anymore—she'd changed into a comfy-looking T-shirt and longsleever combo, with some Internet meme printed on it. Baggy sweat pants were replaced with cargo pants, loaded with as many holes as there were pockets, bursting with tiny tools and measuring tapes and tightly wound bundles of cable.

But most notably, her nearly-white hair had been dyed a deep green. Apparently she did indeed have to wash her hair last night, as announced.

"Oh, I saw them bringing your stuff, so I figured I'd help because I know how to hook all of this up and because the stuff you bought is terrible," she explained quickly, while two burly men adjusted his entertainment center to her liking. "They sold you gold-tipped HDMI cables. I really hope you didn't pay much for those. I have better ones, and a spare hacked cable box so you don't need to pay for a sub, and I'm going to get you some WiFi going, can your phone do N?"

"Kelsey?" he repeated, because he was in no mental shape to make further mental leaps.

She glanced up at her own tattered green bangs, hanging asymmetrically.

"Uh, I thought it was time for a change," she said. "Changing for a time. I bought the dye weeks ago but never had a good reason to... anyway, I'm going to set everything up and—no, no, the couch needs to move too, it has to be centered, it's *very important* to be centered for the best viewing angle, look just move it this way, centered, this way..."

Deciding that the girl next door had his glorious television experience well in hand, Dave fixed himself a bowl of corn flakes, then went and brushed his teeth and stuff.

Technically speaking he was undergoing a home invasion (how exactly did Kelsey get them in through his front door without a key?) but it was more of a breaking-and-decorating sort of offense, which wasn't offensive at all. Best to let them have at it rather than get involved at this point. He might get a sofa dropped on his foot if he intervened.

This strategy paid off, because by the time Dave was fed and presentable, the nice men from the store were gone and Kelsey was relaxing on his couch doing color calibrations on his shiny new television set. Even had her feet up on his shiny new coffee table.

Dave had a seat next to her before realizing he was a bit too close. So, he coughed politely and pressed up against the left armrest a bit.

"Sooo... you're all set," she said, holding out the remote like an offered blade, hilt-first and upside down. "I programmed everything into your new universal remote. It's not yours, it's mine, but you can have it, I already have twelve and this one's not the best one. It's good enough. You can't get Channel 23 but you can get Channel 783 which some people say can show you your heart's desire if you watch at the stroke of midnight on a leap day, and you can get Channel Ninety-Q, which you can't actually get to because this only has numeric inputs but if you want I can manually tune it there, would you like that?"

"I... do not know?" Dave offered. "Would I like to watch Channel Ninety-Q?"

"Oh, absolutely not, they say watching for more than three minutes makes you blind."

"I don't think I'd like that, then."

"Suit yourself. So... who are you?"

Initially it struck Dave as a bit of an odd question. Sort of like if the brave adventurer just swung across the ballroom on a chandelier, striking down the rogue who was about to kidnap the princess, and then as the music swelled and the camera angle got super dramatic, he asked her 'Who're you again?'.

But on his second thought... it wasn't odd at all. Kelsey had talked his ear off the night before about who SHE was, what she did, why he should steer clear of her completely. And then she left to wash (and dye) her hair, granted, but it was still a lopsided balance of power in this neighborly meet and greet.

So, Dave told her who he was.

He explained how he used to be a graphic designer, because two strangers always started off on the career description foot. Of course, that led to explaining how he was apparently living in the Sideways for some time without realizing it, which interested her greatly. He spent more time describing his dramatic rescue by the adventuring odd couple than he did on anything else.

But, eventually he got to his recent career as a FART, and even talked for a bit about his frustration with trying to do anything of any worth whatsoever in his current position. Which was, not coincidentally, why he wasn't rushing out the door to get to his day job today, and had time to sit here and chat with his new neighbor...

"I don't think I'm really helping anyone. Maybe I am, maybe I'm not. I kind of want to help, since I never bothered going out of my way for anyone but myself for so long... so worried about my worries. And all I got for it was a lousy job, a contractual obligation company logo I haven't finished yet, and a one-way ticket to the City. There's... I don't know. There just has to be *more* to life than that."

It was more than Dave would have ever told anyone, long ago. He didn't even open up that much to his father. Granted that was due to there already being considerable weight on his dad's shoulders, and Dave not wanting to add to that... but this felt different. Both Dave and Kelsey were unspoken self-acknowledged social disasters. Perhaps the usual barriers cancelled each other out.

Still, it was hard to tell if he was talking her ear off and/or making her uncomfortable. She had a perpetual aura of being backed into a corner... it was more plain by light of day in an apartment with proper lamps, but it echoed what Dave had felt from her the previous night. Always walking on a wire. If you plucked at her, she might twang. Funny. Dave often thought of himself being the same way, especially during the worst years...

When he decided to bring his overly honest introduction to a stuttering halt, however, she returned the salvo in full.

She started by apologizing for taking so long to let him in the door yesterday—that the only people who ever came knocking were deliverymen.

"Haven't actually been outside in... in... I think it's been a long time," she decided on. "No need. Great delivery services, just great. Nowhere really I need to go. Even when I sell some of my finds, people come to my door to pick them up, or I upload them online. Everything I need's right there. Don't need anything more. Um. This is the first time I've visited someone else in... in... it's been a long time, I think."

Kelsey also explained that she was a "Digital Salvager," finding and selling data from the darker corners of the broadcast spectrum. Plenty of websites got echoed into the City of Angles, in whole or in part, but accessing them was tricky as tricks got. Plenty of TV shows were floating around as well, if you knew how to tune into them, and how to record them. They were elusive.

"I think my best finds were the lost episodes of Lost," she concluded. "Found them in an impossible FTP archive. Bits and pieces that didn't make it into the show, or... maybe they were never actually filmed at all. Never actually made, only dreamed up by the City itself. Either way I've got five DVDs full of 'em. They don't make any sense, though... even when you try to piece it together, it's just... random stuff. Numbers. Bears. Sometimes alternate takes of a shot used in the series. Sometimes long-held still shots of scenery or an actor just staring in the camera and screaming. Um. Is that weird?"

"I suppose? I've never watched Lost. Might be completely normal," Dave said. "Why, do you think it's weird?"

"No, not really. But I'm a bad meter stick for that sort of thing. I do know common wisdom says I'm not supposed to watch them, that those sorts of signals supposedly *cause* cubism, but..."

It was the first danger-tone sounded that morning. Kelsey had warned that her activities were considered creepy and questionable before, and Dave hadn't run away, which must've impressed her... but it did worry him, on some level. Worry for her.

"Is it actually safe?" he asked. "Watching Sideways Signals, I mean. Why chase after them like this if they're dangerous?"

"Because I'm not afraid of them. Because I want to understand them. Understand and not be afraid of them," she rearranged. "It's like white noise. Static. Snow. Snow crash. There's no pattern to it, but sometimes there is. If you stare at it hard enough... um. Anyway. Actually safe? Well. Depends on who you ask. Who you ask matters greatly."

"I'm guessing the Department of Safety says no."

"Yeah. No. I mean, yeah, they say no. City officials say it's horrible and awful and will drive you insane. But I say that... that... chaos isn't *evil*. It's just chaos. You don't need to be scared of it. You just need to be good at riding it out. I'm good at riding it out. I do it all the time. I'm not afraid of monsters under the bed. She's not all that awful. Do you want to watch Revenge of the Jedi?"

"Err, Return of the Jedi? Revenge of the Sith?"

And from one of her many pockets, Kelsey Jones produced a USB drive.

"Revenge of the Jedi," she repeated. "The one they didn't film. Supposedly. It's mythic. They say a Salvager gang found the reels in the Sideways back in the eighties, it's been format-shifted and passed around online ever since. Around and around and around. Studied, verified, unverified, disproven, proven, buried, uncovered. Haven't lived until you've seen an Ewok eat someone alive. ...it's kinda sketchy, though, and you *are* a government official, soo..."

"I haven't gotten past Trainee. And nobody's told me not to watch movies yet," Dave decided. "I'll get us some popcorn."

And so the second day of Dave's forced vacation was spent on the couch next to a cute girl, watching a movie.

It was the first time he got to enjoy Ewok cannibalism and second-reel surrealist Stormtrooper pie fights... and also the first time he'd felt truly comfortable since coming here. True, the film was a pile of headscratching weirdness that would unsettle most people, cobbled together by fans from scraps, but that was fine. It was practically normal, in comparison to everything else in his life. Just two people enjoying time together, letting the hours go by, sharing laughs and microwave popcorn. Hard to get more normal than that.

After the Jedi had been sufficiently Revenganced, Kelsey suggested they rewatch the third Matrix movie. ("Highly underrated. It really speaks to me.") She introduced Dave to levels of film analysis he'd never considered, and possibly were never considered by the filmmakers themselves. Allegories and metaphors about the nature of existence that justified every flop moment in the trilogy, if they were valid. By the end, he'd come around to her perspective.

He picked the next movie, opting for a romantic comedy about a character whose life (which may or may not have been fictional) was being written by a struggling shut-in author. The selection wasn't made with much thought; it was just one of the four movies he'd picked up at the big-box department store where he got the television. Kelsey was oddly quiet as she watched that one. And by that point, when Dave returned from the bathroom and did not sit at the distant end of the couch, neither of them noticed.

When the movie finished, they immediately went on to some episodes of an animated series Kelsey liked. And a few web videos Dave had found recently which made him laugh. (Kelsey wasn't the laugh-out-loud type, and Dave only half-laughed, but she insisted she found the cats to be funny.) And Kelsey wanted to watch something called "Candle Cove" but all that showed on the DVD was white noise, so they moved on.

And on, and on, and on. Pizza delivery. Movies. More popcorn. Heartburn. Antacids.

Eventually, it was one in the morning, and Dave rose from empty sleep to see his screen spraying gently quiet static. It had dropped back to the cable TV when the movie they were watching ran dry.

They'd passed out on the couch. Quite embarrassing, especially since now he had a sleeping body slumped against his shoulder. Any movement would wake her, and put him in a very awkward position. Well. More awkward than this.

So, for the time being, he stayed perfectly still.

This was not how he expected to be spending his mandatory vacation. Okay, maybe he was expecting to watch videos and waste time, but... this wasn't time-wasting, not really. Felt more like time well spent. And he wasn't doing it sitting all by himself on the middle of a too-large couch. Doubly unexpected.

Triply unexpected... it was the witching hour in the middle of his not-home in the middle of the City of Angles and despite the still of night, his pulse wasn't racing upward when he focused on that. No panic. Not even the self-aware panic that comes from wondering if you're about to have a panic attack and as a result causing a panic attack. There just wasn't... anything. Dave had found the calm little center of his new world.

For a minute or two, he embraced that calm. Let it refresh him, like his boss wanted it to. *Come back to work refreshed* was his goal, and maybe not a goal beyond reach...

But in the end, he had to get up. It wouldn't do to snooze the night away like this, for either of them.

First he had to extract himself without waking her, so she didn't wake up with a strange man all over her. No easy task, but he managed it through extreme patience and ninja-like stealth skills borne of not wanting to cause a scene.

Next, he had to wake her carefully. Maybe a gentle-nudge...

Kelsey did not judo-flip him across the room on waking. That would just be silly. But she did awake startled, as if someone had jabbed her with something. Not used to having someone else touch her, maybe. So, Dave backed off quickly (careful not to trip over the new coffee table).

"It's okay, it's okay—we kinda passed out," he explained quickly. "It's really late. Past one."

"Really...? Really. I fell asleep?" she asked. "Usually I only sleep with my white noise generator going..."

"Yeah, well... we've got one of those," he noted, gesturing to the TV behind him, over the shoulder. "I guess we should really call it a day. Hope you didn't have anything important to do, I didn't realize how late it was getting. Not sure where the time went, honestly."

And... the girl smiled. Which was a rare event. Even during the romantic comedy earlier she hadn't smiled much.

"It's okay, okay, okay," she insisted. "I liked—"

Her expression snapped back to nervousness so fast it was like the video of life skipped a few frames. If anything, she looked *more* spooked than Dave had ever seen her, even when he woke her moments ago. Eyes fixed at a point just over Dave's shoulder, mouth open...

Curious, Dave turned to look. Just the television, blasting the static between channels. Nothing out of the ordinary.

"I have to go," Kelsey announced—on her feet, again faster than expected, like she went from sitting to standing without any of the transition one makes through physical space between. "Goodbye."

"Huh? I mean, okay, it's late, I get it," Dave said, glancing back to the unthreatening television, confused. "But is there something wr...?"

He would've finished the word he started speaking, but when he glanced back, she was gone. Not just out the door, because the door did not in fact open or close. He thought he might've noticed if his door opened or closed. Just... gone.

While Dave had been living in the City of Angles for some time now and was starting to get the hang of how strange things were here, he was sadly not naturalized enough to think of anything other than: *It's one in the morning, my eyes must be playing tricks on me because I'm so tired. Nothing out of the ordinary going on here.*

And so he retired to his bed, to enjoy another nightmare-free evening's rest, thinking nothing more of it. The teddy bear by his bedside had fallen down the crack between the end table and the wall, but he didn't think much of that, either. Tomorrow would be another day of lovely vacation—alarm clock, breakfast, washing up, and the day free. Maybe he'd check in on Kelsey then. It'd be the neighborly thing to do.

The walls were thin enough between their apartments for sound to leak through. Dave knew even before he knew who she was that she was a TV aficionado, based on the muffled chatter and game show music and sound effects that floated his way now and then. And if he hadn't been asleep, maybe he would've heard sounds of a heated one-way conversation, followed by soft crying. But probably not.

Dave's teeth were brushed with a bit more jaunt than usual. He used a jaunty angle, far more flippant than the usual straight up-and-down, side-to-side motions he used. Curious. He rolled with it, enjoying the mundane details of life rather than simply burning through them as efficiently as possible. His morning toast was a buttery delight, his morning coffee a dark rich roast despite being the cheapest blend he could afford.

He even put on a rather nice shirt. Not a formal shirt, mind you, but not the generic white T-shirts that doubled as both daywear and eveningwear. This was a parting gift to him from Hollister Avenue, a commemorative concert shirt for a band Dave liked back on Earth. *A rare find in the City!* Hollister had declared, assuming Dave would be a bit more thrilled with the garment than he actually was. But today? Today Dave could find some thrill in it.

It was in this shirt that Dave came calling on the Girl Next Door. Much like the first time he came calling on her, she took her sweet time answering the door. Which was fine; he could stand there poking through his email, smartphone in hand, waiting for her to tidy up or whatever it is she was doing.

After ten minutes, he decided maybe it would be advisable to knock again.

Of course, Dave hadn't thought to get her phone number or her email address or any instant messenger contacts. Probably the most connected person he'd known in this city, even moreso than Penelope who was more of an outdoors-indoorsy type, and he didn't think to get any connections going. Which, on thinking about it, made him feel rather silly.

VERY silly, actually. What was going on here? There was practically a cheerful orchestral accompaniment behind him today, and why? Because he met a nice girl, someone he spent a few hours with, most of which was spent staring at a 16x9 video screen? They were just neighbors. If he wanted to borrow a cup of sugar or loan her the lawnmower, fine, but this *assumption* that he could just skip over next door in the middle of the morning and... do what? Why was he even here?

There. There's the anxiety. Needless worry over nothing at all. Because it was nothing at all. They had nothing, and it was silly to think otherwise—no. The *worry* was nothing. He didn't have to worry. He didn't have to think about this, much less overthink it. Just go with it, like he did yesterday, and whatever happens happens...

One way or another, he'd have an answer. Because her door opened. Just a crack, just like the first time, but—

"I can't see you again," Kelsey mumbled, without even looking at him. "I'm sorry."

And closed, before he could say another word.

Leaving Dave to walk slowly back to his apartment, close his door, lock his door, lean against his door, and realize just how empty the rest of this day was going to be. What a silly thing to bank his hopes on. Silly indeed.

At least now, he had television. That would burn away the pesky hours of his life.

He sat on the couch, and turned on the idiot box, and turned it off again after night fell and it was time for sleep and time to wake up and time to start it all over again.

I think I've been dumped before I even knew I was in a relationship.

I've only had one "relationship" in my life, back in high school. I was always so focused on my grades and my problems and my family and trying not to worry about the looks people gave me because I knew that was all in my head that I never even considered the possibility of dating. Fortunately, one other girl in school had the same problem.

She was a nerd and an outcast and a geek and never, ever talked. Except the one time she walked up to me and asked me to the prom.

Because nobody had asked her and I never considered the possibility of asking anyone. The entire experience was about as awkward and unpleasant as you'd expect, and thankfully quite short. She got married soon after high school and became a mother of five, so I guess she found happiness. And me, well, you know where I ended up.

Actually, this is an insane thing to be talking about with a girl your age. I mean, you probably still think boys have cooties. That's still a thing, right? Cooties? Or are kids these days sexually active really early? I don't know. I don't even know how it worked when I was a kid. By the way don't let your dad read these emails or he will probably shoot me in the head.

Been watching a lot of TV lately, and watching for your email. I guess you're really super duper busy. I'll just stop emailing now, this is getting too weird. I don't blame you, though. I'm the one spamming your inbox because I don't have anyone else to reach out to. My coworkers are my coworkers, Hollister's so busy with his job and his new girl, and there's just nobody else.

In a few days I'll be back at work and this whole mess will be behind me. Everything will make sense again. I did fine alone back on Earth and I'll do fine alone here, once I learn to live with it.

-Dave

Dad doesn't want me emailing you, because we're involved in something very, very dangerous. He says it's dangerous to involve you in any way. So, I'm sneaking this email out from a new account he doesn't know about because I got some weird blips and I think someone's monitoring my main account -- probably dad, that jerk. Honestly, dads, you know? Anyway I gotta be quick so can't write long.

I don't know if you've been mailing me, I'm not risking opening my inbox. I'd like to think things are going well for you, now that you have the job you wanted as a kid! But stay safe. And avoid the Department of Safety. They're super bad news. I'll be able to explain later. Have hope, Dave. Always have hope.

-Penelope

Four more days until the job and normalcy resume.

He'd spent an entire day just sitting there cruising around the channels. Didn't know which ones were the mystery channels unlocked by Kelsey, and which ones were normal. All the shows were a little off-kilter, much like the ones he watched back during Orientation. None of them gave him much comfort. Watching game shows and talk shows and car shows and cooking shows and show shows could certainly drain away a day, though.

Three more days until the job and normalcy resume.

Dave decided it was time to get off his butt and do something fun, rather than mope around his apartment sporadically taking his Alprazolam whenever he was having trouble breathing or thinking. That was absolutely not healthy, stewing in his own anxiety and depression. It was Old Dave thinking, not New Dave thinking. So, he went out to the movies.

Twenty minutes into the movie and he realized he was instinctively tilting his popcorn bucket a little to the right, as if someone sitting next to him might want any. Except nobody was sitting next to him and he felt incredibly stupid when he realized what he was doing. Despite going to some brainless PG-13 comedy with teased boobs and plenty of poop jokes, he didn't really find a laugh.

To make matters worse... on his way out the door, he overheard someone arguing over the price of a large soda at the concession stand. Loudly. Angrily. Both in front of and behind the counter, there was palpable tension. And then a flicker, a glitch, and running and screaming and Dave was out the door ASAP. He didn't stick around for the inevitable Department of Safety quarantine.

Two more days until the job and normalcy resume.

If pop culture was no comfort, maybe high culture was the key. Dave was ostensibly a visual artist; he'd studied art history in enough classes to know his Monets from his Morisots. In his hours of meandering online research he'd come across a website for an art museum, right here in the city. Surely quiet contemplation of paintings would bring some solace to his soul.

It didn't, of course. Not because it was as hectic and tense a scene as the theater—it was a quiet and tense scene. Few people were out today to gaze in wonder at the collected works of Earth and the City. The few that were... well, they kept to themselves. Purposefully hugged one side of the hall or another, to avoid coming near each other.

Sometimes Dave would try to catch someone's glance while standing at a painting, attempting to discuss the color or imagery, but... there was a weirdly *hunted* look in their eyes. A look he'd been seeing around the City quite a bit lately, actually. Like those two who exploded in an emotional outburst of cubism over something as simple as an overpriced beverage...

The only clue as to what was collectively going on came from someone who grabbed Dave by his jacket, while he was on his way out the museum door.

"Are you dreaming? Are you?!" the panicking man asked.

"Wuh, what?" was the best Dave could manage.

"Nobody's dreaming. Nobody. I haven't had a dream in *weeks*," he hissed, tightening his grip on Dave's lapels. "I keep sleeping and sleeping and I don't know if I'm awake or not. You made the sigil, didn't you? You can end this! She's waiting for you! You—"

"HEY!"

And the Safety Officer in charge of screening museum entrants chased the man off. Dave took this as his cue to exit, especially before anyone came asking him for details about what just happened.

Avoiding getting stuck in a dragnet around a theater outbreak. Dodging questioning related to a madman at the museum. Avoid the Department of Safety; *they're super bad news*, Penelope had said. Dave saw no reason to doubt her, even if there was plenty of reason.

Things fall apart; the centre cannot hold.

Probably one of the most overquoted quotes of all time, a vague doom prophecy taken out of context by people who had never actually read... whoever it was that wrote it, Dave mused dryly, since he had no clue either. But the phrase stuck in his head. Repeating, over and over. A mental loop which bounced off the walls of his mind as he bounced off the walls of his empty apartment.

One more day until the job and normalcy resume...

Going out was a mistake. Something was... *wrong*, in the city. Wrong in here, too. Wrong with Dave, wrong with everything. It couldn't just be his own innate sense of ominous horror, the pointless anxiety that rises within to compensate for a life uneventful.

This morning, he decided that as entertaining himself wasn't doing anything, he'd apply his tension constructively. He'd pour his passions into his artwork, such as it was.

He was going to finally finish that damn Lucid Technologies corporate logo. If nothing else came out of this vacation, at least he'd have that.

Nobody was paying him for it, of course. He didn't have to bother, if not for Officer Gilt suggesting the strange shape might make good masthead art for the First Action Response Team of District 23 Weekly Newsletter. Dave's hard work would at last have a home, appearing above stories about new babies born and puppies looking for a home and used cars for sale.

He hadn't been in touch with Lucid in ages, had no proper client instructions to follow. Instead he drew, and redrew, and erased and started over as he felt needed to be done. It wobbled away from where he felt it had to be, then wobbled back, then got blocked for days, then grabbed him by the shoulders when he least expected it...

Today, it was rushing through him. He could feel it like his own heartbeat. He'd jettisoned the latest draft, even stopped using the cheap miniature paint program on his phone. A run to the corner store got him pencil and paper, the only way to properly do this. He would be done with this insane project, this nonsense, this thing, this whatever, this sigil, this who knows who cares get it done *get this out of my head so maybe I can finally dream again—*

Around and around and around and around. Smaller and smaller, towards the centre.

A spiral. That was it. Which was funny, because he'd tried spirals before and they didn't feel right. The key was to make it a spiral at the core, even if it was also a knot or a series of sharp angular turns or whatever. There had to be a base to it, a centre, or it'd all fall to bits...

Hours ticked away as he precisely sketched each line, scratching it in firmly once he felt it was correct. Didn't matter that it had long since left the zone of sensible corporate art and entered crazypantsville. For once it was *working*, this weird thing that had been digging away at the back of his mind since before he even got to the City of Angles. A many-angled path, around and down, down, *down* into the page—

A muffled scream of terror interrupted him. Followed by the distinct sound of broken glass.

The line jittered and stopped.

He almost, almost, ALMOST ignored it in favor of trying to regain the shape that had finally become clear in his mind. But New Dave was already on his feet and out the door, pencil rolling away to be lost under the sofa, before Old Dave could lose himself in his own problems. After all, he knew who was screaming. And he'd be damned if he ignored a friend in need.

This time he had no intention of waiting around for five minutes.

"Kelsey? It's Dave—what's wrong?" he called out, through the wooden barrier that had separated them. "I heard you screaming. Are you hurt? Should I call 911? ...if you don't respond I'm just gonna assume I need to call 911. Kelsey? Getting my phone out. Just so you know. Okay?"

Of course, calling the cops on his neighbor if he was in fact overreacting would put him even more firmly in the doghouse. Where he already was. For some reason which had not been specified. Did he do something wrong? Was he too boring? Was— no. No time for perpetual loops of second guessing. If she was in trouble he needed to act, and if she wasn't, well, better to be wrong than to do nothing.

His finger neatly tapped the 9 before he heard her door start to unlock; a gradual process with five locks to go through.

There was the crack again. He was getting used to seeing her through a tiny gap in the door, by this point. Quickly he looked for any obvious injury... but other than being pale as a sheet and trembling, she seemed okay. At least, not profusely bleeding or anything.

"I... I had a little accident, that's all," Kelsey Jones mumbled. "It's fine. Everything's fine now. Now it's fine. I'll be... it's—"

The door was now open wide and Kelsey was sobbing openly in his arms. This came as a bit of a surprise, given Dave didn't think he'd even blinked.

"I'm ruined," she said into his chest. "Nothing's fine. Everything's not fine now. I broke my computer."

The place looked considerably more lived-in than it had a few days ago.

More empty pizza boxes, empty noodle boxes. Scattered books and manuals. TV remotes everywhere. Couch cushions misplaced, for some reason —why would she take her couch apart? Every television was blasting static now, just meaningless snow. Volume up. It's remarkable Dave could even hear her scream over the background hissing.

And, although he was loathe to actually point it out... she looked terrible. Hadn't showered in some time. Hadn't bothered combing her hair. This was someone coming apart at the seams and making no effort at hiding it. But she wasn't expecting guests today, so why bother hiding it...?

But her computer was in far, far worse shape. And weirder shape.

Keyboards often came in three-segment ergonomic configurations, but this wasn't ergonomic for anyone except maybe Martians. It was twisted and twisted again, as if partly melted. The keys had been completely shuffled around, no longer a friendly QWERTY. In fact, the Q was completely missing, replaced by a symbol Dave couldn't recognize...

The monitor had turned into an equilateral triangle. It wasn't broken or melted—it was triangular, as if it had been manufactured that way in the first place. Fortunately it wasn't functional, or Dave might not have liked whatever it chose to display.

As for the desktop tower itself... well. The window was broken, and for good reason. She'd defenestrated the CPU. It lay in pieces four stories below, in the alley where the dumpsters were kept.

Dave had seen something like this before, specifically a computer doing something like this before. When a Picasso cut a path of cryptic destruction through his old apartment, it transmogrified his computer into cheese. But if a Picasso had been roaming around Kelsey's apartment, presumably it would affect more than just a desktop PC...

She recognized the questions he was about to ask before he could ask them.

"It's from the Sideways," she explained. "Parts of it were, anyway. Memory chips. The keyboard. Ethernet adapter. That's the only way to access Sideways Sites... you need a computer that's been tainted with cubism. Otherwise you can't interface the right way."

"And... the rest of the computer got infected?" he asked.

"Uh... okay, yeah, I think that makes sense," she sort of agreed. "Anyway, it's ruined. I can't do my work anymore, Dave. This is how I can live and make my rent—lost episodes of Lost are okay, but the only real money is in the digital salvage I find. I can't do that without a cubist computer! I can't I can't I can't I don't know what to do now..."

"Count from ten to one, backwards," he suggested.

"What?"

"Do it. And breathe in and out once between each number."

"Dave, I have a problem, this is my livelihood, it's gone, and I'm stuck, and —"

"Kelsey... please," Dave spoke, quietly. "Trust me. Ten to one. Backwards."

For encouragement, he took her hand, and squeezed gently.

Ten numbers later, and she wasn't breathing quite as hard. Wasn't trembling as much.

"Okay. Now. What you need is another computer, right?" he asked. "Where can you get the kind of computer you need?"

"I already know where to get one," Kelsey replied. More stable and centered than before. "I know what to do. I can reach out to the guy who gave me my old computer."

"Oh, you know a guy? That's great!"

"No. No, it's not great," she disagreed. "He's a ganger. Name's Greyscale. Runs the Grey Market Gang, one of the Salvager outfits in this district, specializing in electronics. They may deal in geeky stuff, but they're just as brutal and dangerous as the other gangs. ...sorry. Your neighbor works with the guys who take potshots at you FARTs..."

"I'm familiar with the GMGs," Dave acknowledged. "They knocked over a drug store my team was investigating. It's why I ended up on probation. So... you're afraid this guy will hurt you? Should I call Officer Gilt?"

"What? No. No no. No. Greyscale likes me. ...LIKES me. I traded him a few website dumps for some new cubist computer gear, and now he won't leave me alone. Keeps sending me creepy emails and texts. I keep trying to ignore them but he keeps hitting on me and has severe boundary issues and I'm terrible at confrontations and I can't get him to leave me alone and he scares me so much and this is just gonna make it worse but he's the only guy who can get me the replacement parts and— and. And I'm going to have to ask him for help."

Somewhere deep, Dave's primitive man-brain stirred uneasily at the notion that he wasn't the first man in Kelsey's life. Then the rest of him smacked the man-brain down, hard, in favor of A) not being stupid and B) dealing with the real problem.

"Okay. You don't have to deal with him at all if you don't want to. You've got other options," he suggested. "I told you about my friends who are Sideways explorers. Surely they'd know where to track down some computer parts. They're busy with something but I'd be willing to bug them for this. Or there's Hollister, he's my mentor-of-sorts. Also busy, also willing to bug him. Seriously. Let me see what I can dig up—"

"Can't can't can't. Bad idea, very bad. I... okay. Um. I need to explain something without explaining anything..."

She was looking around for her couch cushions. Unable to find them, she decided to just sit on the floor. So, Dave sat across from her.

"Remember how I... told you I couldn't see you again?" Kelsey mumbled, embarrassed to even bring it up.

"Um. Yeah. You know, if you're not comfortable with me being here—"

"NO! No. Stay. Please stay," she added, to be polite rather than commanding. "It's just that... how do I explain this... I talked to a friend of mine, the night after we watched all those movies. Well, she called out to me, first. Told me that she doesn't like you very much. Um. Actually she kinda hates you. And your friends. Because you hurt her friends."

Another new brain sensation for Dave, being hated. He wasn't used to being hated. Ignored, certainly, but... who exactly had Dave annoyed enough to arouse hatred? He hadn't wronged anybody that he knew of...

"Please don't make me explain more than that because I am dealing with a *lot of things* right now and I don't want to make my life more complicated than it already is," Kelsey begged. "Just... point is, she doesn't like you. She doesn't like you *and* she doesn't want you to break my heart. It's bad enough I'm talking to you again at all, but if you pull your friends in on this problem too, well... it'll just exacerbate things. So that's out. Sorry."

"I have honestly no clue who this person is or why she'd be mad, but... Kelsey, look at us. We're adults, here," Dave said. "We're twentysomethings, even if it sure doesn't feel like it some days, and that means we make our own decisions, and—"

"—and I *wanted* to see you again!" she admitted. "I didn't want to tell you to go away! And for days I, I did my work and I was frustrated and I felt awful and I kept thinking about you and I know this is completely stupid since we just met and we barely know each other really and I don't really know what's going on but—but you're right. I'm an adult and I can see who I want to see, no matter what my friend says. But but but... okay. Compromise. You. *Just* you. I gotta leave your friends out of this. Sorry."

He could've pushed more. Found out who this mysterious friend was... a particularly abusive friend, from the sounds of it. Found out why it was so important to keep Penelope out of things.

But, Kelsey had asked him not to ask. She was pushed right up to the edge, and Dave could see it. Too many things collapsing around her at once. He'd been where she was, knew exactly how little of a push it'd take to cascade that collapse. He'd want to know more... later. When Kelsey was out of the woods.

That meant addressing the immediate issue. And nothing else.

"So you have to ask your stalker for computer parts," he said. "I can be your intermediary here, if it helps. A layer of abstraction between you and him may help. I could do the pickup for you, or call this Greyscale guy if you don't even want to talk to him. Whatever you think will work, whatever will make this happen without making a mess of it."

Kelsey shook her head. Slight snap to it, shaking too fast. "Won't listen to you. Not at all. Only works with people he knows. ...I gotta be the one who calls him. Maybe you can do the pickup, or come with me to get the stuff, I don't know, but I gotta be the one to reach out. ...stay here? While I make the call. Please...?"

This was the real job, wasn't it? The one he was actually hoping for.

Help people out. Help people like himself. People stuck in the tangle of their life, trapped in a maze of problems both real and imaginary, unable to sort out one from the other. Help them, and symbolically help himself. Help sort out the world around him in the process.

I keep going because I'm hoping in the end, it'll all sort itself out. It'll all make sense and things will be okay.

The depths of Kelsey's life-maze ran weirder than Dave could've imagined, and he'd already imagined them to be pretty weird. But he wouldn't shy away from it, wouldn't run in the face of that weirdness. Because that was Dave's one superpower—he kept his head while everybody else lost theirs. For all his lack of skill on every other front, he had that going for him. And now, for her.

"Make the call," he agreed. "And I'm here for anything you need me to be here for. We'll figure out some way through this together."

The good news was that Greyscale the Salvager Gang Leader Creepazoid did indeed have cubist computer parts he was willing to give her. For free, even.

The bad news was that he wanted Kelsey to pick them up in person. She tried to argue for sending someone in her stead to grab them (see also: Dave) but of course, he was quite insistent. Dave didn't hear his end of the very short conversation, as Kelsey mumbled into her phone in pleading tones. He wanted to make negotiation suggestions, or maybe take over as she increasingly grew uncomfortable talking to the guy at all, but before he knew it she was hanging up and heading to the shower to clean up and get ready. Once again, leaving Dave in her living room while she washed her hair.

Dave took this opportunity to head back to his apartment and clean up as well. And try not to let his mind spin away into fruitless predictions of what was to come. Kelsey did tell Greyscale she'd be bringing "a friend," non-specifically, which presumably meant Dave. No way was she going alone—Dave was insistent on that. True, he'd have to go face-to-face with a gang-banger, but that was a day at the office, wasn't it? He felt oddly calm about impending doom. It beat impending *nothing*, which is what really ground into him lately.

Twenty minutes later and they were in the back seat of a taxi, headed towards the outlying streets of District 23. Kelsey didn't feel like talking much, along the way... that hunted look running deeper than ever. Dave didn't intend to push. More information on what lay in store for them would've helped, but he could analyze and think on his feet if need be. That's how he disarmed the situation at that drug store, after all.

The taxi refused to drop them off at their actual destination; this was outer-city gang turf, bad territory, full of abandoned buildings and quarantined structures. They'd have to walk one block to their destination... a large warehouse.

This much Dave had been expecting. He'd researched the typical structure of Salvager gangs, in his wiki-wanderings. After all, they were the natural enemy of the FARTs, in the same way a lion is the enemy of... of... whatever it is that looks after the gazelles while the lions attack. Hopefully with no FART uniform, Dave would be unrecognizable as their prey. Multiple teams were assigned to District 23 and he'd only had that one direct clash with the GMGs.

Salvagers like the Grey Market Gang looted newly arrived buildings, crawling the Sideways looking for valuables, camping out in territory like this warehouse that had fallen into disrepair. They sold their finds to anyone willing to buy at their prices—it's funny how much new imports would pay for a taste of home, or what families would pay for packaged food. Shacking up in a warehouse full of pilfered goods, tagged to hell and back as private territory for the gang, was quite standard for them.

Nonstandard was the enthusiastic greeting Dave and Kelsey got when they made it through the metal detectors at the front gate.

Evening had fallen, and the GMGs were apparently were taking the night off from looting and pillaging to have a party. A whole cluster of folks Dave's age or younger, wearing grey and black. All races, all walks of life mixed in... the City (presumably) didn't pick and choose who got dumped where, and so the Salvagers reflected the City as a whole.

And all of them gave a big "Hey!" Or "Awright!" or "Whoa, hey!" on seeing Kelsey's face, despite her efforts to hide behind Dave.

Immediately, Dave spotted Greyscale. It was hard to miss him, what with his position at the core of the party, surrounded by hangers-on and hot girls and booze. Also, he wore a gold pendant laced with diamonds that read "GREY," which helped. If you took off the flashy jacket and the sunglasses-at-night and the jewelry, he'd probably look completely ordinary... a lot like Dave, for that matter. But he had all those things, which marked him as extraordinary. Nobody had a Hello-My-Name-Is tag that cost as much as the GNP of a third world nation unless they had a name you needed to know.

"Lo and behold, the Troublemaker has arrived!" he declared, in a voice far too ordinary to be intimidating. He waved her in with both arms, thrilled with her arrival.

("Troublemaker...?" Dave whispered.)

("Online h-handle," Kelsey replied, in a voice lower than a whisper. "Will explain later.")

"Kelsey Jones, as I live and breathe. It's like sunshine on a cloudy day when you drop in on me and mine," the gang leader continued....

...before peering over his shades, right at Dave.

"And... who's this?" he asked. "Thought you were bringing one of your girlfriends, or somethin'..."

"I'm just Dave, her next door neighbor," the next door neighbor declared, to deflect attention—and the current topic—from the trembling girl at his side. "I'm here to help carry the computer stuff she's picking up."

"Well, damn man, her stuff ain't THAT heavy," Greyscale spoke, with a smirk. Several of his cronies had a chuckle, on spotting the smirk and realizing it was supposed to be hilarious. "Just some bits and bytes. Kelsey, don't be shy, girl. Come on over. Have a seat, have a drink. T.G.I.S., you know? Thank god it's Sunday, because none of us gotta go into the office tomorrow. Bring yo' neighbor, too! 'Just Dave' is welcome in my kingdom. We are nothing if not neighborly."

"I, I, I, I," Kelsey started, unable to get past the first word. Glancing to Dave, desperate...

"We really can't stay long," he supplied, smoothly. "Sorry to take up your time. We'll take the computer parts and be out of your hair, no need to bother getting up or anything. Where are they...?"

Greyscale scratched his chin, in mock thought.

"It's a biiiig warehouse. The Grey Market's a treasure trove, y'know," he said, nodding to the cavernous, shelf-loaded interior behind him. "I'll send some boys to dig up her gear. But could take some time. So much to sort through. Come here. Sit down. Have a drink. It's a *party*."

The tone, that was something he recognized immediately. It was the same assuring tone that Officer Gilt used in his line of work. *Sir, please remain calm.*

A glance to his partner in crime.

Kelsey looked ready to run... but wasn't running. She stood her ground, even if that ground was unsteady. And was in fact the first one to take a step forward, towards the circle of social gangsters. Having a seat on a crate of DVDs, right near an expensive stereo currently pumping out the hot sound of Oblivion's Advocate, suburban punk rock darlings. Selecting it because it was wide enough for Dave to have a seat next to her.

"I, I, I just need the computer parts," she explained, finding enough courage to speak. "That's all I need. All I need. I just need—"

Greyscale's laugh cut her off.

"You're still doing that thing where you repeat yourself, huh? Man. Forgot how damn cute that was," he said. "Little Troublemaker cutie, sight for sore eyes. Y'know, I missed you, girl. Been some time since you poked your head out of that hole, you know? Holed up in that crummy little place. Dave—it's Dave, yeah?—you live there too. Still a roach motel or what?"

Dave accepted the focus of conversation. He could soak attention to keep it off her, no problem. "It's not bad," he said. "I just added a coffee table. It's looking better now."

More laughter. Furniture apparently being high comedy to the gang.

"The man has a *coffee table*," Greyscale declared. "That's a man who's sorted his life out, right there. Goes to work, comes home, sits at his coffee table, watches the news. A fine, upstanding citizen. Not like us punks and outcasts, right? All we have to do all day is... well, what do we do? Whatever we want, right? Right?"

Concordance from the peanut gallery, as his fellow gang members grinned ear to ear, nodding along.

"We live like kings. Finest things in life, only the finest," Greyscale explained. "I got the best penthouse in this crap slum. Floor-to-ceiling windows, spacious, room enough to party. The best toys, fun times forever. Ought to check it out sometime, Kelsey-girl. I got a cubist computer rig that'll make your eyes bleed. Not literally, I mean. But makes this sad little gift I'm gettin' you today look sad. You could be working on so much better if you'd sign on with the GMGs exclusively... might be safer for you, too..."

A brief silence, from the talkative gang leader. The crazed punk music pulsing behind Dave's ear from a stolen stereo played a weird counterpoint.

It was enough to throw Greyscale off his good cheer. He sat in silence a moment, leaning back in his plush leather armchair of a throne, surveying the two newcomers.

"Whole city's coming apart, you know," he told them. "You can feel it in the air, can't you? Folks cubing out left and right. And the name I hear in the streets... Bedlam. Cult of Bedlam, man. People thought it was the end times in the eighties, too, when the economy was garbage and the homeless were sacrificing people to that so-called demon. But even now, in the era of plenty, that doom's back. I could keep you safe through what's comin', little Troublemaker. You like the sound of that?"

If Kelsey liked the sound of that, she wasn't making a sound in response. The same jacklighted stare, like a deer in front of an oncoming car.

"...it's all the more reason for the Grey Market to party and live it up while everything burns down around us," Greyscale suggested—with a manic grin. "We are HERE, we are ALIVE, and we will run this city into the GROUND if we feel like it!"

That worked to upswing the mood. Despite actually declaring things to be horrible, his buddies took the "let's party" aspect and ran with it—fresh beers popped open, affirmative words blurted out, catcalls, the whole nine yards.

But then, Greyscale held up a single hand—silencing them. And leaned forward, towards Dave.

"So you tell me, Dave-who-has-a-coffee-table... you look around, you look at all this," Greyscale spoke, twirling his hands slightly, gesturing to his hoard. "I've got everything a man could ever want, ever want at all. I run the street. Nobody screws with me. I live the good life. I take what I want—I always get what I want. And my friends, my crew, they soak in the lap of luxury along with me. I can provide everything the Troublemaker's ever wanted. Now, why exactly—and I want you to think this over, really think about it—why exactly would Kelsey give all this up to live in a rotting little hovel next to a nobody like you? What makes Just Dave better than Greyscale?"

The crowd attitude swiveled on a dime. From party to sadness to party to anger... all of it now focused on him.

Better me than her, Dave decided. But he also knew better than to push his luck.

Fortunately timing was on his side. A new ganger had joined the party, now —one holding an open-top cardboard box, with the familiar beige plastic of an old computer keyboard sticking out. With the package ready for delivery, it was time to get the hell out.

"I wouldn't say I'm better than you, Mr. Greyscale, sir," he stated, tacking on terms of respect to supplicate. "I wouldn't say that at all. You've clearly built up a nice business. Family-owned. And it's really been a pleasure doing business with you—if you don't mind, I'll carry that box for her—"

"She chose your world rather than be one of the GMGs," Greyscale pointed out. "You know, I've spent considerable time courting her on a personal and professional level to join forces with me and mine. No joy. Seems she's happy to sit in squalor with YOU all day, isn't she? I knew there had to be something... or someone."

Rapid breathing, right next to him. Panic setting in with Kelsey. Not good, not good at all... this was turning very, very ugly. Dave got to his feet, slowly, nonthreateningly.

"It's getting pretty late," he observed. "Kelsey, do you want to leave?"

"*yesyesyes*," she mumbled.

"Thank you for the hospitality, sir, and the computer gear," Dave suggested. "We don't want any trouble. We'll just be going—"

And then he was on the floor.

In no time at all, the Grey Market Gang was putting the boots to Dave. They didn't even need direct orders from the boss; they were an extension of his will. They knew what to do when someone got in the way of something Greyscale wanted.

I'm being severely beaten, Dave realized, on some distant level. It didn't worry him at all. He was in utter agony, yes—desperately trying to protect his face with his hands, curling into a ball to hide his ribs, things like that—but it didn't matter. They were focused on him. Maybe Kelsey could run for it. Maybe they'd get bored eventually and boot both of them to the street. ...not likely, true, but he could hope...

"STOP IT, STOP IT!"

On her feet. She hadn't stood up, she was just on her feet now. And contrary to her earlier terror... anger had given her enough strength to overcome her fear. She still trembled and jittered, but it was mixed with a fierceness Dave hadn't felt from her before.

As if timed, the punk rock beat had begun to... twist. Strangely, white noise began to flow from the speakers...

With a gesture, Greyscale's team ceased the beatdown. Dave groaned involuntarily, rolling to look up at Kelsey. *Run for it*, he wanted to say. But vocalizations were a bit beyond him, with no air in his lungs at the moment.

"Leave him alone leave him *alone*," Kelsey demanded... in command of the room, now. Someone standing up to Greyscale, an unthinkable thing. "Leave me alone and leave him alone, keep the computer parts, I don't care, but I don't want to b-be here and and I can't I'm scared I can't—"

Two twitches. Then... solid.

"*You're pathetic, Alphonse Grey,*" she declared, in a briefly stable voice.

...which wasn't hers. The pitch was wrong; even with his head messed the hell up, Dave could tell. It was like two overlapping voices, Kelsey's and another....

"Just because I traded you some data doesn't mean you have ANY relationship, working or otherwise. I don't like you. I don't like your world. My world is digital and beautiful and chaotic and perfect. Yours is seedy and repulsive. I'll never love you. And that's how it's going to be."

Looming large, despite not being large. Greyscale, the average joe gangbanger who inflated himself with necklaces and shades, looking quite small indeed. He had to assert himself. Had to downplay this, had to take charge and redirect the room again...

"Don't think I like the new attitude you're copping," he declared. "Not one bit. You know, I first I saw you, saw this cute and sad little thing who deserved a proper patron. Wanted to do right by you, get you out of that apartment and into the REAL world. That so wrong? You hate me for wanting to help you really live your life, girl?"

Stutter, shift, frameskip. Kelsey going from fear to anger to some sort of... weird little smirk.

"I have a patron already," the Troublemaker declared. "I don't // I don't need you."

Noise, pulsing in Dave's ears, like pumping blood. White noise from the stereo which had been playing nihilistic tween punk pop. But now, it was white noise with a pattern. Two notes, over and over. Two words in 4/4ths time, words spoken with a young girl's voice, the same voice that had given Kelsey her dual-toned strength...

do it // do it // do it // DO IT

At last, Greyscale started to notice what was going on. And notice how his buddies, his comrades in arms, were on the verge of fleeing.

"Waste them both!" he ordered. "Hurry up and—"

One foot forward. Not one foot in front of the other, not walking. Kelsey had shifted one foot as in a unit of measurement, now standing one foot closer to Greyscale. No walking. Just... a snap of transition, like a jump cut in film. A flickering video artifact from a signal gone wrong...

Dave wasn't fast enough to do anything, not when he couldn't even pick himself off the floor.

The members of the Grey Market Gang may not have been fast enough either, but they sure as hell were going to try to run for it when Kelsey Jones instantly Picasso'd out in the middle of their warehouse.

The scanline-laced cubist cloud of flickering afterimages where Kelsey once stood was not something you wanted to be near. Now, she was standing in front of the gang leader. She was at his side. She was hanging upside down over the chair, eyes locked and level with his. Pinning him in, jumping from position to position, so rapidly that it looked like multiple Kelseys all over the place, filmed live in front of a studio audience. Screaming and running, gangers grabbing anything valuable they could carry from the hoard before bailing through whatever exits were available...

The only ones willing to go down with this ship while the rats fled were the cowering little king on his throne, the woman he'd wronged, and a useless next door neighbor.

Little by little, the broken images of Kelsey swarmed closer to the trapped Greyscale. At either side, behind, in front, above. Closing in like the inevitability of time.

But... alongside them, pushing them along, there were other images. A shadow of someone else, someone smaller and younger. Through the blur of his eyes Dave couldn't make out details, even after slowly getting to his knees, trying to force his focus into focus... but between that and the vocal trick, he knew enough. Dave could think on his feet, even if he wasn't on his feet.

The spectre urged her on, as Dave struggled to speak.

do it // do it // kill him // do it // he's horrible // he made you live in fear // show him what true fear is—

Despite a body full of liquid agony, Dave got a few words out.

"You don't need him," he spoke, echoing her earlier words. "You don't need this from him, either. Please..."

As if someone had hit pause on the remote, the ghostly afterimages locked in. Somewhere in the morass of them... Greyscale whimpered audibly, squeezing in as deep into his armchair as he could...

Kelsey, sitting on the DVD crate, where she was at the start. She hadn't actually moved, even if she did move in the quantum sense.

"She, she wants me to," his neighbor mumbled. "My friend. Bedlam. She wants me to hurt him. Wants me to leave you alone. Wants wants wants..."

"We're twentysomethings," Dave reminded her. "We make our own decisions."

One by one, the images faded. Only Kelsey remained, whole and unflickering.

Still... Dave could see the shadows which faded alongside the light. And one of them glanced back at him. A face that was almost human glowered at him, displeased. Funny thing was, it looked vaguely familiar...

Less than a minute later, and they were gone. Kelsey collected her box of computer parts, and they left the king of the Grey Market alone in what was left of his Grey Market—picked clean by friends who had abandoned him, leaving him sitting amidst a a pile of empty crates.

She wasn't flickering any more. He wanted to make sure of that, before they took a little cab ride to the nearest emergency room—no signs of cubism. The system had no interest in helping people who were falling apart, not if they were falling apart in that way. Only when it was clear that Kelsey had pulled herself together did he agree with her insistence that he get some proper medical attention for his numerous cuts and bruises.

Sitting there, bleeding and sore in a plastic chair, Dave perused an ancient magazine article about cheese or something and waited for a doctor to show up. Not much chatter... Kelsey had been very quiet. And Dave hadn't pressed her on anything, even if he was full of questions.

Oddly, she answered one of them—the least of them—unbidden.

"It's my middle name," she whispered.

"Pardon?"

"Trouble," she filled in. "Trouble is my middle name. My dad was a bit silly. Kelsey Trouble Jones. The Troublemaker. ...when you said Danger was your middle name, it... kinda spooked me. The synchronicity of it. Patterns in chaos, they dig into me like that, won't let go. Sorry if I spooked you that night..."

"Ahhh. Well... pleased to get to know you, Kelsey Trouble Jones," Dave Danger Smith said.

"And now that you know me... do you ever want to see me again?" she asked. "I'm slightly cubist. Slightly. I broke my own computer by accident, that's what really happened. I can't help it, I soak in chaos and I do it on purpose, and... and you should be afraid of me. I'll understand if you are."

For this, he didn't have to go *Pardon?* or *What?*. Dave even had an answer ready to the conundrum.

"I'm not afraid of you," he said. "Or of her. Or of Picassos, or any of that."

"Why not? Everybody else is," Kelsey pointed out. "Number one thing to fear in this city. Everybody's terrified."

"Really? Are you terrified, then?"

"...no," she admitted. "But that's the thing. I walk in the digital Sideways. I look at strange things and appreciate them for being strange. I decoded Bedlam's presence in the Sideways Signals years ago, I've talked with her, I can feel her in the wires. She likes me. And I'm okay with it all. I understand it and I'm not scared. I don't understand why you're not scared..."

Dave set the magazine down, leaning back in the chair. His spine was unhappy sitting upright, anyway.

"I've been afraid before," he explained. "Afraid of all sorts of things. Sometimes real things, sometimes imaginary things, just to keep that comfortable level of fear up. I maintained a level of anxiety so high when I was younger that I eventually punched right through and out to the other side. Now... do you know what I fear? Being alone. Having nothing worth living for. Just *existing*, day to day. You've got something you live for. Honestly, I admire that. And if it's Bedlam, well... I'm not going to talk you out of that. Maybe you see things in her I can't."

"She's... broken, in a lot of ways," Kelsey admitted. "A child, lost and scared. She's lost some part of herself along the way, I can sense that about her. Maybe that's why she sympathizes with me. ...we're both a bit broken too, aren't we. You and I."

"Maybe," Dave mused. "But at least we're broken together. That's got to count for something."

It was when Dave was exiting the hospital, covered in a wide array of tiny bandages and ordered to stay off the job another few days, that he crossed paths with familiar faces.

Their eyes met only for a brief moment—Dave with Kelsey, the two of them almost leaning on each other for support as they walked out through the automatic doors. And Jackie and Lonnie, the former Grey Market Gangers, previously seen raiding drug stores for anti-anxiety drugs.

She was leading him along, laughing at some joke told previously. Eyes bright and clear. They were likely coming from the urban center, headed homeward. She didn't spot Dave, and if she had, she might not have remembered him.

But Jackie spotted him. Remembered him. And offered, in one tiny moment, a look of absolute thanks for Dave's help in saving his sister from collapsing into cubism.

Despite the official government reprimand for giving away city property, despite being grounded from a thankless job, despite being quite nastily banged up, despite his maybe/maybe-not new girlfriend being best buds with a goddess of chaos... Dave felt complete in that moment. It was a single bit of firm evidence that he had, in fact, made a difference in this city.

I'm assuming you're checking email at your brand new account. But if this is cast into the digital void, that's fine. I'm writing it for myself just as much as I'm writing it for you.

So, I had an eventful day. Eventful week. I can't really summarize properly but let's just say I've been finding things that give me hope in the weirdest of places. Maybe even in the most eldritch bugaboos this city can offer... I'm hopeful about that one, given it directly ties into the well-being of someone who I'm surprised to say I care for quite a bit.

You're having problems of your own, and I get that. Your dad doesn't want me mixed up in them, and I get that too. But you've been there for me to reach out to in the past, and I'm offering the same now. If you're having trouble, I'm just an email away. Not in a "I'm desperately waiting for your response" way; I'm past that. I'm ready to listen if you're ready to talk.

When we next meet, I think you'll find I've got my feet on the ground properly in this city, at last. I'll tell you all about it.

Meanwhile, attached is a copy of the Lucid Technologies logo. More or less finished; either way I think I'm done tinkering with it, time to get on with my life. It's a curious shape, though. Lots of sharp little angles despite having this overall round motif. Completely useless as a logo of any sort. I'm not sure why I was so obsessed with it for so long.

The pain meds are kicking in (long story) and I need to get some sleep. Tomorrow's a new day.

Be seeing you,

-Dave

[**Attachment**: SpiralShape.jpg]

As Dave slept in another room, two eyes peered through the skewed and invisible corridor that connected his apartment to Kelsey's. It was a corridor that hadn't existed until recently, not until it was willed into existence.

Even in the dark of his apartment, the white of his drawing paper gleamed. Perfect little inked lines on perfect white paper, twisting back and forth, down and around. At last, completed.

No matter that this man had stolen away one of her friends, the Scout slipping free of the perfect nightmare-state she had inhabited and fading away peacefully. No matter that he was in league with her enemies, the ones who wanted to stop her from being friends with the whole city. No matter that maybe she'd even lost her little Troublemaker, the one who understood her, to his weird cooties.

In the end, Dave had crafted the one thing Bedlam coveted above all else— a map to the Heart of the City. The funny thing was that he'd crafted it for the other, the bright one, Lucid. Her clever champion Seth Dougal had sniffed out Lucid's plan, turning it into Bedlam's plan. While Lucid pulled together her champions the dark third lurked and waited, to snatch up that prize before Lucid could make proper use of it.

Her friends in the Department of Safety were already on their way. They'd secure her prize. Maybe they'd kill the one who'd bothered her friends so much, which would be neat, but it didn't actually matter. Now, she'd be able to make so many friends. Friends and friends and friends forever, in an eternal world of absolute perfect chaos.

She felt quite smug about it, honestly. Victory over her other selves after so long felt so very, very sweet. The three of them, at odds with each other ever since the fever and division... and in the end, Bedlam would triumph. Her friend Seth had outmaneuvered the ones Lucid spoke to and through. Bedlam would at last have her city of wonderful nightmare. Not a city of dreams, not a city of awakenings. Lucid and Echo collapsing away to nothing, leaving only Bedlam...

Dave slept soundly, as boots marched up the stairs of the Plaza Arms.

//end

Buildings next to buildings, askew or aligned. Buildings sometimes intersecting buildings, for that matter. Walk down a hallway, end up in a ballroom, double glass doors to a subway station, third exit on the left goes to a CDC facility which does nothing to control diseases whatsoever. Whatever you do, don't look in the rooms, because the patients are recursive.

There's no rhyme or reason to any of it—we've got streets which lead to dead ends, roads which criss-cross and loop back around, highways which go nowhere. Literally nowhere, as in "anybody going down that road is not coming back." This is not a good place to wander off unless you like wandering off forever...

Nobody knows where the city came from. Nobody knows how we got here. Nobody knows why any of this is happening. But it's happening. The city exists. We are here now. It's growing every day, and bringing new people with it.

We live a life amidst the twisted yet familiar.

If we're going to survive this, if we're going to stay alive and thrive, we need to learn to live in the City of Angles.

...here's an angle to consider...

There's nothing more terrifying than the truth. We lie to ourselves every single minute of every single day—we pretend the unimportant is important, notably, in order to keep some semblance of order over the chaos. It's very important to go down to the corner mart for a quart of milk, for example. A lot of mental effort is put towards that task, along with monetary resources gained through other mental effort, all of it leading to a frosty glass of milk.

Except the milk is not important—the milk is a lie. The truth is something which would put you straight off your milk, if you stopped to seriously examine it.

The truth about ourselves, the truth about our situation, is paralyzing. The truth about the City, the steady and measured pulse of its beating heart... those are the truths nobody wants to know. So, they lie about what they think matters, to avoid opening the door and seeing who exactly is on the other side.

Except when the one on the other side doesn't give you a choice in the matter. At that time, you will know her heart—and if it drives you mad in the process, so be it.

//008: Heart of the City

As Penelope Yates tried desperately to ignore herself, she briefly pondered having a tall drink of water. That would sort things right out—not the bottled water they'd been buying by the shipping crate lately, but water from the tap. A public drinking fountain. So refreshing. Maybe then, she'd be able to sleep properly... with no dreams.

But no, because her father *insisted* that she avoid whatever the hell Seth Dougal was scheming, she had to dream. Dreams which had been getting increasingly weird, since her life started getting increasingly weird.

Worst part of it? They were, in a moment of either supreme irony or supreme importance, lucid dreams. Just like the name Vivi had picked for their hideout. It'd almost be better if she wasn't aware she was dreaming—maybe then they'd fade away on waking, without mattering in the slightest.

Instead, these were self-aware dreams. She fully understood she was dreaming, nothing she was seeing was real, and she should be able to stop it... except she couldn't. Instead, she did her best to completely disregard it. Stand with back turned, and pretend nothing was happening while waiting for the damn alarm to ring.

This is the second layer. The dream of the city and the city of the dreamer, it's all connected. The dream can be what you want it to be—

"I want it to go away," she suggested to herself. "How about it? Can you make that happen?"

Can you make that happen?

Alas, she could not. Instead, she ignored it. Pointedly.

At the moment, Penelope was ignoring a pair of old-timey television screens with images that extended well beyond the confines of their glass tubes, begging for her attention. Two exemplar moments played on a loop, because of COURSE memory needed to be represented with a recorded-media based metaphor. Ugh.

One screen showed the incident at the Defined Tower... first with her father being murdered right in front of her, then rewinding and replaying, this time identical save for the wound being but a scratch. Dead, alive, dead, alive. Alternate takes of the same shot, like discarded footage from a movie shoot. Sometimes it zoomed in or went for a different angle, really milking it for all it was worth.

The second television showed an exciting bicycle chase through a toy store. No doubt the fine editing work of Flynn-Frisk Funnies Studio, there. It was indeed funny, the way a restroom appeared out of nowhere for them to escape into prior... and then as they were chased out of the store, an infinitely small crack in the walls of the Sideways gave them an exit from impending Bedlam-flavored doom. If she had a remote and could turn up the volume, maybe that television would have a laugh track...

Penelope didn't want to watch either of them. Neither of them made any sense. She somehow remembered her father getting killed, but he didn't get killed... and then an impossible waterfall of cars destroyed the Picasso that didn't actually kill him. And all the lovely spontaneous shortcuts in the toy store? Equally impossible. They formed exactly where and when she needed them most, as if willfully created, which was utterly and completely impossible.

You have to look. You've already agreed to look, been made to look. These things happened.

"No, I really don't have to look," Penelope mumbled, her back turned. "They didn't happen like that. I'm imagining things. I know this is a dream and I'd rather not have it, so I'm not going to pay any attention at all. So there. Nyah. You may as well give up."

You have to understand. Even if only in hindsight, you need and want to understand.

"I already understand. Obviously Dad never died, and those doors were there to begin with and I simply hadn't noticed them at first. That'd make sense," she reasoned.

You have to accept yourself. Just as the oracles have embraced you.

A trinity now, standing behind her. The clack of typewriter keys and the soft rustle of felt. The same force linking the three together, the force of lucidity...

"You mean Gramma Scarlett and Cassie," Penelope recognized—without turning around. "We don't know how they can do what they can do. Scarlett doesn't know why she can see the future in her dreams, and Cassie has no idea who's on the other end of her cosmic typewriter. Maybe they're mutants, like you read about in comic books. Or a secret Department of Safety superweapon program. It's got nothing to do with me, anyway. I'm ordinary. Like Dave."

You believe Dave is ordinary?

"Shut up and let me sleep!" Penelope screamed into her own head.

You believe Dave is ordinary?

Finally whirling about, to confront herself. To face the glowing heart-child, pulsing red with the throb of every life beat in the city—no. Ignore it, even as you stare it it. Don't recognize, don't acknowledge, just... yell at it.

"YES, I believe Dave is ordinary! He's the most ordinary person in the world!" Penelope declared. "You know why I like him? Because he's completely non-special. No crazy dreams, no cosmic coincidences, nothing scary and weird! He's just an average guy trying to live his life. He's trying to make the world a better place—just by being a good person. That's all. There's all this craziness around him but he's not part of it. I want him to be able to float above it all, since I obviously can't manage that myself. I want him to be happy!"

In contrast to Penelope's anger, the other part of her was calm and curious.

And if he's not ordinary? If he is special, in the same way all who are connected to you are? What will you do then?

If Penelope had an answer for her own questions, she couldn't deliver it. She remembered waking up instead.

Quickly rubbing the sleep out of her eyes (despite not getting very much of it) she tried to focus. Snoozing on a cot in the dark of the Lucid Dreamer's basement storage room was hardly restful—and no windows meant it was tricky to tell if it was day or night. Fortunately, her alarm clock—after a quick bash to make its LCD screen read something other than 88:88—announced it to be nearly morning. In fact, it was ten minutes before she was going to wake up anyway.

Another day, another stab at the conspiracy which threatened to... do *something*, even if it wasn't entirely clear yet what that something was. Penelope wasn't really enjoying her tenure as a freedom fighter, but her father was keen on it, and she was keen on keeping him from getting himself killed stupidly.

Hopefully today's plan would be enough to root this mess out. Hopefully this would be over soon, and she could get back to her... relatively ordinary life of crawling the Sideways and drawing maps. Hopefully. Always have hope.

The wide open spaces and blue skies of the Outlands made them ideal for farming and industry, but they were also ideal for people who purposefully wanted to be distanced from the rest of civilization. Or, in the case of Jon Boston, for people who purposefully wanted *him* to be distanced for the rest of civilization.

It probably wasn't a conscious decision. They had plenty of justification for it, after all. *Fresh air is just the thing for your lungs, Pop. You can't risk living alone any more, not with your health. You'll like it there, it's a beautiful retirement community. You can play all the Bingo you want.* And so on. Endless justifications for taking him out of his beloved little apartment in the fringes of the City, and dumping him in a comfortable oubliette.

Then came the lung cancer diagnosis, and the sporadic visits from relatives who wanted nothing more to do with him ramped up ever so slightly... before ramping back down, as he hung in there like a bastard. By this point, no doubt they were waiting for him to croak and cough up the inheritance.

But before he could politely up and die, he had one more thing to do. A burden to set down. Because there was actually a reason Jon Boston himself wanted to stay away from civilization, a person he wanted as much distance from as possible. Today, that particular story was of concern to one Gregory Yates. A story Jon was ready to tell.

After that, if his supposed nemesis somehow found out and took offense? *So be it,* Jon thought. He'd had enough life.

"Don't worry about me," Gregory Yates insisted, taking the guest chair of Jon's tiny convalescent hostel room. "I've already made the enemies I'm going to make. If this enrages them, well... I don't think that'll actually change anything. If anything, it'll make my work easier. Trust me on this. Now. How did it start?"

Fair enough, Jon decided.

"It started in the eighties. A lousy decade, all around," He explained, sitting up in his uncomfortable bed. "Sometimes I think the Earth's a parasite. We feed on its people, it feeds on our souls. It's stupidly morbid, I know, but America was thriving in the eighties while the City was crashing down around us. Highest unemployment rate on record. Homeless squatters all over the outer city fringes. Those were the ones Bedlam found. Men with nothing left, ready to embrace... whatever. Gangs. Cults. Motivational speakers. Same thing."

"My old gang formed around then," Gregory added. "I echoed in two years later. So yeah, I was there. Eighties. Screw 'em."

"Damn right. Lousy time to be a cop OR a robber," Jon said. (Odd, two people from opposite sides of the line chatting so casually now. But both were retired, in their own ways.) "So, I had O-2 clearance in the Department. High as you get without being the head honcho, in charge of my own investigation squad. We got tasked by O-1 to deal with these pockets of desperate weirdoes, cults and such. For instance, the so-called 'Cult of Bedlam.' Understand, they were just rumors... missing persons cases were spiking high, yeah, but 'They're being sacrificed to a chaos god' felt... it felt like hogwash, frankly. Still does, except..."

"Except you were there. You saw them firsthand."

Bad memories, floating up. He'd called them on purpose, though. Jon gritted his teeth through the pain of it—and the pain in his lungs—and nodded, acknowledging the truth.

"Your name wasn't reported in the newspaper article that broke the story, but I have it on good authority you were part of the raid," Gregory said. "You and your men were hailed as heroes. So why all the secrecy?"

"Wasn't how we did things on the job, back then. Not when there was Picasso exposure. Didn't want the stigma following our boys home, have folks in their communities think they got infected. On top of that, it was my only moment in the sun... after that, I kept my head down, stayed uninteresting. Retired early, and I've been lying low. Ever since... that *freak* started running the circus. Dougal—"

As if intoning the name was enough to summon up agony, Jon ran through the paces of a coughing fit. Blood on a tissue. Whatever.

"...I had better things to do than chase down rumors about Bedlam. But a dispatcher I'd come to trust came to me, said she saw a pattern in the kidnappings, swirling around a central point. A warehouse. She'd been on the money about other things... claimed they came to her in dreams. I know that sounds crazy, but..."

"Ms. Scarlett, yes?"

A surprise, there. But this man showing up out of nowhere, asking questions nobody had known to ask him before... should anything surprise Jon, at this point?

"I take it you found her? Is she still alive?" Jon asked.

"Alive and kicking. She's the one who gave me your name," Gregory acknowledged.

"Huh. Yeah, that'd be her. Dizzy dame, nobody at the district station house paid much attention... but I'd gotten mileage out of her instincts before. Figuring I could put this Bedlam thing to bed, I took a few boys with me to the warehouse. Weren't expecting anything, maybe rouse some transients, arrest some ranting loon, but... but what we found there... when we saw *her*..."

Pausing, to make sure his breath was even. He did not want to collapse into a coughing fit, not at this point in the story.

"Bedlam is real," he confirmed. "She exists. A crazy-looking thing, shaped like a little girl. You only see... it's like you only see her *shadow*, but the shadow is alive, so who knows what she really is? Doesn't matter. She was there. Her followers had kidnapped some boy, offering him up to be turned into a Picasso. That warehouse, the things they'd painted on the walls, the walls and the doorways and *everywhere*..."

He jerked, hearing the gunshots again. Not really there, he had to remind himself; just a memory. Memories can't hurt you. At least, not directly.

"...we opened fire immediately. Guns out and unloading on the crazies. We were shooting and shooting and we didn't stop. Papers didn't print that bit, you know... that they didn't fight back. They just screamed and some Picasso'd out —but they all died, left and right. We executed them, flat out executed them all. I think we all went a little mad, that night. Whenever I have a nightmare, it's that one. It's ALWAYS that one."

First time he'd spoken of that night, now thirty years on. Telling a stranger about the spontaneous moment of crazed slaughter was... not easy. But he'd been preparing all day. And why not? What did he have left to fear, dying of cancer? Already happening.

But the truly terrifying part... that he kept for the end.

"It's a miracle none of us shot the kid. Once the smoke cleared, we hustled the boy out of there. The papers reported the basics—officers on scene in shootout with gang, child rescued," he noted. "No details. No names. Cult of

Bedlam, that got out, no way to keep that out, but... no details beyond that. Certainly not anything specific about the minor involved. Not a thing..."

Gregory must've sensed that loose end. Most people would be horrified at the description of the shootings, but he didn't seem to care about that... he'd latched onto the part that Jon truly feared.

"Who was the boy, exactly?" Gregory asked.

"...one thing I left out of my official report... was the boy's eyes," Jon spoke, answering while trying to avoid answering. "Because I saw the look on his face, gazin' on that horrible shadow-child. Both of them the same age. And both of them smiling. The boy... the boy *liked* what he saw in her. I... I almost shot him down with the others, mistaking him for a lunatic. My mistake was in not taking him for a lunatic. If only I'd... if I'd just..."

Gregory allowed him a moment to stop clutching at the sheets, to calm himself, before asking again.

"I have to know... who was the boy?"

Jon closed his eyes, as if expecting to be struck down by a bolt of lightning for this. Not that the lightning would be immediate, of course.

"His name was Seth Dougal," Jon told. "Bright boy. Clever. Immediately devoted his life to learning the job, scaling the ranks of the Department of Safety until he was on the very top. None of the others could see, not like I could... I saw madness behind his eyes, the few times he crossed paths with me at the Department. I saw it pushin' him on, smiling all the way... so as soon as I could retire, I did. I got the hell out of there. I've been nothing ever since, and for that, I'm thankful. They say the cult's back in action, lately. Likely *his* cult, now. I'm glad to be where I am, far away from him."

Sensing the story was done, Gregory nodded to the man. Thankful.

"For what it's worth... I already knew about Dougal's involvement. We've been working this situation, the new Cult of Bedlam, for some time now. I didn't know *why* he threw in with Bedlam, but it doesn't actually matter," Gregory offered.

"...you knew? Then why did you want to hear an old man's rantings?" Jon asked.

"A few reasons. Scarlett thought you might want to talk about it, get it off your chest. And the timing was just right... me here, with you, in the middle of nowhere. Perfect bait for a trap."

Craziness. For a moment, Jon wondered if this young man was just as nuts as the cultists he'd gunned down that night... or himself, doing the gunning. But no—Gregory was calm and collected. Not even the false calm Seth Dougal projected, with inner madness. This was method without madness. But... still risky.

"You, your friends, Scarlett... you're all taking this new cult head-on, then?" Jon asked.

"That's right. Trying to, anyway."

"Then I hope for your sake you finish what we couldn't. Because the old Cult of Bedlam, that was... nonsense. Random kidnappings and disorganized, half-mad men. They were abominable, but ultimately, not much of a threat. A cult with Seth Dougal at the head... well. We'll all be lucky if we're dead by the end of whatever he's got planned."

Lucky lucky lucky lucky. Couldn't believe his luck. The stars were right. Ducks in a row. Luck lucky luck.

Everything was coming up Cartwright.

He'd been having a bad run of it this year, honestly. His career as a police officer took something of a turn for the worse when his boss sacrificed him to Bedlam, driving him completely insane. Cartwright had to admit, in the few times he was capable of admitting it, that going mad was something to be concerned about.

But now, he had a new role—he was a friend of the most wonderful girl in the world, a friend, a good friend, a girl who drove him screaming into his own skull and back again and made him into something strange and powerful and—

Lucky. Lucky. Had to focus on the luck. All this *luck* coming out of his ears, drowning out the orders.

His original orders were very loud and clear: *You know this Yates man quite well, yes? Good. I'm far too busy with the fear campaign to bother with that old fool myself. You know the patterns and personality of Gregory Yates well, which will aid us. Therefore, your task is to observe and report on his activities. Do NOT engage. Bedlam does not want any friends in direct contact with his daughter, little Penelope, and I'd rather not allow indirect risk. I realize this is going to be hard for your feeble little mind to grasp, Cartwright, but observe and report only or I will make you wish I was the one hurting you. I promise you that when the time comes to kill Gregory, I'll let you know.*

But so much luck, luck and ducks and stars. Hated, HATED Gregory Yates, the wife-killer, the gang-banger, the bastard. And here was Gregory Yates, all alone in the middle of nowhere...

This had been such a BORING assignment. Studying Gregory's movements, watching from afar, taking notes... all good police work, made him feel like a proper cop again instead of a minion of the cult. But Cartwright inevitably grew restless... and with Dougal's attention on other matters, Cartwright's brain slid a bit to the left.

The new orders were: *You know this Yates man. You know how evil he is. Observe and report. I'm too busy to kill him myself, and you hate him so much, so I'll let you kill him. Follow Gregory, bide your time, wait to kill him, the time is coming, he's hurting you, kill him...*

Those were the orders, yes, those were his original orders: *Kill Gregory Yates.* Simple and perfect.

The Cult of Bedlam was too chaotic, even when it was working at peak condition, for anyone to even notice that Cartwright's instructions mutated along the way.

With single-minded determination, Cartwright had tailed his prey right out of the City and through the Suburbs and into the Outlands. He kept a respectable distance, avoided notice. Hard to do on the open highway of the Outlands, but he probably succeeded; the target didn't seem the least bit worried about Cartwright's sub-compact following him.

Yates got out at a retirement home, went inside... *observe and report* drifted around Cartwright's mind, a dim and distant sound. Too quiet to matter. Not now, not with this amazing luck.

Because having finished his business here, Gregory was now all alone. Standing in the parking lot of the retirement home, leaning against his car, playing with his smartphone. Probably checking social media, posting photos. *I killed my wife, the most beautiful woman in the world, and oh also here is a funny picture of a cat.*

Perfect. Nobody else was here. Nobody to save him. He didn't really matter, anyway. He could die and it wouldn't hurt Cartwright's new best friend in any way. After all, it was the girl that was the real problem. The girl and the boy...

Cartwright just had to walk right up and kill him and then that would be the end of it. Maintain his human form, so hard to do that lately, but he had to do it. Gregory had to see his human face, right before the end. The end. No more Gregory Yates.

One foot in front of the other. One last walk and then he could unleash the new power he had, the power of being Bedlam's best friend, and tear Gregory apart. Each part torn from each other part, yes, that was the way. One foot in front of the other in front of the asphalt in front of his face in front of—

One foot on his back, keeping him pinned to the asphalt while the injector went into his neck. No time to embrace Bedlam's gift—his human bloodstream accepted the drug immediately, putting him to sleep.

Gregory tapped his bluetooth headset, to cut off the call. No need for long-distance communication, given the ones he was talking to—Archie and Karla—were a mere twenty feet away now, having successfully snuck up behind Cartwright for the takedown.

Cass pulled her delivery truck up on cue, and the living remains of the Seventh Street Scavengers hauled Cartwright's drugged body out of sight.

"Yes, that's how it happened," Penelope agreed. "Of course, he didn't tell me the plan. He's not particularly good at sharing, especially when it comes to putting his life on the line in stupid ways."

You weren't there for that. You didn't see it, how can you remember it?

Nonsensical, of course. She wasn't expecting much sense out of this situation—the many television sets, each showing their own vignettes. The other self. Back and forth, yammering, making no sense at all... but then again, why did dreams have to make any sense whatsoever?

"I don't remember it. It's not my memory—I told you, this is how he explained it happening," she repeated, at risk of redundancy. "Besides, dreams are weird and loaded with warped imagination. I probably filled in the blanks. It's just another type of creative writing, like Cass does. ...well, she does poems, not fictional prose, so I guess it's not the best comparison, but..."

Yes, she does not write fiction. She writes truth. She wrote his truth, yes?

A new television, rolling up on little wheels. Archaic technology. Penelope could barely remember when televisions weren't an inch thick and came in four-by-three aspect ratios. The image on the screen... a filthy-looking fellow, tied to a chair. Bleak and dark.

"Look, are you going to insist on showing me this stuff all night? I'm pretty sure this isn't helping me rest," she said, trying to ignore the new addition to this gallery. "Aren't you me? Don't you have a vested interest in making sure I get my beauty sleep?"

You believe you are asleep?

"Well, duh. I remember you trying to show me things, and I wouldn't turn around to look at them and... wait, no, I... that dream ended, I woke up in the Lucid Dreamer, Dad was gone, a few hours later he showed up with Cartwright, and... huh. Am I napping? That's got to be it, I'm napping..."

You have to understand, she insisted. *You want to understand. Remember how it happened. Know what happened.*

"I already know what happened, I was there!" Penelope insisted. "Cartwright eventually woke up, and that's when we started to figure out what was really going on..."

Swimmy. Swimmy and swimming...

No, wait, no. Opposite. Solid. Solid and swimming. If he was just swimming, if his mind was adrift, he'd probably drift away from humanity as well. In fact, that was his first instinct—embracing the gift that people laughably called "cubism," losing himself in it. But he was too solid for that. Solid and soft.

And tied to a chair. Arms behind his back, human legs lashed to chair legs, securely fashioned.

And, for some reason, there was a teddy bear in his lap.

A bright light had been aimed at his face. That plus his darkened surroundings meant he couldn't see particularly well, couldn't see the ones who had captured him or where they'd taken him...

...but they could see him just fine.

Gregory almost felt a pang of pity for the man. The last (and technically first) time he'd met Officer Cartwright, the man had been sharp and confident. He'd taken some oddly personal pleasure in trying to pin Gregory with a crime he didn't commit, thwarted only by cleverness and a bit of bluster... but even in defeat, he was composed.

This wasted, washed out *thing* was not the Cartwright that he'd locked horns with months ago. Like the other "Shabby Men," as Scarlett had named them, he'd let himself completely go. Scraggly beard, long fingernails, and a distinct shower-free aroma. Not uncommon, for those who fell between society's cracks... but the madness in his eyes, even doped to the nines on sedatives, that was truly pitiful.

"Let me summarize what's going on here, so we can get to business," Gregory spoke, when the man came to. "You can't flip out and go Picasso. Not only do you have enough drugs in your system to put down an elephant, but you've been bear-proofed against cubism. You're stuck here and powerless, so you may as well cooperate."

Cartwright's head rolled around independently on its neck stump a bit, as he tried to focus through the weirdness in his veins.

"Familiar," he managed, with a sputter. "Familiar. It's very familiar..."

"Trust me, you've never been here before. And you're going to be out the door just as soon as we're done."

"No, I mean this. This. This situation," he clarified. "Interrogation. You. I had you in one of these, some time ago. Almost had you, for the things you've done. But you got loose. Now, you have me. That's a funny thing..."

"Trust me, I'm laughing on the inside. Now. We need information about the Cult of Bedlam—"

"Did you bring your daughter with you on this adventure?" Cartwright asked, trying to see past the spotlight. "You'd expose her to all this madness, wouldn't you? It'd be just like you to take *her* child and ruin that little girl forever. I almost got Penelope away from you, back then. Almost. Slipped away—"

The girl's voice, next. Confirming she was there.

"I'm not leaving his side," Penelope declared. "And you're wrong about Dad. Completely wrong—"

"Not now, Penny," her father insisted. "Cartwright. Focus on me, thank you —I'm the one asking the questions. Now. We've picked up others in your merry band of misfits, but always too low-ranked, or too crazy to give us anything solid. You, though? You're Seth's right-hand man. I'd bet you've been following me for weeks now, but lately, you've been pretty damn obvious about it. Probably losing your grip. All that combined means you get to play the weakest link. Good job."

"Won't tell you anything about Bedlam. Not a thing," Cartwright promised. "She's my friend. She showed me things you can't even begin to start to consider comprehending. Won't tell you anything about him. Dougal. O-1. He's given me something wonderful. He's a brave man, a smart man, with a plan for this city, a plan you'll never—"

"You've been diluting Nightmare Fuel into the city water supply," Gregory declared, to cut to the chase. "We know. We found the ruins of a drug lab run by one Doctor Montgomery, which filled in most of the blanks. It's put the city on edge, bottling up their nightmares, giving them dreamless sleep. We haven't been able to shut down the entire operation, given it's just a few of us versus all of you... but it's only a matter of time."

...which was clearly not what Officer Cartwright expected to hear. His prideful ramblings stopped dead... leaving him with a very human look of confusion about him.

"Seriously?" he asked. "You figured all of that out?"

"Seriously," Gregory confirmed, nodding. "Even with Seth running the show, this is the Cult of *Bedlam* we're talking about. Its bedrock is madness. They weren't very subtle in the eighties, and they're not subtle now. You're just too chaotic to carry out a grand scheme for very long without making mistakes. Us capturing you being proof of that."

"Then... what am I doing here?" he asked. "There's nothing left to interrogate me for. That's the plan—drugs in the water supply. People turning Picasso. It's perfect. It's horrible. I'm wondering if I've made a mistake when I was befriended. I made no mistakes. Everything is fine. What? What more is there than that?"

"That's what we're here to find out. Because the drug alone is not enough to transform the city into a cubist paradise—incidents are on the rise but it's not enough to take the whole city down. I don't think Bedlam would settle for a slightly increased amount of cubism when she could bring about a proper apocalypse. We're missing something about this plan. You're going to help us find it."

His head flopped to the side, one eye fluttering shut as he tried to think through the haze.

"I don't think I can help you. I don't think I will help you. I hate you very, very much," he pointed out. "I don't know anything. I've forgotten more than I ever knew. You're a murderer and a thug, Gregory Yates, and I'll never help you. There's nothing I can do in the face of Bedlam. She's my friend. She replaced my fear with grace. I'm terrified of her. I'm not making sense. You won't be able to get anything out of me, you goddamn *bastard*, you killer—"

"Fortunately we've got other means of drawing a confession out of you," Gregory explained. "All you have to do is sit right there and stay comfortable. ...are you ready? Remember, no names. He can't see you, and Dougal doesn't know EVERYONE in our little gang."

On the other side of the blinding spotlight... two figures indistinct from Cartwright's view, but very distinct to Gregory. One of them being distinctly uncomfortable with all of this.

She pulled up a chair... turning it backwards, straddling it, studying the madman in front of her from her safety in shadow.

"Don't know if this is gonna work," Cass the poet / taxi driver / cargo trucker noted. "It's not like telepathy. I just... sometimes read *about* people, when I look at them. Vague things. Whoever's typing to me doesn't dredge up useful specifics..."

The one at her side, encouraging and comforting, rested a small hand on her shoulder.

"Remember what Grandma Scarlett said. Don't think of it as someone typing *to* you; you're the one providing the words," Penelope reminded. "You're the one with the actual insight, like how she controls her dreams. Just look at the guy, and tell us what you read in him..."

Cass adjusted her glasses, peering nice and hard at the drooling individual bound to a chair. Squinted. And clearly got nothing in return, as the developing frown on her lips suggested. So, she tried glancing aside, distracting herself... then glancing back.

A series of near misses, culminating in missing her forever.

"...which tells me jack-all," Cass said, after repeating the roughly typed letters wobbling over Cartwright's head. "Sometimes it's insight into a person's motivations, sometimes it's a wry observation, usually it just makes no goddamn sense. Any clue who he's thinking about?"

"It's not relevant," Gregory immediately declared. "Try again? Could be like fishing. Maybe you'll get something else."

"Not how it works. I get one little blurb, and that's it. It's meant to be a summary, I think. Like a fortune cookie that doesn't care if it seems relevant or not... sorry. Don't think I can help much. ...you're not gonna have to waterboard the guy now or something, are you? Should I be hustling the kid outta here before it gets messy?"

The kid in question felt the need to speak up, before that line of thought got chased any further.

"We can't kill him," she declared. "And Dad promised we wouldn't torture him. Everybody knows torture doesn't actually work like it does in the movies. I still think C— the uh poet, might be able to get something out of him, and without needing to resort to thumbscrews."

"It's a nice thought, kid, but all I can see is what I can see. Sorry."

"But poems are usually longer than one line," Penelope pointed out. "In some ways, aren't you writing a poem about this guy? It should by way longer! Like, one of those Greek epics I had to slog through in my online courses!"

"Well... yeah, but it's not. That's the long and short of it," Cass replied. "I can only read what's there."

"But could you *write* more than what's there? Not read, but write?"

Hanging on the end of her question, Penelope stood on her toes, anticipating. Cass didn't... SEEM immediately dismissive of the idea. In fact, she was thinking about it, having held back her default no-can-do just a moment...

...to swap it for a slow nod.

"Someone bring me my Clark-Nova," she declared. "I've got a poem to write."

Coming up short is a lifestyle choice, a dedication, a final omen which dictates the rest of a life not very well lived.

Coming up short is missing opportunities, going left when you should go right, falling in open manholes you could have seen miles away.

Coming up short is his excuse for everything that has gone wrong in his life.

Coming up short is his justification for everything that has gone wrong in his life.

The father, the mother, missing education, missing job opportunities, missing a chance to get him private education. Missing chances at a better life.

The child, the son, missing life connections, missing social opportunities, missing a chance at love eternal. Missing Elizabeth, the only girl who ever had a kind word for him.

The man, the officer, missing paperwork, missing promotions, missing closed cases. Missing a shot at being anything other than two rungs down the ladder.

The fool, the lunatic, missing his future, missing his chances, missing his mind. Missing any hope for a life beyond the chaotic glory he's been tricked into embracing.

All because one man didn't miss a key detail that he missed.

The fault lies within, the fault lies without, the failure is his own to own, the failure is society's responsibility.

The failure was redeemable, finally having the one thing he wanted, revenge against the one who made him miss his chance with her, the one who distracted her from him so long ago.

The error of omission, of missing observations, being dragged down just short of the mark, dragged away have his humiliating life laid open bare

The final miss, missing his chance, missing his shot, missing the mark, and henceforth Cartwright will not be missed by anyone. Not even himself.

The sharp clack of that final period snapped Cass out of her trance.

Her two companions had been reading over her shoulder, the whole way through. She felt vaguely alarmed that she hadn't even noticed, but of all the things to be worried about today, that probably ranked low.

Despite being the author of the piece, she hadn't actually read it yet. So, she skimmed it, while Penelope and Gregory did their own internal literary analysis.

"Wasn't Elizabeth my mother's name?" Penelope wondered aloud—

"Elizabeth Elizabeth, Lizzie, Liz, third row, second seat over from the window," Cartwright interrupted. "Only one who ever talked to me like I existed. Always wanted to ask her out, never did. Never once. Felt stupid. Didn't think I was good enough. Tried to be good enough. Went with a bad seed in the end, some local hoodlum, not me, not the good guy. Just a friend. Tried and missed—"

"It's not relevant," Gregory declared. "In fact I'm not seeing much of anything in here that's relevant..."

Cass leaned back away from the typewriter, while hanging onto her chair. "This is his life, man. It is what it is. Not my best poem, but I'm under pressure here, y'know? You're lucky I got this much out on paper. I could try for volume two, maybe...? But this seems to be the whole deal, start to finish. I just write the words, up to you to interpret them."

Scanning the lines up and down, Penelope did her best to interpret. But in her online classes, crusty poetry and really old books were not exactly her strong suit. She was better at math and geometry... logic puzzles, pattern recognition, that sort of thing. Colorful metaphors just felt like fluffy nonsense to her...

Patterns. Might be something to that, actually...

First four lines are about shortcomings. Don't focus on the whiny life complaints; count the lines in each block, identify the blocks, see how they fit together. Four on shortcomings. Four which detail his life, step by step. Then one single line on its own which breaks that pattern, then four more lines, then done.

That one single line stuck out. It didn't fit with the others, which meant it called attention to itself.

"One man didn't miss a key detail that you missed." Penelope spoke, looking back up at Cartwright. "Who and what?"

The memory triggered another stream of babble, much as the teenage memory of schoolboy dreams did.

"The key, the key detail, the keys. Keys on a key ring," the former officer replied. "The boy had four keys, not three. Dougal spotted it. Dougal's a clever bastard, rising in the ranks, when I never could. He saw the keys. He also saw something in the spiral, the weird crayon-shape. A drawing on a placemat. *This is the single most important piece of evidence.* The boy. *This is the key*, Dougal said. The key was the boy was the key..."

She should've had a sinking feeling, knowing what the answer to her question was going to be. Not a rising feeling, like something coming to mind which she'd been trying to keep out of her mind...

"What boy...?" Penelope asked.

"Dave Smith," Cartwright recalled. "The key is Dave Smith."

The rising words inside Penelope could be heard loud and clear across her memory, now: *You believe Dave is ordinary?* They weren't spoken in a mocking tone originally, in the dream she kept having every night, but right now they certainly felt mocking...

"We've gotta get Dave out of there!" Penelope declared. "If Bedlam's gunning for him, if the Department of Safety gets their hands on him, I can't believe this, for *weeks* they've been after him and I kept ignoring his emails and calls because you said not to involve him but he's totally involved and always was and—"

"And we'll swing by his place to pick him up right now," Gregory agreed. "Get the truck prepped. We're leaving immediately."

"—what? Really, Dad?"

"Yes, I wanted to keep him out of this. And I'm hardly Dave's biggest fan, but... clearly the boy's important in all of this, for some reason. Whatever that reason may be, I want Dave out of Bedlam's reach. We'll hide him here in the safehouse until we figure out our next move. ...I take it you're going to insist on riding along on this one, Penny?"

Visibly vibrating with energy, Penny grabbed Cass's arm, nearly pulling her from her chair. "Let'sgolet'sgolet'sgo!" the teenager yammered, tugging. "Gotta go! Gotta rescue Dave! Move out move out!"

The young explorer pulled her poetic companion from the room, up the basement stairs and into the Lucid Dreamer above before Cass could say a word.

Leaving Gregory alone with his would-be archnemesis.

Cartwright eyed the trusty sidearm that Gregory had taken to wearing at all times. Eyed the gun, and the man, the man with the gun.

"So, now what happens?" he asked, curiously.

"I'd very much like you out of my life," Gregory admitted, knowing what the man really meant. "Not that I personally care one way or another, but you're a risk factor for my daughter. Unfortunately, she's also the reason why I have to leave you alive. We've got friends here who will keep you fed and watered—and sedated—until we can figure out how to put you back together. So no, I'm not going to shoot you. I'm not the ganger bastard you think I am, Cartwright. I stopped being that long ago... left it behind, for her. Her, and Liz."

With his business here concluded, Gregory turned to leave. Cartwright's plaintive, almost pleading voice gave him pause.

"I have to know," the broken-down man said. "I have to know. Elizabeth. The two of you went into the Sideways together, but one year later, only you and your daughter came back. The official record chalked it up to an accidental death. ...did you kill her? Did you kill the only woman I ever loved?"

The fact that Gregory had to think about how to answer did not ease Cartwright's mind.

"Yes," Gregory Yates confessed.

And then he explained why.

It was the only thing which kept Cartwright going, and now it was gone. Everything else had been stripped away from him. He'd lost each piece of the laughable excuse that was his life... his career, his sanity, and now his hate. All that remained was the also-ran, the pathetic wretch that knew it was pathetic.

No point anymore. The shining glory of Bedlam didn't even feel glorious anymore; that illusion had been stripped away when the anger that powered him had faded.

Fortunately for Cartwright, amidst the cots and boxed food and other trimmings of a secret society safehouse, Vivi Wei had brought along a full length mirror. After all, she wanted to look her best, even when she was hiding out. And in this mirror was the blue-eyed answer to his silent prayer for an end to it all.

When Vivi came downstairs to check on their captive, she found a pile of ropes with expertly tied knots loosely draped around an empty chair, with a single teddy bear sitting where Cartwright once sat.

An empty chair, with a single teddy bear sitting where Cartwright once sat.

The fuzzy standard definition image winked out, leaving a tiny phosphorescent dot in its wake. Old technology. It caught up so slowly to her, no matter how tightly she clung to the modernity of the city. Strange, so strange the way the wake moved slowly—

"I never saw that," Penelope realized. "I didn't see that. We came back later and Cartwright was gone, but... but I didn't see how he left. What happened to him..."

You have to understand. You want to understand—

Pulling at her pigtails, twin shots of pain to distract. Turning her back on the vast array of television sets, on the strange images both familiar and unfamiliar. Turning her back on herself.

"This is a nightmare," Penelope decided. "I'm just having a nightmare. I'm imagining things that never happened, mixed with things I remember happening. That's completely normal, the way life jumbles up everything on your mind into a stew while you sleep. I'm completely normal..."

You want to be completely normal. I'm sorry. You're not completely normal.

No more rage at the strangeness of her situation. She was too worn out from the parade of images and that pleading voice, the voice that matched her own. By now, she could barely manage a whimper.

"I want to be," she spoke.

I know. That's why you are, because you want to be normal. But there are things you need to understand, all the same. I'm so sorry. You are who you are.

"I'm... I'm scared," Penelope admitted... daring to look back, at the other self. "Where am I..?"

Now... the bright child was behind her, offering a comforting embrace. An embrace, and a direct answer. No puzzles to challenge her identity, at least this time.

You're in the Heart of the City, she explained to herself. *You're here with those you love. Your father, and Dave. You found him.*

Finding parking for Cass's box truck took longer than the actual trip out to District 23, home of the Plaza Arms and Dave Smith. Looking for a parking meter which wasn't occupied, tied to a ridiculously small space, or broken into by people desperate for coinage proved too much for Penelope Yates... after a few minutes of this she simply jumped out of the truck, breaking into a flat run for the door of the apartment building.

Gregory caught up moments later, while Penelope was mashing the call button for Dave's apartment. And getting no response.

Fortunately the building's buzzer and lock combo hadn't been in proper repair for some time, so nothing stood in her way as she busted down the doors (a process much like opening them, but with more vigor) and bounded up the stairs. Technically she'd never been to his apartment before—they were far too busy to stay in touch outside of email and texts—but he'd offered his address long ago, just in case. She'd memorized it.

And on arrival at the door to Apartment 2B, she found it criss-crossed in red-black Department of Safety quarantine tape. Damage to the wood surrounding the doorknob suggested it had been hammered open at some point.

"No no NO. Arghh," Penelope grumbled, giving the door a bit of a kick. "They got him, Dad. We're too late. Too damn late!"

"Language, honey. And this could've happened days ago," Gregory suggested. "There's no way we could've known—"

"Yes, we could have," she countered. "Because he emailed me last night. He was HERE, Dad. We just missed him. If you hadn't insisted I leave him out of this, if you weren't hacking my email to make sure I didn't reach out to him, maybe we could've—"

"Hold up. What?" he asked. "Hacking your email?"

"I know when someone's hit my account, Dad. I'm younger, remember? I know more about tech than you do. I know you've been reading my email!"

"...honey, I wouldn't do that to you," Gregory said. "I trusted you to keep Dave out of our mess. I didn't need to spy on you. I wouldn't know how to hack an email account, anyway. If someone was listening in on your mail, it wasn't me. Why didn't you tell me about this before?"

"Because you were—! Uh... wait. It wasn't you? Then... who...?"

"Department of Safety," he concluded. "This would've been good to know earlier, Penny. ...look. We can talk trust issues later. Right now we need to figure out why the cult wants Dave. And before you suggest it, rescuing him is out—we don't have the manpower to stage some kind of full-scale raid on a police station, even if we knew where he was. Right now the best thing we can do for him is figure out Seth's plan, fast, and stop it. Let's start by searching his apartment..."

Gregory examined the door. Although it had been clearly forced open, the Department was unusually thorough in sealing it up after. Standard quarantine spikes to permanently fasten the door to the frame, and quite a few of them, had been rammed through at various angles. Usually the red-black or yellow-black tape was enough to keep anyone but a desperate Salvager out of a potentially cubist space, but Seth had ensured this place would resist all but the most determined looky-loos.

"We're going to need a crowbar," he determined. "Hopefully there's one in all the bric-a-brac rattling around in the back of Cass's truck. Let's go figure out where she parked and we'll sort it out from there."

Her neck was mid-nod... before she noticed the briefest of motions, just behind her father.

"Go on ahead," Penelope suggested. "I'm going to look around a bit, see what I can find out."

"Department of Safety could come back, Penny. I don't want you out of my sight—"

"They came and went, Dad. And I know how to hide if I gotta. Don't worry about me," she insisted. "Go get a crowbar. We need to move fast on this, right? We'd have to question the neighbors anyway, may as well split the tasks."

Despite a look of mild suspicion... pragmatism won over, and Gregory decided he indeed needed to move fast. After a few more assurances that she'd stay out of trouble, they split the party.

Leaving Penelope to investigate the one who had been peeking in on their conversation.

The next door neighbor should've been in Apartment 2C, but the number was missing from the door. Curious. Penelope knocked away, politely but enthusiastically. Sort of a two-and-a-half knock.

No response.

"Hello?" she tried calling out. "I'm looking for my friend; he lives next door to you. ...I saw you listening to us, out here. Can you help? Do you know what happened...?"

One full minute later, and the door opened a crack yet again.

Penelope put on her bestest winning smile, for the benefit of the somewhat nervous-looking woman on the other side of that door. The neighbor was clearly on edge, swimming in a little pool of fear and anxiety. It took her a minute to even acknowledge she'd heard Penelope, and those fingers did tremble as they held onto the doorknob... her eyes stayed fixed on the ground, not even looking at the visitor.

"Th-they took him," the woman said. "Took Dave, they took Dave. Police. Safety officers. Late last night they took him..."

I didn't tell her his name, Penelope realized. Whoever this was, she knew exactly who Penelope was talking about. Of course, it was normal for neighbors to be on a first name basis, yes? Not that Penelope would know, never having lived in one place long enough to get to know the neighbors— and her father wasn't the neighborly type, which didn't help, but... Dave's email, the one he sent to her alternate account the other night, DID mention "someone who I'm surprised to say I care for quite a bit." It was a stretch, granted, but... a boy and a girl living side by side, and him worried about the well-being of someone who could be on edge...

It was worth a sympathy gamble, at the very least.

"I'm worried about Dave, too," Penelope spoke truthfully. "I'm trying to figure out why they took him. Anything you know could help me, and help him. ...did he ever mention me? Penelope Yates? I'm a mapper, I specialize in the Sideways...?"

...which might have been the wrong thing to say. Her eyes widened in recognition, finally looking up to see who was at the door.

"Sh-she doesn't like you. Any of you. I shouldn't be talking to you," the woman mumbled. "You look a lot like her. That's weird. But she doesn't like you. She only wants me to be happy, she doesn't want me to get hurt, she knows things are going to get bad with all of you, she doesn't want me getting close to him because I might lose him I don't know I don't know what to do, she took him, I don't know what to do..."

A bad time for Penelope to recall that Dave had mentioned the source of his concern for this woman being "eldritch bugaboos." Bedlam, perhaps...? Which would also explain the "you look a lot like her" comment. Something Penelope had been trying to forget, as a matter of fact. So much here to untangle, so little time...

Focus on the immediate. That was a lesson Gregory had hammered into her, time and time again. Don't overcomplicate when lives are on the line.

"I want to help Dave," Penelope promised. "I think you want to help him, too. Please... please, anything you can tell me that will help him, anything at all, would be... um, helpful."

Conflicting emotions. Conflicting goals, clearly, as the woman pensively gripped her doorknob. Penelope could see the minute wobbles of the door on its hinge, as she pondered whether to close it or open it. Pondered the risks.

Honestly, this whole thing was a risk for Penelope. She thought she was just going to gather intel from a neighbor, not potentially poke someone in Bedlam's camp, if that's actually how far this went. But she'd gone too far in this short but dangerous conversation not to see it through, especially if someone who cared more about Dave than Bedlam could come over to their side. It was worth the risk...

Apparently the woman agreed, as her door slowly opened.

"I'm Kelsey Jones," she introduced. "And I've got my own Sideways shortcut into Dave's apartment, if you want to use it."

By the time Gregory and Cass had found a crowbar, they found the unlabeled door to Apartment 2C wide open, with Penelope waving them in like an airport tarmac director.

One six-foot-long jaunt through the smallest part of the Sideways he'd ever seen later, and the entire group was now in Dave's apartment. Along with an unfamiliar young woman...

"Long story short," Penelope said, "This is Dave's next door neighbor who's a friend of Bedlam but wants to help us help Dave. And the Department of Safety stole a corporate logo sketch that was on this coffee table last night. I saw it sitting there in a photo Dave emailed to me, but it's gone now. We better get back home, fast, and figure out exactly what it is. Come on, time's short."

Exciting music should've been playing. After all, our heroes were setting forth to rescue one of their own—it was to be a grand chase, all across the city and deep into the Sideways, as far as one could go into them.

"We were too late," Penelope recalled. "We didn't know at the time, but Bedlam was already on her way to the Heart. She'd gotten a huge head start. They had Dave, and they had everything they needed to get access..."

Not everything.

The next monitor rolled into play. This one at least made sense—a high angle shot, down into a Department of Safety interrogation room. An actual, factual video camera could've made this recording. How exactly that recording got into her dreams was another story, but she'd given up trying to question exactly what was going on, by this point.

Penelope bit her lip. "I should've been there for him," she said. "We kept him at arm's length. I obeyed Dad, for the most part. And he was being watched by our enemies for every moment we were ignoring him. I keep thinking that if I'd reached out earlier, I could've done something... did... did they hurt him? Is it my fault they hurt him?"

Her other self was curious, now. Leaning on the monitor, displaying the interrogation room. *If you knew what they did, that would be a memory you couldn't possibly have had. Dave hasn't told you what happened. Are you sure you want to know something you couldn't know?*

"Y... yes. I want to know," she decided.

And sat down before the monitor, cross-legged, to watch what was on the tube tonight.

Earlier, much earlier...

...Dave Smith was having a terrible night.

For starters, because it was literally how his night started, he got beaten up by a gang of Salvagers and had to go to the emergency room. He was fortunate to get out of that mess with only scrapes and bruises aplenty; the doctors didn't feel there was a risk of concussion or internal bleeding, so they sent him home. A good night's rest would be enough to at least help him stabilize.

Unfortunately, an hour or two after Dave crashed out on his couch in sleep, he was awakened by a battering ram to his door. Before he could properly object to men in body armor and riot shield helmets storming his apartment and messing up his recently vacuumed carpet, they had him handcuffed and out the door. They only paused to swipe his house keys from a tray by the door and carefully roll up the full-page Lucid Technologies logo sketch he'd left out.

Now he was having trouble resuming his prior sleep, given he was in an interrogation room deep within some Department of Safety precinct. Fluorescent lights, lack of proper bedding, and extra bruises added on top of today's pre-existing bruises meant no more sleep for Dave Smith. Sitting upright in a chair and handcuffed to the desk didn't help matters.

At first he wondered if they came after him for his involvement in the craziness at the Grey Market, but nobody had actually charged him with anything. No mug shots taken, no fingerprinting. Straight from some precinct back entrance into a tidy little room to sit and wait. And wait.

Despite his predicament, he wasn't particularly worried. Which was worrying, since most people would be worried about being bagged without Miranda rights and dragged off to a cell. But what gave Dave some comfort was that Kelsey wasn't here—they'd completely ignored her door, compared to the loving attention they paid to his with a battering ram.

If this was about the gang fight earlier, or her cubism outbreak... they didn't have all the facts. And if they wanted to get those out of Dave, well, he could make up some story that completely omitted her. He knew damn well what the D-o-S did to people with cubism, even the uniquely controllable cubism that Kelsey exhibited. No way he'd help them hurt her.

An hour later Dave learned the truth about his incarceration, gaining the answers he was patiently awaiting. He didn't like them, but hey. Answers.

Despite being a new arrival to the city, Dave knew who Seth Dougal was. Everybody did. He sat on the City Council, representing the Department of Safety. He ran the show. He had great power and sway. And he was smiling quite, quite widely. Maybe a little too widely for a human mouth.

Seth pulled a chair up to Dave's table, opposite him.

"So, I suppose you're wondering what's going on here," he spoke, after taking time to straighten his green power tie.

"Kinda," Dave admitted. Playing it careful, not to admit to anything.

"You're not officially here. You've committed no crimes and done nothing wrong. Oh, there was that Grey Market incident—I'm well aware of it—but that's not really of any concern to me," Seth said. "They won't matter, in the long run. Or the short run, really. No, I had you arrested with no log made of the arrest and delivered here by my most trusted officers so we could torture you for information in an illegal fashion. It's going to be an extremely unpleasant and if you resist us, you will likely not survive."

The champion of Bedlam awaited some sign that the doom that had befallen this foolish young boy was sinking in. A tired and blank-looking stare wasn't really what he was looking for. It wasn't even the blank stare of someone terrified beyond rational thought—Dave Smith was simply rather bored and tired.

"Of course, you could avoid the worst aspects of your miserable fate by cooperating up front," Seth offered anyway, despite a lack of pleading horror. "You have information that we need. Skills we must employ. If you assist us, then I can promise you will in fact survive this night in some shape or another. Given the choice between an agonizing death and a strange existence, most pick existence. It's the only sane thing to do. Wouldn't you agree?"

"Can I get some coffee?" Dave asked, instead.

"...what?"

"Coffee. Brown. Hot," he described. "I've had a very long day. I'm really very tired, and if you want me to stay awake to listen to this, it'd really help me a lot. I'd appreciate it. Thanks."

"Are you... mocking me, son?" Seth asked, puzzled. "I'm telling you you face horrors beyond your comprehension, a terrible end to your miserable little life, and the best you can offer is to politely ask for coffee? Hmm. Perhaps you're already quite mad..."

"No, I'm just really tired. Like I said. I really could go for a cup of joe."

Curious now, Seth studied the boy deeper, looking for all the little tell-tale body cues of emotion. Blind courage? No, this wasn't some playful stance of defiance; the boy looked too slack in his posture for that. Madness? None of the shifting about that normally comes with Bedlam's flavor of neurological miasmic mess. What sort of ploy was this, what game was he playing? Perhaps Seth had found a formidable opponent, at last...

Undaunted, he continued with his explanation. From his coat, he produced a copy of the Lucid Technologies logo.

"You don't know what this is," he noted. "You've been drawing it and redrawing it ever since you got here, but you don't know what it is. I do. And more importantly, my partner knows what it is. She also knows it's incomplete. We had hoped it was complete *enough*, but sadly, the very last part of the pattern is missing. So. Tonight, you are going to complete your work for us."

Dave blinked several times. "You want a corporate logo? Seriously? I already told Officer Gilt I'd give it to him when I was finished..."

"We're accelerating the timetable. Outside pressures, you understand, it throws everything off. Annoying elements are getting closer every day to our operations... but that's not really your concern. This is your concern, this schema of yours."

"But it's a *logo*. Black-bagging me over a squiggly little scribble seems a little extreme."

"Ahh, but it's so much more than a logo... and the 'corporation' you drew it for is something of a rival of ours. We want it for ourselves. We want you to finish the drawing. Do this, and we ensure your survival. You refuse, and we tear you apart until nothing remains but a burnt-out husk capable of nothing *except* finishing the drawing, and then that husk gets repurposed for unspeakable ends. Work with us, or suffer. Will you finish your grand task, Dave Smith...?"

Good. Now the boy was considering this options. Perhaps his surprisingly steely resolve was helping him evaluate this pragmatically; that would give Seth the result he sought. Maybe the boy didn't fear pain, but surely that meant he was rational enough to make the only rational choice—

"Nah," Dave said, leaning back in his chair. Well, as far as he could with the handcuffs holding him to the desk.

"Hmm. I don't think you understand the gravity of your situation, son—"

"A good friend of mine said the Department of Safety was up to no good," Dave explained. "She's in danger because of whatever it is you're up to. Given the way you're describing it, making it sound like a bad Lovecraft novel, I'm thinking Bedlam. I've seen the city get more and more on edge lately, more cubism, which is obviously related. So if I help you, it helps her, and it hurts my friends. That means I'm not helping you. Sorry. I mean, really, it'd be just *stupid* to help you. I can't think of a single good reason to do so."

"Did you not hear me describe the tearing apart and the husk and all that? Don't you want to live?"

"Oh, definitely. I like living. I don't particularly want to be husked or whatever, but I'm going to have to say no. Sorry to be a bother about it, honestly."

The lead of the Department of Safety (and Cult of Bedlam) considered this, hands folded together, tapping his upper lip as he pondered... while the overhead flourescents flickered, and grew slowly dim...

"Mortal fear doesn't seem to be your lever. It works quite well on most, but I suppose we'll need more to tip you into our hand," Seth said. "Very well. We have ways of conscripting the reluctant into our brotherhood. This is a good-cop, bad-cop routine, you understand. And I'm good-cop. It's time for you to meet bad-cop."

Dimmer and dimmer. Darkness in the room. The power wasn't going out, not exactly... the light was being swallowed by something, drowned out. The inverse of shining a light in a dark corner; this was shining a dark in a light corner...

And soon, they were not alone.

The living shadow manifested, sitting cross-legged on the interrogation table. Inches away from Dave's face. Wrapping around his being. Moving through him.

Hello // hello // hello, Bedlam echoed, through the tiny interrogation room. Smiling, smiling away with a million smiles, the cat who was about to swallow the canary. *I've wanted you for some time. // You took away the scout from me. // You put her mind back together, and she faded away soon after. // Murderer. // Thief. // I will murder you. // I will steal your mind. // I will make you serve me, I will take you apart and put you together as my new friend, my toy...*

Unthinkable geometries twisted the room, adding new corners where corners didn't exist before. Living nightmare replaced waking dream, enveloping all Dave could see, replacing all he could hear with the white noise of chaos. Bedlam began to pulse with the sickened throb of a maddened mind, pouring herself into him, filling him with her idealistic night terrors...

You'll know fear few have ever experienced. // I'll remake you in my image. // But the fear, the fear is just a // birth // birth pain. // A becoming. // Becoming my friend // best friends forever. // Once you emerge through fear and out the other side // out in the world of perfect nightmare // on the other side of terror where madness is sanity, you'll see the glory of—

"But I already did that once," Dave pointed out.

Immediately, the twisting shadows froze. Mid-twist.

What. //

"Through fear and out the other side, right? I already did that," Dave explained. "Long ago. My anxiety got so intense, beyond medication, so far beyond anything rational that I just... burst through. Then I didn't really worry anymore. I'm sorry, but I'm just not afraid of you. I'm too broken to be afraid at times like these. I mean, it's really creepy, I think you're doing a great job and I'm quite impressed, but things like this can't shake me. That's sort of the only thing I'm good at, actually."

The burning green eyes of the nightmare child bored deep inside Dave. And found... fear. There *was* fear, it was the core of his being, but... it wasn't fear she could grasp. It was a hollow and shriveled fear, an old one, which now fit him like a comfortable shoe. Useless to her.

Kill you. // I could kill you. // I should kill you for hurting my friends.

"Mr. Dougal already suggested that, and I'd be okay with it," Dave pointed out. "It'd keep my friends safe, after all. I wouldn't enjoy it much, but..."

Kill your friends. // Twist the lucid child in half. // Always wanted to. // Destroy Penelope Yates. // Burn your little sister to the ground. // Nothing but ash in your mouth...

"That's not much of a threat, either. I think if you could do that, you'd have done it by now. I sympathize, Gregory is a pretty scary dude. I can't recommend tangling with him, he even gives me the willies sometimes."

The smiles of Bedlam twisted around into fractal sub-smiles.

Kelsey Jones // Kelsey // The Troublemaker // Kelsey could die. // I could kill her. // You want to keep your friends safe, yes? // You would obey me if I threatened to kill Kelsey Jones.

That should work. Bedlam saw that inside his fear, a fear for his friends. This would be her lever...

"I don't think you'll kill her, actually," Dave spoke, calmly. "You don't want to hurt your friends, either."

I've hurt friends. // I ate Montgomery. // His terror was delicious.

"But Kelsey's different. She accepts you, right? Really thinks you're not beyond redemption," Dave pointed out. "In fact, I'd say she's probably the best friend you have. Unlike Seth here, she's kind-hearted. She also sees beauty and grace in the things you do, in the nonsense of the Sideways Signals. I don't fully get it myself, but I've got faith that she's right about you, that you're not entirely horrible. And I don't think you'd want to sacrifice your only real friend just to push me around."

Now it was Dougal's time to chuckle. "Cute, but wrong. I can have Miss Jones in a cell with the snap of my fingers," he suggested, holding up two fingers to snap for emphasis. "We can have her beaten to within an inch of her life. We can violate her body and mind in ways you can't dream of, and make you listen to her screams all the while—"

// ... no.

The fingers remained unsnapped.

"What?"

// not her. // she is not leverage.

Sensing his chance at prying the design loose from Dave Smith, the chosen of Bedlam chose to make his opinion known.

"Bedlam... listen. Friend. You have to understand the importance of this," Seth suggested. "You trusted me to run your cult, to organize it in ways you can't organize things. I ask you to trust me on this. If we can use that pathetic shut-in's pain to make him ours, we have to do so. This is the process we must go through, if you are to befriend the whole city—"

Now Bedlam was in Seth's face, spinning about, burning with eyes of green flame that briefly turned his immaculate white suit a pale green from the sheer glow.

// NO. // No, // she declared. *// You do not touch her. // You do NOT. // Dave is the key. // Dave has the keys. // He will not go mad and join us as a*

conscript. // He will not save his own skin. // He will not help us. // But we don't NEED him to finish his task. // We do this my way.

"But without the complete design, the last leg of the journey is a blank. Brute forcing a lock is hardly a plan, and we can't even know which lock that key will fit—"

// Don't care. // This city must be saved. // I must befriend all. // So, we will tear that place apart until we find the source. // I will not be denied, not when I am this close. // Burn it all. // Destroy it all. // Every lock, the key in every lock until one opens. // Tear this city apart if need be to put it back together correctly. // We go, NOW. // The road is long. // Bring him. // He may yet be of use. // We are going to the Heart of the City. //

Right before everything went to hell, there was a gathering.

Here stood the ones who knew, on some level, that they were all tied to something—or someone—very important. Few really recognized that connection, or wanted to recognize it. That didn't matter. The words and numbers had followed them around, leading them up to this moment. All of them, under one roof, in one room, to learn what was to come.

An ominous descriptor, one probably worthy of carefully typed poetry by their resident wordsmith, but at the time none of them felt particularly poetic about it. They had a problem on their hands to chew through.

The poet was there, Cassandra the oracle who saw through people and could write their stories. Earlier this year she was perfectly content to drive a taxi and fail to light the world on fire with her long-line poems that aped the style of her mentor. Being nothing of consequence outside of a strange hallucinatory brain fungus was just fine in her book. Now, she was acting as a combination of chauffeur and interrogator for a rebel alliance and not entirely comfortable with that fact.

Her benefactor was there, Scarlett the soothsayer who rose from her pillow each morning with the plight of those in need firmly in mind. Many a decade she'd strolled through this city, and gained a kinship with its stranger side that few would accept. She accepted it gratefully. In fact, she was pleased as punch to be here now, right when things were going to get very strange indeed.

The questioner was there, Marcy the painter who put forward her one-word challenges all over the city. Waking people up to the nonsense of their lives had been her calling, and she fell into the rebel role quite nicely. It had empowered her art these last few weeks, desperately trying to get the word out not to trust the forces of Bedlam who demanded complacency and fear from the masses... even if few paid much attention to her words, which were often painted over by lunchtime the next day.

The empath was there, Vivi the dancer who heard the true and unspoken voice of people. On the surface, joining in this little group had gotten her career truly launched with a club of her own... but she'd come to care of these strange folks who hid in her club's basement, knowing them personally, wishing them well. Even if on some level, having experienced the horror that Bedlam wished to unleash firsthand, she worried about how much of a fool's errand this would be.

The old guard were there, Archibald Tully and Karla Berkowitz and Johnny the Maître d'. Survivors of the old 7th Street Scavengers. Unrecognizable now if you knew them once as Archie Crowbar and Kut-ya-up Karla and Johnny the Icepick, but despite the rotund trappings of middle age, they carried themselves like bulldogs. Cuddly, yet fierce... and ready to swoop in to extract throats if things came to that.

The chaotician was there, Kelsey Jones, the online Troublemaker. And she was not happy to be here. The whole building felt weird, and there were teddy bears everywhere that seemed to stare at her. Scarlett wasn't pleased she was here, either... someone that closely knit with Bedlam, in the heart of the Lucid Dreamer. But Penelope had insisted Dave would want her to be here and be safe, therefore Kelsey would stay. Even if she was having doubts about throwing her hat in with this crowd.

The paternal figure was there, Gregory Yates. Formerly a no-good punk named Kegstand Greg who roughed people over and stole and generally did not give a word-he-doesn't-say-anymore, but that foolish boy was long gone. The man in his place had been changed forever, and now stood by his daughter's side, to protect her from all the evils of the world. He stood ready for a fight, even here in their secluded safehouse.

And then there was Penelope Yates.

"We need to figure out what this is," she explained, setting her tablet computer down on the cheap folding card table. "Dave emailed me the design last night. Whatever it is, this may be why Bedlam's kidnapped him. He's been working on it since... well, even before we found him in the Sideways, he was working on it. And this is the crazy part—he told me once he was hired by a company called 'Lucid Technologies' to make it. Name ring a bell?"

"Th-the club?" Kelsey offered. She tugged at one of the long sleeves of her shirt, as if trying to stretch it out, hide deeper inside it. "S-sorry, didn't mean to interrupt, just... just trying to be useful..."

"No, no, you're right. It's 'Lucid'. Like the Lucid Dreamer. The word's been following us around a lot. I know Grandma Scarlett likes to use it. ...why is that, anyway?"

Scarlett clicked her dentures, once. "It's a fine word," she justified. "It suggests clarity and understanding. No haze of lies or misdirection. And a lucid dream is one that you control... which is what I do. I use the voice within me to guide my dreams, and help children in need. That's why I suggested it as a name for the club to Vivi."

A raised hand, from Marcy.

"Sorry, I was just interping with my sis, and... she says she came up with the name on her own," Marcy explained, while Vivi nodded along. "It was on her list of possible names, right before you came up and suggested it..."

"All the more reason it's important," Penelope said, to bring things back around. "So that means the drawing might be important, too. He's been mailing me drafts of it—and the Department of Safety might've been watching my email. Also, Dave's boss works for the D-o-S and wanted him to finish the design, too. This was the only item we know they stole from his apartment when they kidnapped Dave. So. We need to figure out what this *is*."

The combined minds in the room gathered around the high-resolution photo, studying it. And studying it. And studying it.

"It's a scribble," Gregory decided. "Case closed."

"Daaad! Unhelpful."

"Sorry, honey, but that's what I see. It's a scribbly spirally thing. Like you'd stick to a fridge with a magnet when you just wanted your kids to be happy. — uh, for the record, I loved your drawings. Legitimately."

Cass crouched down, studying the tablet computer closer. Scratched her chin. Frowned. "Not really seeing anything in this, and I'm supposedly the one who sees into things," she said. "Search me. You say this Dave character sent you earlier versions, right? Maybe it's like a flip book animation, or somethin'. You still got them on file?"

"Yeah, uh, hang on, let me..."

Penelope reached over, flicking through her image library. She'd set it up so all email drafts and map files and photos of her friends got dumped into one huge pile of pictures... which actually wasn't very helpful, now that she thought of it. She flipped past photos of Milly and Lucas, EchoMap dumps of Sideways crawls, old drafts of Dave's logo, a photo of Karla passed out drunk on an armchair that she thought was funny which was just sort of embarrassing right now, more logo drafts, more EchoMaps, more...

Her fingers paused, still making contact with the touch-sensitive glass surface. Then flicked back.

EchoMaps. Logo drafts. Flick left, flick right.

"It's a map," Penelope realized.

"That scratchy thing is a map?" Gregory asked. "I'm not seeing it."

"No, no, it is! Here, look, I... just... hang on a minute. I need to do some crazy CSI stuff here..."

She retrieved the tablet from the table, having a seat on the floor and firing up an image editing program. Normally she only used it to color the red out of people's eyes in pictures or put captions on cats, but now it was going to have to pull duty as a collage maker.

For the base, she put Dave's latest draft. On top of it, she pulled in any EchoMap dumps she could get. Make them translucent, start rotating and scaling them. Like a jigsaw puzzle, trying to find where the edges fit... except in this case, it was finding where the line carved a path through existing hallways and rooms...

Penelope didn't even notice the small crowd gathering behind her, to watch over her shoulder. She was onto something here, she could feel it. Downloaded as many maps as she could from the cloud, ones she couldn't fit in on her tablet because they were too huge. Deleted a few games to make room. She could lob birds at pigs some other day—this was way more important.

Fifteen minutes later, and the overlapped ghosts of Sideways maps covered a good portion of the spiral. Very little towards the absolute center, where the line skittered off to nothing—Dave did mention in his email that it wasn't quite finished—but she had a starting point.

"An Outlands Sideways access point at the Gas 'n Eats Diner," she announced. "It's on an endless highway. Dad and I explored it, once. That's where the map starts. Then... follow my finger, here... it goes through some parts of the Outlands branches of the Sideways... and apparently connects to a section I explored in the Suburbs, a toy store. From there it's into the City-level Sideways, and on and on until... well, I don't know where it eventually leads. Somewhere deep. But it's all non-Euclidean connections and shortcuts, using hallways we hadn't explored yet—the overall path probably runs a lot a shorter than it looks. Point is... this is a map."

"A spiral down through the layers," Kelsey thought aloud.

The attention this brought her was not pleasant.

"S-sorry, it's just... I've always thought of it as layers," she explained. "Like network protocol layers. Or better, a cake, a tiered cake turned upside down. Larger to smaller, deeper you go. I mean, think about it. The Outlands are huge, and sit on top. Then one layer down are the Suburbs, smaller... then the City itself, small but densely networked. And connecting it all together are the Sideways. Down and down, spiraling, large to small, like an upended cone, and it spirals down to... to... a point. An origin point. A heart..."

"The heart of the city," Penelope spoke, to complete the thought. "The toy store guy said Bedlam wanted to get to the heart of the city. It's a silly term, I know, but this must be a map that leads you there! Look, it IS like a cone, and that means it all spirals and flows upward from a single origin point at the very tip of that cone. The very bottom of it all. That's what Bedlam's looking for, the City's origin point! Like a river's source! Like... like... I'm out of metaphors here but I think you get what I'm aiming at."

Gregory scratched his chin, unsure. "I don't like putting money down on metaphors and guesswork," he pointed out. "But whatever's at the end of this map, it's something we do not want Bedlam having access to. That's pretty obvious. Here's how we're going to... Kelsey? Something wrong?"

Their newest member was hugging herself with both arms. Trembling.

"I... I think she's on her way already, actually," Kelsey spoke, through clenched teeth. "Getting closer and closer. It's like... like that sick feeling in your stomach when you know things are going wrong. Rises up, from below. I can feel it. I'm. I'm gonna lose it. You need to get away from me. I don't want to hurt anyone. I'm cubist. I'm sorry. I'm messing everything up, I just wanted to help Dave, I'm your enemy, you can't be around me // you can't // I'm lost // I can't—"

Backing away, slowly. All of them, as the girl flickered. Gregory had his hand on the hilt of his gun, ready...

One didn't back away. She put her arms around the terrified young woman. Brittle arms, but warm and tight enough to keep her in place.

"Shhhh. Shhh, child," Grandma Scarlett whispered. "You're not lost. No one is. Be still, be calm."

"You can't // you can't—"

"I can. The bears that we use, our guardians? They are love," Scarlett explained. "I've seen you shy away from them, but you don't need to. Loving dreams were shared with them, and now they share them with you. That shines through the darkness of any nightmare. Shhh. Be still. ...I'd best leave you young folks to this affair. Poor Kelsey needs my undivided attention if she's to make it through this night, I feel."

Slowly, she led the frightened girl away from the others. But did pause... to glance back at Penelope, specifically.

"Remember that, child," she spoke, with determination. "No one is lost. No one."

With that oddly intoned note in her wake, the two departed.

"...right. As I was saying, it's a good old-fashioned Sideways crawl for us," Gregory said, deciding to take over now that the theory portion of the evening was complete. "We beat Bedlam to the heart, we don't have to find out what happens when a chaos god pokes the origin point with a stick. Since it's a non-Euclidean path we're going to have to start at the beginning—the Gas 'n Eats Diner. Otherwise we could stray off track too easily. Good thing we know a shortcut to get there. Archie and Karla, you're with me. I'll need muscle and guns. Johnny, stay here to guard my daughter and the others. Let's move. "

"Do I seriously need to say it, Dad?" Penelope interrupted. "*Seriously?*"

"You're not going with us," Gregory declared. "Honey, I said you'd be with me on this crazy adventure, but I'm willing to break my word when it's this important. We're going face-to-face with Dougal and his pet chaos goddess, and there's no way this ends without violence. I'm not putting you in harm's way."

"I'm going with you, and you can't stop me."

"Actually, yes, I can," he stated. "I've gotten adept at tying crazy cultists to chairs, and—where the hell did Cartwright go, anyway? Ugh, not dealing with that right now—and I'll do the same to my own daughter if I need to, to keep her out of the firing line—"

Before he could stop her, Penelope keyed a sequence into her tablet computer, and its screen went dark.

"Gesture lock," she announced. "My tablet. My map. And now, I'm the only one who can access it. Good luck getting to the heart without me."

Which was enough to test even Gregory's legendary patience with his precocious daughter. Muscles tensed behind his skin as he tried to maintain composure; a headache was not far behind.

"Penny, we do not have time for this," he tried to reason.

"Penelope," she corrected.

"What?"

"My name is *Penelope*. Use my real name," she spoke, glaring him down. "I may be young but I've been through more gnarly stuff this year than most adults. I'm done being treated like a child. If I have to resort to a childish trick to get you to deal with me, that's only because you won't see me as anything other than your little Penny. But Penelope has her own damn good reasons for wanting go with you."

"Really. And what, exactly, are those?" Gregory asked, crossing his arms. "You want to be an adult? Reason with me like one. Why should you go with me into the middle of an assault? ...is it about that Dave character? Please tell me it's not just about Dave."

"Of course not. This about more than Dave. This is about what I've always wanted: to know this city's heart," she explained. "What do you think I've been trying to do during all these years I insisted we crawl around the Sideways? I want to know. I NEED to know and understand the truth of this city. And if this map is right, X marks the spot where I can get some answers. If you don't take me with you... then all that's gone to waste. This may be dangerous, but that doesn't matter. This is my life, Dad, and my dream. Let me have it."

...which left Gregory in something of a pickle.

He'd been struggling with this for a long time. Penny was certainly a kid, being only thirteen years old. But... Gregory had been about her age when he got started with the gang, scouring the Sideways and running wild and being an independent spirit. But... he'd also been pretty stupid about it all at the time, being only a kid. But he valued that independence all the same, and wouldn't he want the same for his daughter? But she was going to make mistakes, and had in fact made mistakes even in recent history. But, but, *but...*

Days like these, Gregory truly wished Lizzie was still here. She was the smart one. She pulled him back from the brink when he was a self-destructive little punk, and he'd been trying to do the same for Penelope. And failing.

But...

It's not like Lizzie was *all* caution and responsibility. Gregory's idealized memory of her was one of poise and maturity, but each day he saw more of Penny in her. After all, Lizzie was the one who wanted to get into mapping and exploring, to put her husband's talents at scavenging to better use. For all her maturity, she was also ready to face foolhardy danger in the name of something greater. And now, so was Penelope.

So, he could either fight his daughter in this over and over, holding her back from the inevitability of growing up... or he could give her room to fly, and do his best to keep her from crashing in the process.

"You're not getting a gun," he warned. "You're staying in the back of the group and we're taking point. And if things go sour you're going to run for the nearest exit back to the City you can find—because as much as you want to follow this map to the end of the road, the end of the road will be Bedlam if we screw up. Understood?"

Penelope was already stuffing her tablet in her backpack by the time he finished.

"Understood," she agreed. Apparently with enough caution and responsibility to know what points to argue, and which ones to roll with. "Let's go... do... thing. Move out? Roll out? I really want to say something cool and badass right now other than just 'let's go,' but I can't think of anything awesome —"

"Let's go," Gregory decided.

As much as Penelope wanted to, she couldn't pause periodically to take EchoMap readings. This wasn't an explorative journey into the Sideways, which were normally slow and calculated affairs, studying every nook and cranny. This time, they moved with purpose, following a line which charted a path through territory both familiar and unfamiliar.

Normally a Sideways crawl could take days... or longer, if your route went non-Euclidean and you weren't paying enough attention to notice. When pathways weren't two-directional and doorways led to different rooms depending on the direction you approached from, the Sideways went from being a curious thing to a deadly thing. Plenty of amateur mappers and even professional Department of Resources mappers had been lost forever from careless wanderings. Even Penelope's dad got lost down here for a year... the same year she was born. The same year her mother died.

So even if they wanted to move quickly—and they did move quickly, at least compared to the speed of an exhaustive survey—they had to move cautiously. The four of them traveled as a pack, loaded with backpacks full of supplies which could keep them alive should they get lost. Although if they did get lost and Bedlam reached the end of the map before them... well, nobody quite knew what would happen, but it would not likely be pleasant.

"Next left," Penelope announced, glancing up from her tablet while carefully stepping around discarded toys. "The back stock room. The Sideways continue through there. I saw it when I was down here with Lucas and Milly."

"Bedlam's been after this for some time," Gregory interpreted. "If she got this far already then they were probably tapped into your email for some time, getting the drafts that Dave sent you, trying to figure out where they were eventually going to lead. We're lucky they don't know about your second account. Maybe they don't know we've got the completed map."

"It's not actually complete, though. Dave said he was *almost* finished..."

"Obviously it's complete enough, or Bedlam wouldn't be making her move now. We get lucky, we can come up behind them, and... stop them," Gregory chose to phrase.

The one-word unspoken question hung in the air, after that.

So, Karla busied herself with distracting Penny. They didn't need some secret plan or hand signal; the 7th Street Scavengers had an odd sense of each other, and Karla knew when to run interference. Giving Archie and Gregory some time to whisper in private, moving ahead of the other two.

"...how?" Archie filled in, speaking the question. "How exactly are we going to stop Bedlam? Three middle-aged former punks and a kid are not a formidable army. What's your plan?"

Making sure Penelope wasn't looking... Gregory unslung the backpack from his shoulder, tugging the zipper down. Then tugging it back up, once Archibald Tully had an eyeful.

"Seriously," Archie replied, unsure if his buddy was serious.

"Seriously," Gregory spoke seriously.

"Grenades? C4? I'm not even going to ask where you got military-grade explosives. We didn't play with toys like that even when we were dangerous dudes," Archie pointed out. "I'm also not going to point out that setting off bombs in the Sideways is an extremely bad idea. You've heard the same tall tales I have. Blowing away walls, holes that lead to nothingness, or weirder than weird things..."

"Fire and explosives are the best ways to take out a Picasso. My sidearm's good for intimidating Salvagers who mess with us, but Picassos are too disembodied for me to reliably find a center of mass to shoot at. Splash and area of effect is the key. Bedlam's the Picasso to end all Picassos, so I brought the booms to end all booms."

"Taking you along with her."

"If that's what it takes, yes," Gregory agreed. "I do what it takes to protect my daughter. If that means asking my best friend to grab her and run for it while I blow Bedlam to hell, so be it. Lizzie would want you to watch over her when I'm gone."

"Yeah, no, that's not happening. Give me your backpack."

"Archie—"

"I'm getting old, Gregory. I've got half my life in front of me but I've also got half my life behind me, and nothing comparatively important to show for it. Yes, I have a fish restaurant which offers gainful employment to our futureless miscreants, that's good stuff... but you have considerably more ahead of you than I do. You've got her. You'll see her grow and move on and have kids of her own, one day. If someone IS going to splatter Bedlam, it's better that I do it than deny you all that."

Gregory let out a trademarked groan. "Look—"

"You know, you're way too used to getting your way. Father knows best, right?" Archie continued. "But this year, things haven't gone your way. Your daughter's turning into an independent young woman. She's making connections that you normally shun, pushing the world away to keep her safe. Just consider this another in a long string of things you are no longer in charge of, and be happy for it. If you'd just *let go* once in a while, maybe you'd be a happier man. You know Lizzie wouldn't want you this wound up all the time."

Defeated, Gregory swapped backpacks with his old friend and mentor.

"All I've been trying to do is what Elizabeth would've wanted me to do. She wanted me to raise our daughter, and protect her."

"No, she wanted you to raise your daughter," Archie corrected, adjusting the backpack straps. "You tacked on the protection racket yourself. Look, man, you're family. Love and blood. You ran with me in the streets, you married my sister, you got me set up good. You did right by her, in the end. Let me do this for you. Assuming I even HAVE to do it. Who knows, we might have a ray of hope in our future."

Hopeless.

Endless.

Terror.

Leaning hard against the wall, Gregory desperately tried to catch his breath. Which was strange, because he couldn't recall how that breath got away from him. A glance through his blurred vision confirmed the others staggering and fading as well... the wave of nausea and anxiety building deep within his belly echoed on them, as well...

Nothing had changed. Just another hallway in the Sideways. No monsters in sight. And yet, something had not so much tickled as throttled Gregory's primitive lizard hindbrain. The fight-or-flight instinct was screaming for flight, even if there was nothing to fly from...

Gradually, the burst subsided... but left tension in the air. Heavy tension where none should exist. Granted they were headed down to the origin point of the city and towards unknown doom, but this felt more like an external tension, something being forced on them.

"What... the... heck?" Gregory mumbled, as he very, very slowly regained control. Control enough not to swear, of course, Lizzie disliked swearing. "What the heck was that...?"

"It was Bedlam! It was Bedlam, she's down there already! You have to move faster!"

Gripping the CRT tube, shaking it by the wood grain frame. Didn't even realize she was doing it, until she did it.

...which immediately made Penelope feel self-conscious. It was like shouting 'Don't go in there!' while watching a horror movie. But this wasn't a movie of the week, this was recent events, playing out in front of her. Conversations she wasn't privy to alongside things she remembered well...

"We were ten steps behind the whole way," she explained to herself. "Didn't know it at the time. We thought we were hot on her heels, but she was already there. —already down *here*, at the Heart of the City. She's here now, isn't she? Down here with me. That's what this really is. I'm disjointed, I'm messed up, I'm... I'm going cubist, aren't I? Picassos lose sense of time and space..."

You could be. It might happen. Surviving her nightmare is up to you—a nightmare and a dream are variations on the same thing, she told herself. *You're afraid. You're afraid to see these things, yes? Aren't you afraid you're slipping further away?*

"Hmm. I don't think I am. Not actually slipping away, I mean," Penelope realized. "I'm seeing what happened, what really happened. I think I'm putting things *together*, not falling apart. ...I know what I want to see. When Bedlam started banging around down here, trying to bust down the doors, and we felt that wave of despair... what happened up *there*? Back home. If Bedlam running wild in the Heart of the City felt like that to us in the Sideways... what'd it feel like to everybody up in the City itself?"

This time, she pulled the TV set in herself. Didn't feel the reluctance she felt before, had no intention of looking away—she needed to make sure her friends were safe. Even if she went completely insane and ended up wandering the Sideways forever as a lonely ghost, at least she would know if the others survived this disaster...

Night was falling on the city, in more ways than one. And the moment the sun went down—by coincidence or perhaps by design, no one would ever know—it began.

The entire City had been on edge for weeks. Nobody knew why; nobody was having unpleasant and foreboding dreams or anything like that, but tensions ran high. Arguments and fights. People confining themselves to their homes, afraid to go out. Cubism incidents on the rise, and the Department of Safety unable or unwilling to keep it all under control. Plenty of dire warnings in the media about it all, safety alerts and recommendations, which did nothing to ease the mind—and in fact were designed for the exact opposite...

One night, the dam started to leak. Which was better than the dam bursting, but when the dam represents the collective psychological state of the world and the water represents reality-twisting madness, even a small leak can be disastrous.

What triggered the leak, no one knew. No one outside the circle that had grown around the Lucid Dreamer, that is.

They could feel it, even in a building lined with Grandma Scarlett's hand-sewn shields of faith. The mood of the entire City darkened—every layer of it, from the City to the Suburbs all the way to the Outlands. That strange feeling that crawls up the spine for no reason began crawling up every spine simultaneously...

Normally, a sudden wave of ominous dread would be a little odd, but not represent a huge problem. But for a populace being gradually dosed every single day in Nightmare Fuel, it was a one-two punch to the sanity that many couldn't take.

The first sign was Kelsey's scream. Scarlett was there, trying to soothe her, but she'd already embraced the chaos long ago... that toehold plus the N.F. in her veins would've been enough to instantly spike her deep into the depths of cubism, if not for the sanctuary she was taking refuge in. As is, she simply suffered and cringed in agony.

"It's over, it's over," Kelsey burbled, through tears. "We lost. Everything's lost. She won. She wants me to be perfect, like her. Wants everybody to become like her. Scared. So scared. I... I don't want to be like her. I want to stay here. With Dave. With all of you. Please. Please, help me..."

"Shhh. Shhh. You are safe in these walls, young one," Grandma Scarlett assured. "We are protected by the purest compassion imaginable. You will not become like her as long as you stay with us..."

Cass did her best not to shiver. "That is *damned* creepy feeling," she admitted, wrapping her arms around herself. "What is this, some side effect of the drug? But we've been drinking bottled water! Freaky... like someone walking on your grave. ...no, like someone dying on top of your grave. Like death on top of death, pushing you down into the dirt. Like—"

"I know you enjoy your wordplay, Cassandra, but I suggest this is not the moment to indulge."

"Uh. Right. Sorry, ma'am..."

Moments later, Marcy and Vivi ran downstairs from the club above, Marcy carrying a laptop computer. She put it down on the table, where the others of their little band had gathered.

"It's exploding all over the net," she explained, with signs for her sister's benefit. "Picassos, everywhere! Out in the open! It's a disaster and a half. The Department of Safety precincts are loaded with them. Nobody knows what to do except stay home and hide. Did... did Bedlam already win? ...I don't know what to do. What the hell are we gonna DO? "

Given that the rebel alliance consisted of a poet, a dancer, a graffiti artist and a guy formerly adept with an icepick... a silent consensus was reached that not much could actually be done.

"Are we boned? Seriously. Just tell me if we're boned," Marcy requested. "Be honest."

The contrary opinion was given by the most helpless of the bunch, the frail old woman trying to comfort Kelsey.

"No, we are not 'boned,' as you so politely put it. So long as we can draw breath, we must. We must *live*, and have faith. Meanwhile... there is in fact something we can do. If the city is falling to chaos, we need to save as many people as we can."

Cass nodded, thinking she'd caught on right away. "The building. It's laced with anti-Picasso bears. We gotta go out there—it's dangerous as hell, but we gotta grab as many folks who haven't flipped out and gone cubist as we can and bring them here. Gotcha."

"Mmmm. Well, no. Rather the opposite, I'm afraid," Scarlett corrected. "I hope you brought your running shoes."

C-average, right down the board. Not the best, not the worst. Unnotable in every respect—not even notably upset about being unnotable. Janice was simply content to be someone who is a person who is alive in a place. Is content. Will be content.

She was content to go out and get the groceries today, despite feeling oddly unsettled by the sky. Janice hadn't been agoraphobic in the past, but lately every action she took had a measure of apprehension behind it. Unsure about going out, could be mugged, could get lost. Unsure about driving on the roads, could get in an accident, could be late for dinner, could lead her family to worry about her, could, could, could...

It didn't make sense. But very little made sense right now. C-average, right down the board. No more homework today. She'd graduated a long time ago.

She was tired and wanted to go home. Why didn't anything make sense?

Her groceries were out of their bag. She'd spilled them, when she lost her mind. Now they were in a state of flux around her; bananas were oranges were milk, eggs were potato chips. Paper or plastic. Maybe both at the same time, hard to say, really... they had a glossy feel and a matte feel. Everywhere, all around her, bagged and ready to carry home.

Going home would be lovely right now. There'd be less screaming at home, hopefully.

So much running and screaming today. Mostly running away from her and screaming. Why? Janice needed help. She needed someone to tell her things were going to be okay, because right now, they didn't feel the slightest bit okay. Everything was wrong in every possible respect. Cars were being shoved or bent or broken as she walked by them, trying to catch up with people, trying to talk to them. *Excuse me, what's going on, did you feel that just now, I'm a bit worried about all this, why can't I feel myself here right now, what, help // help // what...*

I'm a Picasso, some part of her realized. But no, of course not, she couldn't be a Picasso. She didn't go traipsing around in the Sideways, she wasn't depressed, she hadn't been flickering or jittering... there weren't any signs. People didn't just go Picasso out of nowhere. Even if they were feeling oddly alarmed all the time. All the time. Alarm bells. Ringing and ringing—

A half-brick punctured her shopping bag self. Paper or plastic. It became both.

"HEY! Hey, over here! You great big freaky grocery thing!"

Someone threw something at her. She stopped trying to flag down a bystander to ask what was going on, focusing instead on whoever did that...

Kids these days, honestly // Hello, what's going on? // Help me help me I don't understand // two dozen should be enough with the pancake mix, she called out to the young woman.

Moving towards her, now. Not walking, just... moving. She was running away, running away from Janice, but Janice always seemed to be exactly twenty feet behind. That meant moving through a bus stop and a parked car but for some reason they didn't pose much of a hindrance.

Hours or minutes later and Janice was bursting through a wall of glass and neon and staggering and catching her breath in lungs which finally started existing again. All her fresh produce and cereal boxes dropped to the floor around her, scattered... as a blanket was tossed over her shoulders.

"Okay, okay, we got ya," another woman spoke, one with glasses and one of those funny old-timey hats. She moved in to support Janice, as her knees weakened. "Easy, now. You're safe and sound."

"Wh // what... what just happened?" Janice asked, confused. "Excuse me, what's going on? I was out shopping, and suddenly I felt the strangest thing, and... oh. Oh God. I was a Picasso, wasn't I...?"

"Briefly. But you'll be fine in here; nobody can go Picasso behind these walls," Cass explained. "S'why we're rescuing as many of you as we can. I gotta get back out there and bring someone else in. Head to the bar with the others, Vivi's got a teddy bear and some water for you."

Cubism above, spreading through the city like a stain on the carpet. Slow and creeping, but utterly inevitable, and very difficult to get rid of. Penelope didn't know any of that was happening *knew that was happening, she knew, somehow she knew because she was going mad, mad at the Heart of the City, wasn't she* but even if she knew, she didn't have time to worry about it. Because they had their own cubism to deal with.

The last stretch of the map was traversed at a full sprint. A bad thing to do in the poorly lit and chaotic realm of the Sideways—you never knew when the next door would join to a hallway at a funny angle, or when a toppled over piece of furniture shrouded in darkness would trip you up. Normally, Penelope and Gregory crawled the sideways at a, well, crawl. Safety first. But 'safety first' also meant not crawling around when you're being chased by Picassos.

Picassos. Plural. Two of them.

Whether they accidentally stumbled across the stomping grounds of these two wayward souls or if Bedlam sent them on an intercept course, the end result was the same. They had to move it or lose it.

Penelope ran in the middle of the pack, with Karla and Archie behind her and Gregory leading the way. Occasionally they had to give her a little push or help her when she stumbled—reading a map on her smart tablet to ensure they didn't take a wrong turn while running for her life was not particularly easy. And if they did take a wrong turn, if they went through some non-Euclidean one-way connection... they could be lost for good. Then, it'd just be a matter of time before the Picassos hot on their heels got them.

Naturally, one of them spoke with a creepy little girl's voice, echoing down the endless hallways.

Kicker lane active // ball 1 locked // ball 2 locked // no jackpot for you, she chimed, with a voice like the bells and beeps of a pinball machine. *My friend wants you drained out // down the center drain // game over for all of you // over // over and over...*

No doubt there was a very interesting story as to why a child obsessed with pinball was chasing them, a cloud of blinking lights and spinning bits of plastic and steel ball bearings, but Penelope didn't have time to ponder her origin story at the moment.

As for the second Picasso... that one didn't speak. It just screamed. Overlapping screams in some twistedly pleasant four-part harmony, as if the Beach Boys were being electrocuted. Also it was on fire.

A glance down at the map. Her EchoMap software was pulsing rapidly, trying to get a grasp on the surroundings despite their high-speed rampage and the shrieking horrors following them. It wasn't outputting a particularly *good* map, but it was enough to give her a rough idea of what was coming up.

"Next left then one hundred yard dash across open room!" Penelope called out. "Then I think an elevator, then... that's it! End of map! Almost there!" *already there, already in the heart, remembering this tense moment which was just moments ago*

Gregory, gun drawn, kicking down the door ahead of them. Light flooding out, and...

...a fancy, elegant ballroom.

Chandeliers. Hard wood floors, perfect for dancing. Tasteful curtains over windows that showed... nothing. The sky beyond windows in the Sideways always looked completely fake, even faker than the fake sky over the City of Angles, but this deep in the works they didn't even bother throwing up a flat Hollywood set decoration skyline. There was simply nothing out there.

Charging across the room, towards an incongruous looking elevator in the distance. The strip of wall it was embedded in didn't belong to the ballroom; tasteful wood roughly transitioned to painted-over brick, slick like the walls of an old high school. No markings, no indications like "Heart of the City, Right Here!". Dave had mentioned his map was incomplete, but... this was the only way out, the only way through, and they'd have to see where it went.

After dealing with the murderous monsters chasing them, that is. Penelope skidded on the hard wood, stabbing the call button for the elevator—a DOWN button, of course, no UP button at all—while the three adults turned to face the visually distorted things that settled in the middle of the room.

Collect hurry up award // jackpot value is rising, the pinball-obsessed child teased, a matrix of reflective spheres forming around her in a cubical shape...

"You two get moving," Archie said. "Karla and I will keep them off your back as long as we can."

Gregory's grip on his sidearm tightened. "Archie, we don't have time for—"

"No, we don't. Get moving," his old running buddy stated... while slinging his backpack off one shoulder, letting it hit the floor with a heavy impact. "Take her to the heart. You know I've got this."

After less than a moment's hesitation... Gregory nodded in agreement. "Try not to blow the windows. We need to come back this way when we're done. Penelope, MOVE."

She wanted to object to leaving two of their party behind, but by then a soft *ding* had signaled the arrival of the elevator, and they were on their way.

Down, down to the lowest point of the City of Angles. The source of the spiral. The heart of the city.

"I'm here now," Penelope realized. "But it all went wrong. It's all going to go wrong..."

Television sets as far as the eye can see. Every memory she should and shouldn't have. Like the memory of being found in the Sideways, a impossible child that was never actually born...

She couldn't look away from those monitors, now. Penelope had already accepted that she wanted to know, she couldn't turn her back to them and ignore them as she'd been doing. But were they driving her mad? Were they driving her sane? Impossible to say.

For what it was worth, her other self was sympathetic.

This is difficult for you, she told herself. *You know that. And it may very well break you. But it has to be done. You must either break or emerge whole. Those are the only ways out.*

"I'm scared," she admitted. In a voice much smaller than she'd have liked.

You should be.

The elevator only had two buttons, marked L and B. With B being the lower selection, she opted for that. While jamming the DOOR CLOSE button, of course.

Smooth silver doors sliding shut, blocking her view of Archie and Karla, staring down two aberrations of nature. Possibly the last time Penelope would ever see them again. *this is near it, near the moment of Bedlam's rage, did they survive, please show me, it's too close and I can't see*

Gregory, reloading his gun with a fresh clip. He'd sprayed a few in the direction of their pursuers, for what good tiny little bits of flying metal would do against a Picasso. Hitting the brain stem clean on something that was largely non-corporeal was always a bit of a crapshoot, to use an inappropriate term.

"Penelope, I..." he started.

And couldn't think of anything reassuring to say. So he went with honesty.

"I don't know what's going to happen," he mumbled. "I shouldn't have brought you down here. I don't think we can actually do anything to stop Bedlam. Darn... d... dammit. Dammit to hell."

"We had to do something," she reminded him. "We couldn't do *nothing*. I mean... at least this way we're trying, right? I don't know what we can actually do either, but... we had to. We just had to... and I had to come here. It's where I need to be."

Silence. Not even elevator music. Elevator music would've been nice, really.

"How do you know that?" Gregory asked. "How do you know you need to be here? ...Penelope, look, you... I never told you this, but I guess we've come too far now, and..."

"You found me in the Sideways. I'm not really your daughter."

How did I know that? I can't think of how I knew that, is that like how I know things in this strange place I've found myself, but I knew that in the elevator and that was just before now, I'm lost, I don't understand any of this, help me

Gregory couldn't ask how she knew that. He was too shocked to hear her say it outright.

"You're wrong, though," Penelope added... with a tiny, sad smile. "You found me in the Sideways. And I am really your daughter."

ding.

...we came in?

Hallway. More glossy and painted brick walls. Pipes and overhead lights. Cheap industrial design...

The elevator opened to a small lobby. Guard station with monitors and a chair, unoccupied. Coffee mug with a three letter acronym on it. Standard ceremonial American flag, upright and loose, like you'd find in any government facility. Security cameras in every corner of the room...

And a sign mounted on the wall, a single identifier to declare where they were.

Gregory stepped out of the elevator, gun drawn and aimed, checking every angle. Behind him... Penelope slowly emerged, fixated on the sign. Forming the words.

"Centers for Disease Control and Prevention," she read. "CDC. It's even on that mug. I don't get it. This is it? A medical research facility is the Heart of the City? I was expecting something, I don't know, weirder than this—"

The heart trembled.

Something shook the room, shook the corridors in the distance. It felt like a wrecking ball slamming into the side of the building, sending a deafening roar down the boxy hallways of the facility. One impact. Two impacts... lighting flickering, electricity wavering under the strain of whatever was assaulting the place...

And the creepy feeling, that pulse of dread and doom and panic, surging with each hit. Bedlam. She was down here.

Isn't this where...

"Stay behind me, honey," Gregory insisted, gun pointed squarely at the hallway ahead. "We're moving."

Every hallway the same. Door after door after door, each with a keyhole lock, a sturdy 1950s-era metal doorknob, and a room number. Room 5. Room 17. Room 3. Room 21. Not in any particular order, either—certainly not numerical order, and the hallways themselves formed a maze of right angles, which looped back around on themselves in impossible ways. Penelope tried using her EchoMap app, but it crashed outright trying to make sense of the readings it was getting...

This was still the Sideways, even if it was an oddly CDC-flavored Sideways. The occasional fire extinguisher, eye wash station, or emergency defibrillator suggested the basic rigmarole of scientific safety. Plastic folder cubbies were bolted next to each door, possibly for patient paperwork, but they were all empty.

Most importantly, every door was locked. She'd been trying the knobs randomly, as Gregory led the pair onward into the facility. None of them budged in the slightest. If she put her ear to the door, she heard nothing... although the successive series of impacts and roaring waves of darkness from deep within the facility made eavesdropping difficult.

But the doors weren't the only features down here. They passed nurse waystations, pharmacies, supply closets. A break room, at one point, complete with water cooler and a bulletin board with employee-posted flyers for used cars or guitar lessons. This was an echo of some place on Earth, some place where people worked... heavily monitored by cameras and buried deep underground, given no windows whatsoever, but still a living locale.

All of this, from just two minutes of exploration. And two minutes would be all they'd get, because the next open room they reached was occupied.

One man on his knees. And another with a gun behind his head.

Seth Dougal took the time to adjust his tie with one hand, while steadying the grip on his pistol. The muzzle was flush with the back of Dave Smith's head.

Gregory wasted no time in taking aim at Seth, adjusting his stance like a marksman. Steady and strong. But not before making sure Penelope was safely behind him.

For a moment, the four of them remained quiet.

"Hi," Dave offered, weakly.

"This is actually very good luck for me," Seth decided. "You, being here. Dave has been... uncooperative in helping Bedlam find the correct door to the heart itself. Perhaps a few more variables in the equation will help...?"

"Let him go or I drop you," Gregory declared, simply.

"What, and risk me ventilating our dear everyman's skull? I don't think so. This is a classic movie scene, Gregory Yates, a Mexican standoff. Isn't it beautiful, this classic tableau—you the crusading hero, me the psychotic villain? But you know how those standoffs end. Badly."

"Five seconds," Gregory added.

"Bedlam's quite upset, being so close to her prize and unable to reach it," Seth noted, smiling widely. "I can only imagine the havoc playing out up top, with her rage expressing itself down here. Of course, this is nothing. Once she gets to the heart itself, she can *fully* express that nightmare. That plus the my lovely drug will turn this entire world into Picassos. It'll become the City of Bedlam. Perfect and chaotic, immortal madness with nothing more to fear—"

The wall behind Seth turned red.

Bedlam's best friend collapsed like a doll, flopping lazily backwards. The horrific display made by his exit wound smeared as he slumped against it, smearing down the wall as he sank at last to the floor.

Throughout it all, Gregory remained perfectly calm. Unlike the shock and horror on the faces of his companions.

"A Mexican standoff is when three people are pointing guns at each other, not two. When only two people have guns out, whoever shoots first basically wins," he explained. "I had plenty of time to line up a kill shot, so I took it. Now I suggest we get the hell out of here before Bedlam notices what just happened."

The lights didn't go out. Electricity was still pumping through the wires, in that weird way power always flowed in the City of Angles, even down in the Sideways. But nevertheless, the world went dark around them. That's what happens when every shadow in the room becomes the living embodiment of bottomless hatred.

Those discrete pulses of anxiety being sent up through the hallways by Bedlam's efforts, pounding on door after door to try to find the one she desired... those were peanuts. The absolute terror they felt now was like someone unscrewed their scalps and began to pour fear right in.

my friend //

MY FRIEND //

YOU KILLED MY FRIEND //

"Tight" was a word in Penelope's vocabulary, before. But now she knew the definition of it, well and truly, as she curled in a *tight* little ball on the floor of the CDC facility. Screaming and crying, but unable to hear her own voice over the noise of Bedlam ringing through her head.

*every turn // every time // you tried to stop me // I'm trying to save this
city   //*

*hate you so much // ruining everything // I'd been avoiding you // like I avoid
her and her mirrors // but this //*

THIS //

*hate you // hurt you //
your worst fears // I will make you face them //
I will destroy you // but not kill you // just destroy you. // completely.*

No more screaming. No more movement. Just lying on the floor, so tense as
to be locked rigid.

Except for one. The one immune to Bedlam's charms.

"You're not including me in that?" Dave asked, confused.

The shadow child crouched over Penelope and Gregory's prone forms
looked up... smiling at Dave Smith.

you get to enjoy this, too. // because this is your worst fear, isn't it? she
asked. *not pain. // not death. // you can bear any burden because you're
already broken. // but can you bear to see your friends suffer // and be
unable // completely unable // to do anything about it...?*

Face what you fear most. //

He opened his mouth to say something. And couldn't say anything.

Because there it was. That old familiar feel, the oncoming wave of anxious
energy. Control slipping away. Everything right is wrong again...

Little Dave Smith, the boy who feared everything, the boy who made
mountains out of molehills. That boy couldn't handle anything life threw at
him. That boy, who had emerged in the lonely and desperate hours since his
arrival in the City of Angles, was back. Because Bedlam was right; Dave could
swallow anything thrown at him, anything but this.

He'd tried to save Sarah. He'd tried to join the First Action Responders, to
save everyone. To leverage his own problems to solve the problems of others.
And now, there was absolutely nothing he could do to keep Penelope from
drowning in a sea of pain. Nothing at all.

Face what you fear most. //

Bang.

Running in the streets, laughing and throwing rocks at windows. The only
people around for miles.

Archie was a few years older, but he'd taken the kid under his wing.
Nobody else would, after all; he'd run away from the Department of
Orientation, refusing to accept that his family was gone and the foster system
was his fate. He found a new family in the Seventh Street Scavengers. They

350

liked this upstart brat, the wild child that hated this city and loved to defy it at every turn.

"NICE one!" Archie called out, as a third story window shattered on an abandoned building. "Good arm there, good aim. Hey... you wanna see the Sideways?"

"What're Sideways?" the brat asked.

"All sorts of treasure down there. Never know what you'll find, and not many gangs to rumble with. C'mon, let's go salvaging. You'll love it."

Bang.

Disapproving stares. He was used to them from the teachers who knew he'd never amount to anything, but now he was getting them from Liz Tully, Archie's kid sister.

"You're a no-good thug, Gregory Yates, and I don't like you at all!" she declared. "Just like the rest of my brother's friends. And you smell awful!"

For the first time, he didn't laugh it off when someone gave him that look of disdain and pity. He didn't like it at all.

Bang.

Laughing away and throwing popcorn at the screen. It was a private show —he'd broken into the abandoned theater and set everything up a day ahead of time, projector and reels and all. Lizzie didn't know that Karla was along for the ride, running the reels.

Karla seemed to like the idea of Greg and Lizzie together, maybe just to annoy Archie, but hey... if it got him some quality time with his girl, Greg was all for it.

"Hey. You're my girl, right?" Greg asked.

"Mmmmaybe," Lizzie said, with a wry grin. "You're growing on me. Like kudzu, or mushrooms. Kinda grungy and icky but... growing."

"The hell's Kudzu?"

"You'd know if you paid attention in Biology class. ...y'know, I could tutor you, there. It's seriously NOT hard to score on those tests and pull your grades up. I know you're smart enough to do it, if you'd just put in the effort."

"Thought you already had some guy you were tutoring..."

"What, that Cartwright kid? His parents paid me, sure, but this I'd do for free," Lizzie offered. "How about it?"

Bang.

Signature on paper, making it nice and official. Dry rice thrown in the air, which the city official had expressly warned Karla not to do, but she wasn't the sort to bother following the rules.

The former Seventh Street Scavengers emerged from that dusty old government office, cheering on the new Mr. and Mrs. Yates. Archibald gave Gregory a few hearty, manly slaps to the back in congratulations.

"It's all changing, isn't it?" he wondered. "Gang isn't really a gang anymore. We're getting jobs. We're moving on. Honestly feels weird to be... to be... *responsible adults*, now. You ever miss it?"

"A little," Gregory admitted. "But Lizzie's got a good idea for how we can make some scratch and relive the good old days. We're gonna make Sideways maps and sell 'em online. Internet's going to get big, man, information superhighway is HUGE. There's a whole market for independent mappers now. Maybe even get some salvage finds to our name while we're at it."

Archie wrinkled his nose. "I don't like the idea of you dragging my little sis into the Sideways, man..."

"Relax, I got it covered. You know me; I'm hardcore. Only difference is now I can be hardcore *and* legit."

Bang.

Gun in his hand, but wavering. He never wavered. He was a steady hand whenever the guns came out during gangland days, and a steady hand when trying to dissuade Picassos from following them around. But now... but *now*...

Flickering form. Already getting distorted.

"You have to do it," Elizabeth said. "Please, Gregory... you have to. Shhh. It's okay. I love you—"

"Can't. I can't," he spoke... while keeping the gun raised. "Lizzie, I..."

"If you don't, I'm going to lose who I am anyway. I won't be *me* anymore," she reminded him. "I'll be a ghost of myself. And... I might come after you. Picassos are drawn to the familiar, without even realizing they're a threat to their loved ones. I could hurt // hurt you. I could hurt her..."

Her. The baby, mewling away where they set her down, out of sight of the gun with blankets to muffle the noise of the shot. The child they found, while lost in a series of mixed up Sideways. The child Lizzie had grown so attached to...

"I want you to raise her," Elizabeth said, seeing his glance to the side. "Please. She needs a father. That child is something special, I just know it, and I'm relying on you to find your way back to the city and give her a good life. Do that for me, and I'll die happily. Please... I... I'm losing it, it's like, like I'm slipping away // sleeping away // Gregory, don't make this any—"

Through gang dust-ups and Picasso dangers and everything else this City had thrown at him, Gregory had never actually killed anyone. He'd fired his gun plenty, but never actually killed anyone. Not until that day.

Bang.

All the happy memories were brutally painful. That was the point—Bedlam showing him everything he had lost, right up to the moment he lost it. Happiness turned sour. All because Gregory made a decision, and pulled a trigger.

"You didn't have to die," he understood.

"I didn't," his wife agreed, her blood still pooling around her body, her face still smiling.

"We didn't know at the time that people can come back from cubism. We still believed what the Department of Safety said, that Picassos were as good as gone, and once you were infected..."

"I didn't have to die. You didn't have to kill me. Penelope has shown you that I could have been saved."

"I killed you for no damn good reason..."

"That's right. You murdered me for no good reason," Lizzie's corpse said, rictus grin still there, so many teeth, such a bright smile through the blood. "You're a no-good thug, Gregory Yates, and nothing good can ever come of you. Nobody could ever love you. Murderer. Killer..."

The gun didn't waver, now. But it wasn't pointing at her anymore. When did he turn the gun around? Couldn't remember, but there it was, under his chin. He knew how to aim it to make the kill shot.

"You're not a father. Nobody like you should be a father," the many mouths of Bedlam-Lizzie spoke. "You should have given Penelope up for adoption at Scarlett's orphanage. You should have left her where you found her. Better that than let her spend one minute with someone as horrible as you. Cartwright was right. You're right. You deserve to die. You deserve it. You know what to do."

Gregory knew what to do.

Face what you fear most. //

Surrounded by the impossible, now. By moments where Penelope twisted the world in her favor. Even her birth was a twist in her favor... a child from nothing, born of no one, manifesting in the Sideways whole. She wouldn't be surprised to look down and not see a belly button at this point.

Slowly... she rose from the floor of her nightmare, the cloud of images floating away at a comfortable distance, the other self rising with her.

"That's what I'm afraid of, isn't it?" Penelope spoke aloud—at no one in particular, at least no one obviously present. "You wanted to break us down by making us face our fears. You're giving me a nightmare, disjointing my memories, trying to drive me insane..."

Another self, now. One behind her, dark and shadowed and green. It had been watching silently this whole time, watching Penelope interrogate and comfort herself simultaneously.

Now, Penelope was able to see it. Able to see all of herself, really. And somehow... it made her sad for Bedlam.

"I'm sorry, but I think this kinda backfired on you," she admitted. "I wasn't going insane. I was going sane."

The shadow that looked like her... looked confused. So, Penelope explained.

"What I fear most is accepting the truth," Penelope spoke. "The things I'd been brushing under the rug all this time as coincidences or simply outright ignoring. How the city twists around when I want it to... the dreams I've been having... the way I'm connected to all these people I've surrounded myself with. You forced me to to look that square in the eye because I was so scared of doing it myself. I know who I am now."

Jittering shadow. Fear. Green eyes wide.

// no // no...

"I was born an ordinary person, because I wanted to live. I'm the desire to live that's inside all of us, actually," she admitted. "Oh, I'm definitely Penelope Yates. I like being Penelope Yates. But I'm also the one who contracted Dave, hiring him to draw me a map to the Heart of the City, so I could finally learn the truth. I'm the one who helps Cass read the stories of people around her. I'm the one who helps Scarlett save the children with her compassion and her sewing. The dream is whatever I want it to be, because it's my dream. ...I'm sorry to be super dramatic about this, but—"

// NO NO NO NO

"—I'm Lucid."

No red-shift self, now. She didn't need that crutch to explain the facts of life to herself. There was just Lucid, and Bedlam. Two of the three points of view sharing one soul.

But Lucid wasn't gloating in victory. She was sympathetic to Bedlam's shivering terrors... even reached out to rest a hand on her sister-self's shoulder.

"I can't say I totally understand what's going on yet, since I'm also Penelope and she's not quite got this all worked out. She's human because she wants to be, and that's limiting. A good kind of limiting. But even she knows that it doesn't have to be like this," Lucid said. "We don't have to be at each other's throats, you know."

// have to have to. // chaos. life. // can't have both...

"I think we can. We've both been going at the same problem, haven't we?" Penelope said. "I've been mapping the city to try and understand it better, so I can help people live *with* the city instead of against it. I think the city's beautiful—yes, even the Sideways. It doesn't have to be this great big scary thing everybody has to hide from..."

// don't have to hide // not at all, not at all // if everyone just embraces the nightmare, Bedlam suggested. *that's my goal. // to befriend everyone. // nothing to fear. // immortal. // dreamlike. // heavenly...*

"Yeah, but that's kinda the polar opposite, right? If people can't lie to themselves and pretend the city is totally normal... resisting the dream at every turn... they *also* can't dive headfirst into it and go completely crazy. Neither's a really good way to live. There has to be a middle ground."

// chaos in life. // like kelsey...

"Or life in chaos, like me," Penelope suggested. "I think I can do it. If you just give me a chance, I think I can help get this city to where it should be. Not saying it'll be overnight, but... c'mon. Let's give it a try. No more driving everybody insane, *or* trying to force the city to be rigid and ordinary. Enough room for you *and* me. How about it?"

Wavering, the shadow uncertain.

// if I say no?

Penelope glanced around at the accelerated memoryspace they were occupying. Beyond that, she could see the walls of the Heart of the City... or at least the hallways and antechambers leading up to it. Brick and mortar. Echoed stonework of a long lost CDC facility...

"I can collapse this whole place," she suggested. "Neither of us get to the Heart. You don't get to remake the city in your image, and everything continues on as it did before. Not a great outcome for either of us. Especially me, since I'd be dead. Or at least this incarnation of me, Penelope Yates, would be dead. Honestly, I'd rather not to do it. But... I will. If you make me choose between that or letting you ruin everything."

A brief spike of darkness, there. Bedlam hated being denied the things she wanted—even by her own friends, which was what led her to charging down here pell-mell before Seth's plan had fully come to fruition. But... even with her complete lack of impulse control, she had enough sense to know when it wasn't worth hanging on any longer to an idea.

Besides, in the end, she'd likely win anyway.

// still so limited. // still penelope, even if you're also my other self, Bedlam teased, while bowing in defeat. *// a hard, hard road ahead. // unaware of what lies in wait... // the nadir of our trinity, sorrow's Echo. // the distant threat of the bleed. // far worse things than me. // so much simpler to soak the city in nightmare // save everyone, all at once // everywhere...*

"Simple doesn't mean better."

// won't help you. // won't stop you. // will wait patiently for you to fail.

"It's a starting point, at least," Penelope said... offering a friendly smile, and an extended hand to shake. "We can sort the rest out later. For now, I really need to get back to being Penelope. So... are we cool?"

There was no gun at his head. Not in reality—the reality he now was waking to.

Gregory snapped to his senses, feeling a hand taking his. His daughter's hand. All the agony that had been coursing through his mind had ceased... everything crystal clear once more.

"It's going to be okay, Dad," Penelope spoke. "I promise. ...it's over. Bedlam's retreating. We won. Dave? Dave, you okay?"

The young man (still in his pajamas when Seth kidnapped him, much as he was when Penelope first found him) looked up from his seat in the corner. Body shakes starting to subside.

"I... think... yes, I'm okay," he decided. "As okay as I can be, anyway. Is she gone? For real?"

"She's agreed to leave us alone," Penelope decided to summarize. "I can explain more later once I've figured out exactly how to explain it... Dad? You can put that away, she's not coming back. Trust me on this."

Immediately, Gregory holstered his gun. Feeling vaguely self-conscious about having it at all.

"Let's get out of here, then," he said. "Dave, you're with us. Archie and Karla are hopefully still up top, fighting Picassos... we double back to find them and then go home. ...okay, I know that look. It's the 'I'm about to directly countermand your paternal order.' What exactly is more important than getting out of here alive?"

"Getting to the Heart of the City," Penelope spoke. "Like I wanted to do in the first place."

"Isn't this it? It doesn't look like much, but—"

"Dave's map wasn't finished. The Heart's in one of these rooms. Although I don't know which one..."

She found a key ring being pressed into her hand. Dave's house keys. Specifically, he had four keys on the ring: a key to his father's house, a key to his apartment, a key to his old dorm room... and a key which was there all along, even if he never noticed it because it wasn't always actually there. One which was just the right size to fit in the heavy metal door locks they'd been passing along the way.

"I'm pretty sure it's in Room 23," Dave spoke. "I knew all along. I've been seeing that number all over the place ever since I got the city. I just didn't want to tell Bedlam because, well, scary girl destroying city equals bad."

The Heart of the City.

Penelope was good at memorizing the layout of rooms, all the little details that went into urban planning and modern decoration. It was a key skill for a mapper to have. And a boon, given when she tried to record an EchoMap of the actual heart, her tablet bricked itself.

The room suited the facility around it. This was akin to a hospital room... a large bed with raised metal rails, harsh overhead fluorescent lighting, and plenty of beeping or buzzing or burbling devices all around. Tubes and wires and sensor leads, all of them converging on...

Converging on...

Herself.

A girl in a hospital gown, one who looked just like herself. Facial features the same. Hair even the same, although not done in pigtails, and in fact colored shock white like an old lady. But the girl was certainly not old—she couldn't be more than twelve going on thirteen, just like Penelope. They were in sync, age-wise. At least, they seemed to be...

But it was hard to look at the girl in the hospital bed. What was swirling overhead was far, far more distracting.

It was the City. Ghostly and unformed, like the undefined spaces beyond the edge of known space, buildings and street lamps and streets and more... pouring upward with a twisting motion, an upward spiral, upward from some vague space just over the girl's head. Calling this the 'source' of the city was a more apt metaphor than Penelope could have realized (or perhaps exactly as apt as she did realize) as it flowed up and through the ceiling... presumably upward and upward, to generate more buildings for the City of Angles itself.

The patient was dreaming the city. Eyes closed, sleeping away, and dreaming everything around them.

A plastic hospital wristband offered:

- an unhelpful bar code,
- a blood type,
- an age (twelve),
- a date of birth (February 23, 1906),
- and a name of sorts ("Patient 23").

And nothing else.

Gregory got a bit more out of the ridiculously thick pile of papers on a clipboard, hung by a peg at the foot of her bed.

"Patient 23," he read. "She's... apparently been in CDC care since 1918. That's the same year people think the City started to exist. She's been asleep ever since, never waking. The rest is... it's just a bunch of doctor scribbles and notes about heart rate and brain waves and so on, going back and back to before the CDC existed..."

Being both confused and more likely than the other two to overcome his shock at being confused, Dave politely raised his hand to speak.

"I don't quite get it," he admitted. "Who is this? Why does she look like you? Why does she look like Bedlam too, for that matter? Or is it that you and Bedlam look like her? Is she really making the city? Is the city all her dream? How could she be twelve years old and one hundred and nine years old? What's going on here, exactly? Should we wake her up—?"

"NO."

The force of it surprised even Penelope, despite the fact that she was the one issuing the objection.

"N... o. No," she repeated, trying on the word. "No, we should not wake her up. ...I don't understand this even though I really think I should, especially given the other things I've learned about myself today, but... I think waking her up would be extremely bad."

"Really? Why?"

"Because if she's dreaming up our entire world, and we give her a wakey-wakey nudge..."

"Oh? *Ohhh.* Okay, yeah, bad," Dave agreed (while switching to a quieter tone of voice). "I think I see why Bedlam wanted in here. Turn her dream into a nightmare. ...I'm not sure I like any of the implications of what all this could mean but I'm still a bit puzzled about what we should be doing next, all the same."

Gregory looked away from the tightly packed pile of meaningless medical data, to look towards his daughter. His first instinct was to declare *okay, here's what we're going to do, we lock the door behind us and throw away the key and then we go find Archie and then we go home and forget any of this ever happened* but honestly... this wasn't his decision. This was her life, and her decision. It was time he started accepting that.

Fortunately, Penelope had made her decision.

They left the dreamer much as they found her... with a few key differences.

For one, they took her chart and medical bracelet. Those were mysteries that needed to be investigated, if Penelope was ever to find closure on this journey she'd been taking since she the day she was born.

Next, they left Penelope's teddy bear in the dreamer's arms. Her Gregory Bear, the bear she'd made for herself out of a wish and a thought, the ur-bear behind every bear that Grandma Scarlett had ever made. It seemed for a moment that the dreamer smiled in her sleep.

Finally, Penelope closed and locked the door behind them... and slid the key underneath. If even Bedlam couldn't break down this door, nobody would, and with the key inside it would never be opened again. They could've taken the key with them, hung onto it for safety, but that'd just encourage would-be megalomaniacs like Bedlam to kidnap and torture everyone around Penelope to get their hands on the Heart of the City. This way, the dreamer could sleep peacefully, and her city would go on much as it always had. For now.

The city went on much as it always had.

She had a moment to reflect, some weeks later. A visit to That Fish Place, to have some lobster. Father laughing it up with Archie in the back room, leaving Penelope to her thoughts and her seafood.

Thoughts of the night when everything changed, and the days beyond... not the lucid television-monitor memories of that strange experience, just ordinary memories, but clear to her all the same.

At the moment the dreamer was given a teddy bear of her own, Bedlam's influence over the dream shattered. The wave of Picassos and those that turned into Picassos in reactionary terror were instantly returned to their normal shapes. Just as a pulse of fear had started the cascade of chaos, a pulse of calm ended it... a calm that settled over the City, the Suburbs, and the Outlands like a warm blanket. For a night and a day, the city knew no evil. No murders, no muggings, no theft, no fighting, no negativity.

Of course... nothing lasts forever. And soon, the media began the drumbeat of fear anew. *Picasso night! What happened? Where was Seth Dougal in our time of need? What is your government doing to prevent a future outbreak of cubism? News at 11.* Still, not exactly a new tune, and as the Nightmare Fuel burned its way out of blood streams, dreamful nights of rest helped tilt the city back to normalcy.

Archie and Karla reunited with the group. Gregory was surprised to find they hadn't been blown to kingdom come; the grenades were useful in keeping their attackers at a distance, but what settled matters was the strange calming wave from the Heart of the City. Instead of facing two monsters, they faced a very lost-looking little girl and a confused-looking man soaked in gasoline. Both ran away rather than talk the situation through. Penelope wanted to go looking for them, but Gregory insisted they get topside, and she was too tired to argue it.

With no more need to organize a makeshift rebel alliance, Scarlett returned to her orphanage. Cass resumed running deliveries. Sometimes they'd meet at the Lucid Dreamer for a bit of catch-up, but the group didn't have a reason to hang together any longer. Penelope kept in touch with everyone by email and text, but it was clear this moment in their lives had passed. They had their own lives to live, now.

Archie went back to his restaurant. Karla celebrated her husband finally getting out of traction with a night of passionate rekindling that nearly put him back in traction. Vivi took up the mantle of her former mentor Gee Bee, running one of the hottest clubs in the city. Marcy resumed writing one-word challenges all over the city.

None of them really talked about what happened in the Heart of the City. Penelope wasn't sure who to tell about it, even among her friends. Wasn't sure what to tell them, since she didn't fully understand it herself.

She was Lucid. She was Penelope. She was life in chaos. She was just some girl. She knew things she shouldn't know. She only knew what she knew. That strange moment in her life had passed, leaving her with memories and little else. At least, little else she was ready to tap into just yet.

But she wore the hospital bracelet now, like a combination of a good luck charm and a reminder string for her finger. Proof that the city's mysteries ran deeper than she could ever imagine, and she should never look away from that fact.

There were challenges coming. Bedlam had insinuated as much. And Penelope had seen one herself, in her lucid dream at the Heart of the City...

Because she knew how Officer Cartwright, the broken down and ruined man, had slipped free of his captivity. He made the ultimate escape, thanks to a vision in a mirror. A girl, twelve going on thirteen, with brilliant blue eyes and a sad expression of sympathy.

Echo. The third in the trinity of viewpoints, the dreamer's reactions to her dream.

She made an offer to Cartwright, which was gratefully accepted. And then he no longer existed.

Idly, Penelope twisted the bracelet on her wrist, thinking.

"Things are gonna get worse before they get better," she realized.

--- ---

It was ridiculous, honestly. He'd already pulled the graveyard shift twice this week—once more than he had to, just because Wilkins wanted to trade off. And what'd he get out of that? Free membership to the office coffee club? He didn't even LIKE coffee.

That meant he had to be in the facility after dark, when security was even more paranoid than usual. He had to go through the checkpoints, keep his badge front and center, smile and take it when the bored guards gave him more grilling than he deserved. All so he could wander these halls, checking in on the patients, yep, still asleep, still vegetables, who cares, not him, not *anyone*...

Eventually he gave up even pretending to do his job. His boss wasn't on site, so why keep up appearances? Better to take a nap on the couch when nobody was looking. He needed his energy for the day shift, anyway; they were supposedly getting the new MRI prototype today, the one they'd dubbed the Dreamcatcher. If anything was going to shake things up in this going-nowhere project, it'd be that.

So, Doctor Jack Hayes crashed out on a Carter-era couch in a break room that hadn't been redecorated since Nixon, and snored away. The quiet hum of the shiny chrome refrigerator kept him company.

He woke seven hours later, because the telltale sounds of activity hadn't been present.

Peel self off couch, taste horrible in mouth, scratch at unshaven beard. Hate life. Get up, grab clipboard, get back to making rounds before anybody notices...

Except the hallways were different.

The hallway was not actually a hallway. It was a living room. Half of a living room, really—the other half was a high school locker room. And beyond that seemed to be a dentist's office. Three rooms for the price of one, all outside the door of the facility break room...

He knew what this meant, of course. He just didn't want to accept it. So he closed the door, counted to five, centered himself, and began screaming and screaming and screaming and screaming.

There was a knife in the drawer which they normally used to slice bagels. It could slice his throat. Well, no, that'd get messy and dangerous, the best bet would be to use the wrists. Down and not across, down and not across...

Pushing up the sleeves of his CDC-issued lab coat. Skin pale and waiting. Knife sharp and waiting.

Waiting.

The knife clattered into the sink, before Jack Hayes sank to the floor opposite the fridge, pulling at his hair. Unable to do it. Unable to do the only sane thing in an insane world.

Because Jack knew the score, because he'd seen the game playing out in classified prototype MRI scans they'd been performing, he wasn't the least bit surprised to see a creepy girl with blue eyes studying him from inside the reflective surface of the fridge.

"I'm so sorry," the girl told him. "You don't want to be here. You don't deserve to be here, in the City of Angles. It's cruel and unkind..."

"You're the third aspect," he recognized. "Your name's Echo. Oh god. Oh god, I'm here, I'm really here. I'm inside the dream of Patient 23..."

"Split away, echoed into this world. The real Jack Hayes has no idea you're here. He's awake and toiling away in his hateful job, but at least he's real, at least he exists. Unlike you. Doctor Hayes, I'm so sorry. You don't deserve this miserable existence. Nobody does. Nobody in this entire city should suffer this existence..."

Jack's head hung. At least he had the good fortune to meet *her*, of all people. It beat meeting the second aspect, that was for sure.

"It's going to be fine. I can make it so you won't hurt anymore, not at all. You'd like that, right?" the girl asked. "You're only an echo, like me. A dream of a person, not really here. Nobody is real. Once you accept my revelation, it won't hurt anymore..."

"Do it before I wuss out again," Jack whispered.

"...but I'm sorry. I can't do it yet," Echo spoke. "Not yet. I need your help. The city needs you. The Heart has been sealed, but the dreamer must awaken and end this terrible nightmare forever. You can help me do that. Will you help me, Jack Hayes...?"

It's not possible, he was going to say. Because they'd been trying to wake the oddly unaging Patient 23 for almost a century, now. Nothing worked. Brain wave manipulations, chemical stimulants, electrical shocks... nothing got through. His superiors had theorized that if Patient 23 awoke, the city in her dreams would be lost. All the psychic echoes trapped inside it would fade, like... well, to abuse a metaphor, fade like a dream.

But... Jack was one of those echoes, now. He was inside. It wasn't beyond the realm of possibility that a man on the inside could make it happen...

He could destroy the city and "kill" everybody inside, including himself. But would it be killing, really? They didn't exist. He didn't exist. What did any of it matter? Why not wake the dreamer?

Slowly, Doctor Hayes pulled himself from the floor. Resisting the urge to laugh a little.

"Why not?"

//end

\\00a: Are We There Yet?

Billy was only ten when his parents made the decision to take a vacation.

His father worked at an insurance company, where he said he made sure sick people could afford to be well. It didn't pay a lot, but they had a cozy apartment in a nice building near the Zag, which was good. His mother worked as a teacher, working with kids like Billy who schooled from home, over a speakerphone. (Billy had to attend most of the classes his mother taught, because they couldn't afford to hire some other teacher for him. Honestly, he didn't mind, because he was in another room and used a fake name so none of the other kids would tease him for having his mommy as a teacher.)

Billy had never left the city before. He'd rarely gone more than five blocks away from his house, really. Most of his friends were from the same apartment building; he wasn't allowed to wander around outside. (You could fall in the Sideways and get eaten up by a Picasso, people said. Scary stuff.) Fortunately, there was a great rec room in the basement with toys and video games. As long as you got along with the other kids, you'd do fine. That meant if someone was a bit pushy, like Julio who always wanted to play the Atari, you should just let them get their way. It beat having problems with someone you live with.

But now, the boy who rarely left the apartment building was going allllll the way out to the Outlands. They were going to visit a lake!

"It's going to be beautiful, son, simply beautiful," his dad promised when he made the announcement over dinner. "A lakeside resort! A whole house to ourselves. A dock, with a boat. I can teach you how to swim!"

A lake! There was a small lake at a park in the city—sometimes they went to that park, when Dad had time away from work. (He usually worked weekends.) But that was a small lake, Dad said, a fake lake. This would be a real lake!

"John, how can we possibly afford this?" his mother asked.

"It's a newly discovered resort community! It just got added to the Outlands," he explained. "Near the edge of the maps. That means it's nice and cheap! Don't worry, the Department of Safety already surveyed it, it's completely safe. Besides, we don't have to take a charter bus out there. I can drive us and save a ton of money."

Needless to say, Billy was the star of the rec room the next day. He told everybody about the lake they were going to visit, all about the giant house they'd be staying in. He promised to take lots of pictures. Even Julio was impressed, and let him have more than a few minutes with the Atari.

He'd put up a calendar on his bedroom door, so he could check off the days leading up to the trip. Little red X marks, day by day. He made notes to himself of what to pack—underwear and socks, to make Mom happy. His Walkman, and all his cassettes! Tons of batteries! It was going to be a long car trip, longer than any trip they'd ever taken before, and he'd want as much music as he could bring with him. Also, his Polaroid camera, so he could take pictures.

On the day they piled into the car with suitcases and a handful of sandwiches and snacks, Billy was nearly bouncing off the walls with excitement. They had to remind him twice to put on his seatbelt.

A lake! A lake!

Billy insisted the family pose in front of the car, for a photograph. He had to take two—one with himself and his mother, one with himself and his father. He could use scissors and tape to make it a trio after he got home.

The family station wagon pulled onto a major highway that morning, joining the flow of cars headed out of the City and towards the Suburbs.

Only a few highways led to the Suburbs, his dad had explained. You had to know which ones to take, since they all ended up in different places in the Suburbs. He'd bought a brand new paper map from a mapper, and highlighted the route they'd take in red pen. Mom's job was to read the map and lead them the right way.

"Now, it's going to feel a little strange," Dad explained to Billy in the backseat, while keeping his eyes on the road. "You may wanna close your eyes, because sometimes you feel a little sick. But one moment there'll be big city buildings, and the next... whoosh! The Suburbs!"

"Will it hurt?" Billy asked.

"Oh, no, no! It's just going to feel a little strange—"

It felt a little strange.

Billy didn't have time to really think about how strange it felt. He didn't even see the shimmery transition, because suddenly the morning sunshine was in his eyes—the building that had been blocking it was gone.

The Suburbs!

He'd seen pictures, in books and magazines. Houses, whole buildings that had only one family in them. Lots of houses! He could see entire bunches of them in the distance, all huddled together like they were cold or something. But the sunlight was now flickering through *trees*, not buildings. Trees! They lined the roadways, everywhere. So much space, devoted to just trees!

This was worth a picture. He insisted his dad pull over, next to a nice bunch of trees and houses, so he could snap one with his camera. He added it to his family pictures.

With this task complete, Billy popped a copy of the Ghostbusters soundtrack in his Walkman, enjoying the music as he watched the trees and houses and street signs go gliding by. So much open space... kids could run and play and run forever here, and never have to worry about the Sideways, he bet. It would've been nice to live here.

"Are we there yet?" Billy asked. "Is the lake out here? I bet you could fit a whole lake out there. There's enough room for all sorts of lakes!"

"Oh, this is crowded compared to where we're going!" Dad promised. "Just you wait. It's going to be so beautiful!"

Hours later, a highway inked in red, one more "kind of funny" transition and they were in the Outlands.

If the Suburbs were spread out, the Outlands were even MORE spread out. This was the rural countryside, Dad explained. They had farms and factories and endless forests here.

The cars had changed, too. Most of the cars in the City were taxis, and in the Suburbs it was station wagons and hatchbacks and things. Here, they didn't see any cars at all. Every now and then a GIANT truck would pass by them, with wheels and wheels. Carrying important things like Walkmen from factories in the Outlands, all the way back to the City, no doubt.

He even saw cows! They were gathered by a fence, watching the trucks go by. This is where milk and hamburgers came from—they raised animals out here and then shipped them into the city. (Billy knew that they killed animals to make hamburgers, of course. But that was okay, because hamburgers were delicious and there would always be more cows.)

Dad wouldn't stop so he could take pictures, so the photos ended up being kind of blurry. He could probably convince even Julio that those were cows, though.

The second set of AA batteries had gone dead, so Billy popped them out and loaded fresh ones. He'd listened to his tapes twice now, wanting to keep the music going. He wanted to be excited, to stay excited, even as the sun was setting.

(Mom wanted to pull over to eat a late lunch, maybe at one of the rest stops. But Dad insisted they were making great time, and wasn't this why they brought snacks and sandwiches, anyway?)

"Are we there yet?" Billy asked. "This is where the lake is, right?"

"Won't be long now!" Dad promised. "Honey, is it exit 18 or exit 1B? I can't read this stupid map..."

"Here, let me see that," Mom said, pulling the now ragged map away. They'd folded and unfolded and refolded it a dozen times, trying to make sure they were on the right route. "I... have no idea. Where did you buy this? You should have gone to the bookstore for a reputable atlas..."

"I know a guy who knows a guy. And I'm not paying fifty dollars for one of those overpriced things," he insisted. "Atlases are a racket by the mapping companies."

With the batteries reloaded, Billy slipped on his headphones and let the music drown out the increasingly irate chatter of his parents.

The second set of batteries was long dead before Billy woke up.

He must've dozed off, because the sun had gone down. It was really late at night now, dark... the tree line on either side of the highway hard to see against the sky above.

And what a sky...! Stars! The moon! You couldn't see too many stars from the City; it was always too bright there, it drowned out the starlight. He learned that in his classes.

The headlights briefly illuminated a sign, which read EXIT 86 AHEAD.

"Are we there yet...?" Billy mumbled, trying to shake the sleep off.

"Go back to sleep, Billy," Mom ordered. It was her stern voice, the one she used when she was serious. If he didn't obey she'd get mad.

So, Billy closed his eyes. But he couldn't sleep, so he just pretended. Mom wouldn't know the difference. It meant, however, he couldn't show that he was able to hear them. Couldn't react.

"We have to turn around, John," Mom insisted.

"It's got to be up here somewhere," Dad said. "We've been following the map. This IS the right road. Third right after the water tower, that's what it said —"

"—should've bought a *real* map, not something by one of those would-be explorer types."

"I know where I'm going!" Dad nearly growled. "I know where we are. Everything is *fine*."

"We're going to run out of gas! If you turn around now, we can double back, refuel, maybe figure out where we are and ask for directions to the lake —"

"I don't need directions to the lake."

"But you DO need gas. Look, it's almost empty! Just... turn back, we'll refuel, then you can drive all night if you want. Please...?"

And finally Billy did in fact fall asleep.

"Billy? Billy, wake up."

Morning. Sunlight.

Billy's eyes opened and his stomach growled. Slowly, he blinked away the sleep stuff from his eyes, tried to wiggle around to unkink unhappy muscles.

The first thing he saw was a sign reading EXIT 86 AHEAD.

The car wasn't moving anymore.

"Are we there yet?" he asked. "We've stopped..."

"We're going to go have a picnic!" Dad said, with a very, very big smile. "Get all your things, we're going to have to walk a ways. A long ways. But we'll be at the lake soon!"

Billy glanced out the window, to the roadside...

...where Mom was hurriedly emptying out his suitcase, dumping all his socks and underwear. Filling it with what was left of the food they'd brought with them.

"We'll be there soon, champ," Dad said. "I've never let you down, right? We'll be at the lake later today!"

Billy had never walked a mile before, and he really did not enjoy it.

Kids who went to schools, real schools in actual school buildings, they got P.E. classes. In the Suburbs they even had track and field. Billy had none of these things, and long-distance hikes were a new and unpleasant experience for him.

Only when his protests grew loud enough to get him yelled at did they actually stop to eat. But as hungry as he was, they insisted he only eat half his sandwich.

By now, his Walkman was completely out of batteries, and he didn't have any more. He still wore the headphones, because right now, the Walkman and Polaroid and pockets full of photos were the only things he had which was really his. They'd left all their luggage behind; carrying only his little suitcase, now full of food.

Mom and Dad were arguing a ton, so he pretended he had batteries and was enjoying his music. But he heard it all. All of it, even the bad words, and he had to pretend he couldn't hear it. He didn't want to hear it, anyway. In fact, after awhile, he'd convinced himself he wasn't hearing it.

The sun was going down again when they finally reached the rest area.

By now, what was going on was obvious to Billy. The car ran out of gas. They were walking back to buy gas and food, and then they'd need to get a ride back to the car. Once they got to the rest stop, everything would be fine—they'd have gas, food, a ride, and then be on their way to the lake.

Dad was so excited to see the rest stop that he started running ahead. Billy could barely walk, much less run. Which meant he had time to really *look* at the place.

No cars, no trucks. Nobody here. It was shiny, once... like the pictures of 1950s diners he'd seen in books. But now it was a little less shiny. Not completely broken down, but nobody had been shining the shiny parts...

And the gas pumps didn't work.

And there wasn't actually a diner.

There was a diner—a big building, with a sign reading DINER. But inside the diner... was a living room.

Billy could see a library, one room over from the living room. Not like a library in a rich person's mansion, but like a public library, with a Returns desk and a sign reading "New Lender Applications Here!".

Even a kid like Billy knew what this was. When rooms didn't make sense, *really* didn't make sense, you were probably in the Sideways.

But there was no Sideways in the Outlands. Everybody knew that. The Sideways were always a danger in the City, sometimes you'd find them in the Suburbs, but out in the country it just didn't happen. The Outlands were stable. They were safe. They were random, you'd get farms and forests and factories, but it was a good place. Like lake resorts...

No gas. No food. The Sideways.

"We're never gonna get to the lake, are we," Billy realized.

"Nonsense! Everything's fine!" Dad declared. "What a strange diner! Ha ha! I'm sure we can find some food here. And I'll figure out some way to get the gas pumps working. Then we'll go back to the car and be on our way!"

And then the biggest argument ever happened. Because Mom had started screaming and wouldn't stop.

Billy ran into the library room, grabbed a book, and started reading. He didn't care what book, now. Just anything to replace those words with other words.

Billy's Dad pulled him aside an hour later, to explain how things were going to go.

"Now, you and your mother are going to stay here," he said. "It's comfortable, and you have a lot of books, and there's a cozy couch you can sleep on. That's much better than a car seat, isn't it?"

"I'm hungry," Billy said, even though he knew it wouldn't change anything to say it.

"I know, Billy, I know. And I'm going to find food. Now, in the back of the library there's a hallway, and doors. I'm going to go exploring. And I'm going to come back with food and gas and a new map, and we're going to go to the lake. But meanwhile, I need you to wait right here with your mom. Don't follow me. Whatever you do, absolutely DO NOT follow me. Okay?"

Billy said nothing.

"Your mom, she's... a little tired," Dad decided to say. "I'm gonna need you to be the man of the family while I'm gone. Look after your mother. I promise I'll be back soon, champ. I promise."

Dad wasn't back by the next day.

By now Billy was totally starving, but he didn't want to say anything about it. He didn't want to talk to Mom and that was fine, because she didn't want to talk to him. She just stayed on the living room couch, lying down, sometimes groaning.

Mom had started taking her pills, the ones she took when she got nervous. Lots of women in the apartment building took them. They made Mom really sleepy, and Billy was okay with letting her sleep. He was the man now, and couldn't go cuddle mommy for comfort. The man was supposed to be strong.

He decided to pass the time by taking more photographs, and arranging them on the floor of the living room. There were pictures from the trip so far—those came first. The suburbs, trees and houses. Blurry cows. A quick shot he'd snapped of the car, just before the long hike. He'd run outside and taken pictures of the old diner, inside and out.

The best picture, though, was the pair he'd taken at the start. Him and Dad, him and Mom. He'd found scissors and tape in the library desk, and went ahead with a little photo doctoring. He was going to wait until they got home, but... this was a good enough time. Now, it was a photo of Dad and Billy and Mom, together. Better.

Dad never came back.

Mom stopped moving, after awhile. She'd emptied her bottle of pills and went to sleep. She must've got sick when she was asleep, threw up all over the couch, and then just stopped moving.

Billy wasn't moving much, either. He stayed on the floor of the living room, with open books all over the place, and his photo collage. His Walkman and his tapes, arrayed nicely. He couldn't listen to them anymore, but he wanted to be able to look at them.

Why not just go into the Sideways, and find Dad?

Because kids don't go into the Sideways. Never, ever. It was like taking candy from strangers; they beat it into your head from early on, you never ever ever ever go into the Sideways. You stay away from the yellow-black and the red-black. Neither are safe. If you find a Sideways by accident you leave right away and tell an adult.

It wasn't because he was too scared to follow Dad. Not at all. He was just being a good boy and doing what good boys did.

Besides, by now, he was too weak to go anywhere. He had considered leaving the diner before, going back to the road. Maybe a truck would come along. But he didn't want to leave. He couldn't. Couldn't move.

It hurt a lot.

Sometimes he thought he heard things, but he couldn't chase after them. He thought he heard Julio, demanding he move over so he could get a turn on the Atari. He heard his mother crying, but Mom didn't move anymore.

And finally, he heard a girl.

"I'm so sorry," the girl whispered.

"M'hhngry," Billy mumbled. He couldn't see, couldn't really focus... some girl, above him. Maybe his age, maybe a bit older. Hard to say...

"I'm so sorry you had to go through this. But it's okay. I'm here now," she spoke. "Shhh. It's going to be fine. I can make it so you won't hurt anymore, not at all. You'd like that, right?"

Billy could only mutely nod.

"You're only an echo, like me. A dream of a person, not really here. Nobody is real. Your mother and father, they couldn't accept that, so they hurt and hurt and then died. But once you understand, it won't hurt anymore. I can help you see the truth. Are you ready?"

Trying to speak with dry lips, Billy replied at barely a whisper.

"Am I gonna go to Heaven?" he asked.

The voice paused.

"No," she said. "But it won't hurt at all, not existing. I promise."

It didn't really matter. None of it did. Billy could accept that, so long as it all stopped.

The flashlight beam whisked around the room, in a tight search pattern, before falling on the body.

He tugged a paper breathing mask up, to cut the smell.

"Definitely still part of the Sideways," Gregory confirmed. "Entropy's nice and low. Body's hardly fresh but hardly rotten. From the fashions I'd say... I don't know, early eighties? Been here thirty years..."

A young girl stepped out around him. She wasn't afraid of dead bodies. You couldn't be, if you were taking up her line of work. Still, she tried not to inhale too deeply.

"That's probably his wife," Penelope said. "The poor guy who Picasso'd. He was screaming something about his wife and kid... do you see a kid anywhere?"

Her own flashlight swept across the floor.

She saw old plastic audio tapes, laid out in a neat row. She saw photographs... a neat little chronology of events, a vacation from the City to the Suburbs to the Outlands. And finally, a crudely taped together photo of a man, a woman, and a little boy...

But no little boy, anywhere. No sign there ever was a kid here, other than the photographic evidence.

"Odds are he gave up and ran for it," Gregory suggested. "Poor bastards. Go for a Sunday drive, roll down an Endless Road... but you were right. This part of the Sideways DID cut straight from the City to the Outlands. That's a first; the Department of Resources will pay huge bucks for our map."

"I don't think it'll do anyone much good," Penelope said, clicking off her light. "It didn't do them any good—"

Outside, through the glass diner windows.

She snapped the light on again, curious... but the flashlight just bounced off the glass, showing nothing beyond.

"Something up, Penny?" Gregory asked. "We should double back..."

"I thought I saw... just for a minute I thought I saw someone out there. A girl," Penelope said. "Probably just my reflection."

In the end, she decided to collect the photographs. If the Department of Resources came through here they'd just bag up the body and all the evidence and dispose of it, to avoid any chance of cubist contamination.

It wouldn't be a kindness to the boy who took these pictures to let them vanish without a trace. He deserved to be remembered by someone, she felt. So, she'd remember him.

\\00b: Special When Lit

Silver down the ramp, off the wall, straight into the ball drain.

That didn't make sense to her. Good game design meant that you had a chance, that you could have prevented a drain out if you were fast enough or skilled enough. She was fast and skilled; years of play under her belt proved that. But the ball went down that ramp and came to a crashing halt, draining away forever. Game over. No other outcome possible.

Normally that wouldn't bother her. She'd just tap the button her dad had wired up which faked a quarter and play again. But that wasn't working, either. There the ball sat, motionless, at the bottom of the drain. No more game. Didn't make sense.

Zero score at the start of a new game, with the high scores so tantalizingly out of reach. Memory on board to store the last five highs, all of which read TOM.

Tommy. Tomiko. *Tomiko can you hear me?*

Return to start, line up the skill shot. How far you pull the plunger is key.

Standing out is bad. It was better to be one of the flashing lights in the background; otherwise, you were either drop target or flipper. Beat on or beater. And Tomiko wasn't much of a flipper, didn't really aspire to be one. She was content to be unnoticed.

For years she'd been home-schooled. It was a conversation her parents had for many years—not an argument, not a fight. Father was soft-spoken at all times, even when he disagreed. Mother and Father simply conversed about whether or not Tomiko should be home-schooled, when and if she should migrate to public school, and so on.

It wasn't a matter of money. It was a question of fear, because Mother was afraid. It cost more to take classes online, yes, but most kids did it anyway—otherwise you'd have to be driven out to a public school or worse, take a public school bus. Tomiko had heard horror stories of that, of buses with bad drivers that drove off with lots of kids and never came back. ("That only happened a few times, Tomi. It does not happen every day. But it scares people to think about it.")

But Father was public-schooled, and he saw it as important, a way for quiet Tomi to make more friends. He survived public school. He'd even taken the bus for years and never vanished. Why should Tomi be denied the life experience?

In the end, the conversation always ended with Mother's worries being declared the winner. Father didn't want to upset her. And so, Tomi was home-schooled.

Line up for the jet bumpers. The chaos of the bumpers is dangerous, it can knock the ball down a drain if you aren't careful, but risk means reward. *Don't fear the chaos. Embrace it.*

Drop targets falling, a bank of six. Complete all six for a bonus. Knock them down until they're all gone. F-A-T-H-E-R. Fifty thousand points, orange L.E.D. letters lighting up in victory, screaming out that he is gone.

The new targets appear. J-A-K-E.

Jake was not as quiet as Father. Jake was very loud, and when he was loud, it was best to go down to the basement and play pinball rather than get in his way. He'd break things when he got loud. Mother would cry. But it was better than the alternative, she insisted—they needed a man. Mother did not have a job. They would have lost the house. Father made money, but not enough money for them to stay alone (only fifty thousand points) and now this was the only way.

Drop target or flipper, beat on or beater.

Public school. Couldn't afford home-schooling anymore. "A bright new opportunity," Mother said, using Father's words to convince herself. "You'll make so many more friends. You won't be playing on that machine all day, you can play soccer after school or make music."

Every day Tomiko came home and played pinball instead of soccer or making music. She had to sneak off as quietly as possible.

Ringing bells and buzzers, a mixture of electro-mechanical and digital. The cusp of transition in the pinball industry, before games went to dot matrix. Plenty of voice samples. Voices calling out. *They're coming for you, they laugh, they hate you, you are afraid. But you don't have to be afraid.*

Nobody in the Suburbs was really poor, except for the really poor people. Tomiko's house was lovely when it wasn't broken and even if Father never made a lot of money they never wanted for anything.

For instance, she had three pinball machines in her basement, purchased by Father, after he got his first promotion. She was barely tall enough to play when they arrived.

"I used to play these games when I was your age," Father explained. "I loved them, but the arcade at the mall shut down one year and I never got to play them again. I am grown, I can buy the games for myself—and if you like them too, you can play them whenever you want without spending a single quarter. You can be my little Pinball Wizard, Tomi."

She owned pinball machines and lived in a nice house in the Suburbs, but now with Father gone and Jake in the house, she was in public school with the kids who didn't have any of those things. And they did not like that she had them.

Tomi had tried to make friends. She invited some girls over to her house at first, to play pinball or watch cartoons from her library. It seemed to go okay. They were friendly enough. Mother made snacks. Jake was out working and drinking so there was no chance he'd scare them off.

Then the next day they had a new name for Tomi: "Rich Bitch."

Score going up, higher and higher. Combo multiplier for hitting the four-loop sequence.

They're coming for you, they laugh, they hate you, you are afraid. You're looking for a way out.

No way to placate them. Sarah had rounded up the others and turned them against Tomi, made her out to be an outsider, someone who shouldn't be there with the rest of them in that dirty little classroom with the teachers who were bored and hateful and lessons which were easy compared to home-schooling. Tomiko didn't belong, not in any way, shape, or form.

She'd keep going for the center loop and missing it, every shot she made. She brought toys in and offered to share them—Sarah broke them. She brought vacation slides in from back when her family took vacations, tried to tell exciting stories—Sarah and her friends stole Tomi's things and dumped them in the toilet.

Tomiko had no idea how to make the shot, how to finish the goal and earn the bonus. Even avoiding the center loop entirely didn't help; Sarah made sure that Tomiko couldn't fade into the background, couldn't be just another blinking light or painted on decoration. The teachers were of no help, telling Tomiko to sit down and do her work and quit bothering them.

Eventually she decided to aim for the jet bumpers. Risk and reward. Tell the principal about the bullying directly.

It seemed to work, flashing lights and spinners, parent-teacher meetings. Sarah's parents scolded her, and Sarah swore she'd never do it again and she was so very, very sorry.

But Jake was very, very loud. Because Tomiko had pulled him away from his boys to go to the stupid meeting and waste his time with this nonsense. He was so very loud and this time he was the flipper.

Combos broke again the next day when Sarah and her friends beat Tomi for being a tattletale.

She never tattled again. Besides, things were getting worse at home.

Chaos, now. Ball all over the place, missing every shot, kicking off the bumpers, dancing near the drains. Can't make a single shot. *All this needless suffering. You're terrified, you're confused. Hard work should mean a reward, right?* Every goal she started timed out.

The voice in her closet was getting louder. Giggling. Scary. Like Sarah and her friends. Mom said never to tell Jake about the voice in the closet and in fact, to never talk to Jake if it could be avoided. Because Jake just lost his job.

That meant Jake was there all day, every day, not just in the late evenings. He'd sit in the living room and drink and watch television. If Tomiko walked through, if she blocked his view of the television for even a second, he'd be loud. If Mother ever pointed out that he had no job and needed another, he'd be VERY loud, and then jet bumpers at maximum and another piece of furniture would break.

It can always get worse.

Because after a few days of this, Tomi started to glow in the dark.

It was her fingers, at first. They flickered when she moved them—just a little, a very little, but enough to be noticeable. She was lit like a special lane that had just been activated, with the promise of fresh bonus points. In fact, something about the way her hands were starting to be blurry and bright was exciting to her. Even if they were also very, very itchy.

One night she dared to show Mother.

Tomiko didn't go to school the next day. ("She's sick and cannot attend," Mother had told the school on the phone.) Mother wanted Tomi to stay in bed all day, to rest, while she found a cure. Mother on her laptop computer, desperately searching the Internet, while her daughter stayed in bed and was completely bored.

Eventually Tomi snuck away. Snuck by Jake, who was sleeping in his armchair. Down to the basement.

The pinball machine was so bright and welcoming. Those familiar noises and beeps and music loops, the digitized voices encouraging her and telling her what goals to shoot for... it was all so wonderful. No loud Jake, no sad Mother, no spiteful Sarah, no bored teachers, nothing bad. Even the giggling girl in the closet wasn't scary to think about when Tomi was the Pinball Wizard.

Day after day Tomi would stay out of school. Jake didn't care; he was drinking more than ever and that meant sleeping more than ever. Mother looked scared, but Tomi wasn't afraid anymore. She had her pinball. It was always the comfort in her life, the one thing which was never bad. Father's gift to her.

Eventually Tomi stopped going upstairs. She'd stand there, playing game after game. Sometimes she'd ignore the plates of food that Mother was leaving at the bottom of the stairs for her. Funnily enough... Tomi wasn't hungry anymore.

It's all around you now, isn't it? Steel wires and blinking lights behind painted glass. No fear. Just the chaos.

"Yes," Tomi agreed with the giggling girl.

Soon the limited little rectangular box of the game wasn't enough. Tomi needed more.

The game filled the basement, now. It filled her world. Multiball, jackpot, super jackpot. Rolling and spinning as the flippers played in a blur, like blurry fingers, keeping the ball in play forever. She hadn't tapped the button which inserted a fake quarter in some time. She wasn't even playing one game, she was playing all three of the pinball machines at the same time, they were all the same game, there was so much of it and it was all she really needed in life...

Loud Jake. So very loud, even louder than the jackpots and the rattle of the jet bumpers.

"Dammit, this has gone on long enough! There is NO CURE!" he was screaming. "Your little brat is a Picasso. That's enough. I'm calling the Department of Safety."

"NO! NO!" Mother. "NO, I won't let you!"

"OUT OF MY WAY!" Loud Jake shouted.

Silver down the ramp, off the wall, straight into the ball drain.

Mother down the stairs, off the wall, flat on the basement floor.

Good game design meant that you had a chance, that you could have prevented a drain out if you were fast enough or skilled enough. Tomi was the Pinball Wizard now, in flesh and mind and chaos. She should have been able to win the game. And she didn't.

Game over for Mother. New high score, LJK, looming large at the top of the basement stairs.

LJK.

Tomi, can you hear me? Can you feel me near you? the green child whispered in her ear. *You don't have to be afraid of him any more. You don't have to be afraid of monsters, not when you ARE the monster. Show him what that means.*

Forget the skill shot; pull the plunger all the way out. Launch the ball down the stairs. Jet bumpers to maximum.

It was the finest game Tomiko had ever played. The bells echoed with his screams, becoming a music unlike any she had ever heard before. Multiplier after multiplier racked up until she had finally broken a hundred million points. And when the multiball kicked in... when he was torn in three and battered about the playfield, sent up ramps and through loops and down sink holes... it was perfect. Completely and utterly perfect.

All games end eventually. This one ended to the sound of sirens.

Her new best friend forever opened the doorway for her.

We'll play as much as you want, playing forever, she promised. *Come with me to my home and I'll never make fun of you like the other kids do. We'll be perfect together in a wonderful nightmare. We'll live forever and nobody will ever hurt us.*

Tomiko was brilliantly lit, now. All lights and silver and springs and bells. A special girl, Father's special little girl, Mother's cherished little girl. Finally finding her place in this world. Special when lit.

The *crunch*ing and *squelch*ing made for a very interesting combination of sounds, he thought.

Seth Dougal, O-1 of the Department of Safety, had made a special point to be here at this crime scene. It was a rather extreme one, a spray of blood and organs and pinball machine parts—almost like a piece of modern art. He resolved to have the official photo record reproduced for his later amusement and edification.

The O-2 who was in charge of the scene picked his way across the disaster zone in the basement, wearing rubber shoes already ankle-deep in stains and muck.

"Looks like an entire arcade exploded in here," he said. "Manifestation of physical objects which couldn't have actually been present at the time of the Picasso's emergence. We've counted twenty-three flippers alone and there's probably more out there. Whatever swept through here it was a hell of a powerful distortion compared to most Picassos..."

"What about the occupants?" Seth asked.

"You're looking at them, it seems," the officer said, gesturing to the mess with his clipboard. "The woman's not particularly mauled, just incidental postmortem injuries; she fell down the stairs. The tissue samples are from an unidentified male, and we only know that because we found his... uh. Anyway, we found her laptop upstairs; lots of conspiracy theory websites and crackpot home remedies for cubism. We're guessing the daughter was infected and she's responsible for this, since she's M.I.A. Probably slipped into the Sideways; we found an unregistered opening. Not sure how recently it manifested..."

Disappointment swept over Seth. Not sadness, not exactly, just... disappointment.

"So she was trying to 'cure' her daughter, and the situation spiraled out of control," he said. "It's a shame, a downright shame. I keep telling the Mayor we need to crack down on these websites encouraging people to take care of their infected loved ones, trying to give them hope that it can be reversed. There is no cure. Conversion to a Picasso is simply... inevitable."

"Family's family, sir," the officer said, tucking his clipboard under one arm, having finished his notes. "And desperation drives you to strange ends."

With the Picasso gone and no survivors, the case was promptly closed. The house was cleaned up by the Department of Resources and put on sale at a deep discount, owing to the entrance to the Sideways in the basement. There would always be some family out there living in fear of the City that would be willing to buy a scary house, if it meant escape to the Suburbs.

Fear was a powerful motivator, after all. And Seth would have it no other way.

\\00c: Hollow

She danced around him in a way that was extremely distracting. Which was a bit of a pain, since he was very busy at the moment; this was delicate work, and he'd had to start over three times already. It was difficult to focus on your work when some kid was doing her best to try and grab your attention.

Eventually she just interjected herself completely between himself and his work.

"Boo!" she chirped, from behind the mask.

"Must you do that?" he asked, trying to brush her aside.

"Of course! It's Halloween," she exclaimed, worming away before he could nudge her away. "It's the scary evening of scary stories and treats and fun! My favorite, most favorite-avorite-avorite time of year. Come on, can't you get into the spirit of it?"

"Absolutely not," he replied. "Halloween is a pointless cultural diversion which has no applicable use in the City of Angles. I don't understand why people still pretend to celebrate it. It's not like kids go door-to-door in the middle of the night, the way they do on Earth..."

"There's more to it than trick-or-treat, though," she protested, hopping up to have a seat nearby. "There's the costumes! You get to pretend to be a monster. It makes monsters friendly. And there's the spoooooooky stooories..."

"Both of which are valuable tools for inoculating the young against emotional trauma, yes," he decided to concede. "I'll grant it serves that purpose. But again, is that appropriate for this world? Do we really want our children to believe that the dangers which lurk in the dark aren't as bad as they may think?"

"I like to think there's nothing awful under the bed," the child said, with a pout behind her smiling mask.

Realizing he just wasn't going to get anything done tonight, he decided to put aside his project and focus on the girl instead. Maybe then she'd leave him alone, once he proved exactly how boring he was. How boring this evening was, in essence.

"You're in a very unique position in that regard," he reminded her. "For most, the Sideways pose a considerable threat. Why are we using stories designed to tease a fear reaction and then ultimately neuter it with laughter to downplay that threat? Even the scariest story or the most gruesome movie is just an excuse for us to harmlessly experience fear, so that we can release the stress without coming into contact with true danger. It's an outlet for steam which I don't feel is healthy in the long run."

"So you don't enjoy scary stories?" she asked. "C'mon. Everybody likes scary stories."

"Consider both possible outcomes from the telling of a traditionally 'scary' story," he said, applying quotes to the air with his fingers. "One outcome is that the story falls flat and does not scare. Honestly, that's how it is for me—I've been a professor of literature long enough to hear every tale in the book. I'm just never going to be afraid of someone's crazy made-up tale. In my case, it's not even serving the base purpose of entertainment. Second outcome is a fear reaction, climaxing in a cheap thrill, ending in emotional recovery. Each time this happens, it lessens the chances you'll react properly with true fear when there's justifiable cause for fear."

"Soooo... the more scary stories you hear, the less likely you're going to be afraid when it counts?" she replied, trying to work her way through his long-winded explanation.

Finally, he thought.

"Precisely. For someone living in a dangerous environment, day-to-day danger is more than adequate—additional false danger on top of that only serves to water down the true danger."

"And you've heard all the stories, have you?"

"Well, I don't like to brag," he lied. "But I suppose so, yes. The number of actual stories is quite limited; most are just permutations of a basic story structure. Once you see that structure, there's no surprise left. Certainly no horror."

The girl cocked her head to the side, curious behind the mask of perfect normalcy.

"What if I told you I could scare you with a story?" she asked.

"I rather doubt you'd be able to. And I am quite busy, you know..."

"I know. You've been busy for some time. Why not take a break?" she suggested. "It's Halloween. That makes it scary story time! And I bet you I could scare the bejeebers outta you, if you'll let me. You're so sure of yourself, why not take the bet...?"

He gave it due consideration. It wasn't like a young teenager could possibly come up with the sort of tale which the greatest masters of English literature hadn't already dreamed up a thousand times already. Plus, there could be a benefit...

"If I listen to your story and it doesn't scare me, you'll leave me alone?" he asked, to place his bet.

"And if you hear it and you get scared, you need to go trick-or-treating with me so we can get candy," the girl offered, a double smile of mask and flesh. "It's boring hanging around down here all the time. I'm sure we could find someone with candy. Is it a deal?"

"Fine, if it'll get you off my back," he agreed. "What's your story?"

The girl giggled brightly behind the bright mask. She took a bow, formally, to introduce herself as a storyteller. And then spoke.

"My story begins six months ago, far above in the bright and wide world," she said, setting the stage. "It began with a woman and a boy and a man. But it didn't really begin with them—it really began when another man entered the picture—"

"And the man caught his wife cheating on him and there was a murder-suicide somewhere in the mix, and maybe a bloody hook on a car door. I've heard this one before—"

"No, he never clued into the wife's infidelity. He kept going to work, day in and day out, without suspecting a thing," she countered. "In fact, even when she left him, he never figured out why. That's how little he really cared about her. And the boy was a bad boy, very bad, and eventually ran off and joined a Salvager gang. That left the man aaaaaaaall alone..."

"I'm not sure how the family is relevant to the story you're trying to tell. Are you trying to inject some real-world drama into it?" the man wondered. "Ask yourself if you could cut the characters from the story and end up reaching the same plot conclusion. If so, they weren't even needed."

"I'm telling this story, not you, because you don't like to listen to stories. Now hush," she scolded. "The man! The man was all alone. He was sad, even if he never could understand why, because he hadn't paid much attention to the ones who left him and assumed he was far too intelligent to let loneliness affect him. And then he lost his job. And then he lost his apartment. And then he lived in an alley. And he annoyed all the homeless people with his prattle until they wouldn't be near him..."

"Not seeing the scary story aspect yet. This reads like a bad TV movie."

"One day he was trying to escape the rain, so he went into the Sideways, because nobody else would take him in. Why go there, you may ask? Because the man was very clever and decided that he could outsmart the dangers, could learn his way around and make his own life there. Nobody else wanted him, so why not make a new home, a new place for himself?"

Understanding came to him immediately.

In the form of a groan, pressing a wet palm to his face, shaking his head.

"I'm going to stop you here, because it's patently obvious where you're going with this," he grumbled. "You're doing a standard tale of The Fool. Someone who runs contrary to society's established patterns and standards, repeatedly making the same mistake, and is punished for it. In this case, The Fool is running afoul of the 'no man is an island' aesop. Let me guess—in the end, he becomes a Picasso, the ultimate realization of the monster within humanity and thus this scary story stands to help silly young children realize they need to love their family and so on and so forth?"

To which the masked child simply giggled.

"Naw, I don't really have a point," she said. "I'm jus' tellin' a story, you know?"

"Really. Okay, let's skip ahead a bit and get to the jump-and-scare moment," he suggested. "In fact, let me fill in for you, so I can save my time and get back to what I was doing. The man goes mad with despair and loneliness, and instead of returning to society to mend his fences and embrace civilized behaviors, he starts taking apart any poor bastard unlucky enough to wander into HIS Sideways and, I don't know, makes tiny model houses of out their bones and sinew. How's that sound? Is that creepy enough?"

"Wow. You really do know all the stories!"

"I told you I did."

"Well, maybe you can explain something for me about the story?" the child guessed.

"Likely, yes. But you said you'd leave me alone if I wasn't scared, and as you can see, I am not scared in the slightest, so..."

"Aha! The story's not reaaaaally done yet, is it?" she asked. "Because if the lonely Picasso really is pulling people apart and making little houses out of their bones, isn't it important for the audience to know *why* you're doing it?"

"But it's completely obvious!" he protested. "It's a blatantly direct symbol, which anyone can understand! Broken home? Cheating wife? Delinquent son? Lost job? Cast out even by those who were cast out, living in the worst place imaginable, driven to madness in perfect isolation? I am making replacement houses, and trying to symbolically repair my life in the process! It's such a clear-cut message. How could anybody possibly be scared by this!?"

This, being the perfectly formed model house of femurs and ligaments that he'd been working on all night.

Just like the night before. And the night before. And the night before.

There's always more bones. More people like him, lost and afraid and refusing to accept what was in front of them. Was he really to blame if he had such important things to do with his time? He was important. He still had a place, *this* place which the child of shadow had given him on the day she found him. His Sideways. His home. The only one he ever needed.

The child pulled her smiling mask of normalcy up to her brow, to reveal the green smile of madness beneath.

"I can't see any reason why anyone would be scared of your blood house," she agreed.

"Exactly. Which, I believe, ends the story and I have won the wager. So if you don't mind, please, I really need to get back to it," he concluded. "You can go now."

The mask slipped back into place, the child rocking back and forth on her heels.

"'kay. I'm sorry, I just was bored," he said. "I guess I can go looking for the heart of the city again. Or play with one of my other friends. Or make new friends. I can always make new friends."

"Yes, you go and do that," he suggested, pulling a forearm from the pile, stripping it down with a thought. The flesh neatly compressed itself into a tiny super dense wad, to be stacked alongside the others. Very tidy and organized, that was the key to a life well lived.

"Dooo me a favor...?"

Closing his many eyes, he tried to hold back the frustration his discombobulated body pulsed with.

"If you see a girl like me down here, let me know," Bedlam asked. "Like me, but with red hair. I want to make friends with her. I really, really do."

"Yes, fine, whatever."

"I'm going to make friends with everybody, eventually. Once I find the heart. But she might not like that. So I need to make friends with her first. And then we'll play forever, just like you and I play."

And then he made it a point to ignore her. Because it seemed the only way the child would leave him be. Leave him to what he needed to do.

It wasn't insanity. He wasn't insane. His mind was ordered and time was a clear sequence to him, even when it wasn't running perfectly in sequence. Time. Memories. Things like that, ghosting in and out and repeating—he could sort through it all, in time. Perfectly sane.

After all, that was just a scary story, that being in the Sideways drove you insane. That losing everything you had in life without realizing what it meant to you could drive you to this psychosis. An educated man, a man of reason, had nothing to fear. Had no reason to actually experience the horror of what he was doing, to let it reach him, because to do that would be to give in to the basest of societal compulsions. Fear was beneath him. He rose above such childishness, and found peace...

A shocked gasp.

Not from him. He wasn't shocked anymore. He was unshockable.

The shocked gasp came from the one who wandered into his home, three days later, when he was unfocused and not paying attention.

Looked like some street urchin. Probably came in through the alley entrance, the same one he used, six months ago.

Fine. His house needed a new wing.

Author's Notes

//001: STARTING OUT SIDEWAYS

Starting Out Sideways always had the same overall shape -- man is in a time loop without realizing it, woman enters his life and brings a horrible monster with her, they run away, he solves the problem, the end. But it went through a lot of changes as the writing progressed and I started feeling out what I wanted City of Angles to be, overall.

PENELOPE'S AGE

Initially, Penelope was going to be 22, to match Dave's age. This would also make her a prime candidate for web advertising, which typically focuses on your most desirable female protagonist. (Sad, but true.)

Problem was, her character was never intended to be seen as sexy, never really destined for a romance angle, and simply felt WRONG being a grown adult tromping around with a controlling father figure. If her personality was going to be centered on innocence and hope, being an adult didn't feel right thematically -- and a teenager would be even worse, since odds were low a teenage daughter would have good sync with her father.

Don't get me wrong, it could technically be done at those age brackets. It's not like passing a certain digit counter makes you a cynical jerk. This was more a matter of how the character felt to me, what shape she should take in order to stand tall in the way I wanted her to. And for that, making her younger felt like a much better fit.

In the end I dropped her back to 13. With youth comes the promise of a new day and bright-eyed idealism which hasn't been trampled upon by adult reality. It strengthens the bond of father-daughter, adult-child I was looking for. And it positioned her to be a unique voice in the largely adult world of City of Angles, by presenting a young perspective which has none of the emotional baggage that older refugees from Earth carry with them.

It also made the teddy bear she carries around (which I have big plans for) more of a sensible choice. That was seriously a big deal, believe it or not.

DESIGNING DAVE

The intention from the start was for Dave to be an "Arthur Dent" style character, but that's only a starting place -- a challenge to myself, to begin with a familiar framework but run wildly in another direction to make Dave feel unique and original. He started out as your typical bumbling confused guy who was being dragged along for the ride, then went somewhere else entirely.

For much of early 2012, I was dealing with anxiety attacks due to an undiagnosed sleep apnea condition which was interfering with my sleeping patterns and screwing up my mental frame of mind. Eventually, it got so intense that I gave up worrying about it and just adopted a stance of grim acceptance of the unpleasantness I was going through.

My problems eased down in the middle of the year to the point where I was doing quite well -- but for Dave, his problems did not. At a young age he was hyperanxious, easily scared, and lived in a perpetual state of dread as one thing after another went wrong in his life. Nothing huge, but enough little complications that he was having trouble rolling with the punches. When his mother finally died, it pushed him through to the other side... numbness, unflappable calm, and a dampening down of his personality.

THAT was the establishing factor that moved him beyond Arthur Dent, his unusually high tolerance for craziness due to being so unsettled he became crazily settled. This was the personality trait I'd use to move him beyond being traumatized and into using that trauma to help others, much as he did when faced with the Girl Scout Picasso.

SEEING THE SIGHTS, BREAKING THE LAW

Originally the story was going to go from the Sideways straight into Dave's orientation. However, this would mean we never got a feel for the City proper... just for the most twisted, darkest corners of it. I wanted to show the reader what city living was like, not just the layers of horror underneath it.

This led to developing the second act, where they're being tailed and have to walk the streets a bit to try and lose the tail. Originally, Gregory would've known from the start that they were in a quarantined section of the Sideways (and in fact, originally ALL of the Sideways were illegal!) The Department of Safety was going to tail them, and Gregory would be focused on dumping any data they had on them proving they were in the Sideways, to avoid having any evidence on hand when caught.

Problem here is that if all of the Sideways are illegal, that means every mapping excursion is illegal, and Penelope and Gregory would be dodging the law their entire lives. I couldn't see Gregory willfully breaking the law and putting her in blatant danger. Also, I couldn't see the Department of Safety "tailing" them; they'd jump the pair right away rather than let them sneak around.

The solution was to have them UNKNOWINGLY breaking the law -- and that it was a trap set up explicitly to catch them. Also, their tails wouldn't be Department of Safety, but Cult of Bedlam... an organization which had corrupted the Department of Safety, without anyone realizing. Now it felt better for their pursuers to keep back a distance, and for the cops to only swoop in when they'd avoided capture.

RANDOM NOTES...

...the very first thing we see is reality being horribly broken, with the clock reading 88:88 AM. (8 representing infinity, and representing double loops..) This was inserted into later drafts to ensure the mundane nature of the first scenes didn't lose readers.

...there's TONS of hints at Dave's destiny littered throughout his introduction. The logo he's designing and the company he's designing it for are not random but quite intentional. It's the only aspect of his time loop that changes every day, as he continues to refine the logo at the request of Lucid Technologies (lucid dreaming being a state of controlling the wild chaos of dreams).

...on top of all that, even in his downtime he's working on the problem (the video game where he's trying to escape a maze).

...the design on Dave's t-shirt in the official character art is very similar to the logo he's creating, as evidenced by the "Make it look more/less like a Celtic knot" request by Lucid.

...the first hint that Dave's key ring is strange comes when the narration mentions he has four keys, but only three are described. This was also done in other stories I've written, such as Unreal Estate, to show where reality is broken -- in hopes the reader will simply assume it was a typo.

...I'm purposefully avoiding the Little White Blonde Girl In Peril trope with the Girl Scout Picasso. Because it shouldn't matter; a child in pain is a child in pain.

...the scene where Penelope talks with her father before bed was inserted late in the draft process, to try to break the 3rd person away from being centered on Dave exclusively. We still haven't passed the Bechdel Test, but that'll be coming!

...when Penelope pops in on Dave to chat at night, the scene felt very strange when she was written as adult or late teenage, particularly since it ends in a hug. I was able to deflect the assumption that this was headed into weird romance territory with lines like "Okay, sure, you're a really old guy..."

...the O-n rankings of Department of Safety officers are a tribute to the SCP Project, a horror story series which also deals with containing nightmarish things.

...I seriously debated including the lyrics for Spongebob Squarepants to avoid being sued, but it just felt SO appropriate here. It was also one of the sticking points which convinced me to drop Penelope's age back a bit, since it was one of the clearest moments of the story in my mind and would only make sense coming from a kid. Or a hipster, I guess.

...Bedlam is specifically referred to as a "she," to help hint at her true nature which will be revealed later.

//002: ORIENTATION EXPRESS

The idea behind Orientation Express was simple -- continue the story of Dave as he learns more about the city, and in turn allow the reader to learn more as well. It's a simple framing device, allowing me to deliver exposition without feeling unnatural.

However, all of that ended up taking a backseat to the character interplay and depicting the spectrum of reactions new arrivals can have to the nature of the City of Angles. In the end that became more important than explaining how the government is organized or how the city is laid out. I suppose all that stuff will have to be gradually revealed as we go.

HOLLISTER - ONE OR TWO CHARACTERS?

Originally Hollister was going to be two different characters; a bored and disinterested seminar teacher, and their 'camp counselor' aide known as Hollister. He was only going to be in the story at all so I could introduce him prior to coa//003, and so there'd be at least one friendly face in the generally impassive front of the Department of Orientation. He'd only be there as part of his 200 hours of community service after a minor criminal charge (since he was always intended to be a wannabe underworld mover and shaker).

In the end, I decided to consolidate the characters from two to one, and make Hollister's actual day job be working for the Department of Orientation. It made sense; he's a guy who likes to help people get what they want, even if his tact and timing need work. By being the only friendly face they see despite his sloppiness, it reaffirms his helpful nature.

DANGER IS MY MIDDLE NAME

What started as a one-line throwaway joke became a runaway plot point for Dave Smith. I was trying to decide his future direction, to decide what changes he would be going through that would elevate him from grey nobody into a genuine individual.

He was always slated to be compassionate -- pulling on the overall theme of City of Angles, "Community and Compassion vs. Isolation and Indifference." By making his middle name actually be Danger, I then came up with the "I always wanted to be a fireman" joke, which led into what he would transform himself into given the fresh start the city offers.

OF MY DREAMS

Both dream sequences were not in the original outline for the story. I came to the point where I needed to bridge one day's events with the next day's events, and had no means to do it. When I decided Dave needed to miss all his opportunities to talk to Penelope until he was truly in dire straights, I realized having him sleep through these moments -- and playing it into the ongoing "Dreams, Nightmares, and Wakings" theme of City of Angles would benefit the long term goals of the story.

SCARY BLACK MAN

I've very rarely written a person of color, much to my regret -- I try to draw upon and depict a wide spectrum of characters. It presents a challenge to me as a writer and better illustrates my usual themes of community to show people from all backgrounds working together.

However, to this day, I'm still not sure I wrote Jayden's dialogue very well. I didn't want him to be poorly spoken but he had to reflect the bad neighborhood he grew up in as well. This is a thoughtful young man who tries to make the best of bad situations, and showing aspects which run with and against media stereotypes was key to fleshing him out. Hopefully I did a decent job; I'm too close to my writing to know for certain.

RANDOM NOTES...

...despite Dave offering up his mother's maiden name, she wasn't found as a contact for him. The reason why is explained later, but this sets the seed for that story.

..."nobody pays you not to react to things" foreshadows Dave's chosen career.

...Hollister clarifying City of Angles vs. City of Angels comes from several people realizing only after reading the series for some time that it was spelled that way.

...Hollister is very vague in explaining when Yvonne got to the city, as he's under orders not to reveal the echo theory until later in the seminar. His discomfort may also be why he called the meeting short.

...the dream contains numerous long-term story arc references; the crafting of the Lucid logo, the spiral nature of it, the word "lucid" playing into Dave learning to control his dreams, Penelope's role in the crafting of dreams, etc.

...Penelope's hair is red, carrying through the arc colors (Penelope / Red, Bedlam / Green, Echo / Blue). Similarly the flyer under the door is on blue paper and in Dave's nightmare about Seth Dougal, he wears a green tie.

...I debated for some time how Sarah would die, or if she'd back away from her suicide attempt successfully, etc. In the end I decided it'd be best if Dave had a chance to show he wanted to save her, even if a random confluence of physics prevented it (as might realistically happen).

...the arc number 23 is continued here, with a 23 minute phonecall. That's a happy coincidence; Lirazel pointed it out on my blog that I'd used 23 several times. I liked it so much I decided to keep using it.

//003: KILROY WAS HERE

The Wei Sisters evolved out of a rather embarrassing and slightly sexist issue -- that if I wanted to advertise this series in web banners, I needed some Hot Chicks to use in those ads. All my research pointed me to the fact that featuring sexy girls up front in your ad campaign would draw folks in, and then you could present them with reasonably humane portrayals of women to make up for it.

Still, their personalities and hobbies and so on grew out of things I wanted to try depicting in writing. I'd worked with graffiti writing and the pillars of hiphop before, and using it as a tool for expression in the face of the puzzle the City of Angles presents was appealing. Balancing that out with someone who was tied into the social night life of the city would give me opportunity to present that side of the urban experience. Finally, I could depict a sister bond, a family connection despite not being sisters by blood -- perfect for the ongoing themes of using strong relationships to stand tall in the city.

SEXUALITY AND VIVI WEI

Stop me if you've heard the joke before. Guy is jonesing for a girl. Someone says, "I'll teach you how to flirt with her." He asks "Will it help?" and she says, honestly, "Can't hurt your chances." Because secretly she knows he has no chance in hell, BECAUSE...

...and I couldn't fill the punchline. Not without dipping into tired old cliches, or sexist "friend zone" interpretations, or changing Vivi's character to something that just felt wrong for her.

I struggled with this one for a long time. It was a great setup, and made sense for Marcy; she didn't like Hollister, but she knew this was a harmless red herring of an offer, because... because... because Vivi was gay? No, that was too easy, and also didn't suit someone who I felt would be more 'free love' themed than Marcy was. ...because Vivi was biromantic asexual? It would fit the punchline, might even fit her humanist attitude, but felt a bit too extreme and still didn't suit her.

At first I thought I found an answer -- that Vivi was actually a very discriminating partner and has very high standards -- and I finalized the entire story with that. Hollister was okay with it for the same reason he's okay with it here, that he wants something else from her regardless. But... then when 006 came around, I rethought things.

The original idea for Vivi was a polyamorous sort, someone who cherished humanity in all forms. Having her be quite closed off physically just to make the punchline with Hollister's situation work didn't fit. I needed a way to make Hollister clearly and obviously inappropriate as a potential partner for her, but very appropriate for a friendly relationship.

After working on the series timeline for a bit, I realized Vivi was actually brought into the city around age seven... old enough to remember having a younger brother, even if that era of her life was still largely behind her. And having Hollister crash head on into that memory seemed to work, particularly since Hollister was immediately accepting of the idea rather than defeated by it. I could avoid the tired "friend zone" idea, and I could keep Vivi sexually open (and ironically healthier about it than Marcy, who treats her partner like crap).

I SAW THE SIGN

The second major decision I made for Vivi after her initial design was her deafness. It was directly inspired by a guest strip in the webcomic Girls With Slingshots, where a group goes out to a dance club -- and ultimately only the deaf woman has fun, because she could enjoy the experience in a unique way while the others had to deal with noise and headaches. It was a fascinating dichotomy and I felt it wouldn't change my design one bit for Vivi, she could still enjoy dance and socializing... in a different way, one which would be fascinating to write about.

I used my friend David as an invaluable resource here, and he taught me a lot about the structure of sign language and the challenges of lip reading. I wanted this to be as authentic a character as possible. Having dealt with my own disability issues such as mobility impairment all my life, it was important to get this right when reaching out to a different disability experience than my own. She had to be genuine.

This curious mix between the sisters of signing, writing, dancing, intimacy, social connections, and how it all tangled up and played against each other... it really made the Wei Sisters stand out in my mind as characters I really, really wanted to write about. My hope was they'd also be characters the reader would want to read about, as well.

RANDOM NOTES...

...the number 23 makes a return appearance (don't go to floor 23, it doesn't exist).

..."Ghostwriter" was also the name of the lead singer in my virtual band in the game Rock Band by Harmonix. He was more of a hipster type, though, and better resembled Cass from //004.

...the homeless man's sleepy rambling foreshadows the rise of Bedlam, and her ultimate goal to find the spiral Dave is drawing and the bed that lies at the end.

...I agree with Slyck and Marcy's interpretation of "YOLO." It's a contradictory concept; if You Only Live Once, why throw that life away doing some stupid thing in order to "live"?

...originally the Defined Tower was going to be 30 Rockefeller Plaza, which is often shown lit up at night. However, its windows are TINY and unsuitable for the story, so it's an unnamed building.

..."Up with this I will not put" is paraphrased from Winston Churchill. It was also featured in the pilot episode of Phineas & Ferb. Always struck me as a good twist, a clever way to take a defiant stance.

//004: TURN LEFT

Turn Left is a story which went through a considerable number of changes. For this one, I think it'd be best to go over each major revamp, in order.

THE EARLIEST IDEA

A literate and soft-spoken urbanite taxi driver who gets odd premonitions in his dreams gets into an accident and loses his job. He's hired on instead by a trucking company, and ends up in a massive culture clash with the Outlands truckers. Eventually he wins their trust by rescuing one of them when they get trapped on an endless loop road, using his strange visions to guide him. The end.

THE NEXT IDEA - CASSANDRA

The taxi driver is largely the same, but is swapped to a female character. Similar to 003, this was me attempting to inject a few more female characters into the series, which in the early stages was dominated my men like Dave, Gregory, Hollister, Seth, etc. One unfortunate loss was that my original concept was for the driver to be a person of color (see 002 and Jayden). In hindsight I could have kept the race the same and just flipped the gender, but I think introducing the African-American Reg (as a clueless and rich but friendly socialite) helped me keep the same idea of a compassionate protagonist within Cass's inner-city urban circle.

This generally worked -- hipster girl contrasts against country drivers -- but wasn't really interesting enough. Also, there had been some feedback in 003 that people were looking for more surrealism, seeking study of the city itself and the strangeness within it. A whole chapter devoted to something that could easily be done on Earth wasn't feeling right.

THE BIG IDEA - BEAT GENERATION X

Two major changes happened at this stage. One, Cass was cast as a beat poet, tutored under an echo of one of the original beats. After watching documentaries about the beats and reading Howl, I realized Allen Ginsberg would be perfect for this. It would give Cass an internal struggle to either embrace the weirdness of the city (very in tune with the beats) or to stubbornly insist on a normal life.

Second, Grandma Scarlett was introduced as Cass's boss. Before, the trucking company that would hire her would be completely ordinary -- now, she had a far more interesting employer, one which directly tied in the ultimate finish of the first volume. This was the overarching plot hook I needed to make this story shine instead of sink as a complete standalone with no interesting twists.

One more critical thing which changed was that the "future visions" aspect was moved off the driver and onto Scarlett. This meant her name was no longer applicable (Cassandra, the one whose prophetic visions are ignored) but I'd grown to love Cass's name, so I kept it. Cass had a constant companion in the form of Lucid's words, anyway, so was still slightly applicable.

THE FINAL IDEA - THE TRINITY WAR BEGINS

The ending I had in mind was still a simple one, where Cass uses her connection to Lucid to help get Eddie out of an Endless Road. Perhaps the bears would play into it, talking to her, encouraging her. But... this didn't feel very exciting. Sure, it resolved the culture clash angle, but the culture clash angle just wasn't important anymore. It wasn't the core conflict of the story.

It seemed a bit extreme at first, but pitting her against the Shabby Men and introducing the nightmare drug one story ahead of schedule worked. I could keep the culture clash angle in by having Eddie come to her rescue, realizing that truckers are truckers and no matter how strange Cass may be to him, he wasn't going to let someone hassle one of his own.

ONE LAST TWEAK - THE SACRIFICIAL BEAR

So, Cass is being chased by the Shabby Men, and when it looks like she'll be okay the car goes Picasso on her and... what?

Originally I was thinking it would chase her onto an endless highway, and we'd be back to Cass using her connection to Lucid to escape the loop. But... that wasn't really needed anymore. It wasn't going to be a major reveal, having her do that.

Instead, I decided to dig deeper into the purpose of the bears as shields against the forces of Bedlam, and use the bear on the dashboard as a weapon. In a final, final, FINAL edit that bear was no longer just a random decorative dashboard toy and was the bear Scarlett gave Cass in the first place, to bring things back around.

In the end the story ran WAY longer than planned, went in a completely different direction, changed the protagonist several times, and worked much better as a result.

RANDOM NOTES...

...the first poem, Dreams, ties heavily into the overall themes of the story. Buried in the metaphor are some directly relevant phrases. Line two is about the Sideways and Bedlam's children. Line three is about the Department of Safety. Line four is about the trinity of Lucid, Bedlam and Echo -- and then the 'trinity within the trinity' of Penelope, Lucid, and the City of Angles itself. Finally, the reference to Tommy Westfall is the first major hint that the entire world is a dream within someone's head.

...Cass running out of steam during the recital matches the words Allen Ginsberg used when he gave up in the middle of his first recital of Howl.

..."every path leads me to nowhere" is a line from Rooster by Alice in Chains. Lucid uses the common culture of America when she teaches, perhaps.

..."Turn Left," the title of the story and the first time Lucid directly addresses Cass, was not the original title of this story. Several other titles were considered, like "Long Strange Trip" and "Words on the Street." "Turn Left" felt shorter, punchier, and more ominous. Originally the instruction was to turn right, but left felt more awkward and dangerous and thus more appropriate.

...Rockford and Greystone were mental hospitals from Allen Ginsberg's past; Naomi was his mother, who had been consigned to hospitals herself.

..."Live without warning" is a line from Warning by Green Day.

...Dave's cameo was a spur of the moment decision; it seemed a good way to keep him in the series despite not making a return appearance until 007.

...the Clark Nova typewriter made an appearance in the movie version of Naked Lunch, which was partly an adaptation of Burroughs classic novel and partly a study of the beat generation itself. "It has mythic resonance" comes from the movie. The Clark Nova never existed as a brand of typewriter; the prop department doctored up a Smith Corona Sterling to represent it. Scarlett's response about the world being a sham and who gets to decide if it's real ties back into the overall theme of the city as a dream.

...I debated for some time how to resolve the conflict at Melba's Diner. Early drafts had Cass casually using a can of mace over her shoulder and then walking out the door. Ultimately as I developed Cass, making her someone who reads a situation and adjusts her actions accordingly, I decided she'd cut the legs out from under the more threatening aspects of the situation and then simply leave. It felt more appropriate. I do feel like I should've done more with Melba herself, however; her and the diner were more important in earlier draft plans.

...the Department of Safety warning not to accept unsolicited toys is a clear attempt by Seth to stop Lucid from spreading the bears around the city. It doesn't work thanks to Cass's tenacity.

...how to get the girl out of the house was a bit of a conundrum. The original draft had her escaping while Cass talked with the shabby man, and appearing back in the truck begging Cass to drive and drive fast. Ultimately I realized Cass needs to take proactive action here and make her decision to go all-in or walk way from the situation (the same decision Eddie had to make, once).

//005: WOUND UP TOYS

What a crazy process this one was. //005 was originally meant to be Cleanup on Aisle Ten, a story about a repeating grocery store. However, as I developed the idea, it became clear it was a better match for vol//002 of the series, when Echo would take the stage as the primary antagonist. That left me with no story for //005, and a deadline rapidly approaching to have something up on the website...

WHAT TO DO, WHOM TO DO IT WITH

The obvious choice would be to go back to the Yates family. Otherwise, the next time we'd be focusing on them would be near the end of the volume. Telling a story about Penelope and Gregory would allow me to check in on their progress. But what story to tell? A typical outing for them? Did that already. A boring day at home? Meeting their neighbors? What?

Eventually, I decided to take an idea I had put on the backburner and adapt it for Penelope. I had a vague story idea titled "The Strange But True Tale of Old Man Jenkins," which took a group of suburban kids with zero experience with the world and ran them through a Scooby Doo style investigative story surrounding a suburban legend. Haunted houses and childish superstitions could have a firm root in reality in the City of Angles, of course.

The original story idea had three kids in it, or rather three basic ideas for kids. One would be a walking pile of anxieties inherited from parental fear, one would be a rich kid with a lot of toys, one would be an oral history shaman who reveres the weirdness of suburban lore. Not much to go on, but enough of a starting point that it could be adapted to be a Penelope story, where she meets these characters and they go off on an adventure.

This eventually was adapted to three different kids. Milly Frisk became the anxious one, Lucas Flynn became a combination of rich kid and oral historian... and a third kid was introduced, the moody cousin of Milly, named Ryan Sullivan.

Ryan, a troubled youth forced into Milly's family because he had no other living relatives in the city when he was copied over, would be there as a possible love interest for Penelope and another example of giving in to despair rather than living your life.

However... after writing the introduction scene for Milly and Ryan, in which Ryan basically said nothing, the problem was clear: he's boring. He's a standard character, a stock one, which exists only to drive home a point and to eventually lead to a big speech about the importance of life yadda yadda. The story did not actually NEED him, and he dragged things down.

So, I chopped him out, and the story finally flowed smoothly as a result. Adding a quasi-love triangle between Penelope, Milly, and Lucas made the whole group more cohesive and completely eliminated any need for Ryan.

GREGORY'S OFFSCREEN ADVENTURE

I didn't feel like that would be enough for a story, however. If Penelope's off on an adventure, where's Gregory? Since her story wouldn't tie into the overall series plot, his jaunt could -- he could investigate the men who followed them around since //001. I even had a great confrontation designed for when he comes to the end of his investigation and learns the truth about the Cult of Bedlam incident in 1982...

But that's the thing. I had the final confrontation, and nothing planned between the start and the finish. Endless scenes of Gregory shaking people down for intel would get tiresome fast.

In the end, I decided his investigation could happen entirely offscreen. He'd be off doing his thing, whatever it was, and the details didn't honestly matter. What would matter would be the results, which I didn't even need to work into this story -- they held revelations best kept for later in the series.

That allowed me to focus entirely on Penelope, expanding the scope of her story to include an encounter with Bedlam herself, and... there we go. //005 had finally taken full shape.

RANDOM NOTES...

...this is the first time we're told that Penelope was found, rather than born. Honestly, I hadn't completely decided whether her mother died in childbirth or whether Penelope was found as an infant in the Sideways and her mother met some other fate. By this point, I'd solidified my plans (mostly).

...Roland Fletcher Middle School is named after Mayor Fletcher, who was responsible for the new deal reconstruction project which ended in disaster in the 30s. (Using 'Flynn' and 'Fletcher' in the same story was also a shoutout to animated series Phineas & Ferb, which I adore.)

...Penelope's brief dream sequence refers to the door from Heart of the City, with Bedlam following her down there (piggybacking off Lucid's efforts to get Dave to find the place) and hints at what she'll find there ("she was already on the other side").

...the layout of the toy store, including the S-curved gauntlet of cheap toys, is based on a real retail chain toy store where I grew up. Modern toy stores often have the same initial aisle you must pass through, but rarely as lengthy and egregious as that one was.

...the story about Duke and GI*JOE is legit, although I have no idea if the actual toy was really rare. Hasbro tended to phase out characters on the TV show in an effort to push the next wave of toys, which is also why the Transformers movie had such a high body count. The EIGHTIES! It's sadly what passes for culture for people my age.

...Penelope used her ability to manipulate the city to subconsciously create a bathroom they could take refuge in, much as she used it to save her father in //003. Originally this scene was going to take place in the locked cage room / ticket claim desk where expensive items like video games were stored back in the 80s, but I couldn't figure out how they'd bypass the lock quickly.

...when Bedlam taunts them with "Row, Row, Row Your Boat" she's also hinting at the true nature of the City of Angles. ("Life is but a dream...") Which the essence of Lucid within Penelope recognizes, realizing the dream can be what she wants it to be. She creates the passage out of the Sideways from nothing.

...the arguement between Penelope and Gregory stayed the same from my first draft on, even though I wasn't sure it worked. Writing the dynamics of parent/daughter, adult/child on top of the craziness of the Cult of Bedlam was a chore and a half. Prereaders were extensively used to verify I hit the right tones.

...although the cliffhanger note at the end suggests an "Evil Twin" trope, the audience has yet to find out that Penelope ALSO greatly resembles both Echo and Patient 23. WHAT A TWEEST etc.

//006: GLITCH BEAT

This story changed little from the original plans. The core concept remains -- a dubstep artist goes Picasso in the middle of Vivi's club, and an investigation leads to revelations about what the Cult of Bedlam is up to. However, many aspects of the investigation changed as the story was developed...

A MATTER OF PERSPECTIVE

Originally this would be another tag-team of Marcy and Hollister, similar to 003, in which they venture into the unknown. Vivi was going to be suffering from depression, having lost her job and her second home (the club), and fearing she might go Picasso from despair Marcy would be driven to look into matters.

However, after Vivi had little to no actual presence in 003 -- and what little we saw of her was "fanservicey," I decided I needed to do a proper story from her perspective. It'd be difficult given the communication barriers in front of her, but those barriers could be worked into the story itself. This would let me explore Vivi as a character and not just as a princess to be saved by a crusading sister.

LA RESISTANCE

Originally, Vivi and Marcy were NOT going to connect up with Gregory and Penelope. There wasn't even going to be an organized resistance against the Cult of Bedlam, and most of the revelations about the cult's plans would be stumbled across by the time it was too late to do anything.

But when it came down to it, I realized the Wei sisters had no role to play in the future if I didn't work them in with the other protagonists. That, plus my decision to ally Cass's truckers and the 7th Street Scavengers together, said that rolling all the protagonists in a ball might not be a bad idea. Of course, I still needed a reason to keep Dave out of it... which is explained in 007 and 008, as Gregory tries to keep him out.

A HALF-HEARD CONVERSATION

I wrote out the complete discussion between Montgomery and Dougal, so that Dougal's body language and Montgomery's words would mesh. This also included critically important words Vivi couldn't properly translate. Here's the complete discussion, for your amusement.

> Montgomery: "We're still on track, Mr. Dougal."
>
> Seth: "I'm not so sure we are. You had to deliver a massive overdose to get the results we wanted. We obviously can't funnel that strong a concentration into the water supply."
>
> Montgomery: "It won't be a problem. I had to spike the Nightmare Fuel dose to trigger their transformations, but that won't be needed when her influence is applied. You can dilute without issues."
>
> Seth: "There's also a question of supply. Many of the men I assigned to

your team have had their cover blown, thanks to those obnoxious blue collar dimwits in the Outlands..."

Montgomery: "Their loss won't impact matters. Between the supply I've stockpiled here and at the other facilities, there's more than enough. Granted I wish I had more time to research and refine the formula..."

Seth: "I'm suspecting that by this point, your 'research' is more for your own enjoyment than for the furthering of Bedlam's advent, Montgomery. And it's growing difficult to keep it away from the third estate."

Montgomery: "Your men are responsible for those leaks. They were too... unstable. Conscripts and madmen. If I had more true believers this would be far quieter. But I've taken care of my own problems, and will continue to do so. You don't have to concern yourself with me."

Seth: "Fine. I'll have a truck by to pick up delivery tomorrow. After that, it'd be best to shut down this facility, I think. Too many of your little experiments, too much structural cubism. We're moving on to the next phase. For the coming of Bedlam and the glorious chaos."

Montgomery: "For the coming of Bedlam and the glorious chaos."

RANDOM NOTES...

...the breathing exercises and memory walk in Vivi's morning routine were written in expressly to be a bookend with how she recovers from cubism. Bookending the same actions under a different context and highlighting the differences also came in handy in 007.

...Gee Bee is named not after the Bee Gees, but after C.B.G.B., a legendary club in New York that birthed the punk scene. It also fits the pattern of most characters having a true name in addition to a colloquial name used with friends (Penelope/Penny, Gregory/Greg, Cassandra/Cass).

...the dubstep DJ is a rather poorly masked celebrity cameo. His full name or stage name are never given to avoid lawsuits, but folks familiar with popular music around 2012 will know who it is.

...I researched club layouts, to make sure Vivi would be in position to have a difficult time getting to the exit when it hit the fan. The club where the Great White fire incident took place was a key model here, but I had to add a green room behind the stage area with a private bathroom for Vivi's use.

...I debated if Vivi's job offer would really be at a strip club or not. It's an abused trope, being "forced" to debase yourself for money. I didn't want to annoy the reader by continuing to abuse it. I realized though that the problem is not with Vivi, but with her friends reactions to it; Vivi would be willing to do it, but recognizes that THEY see it as beneath her and depressing. Vivi is far more sex-positive and while it's not ideal, she could live with it.

...at the Plaza Arms, they see doorbells for Dave Smith and Kelsey Jones. Similarly, the DJ's notes mention typing on keys that don't exist, which is similar to how Kelsey finds Sideways websites.

...originally the electrified prison cell was going to be a "malevolent murder maze," a confusing funhouse of hallways and doors designed to terrify the experimental test subject. However, for simplicity's sake, I focused on the drug's effects and a single cell instead.

...as Vivi is passing out from the effort of restoring her body, she sees a vision of Bedlam AND Lucid (the identical girl with a red glow).

...the movie reference in question (Rick Blaine) is of Casablanca, where Rick ran a bar and was trapped between German occupation forces and local resistance. Eventually he sided with the resistance, but Scarlett points out he did have a choice to remain neutral, and so does Vivi.

...originally my plan was for Vivi to run an underground rave, constantly on the move, because they were on the lam from the Department of Safety. I realized however it'd be too difficult to explain how Seth couldn't catch them easily, so I prevented Seth from learning what really happened by knocking off Montgomery and destroying the building. As for Bedlam... well, they don't always see eye to eye.

//007: WELL ENOUGH ALONE

The final version of this story is a mix of ideas old and new. Originally, //007 was to be titled "Free Cable," and would deal with three things -- Hollister getting a hacked cable box for Dave which serves up creepypasta style programming, Dave's new career with the FARTs, and a plot regarding Dave's lineage which I decided felt more like an "Echo" story and got shelved for later writing.

What carried through was the idea of Sideways Signals, and a BIT of exploration into Dave's job. But a throwaway joke about 'Smith' being next to 'Jones' at the Plaza Arms evolved this story into so much more...

THE TROUBLEMAKER

Kelsey Jones represented a wide array of plot hooks and character concepts I had wanted to explore at one point or another, all balled up into one bundle of nerves. Let's look at the checklist...

A) She suffers from a form of anxiety disorder, but a different flavor of it. I wanted to do a proper exploration into anxiety, and Dave's bizarre and personal blend didn't allow for that.

B) She represents the positive side of Bedlam; someone who comes to the same conclusions Lucid did, but from the other side (chaos in life instead of life in chaos). This gives Bedlam an ultimately sympathetic angle.

C) She works as a love interest for Dave, by being similar in many respects but quite different in others. They mesh. This opens up relationship stories going into the future, ones which will differ wildly from the only other possible relationship pairing so far (Vivi and Hollister).

I felt drawn to Kelsey as a character, quite intensely. Here was someone who was completely broken in so many respects, twisted by her passions... the Lovecraftian protagonist who is driven mad by forbidden knowledge. And yet those passions drive her, push her past the point others would shy away, giving her extraordinary ability to compensate for the many flaws she suffers due to this chase. She has so many mirrors to other characters like Dave and Penelope which are worth exploring.

THE MIRRORED CONFLICT

Once I decided the meat in this sandwich would be Dave's developing relationship with Kelsey, I needed bread to go with it. In particular, if I was going to depict Dave's career as a FART (apparently I am twelve years old) I needed to show how they came into conflict with their opposite number, the Salvagers.

Not much had been said about Salvagers by this point. We've shown Greg and the rest of the middle-aged gang bangers from the 7th Street Salvagers as a positive force, but before mellowing out they started the way all Salvagers start -- looting, stealing, getting into turf wars, etc. Hardly positive. That side needed to be shown as well.

Staging two different action scenes, both involving the same Salvager gang, was the key. The first is a smaller and more intimate affair, where Dave's innate Dave-ness makes the difference in disarming things. In the second, Dave ultimately solves the problem (calming Kelsey down) but the gang is clearly in the upper hand position. The two conflicts show two different sides to the gangs... desperation and greed.

There was one major difference between the final version and early sketches I made, however. Originally the relationship between Kelsey and the gang leader was going to be far more complex -- her brother was once a gang member, and the leader wanted to have him killed for being a snitch. She pleaded for his life, and the leader only spared him if Kelsey agreed to be his new girl. But... that felt way too, to put it bluntly, "rapey" and unpleasant. Ultimately it worked better for the leader to simply covet Kelsey, with her feeling pressured and powerless. She saves herself from this mess; Dave isn't much of a white knight. In the end, he has to save her from herself before Bedlam's influence causes her to go too far.

RANDOM NOTES...

...the title, "Well Enough Alone," has a double meaning here. Numerous people advise Dave to mind his own business and look after his own interests (leaving well enough alone), while Dave and Kelsey struggle with the problem of social isolation (is he well enough when alone).

...owing to the shutdown of over-the-air analog broadcasts, I had to specifically mention that Carlos replaced his antennae with digital ones. Even so, video snow is an artifact of a bygone age.

...the "cubism remedy" websites Dave browsed are also mentioned in the VIP story "Special When Lit."

..."Sometimes I wish things were less gonzo" references the works of Hunter S. Thompson, who personally knew Allen Ginsberg, Cass's mentor.

...Candle Cove is a reference to the amazing horror short story by Kris Straub, of Starslip Crisis fame.

...Greyscale was originally named Jessie, and referred to Kelsey as one of "Jessie's Girls." This was before he was changed from a manipulative pimp into being a creepy stalker.

...Oblivion's Advocate makes their first appearance in the narrative here, playing in the background at the GMG party.

..."And that's how it's going to be" is a reference to the Brain From Planet Arous, and was sampled by deadmau5 for his song "Moar Ghosts 'n Stuff." Always liked how bitterly final it sounded.

...Bedlam's internal narration hints at the cosmology to be explored next; the trinity of Lucid, Bedlam, and Echo. Mentions are also made of the "fever and division," the moment where she first created the city in her mind and then split into three viewpoints.

Of all the chapters in the first volume, this one was both unchanging and ridiculously fluid.

I always knew how the series would end -- a showdown at the Heart of the City, where revelations about Patient 23 would answer some questions, but raise many others. I knew Bedlam's scheme would be stopped... somehow. I knew Dave's map and key would come into play. But the details of it all were quite tricky to figure out...

DREAM FRAMING DEVICE

Two draft updates in, I introduced the framing scenes with Penelope's dream, where she was trying to deny her nature as Lucid in order to remain simple and ordinary. This solved a lot of problems. For starters, it made the story more interesting; more than a simple series of events where This Happens and then That Happens. But more importantly, it solved the ultimate conflict of the first volume.

By tying it into Bedlam's attempt to drive the group insane, the dreams gave me an angle of attack on Penelope, a way out of that attack, AND a way to turn the tables on Bedlam. I knew Penelope would somehow stop Bedlam cold but couldn't "kill" Bedlam, since Bedlam was technically a part of her and a part of Patient 23. But how could she be stopped, then? The answer was to use Bedlam's attack to force Penelope to accept the Lucid side of herself... and once accepted, it flips the script on Bedlam, forcing her to contend with a fully realized avatar of Lucid. A stalemate occurs and the two forces agree to pull back to their respective corners. (Bedlam, in particular, is willing to agree to this because she's aware of the likely events to come in the next two volumes and wants to watch Lucid dance on a hot plate dealing with them.)

Ever since Sailor Nothing, I've been a fan of couching real-world memories within a loose dream framework. It's a good way to depict both an internal struggle and the concrete details of what's going on. A bit gimmicky, I'll admit, but it helped me give shape to the narrative of //008.

NUTS AND BOLTS

Other issues with this chapter were seemingly minor, but kept me stumped for days. For instance, the opening scenes with Jon at the retirement home.

The idea of Cartwright ambushing Gregory after he uncovers too much of the truth had been hovering in my head all through this volume. Originally this was going to be the "B-Story" to Wound Up Toys, that while Penelope was having fun with the kid brigade, Gregory was investigating and got into a mess with Cartwright. But I decided that side of the story would be kind of boring, especially compared to the A-Story which was red hot, and it wasn't worth depicting. Still, the encounter with Cartwright stayed in my mind as a future scene.

Here, it made sense. It laid the last groundwork for Seth Dougal's backstory, filling in his origins -- but beyond being a pile of exposition, I could use it to move the plot forward, by turning Cartwright's ambush into Gregory's ambush. Gregory didn't particularly need the details of Seth's rise, but knew that digging into them would bait Cartwright into a trap. This let me use the overall idea, but have a very different outcome.

Another example of a minor-but-critical issue was Kelsey's involvement. Kelsey was a very late addition to the series in general; I wasn't sure what to do with her during the planned event of Dave's kidnapping by the Department of Safety. Would she get kidnapped too? How would that play into Bedlam's friendship with her? If she stayed behind, how would that work? How could the DoS have missed her? What role would she play?

I went through plenty of permutations of Dave and Kelsey's circumstances, before arriving at the combination I felt worked best. Dave obviously had to go; he was the key (quite literally) to unlocking Patient 23. But Kelsey going with him would overly complicate matters -- and leaving her behind would help move the protagonists forward, much like Cartwright's kidnapping helped move them forward. A lot of our heroes investigation into the Cult of Bedlam happens off-screen through the second half of the series, and this was a chance to bring it to the forefront before everything went to heck.

PICASSO FRIDAY

Finally, and this one stymied me for some time... the timing of Picasso Friday, the unleashing of Bedlam upon the Heart. In the initial plans, Bedlam actually managed to get into Patient 23's room, and was curled up in bed next to her (as the babbling man on the subway in Kilroy Was Here suggested). Her direct access to Patient 23 let her change the "mood" of the entire City, causing a massive outbreak of cubism. This posed way too many problems, though...

For one, originally the cubism outbreak was going to be what pushed our heroes to journey to the Heart themselves. But the journey was described as a long and winding spiral through all three layers of existence! How could they possibly get there in time before it was too late for the City? I had to move the outbreak's timing to happen in the MIDDLE of that journey, rather than the start, to keep it plausibly menacing without being implausibly destructive.

Also, if Bedlam got direct access to Patient 23, that meant the final showdown had to happen INSIDE the hospital room. Not a lot of physical space to move around in, there... and we'd need to have the revelation of Patient 23 happen simultaneously with the high-tension staredown with Bedlam. You can't pack two huge events like that into the same narrative space. There's no room for it; having enough time to get reactions from everyone to the revelation of Patient 23 AND having enough time to fight Bedlam, both more or less simultaneously? One event waters the other one down. I had to split them up; showdown first, THEN the patient reveal.

In the end, the compromises I made allowed the end results I wanted. Bedlam's proximity to Patient 23 while beating down her door was enough to shake the City up, the beatdown didn't start until there was just enough time to stop it, and the final confrontation didn't interfere with the quiet and reflective moment on realizing the City is one huge dream.

RANDOM NOTES...

...Lucid's discussion of the "second layer" plays into revelations in the second volume of the series, about the dream of the city which connects to the city of the dreamer.

...Penelope's alarm clock reads 88:88, the same as Dave's clock in //001.

...originally my plan was for Archie to blow himself up to save them from the Picassos, hence the foreshadowing with the C4. However, there wasn't enough narrative space to have a showdown, a revelation, AND a mourning period back to back to back. So, I figured I'd buck tradition and allow the tease but NOT end up in a noble self-sacrifice, which I've always felt was overrated, anyway.

...one of the two Picassos that attack them outside the Heart is indeed Tomi, from the bonus story Special When Lit.

..."We came in?" and "Isn't this where..." are the first and last things heard on Pink Floyd's "The Wall."

Artist's Sketches

These early and unused poses show the process through which Allison Barraza, the official artist for City of Angles, developed the characters.

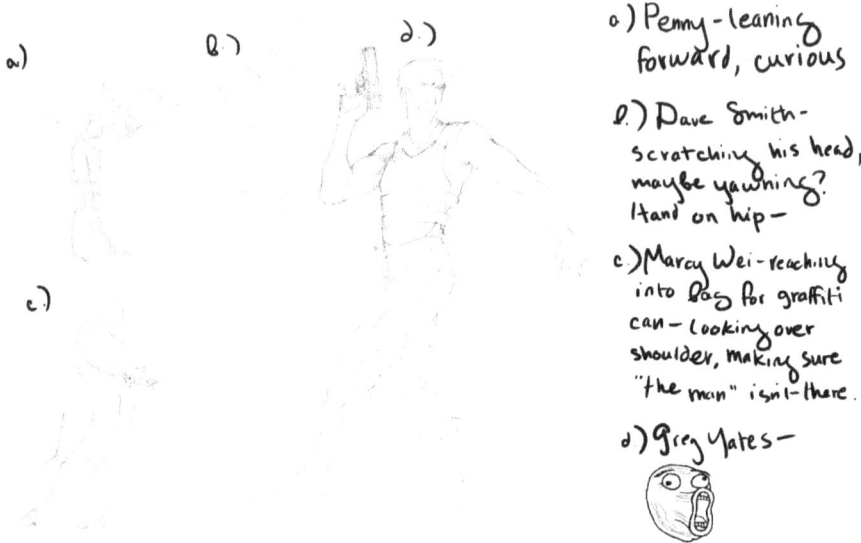

a) Penny - leaning forward, curious

b) Dave Smith - scratching his head, maybe yawning? Hand on hip —

c) Marcy Wei - reaching into bag for graffiti can — looking over shoulder, making sure "the man" isn't there.

d) Greg Yates —

The first art produced for the series. Pose examples for Penny, Dave, Marcy, and a more fleshed out Gregory. The latter of which was right on the money.

Two more possible poses for Penny. Since she was our main character I decided a more upright pose would be best, since it could be easily repurposed for merchandise and so on.

CASS   **VIVI**

Cass and Vivi. We decided it'd make for a better thumbnail if Cass was wearing her hat, rather than holding it. Also better for web banner ads and the like.

Two possible poses for Hollister. The second expressed the cocky young man attitude I wanted perfectly.

A series of thumbnails to determine pose and positioning of Dave and Penelope on the book cover. Since Penny is our main character I wanted her to be front and center, so we used a combination which kept her in focus while moving Dave back a bit.

www.ingramcontent.com/pod-product-compliance
Lightning Source LLC
Chambersburg PA
CBHW060811030726
47503CB00002B/438